THE TAGGER HERD
COLLECTION THREE

From Book One
The phone call that changed their lives forever

The phone was still ringing, so she hit the answer button and raised it to her ear.

"The Stables," she answered.

There was hesitation before the person spoke. When she did, Dru could tell it was an older woman. "Can I speak with the owner please?" She said quietly.

"I am one of the owners, Dru Tagger."

There was more hesitation. "Oh…good. I'm so sorry to bother you."

She hesitated long enough that Dru could add, "No bother at all, how can I help?"

"Well," another hesitation. Even over the phone Dru could tell she was upset.

"I'm not really sure how to start," the woman paused. "My name is Cora Smith and my husband, Wes, passed away a little over three weeks ago."

Well that was a start, Dru frowned. "I'm so sorry."

"Yes, well, thank you. I received a phone call a few minutes ago," she hesitated again, "I'm a bit confused about the call."

"Was it from someone here at The Stables?"

"No, I got your number from a card my husband had in his wallet."

"Do you have horses? Was your husband looking for somewhere to board them?"

"No horses. We sold all our horses a couple years ago."

"OK…" Dru walked away from the arena and the excited chatter from the two teenagers talking about the last day of school.

"That's what's so strange about the phone call I received. The man who called said he would be delivering the hay in the morning."

"Did they call from Tagger Enterprises for the hay?"

"No."

Dru quietly exhaled in rising confusion. "Hay for what?"

"I don't know; we don't have any animals. I canceled the hay order from the man, but now I'm worried," The woman's voice trembled as she continued. "My husband was being very secretive before he died. He even shipped me to Seattle to spend time with my sister for a couple weeks."

Dru still wasn't sure what this had to do with The Stables.

The woman on the phone continued, "We live in Lenore, but I haven't been there since a week before he died."

"Mrs. Smith," Dru leaned against the back of the building. "I'm a bit confused. How can The Stables help?"

The voice let out a frustrated sigh, "I am afraid my husband bought some animals without telling me and they have been at our home in Lenore, unattended, for over three weeks."

Dru slowly stood away from the building, "Horses, sheep, cattle, chickens…a lot of animals can forage for themselves for three weeks."

"Yes," The woman's voice was a little stronger since she had finally voiced her concern. "After my husband died, we had him brought to Seattle and buried here, with family. I haven't been to our home now for over a month. I have no one there to call to go check the property. With your card here… well, I thought maybe he had talked to you about this."

"No, not with me," Dru frowned. "I'll talk to the manager here to see if he spoke with your husband. If not, then we'll take a drive and check." This could be a total waste of time… she HOPED it was a total waste of time. "You have no idea what kind of animals he may have bought?"

"No," she sighed, "I'm just so worried. The man with the hay was so adamant that my husband had bought the hay AND that it was scheduled to be delivered in the morning."

"Did he say how much hay he was delivering?" It was coming on summer when most large animals would be grazing in pastures and not be dependent on hay. The first hay crop was coming off the fields. He could have been stocking up for winter.

"He didn't say."

"OK, I'll go check it out," Her parents and grandparents had taught her to have respect for animals. Something in her gut told her to make the drive. She wouldn't be able to forgive herself if there were animals suffering because she didn't have time to take a drive 30 miles up the river.

www.thetaggerherd.com

ISBN: 978-1-7339528-5-9

THE TAGGER HERD

Collection Three

Book 11 – Reilly Morgan - Epic

Book 12 – Sadie Tagger – Heart & Soul

Book 13 – Matt Tagger – Rescue or Recover

Book 14 – Nora Tagger – Three Horses & a Dream

Book 15 – Grace Tagger – The Past & the Future

A Series by

Gini Roberge

The two men below were the first to know the book existed and were the first to read it. Through their encouragement I continued with the series.

Our 'courier' Emily is Ben's wife and now a good friend of mine as well as their daughter Kenzie.

SPECIAL THANKS TO

BEN SMITH, DVM

For Your Input and Editing Expertise

And the courier Emily!

AND

STEVE ROBERGE, BRO

My sounding board, encouraging voice, and special editor

THE TAGGER HERD SERIES

Reilly Morgan

EPIC

Gini Roberge

CHAPTER ONE

"You want me to do what?" Reilly turned and looked at Kelly.

"Climb on the fence, hook your legs over the top rail and hang upside down." Kelly giggled, her eyes were lit with a sense of fun. The white coat, with the fur trim around the hood, seemed to highlight her red hair and green eyes.

Reilly looked at Kelly to see if she was serious; she was and a sigh escaped him. "OK, but no more weird ones like this."

She giggled. "Depends on if we like it."

Reilly climbed to the top of the fence and looked across the arena to the barn. He wanted to make sure no one could see them.

"There's only a couple people home and they're in the house." Kelly laughed when she realized what was taking him so long.

Reilly did as she asked and hooked his feet around the second rail and leaned back; his knees bent over the top rail. He hung upside down and tried to keep his jacket from falling to his armpits. The field was slanted next to the fence, so Kelly's head was even with his when she knelt next to him.

She leaned in for the kiss. He tried to remember what it looked like in the movie and tried to kiss her back with the blood rushing to his head. In the movie, Spiderman didn't use his hands when kissing the girl, so Reilly held onto his jacket and tried to concentrate on the kiss and not the pressure building behind his eyes and the top of his head. It didn't work.

He turned his head with a chuckle. "OK, this one's out."

Kelly's laugh made him smile even more. "Well, it looked good in the movie."

"Too much pressure in my head," He told her as he sat up and crawled down from the fence. "That's about the 10th movie kiss we've tried to duplicate."

"And I liked them all," Kelly giggled.

"I liked them all except that one." Reilly leaned in and kissed her cheek. "So, now which one?" He was enjoying their new game. It turned out to be one of the best ways to kill time on a wintery afternoon.

"Your turn to come up with one."

"How about the old western ones? I've seen it in a couple movies."

"Show me." She looked up at him and smiled.

"OK, you have to act like you're trying to walk away from me and I pull you in and we smash faces."

"Smash faces?" She gasped, her eyes wide in disbelief. "That sounds romantic!"

Reilly chuckled. "Here, I'll show you."

He took her hand and she walked away from him, pulling her arm hard, she flew back towards him and he bent in for the kiss. Her back was stiff and she was leaning away from him so he missed her lips and hit her jaw causing another round of giggles.

"You can't be so stiff." He told her with a grin.

"You were going to smash our faces! What did you expect me to do?" Her giggles were like chimes in the winter air.

"Let's try it again." He said.

She walked away from him and he pulled her back hard, this time she flew back at him, leaning towards him and they connected so hard they both jumped back, hands at their sore mouths.

Laughing, they repeated the move until they got it right.

"That one's fun," Reilly grinned at her.

"Once it didn't hurt," Her green eyes sparkled in amusement.

"Your turn this time."

"How about the one from The Notebook?" She took his hand, lacing her fingers in his and they walked toward the barn.

"I don't know that one."

"My phone is in my car. Do you have your phone? I can look it up and show you."

Reilly shook his head. "It's in the house. Let's go look it up on the computer."

Hand-in-hand they walked to the house, laughing at their kissing experiments.

No one was in sight as they made their way to the computers in the library.

Kelly researched the kiss and showed it to Reilly.

"So I grab your head as we start the kiss and you jump up and put your legs around me." Reilly watched the scene again.

"Yeah, can you hold me up?" She asked in concern.

"I guess we'll find out," he chuckled. "Since we're on the verge of a snow storm, there isn't much we can do about the rain…unless we stand in the shower."

She giggled again. "I don't think we should go that far."

He moved the chairs out of their way and he placed his feet apart, faced her and braced himself. She stepped up to him and they moved together for the kiss. He placed a hand on both sides of her face and pulled her into him the final couple inches. As their lips touched, she jumped to wrap her legs around him and he stumbled backwards, tripped and rolled to the ground, ending the kiss in a burst of laughter.

When Reilly looked up, Dru was standing over him, amusement in her eyes.

"Hi, Mom." He stood and helped an embarrassed and giggling Kelly to her feet.

"What are you doing?" His mom smiled.

"We're re-enacting great movie kisses." Kelly explained, trying to contain her giggles.

"Well, that sounds like fun." She was wearing her hair in Reilly's favorite style; loose down her back and no hat. Her blue eyes shined in amusement.

"Which was your favorite movie kiss?" Kelly asked.

"John Wayne and Maureen O'Hara in the Quiet Man, when the storm was coming in." Dru said without hesitation as the three of them walked to the kitchen. "Very emotional…very epic…and they were a spectacular couple."

"I like that one too." Reilly nodded. "We hadn't thought of that yet."

"Dru?" Kelly turned to her. "What's an epic kiss?"

"An epic kiss…one that rocks all the others." She explained with a knowing grin.

"Do you have an epic kiss?" Kelly asked hesitantly.

Dru smiled, from the inside out. "Yes."

"Do tell!" Kelly said excitedly.

"I'm not sure I want to hear this." Reilly grimaced.

Dru chuckled and leaned her hip against the kitchen counter to face the teenagers. Kelly was seventeen and Reilly would be seventeen the next month.

"It was the first kiss with Jack."

"Good to hear!" Reilly placed a hand over his chest in feigned relief.

"Is it too personal to share?" Kelly asked politely.

Dru shook her head and shrugged, "I don't think so. It was the night before Rooster's surgery. I was in the living room looking out the large window to the front pasture, thinking of what it would be like to lose another one of the herd." She sighed. "Scott had just told us how Wade broke his arm…it was horrible thinking of Wade going through that…and Rooster? If we lost Rooster, too?"

"Sounds depressing," Kelly whispered with a lifted brow.

Dru chuckled. "When I heard Jack come into the room, I turned, then he did the one thing I had wanted him to do for years…he held out his arms to hold me…console me." She smiled softly, her eyes looking beyond the teenagers and into the past. "After a few minutes of holding him, enjoying the warmth of him, finally knowing what it was like to have his arms around me…I leaned back, looked into his eyes, and all the emotions I'd held back for years rushed to the surface, his lips were right there…and I just couldn't stop myself. I leaned in and kissed him. Soft and nervous at first…but then…I just melted into him. For years I'd stopped myself from even touching him, but it was time and we gave in and…it was like we'd been together forever and would never be apart again."

"How long did it last?" Kelly asked breathlessly, entranced by the emotion in Dru's voice.

"For hours," Dru smiled at the two of them. "We didn't talk, didn't ask for anything more…we just held each other and kissed…making up for the years we had wanted to be together but were afraid to take the chance."

"Hours?" Reilly's eyes shot up in surprise.

Dru chuckled and nodded. "Somewhere in the night we fell asleep on the couch. Scott and Grayson woke us up…grinning down on us. Grayson said 'It's about dang time' then walked into the kitchen."

Reilly leaned back and looked at his stepmother. "That is epic."

"It was epic." She sighed, her eyes still misty from the memory. "And, now, every time I'm away from him, and then I see him again…I remember that first kiss and fall in love with him all over again."

"Dang, Mom." Reilly exhaled.

Dru shook her head lightly and stood up from the counter. "Alright, enough with the past, I have work to do." She grinned at the teenagers then walked to the back door. "I have to run in to town for supplies for this weekend and Christmas at the ranch. I'll see you two later."

The teenagers followed her out the back door and stood on the porch to watch her leave.

"Let's go back out to the barn." Reilly took Kelly's hand and they walked to Rufio's stall.

The last two summers and this Christmas break, kissing Kelly had been great; he loved every minute of it. But they had gotten to the point that kissing wasn't enough, he wanted more…but he wasn't sure he was ready for more or that she was. He wasn't sure. He'd never had the feelings for Kelly that his mom said about his dad.

"Reilly?" Kelly looked up at him, the amusement of the day gone, replaced by doubt.

"Yeah?"

"Do you think we can ever have that?"

"I was just asking myself the same thing." He admitted with a sigh.

Rufio stuck his head over the stall door, looking for treats or attention. They gave him attention.

"I like kissing you, Kelly…always have."

"It's always been fun." Kelly agreed. "But, I've never had the emotion that Dru was just talking about."

He shook his head with a tinge of impending doom. He looked into her concerned green eyes and told her the truth. "I haven't either."

"Kiss me, Reilly." Kelly stepped to him, a hint of desperation in her eyes. "Kiss me and see if we can get that emotion."

Reilly wrapped his arms around her and leaned down, as their lips touched, he tried to feel the emotion of love, instead of just the enjoyment of kissing her.

They broke the kiss at the same time, took a step back away from each other, then looked into each other's eyes…realizing there would never be that emotion…they would never love each other as more than friends.

Reilly's heart hurt as he saw the tears in her eyes.

"If we don't have it with each other…" Kelly started, the loss already trembling in her voice.

"Then we need to move on…to find the right person." Reilly nodded, a sadness overwhelming him, the tears starting to rise. How could this happen so fast?

"I can't kiss you again, Reilly." A tear slowly trickled down her cheek. "I would think of every one as our last and I just don't think I could do that. It wouldn't be fun anymore, it would be…heart breaking." She gently wiped the tear away, the sadness of the situation realized.

He nodded, his shoulders drooping, understanding because he couldn't do it either.

Reilly reached out and pulled her to his chest and wrapped his arms around her, for what he knew…was the last time. She wrapped her arms around his waist and lay her head on his shoulder. They held each other tightly.

"I remember the first time I saw you." She said, her voice shook with emotion. "You handed me the lead rope to a horse you brought back from the ranch."

Reilly nodded. "I remember thinking how pretty your red hair and green eyes were." It was if it was the day before. He remembered how just touching her hand made him jump…stumble into the horse trailer. His eyes glistened with tears. "You were my first kiss."

"O'Reilly…" She smiled hesitantly and he smiled in return at the memory.

"I will love you forever." He swallowed hard to keep the emotions in check then buried his face into her shoulder. "You'll always be my first love, Kelly."

"And you mine," She whispered with a breathless sigh. "But somewhere, out there, is our epic love."

CHAPTER TWO

Reilly sat on the tailgate of his blue truck and watched Kelly's car make its way down the long driveway.

"What's up with you?" His dad asked as he leaned against the truck.

"Kelly's gone."

"I thought her Christmas vacation with her grandparents was all weekend…not leaving for home until Monday?"

"No, she's gone." Reilly looked at his dad sadly. "She's headed to The Stables to tell Grace goodbye, then she's gone."

His dad looked at him in surprise. "You broke up?"

Reilly nodded.

"Three days before Christmas and the two of you break up after a year and a half?"

Reilly nodded again.

"Are you alright?"

Again, a nod.

"Do you want to talk about it?"

Reilly shrugged.

His dad moved from leaning on the truck to sitting on the tailgate next to him.

"Do you have an epic kiss?" Reilly asked him.

"What?"

"Do you have an epic kiss? One that rocks all the others." Reilly said, using his mom's words.

His dad was quiet for a while before he spoke, "Well, I would say I had two."

"Two?" Reilly looked up at him in surprise.

"I've had two loves; your mother and Dru."

Reilly nodded. "Can you tell me about them?"

"With your mother; it was when she was pregnant with you. Right after we found out about it actually. She went swimming, which wasn't an exercise she usually did, but she was concerned about gaining weight during the pregnancy." He paused and sighed. "That evening, she started having stomach pains, really bad. I rushed her to the hospital thinking she was losing you, but it was just a pulled muscle."

"You can pull a muscle swimming?"

"Yeah, she over did the new exercise, is what the doctor said. That night, when I brought her home, we stood in the middle of the kitchen still scared and I was holding her." He looked at Reilly. "I told you that you weren't planned."

Reilly nodded.

"It was that night, while I was holding her, that we realized how much we actually wanted you and that we were going to be a family…a real family, forever."

Reilly looked at his dad sorrowfully, it was her forever…not theirs. Forever for her was 5 and a ½ years, until she died in her sleep.

"We stood in the middle of the kitchen floor and I kissed her…she kissed me, and we let each other know that we were there for each other for the long run." Jack sighed. "One kiss said so much…it was epic."

Reilly sat quietly thinking how wonderful and how sad the story was.

"What about the second?" He finally asked his dad. "With Mom…she told us her epic kiss earlier." Reilly half smiled at his dad.

"Please let it be with me and not Nick." His dad laughed.

Reilly chuckled. "Really, Dad? I thought you didn't have a problem with Nick."

"I don't, but if she has an epic kiss, that isn't with me, it shouldn't be with someone I know or with a guy like Nick."

Reilly chuckled again. "Like Nick?"

"We all see the way women look at him. I think the word handsome has been thrown around a couple times or a hundred." He laughed.

"From what I understand, women seem to think you're handsome, too." Reilly felt the sadness start to lift. "Grace said you two are different kinds of handsome."

"And what are those?" His dad seemed amused.

"She said you're a charming, sophisticated handsome."

"Well, that's not bad." His dad grinned, then looked at him with an 'I'm not sure I want to know this' look. "And Nick?"

"Grace says he's ruggedly handsome."

"Ah, man…" His dad whined.

"Which one would you rather be?"

"Both! Every man wants to be both." His dad shook his head in amusement.

"It doesn't matter anyway, she said her epic kiss was with you." Reilly grinned.

"Oh, thank goodness." His dad said in mock relief.

"So what was yours with her?"

"The first kiss," His dad grinned, the light in his eyes was the same as Dru's had when she told her side of the story.

"The night before Rooster's surgery," Reilly nodded.

"I was upstairs with you and Wade, making sure you were alright for the night. Wade asked if I would check on Dru, said she was sad and had been there with Rooster from the beginning. As I walked down the stairs, I knew she was in the living room alone. I had spent years not touching her…not wanting to cross the line with her, if it didn't work out…" He shook his head at the thought. "I was terrified as I came around the corner and saw her sitting on the end of the couch looking out the window. I knew she was emotional when it came to the horses, and just hearing about how Wade broke his arm…she was in a very vulnerable state of mind, which is extremely rare for Dru." He paused and looked down the driveway as if looking into the past. "When she looked up at me, with those beautiful blue eyes shining from the tears, I had to take that chance; the chance to contain my feelings to help her, to hold her and let her know it would be OK." He looked at Reilly then back down the road. "I wrapped my arms around her, she lay her head on my shoulders and I stood there trying to focus my brain on anything but the way she felt in my arms."

He shook his head. "It worked until she looked up at me, with those mesmerizing eyes of hers, and we were just inches away… Before I knew it, we were kissing…she pulled me tighter, and I realized she'd wanted it as much as I did. That first kiss, lasted forever…hours. Hours of trying to make up for all that time we'd lost by not taking a chance. I don't think we spoke one word to each other…afraid to break the spell, I guess."

"It was epic."

"It was." His dad nodded with a loving smile.

"It was epic for both of you."

His dad chuckled. "Good to know."

Scott's truck turned into the driveway and they watched him approach. Reilly's dad turned to him. "Epic kissing have something to do with you two breaking up?"

Reilly nodded but didn't explain.

They remained on the tailgate as Scott stepped out of his truck.

"Isn't it a bit cold to be hanging around outside?" Scott asked as he approached with his hands deep in his pockets.

Reilly shook his head. His dad turned and looked at him and Reilly nodded.

"Reilly and Kelly broke up." His dad told Scott.

"Dang, Reilly, you guys were together for a long time." Scott frowned.

Reilly nodded.

"Never really sure what to say in these situations," Scott sighed.

"Did you ever have an epic kiss?" Reilly asked him, somewhat embarrassed, but they could blame it on the breakup later.

Scott looked at him in amused disbelief then looked to Reilly's dad who answered. "Epic kissing had something to do with the breakup."

Scott nodded, then stared at the ground while he thought about the question. Finally he looked up. "Two of them. Halloween a couple years ago…"

"Tinkerbell?" Reilly's dad looked at him in disbelief. "You're not telling him about that!"

Reilly chuckled at his dad's expression and Scott shook his head.

"The first kiss," Scott explained.

"You call Jordan, Tink." Reilly said. "So she dressed up like Tinkerbell?"

"Scott…" Reilly's dad shook his head.

"Chill, Jack." Scott laughed. "Yes, I call her Tink because she's so tiny, she looks like a pixie. A couple years ago, we decided to go to a Halloween costume party. Jack, Grayson and I dressed in white shirts, black hats, blue jeans, and cowboy boots."

"Original." Reilly teased.

"We were George Strait times three." Scott chuckled. "Dru and Leah were dressed in the exact same thing but they were Loretta Lynn. We're all standing in the kitchen waiting for Jordan, who was supposed to be wearing the same thing but wearing a blonde wig."

"She walked down the stairs in that Tinkerbell costume and I just about lost it." Scott exhaled loudly with a glint in his eyes. "But the whole thing, what made it so epic? It was…how…vulnerable she was…the risk she was taking…the chance in wearing the costume, knowing that she would be teased that night and for years to come…but she did it for me, left herself out there emotionally….for me. That was, just…" He sighed again. "The first kiss was telling her how much I loved her and understood what she did for me." Scott shook his head and looked at Reilly. "It was epic…and end of that story."

"They didn't make it to the Halloween party…and none of us have said a word to her about it." Reilly's dad said with a chuckle.

They all three smiled.

"I won't say anything to anyone." Reilly assured Scott. "The second?"

"The night she fell into the fire at the ranch," Scott's eyes glazed over from the memory. "We were on the hillside. I had her sitting on the ground between my legs and was leaning over her to protect her from the rain. She looked up at me and we both realized just how bad it could have been. At that moment, in that kiss…we were the only two people in the world and just let each other know…" He stopped when his voice cracked from the emotion.

Reilly turned away from Scott and looked down the driveway.

They all turned as Grayson walked out of the house carrying a large box full of Christmas gifts to take to the ranch. All three moved from the truck and to the house to help.

Once the truck was loaded, packed tight with Christmas gifts, they loaded the stock trailer with six of the Tagger Herd including Rufio and Cooper. The rest would be loaded into Dru's trailer the next day.

Reilly waited until Grayson latched the back gate of the horse trailer before he asked the same question to him. "Do you have an epic kiss?"

"What?" His uncle looked at him curiously.

"Reilly and Kelly broke up…something to do with epic kisses." Scott told him.

"Dang, Reilly, sorry to hear about that. I like Kelly…does Grace know?" He asked, clearly concerned.

"Kelly was going to The Stables to say goodbye to her." Reilly answered sadly, his eyes dropping to the ground to hide the glisten the rising tears were causing.

"Why don't you ride to the ranch with me? Change of scenery always helps." Grayson told him.

"I don't have anything packed yet." Reilly answered and looked to his dad. He really wanted to be alone and away from the rest of the family when they all found out.

"I'll get everything and bring it up tomorrow." His dad offered.

"Thanks Dad," Reilly smiled then hesitantly gave his dad a hug. "For everything..."

Reilly quickly turned and jumped in the passenger side of the truck.

They rode the first half hour in silence. Reilly tried to figure out how, within a half hour, he and Kelly were kissing and having fun, then she was gone…forever… without a bad word being said between them.

"Do you want to talk about it?" Grayson asked.

Reilly shook his head and stared at the passing scenery.

"Well, to tell you about my epic kiss, I have to tell you something that not even Scott and Dru know."

Reilly turned to him in surprise. "I won't tell anyone…if you're sure you want to tell me."

Grayson nodded, "There should be someone else out there that knows what a wonderful, beautiful woman Leah is, besides me."

"We all know that." Reilly looked at him.

"Not the way I mean," Grayson shook his head and continued to look straight ahead at the road. "If she wasn't the special woman she is, we wouldn't have Gracie and Sadie in our lives."

"That would suck." Reilly smiled.

"Yes, it would." Grayson chuckled, then sighed.

CHAPTER THREE

"After our parents and grandparents were killed in the accident, and I relented to staying in college, I went through a really angry stage of my life." Grayson started. "Dealing with the loss, dealing with Dru having to bear the brunt of all the work…which, even though I was only 19, I was the oldest son, and I should have taken it on. I spent every minute in books or ranch work, and feeling guilty the whole time…it just got to be too much."

Reilly kept quiet, using Dru's example of knowing when to speak and when not to…so the person could tell their story at their own pace.

"The first time I saw Leah was the morning of the accident. I was late for class and ran in, taking a seat next to two beautiful girls. But it was the blond one…her eyes lit up when she smiled at me and sparkled when I winked at her…she was the one." He took in a breath and let it out slowly. "Seconds later the professor is telling me about the car accident.

"I was out of school for a week and when I returned the last thing on my mind was girls. But, Leah had already decided it wasn't the right time and had moved to the back of the room, I only saw glimpses of her until spring.

"Then the holidays…we tried so hard to make it good for Nikki and Matt. Nikki was three and excited about Santa and all the lights…we tried." He sighed again. "Luckily, Matt was too young and Nikki was too enamored with everything else to notice how mentally lacking all three of us were that Christmas.

"By spring break and branding, I had blown my top a couple times at college, getting into fights and screaming matches with people. Busted a couple holes in walls when I just couldn't hold in the anger. I'd go back the next day and fix them.

"A couple professors had tried to talk to me but I wouldn't listen, I'd just walk away like they weren't talking to me…figured it was better than hitting them to make them shut up.

"Spring break came, and I used one of the younger ranch horses, and paid the price by getting my head smashed against a tree and getting knocked out for about five minutes. Scared Dru and Scott…so, that made me even guiltier and angrier."

"When I got back to school, I started drinking on the nights I didn't go to the ranch. It put me in a haze, numbed the pain…until the next day. And that made me feel guilty and angry."

Grayson sighed and remained quiet for a few minutes. Reilly was silent; wondering how a story like this could end in an epic kiss.

"Leah approached me while my face was still black and blue and swollen. Brave woman, I thought, and asked her out. I enjoyed dinner, which made me angry…that I should be having a good time, knowing that Scott and Dru were working so hard and I was having a good time. I didn't even try to kiss her that night, nor the next three times we went out. Then I did…boy that was…"

"Epic?" Reilly asked then saw Grayson shake his head.

"Awful…worst kiss ever," Grayson chuckled.

"Serious? The way you two are now…I figured every kiss was perfect."

"Not even close," He glanced over at Reilly. "Don't ever kiss a woman when you're drunk and mad at the world."

"OK, noted." Reilly nodded.

"Just before the date, I called Dru and she had been fixing fence where elk had broken through…in the dark with just the headlights from her truck. Guilt and anger for not being there just exploded in me. I drank too much at dinner…to the point that Leah even took the chance to mention it. I just grumbled at her and told her if she didn't like it she could leave."

"Did she?"

"No, she just got pissed at me and said she didn't wait around for six months for me to walk away when it got too tough. So I kissed her, an angry drunk kiss that cut and bruised her lip."

"More guilt and anger?" Reilly nodded.

"Exactly," Grayson nodded. "The next day, when I saw her lip, I just about died…started crying right in the middle of campus. She grabbed my arm and pulled me to the side between a tree and one of the buildings. All the emotions I'd been holding in since the accident just started flooding out of me. She just stood patiently, holding my arm and waited.

"Once I stopped and apologized for hurting her, she walked me down to the fitness center where they had the boxing bags and told me to hit it. I'm still in my jeans and cowboy boots, hung over, eyes red from crying and she has me punching this bag hanging from the ceiling. So I did. For about an hour I tried to beat out every bit of anger I had in me. She fought off anyone that dared come near me to try and make me stop. Once I couldn't lift my arms anymore, we went to the cafeteria where she made me eat." He chuckled softly. "I think I ate half the food there that day.

"Then, she got my books. We did all the work we both needed to have done for the next day and then went for a walk. She hadn't met Dru yet, but she told me it sounded like Dru needed to have the overload of work in her life to fill the void left by our parents and grandparents death. I would be selfish if I took that away from her."

Grayson glanced at Reilly. "She was dead on. Dru had to have that…so did Scott." He was silent for a while. "Leah had a tough time when she went through the loss of her parents, so she understood we all needed something."

"What happened to her parents?"

"Leah doesn't talk about it…it's her story to tell."

"I understand," Reilly nodded.

"For the next couple of months, until we were out of school, I went to the fitness center and punched the bag every night."

"What about the kiss?" Reilly frowned.

Grayson smiled. "She wouldn't let me kiss her again until the anger was gone and I was back to being myself again. Until classes were done that year, we were nothing more than friends. She stuck by me for MONTHS, helping me finish my classes that year, and working through the anger.

"The first time I took her to the ranch we drove straight to Rider's Point, where we had spread the ashes, and I introduced her to my parents and grandparents. On the tallest point of the ranch, with a breeze in her hair, and nothing but the mountains and sky to witness, I swept her into the first kiss, what you kids call the movie kiss, and let her know how much everything she had done for me had meant, for us then and into the future…to our girls.

"That, Reilly, was epic."

Reilly felt the goose bumps raise on his arms and the tears well. He glanced at Grayson, his were glistening too but he had a smile on his face.

"Every time I kiss her like that, I'm apologizing to her for the first horrendous kiss and thanking her for everything she has done for me since."

"You're right," Reilly said. "Leah is a wonderful and beautiful lady."

They sat quietly a moment then Reilly looked over at Grayson and smiled. "So what you're telling me…is Sadie gets her angry streak from you…not Dru?"

Grayson chuckled. "Don't tell Dru that."

"I won't."

"So, now that you know my story…can I ask what happened between you and Kelly?"

Reilly sighed. "We realized that we weren't…the right one's for each other. We enjoyed kissing but we wouldn't be anything more."

"Did you ever…"

Reilly shook his head. "No, not that I didn't want to, but it never seemed right and we agreed we were too young. Honestly, I was afraid that it would ruin our make-out sessions." He smiled. "I just really enjoyed kissing her, but it was time to move on…she should have the guy that makes her feel special" Reilly let out a long wishful sigh. "Kelly should have an epic kiss every day."

He returned to staring out the side window. He let the sadness take over, wishing he could force himself to love her enough to give her the epic love she deserved.

###

Reilly, riding Rufio, looked down the hill and saw Matt headed back up; Trooper slipping in the deep snow with each step. Bart, head down against the wind and swirling snow, was trotting alongside the horse and rider. Both Reilly and Matt were wearing long full-length coats to keep themselves warm. Scarves were wrapped tightly around their faces and over their cowboy hats. The wind was strong on the side of the mountain.

"That snow is slicker than snot," Matt yelled up at him as the trio of rider, dog, and horse finally reached the top.

"It's coming down hard, too." Reilly looked up at the sky, the brim of his cowboy hat protecting his eyes from the large snowflakes.

"I'll feel better when the family finally gets here." Matt nodded and they turned down the road towards Circle 50.

"No doubt it will be a white Christmas." Reilly grinned, but it went unseen behind the scarf. "At least here, sounds like we're going from snow to 70 degree weather in Texas…too hot for this time of year."

"I agree." Matt nodded then pointed at a small herd of elk walking along the fence line, heads down against the cold wind.

"It never gets old." Reilly nodded. They all loved seeing the animals on the ranch.

Then Matt pointed again. In the distance were three trucks pulling horse trailers moving slowly along the snow covered road. The family had arrived for Christmas.

"Let's get the horses to Circle 50, then we'll go over to the ranch." Matt yelled over the sudden gust of wind that blew snowflakes in a tornado around them.

"They should have the fire ready for us when we get there." Reilly hollered back, not sure if Matt heard him.

When they arrived at Circle 50, they left the horses in the barn with food and water then loaded into Matt's truck for the drive. Bart nestled comfortably in the back behind Matt's seat.

"Did Lucas make it?' Reilly asked as he buckled himself into the truck.

Matt nodded. "Should be in one of those trucks. Tessa and Alex should be there, too."

"Going to be a full bunkhouse this year." Reilly smiled. Having everyone together was always fun, especially at Christmas.

"Sorry to hear about you and Kelly." Matt glanced over at him.

Reilly just nodded. It was better today than yesterday, and tomorrow, especially being Christmas Eve, would even be that much better. The sense of loss would come in June when she didn't come to town to work at The Stables.

"We'll stay in touch on Facebook." Reilly sighed.

"Not the same as having a kissing partner though." Matt grinned. "But, you turn 17 next month…you'll have plenty more."

"And you turn 21 next month…how many have you had?' Reilly asked with a raised brow.

Matt chuckled. "More than a couple, thanks to Nikki. She kept introducing me to girls when we were in college…now that's a sister!"

"Any of them, you have an epic kiss with?" Reilly asked, his face warming.

"A what?"

Reilly explained the kiss. "I asked Grayson, Scott, Mom and Dad yesterday about theirs."

"I don't think I've had mine yet." Matt nodded with a frown. "What did you figure out, knowing their answers? Did it help?"

Reilly shrugged, he had been analyzing the stories all day. "Well, except for one of Scott's, that was borderline…and led to more…none of them have anything to do with sex and everything to do with love, emotions, feelings, history, caring, one or both people being vulnerable for the other person."

"A relationship," Matt nodded.

"Yeah, but…" Reilly sighed. "I had all of those with Kelly, except the 'right' kind of love."

"I haven't even had that." Matt said gloomily. "And I'm 4 years ahead of you."

"Why?"

Matt shrugged. "The last girl said I wanted too much out of her."

"What does that mean?"

"I wanted to go and do and adventure. She wanted to go for strolls, or watch a movie, or just sit and 'be' together."

"Sounds boring."

"Exactly!" Matt nodded vigorously. "I'm not ready for that nesting stuff yet, I want to play, and would love to have someone to do that with."

"Where are you going to find a girl that wants to sky-dive, dangle off of cliffs, scuba-dive, bike, kayak…and all those other things that you do?"

"I've found a couple, but they just don't…" Matt shook his head. "I don't know."

"Hold your interest?"

"Yeah, that's it…I just get bored with them." Matt nodded and pulled in next to their mother's truck.

They quickly jumped out to helped unload all the horse trailers.

In the middle of the driveway, with large snowflakes falling around them, his mom stopped him. Her eyes were full of love and concern.

"What happened yesterday? I find you guys laughing on the floor one minute and fifteen minutes later she's driving away, forever?"

Reilly didn't answer, he just shrugged and threw his arms around her.

"Thanks, Mom." He whispered.

"For what?" She asked when he stepped back.

"For loving me and loving dad. You are both….epic." Reilly grinned at her.

She looked at him like he had lost his mind then she sighed. "So all is good? You're OK with this?"

Reilly nodded. "It was the right decision. Kelly deserves more than I can give her."

"And you deserve more." She returned his smile.

"We all deserve more." Reilly grinned. "We all deserve to have epic loves and lives. You and Dad have that."

"We do." His dad said as he walked up behind Dru and wrapped her in his arms, kissing her cheek. Then he picked her up and threw her in the snow.

CHAPTER FOUR

Reilly walked out of the barn and walked quickly to his waiting family and friends. Most of them were standing in the driveway between the ranch house and the bunkhouse. Wade, Nick, and Alex were still in the barn.

Christmas at the ranch was always fun but this time it was going to be OVER THE TOP! So many surprises! And this one was big!

Christmas at the ranch, the previous year, was Nick's first real Christmas and he wanted to make this year even better with their surprise.

A month before, Nick had approached Wade and Reilly about helping him with a Christmas surprise. Once hearing the project they said yes immediately. Since the project was at Nick's property in Lenore, and would take up most of their weekends prior to Christmas, the challenge was getting Tessa's approval to let Alex help. Alex would have been very disappointed if he was the only boy, going to the ranch for Christmas, that didn't get to help.

Not taking any chances, Nick had Reilly and Wade ask Tessa if Alex could join them. Luckily she understood how important it would be for Alex to be part of the project, even though she didn't know what it was.

While they worked on the project, Nick told the boys about his bull riding days. To Reilly, it sounded like a great adventure and made him that much more excited about going to college with Grace and going on adventures with the rodeo teams.

Reilly turned and looked back at the barn. No sign of them. He quickened his pace.

"It's a good thing it's warm out here in the snow." His mom smiled at him.

"I'm just glad we have lots of snow this year." Nora added. Reilly chuckled at her comment.

"So what's going on?" Grace asked with a frown. She had been upset Reilly wouldn't tell her the secret.

"In just a minute," Reilly said. "Everyone here?"

They all looked around. The Tagger Trio and all the family, Lucas, Tessa, Jessup, and Cora were all there.

Reilly lifted his phone to record their reactions for the group in the barn to see. He turned to Lucas and Nikki. "Whistle!"

The two looked at him and laughed but did as he said. The two loudest whistlers made a competition out of it and tried to out whistle each other.

"Ok!" Reilly grimaced with a smile. "That's going to be loud on the recording."

Holding the camera on the family he turned his head to the barn and watched Nick walk straight out of the barn about thirty feet, he turned and looked at the family waiting patiently for the big surprise. Reilly waved to let him know everything was a go.

Nick waved back, looked into the barn and nodded.

The first thing they saw was Nick's horse, Blue, walking out of the barn. The blue roan was wearing a black shiny harness and he elegantly pulled a restored antique sleigh behind him. It was deep green, with gold trim and had a tall driver's seat up front and two bench seats in the back that faced each other. They had placed large wreaths with red bows on the sides to decorate it for the holiday. Bells could be heard ringing with each step of the horse. Large flakes of snow fell quietly completing the vision.

Wade and Alex were on the driver's bench. Both were grinning and Alex was proudly holding the reins.

"Oh my!" Reilly heard Tessa over the top of everyone else's exclamations and shouts. He turned quickly and looked at her shocked expression as her son drove the sleigh towards them. "Alex…" Tears ran down her cheeks as she smiled proudly at her son.

Reilly grinned; it was worth all the hard work they put into the sleigh just for her reaction.

He turned and watched the majestic sight of the horse and sleigh slowly making their way up the drive. The snow covered mountains, barn, and fences behind them gave the horse and sleigh a spectacular backdrop. Nick was walking next to them, just close enough to jump on the sleigh if something happened.

Wade and Alex's grins were electrifying as they reached the group and Alex pulled the horse to a stop, with a "Whoa".

"Merry Christmas, ya'll!" The two boys yelled at the happy and excited group.

"You look like one of those Christmas cards!" Nora yelled, as Nick helped her and Sadie into the back of the sleigh; after hugging him first.

Reilly kept the recording going as everyone greeted the two boys.

Nick stepped back and let everyone check out their surprise. He was grinning happily which made his brownish green eyes under the brown cowboy hat shine.

Tessa walked up to Alex and smiled up at him. Alex couldn't have been happier, or prouder, as he looked at his mom.

"Crying again, Mom?" He teased with a grin.

"Of course." She laughed.

Reilly zoomed in to get the beautiful expression on her face. She turned quickly, stepped up to Nick and threw her arms around his neck. Reilly chuckled at the surprised look on the man's face as he returned her embrace. She stepped back, looked up at him, then leaned in and gave him a kiss on the cheek.

Nick smiled down at her then laughed at something she said. Her eyes were shining in happiness. Before Reilly knew it, Nick had bent over, swooped her up in his arms and set her up in the sleigh behind her son. Everyone laughed at her scream of surprise.

For hours the boys took the family for rides. Blue was a perfect gentleman and accepted all the attention from the kids and adults.

The barn was full of happy family and friends as Nick and Reilly removed the harness from the blue roan.

"Where did you find it?" Grayson asked while running a hand over the back of the sleigh.

"Sandpoint," Nick answered. "I saw it advertised on the internet and went up and bought it the first of November."

"It looked really bad when I first saw it." Reilly added. "But every weekend it looked better and better."

"When it came back from the painters…" Nick shook his head and grinned. "It was worth all the time sanding."

"It's beautiful." Dru smiled. "I've always wished we had one up here."

Nick smiled at his ex-wife. "I can't believe how much I enjoyed last year. I wanted to do something special for this year."

"Well, you accomplished that." Nikki slid her arm through his and squeezed. "I want an evening ride in the moonlight with my beau."

"I'll make sure you have that, with someone else driving besides me." Nick chuckled. "I also bought an old buckboard wagon to restore. I thought you could use it for the kid's clinics at The Stables."

"Can we help restore it too?" Alex asked excited.

"I think the four of us made a great team," Nick nodded. "If your Mom says yes."

"Mom?" Alex turned.

"Of course," Tessa answered. "This was such a great surprise for us, I can't imagine how the kids are going to react at the next clinic."

As Alex and Wade celebrated and made plans, Reilly glanced over at Grace. She was across the barn sitting on a bale of hay talking with Leah and Sadie. A number of times, the last eight years, he would look at her and try to mentally tell her to turn and look at him. It didn't work very often, and he was pretty sure when it did it was just a coincidence. He dipped his head down and stared at her, thinking her name over and over. Chuckling internally, he was about to give up when she actually turned to him and tilted her head.

"What?" She mouthed.

Reilly laughed openly, confusing everyone around him.

He shook his head and walked towards her. Halfway over, his stomach started to ache. It wasn't a sick ache, it was a foreboding ache. One of those 'gut feelings' he'd had before.

Grace was wrapped in her mother's arms…safe and sound…so why the foreboding ache now?

He mentally shook it off and joined the happy group.

CHAPTER FIVE

The moonlight on the snow caused a natural light that reflected through the windows. It looked like daylight in the bunkhouse and Reilly could see everyone clearly.

His parents were snuggled in the bed below him. On the same wall, in the next bed was Alex in the upper bunk and Grayson and Leah in the lower. Then the top bunk was empty with Scott and Jordan in the lower. Lucas was in the lower bunk of the last bed with no one in the upper. Across the aisle was Nora in the top bunk and Nick in the lower. Then Sadie and Nikki; Wade and Matt; then Grace and Tessa by the door, directly across from Reilly.

Bart was snuggled next to Matt and Mavis was snuggled next to Nikki.

It was Christmas morning. Pretty soon the coffee pot would click and the aroma of coffee would take over the smell of the pine tree that held their freshly crafted ornaments and topped their gifts.

One big Christmas surprise was done and everyone delighted by the sleigh. Reilly was involved in one more…and he was so excited he could barely contain himself. He reached under his pillow and touched the box that hadn't disappeared while he was sleeping. The excitement was too much!

Reilly giggled, which caused Grace to giggle, because, of course, she was awake, too. Then Alex giggled…Tessa giggled…then Wade and Nora together. Sadie didn't just giggle, she laughed, which caused a round of giggles and laughter from the rest of the family and friends. The whole room was awake, only needing a giggle as an alarm.

All the kids sat up and waited as Matt handed each their Christmas stocking. Laughs and giggles filled the air as they emptied their stockings and found their candy and gifts. Cora and Jessup walked into the bunkhouse from the house, Cora carrying a huge plate of cinnamon rolls. Everyone's favorite Christmas morning breakfast.

They elected Lucas as the person of the year to hand out the gifts. Nick had done it the year before.

Using his accent to entertain, the Christmas merriment continued as the gifts under the tree slowly disappeared.

Reilly sat up excitedly. Now was the big gift. Always the fun one of the year; it was the gift between the Tagger Trio. Two years ago Scott bought all the adults a rafting trip, which ended up as a honeymoon for his parents.

Last year was Grayson's turn and he gave mini-vacations to each of the Trio and spouses. Scott and Jordan's trip was the Texas cutting clinic they attended. His parent's was a trip to the Kentucky Derby and Grayson took Leah to San Francisco, where her parents had met and married.

This year was Dru's turn and she had been exceptionally quiet about her gift.

"OK." She grinned as she took her place in front of family and friends. "My turn!"

Dru nodded to Matt and he stepped to the door.

"This year we have had some pretty good battles." She said to her brothers.

"About what?" Grayson asked.

"There's only one I can think of," Scott laughed. "That was the ride back from looking at the Zanger bull in Riggins."

The Trio laughed at their inside joke.

"I still say it was you, Scott." Grayson laughed.

"Not me, it had to be Dru." Scott turned to his sister with a raised brow.

"I'd admit it." She chuckled. "I know it was Grayson."

Reilly laughed along with them…it was the classic skunk or human debate.

"But anyway," Dru grinned. "Back to THE battle of the mountain."

"Which is?" Leah asked.

"Patience," Dru giggled, her blue eyes danced in mischief as she nodded at Matt.

Matt stepped out the door and was gone for a couple of minutes. The whole room was quiet as they anxiously awaited his return.

Dru opened the door and Matt walked in with a huge box that barely fit through the door.

"Careful, it's breakable." Dru told him as he set it down in front of her.

"It?" Grayson shook his head.

"You bought one thing for all three of us?" Scott exhaled. "That never works out well, Dru. You don't share well with others."

Dru giggled again. "I'm the oldest, I shouldn't have to share."

"No, I'm the youngest." Scott chuckled. "I shouldn't have to share."

"You've both got it wrong." Grayson corrected them. "The poor middle child shouldn't have to share."

The whole room laughed.

Reilly started bouncing on his bed. This was SO exciting and fun.

"Well, we don't have to share this." Dru reached down in the box. As she rose, she continued. "It was the battle between Circle 50 and Tagger Ranch…who got Mavis and Bart."

When she stood, she had two little Australian blue heeler puppies in her arms.

Reilly laughed and bounced even more.

Grayson and Scott were both grinning as they reached for the puppies. Leah and Jordan were just as excited. Bart and Mavis' heads turned and looked at the new additions, but stayed comfortably tucked in by the legs of the Circle 50 owners.

Reilly looked down at the rest of the adults and kids who were laughing, oohing, and awing.

Alex's face was just plain jealous. Tessa's had a beautiful relaxed smile. Lucas and Nikki, who were sitting together on her bunk, laughed as the puppies began licking their new owner's faces. Cora and Jessup sat in chairs at the farthest end of the aisle, both laughing and looking excitedly at the new family additions.

Nick was on the bed next to them, leaning against the wall with his legs stretched out in front of him. His second Christmas, and he looked as happy and content as Reilly had ever seen him.

A whine came out of the box which caught everyone by surprise.

Reilly turned and watched Dru reach down and lift two more puppies out of the box. Both of them were red heelers. They looked like miniatures of Mavis and Bart.

"Who are those for?" Wade asked excitedly as he petted his dad's new puppy.

"Well, I need one too." She smiled at him and handed a puppy to her husband.

"And the other?" Reilly asked as he climbed off the top bunk and sat next to his dad to greet the puppy.

Dru's smile was wickedly amused. She lifted the puppy in the air and made kissy noises to him. It licked at her, not quite touching her, and wiggled excitedly.

"Who do you think you belong, too?" She asked the puppy, then finished with an evil giggle.

Matt moved the box quickly so she had clear access to the aisle between the beds.

She began slowly walking and giggling mischievously, her head down looking at the puppy cradled in her arms.

Finally, she glanced up at her intended destination.

The look of shock registered on Nick's face. "No, Dru."

"Yes, Nick." She lifted the puppy towards him. "How can you say no to this adorable little face?"

"I've gone all my life without a dog." He shook his head and sat up, no longer relaxed and content.

"And that's 41 years too long." She informed him with a chuckle. "Or is it 42?"

"Three months younger than you, Dru. You do the math." He grinned back while shaking his head.

Nick started to rise out of the bed as Dru got closer, but Sadie and Nora jumped on his legs to hold him down, their laughter matching their aunts.

"You two!" He bounced his legs trying to get them off.

"Too, late." Dru laughed and handed the puppy over to his very reluctant owner.

Nick looked down at the puppy in his arms. "I travel too much."

"Dogs are portable." Dru argued, as she walked back to the front; giggling like Sadie and Nora.

Reilly laughed, as much as his mouth was saying no, Nick's expression was saying yes as he smiled at the puppy. It was looking innocently up at him.

"I hate you, Dru." Nick looked up at her with a smirk.

"I hate you too, Nick." She laughed.

"And the new battle begins." Nikki announced. "What to name the dogs so they don't sound too much alike."

"Well, I'm out of that battle." Nick said, everyone looking at him in surprise. "I have a Blue and a Bay so I might as well have a Red."

"Wow, you sure named her quick, for someone that didn't want her 30 seconds ago." Tessa teased with a laugh.

"Must be the little kid in me." Nick grinned at her and winked at Nora.

"So, that's only three more names." Alex said as he sat next to Nick and played with the puppy.

"Make that two." Scott turned to his wife. "This is Spur."

"From *The Man from Snowy River*!" Jordan exclaimed happily. It was her favorite movie.

"Any ideas for you Grayson?" Reilly glanced over.

Grayson shook his head. "None that come to mind yet, for a female blue puppy."

"You can call her Smurfette!" Sadie giggled, then laughed at her father's expression.

"That's as bad as telling people I'm riding a horse named Buttercup." Grayson shook his head with a chuckle and a wink at Grace.

"How about you, Dru?" Tessa asked. "You've known for a while."

Dru shook her head. "I have a couple ideas but thought my youngest son might help me out." She grinned at Reilly.

"Oh, cool!" Reilly said excitedly, bouncing again. "I've never named a puppy."

"Well, take your time." She gave him the smile that always warmed his heart.

He nodded and started thinking of names. Duke, Sparky, Max…no those wouldn't work.

"Ok, everyone." Dru hollered over all of the excited family. "We have one more gift."

"Really?" Scott asked.

She nodded with an excited smile. "Everyone take your seats."

Once everyone was reseated and looking at her curiously, Dru nodded over at Reilly.

Excitement ran through him as he crawled back up on his bed and retrieved the small box from under his pillow.

He jumped down and looked up to see Sadie, Wade, and Nora hurrying up the aisle to stand next to him. Grace was already alongside of him and Dru had returned to her seat next to his dad.

Once the five were standing together, they grinned at all their family who were looking at them with confused smiles.

Reilly nodded as he turned to Wade.

Wade: "We have a very special gift to give today." He grinned.

Sadie: "This is to show the love and appreciation we have for a special someone." She giggled.

Nora: "Someone works very hard for us and we want to make sure she knows that we understand how much she does for us." She looked at her mother whose eyes opened wide in surprise.

Grace: "Jordan, while we are competing and hopefully receiving awards and prizes, you sit on the sidelines and cheer us on, whether we are doing good or bad. You encourage us every step of the way. " Jordan's eyes glistened.

Reilly: "So, we are presenting you with a gold belt buckle as a trophy for being a world champion aunt, mother, driver, schedule manager, horse wrangler, and supporter."

Reilly held the box out for a very shocked Jordan. She slowly rose and walked to the kids. She kissed and hugged each one of them as she made her way to Reilly.

"I love you, Aunt Jordan." Reilly whispered as she hugged him.

A tear escaped and she quickly wiped it away as she took the box from him and opened it.

"We all designed it and Aunt Dru helped us order it." Grace said proudly. "It has your name across it, of course, but it also has five hearts inside five horse shoes to represent all five of us and the horses too."

"I can't believe you kids did this." She said as more tears fell. "I love all of you."

Hugs and kisses were given again.

Scott already had her belt ready for her to snap it onto. After showing it to everyone, she quickly attached her buckle to the belt and wrapped it around her waist, over her pajamas.

"I love it!" She yelled and grinned at the kids.

Reilly lay in his upper bunk and looked down at his parents snuggled in the lower bunk. They were facing each other with the puppy curled in between them.

He wanted a special name for the puppy, something that had meaning. He thought back to some of the happiest times he'd had which included the Memorial Day weekend ride that he and his parents, along with Jessup had taken. It was just before they got engaged and they had ridden to the ghost town and the hidden cave above the river.

"I have an idea for the puppy name, Mom." Reilly smiled down as they both turned and looked up at him.

"What did you come up with?" Her voice was soft and her eyes looked at him with contented love.

It warmed his heart every time she looked at him like that.

"Name him after the one thing Dad isn't." Reilly grinned.

"Oh, Reilly." She smiled up at him, then looked at his dad and touched her husband's chin lightly with a fingertip. Their eye's radiated with love as they looked at each other. "Your father is everything to me."

Reilly chuckled. "That's corny, even for you, Mom."

They all three laughed.

"Dad's everything but one thing." Reilly said in false seriousness.

"And what am I lacking in, Son?" His dad grinned up at him.

Reilly nodded and frowned. "You'll never be her Indiana Jones."

His mom burst out laughing, her head tilting backwards into the pillow, which was covered in her blonde hair.

His dad laughed too…with a nod. "I have to agree with him on that."

"You're adventurous." She said to her husband.

"To a point." His dad smiled.

Her eyes turned back up to Reilly. "So we call him Indy?"

Reilly grinned and nodded.

"Do you want to go introduce Indy to the group?" She asked.

Reilly quickly slid off the bed and took the puppy out from between his smiling parents. He walked down and announced the puppies name to all the family playing different games throughout the bunkhouse.

Sadie's arms were tightly wrapped around an extra- large stuffed dingo that Lucas had given her for Christmas.

Alex and Wade were supervising Jessup as he tooled the leather in Wade's new roping saddle. He'd outgrown the birthday saddle already that Jessup had tooled a dollar and a rooster into the skirt. A new dollar and rooster were coming to life on the new saddle.

Grayson, Nick and Scott had taken their puppies, tucked warmly into their jackets, out to feed the animals.

By the time he walked down the bunkhouse and back. His mom had moved in closer to his dad, their arms wrapped around each other. They were asleep.

Reilly climbed back onto the top bunk, sat with his legs crossed in front of him, and cradled the puppy in his arms. He glanced down at his sleeping parents, then laughed as the snow covered Grayson, Scott and Nick entered the building and pulled their puppies out from inside their coats.

Reilly sighed at the sight of everyone playing games at the other end of the bunkhouse.

Love wasn't just epic between couples, love was epic within families, too.

And this…was an epic moment.

CHAPTER SIX

"Why are you here?" Grace asked from her bunk across the aisle.

"Well, isn't that a nice greeting." Reilly grinned at her.

"Geez, and she's supposed to be your friend." His dad said from the lower bunk.

"Why are you here? Seriously?" Grace frowned down at his dad too. "You guys are always gone when we wake up the day after Christmas."

"Don't you love us anymore?" His dad chuckled as he snuggled into Dru.

"Of course," Grace looked worriedly between them. "But why?"

"Look outside, Grace." Dru smiled.

Grace leaned over the edge of the bed and looked out the window. "There must be five feet of snow out there!" She announced loudly.

"It's more like three." Grayson laughed from his bed, snuggling with Leah. "But it's still snowing."

"Have you ever had this much snow up here before?" Alex asked from his mom's bed, below Grace. He had left his upper bunk and was laying peacefully with her as they looked through a book of Australia that Nick had gifted him.

"A couple times, when we were kids," Scott answered.

"It usually doesn't come down all at once. It gives us time to plow in between." Grayson added.

"What about the cows?" Alex asked in concern.

"We filled all the round feeders with new bales late yesterday in preparation for the storm." Grayson told him. "We'll wait until it lets up and start plowing and check on them."

"Can I help?" Alex asked anxiously.

"Alex." Tessa frowned.

"It's OK, Tessa." Grayson smiled. "It's good to have company. I'll show him how to drive."

"Really?" Alex jumped up. "Can we go now?"

They all laughed.

"We'll wait until it slows down." Grayson nodded.

"Can I help too?" Wade sat up in his bed.

"You can go with me, Buddy." Scott smiled.

Nick walked down the aisle. "Plow us a good route and we'll hook up Blue and do sleigh rides today."

"Awesome!" Grace grinned.

"What do we do until then? There's no TV." Alex looked around.

"There's a TV and DVD player in the house." Dru told him. "Jessup has a ton of movies he's collected over the years."

"*The Cowboys?*" Alex grinned.

"Oh, yeah!" Wade nodded.

"Let's go!" Alex grabbed his coat and started to put his boots on.

"Alex," Scott laughed. "You can't make it through the snow until we shovel a path through."

"Well," He turned back with a roguish grin. "What are you waiting for...John Wayne's awaiting!"

The room laughed as all the men stood and started putting on their winter gear.

"You wait here," Scott grinned at Alex. "We don't want to lose you in a snow drift."

"OK, but hurry." Alex ran to the window to watch.

They plowed and shoveled all morning.

Reilly made it back to the bunkhouse with Lucas, Nick, and Matt. Jessup was on the ATV with the snow blade, Scott and Wade were in the truck with the plow attachment on the front and Grayson and Alex were in the front end loader pushing the snow off the road. They were headed down the main road and to the neighbors to see if they needed help.

After lunch, Reilly helped Nick harness Blue and the sleigh rides began. They took off the bells so Blue didn't have to listen to them all day.

Reilly was the first driver of the day and he excitedly took the reins and picked up his first passengers; Tessa, Leah, Jordan and Dru.

Half way around the plowed loop Reilly had to turn around and look at them since none of them had spoken. They were all relaxed into the benches; coats and hats on, with blankets over their legs. They quietly watched the winter scenery go by.

"Is something wrong?" Reilly asked.

They all shook their heads.

"It's quiet." His mom whispered.

Reilly nodded and turned back to the road. He had been thinking the same thing. The only sound was the distant hum of the loader plowing the roads, the hoof beats from Blue's walk, and the swish of snow as the sleigh slid over it.

He glanced around the majestic view. The dark green trees with boughs hanging low from the weight of the snow were on the left and the endless mountains on the right all covered in winter white. Pockets of blue sky allowed the sun to shine through and caused the snow to glisten like a carpet of diamonds.

It was just peaceful and heaven on earth.

He was nearing the end of the loop before anyone spoke.

"I'll give you twenty bucks to take us around again." Leah chuckled.

"I'll throw in another twenty." Tessa sighed.

"From me too." Jordan added.

"I'll let their sixty pay for me, too." His mom giggled.

"Deal." Reilly laughed softly and waved at the waiting kids as he passed.

His next riders were all the Tagger girls; Nikki, Grace, Nora, and Sadie.

Half way around, they hadn't spoken either. Reilly turned and looked; they were all relaxed and enjoying the scenery.

He chuckled to himself. Everyone needs peace and quiet sometimes, adult or kid. Even without the bribe, he took them around twice; no words were spoken.

When he stopped, Nikki surprised him by crawling onto the bench next to him. The other three girls hurried into the bunkhouse.

"What's up?" Reilly asked with a quizzical smile.

"Buttercup!" Nikki giggled. "Get moving before someone else gets out here."

"Ok..." He flipped the reins so Blue would move out.

He waited for her to speak.

"I just wanted to make sure you're OK with the breakup." She spoke softly, glancing at him.

Reilly sighed inside. Since he was little, he'd admired her, but since she had become his sister...he felt the emotions begin to render him speechless. She just killed him!

"I'm fine." He managed to get out.

"Ahh, Reilly." She turned saddened eyes to him, her voice full of tenderness. "I was told you were handling it well."

He shook his head. "It's not about Kelly."

"Then what?"

He rolled his lips together and cleared his throat in an effort to control his emotions.

"You." He smiled, a little embarrassed.

"Are you mad at me?" She gasped in surprise. "Because I hired her?"

"No…never, I'm very thankful Kelly was in my life and I couldn't ever be mad at you."

"Oh, the day will come, I'm sure." She chuckled.

They rode quietly, letting Blue pull them through the winter snow scene. He knew she was waiting for him to speak.

"It was a bit overwhelming to have the sisterly concern." He admitted. "I've never had that before."

"I've always been concerned about you."

"But not like this…not about stuff like this… emotions and all."

"That's true. Unfortunately, you're at the age when the emotion stuff comes at you often and it gets really confusing."

Reilly nodded. "Yeah, but this was different."

"How?"

"In the year and a half I've known Kelly, we never, ever, spoke a bad or disrespectful word to each other."

Nikki smiled warmly at him, just like Dru always did. "That is wonderful, Reilly. I'm so glad to hear that. Which is also confusing…why did you break up?"

"We just realized that we weren't "the one" for each other and we needed to move on."

"So you really are good with it?"

"Yeah, I only want the best for Kelly, and I'm not her best."

"How did you end up so awesome?" She chuckled.

"An awesome dad," He grinned. "But don't tell him."

"I love Jack."

"Yeah, I kinda like him too."

Reilly saw a movement to his left, just on the edge of the trees. An elk, with huge antlers that stretched back to his tail and hung over the edges of his massive body, was jumping through belly high snow causing it to fly around him.

Reilly pulled Blue to a stop. The horse was watching the elk with head held high and ears twitching towards it. Nikki looped her arm through his and squeezed tight as she leaned into him.

They silently watched the majestic animal hurdle the snow until he stepped onto the plowed road. He turned his head towards them then turned away and walked peacefully on his new cleared trail.

Reilly flipped the reins and they followed the elk down the road.

The elk led them down the road until they reached the mid-point of the loop. The elk continued straight and Reilly turned Blue to follow the loop.

"That was cool." Reilly chuckled, always in awe of the animal's strength and beauty.

"Yeah, it was."

Again they were quiet, just enjoying the view and each other's company.

"I don't think we do this enough." Nikki finally broke the silence.

"Gliding through the snow in a restored antique sleigh, pulled by a big blue horse and following an elk down the road?" He snickered.

"That, too," Nikki giggled. "Spending time together as a brother and sister."

Reilly nodded. "It's about time we do a little of that."

"What do you want to do?"

"You can introduce me to girls, like you used to with Matt." He laughed.

"That's when we were in college." She grinned. "I'm not around many anymore. But, I promise if I find one worthy of you, I'll hook you up."

"Like a good sister should," He returned her grin. That's a Tagger girl for ya!

They talked about her future horse rehabilitation business as they made their way around the loop.

The ranch buildings came into view.

"You really are OK with the breakup?"

"I am. We made the decision together with no hard feelings. I'll always miss her, but at least we have rodeos together and Facebook to chat."

"She's not gone forever."

"Nope."

"Well, if you ever need to talk, you just come to your big sis."

"I'm bigger than you."

"Figuratively…not literally…thank goodness." She chuckled. "Would you mind if Lucas drove? I'd like to do a loop, just the two of us."

"Sounds romantic."

Lucas, Nick, Alex, and Tessa stepped out of the bunkhouse door as they slid into stop.   Alex was carrying Nick's puppy, Red. Reilly was surprised to see Alex had returned.

Lucas happily climbed on the sleigh, kissed Nikki and with a quick flip of the reins they disappeared down the road together.

Reilly chuckled and turned to Nick. He was watching the couple drive away with a slight smile on his face.

"They're good together." Tessa commented.

"That they are…" Nick answered. "Don't tell Lucas, but I don't think there is anyone out their better suited for Nikki then him."

"Well, I'd never tell him that." Reilly grinned.

"Your secret is safe with us," Tessa giggled as she flipped her hood off her head. "It's warmer out here than I thought it would be."

Alex placed Red on the ground and the puppy took off at a run. The twelve-year-old laughed and quickly limped off after him.

"Alex, be careful." Nick and Tessa called out in unison, looked at each other, and laughed.

Nick followed Alex and the puppy with Alex trying to move faster.

"You're going to land on your butt, boy!" Nick called out.

"Wouldn't be the first time!" Alex laughed over his shoulder as he closed in on the puppy.

Red ran up to the edge of the corral. Eli was on the opposite side of the fence and put his nose down to the puppy. Red stretched out to investigate the large animal.

The puppy barked and Eli bounced his head, which made the puppy jump back and run for Alex. Alex and Nick started laughing.

Reilly glanced at Tessa and was surprised to see her frowning at the pair.

"Are you OK?" He asked her.

She just nodded, turned abruptly, and walked into the bunkhouse.

CHAPTER SEVEN

Nick and Alex walked back down the road so Reilly decided to head to the barn and wait for the sleigh to return. There was no one else in the barn and the horses were lined up on the outside open stalls eating. Their heads popped up as he entered. A fresh layer of white snow decorated the backs of the horses. It helped insulate them and keep them warm.

Reilly tossed a few flakes of hay into the feeders as Nick and Matt walked through the small door.

"What happened to puppy chasing?" Reilly grinned at Nick.

"Wade showed up," Nick answered. "He trumps me every time."

"I thought I'd wait in here for Lucas and Nikki to return. I didn't want to disturb anyone trying to sleep in the bunkhouse." Reilly told them.

"Might be awhile," Matt grinned. Reilly joined the grin but Nick didn't…which made both of them laugh.

Reilly climbed up on the hay bales to sit and wait.

"Did you ask Nick?" Matt turned to Reilly as he made himself comfortable on the hay.

"No." Reilly admitted and glanced at Nick.

"Ask me what?" Nick sat next to Reilly. "This have to do with your breakup?"

Reilly nodded then glanced to Matt, not sure how to approach it with him.

Matt shrugged a shoulder. "Had to do with kissing." He started to explain.

Reilly shook his head. "Epic kisses." He felt himself blush.

"He's asked all the adults." Matt chuckled at his brother's embarrassment.

"Well, I hope Dru's was with Jack, because it sure wasn't with me."

"Why?" Reilly was surprised.

"We were young, dumb, and just having fun." Nick explained with a wide grin. "Other than one kiss, which she…probably to this day…doesn't understand the true meaning, we were just kids having fun."

"What do you mean?" Matt asked.

"The one kiss?" Nick said.

Matt and Reilly nodded.

Nick leaned back on his chair of hay. "When I met your mother she was everything any bull rider had ever wanted or dreamed of. I remember the moment I saw her. She was just finishing a run on this big black mare, Jet, and came out of the arena with a huge grin…lit up her blue eyes, her face, blonde hair flying…she was laughing and I was mesmerized." He grinned. "Every single, and some married, cowboys were jealous that I caught her attention." He shrugged. "I was oblivious to it all, I fell head over heels for her."

Reilly glanced at Matt who was as entranced with the story as he was.

"We went from rodeo to rodeo just laughing and having fun. Grayson and Scott joined us a number of times and we got along like brothers…except I didn't know it at the time because I didn't know what having a brother was like. They were the best months of my life. Dru and I were both twenty when we met, she just turned twenty one when I asked her to marry me." Nick paused and looked between Matt and Reilly. "That was the day…that was the epic moment…kiss for me." He shook his head and sighed. "She had no idea what my past was like, she thought I had grown up just like her, in a loving family in New Mexico. She also didn't know about Nikki and I was too terrified of losing Dru to tell her."

Reilly remained silent, he didn't really understand that part; Nick never talked about his past before.

"Do you know where Palouse Falls is?" He asked them. They both nodded. "We were coming back from a rodeo and decided to stop at The Falls. We're standing at the base of it, looking up at in in awe and I turned to her and realized that she was my happiness. The three months I had been with her were absolutely the best I'd ever had and I couldn't imagine it ending."

He looked at the ground then back up to Matt. "I got brave enough when she turned to me with the light and joy radiating out of her, to ask her to marry me, right there…hadn't thought of it before that moment but I knew she was my chance of a happy future."

He looked at Reilly. "When she said yes, I took her in my arms and kissed her longer and more intense than I ever had before…I was saying goodbye to my past and kissing my future." He shook his head with a wry grin. "She knew it was different, but thought it was only because of the proposal but, to me, it was so much more." He sighed. "We got married a week later, and three months after that I was running out...my past was more of a hurdle to get over than I realized."

Nick looked up at Matt; "And you know the rest of it."

Matt nodded.

Reilly was curious about the rest of it, but was fine not knowing, too.

The small barn door opened. Wade, Alex, and Scott walked through.

Nick turned to Reilly. "You're OK with the breakup?"

Reilly nodded, glad that everyone was concerned about him, including Nick. "You'll find yourself a new girl." Matt smiled.

"Nikki said she'd try to hook me up if she found a girl 'good enough for me'." Reilly chuckled.

"She's either at Circle 50 or at The Stables." Nick shook his head. "She won't be finding you many girls there."

Reilly looked over in time to see Leah and Grayson walk through the door. Grayson's puppy rested in his arms but was in a fit of sneezing.

"What's wrong with her?" Nick looked concerned.

"She just earned her name," Grayson chuckled. "Pepper."

Leah giggled. "Cora dropped a pepper shaker on the floor and before she could pick it up, little blue pup decided to take a big whiff."

The rest of the family walked through the door.

"Looks like this is the place to be." Matt laughed at the group.

Nick turned to Reilly with a devilish grin, "You want to know how to get a girl?"

"Of course," Reilly nodded.

"Me, too!" Matt raised a hand which made them laugh.

"You have speakers for the music on your phone?" Nick asked Reilly.

"Yeah," Reilly stood. "I'll go get them."

He returned and handed them to Nick.

Nick scrolled through the music on Reilly's phone and nodded approvingly. "You got some good ones on here."

Reilly grinned. "Country boy at heart, with a little rock and roll here and there."

The front half of the barn had been cleared to store the sleigh which Lucas and Nikki were still riding in. The rest of the family members had joined them by sitting around the hay stack.

Nick chose a song and looked around the room. He smiled then turned to Reilly. "You learn to do this…and you'll get a girl or two." He winked and walked across the room stopping in front of Leah and turned to Grayson. "Mind if I steal your wife for a demonstration?"

Leah and Grayson just shook their heads curiously and she took his hand as he led her to the middle of the barn.

"Ready?" Nick asked Leah and she nodded cautiously.

Nick nodded at Reilly, who pushed the play button and turned the volume up.

The music boomed through the room as Nick grinned at Leah.

Within seconds he had her swing dancing across the barn floor.

The room erupted in laughter and clapping as he swung her around his back then under his arm; twisted her the other direction, back again…over and over again. Leah was screaming in delight.

"You know how to two-step?" Nick asked Leah who nodded excitedly.

"Here we go." Nick laughed. Eight beats later they were two-stepping across the barn.

The feeling of doom crossed over Reilly. His hand went to his stomach as if to quell the sensation. He searched for Grace and found her pulling her dad out onto the dance floor. They were both laughing as he twirled her around making her hair fly. Reilly shook his head to erase the feeling then turned to Tessa.

"I don't know how to do that." She leaned away from him, but the look in her eye as she watched Nick and Leah said she wanted to.

"I don't either." Reilly laughed and took her hand. "So we'll learn together."

They watched as the two dancers returned to the swing dance and Reilly copied their moves. Pretty soon he and Tessa were dancing across the floor as he was swinging her around him and under his arms then out away from him…back and forth and all around.

Alex and Nora started dancing. Alex would stay in one place and swing Nora around him. They laughed every time their hands broke apart and Nora would go flying.

Reilly's parents were dancing and Sadie had grabbed Matt while Scott and Jordan danced together. Everyone was watching Nick and Leah as they demonstrated new moves, then trying it out with their partner.

Jessup and Cora had just started dancing when the large barn doors opened revealing the impromptu barn dance to a pleased Nikki and Lucas. The pair quickly joined in.

They spent the afternoon switching partners and learning new moves from Nick.

"How did you get so good?" Reilly asked him as they took a break to watch Matt and Nikki and Wade and Cora dance around the room.

"I spent a few nights in a few beer joints while I was bull riding." Nick grinned with a twinkle in his eye. "It's the fastest way to break the ice with women, whether they know how to dance or not."

Reilly returned Nick's grin as Grace came running up to him.

"Alan and Levi invited us to a New Year's party." She said excitedly.

Reilly felt nauseous…

"It's just karaoke and dancing, we can show off our new moves! Mom and Dad said I could go if you were going." She was bouncing in excitement, her blue eyes lit up. "ASK JACK!"

Reilly stared at her with the nauseous feeling running rampant in his stomach.

"Come on, Reilly, ask him!" She said and pulled him to his dad who was dancing with Dru.

Reilly didn't say a word as Grace asked Jack for him. Of course, his dad said yes.

Reilly wanted to throw up, but didn't know why.

They spent two more days on the mountain until the snow stopped and the roads were cleared enough to get the truck and horse trailers down the steep grade.

Reilly had two more days to talk Grace out of going to the dance. But he knew it was useless.

He sat up in bed the first morning back at The Homestead and looked around his and Wade's room. He was surprised to see that Wade wasn't lying in bed.

Wade stepped out of the bathroom and Reilly could tell something was wrong.

CHAPTER EIGHT

"Wade?"

"Morning."

"What's wrong?"

"I gained weight over the holiday."

Reilly laughed. "Everyone did."

Wade sat on the edge of the bed and sighed. "I'm 123 pounds."

Reilly leaned back against the wall. "Wade, I don't know what to say. You've wanted to grow but…"

Wade nodded, "It's time though."

"Are you sure?"

"Yeah, I can't take any chances. We said 125 was the weight limit. So…it's time."

"When?"

"Now," Wade stood. "It's a nice day outside, just a dusting of snow which will melt as soon as the sun is up high. This morning…is my last ride on Rooster."

Wade straightened his back and walked to the door. He stopped and turned.

"I think…if you wouldn't mind…could you ride Dollar with us?" Wade's dark eyes shimmered. "Our two brothers riding with us on our last ride."

Reilly threw the covers off and jumped out of bed. After getting dressed as fast as he could, he followed Wade down the stairs.

Only Cora was in the kitchen. Wade walked to her and wrapped her in a huge hug.

The older woman could tell something was wrong but remained quiet and hugged him back. Her eyes went to Reilly.

"Wade?" Reilly asked, he didn't want to say anything if Wade didn't want anyone to know.

"After I leave.," Wade kissed Cora on the cheek and walked out the door.

Cora turned quickly to Reilly.

"He weighs 123."

Her eyes opened wide. "Rooster?"

Reilly nodded, "We're headed out for the last ride."

"I'll make sure no one goes out…give you time."

They hugged briefly before Reilly followed Wade.

As they walked into the barn and towards the two red horses, Wade stopped and turned to Reilly. "I don't want this to be sad. This is what we all expected. Sadie's last ride on Milo was getting Nora's saddle out of the brush. When she looks back on it now, it was a sad ride, not a good one."

"I understand."

They continued to the horses.

"I have an idea." Reilly said.

"What?" Wade opened Rooster's stall.

"I'll be right back." Reilly turned and ran out of the barn and to the house.

Cora was standing on the back deck watching the barn so he told her his idea and she smiled.

"I'll handle it," She turned into the house as Reilly returned to Wade.

"That was quick," Wade chuckled. "Your ideas usually aren't so short."

Reilly grinned. "Cora's handling the details."

By the time they had the horses saddled Grace, Sadie and Nora were walking in.

"Tessa is bringing Alex over." Nora told them.

"I'll saddle Rufio for him." Reilly nodded.

"We have to stay in here until Alex arrives." Sadie told them as she walked Little Ghost out of his stall.

Nora walked to Arcturus' stall and Grace went to Buttercup.

"Why?" Wade frowned.

"So we all start at the same time." Sadie answered.

"Start what?" Wade looked confused.

Sadie laughed. "Didn't Reilly tell you?"

"Tell me what?" Wade turned to Reilly.

"We're playing Dice." Reilly grinned, it was one of their favorite horse games.

"Cool!" Wade looked excitedly at Rooster, running his hand over his nose. "That's a great last ride."

They heard a car stop and Alex appeared limping to them as fast as he could. "I love Dice!"

They walked the horses out of the barn and to the mounting block where Wade swung a leg onto Rooster's saddle one last time. He closed his eyes tightly then took a deep breath.

Wade looked over at his brother-cousin, sister, cousins, and friend. "That was a tough one." He admitted.

They all nodded in understanding and mounted their own horses. They walked towards the front pasture and found Cora and Tessa standing next to the house.

"New rules!" Cora told the excited group. "No one can go faster than a walk. There are four dice stations; Leah and Grayson, Dru and Jack, Scott and Jordan, then me and Tessa." She looked up at the kids to make sure they understood. They all nodded. She handed them each a pen and blank white notecard. "Use these to track your points. You roll two dice at each station and your total number will be written down. The first one to reach 50, wins $10."

"We're playing for money?" Sadie yelled with a grin.

"Yep, but…we'll go around for an hour…with as many $10 winners as we can get…but the one person with the most money gets to keep their money and everyone else forfeits theirs."

"Ah…man!" Alex complained.

"And one more thing!" Cora laughed. "The money can only be spent at Red Lobster!"

"Cool!" They all cried out.

"I'm hungry already!" Wade laughed and cued Rooster forward and down the driveway.

Tessa and Cora were at the big water trough by the gate into the front lawn.

"You have to pair up and go to different stations so no one knows your points!" Tessa smiled. "You also have to change who you ride with after each round."

Reilly and Wade threw the dice at Tessa and Cora's station, giggled as they both got 4's then headed for Dru and his dad who were enjoying the southern pasture island with puppy, Indy. Each of the other teams threw at Cora's station first then Nora and Alex headed to Leah, Grayson, and Pepper the puppy who were in the northern pasture island. Sadie and Grace headed to Scott, with Spur tucked in his jacket, and Jordan who had setup lawn chairs next to the already lit fire pit.

The first round went to Alex…then Grace…then Wade won three times in a row before Alex won again. Wade and Alex were the final winning pair with $50 together to spend at Red Lobster.

The riders and parents gathered in the arena.

"Ready for the next game?" Cora asked.

"Yeah!" The kids hollered in laughter.

"Get your lariats ready." She told them. "Line up in the middle, side by side, and facing the chutes. You can only walk."

"And do what?" Sadie asked her and received a chuckle from all the adults.

"Ready?" Cora laughed.

"Yeah.." The kids said cautiously.

Leah and Jordan appeared with the extra-large beach balls they used for training horses. They tossed them out into the arena to the roar of the kid's laughter. All the horses watched the balls alertly but didn't react…they were used to them.

"Good thing we don't have snow down here!" Nora laughed.

They all took turns trying to rope the big balls as they bounced and rolled around the arena.

"Good thing I've been practicing!" Alex swung the rope and missed. "But I need more!"

"What do we get if we rope one?" Grace asked as she threw a loop at one. It bounced off and slid to the side.

"If the miracle happens? $25!" Cora announced.

"At Red Lobster?" Sadie asked as she threw. The rope floated perfectly over the top of the ball, she pulled at the right time and the rope tightened around the middle of the ball. She tugged the ball and it bounced off of Little Ghost's legs. The horse pushed the ball with his nose.

"Twenty five bucks! That's a lot of shrimp!" Sadie hollered which made everyone laugh and the kids start throwing with more determination.

Grace won herself $25 too.

Reilly had watched her throw and saw her throw the rope higher than he had been and floating it over the ball instead of throwing at the ball. He followed her technique and won himself $25!

"Dang!" Nora hollered, "I'm the only one without any money!"

"You're not done yet!" Cora hollered. "Ready for the next game?"

"Yes!"

"Put the ropes away and head to the top of the driveway." Cora yelled to them.

All the adults had disappeared in front of the barn before the kids got to the arena gate.

Reilly glanced over at Wade. His brother-cousin was leaning over and stroking Rooster's neck and laughing at something Sadie said. Reilly felt his throat constrict in emotion. Wade couldn't ask for a better last ride on his special horse.

They rode around the front of the barn and all the adults were lined up across the driveway. Cora was at the top holding their equipment.

"What is she holding?" Alex asked.

"Polo mallets." Grace laughed and Buttercup pranced.

"We're playing polo?" Sadie said in disbelief.

"Nope!" Cora answered. "Line up across the top here." She pointed to a line scratched out in the gravel. "Paul brought over a couple mallets and balls that were left at The Stables. Remember to thank him next time you see him, because none of us wanted to miss a second of the fun and go get them." Cora laughed.

"What are we supposed to do?" Wade asked as she handed him a mallet.

"The driveway gate is closed at the road. In front of it is a hole dug in the ground, just a shallow one so the horses can't get hurt." She pointed. "Now, you have to start here and try to get the ball in the hole. The person with the least amount of hits to get it the hole wins….fifty bucks for Red Lobster!"

"Oh yeah!" Wade yelled and looked down the driveway. He turned Rooster head first down the driveway to get a good lineup. He swung the mallet; the ball only rolled twenty feet. He grinned back at Cora. "This may take a while."

"You already have thirty for the restaurant, Wade." Grace yelled. "You need eighty?"

"That's a lot of steak!" Reilly laughed.

Wade turned with a wide grin and his eyes sparkled. "Lots and lots of desert! I'll put on the other two pounds and make it 125 even!"

It took Wade sixteen hits to get the ball in the hole. Grace did it in fourteen hits, depressing her cousin. Sadie got impatient and hit the ball into the pasture. It took her five hits just to get it back on the driveway, she finished with twenty one. Alex took fourteen hits, tying with Grace.

Reilly and Nora were next. Reilly took the mallet and lined it up so Dollar was pointing head first down the driveway, just like the other kids did. He swung the mallet hard and it rolled about twenty five feet.

"That wasn't much better than mine." Wade teased with a chuckle.

Reilly lined up again, head first down the driveway, and hit it again. This time it rolled to the halfway point. It only took him six more times; he was ahead with only eight hits.

"Beat that Nora!" Reilly turned and yelled up the driveway.

"I will!" She yelled back.

She lined Arcturus along the line. Instead of head first down the driveway she turned the horse to the side so the target was to her left and the horse was sideways to the ball. She kicked a foot out of a stirrup and put the toes of both feet in one stirrup…the driveway to her back. She was able to lean over the saddle on her stomach and use both hands to swing the mallet down towards Arcturus' belly. She smacked the ball hard and it shot out from under his body. The black horse didn't move when the mallet bounced off him.

Nora turned quickly to see the ball was still rolling at the halfway point.

The crowd erupted in cheers and laughter.

"That's my daughter!" Scott yelled with a fist pump in the air.

The whole group walked with her to the ball.

Nora turned sideways again, put her back to the target and swung the mallet to the ball with both hands. A smack rang out and she turned.

They all watched the ball roll nearly the rest of the way…it stopped within a foot of the hole.

"Dang!" Reilly yelled and shook his head.

With a one-handed, light tap, Nora put the ball in the hole.

Cheers rang out as Nora turned to Reilly with a tilted head and raised brow. "Beat that Reilly Morgan!" She teased with a wide grin.

Reilly just shook his head in amazement at his cousin. She was something.

He stepped out of the saddle and kicked the dirt back in the hole. Wade waited for him as everyone else walked back up the driveway.

Reilly took his time opening the gate and chaining it to the fence so it wouldn't swing in the wind. He glanced up the driveway and once everyone was at the top, he stepped into the saddle.

Wade looked at Reilly, nodded his head slightly, his eyes were glistening. "That was perfect."

Reilly nodded, his own eyes getting misty.

"Let's take the last walk." Wade sighed.

They laughed about the games as they walked up the driveway and into the barn. Wade walked right up to the mounting block, quickly stepped off of his horse and patted Rooster on the neck. The horse tucked his nose into Wade's side. Wade leaned into the horse's ear, whispered something, then turned into the barn and unsaddled the horse.

Their spirits were high as they joined everyone in the driveway.

"Come get your winnings then you can head out to the restaurant." Cora called out to the kids from the deck.

"Reilly!" His dad hollered.

Reilly turned in time to catch the keys that were thrown at him.

"Take my truck and you kids have fun." His dad grinned.

"Just us kids?" Sadie hollered, eyes wide in disbelief.

"I think you guys can handle it." Grayson laughed at her.

It was one of the best lunches they would ever have. After deciding to pool their money, they laughed and ate until they couldn't eat anymore. They raised their glasses for a toast to the most special red horse that ever lived. To Rooster!

CHAPTER NINE

"Remember what I said."

"I know. Nothing's going to happen." Grace said.

"Take it from me, it's tough to back off and say no."

"Reilly, I'll be fine. I won't be doing anything like that."

"Don't drink if anyone has anything."

"Reilly, I said I would be fine. I have no intentions of drinking."

He looked at the frustration in her face, nodded and turned off the engine to the truck. Glancing up at the house, he had the uneasy feeling in his gut again.

"It's our first New Year's party away from home." Grace smiled excitedly. "Let's just enjoy it. Levi and Allen are the only guys I know here, and they're gentlemen, they'll treat me that way…besides, you're here." She grinned. "We're just going to dance and karaoke. Let loose, Reilly!"

Reluctantly, he followed her lead and opened the truck door. They could hear the music vibrating out of the house.

"Dang, that's loud." Grace turned; the excitement lighting her face. "Come on Reilly, smile, have fun, maybe you'll find someone in there you like as much as or more than Kelly."

Reilly rolled his eyes; that wasn't going to happen.

The front door opened and they were assaulted by the loud music and Levi's grin.

"I've been watching for you two." Levi hugged Grace as she walked past him and into the house.

"This is a big house," Reilly smiled at their roping friend.

"Belongs to my grandparents…that are on a cruise right now," Levi grinned mischievously.

"Do they know you're throwing a party here?" Reilly frowned, the uneasy feeling just doubled.

"Of course not," Levi laughed and pushed Reilly into the house.

Grace was already at the karaoke machine singing a song with a couple other girls; Allen was handing her a drink.

"Is that alcohol?" Reilly yelled over the music at Levi.

"No, none here, but all the other beverages are in here." Levi turned quickly and walked down a hall.

With a glance to Grace, Reilly followed him into the kitchen. He looked around but didn't see any alcohol; but he knew teenagers well enough that there had to be some at the party somewhere.

"Hi," Came a voice behind him.

He turned to see a pretty redhead smiling at him. Her hair was a deeper red than Kelly's and she had blue eyes instead of green. Reilly quickly realized he had instantly compared her to Kelly, and made himself stop.

"I'm Christy," She said loudly while leaning towards him. She wore a black dress that made her eyes stand out. The black boots she was wearing made her nearly as tall as him.

"I'm Reilly." He smiled and yelled back.

"Levi said he had invited a cowboy with black hair and blue eyes that I might like." She grinned. "Are you that cowboy?"

Reilly laughed. "I hope so."

"What makes you a cowboy?" She flirted with a sweet smile.

"Well, I have horses. I rope in the rodeo and at a cattle ranch."

"Well, you must be the cowboy he was talking about then."

He spent the next hour talking with Christy. They hadn't even made it out of the kitchen.

"Well, I'm glad Levi told me to look out for you."

"Me, too."

"He said you were Allen's girlfriend's cousin."

"I don't know if she would call herself his girlfriend, they're just friends."

"Well, he sure wanted some time with her tonight."

"What do you mean?" Reilly frowned, the uneasy feeling returned. He looked back towards the big front room but couldn't see anything but hallway.

"Levi pointed you out to me as soon as you walked in the door. Wanted me to come talk to you in the kitchen."

Reilly stared at her. The uneasy feeling just tripled. Something wasn't right.

He quickly walked past her and went right to the karaoke machine. The mixture of the loud music pounding in his head and the queasiness in his gut made him want to throw-up.

"What's wrong?" Christy asked as she followed him.

Grace wasn't singing anymore. He looked around the room, searching for her but the house was too big and there were teenagers everywhere.

Levi appeared before him. "I see you met, Christy."

"Where's Grace?" Reilly hollered over the music.

"She's OK, Allen will take care of her."

"What does that mean?" Reilly's heart started pounding. "Where is she?"

"Reilly, seriously…" Levi frowned and cocked his head to the side. "She's OK, she's with Allen…he wouldn't hurt her."

Reilly started to relax, Levi was right. Grace said he'd been a gentleman with her…why would things change now?

Then he thought of the night so far…Levi met him at the door, led him into the kitchen, and arranged for Christy to distract him in there for an hour. Allen had given Grace a drink within minutes of her walking in the door.

Reilly looked intently at Levi, his eyes narrowing in doubt. "Where is she?" He said slowly and deliberately.

Levi grinned and shrugged. Within three wrestling moves his father had taught him, Reilly had Levi flipped, smashed into the ground on his face, and his arm pinned high up his back.   Levi screamed in pain causing the people surrounding them to step away, creating a circle.

"Where is Grace?" Reilly asked; anger and stress causing his voice to go low and gruff.

Levi stopped screaming long enough to yell; "She's upstairs and down the hall."

Reilly let him go and sprinted towards and up the steps, taking them two at a time. He heard someone running behind him but didn't turn to look, his focus was on finding his best friend. If anything happened to her, he'd never forgive himself.

"Grace!" He yelled as he opened the first door. It was a bathroom, the next door he opened was a closet. He was still being followed, but the panic was rising and didn't turn to look, he continued to the next door.

"Grace!" Reilly flung open the next door, it was a bedroom. He flipped the light switch to see a guy on top of a half-undressed girl. Both looked up at him in alarm.   It wasn't Grace, so he moved to the next door and found it locked.

He pounded on the door. "Grace!"

There was a muffled sound, but he couldn't tell what was said. His heart was pounding, his breathing nearly panicked.

He stepped back and finally looked around him. There was a large teenager on each side of him. Both well over six foot tall and as broad as Grayson. Reilly recognized them as the twin brothers that were linebackers for the Lewiston's varsity football team. They looked at him in concern.

"We got your back." The big one on the left nodded.

"Grace!" He yelled again, leaning against the door and staring at the two linebackers.

"Reilly?" He heard muffled from inside.

"Talk to me Grace." Reilly yelled through the door.

"Cooper." He heard her say…but just barely.

Reilly took a step back and stared at the door.

"Allen, you have ten seconds to open this door." Reilly yelled as loud as he could.

"What does Cooper mean?" The linebacker to his right asked.

"It's her distress word." Reilly answered.

"The hell with ten seconds," The linebacker said.

Within a split second, a foot from each linebacker hit the door as they kicked their way into the room. The door splintered as it came open and dangled from its hinges.

Reilly ran between them and into the room.

The lights turned on.

Grace was lying on the bed, her top shirt was off but her tank top was still tucked into her jeans. Her hand was at her head, as if dazed and confused.

Allen was on the bed hovering over her, his shirt unbuttoned but still fully clothed. His eyes wide in alarm.

Without a second thought, and in only two moves, Reilly had him flipped off the bed and was jamming his face into the carpet and had his arm up around his back.   As hard as he tried, Allen couldn't get free, nor talk.

"I got him." One of the linebackers said and took over the hold Reilly had on him.

Reilly nodded and turned to Grace. The other twin was helping her sit up and putting her shirt back on.

"What happened?" Grace slurred as her head flopped backwards.

"Is she drunk or drugged?" Reilly asked the linebacker.

Picking up the glass on the table, the linebacker sniffed then tasted it.

"It's called an Apple Pie, tastes non-alcoholic, but it's loaded with alcohol." The linebacker looked at Allen and shook his head. He stood with a nearly unconscious Grace in his arms. "Where to?"

"I have a blue Toyota out front." Reilly walked to the door, one last look at Allen, the friend they had known for over a year. "Don't call her or contact her or me again. The last thing you want is her father tracking you down…or her uncles…or her mother and aunts."

Reilly left the room and led the linebacker carrying Grace, down the hall and out the front door. Once she was buckled, he turned to the linebacker.

"Thank you. I'm Reilly Morgan." Reilly stuck out his hand and shook hands.

"Brady Mattson and I think you had it well in hand." He smiled grimly. "Nice moves."

Reilly nodded. "Can you get your brother out of there?"

"Billy? Yeah, I can, why?" He pulled out his cell phone.

"I'm about to bust this up." Reilly walked back towards the house.

Billy was walking down the stairs as Reilly reached for the house phone, dialed 911, waited for someone to answer, then hung up.

Levi walked towards him with a worried expression, "Reilly, what's going on? Christy just said Grace was carried out the door."

He held out a hand, which Reilly took and, within two moves, used it to put Levi onto his face again, harder this time than before. "Don't ever reach out to either of us again." Reilly said angrily.

Everyone had stopped singing and dancing and were staring at them. The house phone rang but no one answered it.

Once the phone stopped ringing, Reilly let go of Levi, reached for the phone and called 911 again, waited for someone to answer, and hung up.

He turned and walked out the door with Billy right behind him. The music started again.

As they walked to Reilly's truck, Billy turned to him.

"What was with the phone?"

"Standard protocol for police departments…since someone called 911 and no one answered when they called back they have to send police out here to check on the house. They'll take it serious with two hang-ups."

"We best get out of here." Billy nodded to his brother and they jogged to their truck.

Reilly quickly started the Toyota and pulled away from the house. A mile away he passed two police cars with their lights flashing.

Watching the lights disappear behind him, Reilly pulled over and looked at Grace. Brady had leaned the seat back to try and make her comfortable but her head was to the side, dark blonde hair covering her face and her breathing deep.

How much did she have to drink? What was Allen going to do? And now what was he supposed to do?

The Mattson brother's pulled in behind him and walked to his window.

"You need anything?" Billy asked.

Reilly looked at the clock. It was only eleven o'clock; two hours short of their one o'clock curfew.

They were in Orofino, over an hour's drive from The Homestead. Or he was within a half hour of Nick's place.

Reilly looked up at Billy and stuck out a hand, "Thanks."

Billy shook his hand and nodded. "I can't believe he did that. I've known Allen for years."

"I'm pretty surprised, too," Reilly sighed.

He quickly told the brothers of the night's event.

Brady had turned red in anger. "I'll be calling his parents in the morning. Don't know if it'll do any good, but they should know what he's doing."

Reilly nodded and looked over at the sleeping Grace. What if he hadn't been there?

"What are you going to do now?" Billy asked.

"We have an uncle that lives in Lenore. I'm going to his place…try to figure out what to do next."

"Do you want us to follow? Help explain?" Brady asked.

Reilly shook his head. "No, you guys have done a lot already. I really appreciate your help."

"It's not something we could stand by and just watch happen." Brady frowned then smiled. "But we did get to kick down a door…I've always wanted to do that."

All three chuckled.

"We'll see you at school on Monday." Billy nodded then the brothers left.

Reilly drove straight to Nick's; hoping he was home. He was and by the time Reilly turned off the engine, Nick had walked out of the house with the puppy in his arms.

"What's up?" Nick asked with a frown as he leaned down and saw Grace in the passenger side. "Is she asleep?"

Reilly shook his head with a worried look; she wasn't asleep…she was passed-out.

Nick looked between Reilly and Grace, handed him the puppy, then opened Grace's door. He lifted her out as Reilly opened the house door.

He placed the puppy in its bed and stood in the middle of the front room and waited for Nick to lay Grace down on the bed in his spare room.

When he returned, he motioned for Reilly to sit, then waited for him to talk.

Reilly told him every detail.

"You called the police to break up the party but not what he did to Grace?"

Reilly nodded.

"He attempted to molest her?" Nick asked through gritted teeth.

"I don't know…that's what it looked like to me…at the time." Reilly was near tears from anger, his whole body trembling.

"Then why didn't you call them for that?"

"I called the police to make sure they knew there was a party there, whoever they arrest will be able to witness my taking Levi down twice and Brady carrying a passed out Grace down the steps and to the truck. Some of the kids probably have video of it on their phones." Reilly sat up in his chair, knowing he did the right thing. "Billy and Brady will testify what happened in the room and Grace's condition. If Levi and the girl will testify…"

Reilly stopped and sat back in his chair.

"My first thought was to get her out of there, I did as fast as I could. Then she needed to be somewhere safe, you were the closest place, I knew you'd make her safe."

"Her parents should know."

"I agree." Reilly said and pulled his phone out of his pocket.

CHAPTER TEN

Grayson and Leah arrived a half hour later…not knowing why they were there, just that Grace was OK, but Reilly needed to talk to them.

They started out by looking in on a sleeping Grace, making sure she was OK.

Grayson was sitting down at the beginning of the story, but by the time Reilly got to his sprint up the stairs, the man was standing, hands balled into a fist, eye's looking like they were ready to kill someone.

By the time Reilly got to the end, Leah was standing too; a hand gripping her husband's arm tightly, her face tense and angry.

When he finished, Reilly sat quietly, not knowing what to do next. His phone rang, glancing at it, he didn't recognize the number.

"Hello?" He answered while staring at Leah and Grayson's angry faces.

"Is this Reilly Morgan?"

"Yes."

"This is Levi's father…I think we need to talk."

Reilly was stunned and wasn't sure what to say.

"My son is at the hospital with a broken cheek bone and he said you did it."

"Yes, I did." Reilly answered firmly.

"I'm willing to handle this without the police, since I already had to deal with them tonight at the party at my parent's house."

"Actually, if we're going to talk, then I want the police there…you may want to talk to your son first."

Reilly didn't hear the answer as Grayson ripped the phone out of his hand, stepped out the front door, and yelled into the phone.

Reilly turned to Nick. "Can you call my dad? I might be in trouble for breaking Levi's face."

"It's better than what I would have done." Nick answered and reached for his phone.

His dad and Dru arrived at the same time as one of the sheriff's officers that had responded to the call at the party.

Nick and Leah had tried to convince him he wasn't in any trouble with the law, but Reilly was still shaking as his parents reached him, confused and concerned.

"You got in a fight?" His dad asked.

"Not really," Reilly answered but didn't have time to explain as the lady officer walked up to him.

"Are you Reilly Morgan?" The lady officer asked.

"Yes, ma'am," He answered with a shaky voice.

"I've talked to a number of the kids that were at the party, as well as looking in the room with the busted door." The officer told him.

"What?" Dru turned startled eyes to him.

"The two Mattson brothers have been called and I talked to them, too. They are willing to come in and sign anything needed stating you were provoked."

"What?" Reilly's dad turned to him, then to the officer.

The officer continued; "It seems as though Levi has a broken cheek bone and a strained shoulder. Allan has a broken wrist and a nasty carpet burn across his face."

Reilly didn't remember breaking the wrist…he could have…or Billy did, but he wouldn't tell anyone that.

"Allen and Levi attacked you?" Dru turned to him, her eyes wide in shock.

"No," Grayson said gruffly as he walked up to them. "Reilly attacked them when Allen tried to molest Grace."

"WHAT!?" Reilly's parents yelled out.

Reilly didn't know what to say or do…his nerves were about shot. He looked to the officer. "Am I in trouble?"

"No," She answered. "I can't imagine either boy pressing charges due to the circumstances."

Reilly looked back at the house.

"I'll check on her." Leah nodded and turned into the house.

"Can I take a minute and tell my parents what happened?" Reilly asked the officer.

"They can listen while I take your statement." She answered.

They stood in the cold night air as Reilly repeated the story. Bouncing, he told them every detail he could remember. Grayson and Nick paced to the side as they listened. Dru held his hand and squeezed as he told the events of the night.

"Reilly?" It was Grace, behind him, standing at the door wrapped in her mother's arms. Her complexion was pale with a hint of green. Her hair was a mess, makeup a mess, and she was holding her head. Her chin started quivering as she fought off the tears. "He said it was apple cider."

"Do you know how many you had?" The officer asked.

"I drank the first one down really fast, then he handed me another, it was good…it went down fast too." Grace answered through squinted eyes. "Then, I think one more…I'm not sure."

"Do you know how you got upstairs?" The officer continued.

"Allen," Grace answered with an embarrassed look at her dad. "I wasn't going to do anything, I didn't want to, just ask Reilly. We talked about it before the party."

"We did, and she wasn't going to." Reilly confirmed while looking directly at the officer, not daring to look at Grayson.

"Why did you go up the stairs?" The officer asked.

"That's where Allen took me," Grace frowned. "I wasn't feeling well and I told him I wanted to talk to Reilly. He said Reilly was upstairs with a red head."

Reilly's bouncing stopped and he felt like he had been kicked in the stomach. Allen had used him to get to Grace. "I was in the KITCHEN with a red head."

He felt his dad's hand grip his arm; his dad understood how the words must have hurt.

"Did you see Levi any time after the first drink?" The officer asked.

"No…" Grace answered with a frown. "I don't really remember."

 "What do you remember about being upstairs?" The officer continued with a glance at Grayson.

"He opened a door, and let me sit down. He said he would go get Reilly. I laid down, because my head was spinning…then I remember Reilly yelling from somewhere. When he said our code, I responded with Cooper and next thing I know a light was coming in and Reilly and two really big guys were standing next to the bed…then nothing."

"The code?" Grayson turned to Reilly.

"'Talk to me Grace' is the code." Reilly answered nervously. "If everything is OK she says Buttercup. If she's in distress, then it's Cooper."

"I have to ask just a couple more questions, personal ones, do you want to speak privately with just your mother?" The officer asked Grace.

"No, I don't need to." Grace answered with a frown. "I made-out a couple times with Allen, that's all, no sex. I'm sixteen, still a virgin, going to keep it that way for a long time, and I'm very proud of it."

Tears started falling as she looked at Reilly.

"Do you want to press charges?" The officer asked Grace.

Grace nodded then frowned at the motion. "Absolutely! He's not going to get away with this."

The officer nodded and smiled. "Then I have enough for tonight. I will call you when we need anything."

"What about Reilly?" Leah asked nervously.

"That's up to Levi and Allen's families." The officer answered.

"Levi won't be a problem." Grayson answered gruffly.

The officer turned to him with a questioning look.

"His dad called Reilly, and I talked to him." Grayson answered; his expression telling her that he let the father know exactly what happened.

The officer nodded and walked away.

Grayson turned to his daughter. "Are you alright?"

Her pale expression was turning green again. "Yeah, I'm fine."

Reilly tilted his head at her and smiled. "There you are, getting drunk and saying stupid things again." His blood froze, his mind tingled in disbelief…why did he say that?!

There was dead silence, then deep sigh from Grayson as he took his daughter's arm. "You throw up yet?"

"No." She answered as she stumbled next to him.

He picked her up and walked through the front door. "We better get you to the bathroom because it will happen any minute."

"Good thing the cleaning lady was here today." Nick said.

"What? You don't clean yourself?" Dru asked with a strained smile.

"No, really can't say that I do." Nick shook his head and shut the door behind everyone.

Reilly stood in the middle of the floor, again looking around at everyone. Nick walked to his large monitor on his desk, sent an email, then turned the computer off.

"You were working?" Reilly asked.

Nick shook his head. "It's 7:00 at night in Australia. Nikki and Lucas were in Sydney for the New Year's celebration…they put on quite a show. I was chatting with an excited daughter."

"I'm sorry we interrupted." Reilly looked concerned.

"Reilly, do you really think I care…or that Nikki would?" Nick asked.

"No, I guess not." Reilly sighed and looked back towards the bathroom where Leah and Grayson were with Grace…who had started throwing up.

Reilly looked at his mom and dad who were also looking down the hall.

"Dad?" Reilly whispered, his nerves starting to relax and making him nauseous.

His parents turned to him.

"I don't know what I could have done different." Reilly said, glancing between his dad and mom.

"Reilly, you quite possibly saved her from being molested." His dad said in exasperation. "You did everything right. Watching out for each other, the code, safe word…there are very few kids out there that have that."

"Then there are the outstanding wrestling moves someone brilliant taught you." His mother smiled reassuringly.

Reilly nodded and half-smiled at his dad. His eyes shot up as Grayson walked down the hallway and straight at him. His eyes were narrowed; looking angry.

Images of Grayson working out his anger on a punching bag for hours each night at college flew through his mind.

Reilly's eyes got wide and he shook his head in panic. "I'm sorry Grayson, I tried, I never wanted her hurt…"

"Shut up, Reilly." Grayson said gruffly. Gruff enough that Reilly's dad took a step between them, a hand up to stop his forward movement.

"This isn't Reilly's fault." His dad said firmly.

"Grayson!" Dru yelled at her brother in concern, stepping towards him.

Reilly's heart was racing, disappointment running rapid in his veins. How could Grayson, of all people, blame him for this? He knows he'd never hurt one of his girls.

"Grayson, I'd die for your daughters." Reilly's voice shook as tears welled.

"Jack, get out of my way." Grayson turned to him. "I'd like to thank the man that saved my daughter."

A gasp escaped Reilly as his dad stepped aside and Grayson stepped to Reilly.

"I swear, Grayson, I'd die for them." Reilly whispered in despair.

"I know… so would I." Grayson said as he wrapped his arms around Reilly and squeezed him so hard Reilly thought his shoulders were going to break.

CHAPTER ELEVEN

"She wants your phone number," Grace smiled from the back of Buttercup, throwing the lariat and missing the target.

After spending the night at Nick's, so Grace could recover, they went immediately to the horses for equine therapy.

"How do you know?" Reilly asked as he twirled the rope over his head.

"Friends of friends that heard what happened." Grace answered as she coiled her rope.

"I couldn't go out with her," He missed the calf.

"Why not? Levi told the sheriff that neither he nor Christy knew what was going on. They just thought Allen wanted time to make-out again and try to talk me into being his girlfriend, without you interrupting."

"Do you believe him?"

Grace shrugged and tossed the loop and missed again. She slowly coiled the rope again.

"I couldn't go out with her anyway." Reilly tossed a loop and missed again.

"But she really likes you, Reilly."

"And every time I looked at her, I'd think of what Allen was trying to do to you upstairs."

"Well, that's a bummer." She threw and missed again.

"I turn 17 in a couple weeks, I think there will be plenty other girls out there before I get too old for them." Reilly chuckled and missed his throw too.

"Maybe you should go out with a girl that's not a redhead." She threw and missed again.

Reilly laughed. "Grace, I've only gone out with one girl my whole life."

"That's not true." Sadie said from Scarecrow as she made her way into the field next to the arena. "You've gone out with blondes and a brunette too."

"I have?" Reilly turned to her confused.

"Sure!" She grinned. "Me, Grace, and Nora! You go out with us all the time."

"Not quite the same," Reilly laughed.

"He needs to find someone new, outside the family." Nora, on Arcturus, said from behind Sadie.

"Well, that shouldn't be too hard." Sadie looked at him and smiled. "You have two horses and a cool truck."

"That's all it takes?" Reilly teased.

"It would be for me!" Sadie laughed.

"Oh, heck, probably for me, too." Nora joined her cousin's laughter.

"Don't try to impress them with your roping, though." Sadie said with a lifted brow.

"What? Why?" Reilly asked.

"Because, today…you two are awful. Neither of you have caught a calf that's standing still and is plastic."

Reilly and Grace looked down at the dummy calf attached to the parked four-wheeler then up to each other…they nodded.

"You're right." They said in unison.

"We need to do something else. What to do on a cold January 1ˢᵗ?"

"I'm gamed out from last week." Nora said.

"No more movies either." Grace nodded.

"I'm glad there's no snow!" Sadie hollered.

"So what's that leave us?" Reilly looked around at them.

"Where are Wade and Alex?" Grace asked the two girls.

"They helped Tessa move into her new apartment." Nora answered. "It's only about ten minutes away…Alex and Wade are pretty excited."

"They need any more help?" Reilly asked.

"No, I guess she didn't have much," Nora responded.

"Well," Grace started. "I want to do something physical to get rid of all this stress and headache."

"Stress from what?" Sadie and Nora asked in unison.

"It was a long night." Reilly said, then changed the subject. "I know today is supposed to be a no work day…but I think I'm going to go clean the horse stalls. I haven't since we got back."

"Sounds good," Grace nodded and followed him as they made their way to the barn. Sadie and Nora were right behind them.

Reilly swept out the last remnants of the old bedding. He looked around and smiled. It was probably the cleanest that Rufio's stall has been since they built it. He'd already cleaned out Cooper's stall.

He walked out to get the first load of wood shaving they used for bedding. When they enlarged the barn they started buying the bedding in bulk instead of in packages. After the third wheel barrow load he nodded in satisfaction.

"How are you doing over there ladies?" Reilly yelled out to the three Tagger girls.

"Almost ready for bedding," Grace yelled out.

"Me, too," The two younger girls said in unison.

Reilly walked over to Grace who was cleaning Buttercup's stall. She was sweeping with a deep frown on her face; her eyes were red-rimmed from crying.

"You OK?" He whispered, his heart aching for her. There was nothing he could say or do…she would have to deal with her demons herself, but he would be ready when she wanted to talk.

She nodded, but didn't look at him.

"I'll start hauling the bedding." He sighed and turned.

As he walked to the pile of shavings, his mind replayed the events of the night before. What if he hadn't been there? How far would Allen have gone?

He shoveled the shavings into the wheelbarrow. He couldn't protect her all the time…luckily he did this time…but what if he wasn't there? The question haunted him.

As he started walking towards the barn, he heard Nora and Sadie laughing. What if it was them? Reilly stopped halfway to the barn, holding the full wheelbarrow, and stared at the building. How could he protect them?

He started walking again as an idea started to form. He walked to Rufio's stall and dumped the shavings on top of the shavings he had just placed. Three loads later, Grace walked out of her stall and looked at him.

"I thought you were done with Rufio's."

"I am." Reilly headed back out for another load.

Grace was standing by Rufio's stall looking in when he returned.

"What are you doing? It's thick enough…too thick."

"Nope," Reilly shook his head but didn't look at her. "It needs to be deeper."

Sadie and Nora finished Scarecrow and Arcturus' stalls and stood watching him.

Three more loads of shavings on the stall floor and Reilly stopped, kicked it around then jumped on the shavings to see how cushy it was.

He nodded in satisfaction, then looked at the three confused bystanders.

"Nora and Sadie stand in the doorway and watch." Reilly ordered. "Grace, come here."

Grace hesitantly walked toward him to the middle of the stall. Nora and Sadie did as he asked and stood in the doorway.

Reilly held out his arm to Grace. "Flip me…just like I showed you before."

"What?" Grace asked with a puzzled expression.

"I want you to flip me, like we practiced before."

"Why?" She asked.

"Because, we're going to teach Nora and Sadie some of the moves that may help them in the future." He said firmly, hoping she understood.

"It wouldn't have helped last night." Grace said softly.

"No, but if you were in control of all your facilities, and he tried something, you could have taken care of him, just like I did." Reilly argued. "You've flipped me a couple times, pretty good, too."

Grace stared at him for a moment, then nodded. "I could have."

Reilly nodded to the two girls in the doorway; they were looking at them in concern. "We teach them, like I taught you, to protect yourself."

"What happened last night?" Nora whispered.

"Details, Nora…" Sadie said quietly, staring at her sister. "Someone tried to hurt Grace last night and Reilly protected her. Why couldn't you protect yourself? Why weren't you 'in control of all your facilities'?"

Reilly glanced at Grace. They hadn't talked to the parents on what would be said to the rest of the kids or family.

Grace stared at her sister, rolled her lips, wiggled them side to side, then sighed. "Someone gave me a drink last night that had alcohol in it." Grace started and the two younger girl's eyes opened wide. "I didn't know it and got drunk really fast…and the person tried to…" She stopped.

"It's OK, Grace. We understand." Nora nodded sadly. "But they didn't? Reilly saved you?"

Grace nodded, near tears.

"You're OK?" Sadie asked softly, staring at her sister with tears in her eyes.

"I am, thanks to Reilly and him knowing the wrestling moves that Jack taught him." Grace took a deep breath then spoke with more conviction. "Reilly's right. We're going to teach you two the same moves."

Both girls nodded silently as Grace stood in front of her best friend, took his arm, and flipped him over her back.

"Cool!" Both girls yelled as Reilly landed with a soft thud in the deep bedding.

"Do it again!" Nora shouted.

Reilly smiled at Nora's enthusiasm then held out his arm to Grace. She flipped him again.

"Can I try?" Sadie asked with a grin.

"I'm 5' 10" and weigh 165 lbs." Reilly said, "Grace is…"

"I'm 5' 9". She answered.

"I'm 5'6". Sadie added. "Wade is too! With his growing spurt, he caught up with me. He's grown 3 inches in the last three months."

"I'm 5'2"." Nora smiled. "I'm already two inches taller than Mom!"

"You better be thanking Scott for being so tall." Reilly teased Nora. "I might be too big for you, but it doesn't hurt when I land, so you may have to flip Sadie.

Nora and Sadie's eyes turned to each other in surprise.

"OK!" They shouted in unison.

"I'm going to flip Grace this time." Reilly smiled at his best friends raised brows of surprise. "Nora, you'll flip Sadie first, then take turns. Just follow what I do."

Reilly walked them through the steps, and Sadie rolled over Nora's back and landed with a thud. Both girls started laughing.

Once they moved, Reilly flipped Grace, who started laughing before she landed.

Fifteen minutes later, and, what seemed like half the stall bedding collecting in the girls hair, Reilly switched them to the next move.

"Once you get them flipped on their faces…run if you can." Reilly looked at the girls, and they both nodded. "Scream if you're still in danger…as loud as you possibly can." Again they nodded.

"If you can't get away, then once they're flipped, bend their arm like this, and twist the wrist like this." Reilly demonstrated on Grace.

Nora and Sadie took turns practicing the moves on each other.

They were all so intent on what they were doing, that none of them noticed the three sets of parents standing on the outside of the stall watching them.

"Now, Sadie, lay on the ground on your stomach, Nora kneel over the top of her like this…" He demonstrated with Grace on the ground. "If you're down like this then you grab here and here and twist here…if you have to bite, poke, kick, whatever you have to do, to get them to let go…then do this."

Grace did all the moves Reilly showed them, and within seconds she was standing over Reilly.

"Then you run!" Grace and Reilly said in unison.

"And scream!" Sadie and Nora added loudly.

"Very good." Grayson said from behind them and they all jumped.

"My turn." Jordan said as she walked through the door. She listened to Reilly's instructions and flipped her own daughter over her back to roars of laughter.

CHAPTER TWELVE

"Have you ever thought of playing football?" Billy asked.

Reilly shook his head. "No…." He looked over at Brady then back to Billy. They were standing behind Reilly's truck as he sat on the tailgate. "I don't particularly want guys like you two trying to smash me into the ground."

The brothers laughed, "We're kind of rare at this age." Brady grinned.

"We're 6'4" and, depending on the time of year, we're usually around 270, but you're about average size to all the other high school players." Billy added.

"You going on to play college ball?" Reilly asked them.

They both nodded, and Brady answered. "Colleges have been looking and offering us scholarships since we were in 9th grade."

Reilly nodded. That was impressive. He looked around the high school campus at all the kids walking to their classes. Lunch was almost over.

"Where you going?" He asked them.

Both brothers shrugged.

"We haven't decided whether to stay together or go to different colleges." Billy answered with a sigh.

"Plus, I have to get my grades up." Brady frowned. "I'm struggling in algebra…can't stand it…let alone UNDER-stand it."

Reilly grinned, "I didn't either but I'm getting a solid B now."

Brady's back straightened and he looked at Reilly with interest. "How? What's your secret?"

"A dingo," Reilly laughed.

"A what?" The brothers asked in unison.

Reilly chuckled. "My cousin, Sadie. We call her Little Dingo…due to her temper. But, she's a math wizard and has helped me keep my grades up. We have to have good grades to be in the high school rodeo association…plus for college."

"You going? Where?" Billy asked.

Reilly shrugged, "I've had a couple colleges call offering a rodeo scholarship."

"Does Sadie tutor?" Brady asked.

"Just family. I'm not sure how her parents would react to her helping anyone else." Reilly shrugged again. "I guess we could ask…since you did her sister a huge favor."

"Her sister?" Brady asked.

"She's Grace's sister." Reilly explained.

"Really?" Brady asked in excitement. "Who do I have to call?"

Reilly shook his head with a grin just as the bell rang for them to head back to class.

"I'll ask her and her dad." He jumped off the tailgate and closed it.

"I'm willing to pay." Brady said earnestly.

Reilly laughed. "It would have to be on the weekends though or in the evening after dark…and not interrupt her racing practice."

"Why?" Billy asked as the three walked into the building.

"She's twelve." Reilly chuckled, then laughed at their surprised expressions.

"Twelve!" Brady cried out. "And she helps you with 11th grade algebra?"

"I told you, she's a wizard." Reilly waved, as he walked the opposite direction than the brothers.

Reilly looked around the hall, no sign of Grace. She was in the classroom next to his and they usually spent lunch at his truck then walked to the two classes together. Just as the bell rang, he saw her…head down, walking fast, and typing feverishly on her phone.

She didn't look up once as she turned into her classroom across the hall from him. She walked within three feet of him.

"Reilly, in the classroom please." The teacher called out.

He stared at the door across the hall. He slowly walked into his classroom with a real bad feeling in his stomach.

"Where did you go for lunch?" Reilly asked casually as he drove Grace home after school.

She shrugged, "I saw you with the twins, so I just hung out with some girls in the lunch room."

"You could have come over and talked."

She shrugged again, then started typing on her phone. They rode the rest of the way in silence.

Reilly walked to the barn as Grace walked into the house.

He had no idea what to do…how to help…who she was texting…or why she wasn't talking to him.

He quickly saddled Cooper. There was only about an hour's worth of daylight to ride after school.

Most of the hour, it was just Reilly and Cooper in the arena. It didn't happen very often, so he took the time and used the entire arena, just walking, trotting, and galloping in circles, figure eights and even played with Sadie's barrels. As the hour started to diminish, he ran the horse around the parameter of the arena as fast as he could. Cooper loved to run, the energy just vibrated out of the horse.

As he rode, his mind went back to the first time he had seen Cooper run at high speed. Grace was riding him during practice. She bolted out of the roping box; Reilly didn't have a chance to catch them. Grace had grinned and laughed, her eye's shining, as she ran the horse until Grayson told her to stop.

Reilly slowed down the black gelding and trotted around the arena. He looked up to see Nora sitting on top the fence watching him so he trotted over to her and stopped. Then he slid behind his saddle and, with a smile, Nora slid on the saddle in front of him. He let her take control and moved with the motion of the horse. He was surprised at how relaxing it was.

They moved into a slow jog around the arena once before she stopped the horse in the middle. Using just her legs and feet, she turned him left, then right, backed him up, and then made his hind quarters move left then moved them right, then his shoulders. She finished with side stepping him to the left and then to the right.

"He's rusty." Nora finally said as she moved Cooper back into the slow jog. They completed a large circle, a smaller circle, then she moved into a figure eight.

At the farthest part of the arena from the barn, she slowed the horse into a walk, and zig-zagged across the arena to cool Cooper down.

By the time they reached the other end, Cooper's breathing had returned to normal. She sidestepped the horse into the gate and Reilly reached out to open it. She cued the horse around the gate and sidestepped him in the other direction so Reilly could latch the gate.

"You're amazing." He said quietly.

"It's fun. But he needs more work."

"I know, this time of year it's tough."

"I wish we had an indoor arena."

"Heated."

"Absolutely."

"Maybe we should look into the rodeo indoor arena, it's only five minutes away, and we can ride at night."

"Good idea." Nora nodded. "Need to keep them in shape for the Wednesday club nights."

They rode down the short distance to the barn, then through the open doors.

At Cooper's stall, Reilly slid off the back of the horse, then Nora off the side.

"I'll get his grain and hay." Nora offered.

"Thanks."

Reilly unsaddled the horse and put the gear in the tack room. She was already back with the grain, and headed for the hay.

He led Cooper into the stall to eat the grain while he brushed him down.

Nora placed a stool by the barn door and watched.

"I want to do something in the rodeo besides poles." She announced.

"What do you want to do?" Reilly asked.

"I know what I don't want to do."

"What?"

"I don't want to use Arcturus or Isaiah."

Reilly nodded. "Are you still going to show?"

"As often as I can, so I can't get them hyped up one weekend then want them to be calm the next. With Libby and Kit both pregnant I can't use them either."

"Coopers done roping, cutting and poles." He finished brushing the black horse and stepped out of the stall.

They turned off the lights and walked to the house in the dark.

"How about goat tying?" Reilly suggested. "Cooper could do that."

Nora frowned. "I'm not sure on that one…I would have to practice getting off the horse at a run first."

"How about this weekend? If the weather holds, I'll help you. Wade's been doing it too, getting ready for calf tying this spring."

"I don't even know where to start."

"Let's go hit the internet."

Grace was in the kitchen when they walked in. She looked up at Reilly then quickly turned away. His stomach started to hurt again…something was wrong.

Sadie and Wade were both on a computer when they entered the library.

"Thank goodness we have three." Nora said to Reilly as they slid into chairs in front of the machine.

"Let's go look at the youth rodeo website first." Reilly suggested. "See what all the events are that you have choices for."

"I don't want any roping ones." Nora frowned. "I love watching you guys, but I'm just not interested for myself."

"What are you doing?" Wade asked turning his chair to watch them.

Reilly quickly filled him in as Nora navigated the website.

"No barrels either." Nora glanced at Sadie who smiled and turned her chair to them too.

"Why?" Sadie asked.

"Because that's you and Scarecrow…and Grace too."

"We're in different divisions most the time." Sadie reminded her. "So we wouldn't be competing against each other."

"Click there," Reilly pointed to a tab on the website.

"Cutting?" Nora nearly yelled.

All four kids laughed.

"I take it…you would be interested in cutting." Reilly teased. "Jordan's been competing with him, along with Scott and Little Ghost, they've been doing pretty good. She took him to the clinic last year in Texas."

"I'd love to do that!" Nora nodded excitedly. "And Mom and Dad could teach me!"

Sadie nodded then she inhaled loudly. "That means, I can compete with Little Ghost soon too!"

"Jordan's gonna need a bigger horse trailer." Reilly laughed. "You can use Cooper for poles, goat tying, and cutting…none involve roping."

They spent the rest of the afternoon on the computers watching videos.

"Look at that," Nora laughed. "It's a plastic goat."

"Let's order it, it's only Monday, maybe we can get it here in time for the weekend." Reilly suggested. "I'll go ask a parent."

Reilly walked to the kitchen to see if there was anyone there…no one. He looked out the back window and saw Grayson and Scott just stepping out of a truck. He knew they liked a beer at the end of the day, so he grabbed two and a soda for him and sat at the kitchen table waiting for them.

They both grinned at him as they walked into the kitchen and took a chair in front of the beer.

"So what's the ambush for?" Scott asked as he leaned back, stretched his long legs out and relaxed.

Reilly told them of his and Nora's plans.

Scott nodded, "Rufio, Cooper, Buttercup, Dollar, and Scarecrow on the road, we may need to look at a bigger trailer, especially with Little Ghost joining soon."

"We might as well order a couple of the plastic goats." Grayson added.

"Wade will be moving to tie-down pretty soon too so it wouldn't hurt him to add the goat tying to prepare for the calves." Scott nodded.

Reilly looked down at his drink and smiled. He was six days short of being seventeen, but they still treated him as an adult. He really liked moments like this.

"How's Grace doing?" Grayson asked.

Reilly shrugged, he didn't want to tell him about her weird behavior until he understood it. But it did make him think of the twins.

"I talked to Brady and Billy today." Reilly told his uncles. "They have both been offered scholarships for football."

The men looked surprised.

"Aren't they still Juniors?" Scott asked.

Reilly nodded, "But they're huge, and good." He looked at Grayson. "But Brady is having a hard time getting his grades he needs in math. I told him I use Sadie. So he wants to know if she can tutor him."

Grayson laughed. "Does he know she's only twelve?"

Reilly grinned. "I told him, but he really needs his grades up so he can get the scholarship. He's had some adults try tutoring him with no luck. He thinks maybe a twelve-year-old will teach him at an uncomplicated level."

"For what he did for Grace…" Grayson nodded. "We'll ask Sadie if she's interested."

###

Grace basically ignored Reilly the rest of the week. If she wasn't in her room, her head was down typing on her phone. She barely spoke to him on the drive into and from school.

"Who is she texting with?" Leah asked Reilly at breakfast on Saturday morning.

Reilly shook his head which made her frown.

"Maybe it's time I pull the parent tech rules out and check." Leah sighed.

"Have you ever checked her texts before?" Reilly asked in concern. His dad had made him agree to the parent tech rules, too. Which let his dad go in and review Reilly's phone and computers, including Facebook, at any time. As far as he knew, his dad had never done it.

Leah shook her head. "I think the only one that has, is Scott and Jordan after Nick gave Nora the phone. Not that they didn't trust Nick, it was more seeing what Nora was sending him."

"Was there ever an issue?" Reilly frowned.

"Not once. Poor guy, some of the pictures she sent him were ridiculous, her toe nails after she painted them each a different color was one of the funniest." Leah giggled, making him relax. "They trust Nick with Nora, the same as we would with Grace or Sadie with Scott."

"I'm not sure how Grace would take it then."

"Well, she's never gone through what she did last week, and as far as I know, she isn't talking to anyone about it. Is she talking to you?"

He shook his head.

Leah sighed, "She left early this morning, taking Trail Boss into town for something Grayson needs when they get back from the ranch. She should have been back already."

A half hour later, Leah walked in as Reilly and Nora were reviewing goat tying videos again and getting ready to head to the barn for the first practice.

Reilly glanced up and knew what she wanted.

"I'll go see if I can find her," Reilly sighed. "Where was she going?"

"Home Depot…she left at 6:45 to be there when they opened at 7:00." She said worriedly. "She isn't answering her phone."

Reilly sighed and turned to Nora. "We'll go to the barn when I get back."

Nora nodded with a concerned frown.

Grace's Trail Boss truck was in front of Home Depot when he arrived.

With an ache in his stomach, he walked to the door with long strides. He didn't know what her problem was…but she dang well knew her mother would be worried about her.

Quickly glancing around, he didn't see her, so he walked to the far right of the store then he walked up to the middle cross aisle. He started walking across the store looking left and right.

She was standing in the back corner, opposite from where he started. Reilly couldn't tell who she was talking to at the end of the aisle; the person was around the corner from her,

With long strides he walked towards her. With each step, the concern grew. She was obviously hiding...there was no other reason to be in the back corner of such a large store. It was the house insulation aisle, and Grayson wouldn't have any need for any of it.

His boots echoed down the aisle as he walked, giving her a warning someone was approaching them.

She turned…her eye's grew wide in shock. A head popped around the corner just behind her…it was Levi.

CHAPTER THIRTEEN

Reilly stopped, frozen in shock. His eyes moved from Grace to Levi's bruised and swollen face. Levi's eyes widened and then he disappeared around the corner.

Reilly turned to Grace. She looked at him defiantly, which instantly pissed him off.

"You owe your mother an explanation. I would suggest you call her immediately." Reilly said flatly, then turned and walked away…his boots hitting the ground hard from anger.

He was already in his truck and pulling out of the parking lot when she walked out the front of the store. He could see her in his mirror as she stood and watched him drive away.

The longer he drove, the more pissed off he was. What was she thinking? She knew it was wrong…other than Reilly being mad…he could just imagine what Grayson was going to do…and Leah! Grace was hiding it…so she knew!

When he was within sight of The Homestead, he recognized the truck following him. It was the twins. He'd forgotten they were coming out for Sadie to help Brady.

Taking a few deep breathes to relax, he decided to focus on them and Nora.

There wasn't anything he could do about Grace… the only choice he had would be to break her trust. He sighed. Maybe this was one of those times he should.

He turned into the driveway with the twins following.

Leah was waiting for him on the back porch when he stepped out of the truck.

"Did she call?" He asked.

She nodded with a troubled look. "What do I do?"

"What you talked about this morning." Reilly glanced at her. She sighed heavily and nodded.

Taking a deep breath, he placed a grin on his face as he turned.

"Nice place!" Brady smiled as they shook hands.

"It belongs to my mom's family; built for three families." Reilly explained.

"All in one house?" Billy looked up at the house.

Reilly nodded. "When you think of it as 1 house for 3 families, it doesn't seem like its big enough."

"Nah…it's big." Brady laughed.

"I'm working with Nora this morning on some horse stuff." Reilly told them. "I figured we'd get Brady and Sadie working on algebra, and we'd go play in the arena." He said to Billy.

"An arena, too?" Billy shook his head.

They walked into the house and found Sadie and Nora waiting for them in the library.

Both girls stood, eyes wide and looking up at the twins.

"Dang." Sadie grinned up at Brady as Nora just stared with a stunned look at Billy.

"You're the math wizard?" Brady smiled down at Sadie.

"I love algebra!" Sadie said excitedly and grabbed the books he was carrying. "You just have to pay attention to the details; one at a time. Come on, let's get started."

Brady looked worriedly at Reilly then to his brother; he turned to Sadie. "OK, be easy on me."

Reilly laughed as they turned.

On the way to the barn, Nora and Billy walked in front of him. Nora was telling him about Arcturus and Isaiah. Reilly grinned as he looked at them. She was 14 inches shorter than Billy, just short of 3 years younger. The size difference reminded him of Scott and Jordan.

"So what are you practicing today?" Billy asked as they stepped into the barn.

All the horses stuck their heads over the stall doors. Reilly and Nora grinned, it was one of the best sights to see!

"Look at all of them!" Billy gasped in surprise.

"Have you ever ridden?" Nora asked him.

He just laughed and shook his head, "Been a city boy…no country living for me. Besides, I'm too big for them."

"No, you're not." Nora smiled up at him. "There's been lots of big riders, you just have to have a big horse."

Billy returned her smile. "That's a positive attitude, but even as tiny as you are…you're a whole lot braver than me to get on one of those."

"Billy, that's silly." Nora giggled softly. They all laughed at her unintended rhyme.

"So what are you practicing?" Billy asked again.

"I'm going to try goat tying." Nora told him.

"You're going to tie a goat?" He looked down at her in bewilderment, which made both Nora and Reilly grin.

Reilly pulled up a video on his phone and showed Billy what they were doing.

"You're going to jump off your horse like that?" Billy looked at Nora in concern. "You're too little, you'll get hurt."

"Well, we'll find out," Nora shrugged. "I imagine I'll do a face plant or ten. We're going to use Cooper. He's Reilly's horse."

They saddled the horse and made their way to the arena.

Reilly placed a saddle blanket in the middle of the arena in case she fell on her target. "Start in the box and just walk a couple times and step off, then we'll speed you up."

An hour later, Nora was galloping down the arena, bringing her leg over the horse and stepping off the horse and trying to get as close to the blanket as she could, without hitting it.

"That was awesome and crazy," Billy told them as they took a break.

"You run around with other guys trying to tackle and hurt you." Nora shook her head. "I'm just jumping on the ground."

"But I start from the ground." Billy grinned down at her.

"Anyone hungry?" They heard from behind them and saw Brady and Sadie walking up to the arena.

"Cora wanted to know if we were going in or if we wanted to eat outside." Sadie told them.

"I'll start a fire in the pit." Reilly grinned at the group. As he walked to the pit he glanced over at the driveway. Trail Boss was parked in its usual spot, which meant Grace was home.

"She and Mom have been locked in the no-media room for an hour." Sadie said quietly as she walked with him. "Do you know what happened?"

Reilly nodded but didn't explain.

Billy and Nora put Cooper in his stall, as Brady and Sadie went back in to grab their lunch.

Reilly stood and watched the flames grow and flicker. He was out of sync with Grace. He couldn't connect with her to know if she was OK. Why would she avoid him, yet meet up with Levi? Levi was responsible for what happened to her!

"You're right, Reilly." Brady said from behind him.

Reilly turned to watch the four walk to him.

"She's a wizard," Brady grinned down at Sadie. "I actually understood what she was saying to me."

"It's easy." Sadie laughed.

"No it ain't, Little Lady." Brady shook his head with a chuckle. "And, I'd sure appreciate if I can come back tomorrow for some more tutoring. I know we have a test sometime this next week."

"Sure!" Sadie said excitedly. "You're easy to teach."

"Depends on what you're trying to teach him." Billy laughed at his brother.

"Reilly turns seventeen tomorrow." Nora informed them.

"Well, how about Monday?" Billy asked.

"No, tomorrow's fine." Reilly shook his head. "Nora and I will be working on the goat tying again, we'll just do the same thing tomorrow."

"Are you sure?" Billy asked.

Reilly nodded. "It's Sunday, so Grace and Jack will be making breakfast. I'll just ask them to make more."

"LOT'S more!" Sadie laughed while looking between the twins.

"You know what the best thing is about birthdays in our family?" Wade asked Reilly as they sat on their beds. They had decided to have some guy time before dinner.

"What?"

"All the family makes an effort to be in the same place. That doesn't seem to happen very often…except Christmas and branding."

"I agree, Nikki came back for Matt's birthday, and now Lucas is here."

"And Jessup will be down in the morning." Wade smiled. "I think he's coming more for Kate than for your birthday."

Reilly nodded with a smile. "Her family from Oklahoma left on Wednesday, so now they can spend some time together."

"Do you remember Jessup being with any other lady before Kate?"

"Not for this long. I know he went out a couple times with a lady from Grangeville." Reilly shrugged. "Honestly, I just didn't really pay much attention before."

"Sadie said Billy and Brady will be here?"

"They will, coming for tutoring again."

"Cool. Going to be a fun barbeque."

The door opened and Matt walked in.

"What are you two doing?" He asked and leaned against the door frame.

"Just getting away from people and girls." Wade smirked.

"It's been me and Nikki, home alone at Circle 50 for the last 10 days…I think I'm ready for some family time."

"Dinner!" A voice echoed down the hall.

Reilly and Wade followed Matt out the door. They lined up, took off at a run…half way down they jumped into a slide and they slid all the way down the hallway, stopping at the rail in a roar of laughter.

"It's a full table tonight!" Nora called out with a grin as they walked down the stairs.

Reilly and Dru's eyes connected and they grinned at each other. She looked extremely happy about the busy dinner table.

He turned and looked around the room. Grace was already sitting next to Dru with a blank expression. He hadn't talked to her since he walked out of Home Depot that morning.

"Since you've been sitting next to Nikki for the last 10 days, I'll switch places with her so we can sit together." Reilly offered.

"Sounds good, love Nikki, but enough is enough!" Matt said loud enough for his sister to hear.

"I agree!" Nikki laughed and sat in Reilly's normal chair, next to Grace.

Half way through the dinner Matt turned to Reilly.

"What's going on between you and Grace?"

Reilly shook his head.

"Reilly, there is something obvious going on…Grayson told me about New Year Eve. Does it have something to do with that?"

Reilly nodded.

"Is she OK?"

"I don't know." Reilly whispered.

"What do you mean you don't know?"

"We can't connect…we're broken." Reilly answered, hoping he would understand.

"What happened?"

"I found her with Levi this morning at the hardware store."

Matt's head lifted and he stared across the table at Grace. "Why?"

"I don't know."

"She didn't explain?"

Reilly shrugged and stared at the food on his plate. "Maybe she did to Leah."

Matt was quiet as he stared at Grace.

"Go into the hall," Matt told Reilly in a low voice.

"Why?"

"Just go."

Reilly stood and was surprised when Matt did, too. When he reached the archway into the kitchen he turned and saw Matt had walked around the table and was approaching Grace. She looked up at Matt in confusion, then, when he spoke, her eyes widened and she shook her head.

"Yes." Matt ordered and grabbed her arm.

No one at the table moved or spoke. They just watched Matt pull her from her chair and drag her out of the dining room and towards Reilly in the hall.

"Matt, let me go." Grace uselessly tried to pull her arm from her cousin's grasp.

Reilly stood confused…not sure what Matt was doing as he drug Grace passed him and down the hall. He stopped part way down and turned Grace to the wall that was lined with framed prints.

"Reilly, come here." Matt ordered.

Reilly walked to them and looked at the picture that Matt had drug Grace to.

It was the picture of Grace riding Buttercup through the wildflower meadow in the Weitas the day before they watched the plane crash.

"What did I tell you that night around the campfire?" Matt asked them.

"I don't remember," Grace muttered.

"Yes, you do." Reilly and Matt said in unison.

"It's not the same," She sighed.

"Yes, it is," They replied in unison again.

"You're choosing to talk with and meet with Levi, over me." Reilly said; the hurt evident in his voice.

Grace didn't answer.

"I told you that night not to let anyone come between what the two of you have." Matt let go of her arm. "How can you say it's not the same?" He asked her.

"Levi isn't a boyfriend." Grace frowned at him.

"It doesn't matter, he's coming between you." Matt answered.

Grace stared at the picture then turned away. Instead of going back into the dining room she went up the stairs instead.

Reilly looked at Matt and shrugged. "It's broke."

They joined the family at the table; no one asked what happened.

With as much strength as he could muster, Reilly pulled on the barn door. It was no use, the pile of mud in front of it didn't budge. He tried pushing it with a boot and was surprised at how easy it gave way. He gripped the door handle again and pulled…a cool waft of air touched his warm skin.

The barn was dark but the smell of mud, urine, and manure was horrendous. It was a familiar odor that made his stomach tighten at the memory. He hesitantly took a step through the door and into the darkness. The flies buzzed around his head and he futilely tried to wave them off.

There was a sound towards the back of the barn so he took a step to it as his pulse raced and his back stiffened. He knew what he was going to see but had no choice…he had to get to the back stall. Forcing himself to continue to move forward, Reilly glanced into the stall to his left…it was empty. He moved to the next one…it was empty.

He closed his eyes tightly, anticipating the vision, not wanting to see it, but knowing he had no choice.

Eyes opened, another step and he was next to the stall. His hand went to the latch and he slowly unlocked it. Gripping the wood handle tightly, he pulled and opened the door.

One step and a hesitant turn…the sad, sunken eyes stared at him. Rufio, leaning against the stall wall, emancipated and forgotten, he was lost…Rufio was lost again.

Reilly's eyes shot open, his body tense. Taking a deep breath he forced himself to relax. The tension left his muscles but the feeling the dream left in his heart was still there. He was lost. That had to be the reason he had that horrible dream of finding Rufio again. He wasn't supposed to be lost anymore…he'd found his purpose…found his life.

He needed Rufio. He needed to put his hands on the horse.

Reilly sat up and grabbed his phone. It was 2:15 in the morning. He didn't care…he needed to go to Rufio. He silently left his room and made it down the long hallway and stairway. Making his way down the hallway to the back closet, he pulled on his boots and his coat.

The need to be with his horse was so strong, as soon as he pushed the door closed he turned and jogged down the steps and ran to the barn.

CHAPTER FOURTEEN

Rufio's stall was the second one in the barn. The horse's head appeared as soon as he stepped into the door.

"Hi, Boy." Reilly whispered to him and felt a sense of relief run through him as his fingers touched the horse's nose. That's what he needed; just to let himself know Rufio wasn't lost.

Then, he saw her. She was in the back of the stall, two bales of straw placed at the back wall. She was holding a bowl of bananas and peanut butter.

Grace smiled nervously, her eyes full of relief.

"I brought blankets, too." She said meekly. "I knew it would be cold out here."

Reilly pushed Rufio back and opened the door. He rubbed the horse down before taking a seat across from her and wrapping one of the blankets around him. Rufio stood next to him; the horse's head leaned against his shoulder.

He nervously stroked the horse's leg and waited for her to talk.

"This is a good sign," She smiled anxiously and held the bowl out to him.

"What?"

"You're here."

A sense of relief ran through every inch of his body. He sighed. She was right, they connected.

"What happened?" He reached out for a banana chunk.

"Matt was right," She admitted with a sigh. "I just never thought of it that way until he pointed it out. I thought it just pertained to boyfriends and girlfriends."

Reilly jammed another banana chunk in his mouth and waited for her to talk.

"Levi called me, I didn't answer, it went to voice mail." She sighed, leaned her back against the wall and pushed the buttons on her phone.

She played Levi's message. "Grace, this is Levi…you probably know that. I cannot tell you how sorry I am for what happened. I never would have agreed to distract Reilly if I thought anything like that would have happened. Please forgive me. I haven't talked to Alan since New Year's, but I talked to his mom. She was pretty upset because Brady had called and told her what happened before the sheriff got there. I verified it for her…she's pretty devastated. She said Alan told her that he wasn't going to hurt you…not go farther than he already had. He realized what he was doing and stopped just before Reilly hit the door."

The message ended. Grace pushed more buttons and played the next message.

"Sorry, message time ran out. I don't know whether to believe Alan…I never would have believed he'd do what he did…his mom thinks it's because he had been drinking, too. Teenager's do stupid things when they're drunk…I guess, not just teenagers. I doubt you do, but if there is any way you would agree to talk, I want to personally apologize to you. This has changed my life forever…the guilt will be with me forever. I don't want it to do the same to you. You did nothing wrong." There was a long pause. "Grace…if you don't text or call…just…I am so sorry…please tell Reilly I am sorry… your friendships are a great loss to me."

Grace held out the phone to Reilly. "You can read all the texts…Mom and Dad did."

Reilly shook his head so she tucked her arm inside the blanket and pulled it around her closer.

"I texted him the next day," She explained. "I didn't see him or talk to him until Home Depot."

Reilly's emotions were running rampant. He was still angry, but now…almost feeling sorry for Levi. His voice had been full of dread and regret.

Reilly remained quiet and waited for Grace to continue.

"Once I texted him, I couldn't stop." She rolled her lips together and sighed. "I didn't realize that it would consume me like it did. I just needed to understand…" Her eyes shimmered from rising tears. "I needed to know what EXACTLY Alan did before you and the twins came through the door." She looked at Rufio then back to Reilly. "I'm a control freak…I'm the one that takes charge."

Reilly nodded. "We all know that."

Grace took a deep breath and let it out slowly. "He took me out of control…I'm having a hard time with that."

"Why didn't you talk to me?" He couldn't keep the hurt out of his voice.

"Because I didn't want you to know what Alan did…" Grace sniffed. "I didn't want Mom and Dad to know the details…I didn't want anyone to know, until knew and I could deal with it."

"And now?"

"That's why I met Levi at Home Depot. At my request, he went and met with Alan. He was telling me what happened."

Reilly's back muscles tensed in anticipation.

"Alan said he didn't do anything…he stopped, when he realized how far gone I was. He didn't realize I would get drunk so fast. He only gave me the drinks to 'loosen me up'."

"He had no intentions of…"

She shook her head. "Not with me as far gone as I was."

"I will never forgive Alan." Reilly told her firmly.

She nodded. "But it isn't just giving me the drinks and getting us in that situation…but it's for taking me out of control. THAT I can't handle…and am still having a problem with it."

"Your parents?"

"They are trying to understand why I kept it a secret. Both are pretty upset with me but they promised to help me, get me help if I need it. They'll stand by me, but don't want me to talk with Levi anymore…until my head is on straight."

"You have a problem with that?"

She shook her head. "No, I don't need him anymore…I've forgiven Levi and I'm trying to move on."

"I don't know that I can forgive him." Reilly was honest. "He was your friend, too. He should have had your interest in mind as well as Alan's, cousin or not. By purposely distracting me, he betrayed both of our trusts."

She nodded, "He knows that…doesn't expect us to be friends anymore. He just wanted us to know he was sorry."

"Levi didn't mention his injuries." Reilly pointed out.

She shook her head. "He never mentioned them to me at all and I didn't to him."

Reilly relaxed against the wall, Rufio stepped closer and rested his head against his chest. Reilly's hand automatically went to the horse's round jaw and he stroked it softly.

"How are you Grace? What can I do to help?"

"Forgive me?"

"Done."

"No, Reilly, I know I broke our connection…your trust." She frowned.

"I broke your trust too." Reilly admitted. She deserved to know the whole truth.

Her eyebrows scrunched together in confusion. "What?"

"Leah came to me, asked me what to do. She and Grayson were…"

"You told her Levi was at Home Depot?" Her head tilted.

Reilly shook his head. He hoped she would forgive him.

Her eyes opened wide. "You told her to in-force the tech rule?"

"Only because we were broken and I couldn't help you in any other way." Reilly said quickly. Now he was on the defense. "I couldn't think of anything else…I only did it because I was so worried about you. She asked me about it and I couldn't think of anything else."

Grace's shoulders drooped and she rolled her lips. "I'm not sure what to say…but I'm sorry."

Now Reilly was confused. "You're sorry I broke your trust?"

"I'm sorry that it got so out of hand that it was your only alternative to help me."

"Grace…"

"Reilly," She stopped him. "I would have done the same thing."

They sat quietly and looked at each other, both processing the new information.

"Where do you go from here Gracie?" Reilly asked. "How can I help?"

"I need to get a handle on my control issues…or my momentary lack of…" She smiled slightly.

"You can't control what other people do to affect your life. You can only control what you do…to yourself and what you do to affect other people, positive or negative."

She nodded.

"You are in control of how you handle the situation…what Alan did and what Levi did."

"I know." She tried to smile. "And I'm working on that. With you, Mom and Dad, I'll handle it."

"You will Gracie."

Grace grinned. "I've really missed you calling me that."

They stood. After one last stroke down Rufio's side, they exited the stall to walk back to the house.

He put his arm around her shoulders and held her tight, thankful for her friendship.

"We're OK, Gracie. You're going to be OK."

"I know," She leaned her head on his shoulder. "I just needed my soulmate back."

CHAPTER FIFTEEN

"So, you are a Queen?" Billy asked.

Nora nodded, "For the Winchester rodeo last year."

"Nice!" Billy turned to her while holding the arena gate open. "What's next year?"

"Grace, Sadie, and I are going to try out for the club royalty court." Nora answered as they left the arena.

Billy nodded, impressed. "So should I be calling you 'Your Highness?"

"No!" Reilly and Wade said in unison and they all laughed.

Nora giggled. "I think I'll pass on that one."

"How often do you practice?" Billy asked as they walked back to the barn after a couple hours of Wade dismounting from Dollar and Nora dismounting from Cooper. They practiced tying the plastic goat. Reilly rode Rufio and practiced roping.

"Every night we can after school." Nora answered. "Every chance I can when I'm not at 4H, or my rodeo club activities and the royalty court events."

"If they would let us, we'd ride and practice every minute of the weekend." Wade grinned up at him.

"I understand that." Billy smiled back at him. "I'd play football all weekend if I could."

Billy carried Nora's saddle to the tack room for her.

"She doesn't let anyone do that." Wade shook his head with a chuckle.

"Do what? I just carried her saddle." Billy looked confused.

"That's what I mean." Wade said. "She, Grace, and Sadie don't let people help them unless we're at an event and in a hurry."

Nikki was the same way. Not all cowgirls were like that. Reilly had seen many girls that insisted their parents take care of the horses for them. But, not the Tagger girls.

Billy looked at Wade and nodded, then looked over at Nora as she stepped out of the stall and turned toward the feed room. As she walked, she turned to Billy and smiled.

"I'm glad you stayed for the barbeque lunch," Wade said.

"Yeah, just about all the parents invited us to stay." Billy grinned as he sat down on one of the straw bales they used for chairs. "After the fourth one, we kind of felt obligated…and very welcome."

"They're like that." Reilly smiled and leaned against Rufio's stall door.

"I'm gonna call and see when Alex is gonna get here. I'll see you inside." Wade turned and walked out of the barn.

Reilly watched Nora carry the grain bucket into Cooper's stall. Her hair was down today, flowing down her back with just a wide black headband holding it out of her face. She had on a blue denim Tagger Enterprises jacket with a pink hoodie underneath. It made her look sporty and cute.

"I'm glad the weather held for the weekend." Reilly turned back to Billy. He had been watching Nora, too.

Billy nodded. "Fifty for the middle of January is pretty good."

"What do you normally do on weekends in the winter?" Nora asked as she stepped out of Cooper's stall and replaced the bucket in the feed room.

"Spend most the time at the gym. I have a little brother that wrestles, so we'll spend time at his matches." Billy answered.

"How many of you mountains are there?" Nora laughed from inside the room.

"Just the three of us," Billy answered, then chuckled. "I think Mom had enough after Chad."

"Brady, Billy, and Chad." Nora stepped out and closed the door. She turned to him with a slight smile and stopped in front of Billy. She wasn't much taller than him when he was sitting. "No sisters?" She asked.

"Nope, Mom's the only woman in the house." He answered.

A loud bang rang out from the back of the barn.

"I'm gonna check that out." Reilly sighed and walked back farther into the barn.

Buttercup was in the far stall, probably bored to tears since she hadn't been ridden since New Year's. Reilly walked in and picked up the bucket she had kicked over. He ran his hand down her back and gave her some needed attention. He thought of Grace and their morning conversation. He was relieved they were back on track and so were her parents…when he'd quietly informed them.

Reilly stepped out of the stall and closed the latch. As he turned and looked down the aisle he could see Nora silhouetted against the open barn doors. She was still standing facing the sitting Billy…then everything changed to slow motion. Reilly took a step down the aisle…Nora took a step toward Billy…Reilly took another step…she placed her hands on Billy's shoulders…another step… she leaned in…another step and she kissed him!

It wasn't the fast kiss, like Kelly had first kissed Reilly. It was long enough that Billy brought his hands up to her elbows and tilted his head sideways to return the kiss.

Reilly was so shocked he didn't know what to do but freeze in place.

Nora stepped back, her eyes wide in disbelief, brought her hand to her mouth, then turned quickly and walked as fast as she could out the barn door towards the house. Her boots hitting the ground hard caused an echo throughout the barn.

Billy watched her walk out until she disappeared. His head turned and he looked at the ground.

Reilly started walking towards his new friend who seemed as stunned as he did.

Billy's head turned quickly to Reilly, his eyes wide in surprise. "Reilly, I…"

"It's OK…I think…sort of…I…think she shocked all three of us." Reilly just shook his head in astonishment. She is fourteen, he thought to himself. That was old enough for kissing…wasn't it?

"Dude…I just don't know what to say." Billy looked embarrassed.

"I don't either." Reilly sighed heavily.

These Tagger girls were just killing him!

"I won't say anything…not even to Brady." Billy stood. "But, …"

"Billy! We gotta go!" Brady yelled as he walked in the barn.

Reilly and Billy exchanged a bewildered glance then walked out of the door.

"Sunday night is home night for the family." Brady explained to Reilly. "Everyone has to be home by five o'clock."

Reilly nodded, smiled, and waved as the brothers climbed in their truck. As Brady drove by him, Reilly could see Billy in the passenger seat. His head tilted back and a hand over his eyes as if he had a headache.

Reilly turned and looked at the house. Now what? Was he supposed to ignore it? Was he supposed to talk to her? Should he tell Jordan? No, that wasn't going to happen.

He reluctantly walked into the back of the house, glancing around for Nora. She wasn't in the kitchen, dining room, living room, library, or in the no-media room. Which meant she was upstairs…alone? Wade and Sadie were in the library talking about Wade practicing jumping off of Dollar. Another glance in the living room and he saw Grace curled up between Grayson and Leah on the couch watching TV.

With all the kids accounted for…it meant Nora was alone.

Reilly sighed as he walked to the steps. He had to at least check on her, she'd looked and acted like she was shocked about the kiss.

He climbed the stairs trying to decide what to say; making his way to her door, which was closed, he still didn't know what to say.

He knocked.

"What?" He heard from inside. She didn't sound mad or upset.

"It's Reilly."

"What?" She answered in a lower voice.

"Can I come in?"

"Why?"

"Nora, can I come in?"

There wasn't an answer.

"Alright, fair warning, I'm coming in on the count of three."

Still no answer, so Reilly reached for the door handle with a big inhale then slow exhale.

She was sprawled out on her bed, face down in her pillow. Her black hair was a mass around her head.

"Nora?" Reilly smiled at the sight.

"What?" Came the muffled answer.

"Are you alright?"

"Why wouldn't I be alright?"

"Nora, I was in the barn." He answered, hoping she would know what he meant.

She lifted her head just enough he could see her very red face and anguished dark brown eyes.

He tried to keep the smile from spreading across his face but couldn't.

"Oh! Reilly!" She turned and yelled back into the pillow.

"I'm sorry." He chuckled. "Do you want me to leave?"

"Yes…no…yes…no." She said quietly into the pillow then, with an exaggerated sigh she turned around and sat with her legs crossed in front of her.

She looked at him in embarrassment. "I can't believe I DID THAT!"

Reilly closed the door behind him and sat in the chair next to her bed.

"Well, you surprised me, too." He grinned.

"Stop grinning!" She shook her head angrily. "I'm so embarrassed!"

"Why?"

"Because I don't kiss boys." She rolled her eyes.

"Do you kiss girls?" He chuckled.

"No…I don't kiss anyone. I've never kissed anyone."

"That was your first kiss?" Reilly asked, surprised.

"Yes. Why would you even ask that?" She tilted her head in exasperation.

Reilly grinned again, "Because you did pretty good for your first kiss."

"Reilly!" She buried her red face in her hands.

"I'm sorry." He apologized, still trying to wipe the smile off his face.

"What must he be thinking?" She sighed into her hands.

"Well, if I was him, and I had a girl as pretty as you kiss me…I'd be thinking I was pretty lucky."

"Reilly! Don't say things like that!" She still had her head down. "I don't want a boy in my life."

"Just because you kissed him once, doesn't mean he has to be in your life."

She tilted her head up, just enough he could see a confused eye looking at him.

He smiled again. "But you want him in your life."

"No!" She shook her head and buried her face again. "Yes…NO! Stop laughing!"

"I'm not laughing at you, Nora." He tried to assure her. "I'm laughing at your predicament."

She lifted her head up and sat in despair. "I kissed him Reilly…I KISSED HIM!"

"And he kissed back."

Her eyes grew wide and her face turned red again. "He did…he kissed back…which means he didn't hate it."

Reilly tilted his head and scrunched his brows in confusion. "Why would you think he would hate it?"

"I don't know…I've never kissed a boy before."

"So why did you kiss him?"

"I don't know…I was just standing there…then suddenly I was kissing him…I don't know why." She looked totally perplexed. "I've never done anything like that before."

"You've never wanted to kiss a boy?"

She frowned, "I've been curious as to what it was like…but I haven't known anyone that I wanted to kiss."

"Not even at school or a rodeo?"

"No," She turned confused eyes to him. "I was lying here last night wondering why I like Billy more than I like Brady…they're twins, they look the same."

"You thought of kissing him last night?"

"No…I had just realized I was looking forward to seeing him today…more than Brady."

"Maybe it's because you spent more time with Billy."

Nora shrugged, still confused she looked at Reilly. "Why did I kiss him?"

Reilly sighed and shook his head. "I don't know."

"Why did Kelly kiss you the first time?"

"Because we liked each other as soon as we met. She was thanking me for a good day at work."

"Did you kiss back?"

"The third time…the first two times happened so fast, and I was frozen in place." He chuckled.

She smiled slightly. "But, Billy kissed back."

Reilly nodded. "The tilt of the head is a good indication."

Her face turned beet red. "That is so embarrassing."

"What, that he tilted his head?"

"No…that you saw it!"

"Well, it could have been Sadie or Wade, who would probably have announced it to everyone already."

Her eyes grew large. "Do you think he'll tell anyone?!" She buried her face in her hands again.

"No, he said he wouldn't say anything…not even to Brady. And you know I won't…not even to Grace."

"Oh, Reilly…." She lifted her distraught face to his. "I am so confused…what do I do?"

"About what? It was just one kiss."

"But I don't want it to be just one kiss and I don't want a boy in my life complicating my plans."

Reilly shook his head in amusement.

"You're not the only one with plans. Billy's going to college on a scholarship, then he wants to play in the NFL."

"Maybe that's why I like him." Nora sighed. "He has plans and goals…like me."

Reilly nodded in agreement then looked at her concerned. "It was one kiss…"

"I know." She lay back on her pillow and stared at the ceiling. "I wouldn't be able to try out for Miss Rodeo Idaho if I was married or had ever been pregnant."

"NORA!" Reilly cried out in concern, his heart skipping ten beats!

She started giggling and turned to look at him.

"Why would you say such a thing?"

"I don't know…it just popped into my head." She grinned and he could see she had been teasing him.

"Seriously girl…that nearly killed me."

These Tagger girls!

Nora laughed then sighed gloomily. "Seriously though…" She giggled again at his strained face. "No seriously!"

They both laughed.

"What do I do? What do I say when I see him?" She asked in confusion.

Reilly didn't have any idea. "Just be you…like before the kiss, I guess."

"I don't know if I can." She said honestly. "Every time I think about the kiss or him…I want to kiss him again."

"Nora…" Reilly sighed. "I thought you didn't want him in your life."

"I don't." She sighed looking back up at the ceiling. "But I do."

"Being a teenager is tough." Reilly concluded.

"I agree."

CHAPTER SIXTEEN

"Have a good birthday?" His mom asked as they started to sit down at the full table.

"Long and busy." Reilly grinned at her.

"Everything good with you and Grace now?" His dad asked and pulled out Dru's chair which was between him and Grace.

Reilly sat in Dru's chair with a grin. "It's my birthday. I should be able to sit where I want."

His dad laughed, "Well, it's good to know that even at 17, you still want to spend time with your dad."

"It's good to know, after 17 years, you aren't tired of me." Reilly teased his dad.

"And where am I supposed to sit?" His mom asked with a raised, amused brow.

Reilly looked past her then up to her twinkling eyes. "Well, since Grace is sitting in my chair, you can sit in hers."

Dru turned quickly and looked at a laughing Grace, then chuckled and took the seat between the two teenagers.

Reilly looked up at Dru's happy eyes as she looked around the table full of family and friends.

"I love you, Mom." Reilly smiled at her.

"I love you, too." She leaned over and gave him a kiss on the cheek.

"What about me?"

"I love you, Dad."

"What about me?" Grayson asked with a smirk on the other side of Reilly's dad.

"I love you, Grayson." Reilly chuckled.

"What about me?"

"I love you. Leah."

"What about me?"

"I love you, Sadie."

"What about me?"

"I love you, Scott"

"What about me?"

"I love you, Jordan."

"What about me?"

"I don't know why, but I love you, Nora."

Nick just shook his head with a grin.

"I love you, Nick."

"What about your sister?"

"I love you, Nikki."

"What about me, Mate?"

"I love you, Lucas." Reilly answered in an Australian accent.

"What about me?"

"No, I don't love you Matt." Reilly grinned.

"What about me?"

"Absolutely, Cora."

"What about me?"

"I love you, brother-cousin."

"Don't tell me that."

"I love you anyway, Jessup."

"What about me?"

"I love you, Tessa"

"What about me?"

"I love you, Alex"

"What about me?"

"I love you, Gracie."

Silence…then a loud burst of laughter from the entire table.

Corny, but epic, Reilly chuckled…just epic.

"Let's go to the no-media room and do presents before cake." Dru called out after dinner. Everyone rose and carried their plates into the kitchen then walked down the hall.

Reilly sat in front of the fire and looked around at his entire family and extended family. This weekend sure ended better than it started.

Shirts, jeans, seat covers for his Tacoma, new hat band for his old hat, two new lead ropes, survival watch, a new phone, and then a brand new pair of cowboy boots from his parents; Reilly was gifted out.

"That's got to be all!" He grinned around at the family. "Thank you everyone. I love birthdays!"

"One more." Leah announced.

"Really?" Reilly just shook his head in amazement.

Sadie handed her dad's puppy to her mother, stood, reached behind a chair and picked up three packages. Her pale blonde hair was loose hanging down to her waist. She wore a light blue turtle neck shirt that made her blue eyes even bluer.

With a grin, she walked the packages to Reilly and set them on the side table next to him. She walked back over to her chair, took her dad's puppy back and curled back up comfortably and cuddled the puppy. She was smiling with anticipation.

Reilly looked at her then to the packages, that were numbered 1, 2, 3. There was a small card on top.

The card read: Don't answer anyone's questions, if they ask. Open the small package first, put it on, then open the second package (it's from your parents) put it on, then open the third package (it's from me). It was signed by Sadie…in perfect hand writing, of course.

Reilly glanced at Sadie, she just smiled, her eyes twinkling in humor.

He opened the first package. It was black silky material. When he picked it up, he started chuckling. It was a black mask that wrapped over his head and tied in the back.

He looked at Sadie, she grinned brightly, as everyone else started laughing.

Without a word, he put the black mask on. His dad tied it in the back for him, nice and tight.

"Wow, it sure makes your blue eyes stand out, you may want to wear that out on dates." Nikki teased.

"That's awesome!" Grace laughed. "What's it for?"

Reilly just smiled at her and following Sadie's orders, remained quiet.

He opened the second bigger box. It was a brand new black cowboy hat. He put it on…it fit perfectly of course.

"Nice!" Wade yelled.

"Goes well with the black mask," Nick chuckled.

"You look like a bank robber." Lucas added.

Reilly turned to Sadie, she sat quietly smiling as she held the puppy close.

He reached for the third package and opened the top.

He frowned at first…then realized what it was and a confused smile crossed his face as he looked up at the blonde gift giver.

"What is it?" Nora asked.

Reilly reached in the box and pulled out a figurine of Zorro, mounted on his rearing black horse, sword raised high in the air.

"Zorro!" Was yelled from the family amid the laughter.

Reilly tilted his head and looked at Sadie.

"Read the bottom." She said softly.

Reilly tilted the figurine over. There was a note attached.

The note: You saved Amy, Adam, and now Grace. Zorro was the best hero because he rode a black horse…like Cooper. You are my Zorro, Reilly. Love Sadie

As he read, Reilly felt the emotion tighten his throat, rendering him speechless…the pride that she would think of him that way. His blue eyes glistened through the black mask.

He didn't hear any of the laughter or comments around him, he just looked across to Sadie. She smiled softly, tears in her eyes as she looked at him proudly.

These Tagger girls were just killing him!

THE TAGGER HERD SERIES

Sadie Tagger

HEART & SOUL

Gini Roberge

CHAPTER ONE

From Scarecrow's back, Sadie could see Nora ride through the door of the arena building. She was perched perfectly on top of Isaiah. The newly appointed princess of their horse club, Nora was in full-on royalty mode. Her long dark hair curled, fluffy, and sticking way outside the brim of her black cowboy hat with the wide shining crown. Her dark clothes and hair matched with Isaiah perfectly. Sadie smiled at the sight of the pair. They sure looked good together, just as she knew they would.

And then Queen Grace appeared at the door riding Eli. Her smile lit up her face and within seconds she was laughing and so was everyone else around her. Her hair, just long enough to touch her shoulders, was straight and held behind her ears by her black hat that was adorned with the silver and gold crown.

Eli's tan and black buckskin coloring matched Grace's dark blond hair, black hat, and dark clothes.

She used Buttercup in the first event, but Grace's energy was mirrored in the prancing horse. Grace was worn out from having to hold onto the reins tight all day, plus having to watch anyone that came too close to the prancing horse so they didn't get stepped on. Eli was the total opposite, and behaved like a perfect gentleman for her.

Princess Nora glanced over and saw Sadie. After a quick wave, Nora said something to the people around her and made her way to her.

"You look awesome," Sadie grinned at her cousin's sparkling shirt that matched the sparkling smile.

"Thanks," Nora sighed happily. "I still wish you would have made it, too."

Sadie laughed and shook her head making the long blonde braid swish across her back. "I guess it wasn't meant to be."

Nora rolled her dark brown eyes. "You can't tell a judge that he doesn't know what the heck he's talking about…embarrassing him…in front of everyone…and expect to be appointed."

Sadie smirked, "Well I was right, wasn't I?" Nora nodded with another roll of the eyes. "And if he would have just listened to me, instead of assuming a twelve-year-old doesn't know what she's taking about, then I wouldn't have gotten pissed."

"And you would be here next to me." Nora shook her head.

"But I am here next to you," Sadie laughed. "Just not with a crown on my head and all gussied up."

"Well, I think you would have liked getting all gussied up." Nora smirked.

"Not in the dresses!"

"Girls!"

Sadie turned to see Aunt Jordan calling from the bleachers.

"What?" Sadie asked.

"The first round of barrels is about to start and Sadie is second. So quit talking and go get in line." Her aunt ordered with a smile.

Sadie nodded and turned her palomino.

"Good luck!" Nora called out.

"I'm gonna need it." Sadie frowned looking out the tractor making a final round in grooming the dirt for the race.

"Why?" Nora stopped her.

Sadie pointed in the arena. "Look at the ground; it's hard, pebbly and kind of shallow."

"You'll be OK," Nora encourage. "Scarecrow will take care of you."

Sadie waved and slowly made her way to the entry ally for the barrels. She smiled at all the girls and a few boys who she had been competing against for the last two summers on Scarecrow. Some smiled and said 'Hi'. Others just looked at her and the horse then sighed and turned away.

She was running just behind a little bay horse ridden by a racer she didn't recognize; it was the girl's first year competing.

Sadie leaned down and stroked her beloved horse's neck. Scarecrow turned her head, making the horse hair tassel that was attached to the horse's bridle swing. Sadie smiled; her thoughts going to Little Ghost and Angel. It was a gift from Aunt Dru and had been one of the best gifts she'd ever been given. It always made her feel that they were there with her.

"One more ride, then in a couple weeks you get to be a ranch horse." She ran her hand through Scarecrow's mane as she thought of the upcoming weeks.

Branding time! Just listening to the adults talk about all the plans, Sadie was having a hard time sleeping at night. She was so excited! It was her absolute favorite time of the year and this year there was double the excitement, it was Circle 50's first branding! Sadie had been ecstatic when she heard that Nikki and Matt owned Andy's ranch...because it doubled their branding time.

The announcer called out the first rider's name and Sadie stood on her tip toes in the stirrups as high as she could. She had to look over all the fencing between her and the barrels to see how the horse ran in the arena dirt. Sadie didn't like it. When she was warming up there was no solid footing for Scarecrow to dig into.

The first rider started at a run down the ally and headed for the first barrel. The horse was wide and a back hoof slid out behind him causing his back hindquarters to dip. The rider flopped to the side of the horse and had to pull herself up by the saddle horn. Sadie held her breath as the girl approached the second barrel…she reined the horse in to slow him down but he still slid with a back hoof then a front after the turn. Sadie cringed. By the third barrel, the girl had slowed down the horse so they were at fast trot as she went around the barrel. Instead of running to the end, the rider pulled in even more to finish at a slow trot.

The girl's face was white as she made her way down the ally and next to Sadie. Was it because it was the girl's first competition or was it the ground? She wanted to ask the girl but her name was being called.

Scarecrow pranced excitedly to the opening…Sadie hesitated…it was the first time she wasn't really sure. The first time she had ever doubted the ground. Was it the inexperience of the rider or was it the ground on the first run? The girl's little bay horse didn't run near as fast as Scarecrow.

They called her name again.

Sadie pulled back hard on the reins but Scarecrow was excitedly prancing to the left, then the right. Run or not? She reached down and patted the horse's neck.

"Are you going or not?" She heard the gate man yell at her.

Third time her name was called.

Sadie took a deep breath, released the grip on the reins, and Scarecrow took off down the arena ally. As she hit top speed heading for the first barrel, the horse slipped causing Sadie to fall slightly to the left. Her hand gripped the saddle horn tightly.

Around the first barrel…the horse's back hoof slid out from behind her causing Sadie to fall backwards. She pulled herself up and regained her balance just as Scarecrow tried to dig in but she slipped again, Sadie's body slid back on the saddle, nearly up and over it. Her lungs tightened…something wasn't right.

The palomino continued and pushed with her back hoofs as deep as she could to run to the next barrel. Another slip jostled Sadie to the left and she forced her heals down further into the stirrups to stay in the saddle. For the first time ever, she felt her nerves screaming at her to stop as her stomach clenched. After another slip she finally listened; Sadie was done and started pulling the horse's reins. A confused Scarecrow didn't initially react.

The hair raised on the back of Sadie's neck. Her stomach quivered making her pull tighter and nearly scream. As they neared the second barrel Scarecrow finally took the cue. The horse lowered her hindquarters to come to a sliding stop, but her front legs slid to the side causing her shoulders to dip. With the momentum of the run, the horse couldn't get her front hooves under her; Scarecrow was going down.

Sadie's body lunged forward and she gripped the saddle horn even tighter as the horse's shoulder hit the ground. She was thrust forward over the horse's neck with the long blonde mane flying into her face and whipping at her skin. They hit hard enough to slide five feet with Sadie's leg pinned under the horse; the hard dirt tearing at her jeans and causing shoots of pain up and down her leg. Fear rose in her as she felt Scarecrow's body start to roll…she leaned into it trying to keep the saddle horn from digging into her stomach.

With rising terror, Sadie realized that Scarecrow was going to roll on top of her, smashing her to the ground. Her whole body stiffened as she prepared to be crushed but at the last moment she slid safely to the side of the long neck, her leg was released from under Scarecrow, but she felt the pebbles and dirt digging into her back.

The force of the roll sent Sadie propelling forward and flying out of the saddle. She looked up and fear gripped her heart when she saw the hard wood wall coming towards her…the reins fell out of her hands as she tried to lift her arms to cover her head. She wasn't going to make it in time. Her whole body tensed to prepare for impact as she slammed into the wall; shoulder and head first. Intense pain ran through her body, flashes of light…then total darkness.

***

Sadie forced her eyes open, at first they seemed to roll back into her head but she managed to finally get them to focus…she blinked and blinked again as she tried to decide what she was looking at; finally coming to the conclusion it was a metal ceiling. She tried to turn to see where she was but her head wouldn't move. She tried her arms…they wouldn't move. Her legs wouldn't move. Her breathing increased as the anxiety took over her.

"Sadie?" A man's voice she didn't recognize…an uneasy feeling started growing in her stomach. "Sadie?"

Her eyes widened in fear as a strange man leaned over the top of her. Panic took over and she tried to crawl away from him, but she couldn't move. Her heart was racing…the sound thumping in her ears.

"Sadie, it's OK." It was Aunt Jordan's voice then her worried brown eyes appeared over the top of her too. Sadie stopped her futile attempt of moving. "It's OK, Hon, you're in an ambulance."

Sadie's eyes widened in terror. "Why?" She tried to say, but nothing came out.

She was riding Scarecrow…so why was she in an ambulance? The panic increased as she thought of her horse. Was she hurt too? "Scarecrow?" She tried to say but it wouldn't come out either.

Sadie looked desperately at her aunt, tears building. Where was Scarecrow!?

"Scarecrow is fine, Reilly said to let you know he would take care of her." Aunt Jordan told her with a shaky voice and tears in her eyes.

Reilly would take care of her…Sadie relaxed…her eyes rolled up again…the darkness swept over her.

***

Her eyes fluttered open. The ceiling was white this time but there was a large white machine over the top of her.

"She's waking up," A voice from somewhere.

She didn't recognize the voice, her heart began to race and she tried to lift her arms…panic gripped her as she realized she still couldn't move. What was wrong? Why couldn't she move?

"Sadie, we need you to relax. Everything is OK, we're just doing some tests." It was a woman's voice this time.

Sadie struggled, trying to move, tears started streaming down the sides of her head and into her hair.

"Sadie, its Jordan." Her aunt's voice rang out from somewhere, making her quit fighting, but the tears continued to stream and her heart raced.

"I want to go home." Sadie cried to herself. "I want to be home."

"Hold as still as you can, Sadie, and this will be over real quick. You're going to feel yourself moving and a big circle will come over the top of you." Aunt Jordan's voice was shaking. "Hold still Hon, just like you're playing statue with Wade and Nora."

Sadie felt the sobs start to rise, it just scared her more.

"Take deep breaths Sadie, it will help you relax." The strange voice said.

Sadie took in a quivering breath then another. It didn't help, the sobs came out causing her to choke then gag. Terror ran through her body when she realized she couldn't move or turn to throw up. Her heart beat faster, her whole body trembled. She cried out in terror.

"She's panicking; we'll need to sedate her." The ladies voice said.

Sadie rolled her eyes as she saw a lady with a bright pink shirt walk up next to her. Then nothing…darkness again.

***

"Come on, Sadie!" It was Wade's voice calling to her but she couldn't get her eyes to open. A tingling sensation came from her hand; it had to be him so she tried to grab it but the sensation started to leave. An overwhelming sense of loneliness ran through her. She desperately wanted to keep him with her so she gripped as tight as she could.

***

Somewhere she could hear beeping but nothing else. Her eyes opened and looked at the ceiling again. This time, it was white…a regular ceiling…she wasn't home…but she was lying in a bed.

Sadie tried to turn her head but something under her chin kept her from moving. She tried her legs and with great relief, they moved. She tried her arms…only one moved, the other seemed heavy and pain tingled in it. There was a dull, thumping ache running through her entire body.

With just her eyes, she looked around the room and saw her mom and dad sitting in a chair next to her. His head was back as if he was looking at the ceiling, but his eyes were closed. She knew he wasn't asleep because his breathing wasn't steady and deep. Her mother's head rested on his shoulder and her eyes were closed too.

Sadie looked around the room the best she could and out the window…it was dark outside.

She lifted the hand that could move and stretched her arm out to reach her parents, they were so close. The need to touch them was overwhelming, she wanted them to reassure her, let her know everything was OK and tell her why she was there. An ache of need swelled from her stomach to her heart. The metal rail on the bed kept her from touching them so she pressed harder until it squeaked and both parents jumped.

"Sadie!" Her mother cried out and reached to grasp her daughter's out-stretched hand.

The warmth of her mother's touch quenched the ache inside her. She smiled up at them. For some reason it made her mother cry.

"Mom," Sadie tried to say, it came out as a whisper.

"They are good tears." Her mother assured with warm loving eyes that made her body relax into the bed.

Sadie smiled at her, then up to her dad, his blue eyes strained but smiling. "Hi, Daddy." Her voice was barely audible but it made his eyes glisten.

"Hi, Sadie Girl," His voice quivered.

She moved her eyes as her aunts appeared in view on the other side of the bed; Jack and Uncle Scott smiling gently from behind them.

When she saw Aunt Jordan the memory of the scary room came back to her. "I'm sorry." Sadie whispered.

A sob of disbelief released from her aunt. "You have nothing to be sorry for."

"I tried to hold still, like you said." Sadie's voice shook at the memory of the fear, her stomach trembled. "I was just so scared."

Aunt Jordan leaned over and kissed her on the forehead; her warm hand cupping the side of her face. "I was so scared they almost had to sedate me, too."

Sadie felt the threat of the darkness coming over her but fought to stay awake. She wanted her mom and dad.

"What happened?" Sadie asked her dad.

"You don't remember?" He frowned at her.

"Just a little…" She closed her eyes and tried to remember.

Scarecrow was running at the first barrel and slipped, then slipped again. Sadie's heart started racing again and her body shook as she remember running to the second barrel…the nerves…the fear…Scarecrow falling…the roll…then seeing the wall come at her.

"Sadie, calm down." Sadie's scared eyes turned to her mother's voice.

The mane flying at her…the pain…the wall…more pain.

"Baby Girl," Her dad leaned closer to her and whispered. "Calm down, it's all over, we're here and you're safe." His soothing voice stopped the trembling.

"Where's Scarecrow?" She cried.

"She's at home in her stall," He said calmly. "She's just fine. Reilly and all the other kids will take special good care of her."

"Just relax," Her mother smiled.

Her anxiety started to decrease as she looked at her parents. The warm gentle touch of her mother's fingers wiped away the tears that had escaped. The motion warmed her inside but made her eyes want to close. She lifted her arm but it didn't move.

"What's wrong with my arm?" The fear started rising again.

"Relax," Her dad whispered. "It's broken…just like Wade had, so you'll be fine."

Sadie took a deep breath and let it out slowly to try and calm her stomach. Her blinking slowed down as she started to fall back into the darkness. Lifting her good arm she touched the side of her face where a dull ache radiated. It was tender, the pain made her grimace.

"It's bruised, Hon." Her mom whispered. "It's swollen and you'll have a good shiner." She nervously teased.

Sadie closed her eyes then nodded. A shearing pain pierced through her head and down her back. Her whole body stiffened and a scream escaped.

"I'll get the nurse." Aunt Dru said.

Sadie tried to open her eyes but the pain wouldn't let her…there was darkness.

CHAPTER TWO

Her eyes opened; Nikki was placing a cool cloth on the swollen side of her face. The skin was hot but the cloth made the heat and pain subside.

"Hi," Nikki whispered with a tender smile; her brown eyes shimmered with tears. "You sure scared the heck out of us."

Sadie smiled; she was too tired to talk.

"Hey, Blondie," Matt leaned over her and kissed her forehead.

The warmth and personal touch felt good, she sighed and closed her eyes.

***

She heard singing somewhere in the distance and forced her eyes opened. Grace was standing by the window looking out into the daylight. She was singing softly...just loud enough to be heard. Sadie just lay quietly and watched her until her sister turned.

Grace quickly walked to her, gently taking her hand. "Are you hurting?"

"No." Sadie tried to smile but wasn't sure she did.

"Good," Grace smiled. "Can I get you anything?"

"No," Sadie's eyes started to close again. "Just sing...I like to hear you sing..." She fell back into darkness as her sister continued her song.

***

"There's my Tagger." Dr. Mark smiled down at her through his mustache. Tenderness radiated out of his eyes.

Tears instantly filled Sadie's eyes when she finally got them both open.

"You're here." She whispered; he made her feel so safe.

"Wouldn't be anywhere else," He sighed and smiled warmly at her.

"I love you, Dr. Mark." She closed her eyes missing the tear that escaped and slowly slid down his cheek.

***

Warmth spread up her hand and she opened her eyes. Cora was standing next to the bed holding the hand gently in both of hers.

The older woman's smile was full of tenderness. Sadie tried to keep her eyes open but the eyelids slowly lowered.

***

It was Reilly she saw this time when she woke. Grace was sitting next to him, leaning on his shoulder sleeping but he was staring at Sadie.

"It's about time." He smiled.

"For what?" Sadie whispered, her head still tired and hurting.

"Finally waking up," Reilly grinned. "I've been sitting here staring at you…mentally telling you to wake up."

Sadie giggled softly. "I'm sure that's what woke me. How long?"

"About ten minutes." He chuckled.

"We'll have to work on getting that time down." Sadie sighed and closed her eyes tiredly. Then they shot back open. "How's Scarecrow?"

"She's OK. Just a good scrape along her shoulder that Dr. Mark and Kate said would heal just fine, no scarring."

"I don't care about scarring."

"I know, but there won't be any."

"Did you see me crash?"

"Yeah," He paused, sighing heavily. "After you didn't come out, when they called your name the second time, Jordan told me to run and stop you from running at all. I was almost to the end of the ally just as they called it a third time. I was yelling at you just as you kicked Scarecrow." He sighed. "I ran to the end of the ally and saw the slip around the first barrel and saw you trying to slow down. When you fell…when Scarecrow rolled…I just about died." His voice quivered.

"I'm sorry, Reilly." Sadie whispered, with the first tinge of guilt.

He shook his head. "I was already running to you before you slammed into the wall. Scarecrow was up and standing protectively over you by the time I got there."

"You're sure she's OK?"

"I wouldn't lie to you about that." Reilly nodded firmly. "It took all my strength to pull Scarecrow away from you so the medics could get to you. She knew something was wrong."

Sadie started to nod but remembered the pain the last time and froze. She leaned back on the pillow and relaxed. "Then what happened?"

"When I was running, I heard Jordan scream. She was there before the emergency crew got there and wouldn't leave your side. They tried to leave her behind but she climbed into the ambulance so fast they couldn't stop her. She may be little, but she's a ball of fire. You should have seen the fierceness come out of the woman."

They chuckled softly.

"She told them that she didn't want you to wake up and be surrounded by strange men. That it would be terrifying for you."

"That WAS scary. That and not being able to move. Then there was this little white room and this scary machine…Jordan's voice came from somewhere and told me to relax, but I just couldn't."

"She was really scared."

"I feel so bad…" Sadie sighed, feeling the tears and more guilt.

"It wasn't your fault," Her dad was standing at the door.

"Yeah," Sadie started to nod again and stopped. "I knew it was bad ground, I shouldn't have run. If I hesitated, I shouldn't have done it."

"Sadie, that may sound logical to you but it's not your fault." Her dad told her as he walked to her bedside.

"Did anyone else get hurt?" Sadie asked, worried.

He shook his head. "They shut the rodeo down when all the competitors refused to run."

"The whole rodeo?" Sadie was amazed.

"Yes, the ground was dangerous for anyone having to run fast," Reilly added. "All the riders put in a complaint with the rodeo association then packed up and left."

Sadie yawned again which made her head hurt. "How come my head hurts so much?"

"You had a pretty good blow," Reilly shook his head. "First Scarecrow rolling over you, then you smacking the wall."

"You have a concussion," Her dad informed her. "Plus you have tissue damage in your neck and torn tendons in your shoulder that will take some time to heal. Your spine took a bit of a jolt but nothing's broken. It will take some time to heal too. Your leg is bruised and scratched from being under Scarecrow as she slid and rolled over it. Then, of course, you have the broken arm and a bruised and swollen face." His face had turned white while he spoke.

"Can I see?" She asked, a little curious what her face looked like.

Reilly shrugged, forgetting Grace was asleep on his shoulder. She woke up with a start and cried out when she saw Sadie smiling at her.

"Oh, Sadie." Her sister came to the bedside.

Sadie squeezed her sister's hand when she felt it slide inside her own. "Do you have a mirror?"

"No, but I can go ask the nurse for one." Grace answered.

"Thanks, I want to see how bad my face is." Sadie tried to smile, her eyes starting to get heavy again and she yawned.

"You have some more visitors." Her dad said.

"Who?" Sadie asked in surprise.

"The waiting room is full of Taggers and friends. I would say there are about 25 people jammed in a room meant for 10." He smiled. "Are you up to a visit?"

"I don't know if my eyes will stay open." She admitted.

"I'll bring Nora and Wade in so they can see you before you fall asleep. They've been pretty worried." Her dad turned.

Grace returned with a mirror.

Sadie lifted it slowly and looked at her bruised and swollen face. She hadn't realized that she wasn't looking out of the whole right eye until she saw all the swelling and the discolored red, blue and yellow skin. The swelling and bruising went into her hair above her ear and up into her forehead.

It looked awful and all she wanted to do was cry, but knew her cousins were coming in and she didn't want to scare them. She quickly lowered the mirror and tried to forget what she saw but felt her chin quiver.

"The swelling will go away." Reilly told her with an understanding grimace. He took her hand and squeezed tightly for support.

Wade and Nora appeared at the door, both silent and looking worried.

"Go on in." Sadie's mom was standing behind them.

"Aunt Leah, are you sure?" Nora hesitated.

"Come in," Sadie called out to them. Hearing her voice, they stepped into the room and slowly walked to the bed. Reilly stepped back to make room for them.

"Last time we saw you, they had you on a board and they had you strapped in, like in the movies." Nora told her, tears in her eyes and quickly grabbing Sadie's good hand.

"You look better now." Wade added and touched the fingers that were sticking out of the cast.

They visited until Sadie's eye lids fell and she slept.

***

"I want to go home." Sadie tiredly told her parents who were sleeping in the chair next to her bed. Her voice woke them up. "I want to go home." Sadie repeated.

"We want you at home." Her mother informed her with a tired smile.

"How long have I been here?"

"Two days." Her dad answered.

"When can I go home?" She asked.

"The doctor will be in pretty soon," Her mom answered. "He wants to check you one more time, and then he'll probably release you today."

"Oh, good, I don't want to be here." Sadie whimpered. "How long will it take?"

"An hour to get released then a couple hours to get home," Her dad answered as he stood and stretched his long arms in the air.

"A couple hours?" Sadie asked in surprise.

Her mother chuckled. "You're not in Lewiston, Sadie. We're in Spokane."

"Really?" Sadie couldn't believe it.

"Yes, you were closer to Spokane than to Lewiston." Her mom told her.

"But all those people that were here?" Sadie looked at her in disbelief.

"They drove up here to see you." Her dad smiled.

Sadie sighed, that was a lot of people…every time she had opened her eyes there was someone there to visit…and they came for her…it was her fault…more guilt covered her heart.

"Let's have you sit up again." They stood on each side of the bed and helped her sit up without putting too much of a strain on her neck.

She grimaced through the pain; it wasn't as piercing as the first couple times.

"If I move slow, it's not bad." Sadie sighed.

"Well then, be a turtle." Her dad chuckled.

"Dingo turns into a turtle." Sadie looked at them forlornly.

"Only for a little while." Her mom assured her.

***

She was sitting on the edge of the hospital bed, with Grace by her side when their mother walked in.

"He said you could go home but he has a lot of conditions." She stood next to the bed and took her daughter's hand.

"Anything," Sadie sighed in relief. "Just get me home."

"No stairs, so you'll sleep in the guest room." Her mom started.

"Done," Sadie smiled, she liked sleeping in there.

Then her mom said the worse thing she could. "Absolutely no going near the horses until your doctor's visit next week."

"WHAT!?" Sadie cried out, pain shooting up through her neck and head, she grimaced.

"He's afraid they'll accidently bump into you and hurt you more." Her mother said sadly, understanding Sadie's distress.

"MOM! Not for a whole week!" Sadie's tears started falling.

"Honey, you said anything." She reminded her.

Then her dad appeared behind her mom.

"Sadie, you're taking pain killers right now. I've had my head bashed into a tree with the same bruising and swelling. I know how bad it hurts," He said with regretful eyes. "You don't realize what your body is going through and the next couple days, as your body begins to react to the trauma of the fall, it's going to be worse."

"Daddy!" Sadie sobbed. "I can't be away from Little Ghost and Scarecrow that long."

"It will go by really fast. You'll be sleeping most of the time because of the pain killers." He tried to comfort her.

Sadie closed her eyes, knowing she couldn't change their minds. She just didn't want to see them for a second, keeping the reality away for as long as she could.

"There's one more thing." Her mother sighed. "No school until after spring break."

Sadie didn't answer or open her eyes. She loved school, loved learning, but it wasn't near as bad as staying away from the horses.

"Your carriage awaits," She heard her mom say and opened her eyes.

There was a wheel chair with a nurse behind it. Sadie looked at it like it was a torture chamber.

Her anguished blue eyes looked up at her dad. "Can't you just carry me?"

"You have to leave in the wheelchair." The nurse informed her.

Sadie looked dejectedly at her, then up to her dad.

In one smooth motion, he bent down to gently pick her up, turn, and walk out the door.

"Your mom will deal with the nurse." He chuckled as his long legs moved down the hall faster than the nurse pushing the wheelchair. Grace ran ahead of them to open the door.

"Mr. Tagger!" The nurse called from behind them. "You can't take her out of here like that."

"Yep, actually, I can." He said and walked out the door.

***

Sadie rode in the front passenger side of the truck with the seat all the way back. Her mom and Grace rode in the back seat. Sadie smiled up at them from her reclining position.

"Dad's my hero." Sadie grinned tiredly.

"Mine too." They said in unison.

Her dad chuckled. "How about I do one more heroic thing?"

"What?" Sadie rolled her eyes to him; the neck brace was awkward in the truck seat.

"What do you say to a milkshake?" He quickly glanced at her with a grin.

"Oh yes!" Grace and Sadie agreed.

He stopped and purchased the milkshakes and after many attempts to position Sadie to drink the milkshake herself, it was decided Grace would just have to feed it to her from the backseat.

They giggled and laughed as they drove toward home, Sadie drank her milkshake like a little bird being fed dinner.

She slept the rest of the way home. Her eyes opened as they drove down the driveway to The Homestead. Sadie turned as much as she could towards the horses in the pasture.

"Can I just watch them for a minute?" She asked with the tears returning.

He stopped the truck and her mother opened the door to adjust the back of the seat so she could see.

As she looked at each one of the horses she quietly whispered their names; Libby, Kit, Rufio, Cooper, Eli, Buttercup, Rooster, Dollar, Isaiah, Arcturus, Scarecrow…then she yelled as loud as she could, making her head hurt and her mother jump. "Little Ghost!"

The grey horse's head lifted instantly and looked at the truck.

"Little Ghost!" She yelled again letting him know where her voice came from.

The horse started walking to the truck.

"Sadie, you're just making it worse for yourself." Her dad told her.

"I know, but I just need to see them closer." She said quietly as a tear escaped.

The horse reached the fence with his large brown eyes searching for her.

"Grace, can you love on him for me?" Sadie asked sadly as another tear slid down her cheek.

"Of course!" Her sister quickly jumped out of the truck.

Sadie watched as Grace loved on Little Ghost until her eyes grew tired and she fell asleep.

CHAPTER THREE

It was the middle of the night when Sadie's eyes opened. Her bruised and swollen face was hurting, which caused her shoulders to tense and make her neck and arm hurt. The combination of all of them caused shoots of pain down her back. Again, the tears stung at her eyes then slid silently down her face as she lay hurting in the dark.

She could hear someone breathing, but couldn't see who it was. She lifted her good arm and touched the side of her face, it seemed hot. More tears…

A small sob escaped her, her chin trembling.

"Oh, Mini-me…" Aunt Dru appeared at her side to place a cool cloth over her sore face.

Sadie's hurting, tear-filled eyes looked up at her aunt's distraught ones.

"Here," Aunt Dru gave her the pain medication, sat on the bed and cried with her until she fell back asleep.

***

Sadie heard voices but couldn't tell what they were saying. As hard as she tried she couldn't open her eyes. The voices were whispering, so she lifted her good hand to let them know she was awake.

"Are you OK?" It was Uncle Scott.

"I can't get my eyes to open." She said…her voice a hoarse whisper.

"Are you hurting?" He asked.

"Only if I move."

"Well, don't move." He teased.

"Ok, good plan." She smiled and tried her eyes again. Her eyebrows lifted high but her lids only enough to barely see out of them.

"Do you want me to hold up your eyelids?"

Sadie giggled tiredly. "Maybe tape."

He chuckled.

"Who were you talking to?"

"Jordan."

"I thought you two were going to the cutting competition this weekend."

He shook his head. "She wants me to cancel it."

"Why?"

"Sadie, that's a pretty silly question."

"But, Uncle Scott, I feel bad enough that this happened, and I scared her, and please don't cancel because of me." She felt the tears swelling, the guilt filling her heart again.

"Sadie; I can barely get Jordan out of your room."

"But that's the point," Sadie pleaded…wishing she could get her eyes all the way open. "She needs a break and Little Ghost and Cooper should compete, and you two are good and…"

"Sadie, calm down," He whispered.

"But I feel so bad," The tears fell.

"What's the matter?" Jordan said from behind him, nervously rushing to her side.

"Please go cutting this weekend." Sadie pleaded.

"Sadie, I just don't…" Her aunt's eyes filled with tears.

"Aunt Jordan," Sadie made herself stop crying and rubbed her eyes with her good hand until they finally came open. "It's not your fault this happened, it's mine, and I don't want this to stop you from going. I feel bad enough already."

"Sadie, it wasn't your fault," her aunt whispered.

"Please go, Aunt Jordan. I'm just going to lay here and sleep anyway. I just need you to go and have fun."

"I can't have fun with you laying here." Her tears fell.

"Then don't have fun," Sadie half-smiled. "But go compete and get the horses out and let Uncle Scott win with my horse."

"Sadie…"

"Send me pictures and a video of Little Ghost." Sadie said firmly.

Her aunt smiled at her and just shook her head.

"Promise me," Sadie pleaded. "I really feel so bad already."

"OK, I promise," Her aunt whispered and kissed her on the good side of her forehead. Within minutes she left to get ready.

Uncle Scott smiled down at her. "Good job, she really needs to get away."

"So do you," Sadie smiled up at him. "Is Mom here?"

"She's in the kitchen. You don't like me anymore?"

"I have to go to the bathroom."

"Oooohhh…I'll go get her."

***

Sadie bent her good arm at the elbow so she could see the fingers, then slowly lowered it, then repeated. It was the only thing she could move without hurting.

"How long have I been in here?" Sadie asked her current family nurse.

"Three days." Aunt Jordan answered.

"So, it's been five days since the accident?"

"Yes."

Sadie watched her arm go up and down. "I'm sorry."

"We've been through this, you aren't to blame."

"Yes, I am."

"No, you're not."

"Why does everyone say that?"

"Because you're not at fault, Sadie. The person responsible for the arena is."

"No, it's my fault."

"Sadie."

"Aunt Jordan."

"Are you arguing with me?"

"Yes."

"Why?"

"Because I am the one that made the decision to run, no one else. I knew the ground was bad…but I took the chance anyway."

"Why did you take the chance?"

"I didn't know if the first rider had problems because of the ground or because it was her first competition and she was nervous."

"So you chanced it."

"Yeah…I figured I would just stop if I didn't like it, once I got out there."

"And you did try."

"Yeah."

"And you would have been able to stop if the ground wasn't bad and Scarecrow didn't slipped."

"But, I wouldn't have had to stop if I didn't run."

"Do you think there is an end to this argument?"

"Yes."

"What is it?"

"That all of you quit telling me it wasn't my fault and admit it was."

"You know that won't happen."

"That's the only way it can end."

"That way, or we just quit arguing."

Sadie let her arm rest on the bed, closed her eyes, and let the pain killers put her to sleep again.

***

"I stink." Sadie smiled at Jack.

"Well, I was trying to be polite and not say anything." His black hair made his blue eyes brighter and his grin made his dimples deepen.

"Aunt Jordan said I've been in here three days."

"That's right."

"So, there is the day of the fall, two days in the hospital and three days in here."

"Yeah, six days of stink on you." He chuckled.

"Have you ever gone six days without a bath or shower?"

"No, I think the longest was four."

"What were you doing?"

"Spring break when I was in high school. A bunch of buddies and I went camping and riding in the mountains."

"Your spring break was only four days? Not a week?"

"Full week, but after four days we couldn't stand the smell of each other so we hiked around and found a big creek to swim and bath in." Jack grinned. "It was the only way we could stay out another three days."

Sadie smiled and had to work on not laughing, it hurt to laugh.

"I can help you to the bathroom then go get Leah."

"I might get my stink on you." She warned him with a grin.

"That's OK, if you do, I have a shower upstairs and I can go outside and burn the clothes."

Again, she had to stop from laughing.

She started to nod then thought of the pain it caused in her head. "It's not until you hurt your head, do you realize how many nods you do in a day."

"I've never thought of that." He answered as he helped her stand.

"I have to think of it a lot now."

He held her good arm and had an arm around her waist to hold her up as they walked. The leg that had been pinned under Scarecrow tingled in pain making her grimace.

"Wouldn't it be easier if I carried you?"

"Probably, but my feet are forgetting what it's like to walk."

He chuckled as he set her on the edge of the tub.

"I'll go get Leah."

"Thank you, Jack."

"You're welcome, young lass."

Her good hand reached up for the hundredth time and touched the neck brace she had on. It was getting to be quite the annoyance. The cast was annoying, too. It was from her finger tips up to her elbow. Wade's had been all the way to his arm pit but it was broken on the upper part too.

Sadie moved the door so she could see the mirror on the back of it. She sadly stared at the image in front of her. Blonde hair sticking out of her braid; spiking out to the sides and to the top of her head. She had pink pajama bottoms on and a blue t-shirt. She turned her head as far as she could to see the swelling around her eye had gone down but the top quarter of her face was black, blue, and yellow.

"I hear you stink," Her mother smiled from the door.

"How is the pain?" Aunt Dru asked from behind her mother.

"OK, right now. My arm quit hurting so much and my face."

"I hate it when my face hurts." Her aunt teased.

"Believe me," Sadie grinned. "It ain't good."

"Well, Jack was thinking you might like our bathtub with the massaging jets better." Aunt Dru told her.

Sadie's eyes widened in hope. "Oh, yes. I love your tub."

Aunt Dru stepped out of the room and Jack stepped in.

"Walk or carry?" He asked.

The image of the really long hallway and stairs flashed threw her mind. "Carry."

"Good decision." He smiled and scooped her up in her arms.

"Bubbles?" Her mom asked.

"Of course," Sadie answered, again reminding herself not to nod.

It was a huge tub so Sadie could lie in the middle and float like she was in a lake. While her mother washed her hair, her aunt held her cast out of the water.

The bubbles surrounded her like a cloud and Sadie closed her eyes. In the darkness, she could feel the water's warmth soak into her skin and reach inside her. The air jets were shooting swirling water against her sore and hurting muscles; it softly tickled her skin making her relax into a warm haze; her mind was entranced. Tiny bubbles from her cloud popped softly on her skin.

Somewhere in the distance she heard her mom; "Don't fall asleep."

"Shhhh…I'm floating." Sadie whispered while looking down at the horses from her cloud. She soared in the air above them and whispered their names; Little Ghost, Eli, Rufio, Buttercup…

***

Dr. Mark sauntered into her room and slowly took a seat in the chair next to the bed. "I brought you something to fill your time while you lay around in bed."

"For me?"

"Yep, I found it in some of my old books…knowing how you like to read and learn, I thought of you."

With her good hand, Sadie excitedly took the book he held out to her. The neck brace was finally gone making it easier to reach.

"It's not a normal book for a twelve-year-old." Dr. Mark's eyes showed a smile since she couldn't see his mouth through the mustache. "But you're not a normal twelve-year-old."

Sadie set the book on her lap. There were running horses across it but it wasn't a *story* about horses…it was a book *about* horses…it was about equine sports medicine.

Sadie grinned at the veterinarian she's known all her life and thumbed through the pages. "I might need the computer to look up some of these words…but that just makes it that much better!"

"I knew you would like it."

***

"It's time for the changing of the guards." Reilly grinned as he and Grace stepped into the room.

Sadie glanced at her dad as they sat on the edge of the bed and smiled.

"I'm glad you were awake this time." He stood and kissed her forehead.

"I love you, Dad." She whispered to him, her eyes shining with adoration.

"I love you, Sadie Girl." He said with tears stinging at his tired blue eyes.

He rose and slowly walked from the room, without a glance or word, to Grace and Reilly.

"So how long have you been awake?" Grace asked.

"A couple hours," Sadie answered. "Dad and I did some walking up and down the hall."

"That's awesome." Reilly said excitedly.

"My back aches when I walk. Dad said it was the jolt to my spine." Sadie told them.

"We have a surprise for you." Grace smiled as she and Reilly moved the bedside table.

"What are you doing?" Sadie asked in surprise.

They just grinned in response as they each reached down, grabbed the bottom of the bed and pulled. The bed was twisted so she was right next to the window.

Grace stuffed more pillows behind Sadie so she could sit up higher and relax against them.

When Sadie turned to the window she saw the horses grazing in the pasture. Her hand reached out as if she could touch them but she just touched the glass. "Ohhh, I can watch them." She was quiet for a while then turned to Reilly. "They are so far away. The door is…"

"Don't ask him, Sadie." Grace ordered sharply.

"What?" Sadie looked at her sister in surprise.

"Dad and Jack threatened him with dire consequences if he took you to the horses." Grace answered.

"Why?" Sadie frowned.

"Because they knew…if you asked…he would." Her sister glanced at Reilly who was standing quietly looking out the window at the horses.

"I promise, I won't Reilly," Sadie leaned on the pillows and looked out at the horses; her fingers lightly touching the glass. "They'll make it up closer pretty soon."

"I'll be right back." Reilly said and quickly left the room.

Grace crawled up on the bed and sat next to her sister as they watched the horses wander the pasture.

"So what's going on in here?" The girls turned to see their mother.

Cora and Aunt Dru walked in the door behind her.

"We thought she could watch the horses this way." Grace answered quickly; not sure if they would get in trouble for it.

"I think it's a great idea." Aunt Dru smiled.

"Your dad thought it might be too tough on you to see them. You cried in the truck." Her mother reminded her.

"It's OK now," Sadie smiled at her. "I love seeing them."

"Well, how do you feel about food?" Cora asked. "What would you like next?"

"You've been feeding me pretty darn good." Sadie smiled warmly.

"But you haven't been eating very much of anything I put in front of you." She reminded Sadie. "So, what really sounds good to you right now?"

"I don't know," Sadie sighed; she really didn't have much of an appetite. "I like the little quiches you make with bacon."

"Well, I'll make a whole bunch so you can nibble on them all day then." Cora nodded. "And maybe some of the chocolate chip cookies you love."

Sadie grinned. "Better make a whole bunch of those, everyone else will want to eat them too."

"I think you're right." Cora agreed with a pleased smile.

There was a thumping sound, lots of them and they were getting closer. It was a sound that Sadie recognized.

"That sounds like hoof beats." Sadie looked at her mother, Cora, and her aunt in confusion.

They grinned and nodded to the window. Sadie turned, but didn't see anything.

Suddenly, Reilly appeared with a rope in his hand...then a grey nose, a beautiful, wonderful, grey nose, and then that gentle loving brown eye...Sadie's heart raced with love.

"Little Ghost..." Sadie whispered excitedly and placed her hand on the window. Little Ghost's head was just inches away. Her heart ached to touch him, to feel the warmth of him.

Grace moved the pillows and slid behind her sister allowing Sadie to lean against her for support.

Her mother climbed on the bed and opened the window.

"Little Ghost," Sadie whispered and the horse's head bounced up and turned towards the window, his eyes searching. Sadie placed her hand against the window screen and pushed. The grey horse pushed his nose to her hand, sending streams of love into her hand, up her arm, into her heart and tears to her eyes. His breath ran through her fingers, her skin tingled from the sensation.

"Oh, my boy, I've missed you." Sadie ran her finger down his nose with only the screen between them. The horse pushed harder against her hand.

"Hold on." Sadie heard her dad.

With difficulty, he pushed the horse's head away from the window and quickly stepped in front of it to remove the screen. The second he moved away, Little Ghost's head swung into the window and into Sadie's awaiting hands.

Sadie giggled excitedly as the horse's nose ran from the top of her head, to her neck, and down her arm, his breath caressing her skin gently. He finally just stood still and let Sadie run her good hand down his nose, over his eyes, around the jaw line and to the soft velvety muzzle. She spoke to him softly, telling him how much she missed him and loved him.

The horse stood with his eyes half-closed as she leaned forward, resting her forehead on his neck and breathed in that smell that she had come to love. It filled her lungs as well as her soul. Little Ghost turned just slightly towards her, returning her love. To Sadie, there was no one else on earth at that moment besides her and this special friend who loved her unconditionally.

She felt the healing of her body, the same as when they rescued the horses and she would lean into him, willing her energy and love into him, to help heal his body and soul.

"OK, next." Her dad said from outside.

Sadie leaned back, "You do good this weekend for Uncle Scott." She kissed her equine friend on the nose and Little Ghost's head disappeared.

It was the blonde nose that came in next. Sadie inhaled sharply as she saw Scarecrow for the first time since the fall. She didn't talk to Scarecrow as she did with her grey horse. There were no words

Sadie could say to show the horse her love and ask Scarecrow for forgiveness. Sadie let her hands, breath, and warmth of a shared touch, tell the horse how she felt. She kissed the horse's nose and ran her fingers through the horse's mane and forelock. It was smooth as silk…evidence that Reilly and the rest of the kids were taking good care of her.

Sadie looked down to see the healing scrape marks on Scarecrow's shoulder. She sighed with an aching heart; another coat of guilt wrapped around her heart.

"OK, that's enough for this round." She heard her dad's voice as he backed Scarecrow out of the window.

"Thank you, Dad." Sadie smiled when she finally saw him.

"It was Reilly's idea." He answered with a smile as he led Scarecrow away.

Reilly stood outside the window, holding Little Ghost's lead rope and grinning at her.

"Thank you, Reilly." She grinned back.

"You'd do it for me." He said softly as he turned to follow her dad.

She knew…she would.

"Alright, young lady," Her mom sat at the end of the bed. "How is the pain?"

"It's just achy." Sadie answered and snuggled into her sister. Grace's arms wrapped around her and hugged gently.

"I think we can leave the bed just like this so you can watch them." Her mom smiled.

"Can they come visit again?" Sadie asked hopefully.

"As long as the boards on the deck hold out," Aunt Dru chuckled.

"That was awesome." Grace sighed and slowly slid out from behind her sister.

Her mother shut the window and repositioned Sadie onto the pillows.

"You're sure you're not hurting." Her mother questioned.

"I'm OK right now, Mom. Just getting tired all the sudden." Sadie answered. Her mom's eyes looked as tired and strained as her dad's.

"Just a little excitement wears you out." Aunt Dru squeezed her hand, kissed her forehead…her eyes were tired, too.

"I'll have those quiches and cookies ready for you when you wake." Cora smiled gently.

"You let us know if you need anything." Her mother said before the three women left.

Sadie's eyes closed and she fell asleep.

When she woke, it was only Reilly sitting in the chair. He had pulled it along the bed and was facing her; his feet resting on the mattress next to her pillows. His eyes, distant and searching, were staring out the window that became the portal to her horses.

A plate of mini-quiches and chocolate chip cookies sat in his lap.

"Have I been asleep that long?"

He turned and smiled, causing his dimples to deepen just like his dad's did. "Long for what?"

"That Cora made all the quiches and cookies."

"I guess it doesn't take long, it's only been an hour or so."

He held out the plate, close to her good arm.

"I'm not hungry." She smiled.

"I don't care, eat anyway." He ordered.

"What?" Sadie giggled in disbelief.

"Everyone is worried because you've lost weight and you're not eating." He lowered his feet and leaned forward, resting his elbows on his knees. His blue eyes stared at her in concern. "So, since I can't help with anything else, I am taking it upon myself to feed you, and make sure you eat."

"You helped bring me my horses…that's everything."

"If you want to get out there to them," He motioned to the horses grazing in the pasture. "Then you have to be strong, Sadie. If you don't eat, you can't keep up your strength…it will keep you away from them longer." He pushed the plate closer to her.

Sadie ate three quiches and a cookie.

CHAPTER FOUR

"Adenosine…" Sadie read out loud, hoping she pronounced it correctly. She quickly typed the word into the tablet her mom had given her and read the definition; *Adenosine is a nucleoside that occurs naturally…*

"Nucleoside…" Sadie read out loud again as she typed it into the tablet; *…consisting typically of deoxyribose…*

"Deoxyribose…" Sadie read out loud again as she typed it into the tablet in her search for definitions; *…any of certain carbohydrates derived from ribose by the replacement of a hydroxyl group…*

"Hydroxyl…" Read out loud and typed upon the tablet as she continued her search.

***

For the first time since the fall, when her eyes opened, no one was in the room with her. They must have thought she was sound asleep. Looking at the clock, it was seven o'clock at night. She looked at the book that Dr. Mark had brought her; she'd read it every time she was awake for the last two days.

She looked around and suddenly felt lonely. The house was completely silent. She was sure everyone was out on the deck having dinner, so she rolled on to her side and pushed herself up. Waiting until the dizziness went away, she attempted to stand. The sore leg was bent and stretched then tentatively she stepped forward using the wall to brace herself.

She was wearing a yellow t-shirt and white pajama bottoms; her hair pulled back in a long pony tail with multiple bands to hold it together. The neck brace was long gone but the bruising on her face was now a swirl of black, blue and yellow as it healed.

On wobbly legs and bare feet, she took a trial step, then another; her back ached but she was OK. Keeping a hand on the wall she stepped toward the door.

When she reached the door and looked down the long hallway, she groaned. The fun long hallway now looked like a long endless tunnel. A hand on the wall, just under the line of picture frames, she slowly made her way down the tunnel. Halfway down was the picture of Scarecrow and her winning the PeeWee division championship. The horse's long neck stretched out as they were running home. Sadie was sitting forward encouraging her to run faster.

She could feel the tears welling in her eyes as she stared at the photograph. It seemed so long ago, she thought. She was so happy, Scarecrow ran faster that day than any other ride…she must have known what was on the line. Then, the crash…Sadie closed her eyes as the vision of Scarecrow's mane flying into her face and the feel of the horse pushing her into the ground, the terrifying flight into the wall.

She reached up and touched the injured area around the eye and found tears she didn't realize had fallen.

"Sadie!"

She opened her eyes and looked up to see Nick, face tense and shocked, walking quickly down the hall towards her. He picked her up and cradled her in his arms. With a deep sigh, she rested her head on his shoulder. The warmth and strength felt good…like they were healing her sadness.

"What are you doing?" He whispered worriedly.

"I don't know. I just didn't want to be in there alone."

"Sadie, you can't just walk around by yourself right now. One fall could injure your neck even more."

She felt the tears silently sliding down her cheeks. "I'm sorry, I know you don't like it when I cry."

"You're hurting…" He said gently. "It's when I don't understand the tears that I can't handle now, but you're hurting, I understand…I can handle it this time."

"Thank you."

"So where do you want to go?"

Sadie relaxed into the arms cradling her. "I think I just needed a hug. This cradling is working too."

He chuckled. "So, you want me to just stand here in the hall and cradle-hug you?"

She giggled softly. "If I tell you where to go…then you may stop cradle-hugging me."

"And if I promise I won't? Will you let me take you somewhere besides the hallway?"

"Promise?" Sadie said, needing the warmth and compassion right now.

"Absolutely, I'll cradle-hug you for as long as you want. But are you sure you don't want me to get your mom or dad?"

"No, they've been with me for days, I think they need a break from me."

"Sadie, your parents will NEVER need a break from you."

"But they are so tired...all of them." She sighed.

He nodded, "Well, I promised I'd cradle-hug you as long as you wanted, so where to?"

"You probably want to sit down."

"I could stand for a while but sitting I could hold you longer."

"OK, can we go to the couch in the living room?"

He turned and headed for the room but stopped in front of the couch. "Now what?"

"Just turn and sit, silly."

"Turning and sitting…"

Sadie felt him lower down to sit on the couch, he gently held her away from him to keep from hurting her. When he was down, she wiggled into a comfortable position and rested her head into his neck so her eyes were covered.

"That's an interesting position." He chuckled.

"Your neck is warm and when I close my eyes, it adds extra darkness."

"Interesting theory, but does it hurt your neck?"

"No, only if I move it quickly. Are you comfortable?"

"I'm just fine. I have a ten-year-old keeping me warm."

"I'm twelve."

"Nora's twelve."

"Nora's fourteen."

"You girls have got to stop getting older, I just can't keep up." Sadie giggled.

"So, why were you crying when I found you in the hallway? Were you hurting?"

Before she could answer, they heard footsteps in the hallway.

"It looks like you have a visitor." Nick told her. Sadie could feel Nick's pulse beat faster.

"Who is it?"

"You have to unbury your eyes to see." He chuckled.

Sadie sank down on his lap to peek under his chin, but all she saw was the living room. "I don't see anyone."

"I'm right here," Tessa's voice was low and soft as she stepped to the end of the couch.

Sadie smiled. "All I can see is your legs, would you mind sitting so I don't have to turn my neck? Please?"

"Ok…" Tessa answered hesitantly and slowly sat on the edge, at the far end. Her curly light brown hair was tucked behind her ears; her brown eyes looking hesitantly to Nick.

Sadie was greeted with a smiling, tense face.

"It's OK, I'm alright." Sadie said reassuring her.

"I know; your parents have been keeping me updated. I wanted to come by, but I've been taking care of the B&B while your family was with you." Tessa answered. "I came in to check to see if you were sleeping."

"I was, but woke up. Nick found me in the hall."

"Are you OK?" Tessa asked with a frown looking between Sadie and Nick.

"Yeah…I just needed a hug…so he's cradle-hugging me." Sadie smiled.

Tessa giggled, her face relaxing. Nick's heartbeat increased.

"Are you cold?" Tessa asked.

"Nick's keeping me warm," Sadie answered. "I'm comfortable. His arms and chest are really strong and warm…plus he smells good."

Nick chuckled, "Well, I'm glad I took a shower after riding all day."

Tessa's cheeks turned red and she glanced quickly at Nick then back to Sadie. "What about the side that Nick isn't keeping warm? Would you like a blanket?"

"Would you be too hot?" Sadie asked Nick.

"I'm fine," He answered. "You need a blanket?"

"I guess so," Sadie answered. "It's a little colder."

Tessa disappeared, then quickly returned with the blanket from the chair and a pillow. She knelt down in front of them, placing the blanket over her. Nick's heartbeat grew stronger when she placed the pillow under his arm where Sadie's back was leaning.

"That way he can relax his arm." Tessa smiled at her.

"That's much better." Sadie leaned down into the pillow.

Tessa returned to her seat next to them, closer this time, and placed a hand over Sadie's leg, next to Nick's arm.

"Do you want me to get your parents?" Tessa asked gently.

"No, I'm OK now. They need a break from me." Sadie felt her eye lids start to close as her muscles relaxed.

"They'll never need…." Tessa started.

"I know, Nick said the same thing." Sadie sighed. "But their eyes are really tired, they need a break."

Tessa looked up and smiled at Nick, his heartbeat raced.

"So what were you talking about when I came in?" Tessa asked looking back at Sadie.

"I asked her why she was crying in the hall when I found her." Nick answered, his arms tightening around Sadie. His heartbeat slowed down.

"You were crying?" Tessa asked in concern.

"Yeah," Sadie answered quietly. "I was looking at the picture when Scarecrow and I won division championship."

"I love that picture." Tessa's smile lit up. Nick's heart sped up again. "I love walking down the hallway and seeing all the pictures of you kids and the horses. But why did it make you cry?"

"It made me think of the crash." Sadie admitted.

Tessa glanced up at Nick.

"Do you still have the little horse?" Nick asked.

"Of course!" Sadie said with a smile. "It's up in my room."

"Not in the memory room in the barn?" He asked.

"No, the saddle and buckle are out there, but the horse is special." Sadie answered.

"What little horse and what's so special about it?" Tessa asked.

"It's a little silver horse about two inches tall. Nick gave it to me for my first championship." Sadie explained.

"Really?" Tessa glanced up at him again then back to Sadie.

"I think I should have given it to Nora, she won it for you by taking her pants off." Nick laughed making Sadie bounce.

Sadie laughed through the sleepiness.

"She what?" Tessa gasped.

"You shouldn't say it that way, Nick. It sounds bad." Sadie yawned.

"As far as I'm concerned, it was bad!" She felt him chuckle.

"OK, you two, spill…was this AT the rodeo?" Tessa looked confused.

Sadie grinned. "Yeah, Aunt Jordan took me and Wade to the rodeo and Nick took Nora to her horse show."

"Just the two of you?" Tessa looked at him in surprise.

"I was working a bull event about thirty miles away from her horse show. So we did her horse show during the day and the bulls at night." He explained to a stunned Tessa.

"I was running for the championship and Nora wanted to come watch, so Nick drove all night to get her there in time." Sadie smiled at the look on Tessa's face as she looked at Nick.

"Why did she take her pants off?" Tessa asked as she looked back at Sadie.

"One of the girls ran into Scarecrow and pushed us into a fence that hooked onto my jeans. It tore them from the top to the bottom." Sadie answered. "It nearly pulled me off Scarecrow."

"Her whole leg was visible." Nick added.

"You're lucky you didn't get hurt." Tessa gasped, then looked at Sadie's bruised face and the three of them chuckled at her statement.

"There wasn't time for Sadie to leave and change jeans, so Nora yelled at her and started taking her own jeans off to throw to Sadie." Nick told her. "There, in the bleachers, this twelve-year-old girl taking her jeans off. Jordan and I nearly had heart attacks."

Sadie giggled. "Wade said Nick had his shirt off in a blink of an eye and wrapped it around her."

"The little snot didn't tell me he had two shirts on until I'd been sitting there, shirtless, for five minutes. He handed his shirt over for Nora to cover up just before Sadie ran." Nick chuckled.

Tessa laughed. "And you won!"

"I quit thinking about my leg, and thought about what Nora did and knew I had to win for her. Scarecrow ran faster than she ever had." Sadie smiled. "We got second in the junior division last year, but we had two more years to win in that one."

"Had?" Nick asked.

Sadie didn't say anything. She watched Tessa look up at Nick with a concerned frown. Afraid they would ask her more, she closed her eyes and turned so she could press her eyes back into his neck to make it really dark.

She felt Nick's heart speed up again and opened an eye just enough to see Tessa had placed a hand over Nick's hand. His thumb was lightly running over the top of her fingers.

Suddenly, Tessa jerked her hand out and stood. Without a word, she walked away.

"Tessa…" Nick called out softly.

There was no response as they listened to her footsteps quickly moving down the hall.

"I'm sorry," Sadie whispered.

"For what?" Nick's voice was low.

"I don't know." She felt the tears coming up again and fought hard to keep them from falling.

"Are you comfortable?" He asked.

"Yes." She whispered.

"No pain?"

"No. Are you comfortable?"

"Yes."

"I'm really tired, I might fall asleep."

"That's fine."

"Do you want me to go back to bed?"

"You don't want cradle-hugged?" She didn't respond because she wanted to stay, but didn't want to keep him there if he wanted to go find Tessa. "Then, we'll just stay here and I'll cradle-hug you as you sleep."

"Thank you." She whispered. He pulled the blanket tighter around her and she felt him relax back into the cushions.

Her muscles relaxed and the sound of his heartbeat lulled her into a sleepy haze.

Somewhere, in the distance, she heard her dad.

"Well, that's quite the sight." He said.

"She wanted cradle-hugged." Nick whispered.

"Do you want me to take her?"

"No, I promised her I'd stay here and let her sleep."

Sadie heard her dad chuckle and tried to respond but she couldn't get out of the haze.

"Tessa said you found her in the hallway?"

"She was crying at the picture of her and Scarecrow."

Her dad sighed. "Did she say anything?"

"No, we talked about her win in the picture. She didn't talk about the future as if she was going to run again; she put it in the past tense."

"Dru thought she might have problems like that. When Dru was riding, she had seen a lot of racers crash, many didn't come back…other's had a long mental recovery time."

They were quiet and Sadie started drowning in the darkness of sleep.

"Grayson, if you need anything."

"Thanks. Your work at the ranch has really helped."

"I mean it, every dime…"

"For my wife and girls, I'd take you up on it, but right now, we're OK."

"Just let me know…but for now…you, Leah, and everyone else, go get a good night's sleep; you all need it. I'm sitting here, instead of you, because Sadie's worried about you." He paused, tightening his arms around her. "I got Sadie. Nothing is going to happen while you're sleeping, but you can be assured that if something does, I'll be calling."

"We'll take you up on that. Thanks Nick."

***

She could hear Nick breathing, deep and relaxed, head leaning back, he was sleeping. She had relaxed away from his neck and her head rest on his arm, just above the pillow Tessa had placed under him. It was light outside, but she couldn't hear anyone moving so no one else was awake yet. Her head hurt, and her neck, and her arm, and her face…she was just a mess.

She moved the arm with the cast just a few inches but it was enough his head moved up and he looked down at her.

"You OK?" He asked, with a gruff, sleepy voice.

"Sort of."

"What does sort of mean?"

"It means I'm comfortable…but I hurt…and I have to go to the bathroom."

"Well, let's take care of that bathroom thing first." Nick chuckled. "That could be a mess for both of us."

She tucked into him as he wrapped her closer and moved to stand. She grimaced as she tightened her neck.

He froze. "You OK?"

"Yeah."

He rose carefully, trying not to jerk her up. When he stood, he didn't move.

"What are you doing?"

"Letting the blood flow back into my legs," He chuckled. "Do you want me to get your mother?"

"No, I can go by myself."

He shifted her gently and walked her to the bathroom in the utility room by the back door. Slowly, he lowered and tilted so her feet hit the ground but held onto her until her legs could walk.

When she walked out of the bathroom, her parents were standing next to Nick. She opened her eyes wide in surprise.

"Taking care of the pain part." Nick smiled at her.

"Is it OK if I cuddle-hug you now?" Her dad asked with a smile. She was happy to see his eyes looked rested.

"Cradle-hug." Nick and Sadie said in unison then grinned at each other.

"Alright, cradle-hug." Her dad reached down and picked her up.

Sadie leaned into him and looked at Nick. "Thank you for keeping your promise."

"Any time you need me." He smiled back.

As her dad turned, Sadie saw her mother wrap her arm through Nick's.

"Thank you." Her mother told him.

"Any time you need me." Nick answered.

CHAPTER FIVE

"Are you sure you're going to be OK?" Her mother asked nervously.

"Mom, I walked and wandered this house all day. I promise if I need you, I'll call. Grace's cell phone is right there on the table." Sadie smiled. "I went without pain killers most of today."

"OK," She leaned down and kissed her on the forehead. "I'll let you get to sleep then."

"I love you, Mom." Sadie said as her mom tucked the covers around her for the tenth time.

"I love you, Sadie Girl." She slowly walked to the door, with one last worried glance back she turned off the light.

Sadie looked out the window and watched the stars twinkle until her eyes started to fall.

Something woke her up and she looked around the room. Other than the light streaming into the room from the gap in the door to the hallway it was dark. She sat up and looked around. Maybe it was Cora going to bed and shutting her own door which was right across the hall.

There was nothing there, she told herself. Taking a deep breath she lay back on her pillows. It was so quiet. She had gotten used to her parents or family sleeping in the chair next to her bed. The sound of their breathing was comforting and when she woke, it would lull her back to sleep.

For as long as she could remember she slept in her bedroom with Nora and Grace. When one was gone the other was always there. Now she was alone…and really didn't like it.

It still hurt to turn her head sideways, so she turned on her side and looked at the phone. Being lonely wasn't a good enough reason to call her parents, they needed to sleep. She also couldn't go upstairs either. That was against the rules even if she could make it up the steps.

Maybe she could call Nora and have her come downstairs. No, she shouldn't wake up Nora just because she was lonely.

Then she heard a noise outside her door. She rolled her eyes over and stared at the light. Maybe it was her mom checking in on her. A shadow moved by the light.

"Shhh…you'll wake Cora." It was Nora that appeared at the door.

"Sadie?" Nora whispered.

"Come in." Relief flooded through her. "Who did you tell to be quiet?"

"Me." Wade stuck his head in the door.

Sadie grinned.

"Is it OK if we come in?" He asked.

"Yes! I was just thinking I should call Nora to come down and keep me company. Come in and get under the covers." Sadie said happily.

"Are you sure?" Nora asked.

"Yes, I was getting really lonely. I'm so glad you're here." Sadie shared her pillows.

Her cousins tucked in on each side of her. After a few giggles they fell asleep.

Sadie was the first to wake and lay quietly while her cousins slept.

"Is Nora awake too?" Wade finally whispered.

"Now I am." Nora answered.

"We need to get upstairs before everyone else wakes up." Wade looked over the top of Sadie to see his sister.

"We don't want Mom and Dad to get mad at us." Nora looked worried.

"You two are funny." Sadie giggled.

"Why?" They asked in unison.

"Details, you two…the window shades are closed and so is the door, which means someone has already been in here." She pointed out.

"Dang, Sadie." Wade lay back on the pillow. "You always notice all the details."

"Like the detail that I'm hungry?" Sadie giggled and pushed on Nora to get her out of bed.

"Fine." Nora laughed.

"I gotta lot of school work to catch up on today." Sadie explained as she found her slippers. "Thanks for bringing it home, Wade."

"You're the only kid I know that would be thankful to get homework." Nora laughed.

"I like learning." Sadie said as she walked to the door with a cousin on each side of her, each holding an elbow making sure she was OK.

"We're headed for the ranch Friday after school, and we get out early that day." Wade said excitedly as they made their way down the hall.

"I can't wait!" Sadie announced happily.

"Can't wait for what?" Her mother asked as they walked into the kitchen.

Her parents, Aunt Dru and Jack were sitting at the small kitchen table when they strolled in. Aunt Jordan and Uncle Scott were in Nampa at the cutting competition. Cora was at the stove and grinned when they saw her.

"Can't wait for branding!" Sadie answered excitedly.

Her parents stared at her then looked at each other then back to Sadie. Aunt Dru and Jack leaned away from the table.

"What?" Sadie looked at them in confusion.

"We've been discussing you staying here, away from the cows and horses." Her mother calmly told her.

"WHAT!" The switch flipped inside her and she was instantly mad. She turned her head quickly…too quickly and pain shot through her neck and head. She grimaced and her hands went to her head, grabbing at her hair and trying to get rid of the pain.

"Sadie!" Her mom yelled.

"You can't keep me away from branding! I love branding; it's the best time of year. I love it more than Christmas! I want to go!" Every word increased in volume and in her anger. The pain was shooting down her head and into her shoulders and back. She closed her eyes to try and stop the pain.

"SADIE! Stop right now!" It was her dad yelling at her. He was louder than he had ever been.

Her eyes opened wide and she saw him angry and worried at the same time.

"Lower your voice and change your tone, or there is no way you're going. We'll get you a babysitter and you can stay here." He told her gruffly.

She closed her eyes again and tried to get herself to calm down by taking deep breathes.

"Do you need a pain killer?" Her mother asked.

"No…thank… you…mother." Sadie said as calm as she could.

She felt the anger subside and with it, the pain.

When she opened her eyes she looked right at her dad. "Please, Dad. Don't keep me away from branding. I really want to go. I can't imagine missing out on it while everyone one else is there." Tears started streaming down her cheeks. "I have been trying very hard to follow all the rules while being home. It was so hard to stay away from the barn and Little Ghost and Scarecrow and the rest of them. I was looking out the window at the horses yesterday and knew I could make it out there to them. But I didn't…I didn't sneak out because I knew it was against the rules. And if you let me go, I promise I will follow every rule you tell me. I really, really promise."

"Sadie, we're not trying to punish you." Her mother said with tears in her eyes.

Sadie turned her sad blue eyes to her mother. "But, you don't understand Mom, this is the big one."

"We've always helped Andy with his branding, so it's really the same thing we do every year." Her dad explained.

"But Dad, it's the big one. It's the special one." Sadie said through the sobs.

"Why is it so special?" Her mother asked.

"It's Circle 50's first branding. It's the first time one of the calves will be branded with the Circle 50…a whole new legacy." She looked at her parents through the tears. "Please don't make me miss that…it's special." She added desperately.

Her mom held out her arms and Sadie stepped in for the embrace, but looked at her dad.

"Please, Dad….just please." She sobbed.

"You're right, Sadie." He said taking her hand. "It is special, I forgot about the Circle 50 brand."

"Then can I go please?" She looked at him hopefully.

"We'll talk to the doctor and if everything is OK, then you can." He said and she moved from her mother and hugged her father. "But we will have rules."

"I know," She whispered into his shirt. "I promise I will follow every one of them. Can we go to the doctor right now?"

"Sadie; it's 7:00 on Sunday morning. They aren't open until tomorrow." Her mother told her.

"OK." Sadie sighed.

"Well, we know the fall didn't knock the temper out of you." He chuckled as he took her arms and stood her up in front of him.

"Turtle becomes a dingo again." Her mother sighed.

***

"The video is here!" Reilly yelled down the hallway and everyone hurried to the computer.

Reilly hit the play button to see Aunt Jordan on Cooper. She walked slowly out into the arena and stared at the nervous herd. Cooper's neck was arched and his ears twitched as he watched them too.

Aunt Jordan made her decision and moved into the herd pushing a cream colored steer away from the others. Cooper responded immediately and faced the animal. The cow moved left and Cooper followed, the cow quickly changed directions but not as fast as Cooper, who jumped with his shoulders to the right, blocking the steer's motion. The animal took off at a run, but Cooper was too fast for him and cut him off…again the run to the opposite side but Cooper's speed was too much for the calf. It turned and faced the black horse and rider.

Aunt Jordan pulled Cooper away and went to get another steer; a red one this time that stayed in the middle of the arena; running back and forth. Cooper matched his every move as he danced back and forth with his front legs. The cow ran to the fence and hugged it tightly then took off across the arena to the other side. Cooper quickly followed and cut in front of the steer to block its retreat. The horse's turn was low and sharp but Aunt Jordan held on; relaxing deep into the saddle. She turned Cooper back into the herd to go for a third. They were still working the steer when the timer went off.

"Wow, that was awesome." Reilly said proudly of his horse and aunt.

The picture flickered…Uncle Scott and Little Ghost appeared to the side of the arena next to the cows.

Sadie sat at the desk, her good hand gripped the cast tightly just under her chin. She was so excited to see them.

They chose their steer and Uncle Scott gripped the saddle horn with one hand then lowered the reins to the horse's neck with the other; signaling the beginning of the ride. Horse and steer danced across the arena. Little Ghost jumped back and forth, trotted forward then continued his front leg dance; his long mane bouncing and swinging with each move. Uncle Scott stopped him and went in for a second steer for another dance. This cow was faster than the other but Little Ghost didn't have a problem. Uncle Scott looked like a statue on the horse and they leaned back and forth to waltz with the cow. He was on the third steer when the buzzer went off, signaling the end of his time. The crowd erupted.

"Did they win?" Nora was right behind her.

"They wouldn't say what happened." Aunt Dru said. "They just said to watch the video."

The next thing on the screen was Little Ghost & Cooper tied to a fence and standing side-by-side alertly watching something or someone just off camera.

"He's so beautiful." Sadie whispered.

"You're talking about Cooper, right?" Reilly chuckled.

Sadie smiled, not moving her eyes from the screen, "Yeah, couldn't be that grey horse…he's kind of homely."

Uncle Scott walked into view and stood next to the grey horse. He was smiling. Aunt Jordan walked in next with her back to the camera. After handing Uncle Scott a trophy, Aunt Jordan turned to reveal she had one, too! They both grinned into the camera.

"This was for you, Sadie." They said in unison.

"I told Little Ghost that you'd be watching, so do good, he did, and we won first place." Uncle Scott said.

"Cooper had the same orders…and we won our division too, our first, first place trophy!" Jordan's voice was bubbling from excitement as she raised the trophy.

Sadie clapped her hands excitedly. Grinning she reached out to touch the monitor where Little Ghost stood.

"Thank you for kicking us out of the house, Sadie." Aunt Jordan smiled. "We're on our way home now. See you soon."

"Can we watch it again?" Sadie asked.

She watched it a dozen more times until everyone else had left.

Sadie clicked off the video and looked into the computer folders that held all the downloaded rodeo files. She searched for the day of her crash and found the video. Clicking on it, she waited, but it was protected with a password. She typed in her first guess, a second…it took only six times. Sadie smiled; they were pretty transparent with the passwords.

She hesitated, looked around the room, then listened…she couldn't hear anyone so she turned the volume off and pushed play.

Scarecrow slipped just out of the ally, then slipped on the first barrel. She watched herself pull on the reins trying to stop the horse, Scarecrow's back legs tucked under her haunches then her front legs slipped to the side. The horse went down on her shoulder, they slid, they rolled, and Sadie flew out of the saddle and slammed against the wall. The camera, which had been on a tri-pod, rocked then fell over and hit the bleachers.

Sadie reached up and touched her neck as she replayed the video again. She leaned in closer just as Scarecrow's shoulder hit the ground and they started into the roll, she stopped it just before she came out of the saddle. She reversed it again and played those few seconds over again, then again, then again.

"Are you still watching Little Ghost?" Her dad asked from the doorway.

Sadie's eyes flew up at him as she jumped in her chair; she knew that she looked guilty. His eyes narrowed and he walked into the room and looked at the screen.

"Sadie!" He said gruffly, rolling his eyes.

"It's OK, Dad." She whispered and looked at him in concern.

"Nobody has watched that." He frowned at her.

"That's why nobody said anything." Sadie looked back at the monitor, which was frozen with her arms in the air the split second before she hit the wall.

"Said anything about what?"

She looked up at him, puckered her lips and wiggled them…thinking. "Can you watch just a couple seconds of it?"

"Not the wall." He sighed.

"OK." She turned to the monitor and he sat in the chair next to her, his arm resting protectively across the back of her chair.

"It goes really fast," She told him. "Watch when Scarecrow's front legs go sideways and we go into the roll."

"Alright…."

She played the video, but stopped it just as she came out of the saddle.

"Did you see that?" She turned to him.

"Yeah, play it again." He nodded.

They watched it three more times before he sat back in the chair.

He had seen the same thing she did. Just as Scarecrow's neck should have been crushing Sadie into the ground, the horse had twisted herself up, in the opposite direction of the roll and bending away from Sadie, saving her.

"Wow," He said. "We always said she would take care of you…if the wall hadn't been there you probably would have walked away with barely a scratch."

"What are you doing?" Her mom walked into the room.

Sadie looked to her dad. He nodded to Sadie then motioned for her mom to watch the monitor.

"Is that the…?" Her eye's widened in disbelief as she looked from her husband to her daughter.

"Just watch the few seconds here." He nodded, set her on his knee and wrapped his arms around her waist to watch.

Sadie played the video.

"Again," Her mother said and leaned in closer to the monitor.

"Scarecrow nearly breaks her own neck trying to keep from rolling on you." Her mom leaned back and stared in awe at the monitor. The screen frozen to the second Sadie was covered with horse mane but not the full horse neck.

They sat quietly for a moment.

"Have you watched the whole thing?" Her dad asked.

"Yes, a couple times." Sadie admitted.

He sighed, "We should see what Jordan saw."

"I agree." Her mother nodded.

Sadie turned the volume up on the computer, and started the video over. There was the announcer calling her once, twice, a third time.

Sadie sat up straighter when she heard the distinct yell of her name as she appeared out of the ally. She couldn't see him but it had to be Reilly yelling at her to stop.

The crowd gasped as she slid around the first barrel and yelled when the horse started to slide, then roll, then flying toward the wall. But it was the next sound that would haunt Sadie.

Aunt Jordan screamed Sadie's name in utter terror as the camera was knocked over.

Sadie jumped and hit the mute button as fast as she could, silencing the horrible scream.

She sat quietly staring at her arm where the goose bumps rose as the scream began. She was nauseous, tears sprung to her eyes and she slowly turned to her parents.

Their faces were as stunned and aghast as her own.

She stood and leaned into her parent's arms. Her body was so numb from the shock of the scream that there were no tears. Her parents embraced her, no one spoke, they just held each other until she leaned back and took a deep breath.

"I can watch the video a thousand times, but I don't ever want to hear it again." Sadie looked up at them.

"I agree, that was horrible," Her mom wiped away a tear.

Sadie sat back down, took a deep breath and played the video again without the sound. Both parents visibly cringed as she hit the wall.

Then Sadie clicked on the video of Little Ghost, Cooper, Uncle Scott and Aunt Jordan. She forwarded the video to the last 30 seconds when Aunt Jordan came into view and her aunt and uncle stood staring at the screen.

She turned the volume up and hit play;

"This was for you, Sadie."

"I told Little Ghost that you'd be watching so do good, he did, and we won first place."

"Cooper had the same orders…and we won our division too, we won our first, first place trophy!"

"Thank you for kicking us out of the house, Sadie."

"We're on our way home now. See you soon."

Sadie stopped the video with Aunt Jordan smiling at the camera. She stared at it, trying to get the scream out of her head.

CHAPTER SIX

Sadie leaned against the deck rail and stared at the barn. They had gone in over ten minutes ago! What could possibly be taking them so long?

"Cora, what are they doing?" She said impatiently.

"I have no idea." The older woman shook her head.

"All the horse trailers are lined up and ready. Why are they taking so long?" Sadie tapped her foot on the ground.

"Be patient, Sadie."

"I don't do patient."

Cora chuckled. "Don't we all know that!"

Sadie exhaled loudly, then froze in place.

They were coming!

All the horses, all in a row, were being led out of the barn at the same time.

"Oh Cora!" Sadie yelled. "Look! It's a parade of the Tagger Herd!"

Sadie jumped, which made her back hurt so she quickly stopped and started clapping instead. It was an awkward clap with her cast.

Aunt Dru was first in line, leading Libby and Kit. Her aunt grinned up at Sadie as she walked right up to the deck and paused in front of her.

"Are they going to?" Sadie asked in surprise, both horses were due to have babies in the next couple of weeks.

"No, but I figured they needed your love, too." Her aunt answered.

Excitement ran through Sadie as she greeted the two horses, petting them and kissing on them. It was the first time she was allowed near the horses except the visits with Little Ghost and Scarecrow through her bedroom window. Aunt Dru turned and led them back to the pasture.

Then Jack and Rufio, Grace with Buttercup and Eli, Sadie laughed as she greeted each of them. Then there was Alex and Rooster, Wade and Dollar, Nora and Arcturus, Aunt Jordan and Isaiah, Tessa and Cooper, Sadie's mom was leading Little Ghost and finally was Reilly leading Scarecrow.

"Thank you everyone!" Sadie called out happily. Only Trooper and Harvey were missing but they were already at Circle 50.

Aunt Dru was quickly walking back to her. It was then that Sadie noticed her mom had stopped with Little Ghost instead of walking to the trailers.

Her aunt walked up to the steps and held out her hand to Sadie. She quickly took it, excited and anxious as she was led to Little Ghost's side.

The horse turned and sniffed at her. Sadie reached out with her good arm and stroked his nose. Her other arm went to his scars, she traced them lightly with the fingers sticking out the end of the cast.

"Are you ready?" Her mother asked.

"Ready for what?" Sadie looked up at her.

"To ride him to the trailers." Her mother grinned.

"Really?" Sadie's eye's opened wide, her heart racing.

Aunt Dru bent her leg, and with the help of her mother, Sadie used her aunt's leg to step on, then they lifted her up and she was sitting on top of her grey horse.

Sadie scooted back to his hips then laid forward so her head rested on his withers; her long braid, arms and legs dangled off the sides. The warmth of him, the feel of him, the love for him, radiated through every inch of her body.

"You ready?" Her mom smiled at her.

"Yes." Sadie sighed.

She closed her eyes, wanting to concentrate on every move. As they began walking, she could feel the horse's muscles tense and relax, his hips rise and fall, his shoulders lifting her own shoulders. Her lungs were full of the essence of him. Fingers caressed his fine hairs as her body rolled back and forth. Her mind was in an enchanted haze.

"Sadie?" Her mother's voice intruded into her enchantment.

"What?" Sadie said, smiling with the love of her horse.

"We have to load him now."

"Can I just stay on him in the trailer…all the way to the ranch?" Sadie giggled behind closed eyes.

She heard her mom and Aunt Dru giggle with her.

"Um, no." Her mother answered.

Sadie opened her eyes and saw the two blonde women smiling at her with love in their eyes.

"I just love him so much." Sadie sighed contentedly.

"We can tell," Aunt Dru stepped up to her and bent her leg again. Sadie slid down off the big grey gelding, her mother holding her waist. She stepped on her aunt's leg then stepped down to the ground. She quickly went to the horse's head to pet him and kiss him. He gently tucked his nose into her.

"Alright, you have a whole week with them." Her mother took Sadie's hand. "Let's get you loaded too."

As Sadie buckled her seat belt, Reilly appeared with a grin and a plate of quiches and a bag of cookies.

"Eat them all before we get up there." Reilly ordered her. "I'm riding with Mom." He looked over at Grace who was next to Sadie. "Make sure she eats them herself and doesn't share."

Both girls laughed.

"I won't share, I'll eat them myself." Sadie promised him.

***

Her eyes opened and it was still dark. There was no smell of coffee making its way through the bunkhouse so she knew it was early and no one else was awake. Her body ached as she slowly rolled to the edge of the bed and looked around. She laid the cast on the mattress so it didn't make a noise hitting the metal railing.

Nikki was in the bed below her, Mavis curled up next to her. Nick was in the lower bed to her right, Nora on the top bunk. Red, the puppy, was curled up next to Nick. Across the aisle from Nikki was Uncle Scott, with Spur curled in between him and Aunt Jordan. Sadie stretched as high as her sore neck would let her, to see if she could see Pepper. All she could see was the dog's tail sticking out of the covers next to her dad.

Bart was curled up next to Matt, but Indy was too far away to see in the dark. She was in charge of the puppies for the week. If she couldn't help with riding and branding, at least she got to play with puppies.

She sat up cross legged on top of the bed and leaned against the wall and waited. It was just a few minutes later when the clicking from the coffee pot could finally be heard. She leaned forward and watched to see who got up first. It was Nick! She giggled softly which caused him to turn and look up at her with a soft smile.

He walked the puppy, Red, over to Alex's bunk and placed her next to the boy. Alex's arm instinctively wrapped around the puppy.

Then her dad sat up in bed and looked up at her, shaking his head. He tucked Pepper back under the covers next to her mom and stood.

Sadie happily scooted to the side of the bed and her dad turned to her so she could slide down on his back for the annual piggy back ride to the table.

"Why are you awake so early, young lady?" Nick whispered to her as he set her coffee mug full of milk down in front of her.

"It's branding week." She said softly, "My favorite week of the year."

"How is the pain today? Was the mattress soft enough?" Her dad asked as he sat down next to her.

There was no way she was going to tell him how stiff and achy her back was and that she barely slept at all. "It's fine, Dad."

"You tell me if you need anything, even if it's just some aspirin." He told her.

Sadie smiled up at him; no one could have a better dad than her. "Ok."

A hand rest on her head and Sadie carefully looked up to see Aunt Dru.

"Good morning." Sadie whispered to her excitedly.

"Mini-me today?" Her aunt asked.

"Yes!" She loved mini-me days. They haven't had one for months! She was only three inches shorter than her aunt now…mini-me days were numbered.

Sadie listened intently to all the plans. It was roundup day for the Tagger cows then branding tomorrow. They would take a day off to rest the horses. Then came the Circle 50 cows; rounding up one day, branding the next…five wonderful days ahead of them.

An hour later, Sadie stood next to her Aunt Dru. They were dressed identical; braids, blue and white paisley wild rags peering out of the brown coats, black cowboy hats, chaps and all…Mini-me complete!

"So you're riding to the corrals with Tessa in the Ranger." Her mom was telling her. "Your dad's out giving her lessons on how to drive it."

"Well, that's scary." Sadie giggled then saw Cora step out of the ranch house in her riding clothes. Her smile disappeared. "Is Cora taking over for me?" A pain of jealousy bounced in her stomach.

"Yes. There's lots of work to do. We spent last night making lunch for today so she could join us."

Sadie sighed, as much as she loved having Cora out helping with the roundup and branding, she wanted to be the one helping.

She turned as her mother knelt down beside her. "I know it's hard, Hon, but remember, she helped last year, too."

Sadie started to nod but it still hurt when she did, so she just sighed. "I know." Her arms wrapped around her mom. "It'll be OK. I'm happy for Cora."

"Well, you know it was your idea." Cora said from behind her. Sadie turned and looked up at the older woman who looked at her with understanding. "You suggested it two years ago." Cora reminded her.

"I know." Sadie smiled meekly. "And you were great last year with the applicators. Are you doing that this year too?"

That would have been Sadie's job this year since she was twelve now. Wade should be placing the ear tags into the applicator, too.

"Yes, Miss Sadie, it is…and I hope to do you proud." Cora smiled.

"You will," Sadie tried to sound happier so Cora could enjoy her day. "And I can't wait to see you working this year, too."

"Well, Little Dingo, maybe this will help keep you busy." The Australian accent came from behind her.

Sadie turned to smile at Lucas as he joined the conversation.

"What?" She asked.

Lucas held out a black bag for her.

She excitedly unzipped the bag and looked inside.

"It's a camera!" Sadie's eyebrows shot up in surprise.

"It's important to have memories." Lucas grinned at her; his black hat was low, just over his amber brown eyes. His mustache and goatee were just perfect for a cowboy. "Since you can't come out and play, then you should be in charge of capturing all the memories."

"Oh, Lucas!" Sadie exhaled and looked at the camera in wonder. "I can get the Circle 50's first branding!"

"See, you're the perfect person for it, Little Dingo. You know all the right moments to look for." His accent always sounded like a song.

"Lucas, I don't know what to say." Sadie looked at him with tear-rimmed eyes. He was giving her a way to be part of the branding…that would last forever.

"You just make sure to get a good one of my lovely Nikki that I can take back to Australia with me." He winked and turned away.

Sadie reached in the bag and picked up the big camera. It had a long lens on it with a zoom so she could get close pictures without being in danger of being hurt from the cows or horses. She could hold the camera with one hand and rest the lens on her cast as a brace.

"What a wonderful surprise." Her mom smiled.

Sadie nodded and felt a twinge of pain in her neck. She must have grimaced since her mother frowned.

"Let's get you a pain killer."

"No!" Sadie nearly panicked. "They make me go to sleep. Can I just have an aspirin, please?"

Her mom paused, "OK, aspirin right now, but I'll be watching you all day."

"Ok." Sadie said in relief. That was close!

CHAPTER SEVEN

As she waited for Tessa, Sadie read the camera instructions and watched a couple of YouTube videos. By the time Tessa slid into the Ranger, Sadie had taken twenty pictures of the ranch buildings and people getting ready that were nice and clear. Excitement tingled through her.

"How are you doing with that thing?" Tessa asked as she slowly, very slowly, made her way down the road.

"I got it." Sadie told her as she took a picture of the long dirt road in front of them.

Sadie placed the camera on her lap and looked over at Tessa, down the road, then back at her driver.

"It would go faster if you push your foot down on the petal more."

Tessa chuckled. "Are you saying you have issues with my driving?"

"Not your driving, it's fine. It's your speed I have an issue with." Sadie grinned.

Tessa laughed and pushed the petal harder. "Is that better?"

"You're getting there," Sadie started to nod, then stopped herself. That was getting so annoying.

They finally made it to the top of Dry Creek Valley and watched the cows gather in the middle as they were pushed from the trees by all the riders.

Sadie turned in time to see Alex, Wade, Nora, and Aunt Jordan ride out of the trees next to them. She took their picture as they all smiled at her. They were herding four cows with babies toward them.

She turned and waited for Cora, her mom, and Grace to come out on the other side and got their pictures, too. They were pushing three pairs of mommas and babies out of the trees.

Spur and Red had ridden with Aunt Jordan's group. Indy and Pepper had ridden with her mom's group. Sadie took pictures of the very tired puppies as they greeted each other.

"I'll put the puppies in the Ranger for the next part." Tessa collected the group who were used to riding in the machine and placed them in the back. The puppies quickly lay down over the top of each other for a rest.

"Here they come." Wade yelled.

Sadie carefully turned and took pictures of the valley of cows and riders just as Tessa slid behind the wheel and moved them down the road. The puppies were already asleep from the long morning run.

"We'll do lunch once they all get here." Sadie told Tessa as she turned and watched the cows walk out of the valley and onto the road. "Then after lunch, Dad said we'll go ahead and push them to the branding corrals for the night. They purchased more cows last year so we have more calves to brand. By riding them to the pasture around the corrals it will save time on the ride in the morning."

"Where should we park?"

"Over behind the cattle chute, over there." Sadie pointed. When she lifted her arm a pain ran down her back. She quickly looked at Tessa, she hadn't seen the grimace.

Sadie looked around for the best place to be out of the way but comfortable enough she could rest her back and neck. The Ranger was bumpy and was causing her to tense which made her whole body start hurting.

"Can you help me up on the chute? I'll be out of the way and can sit down."

"Sounds like the perfect spot for both of us." Tessa agreed. "I'll park the Ranger in front of us so the puppies will be at our feet and we can keep our eye on them."

Once they were set and watching the cows and riders approach, Sadie took a chance to help with the pain.

"Can I have some aspirin?"

"Absolutely, Leah told me to watch out for your pain, so you let me know any time you need something."

Sadie sighed in relief, glad she didn't insist on the pain killers.

"And here," Tessa handed her an energy bar. "This is from Reilly."

They smiled at each other.

"It's supposed to be gone before he gets here."

"I'll try."

They sat watching the puppies sleep and the cows approach the pasture.

"Can I ask you something?" Tessa turned to Sadie with inquisitive eyes.

"Sure…if I can ask you one, too."

Tessa smiled cautiously and nodded at the conditional response. "Scarecrow and Little Ghost?"

The smile spread across Sadie's face…her most favorite topics. "What about them?"

"I can see that you love them both, but there's a difference."

"I guess there is, just like loving people different."

"How is it different for you? With them?"

Sadie stared at the upcoming heard and looked for Aunt Dru who was riding Scarecrow since Libby was so close to giving birth.

"Scarecrow is…my heart." Sadie decided as she touched her chest. "The more time I spent around her, when Nora was responsible for her, the more I loved her."

"She was Nora's first?"

Sadie chuckled, "Yes…she actually named her…that's a long story…but she's mine now and I've been mesmerized by her forever, especially the first time I touched her when she was mine. I love every bit about her…and she loves me."

"There is no doubt about that, but what are you going to do with her if you don't barrel race?" Her question was said calmly, not as if she was interrogating her.

Sadie looked at Tessa and tried to decide how to answer the question she wasn't sure she knew the answer to.

"Why wouldn't I race with her again?" Sadie hoped the woman would give her the answer that Sadie had been trying to find herself.

Tessa smiled softly. "When you talked about getting 2nd last year in your division, you said you HAD two more years to win, not that you HAVE two more years to win. There is a distinct difference."

Sadie frowned and stared at the golden horse making her way across the pasture pushing the sea of black and red cows.

"Does it bother you? Seeing Dru on Scarecrow?"

Sadie giggled. "No, especially today, having our mini-me day. It just makes me think of what I'll look like in a couple more years riding my golden horse."

"Doing what?"

Sadie looked over at her again. She and Tessa were the same height so they were eye to eye.

"Did Mom and Dad ask you to ask me that?" Sadie said with a tinge of fear the woman would say yes.

Tessa's eyebrows went up in surprise. "Of course not, why would you ask me that?"

"Because THEY haven't asked me that question."

"Oh," Tessa's brow furrowed in concern. "Am I getting too personal? Crossing a boundary I shouldn't?"

"Depends on why you're asking." The cows were getting closer and their conversation would end soon.

"Because I'm truly interested…and concerned."

Sadie could see she was being honest, so she figured she should be honest in return.

"I think of all the races I've run…" Sadie exhaled loudly. "And I love thinking back to them, remembering them…but they all end with me smashing into the wall."

"But out of all the races…only one ended that way."

"I know," Sadie said quietly; barely audible over the mooing of the cows. "I keep telling myself that."

"But you want to run."

"Yes…but I need to figure out how to get past that…wall."

"Literally and figuratively," Tessa smiled in understanding.

Sadie smiled in return. For some reason, she knew that Tessa had gone through something similar. The look in the woman's eyes told her that.

"Howdy!" Wade yelled from the herd, ending their conversation for the moment.

Sadie grinned at her cousin, who was riding next to Tessa's son. "Alex is having fun."

"The time of his life," Tessa said with love. "I can't believe the difference in him now."

"He's riding Freddy, Andy's main horse…his last horse." Sadie said of the big sorrel Alex was trotting happily towards them.

"That's what Scott said as he reassured me that the horse would be good for Alex during his first big roundup."

The puppies began stirring for the first time since they had stopped. All four stood in the back of the machine with their front feet on top of the cooler and excitedly watching the riders and cows come in.

Sadie quickly took a picture of the four puppies and the cows they were looking at. Nikki and Lucas were riding in next to each other on Harvey and Bay. Lucas reached out to take Nikki's hand. Sadie took the picture just as their hands touched and the love in their eyes was shining. Lucas will like that one.

Nick rode up next to Nikki, and while she held Lucas's hand, she turned and laughed at something Nick had said. They were all three laughing, the camera clicked.

She turned the camera to her beautiful aunt riding the big beautiful palomino. Sadie clicked the camera just as Aunt Dru and the horse looked at her.

The camera turned to Nora, riding Arcturus proudly, click. Her black-haired cousin was laughing at Wade and Alex…the camera turned to the pair of boys, grins across their faces, click.

Sadie and the camera turned to Grace, her sister riding Buttercup, the horse prancing under her, reflecting the joy that Grace was feeling, click.

The camera turned to Reilly on Rufio. Sadie frowned through the viewer. He was looking off into the distance, his eyes shadowed by his cowboy hat but she could see there was something wrong. He hadn't looked like that since the Tagger Herd came into their lives, especially Rufio and Cooper. Click…she wanted the picture to review later.

The camera clicked on each rider again, as well as Mavis and Bart who were still full of energy and trotting next to Matt and Uncle Scott who were riding Trooper and Monty.

Jack, riding Cooper, rode up next to Aunt Dru. Click, Sadie caught the contrast between the two. The blonde horse and rider next to the black haired horse and rider, they were so different but went together so perfectly.

The camera went to her parents who were riding up to her, smiles graced their faces as they looked into the camera; click.

Sadie lowered the camera and waved at them.

"How was your morning?" Her mother asked from on top of one of Andy's older ranch horses.

"It was OK." Sadie said honestly, they wouldn't have believed it if she said it was anything more. They knew her better than that.

"Lots of good pictures?" Her dad asked from on top of Eli.

"Yes!" Sadie answered and looked over at Lucas, who had moved up to talk with Matt, Aunt Jordan, and Uncle Scott. "It was the best surprise."

Tessa climbed off the chute, moved the Ranger and started to spread out lunch on the back of one of the flatbed trucks that had been parked there the night before. Sadie watched from her perch. She didn't want to move in fear her parents would see how much her back was hurting.

All the riders dismounted, loaded their plates with food, and moved over to Sadie to talk about the morning.

As soon as Nick reached the truck to fill his plate, Tessa walked away to the Ranger. There wasn't anything left in the back of the ATV, but Tessa remained there until Nick moved away. Nick had glanced at Tessa, with slightly squinted eyes. His shoulders moved up, then down as he had inhaled and exhaled in exasperation.

Details…Sadie looked around, no one else had noticed. She turned to Reilly who was standing with Matt and Lucas. They were playing with the puppies. All eyes were shining in laughter except Reilly's. He was smiling but it wasn't in his eyes. Sadie turned to her parents. They were standing next to her talking to Aunt Jordan and Jack. They would talk, then glance at Sadie, then turn back to the conversation then glance at her again.

When they looked away, Sadie sat straight up and turned slightly to see if her back hurt. Little ache but no pain, so she turned to slide off the cattle chute, her cast making it hard to maneuver. Her waist was grabbed from behind her and she was helped to the ground. She carefully looked up to see Matt.

"Thanks," She grinned at him.

"Don't take chances, we want you healthy as soon as possible." He told her.

"I won't," She assured him and walked over to her parents, wrapping her arms around their waists. She wanted to assure them she was fine so they could have a better day.

An arm from each of them wrapped around her back, they smiled at her…this time the smile shining in their eyes.

Everyone helped clean up the lunch and put it away, then remounted their horses to push the cows closer to the branding corrals.

Sadie stared at them as they rode away; the riders had spread out across the back of the herd to get them moving again. She wanted to be there. Pushing the cows across the pastures and mountains was a deep passion for her and she hated missing even one ride.

With a deep sigh, she slid in behind the wheel of the Ranger. Her cast wasn't a problem as she gripped the small wheel with one hand and the fingers of the other. Tessa slid into the seat on the passenger side.

The puppies were riding in the back of the machine again.

Once the cows were moving, Sadie pushed the petal to follow.

"So…where were we?" Tessa smiled as she relaxed into the seat. "Little Ghost…"

CHAPTER EIGHT

Sadie wished he was here today so she could see him. Uncle Scott was going to ride him during branding tomorrow so he was at the ranch house.

She told Tessa about the first time she saw Little Ghost in the stall, lying on his side, not able to get up. The blood on the wall and the wounds on is shoulder and over his ribs which caused them to carry him on a canvas. There were the first couple days watching the fluid drip in the IV's attached to him and Angel. Then the terrible night that the little brown colt had died.

"I woke up in Dad's arms and Little Ghost was lying next to me." Sadie felt the tears building and took in a deep breath to ward them off. "I could reach his nose and held my hand there, feeling his breath. Every minute I was home I was in the stall with him, walking him around the driveway or with him in the horse pasture."

"That's some serious bonding time." Tessa said softly.

Sadie smiled. "Aunt Dru took a picture of me lying on a cot at the doorway of his stall. Little Ghost had laid down right next to me and my arm was over his back. It's on my bedroom wall at home...and on the wall in his stall."

"I love that." Tessa laughed.

Sadie smiled in content as she watched the riders in front of her and talked about her beloved grey horse. "I love everything about him, from his big eyes, black mane, his breath, his heavenly smell, and every single inch of the scars on his side."

"What?" Tessa's voice was low, breathless, and surprised.

"His scars are part of who he is…Little Ghost is a survivor…he fought hard to live and he won." Details… Out of the corner of her eye, she saw Tessa turn her head and look out to the mountains.

Sadie continued, "As much as Scarecrow is my heart, Little Ghost is my soul. We heal each other and love each other unconditionally. The three of us are heart and soul together."

They rode quietly for a while. Tessa was deep in thought…near tears.

"Tessa?"

"Yes?"

"When you look at the five horses right in front of us, what do you see?" Sadie tried to get the woman to think of something other than what was making her cry.

Tessa sighed and studied the horses for a few minutes. "Well, Rufio is alert and looks content."

"Alert and content…that sounds funny together but I agree."

"Dollar is walking calmly, like him and Wade had ridden together forever. The horse Alex is riding looks bored."

"Freddy…a been there, done that attitude." Sadie agreed of the horse's manner.

"Nora's horse, Arcturus, is alert and seems like he is walking…arched." She said confused and looked to Sadie.

"Yeah…" Sadie saw it too.

"Jordan's horse seems as bored as Alex's horse."

"Aunt Jordan likes a lively horse, but today she's riding one of Andy's older horses. Usually she rides Kit who is fun to ride, so this one must be like floating on a lake instead of riding a river."

"That's an interesting way of putting it." Tessa had the light back in her eyes. "You asked me about the horses for a reason."

"I did," Sadie smirked in humor.

"What do you see when you look at those horses?"

"Arcturus is walking 'arched' because he is in high alert, he's not fond of cows but he'll take care of Nora."

"Well, that makes sense." Tessa nodded easily which made Sadie jealous.

"If you look at the difference in Alex's horse, just his backend, to Rufio, what do you see?"

Tessa stared intently at the older gelding then at the younger one. "Alex's horses' hips move differently." She turned to Sadie. "Is there something wrong with him?"

"Probably arthritis, he has been used pretty hard most of his life. I think he's around twenty now."

"That's why he is so calm? He's hurting?" Tessa asked in concern.

"A little or he would act out more. He needs some medicine, just like humans with arthritis use, then he should be OK for lighter rides. Now look at the horse that Aunt Jordan is riding and compare to Arcturus."

Again Tessa stared but shook her head. "I don't see anything wrong."

"Look at his hocks…his ankles."

Sadie had barely detected it so she didn't think Tessa would see it without narrowing the search.

"There's just a bit of a kick-out on his back left hoof." Tessa said as she leaned towards the horse.

"He didn't have that when he started this morning."

"So he hurt himself on the ride?"

"Or it only comes out after being ridden for a while…he's older, too."

"That's amazing you saw that."

Sadie shrugged which caused an ache in her back and a grimace.

Without a word, Tessa pulled out the aspirin and gave her a couple.

"Dr. Mark gave me a book last week on sport's medicine for horses." Sadie grinned. "It's such a challenge to read but it finally gave me a goal."

"Sport's medicine?"

"Yeah, I want to help horses be better…whether they are ranch horses like Andy's two geldings, or healthy horses like Scarecrow and Little Ghost."

"A veterinarian?"

"No, I just want to work with horses. I want to help condition them to be better and faster…to be in the best shape for whatever they do…like working with Olympians to be the best in their sport."

"That's a pretty good goal." Tessa looked at her with wide eyes.

"With Nikki's nutritional expertise, Nora's expertise in training and my conditioning expertise, we can create super horses!" Sadie laughed and Tessa joined in.

"But I'm only twelve, so it will be awhile."

"Why?" Tessa shook her head. "You can start now."

"I need to go to college first."

"For other people's horses, not your own. I've heard of your wizardry. I have a feeling if you put your mind to it, all the Tagger horses will be super horses before too long."

Sadie glanced at her companion for the day with a smile. It is always good to know people believe in you.

"It's my turn to ask a question for you to answer." Sadie reminded her.

"OK, shoot." Tessa nodded again.

"Nick."

Tessa inhaled sharply, but didn't say anything.

"I know you like each other…"

"I'm not who he thinks I am." Tessa said softly.

What did that mean? Sadie tried to associate the comment with herself. Was she what everyone thought she was? The math wizard, yes. The learner, yes. The little dingo, yes. The tough girl, not anymore. She hoped someday to be tough again, but inside…she was just a scared twelve-year-old who was trying hard not to let her family suffer any more for the mistake that she made. She hides her fear to protect her family.

"I understand," Sadie said softly. "You stay away from him…to protect him."

Tessa nodded.

"You have a wall like I do, just not as literal." Sadie smiled at her companion.

Tessa hesitantly smiled back. "I cannot believe you're twelve."

Sadie chuckled. "Mom and Reilly say that all the time."

"Which reminds me," Tessa grinned and leaned down to the small cooler at her feet. She rose with a cupcake.

Sadie laughed. "He's fattening me up."

"He's making you stronger." Tessa giggled as she stuffed part of the cupcake in Sadie's mouth.

Once she was finished with the cupcake Sadie turned to Tessa with serious eyes. "I don't know why you have your wall, that's your story to tell, but I do understand it. So if you need to talk or need me to help protect Nick, you just ask."

Tessa nodded thankfully, the tears instantly filling her brown eyes.

"Get rid of those quick!" Sadie looked at Tessa, "Here come the riders."

"Ack!" Tessa said loudly which made both of them laugh and the tears disappear.

***

"So, you're really not going to let me see the pictures?" Lucas asked as he sat at the breakfast table next to Sadie.

"Of course not," Sadie laughed. "Not until we're all done." He had tried hard the night before to get the camera from her to look at the photos.

"That's DAYS away!" He jokingly complained.

Sadie shrugged, then was quickly thankful she had the aspirin in her already to keep from hurting. She had a very tough night on the hard mattress, barely sleeping at all. As she tried to force herself to sleep, the wind had picked up outside. She had lain in bed hearing Aunt Jordan's scream at the end of the video. It made her tense, which resulted in her back aching.

She was sitting at the table before the coffee pot turned on.

"Did you get the picture of my lovely Nikki?" He asked with a tilt of the head.

Sadie let her grin answer his question. She knew there were lots of great pictures of Nikki hidden in the camera.

"Crikey, you are a little tease, Dingo!" He laughed.

A horn blast rang out from outside.

"Mom's ready!" Reilly yelled from the door. "Let's go!"

"We're burning daylight!" Chimed Alex and Wade in unison.

Everyone laughed, put their plates in the sink to be cleaned later, and walked out into the dark morning.

With camera bag in hand, she walked to her dad's truck. Reilly walked by and quickly stuffed something in her pocket then walked to Aunt Dru's truck. With a confused smile, Sadie reached into her jacket and found an energy bar. She was giggling as her dad helped her step into the back seat.

The sun was just coming over the horizon when they pulled into the branding corrals. Sadie sat patiently but excitedly waiting for her dad to park the truck.

"Stay here." He told her as he climbed out of the truck. She frowned and watched him walk back to the horse trailer.

"Why can't we get out?" Grace asked, just as frustrated as Sadie.

"I'm sure he has his reasons." Their mom answered from the front seat.

After a few minutes, their dad climbed back into the truck and drove forward, without the horse trailer. Sadie looked at Grace in surprise. He never unhooked the trailer from the truck during branding.

He drove towards the corrals and turned the truck so he could backup to the fence. Then he got out and repeated his request for her to stay in the truck. Her mom and Grace jumped out on the other side.

Sadie sighed, leaned her head back against the seat and realized she was more comfortable sitting in the truck than she was on her bunk bed. If he didn't hurry, she was going to fall asleep.

She could feel the back of the truck lower; someone had crawled in back. Fighting sleep, she leaned forward and started bouncing her legs. Finally the door opened and her dad stood smiling at her.

"What?" She asked confused.

He started to lift her into her arms and she leaned back.

"Dad, not out here. I can walk." She said embarrassed.

"Well, OK." He laughed. "Little spirited today?"

"I'm better now." Sadie smiled. How is she going to show them she was better if she continued to let them carry her around?

He helped her out of the truck and walked her to the fence. Her mother was standing in the back of the truck, next to a chair from the ranch house. All four puppies were in the back with her.

"What's going on?" Sadie looked at her parents.

"Just making sure you have a comfortable place to sit and take pictures of the branding and watch the puppies." Her mother smiled.

Sadie grinned at her mom as her dad lifted her into the truck bed.

The chair was the big fluffy one that you could sink and relax into. Her mom tucked a thick blanket around her to protect her from the cool April morning air. Pepper and Indy jumped onto the chair with her and curled up at her sides. Sadie glanced down at Spur and Red as they bedded down in the overflowing blanket.

Jessup's supply table was just to her right so she would be able to see all the action, close up, and personal.

She sighed happily, more comfortable than she had been in days. If she couldn't join in the work, at least she was here at the corrals watching and not back at The Homestead missing out.

Sadie rested the camera on her cast, and watched her family preparing the equipment for branding. She quietly waited for it to get daylight enough to take pictures.

Her eyes opened to Matt flipping a calf onto its side then holding the front of the calf and Reilly held the back end while her dad branded it. Nora ran over with the ear tag applicator and Grace gave the calf its shots to keep it healthy.

She had fallen asleep!

Cora was at the calf gate counting the calves as they were removed for branding and Tessa was on the gate counting the calves as they rejoined the cows in the pasture.

"Hey, sleepy head." Aunt Dru rode up next to her on Scarecrow.

Sadie didn't know whether to smile at Scarecrow or frown because she missed the start of the branding. "How long have I been asleep?"

"A couple of hours," Her aunt smiled. "We're just getting ready to take the first break."

Sadie looked around at all the action; feeling disappointment she missed out.

"You didn't miss much, Mini-me." Her aunt said, understanding the frustration. "And you'll feel better the rest of the day after getting some good sleep."

Sadie sighed and nodded, then realized it didn't hurt when she nodded. Her eyes went wide in surprise. "It didn't hurt!"

"You're healing!" Aunt Dru grinned. "And we have a surprise for you."

"What?" Sadie moved the puppies from her lap and stood in anticipation.

Aunt Dru turned, "Grayson!"

Sadie's dad waved. He had a big grin on his face when he turned Eli away from them and motioned to Jessup who was on the ground. The foreman opened a gate to a small corral and disappeared so Sadie could only see the top of his head over the fence.

Trotting out from the corral was a small black cow with a pink tag in her right ear. Sadie's heart raced! There was only one pink tag on the whole property and it belonged to Dusty, the calf she had saved two years before.

The cow turned back to the corral and a small red calf trotted out towards her. It too had a pink tag in its right ear signifying it was a girl too!

"Dusty's first baby!" Sadie yelled in delight. "And she'll have babies, too!"

Sadie's mood sky rocketed. She picked up the camera and took her first picture of Dusty and her new baby. Then she turned the camera on her beautiful aunt on her beautiful Scarecrow…click, click, click…

Then Uncle Scott rode up riding Little Ghost…click, click, click…

After the last calf trotted away with the T3E brand, everyone was given a drink for the annual salute:

"To ranch life!" They yelled and lifted the drinks in the air.

Click, click, click…

CHAPTER NINE

In the back seat of the truck on the way back to the ranch, Sadie pressed the button on the digital camera and reviewed all the pictures she had taken. Hundreds of them!

Aunt Dru was right, she felt good the whole day after her morning nap. She was able to move more, eat more, and her parents had let her walk on the outside of the corral and take pictures through the fence. She had more energy in her than she had in weeks.

She looked up and out the front window of the truck as they pulled into the ranch house. There was a large delivery truck in front of the bunkhouse.

"Who's that?" Sadie asked.

"I have no idea," Her parents said in unison.

They stopped and her dad climbed out of the truck. He helped her out of the backseat before he turned towards the two men that were waiting at the delivery truck.

A concerned Aunt Dru and Uncle Scott made their way towards the two men followed by the rest of the family.

"Just tell me where they go and we'll get them switched out. We'll be taking the old ones with us." The larger delivery man smiled.

"We didn't order them," Uncle Scott told the man.

"They are all paid for and the delivery fee," The man looked around at the group. "This is the Tagger Enterprises ranch?"

They all nodded.

"Well, I'm in the right place. Just tell me where to put them." The man smiled.

Details…Sadie saw her dad turn, realization on his face. She turned quickly to see where he was looking. Nick was looking back at him…other than a slight flicker of humor in his eyes, his expression was calm. Neither man spoke to each other.

"In that building. We'll bring the old out, and help with the new." Her dad said as he turned back to the delivery man.

"Help is always appreciated." The man nodded happily. "Especially with this many."

"What are they?" Reilly asked as he walked with the rest of the adults to the bunkhouse.

The larger man opened the back of the trailer and everyone remaining at the truck gasped.

"New mattresses?" Wade shouted in surprise.

Sadie stared at all the mattresses. Eight double for the lower bunk and eight twins for the upper bunks. Plus three queen size for Jessup's, Cora's and the extra bed in the house.

Her back started to tighten and her energy drained. This was her fault. Nick had to spend a lot of money on them, only because of her. The tears started to rise again, her throat constricted and her lungs hurt. More guilt wrapped her heart.

As everyone moved forward to help unload the mattresses from the truck, Sadie took a step back. She wanted her horses…but they were still in the trailers. Who was in the barn? She didn't know, but she was headed there anyway.

Isaiah greeted her as she walked into the main aisle of the barn where all the hay was stacked for the winter. Sadie crawled on a bale in the back corner and reached through the stall opening to pet the horse. She slowly fed him handfuls of hay as the tears fell.

"Sadie?" She heard her mother call out but was too upset to answer.

She threw a big flake of hay in the stall for Isaiah, then buried her face in her knees and let the tears and sobs take over. The guilt just overwhelmed her. Even the chair in the back of the truck upset her when she realized how much extra work she caused her dad and mom because of her decision to run the barrels.

"Sadie? I can hear you, where are you?" Her mom called out again from a little closer.

She was still too upset to say anything.

When she felt her mom's arms wrap around her, Sadie leaned in and continued to cry.

"Why the tears, Hon?" Her mother whispered as she kissed the top of her head. "You had such a good day."

"It's my fault." Sadie sobbed.

"What is? What happened?"

"He spent all that money because of me."

"You know who bought them?" She asked in surprise.

Sadie nodded, a hint of an ache went through her shoulders. Her body was too tense.

"Honey, he didn't do it to upset you. We realized this morning that your mattress wasn't letting you sleep, and you were too worried to tell us. So we talked about getting you a new one up here. He just reacted before we had a chance to do it ourselves."

"But it's still my fault."

"We've gone through the fault thing before." Her mother sighed.

Sadie closed her eyes to the argument; she was tired of it. Why couldn't they just say it was her fault? The tears continued.

Her mother sat her up straight then released her from the embrace and she just walked away.

Sadie turned to Isaiah, wanting to crawl into the stall and touch him but it was against the rules.

She held out a handful of hay to him, and even though he had a big pile in front of him, he took the hay from her hand. She sniffed, wanting to laugh at how silly horses were, but she was too exhausted all the sudden.

Hearing someone walking towards her, she turned and her heart dropped and the guilt rose; it was Nick. His eyes shone in concern. The tears started, then the panic because she didn't want to upset him with her tears.

She tried desperately to wipe away the tears with her one good arm and the fingers of her casted arm.

"Stop that, you're going to bash yourself with your cast and hurt yourself more." He frowned. "It's hard enough to look at the black eye…don't make it worse."

"But you don't like tears, and I can't wipe them away fast enough with one hand."

"Sadie, you're a gem." Nick sat down next to her on the bale. "Just stop crying and you don't have to wipe them away."

"I tried, but you just made them come out faster."

"Well, I'd leave to make them stop, but Leah said you were upset because I bought the mattresses."

Sadie didn't say anything; she just kept wiping the tears with her jacket sleeve.

"That's probably one of the silliest things I've ever heard of." He shook his head and looked at her like she was nuts.

"It's so much money…and it's because of me…and because I got myself hurt." She took a deep breath and let it out slowly to try to calm herself.

"Sadie, what else do I have to spend money on?" Nick smiled, his brownish green eyes shone with humor.

Sadie crinkled her face and answered honestly. "I don't know."

"And I don't know if the crash was your fault or not, but if it was, I'll thank you for pointing out to everyone how bad the mattresses were."

"What?"

"You're still twelve?" He asked with a raised brow.

"Yeah." She smiled.

"Good, you and Nora keep changing ages on me, I have to keep up."

Sadie giggled and the tears stopped.

"I was a bull rider for many years," He reminded her. "Those mattresses must be twenty-years-old and the one on my bunk seemed to wake up every ache I've ever had. At twelve, you don't know all the aches and pains yet."

"I did the last couple nights." She admitted softly.

"There you go," He grinned and threw his hands in the air to emphasize his point. "I was going to replace them this spring anyway…sneak them in while no one was looking."

Sadie laughed. "I wonder how long it would have taken for them to notice."

"I only buy the best," Nick winked. "They'll notice the second they sit down on them."

"Nobody's going to want to get up in the morning." She grinned back.

"Good thing it's a day off for the horses."

"Oh, that reminds me." She stood. "Andy's horses have problems. I was going to show them to Dad."

Nick stood. "We're good then?"

Sadie nodded…no pain.

***

As Sadie predicted, no one wanted to get out of bed the next morning, even after the coffee aroma filled the air.

"What's on the agenda today?" Aunt Jordan asked from her bed into the quiet room.

"I think Nick deserves breakfast in bed," Aunt Dru answered.

"I agree," Nick chuckled.

"Problem is getting anyone out of bed to make it." Uncle Scott added.

"What time is it?" Reilly asked.

"Six, we're burning daylight." Grace answered.

The room went quiet again.

Sadie rolled from side to side to see if her back hurt.

"What are you doing?" Nikki asked from the bunk below her.

"Checking to see if I hurt," Sadie answered.

"Well?" A chorus of voices asked.

Sadie smiled. "No, I feel good, thanks, Nick."

"Thank you, Sadie." He answered.

"Well, I guess one good thing came out of the wreck." She sighed into her pillow.

"Maybe we should get you on Scarecrow today." Her father said.

Sadie frowned, she wanted back with her horses but she wasn't sure Scarecrow was the one. She wasn't really sure what she needed.

"Scarecrow might be tired after riding the last two days." Tessa spoke. "Little Ghost only worked yesterday."

Sadie smiled, she had a new friend.

"Can I Dad?" Sadie asked while looking at the ceiling, her heart hoping.

"As long as no cows are around." He answered.

Sadie tossed the covers off and slid to the edge of the comfortable bed. By the time she turned to crawl down the ladder, Uncle Scott was up and helping her down the ladder.

"Sorry," She told him with a smile, along with Lucas, Matt and Nick who had also risen to help her.

"Something tells me you really aren't," Her uncle grinned.

She giggled as she collected her clothes out of the dresser and made her way to the bathroom.

By the time she came out, almost everyone was out of bed.

"Sorry," She grinned and slid on her coat. Her cowboy hat was next.

"No, you're not." Her mother grinned back.

"You stay out of the corral until we get out there." Her dad ordered.

"OK," She answered as she walked out of the bunkhouse.

Sadie stood just outside the door of the bunkhouse and took in a deep breath of the cool mountain air and pine trees…it always helped freshen her mind and made her feel better. She walked around the edge of the building, out of view of the windows and stretched her arms up and twisted at the waist. She was testing for pain. It was a little achy but didn't hurt.

"How did that go for you?"

She jumped at her father's voice behind her and smiled sheepishly.

"Pain?"

"No, just achy."

"Promise?"

"Promise."

"OK, let's go get him saddled up."

"Can I ride him bareback?" She asked and followed him to the barn.

"If you're going to ride, then saddle. If you want to be led, bareback."

What a terrible choice to make. She wanted to ride by herself but wanted the feel of the horse on her legs, not leather.

"I'll ride." She finally decided. "Where are we going to ride?"

"Just to the fall corrals and back."

"That's not far."

"It's far enough for the first time."

They rode peacefully, just the two of them in the crisp morning air. Little Ghost walked calmly as Sadie rocked her hips back and forth following his rhythm.

"I can't remember the last time just the two of us rode." His eyes looked content peering out from below the rim of his black cowboy hat.

"We should do it more often."

"I agree."

They made it to the corrals with Sadie enjoying every step her horse took. There was a slight ache in her back when they arrived back at the barn, but it wasn't too bad.

"Is that all? It just wasn't long enough." She sighed, not wanting to see the barn.

Then Scarecrow walked out of the front doors of the barn, led by her mom. The horse was already saddled.

Her back tensed, "What's going on?"

"It's time to ride her, Sadie Girl." Her dad said calmly.

Sadie rolled her lips together, surprised that her switch of anger didn't go off. She wasn't mad, she was just…

Her mother led Scarecrow up next to Little Ghost.

"Just slide from one saddle to the other." Her mother encouraged.

Sadie stared at Nora's saddle, the scratches still quite visible where she had thrown it into the ravine.

"Sadie, just slide, you've done it a million times." She heard her dad.

Sadie turned and looked into his blue eyes. She wasn't sure it was fear she felt…she wasn't really sure what it was…but there was a punch of anxiety in her gut.

"No matter who you blame for the accident…it wasn't Scarecrow's fault." His voice was low, but firm.

"She saved me from being crushed." Sadie whispered…what was it she was feeling?

"Reach out and touch her." He nodded towards the horse.

Sadie slowly moved her eyes from his and turned to the palomino. Her eyes dropped down to the healing scratches on her shoulder. That's what it was…that's the feeling…it was a different kind of guilt. She had hurt Scarecrow, not the other way around, her horse had protected her.

Sadie leaned down and touched the scratches on Scarecrow with her good arm, then placed her casted hand down Little Ghosts shoulder; her fingertips brushing his scars.

Healing…together they needed to heal. As if floating, she moved from one saddle to the other then bent and placed her hands on each side of Scarecrow's neck. The horse turned and looked back at her, just like the first time Sadie had slid in the saddle. The horse's gentle eye looking at her, loving her, understanding, they needed to be together to heal.

"Can we Dad?" Sadie turned pleading eyes to her dad.

"Can you what?" He asked with a concerned tilt of the head.

"Can we be together, walking, the three of us?"

"Is that what you need?" His eyes softened.

"We heal together." She whispered, hoping he would understand.

He stepped out of the saddle, pulled Little Ghost's reins over the horse's head and handed them to her. "Not far."

Sadie smiled and nudged her horses into a walk toward the corrals. They walked quietly in the morning sunshine; to the feel of the breeze on her skin and the sound of mountain birds and hoof beats. She breathed in and filled her lungs with the pine trees, mountain air, and her two horses.

Riding her heart, she led her soul…the two healed her mind.

CHAPTER TEN

Sadie sat up and looked toward the kitchen, waiting for the clicking. Finally, it went off. She looked over the edge of the bunk.

"Nikki?" She whispered.

"What?"

"I knew you were awake."

"Matt is, too."

"Yes, I am."

"You guys are as excited as I am."

"More." They said in unison.

"Circle 50's first roundup!" Sadie called out loudly.

She was greeted with chuckles and giggles.

"Come on!" She yelled out as the aroma of the coffee reached her.

"We're burning daylight!" Rang out from everyone in the room.

Sadie laughed and turned towards the ladder.

Nick made it to her first this time.

"That seems to be the fastest way to get anyone out of bed." Sadie grinned into his amused eyes.

"Aren't you a stinker this morning?" Her mother called out from her bunk.

"I'm just so excited," Sadie felt the energy of the day running through her as she grabbed her clothes and ran to the bathroom.

"Don't run!" Her father's voice reached her as the door closed.

She looked in the mirror while brushing her teeth. The bruising was still evident, but it was lighter and turning yellowish. During the day she would forget it was there until someone mentioned it. It must be hard for her parents to look at. She was so used to the cast, it didn't bother her anymore.

When she stepped out of the bathroom, everyone was up. Sadie grinned, grabbed her coat and cowboy hat and opened the door.

"Don't run!" Her father's voice rang out again as the door closed.

The lights to the ranch house were on so she went in to help Cora prepare all the snacks for the saddle bags.

An hour later, she and Tessa were driving down unfamiliar territory on the Circle 50 ranch. Her camera ready, Sadie took pictures of the very happy ranch owners preparing their horses for the ride.

With Tessa driving, Sadie spent the day taking pictures of all the riders, the new property, and the red and white Hereford cows that were now walking down the road towards them.

"Now what?" Tessa turned to Sadie.

"I don't know." Sadie grinned, "I was helping Cora instead of listening to the plans for the day."

"Well, what good are you?" Tessa giggled.

"Just a photographer, ma'am." Sadie held up the camera and they both laughed.

"Well, let's drive to the side, wait for them to pass, then follow."

"Sounds like a good stalker plan to me." Sadie agreed. "We can let the puppies go to the bathroom."

The puppies bounced and ran, playing with each other until the cows walked by. They stopped and watched the cows in curiosity.

"How many do they have?" Tessa asked.

"Matt said there were only three hundred last spring. It dwindled to nearly half of what it used to be when Andy's health was good." Sadie answered while taking pictures. "But they bought another fifty cows and three bulls last year and want to grow the count back up in the next year or two."

The roundup was over late in the afternoon with the mountain side full of cows and the Circle 50 ranch house full of happy cowgirls and cowboys.

***

Clicking from the kitchen…

"Nikki." Sadie whispered from the top bunk again, with a giggle following.

"What?"

"I knew you were awake."

"Matt is, too."

"Yes, I am."

"Again?" Lucas asked in false exasperation.

"It's branding day!" Sadie called out and headed for the ladder.

Lucas was the only one up this time.

"What?" Sadie looked around. "You guys don't love me anymore?"

"We did rock paper scissors last night to see who had to grab you this morning." Lucas told her with a grin.

Sadie's laughter bounced off the walls causing everyone to join her.

***

Sadie stood on the back of the truck and took pictures of everyone getting ready. She turned the camera in time to see Matt and Nikki riding side-by-side on Trooper and Harvey. They were heading right towards her. She took their picture quickly then lowered the camera.

"What?" Sadie asked as they walked right up to the fence.

Nikki slid behind her saddle and reached out for Sadie's hand.

Sadie looked for her Dad. He was grinning and nodded to her.

"What?" Sadie asked excitedly as she slid onto the saddle. The three of them slowly walked out of the corral and headed towards all the cows. They stopped right in the middle of the herd.

"What's going on?" Sadie looked at Matt.

"Nikki and I have been battling all morning over it and so we decided you could choose." Matt answered.

"Choose what?" Sadie asked.

"Choose the first calf that gets branded with the Circle 50 brand." Matt smiled, his brownish green eyes shining with excitement.

Sadie inhaled so sharply, she thought her lungs were going to explode. She was so stunned she just stared at her cousin.

"Really?" She finally whispered.

"Really," Nikki answered from behind her.

Sadie looked around at all the calves. "It should be a heifer. She'll be around for years instead of getting sold next fall." Sadie looked at Matt…he nodded. "She should be big and strong…a good conformation." Sadie continued as she looked around the pairs of cows.

There were so many, and they all looked the same…except one. She was standing proudly watching the horses and riders.

"That one," Sadie pointed to her.

Both cousins turned and looked.

"Good choice!" Matt nodded and they walked to the cow and calf to push her into the corral.

Nikki helped her stand on the tail gate of the truck and Sadie turned to watch everyone.

"Wait!" Sadie called out.

Nikki turned and Sadie told her what she wanted. Her cousin happily agreed.

Sadie set the camera on the tailgate of the truck and made sure everyone was visible in the viewfinder. The whole group of family and friends stood in the middle of the corral with the first calf in front of them wearing the #1 on its ear tag.

"We have 10 seconds to get in the picture." Sadie told her dad as she pushed the shutter button.

He picked her up and walked quickly to the group and they all smiled happily at the camera as it clicked.

***

"I can't believe that branding week is over already." Sadie sighed as they drove away from the ranch house.

"It's been quite the week." Grace sighed. "In two days…back to school."

"Me, too!" Sadie sat up in her seat and looked up at her mom.

"I don't see why not. If you can walk around and take pictures all day, you can sit in a chair and listen to a teacher." Her mom answered.

"Oh yeah!" Sadie grinned up at Grace, who was scrunching her face.

"You're just weird." Grace rolled her eyes.

Sadie laughed. "Did I tell you I decided what I want to go to college for?"

"No." Grace shook her head.

Sadie excitedly told her parents and sister about her plan for super horses with Nikki and Nora's expertise.

"What about me?" Grace pouted.

Sadie's eyebrows shot up in surprise. She hadn't thought about Grace. "What do you want to do?"

Grace shrugged. "I've been all over the place with that one. I'll be a senior next year so everyone is asking me that."

"What are you interested in?" Their dad asked.

"Not being told what to do," Grace chuckled. "Which ruled out becoming a sheriff's officer."

"You wanted to be in law enforcement?" Their mother asked in surprise.

"Yeah, I thought about it after New Year's." Grace nodded.

Sadie frowned at the memory of Grace's close call.

"What else have you thought of?" Her dad asked, trying to get away from the New Year's incident.

"Nursing…it was interesting to watch them when Sadie was in the hospital…but I don't want to handle bed pans. Grade school teacher…but I don't want to be in school anymore. Architecture but I'm not that good with math." She answered.

"You don't want to work with horses?" Sadie asked in surprise.

"Why would you come up with those careers?" Their dad asked.

"Friends at school want me to do it with them." Grace answered.

"You've got a pretty good mind for business." Their mom commented. "Jack said you've been doing great helping with the business at The Stables."

"Yeah…but what?" Grace sighed.

"How about running the super horse business?" Her dad asked.

Grace looked to the front seat, "What would I do?"

"We will each be doing our part of taking care of the horses." Sadie answered. "We need someone to take care of us."

"And get clients in the door through marketing." Their mom added.

Grace sat up taller in her seat. "You mean…I would HAVE to talk horses all day? I love talking about horses."

"We know!" Her parents laughed.

"And I'd be in charge!" Grace grinned.

They all chuckled.

"So we have a business for super horses." Sadie clapped. "Now we just have to talk to Nikki and Nora, then come up with a name."

Halfway home Sadie was fighting to keep her eyes open. It had been such a great week. She felt so much better, in her heart and her body.

Fighting the sleep, she picked up the camera and started reviewing the pictures.

"You ever going to let Lucas see the pictures?" Grace asked.

Sadie giggled as she remembered him trying to get the camera from her so he could see the pictures of Nikki.

"Yeah, Mom's going to help me put them all together and have a book made for everyone." Sadie grinned at her. "A special one of Nikki for Lucas and one for Matt and Nikki's first branding."

"Plus one for the entire family to enjoy all the pictures," Her mom added. "But it's going to take some time to get them together and the books to be made."

"There are some good pictures in the camera." Sadie told them as she scrolled through all the pictures. "Some really good ones of Nikki for Lucas."

She came across the pictures of Reilly riding in for lunch the first day. He looked so sad. Not one true smile in any of those pictures.

Sadie looked at Grace. She would know, but she wouldn't tell her what was wrong. It would break their trust between each other. She was going to have to figure it out on her own.

CHAPTER ELEVEN

Sadie stepped off the school bus and looked at the long driveway to The Homestead.

"Are you OK to walk that far?" Wade asked.

"Should be," She smiled, "Just walk slowly."

"Why were your parents called to the school?" Wade asked with a frown.

"I don't know," Sadie shrugged…no pain…she sighed in relief. "I got all the homework done from being gone for two weeks. I know it's right."

"You know?" Wade chuckled.

"Yeah, it was pretty easy."

"Not for me. I got most right, but not all."

"Are you going to ride?"

"Yeah, just practice some roping. Are you?"

"Mom said I couldn't unless her or Dad were there."

They arrived at the house and were greeted by Cora.

"Sadie, it's so good to see you almost back to normal."

"I agree," Sadie grinned at her. It couldn't get better than coming home to Cora's warm, welcoming smile.

"And we have mini quiches and chocolate cream pie." Cora's eye's twinkled.

"Awesome!" Sadie and Wade cried out in unison.

"I think Grace and Reilly left you some…well Grace anyway, Reilly didn't eat very much."

"Why?" They asked in unison.

Cora shrugged. "He wouldn't say."

Sadie looked for the pair. Grace was sitting in the living room watching TV. No sign of Reilly, which was really odd. Without another word she marched to her sister and put her hands on her hips…a little difficult with the casted one. This was crazy. For some reason, Sadie knew it had something to do with her…and Grace knew.

"What's wrong with you?" Grace looked at her sister in surprise.

"How?" Sadie asked sternly.

"How what?" Grace asked.

"How do I find out what's wrong?" She asked.

Grace just stared.

"Go to our room." Wade sighed quietly. He had walked up next to her.

Sadie turned and walked to the steps and looked up. She hadn't climbed the stairs since before her crash. The only time she had been upstairs was to soak in Aunt Dru's bath tub and Jack had carried her.

Sadie turned and looked for Cora. As far as she knew, Cora was the only adult home. Going up stairs was against the rules…it would be the first one she had broken.

"Wade, help me." Sadie turned and with her casted arm resting on the rail, her good arm was braced by Wade.

She placed her foot on the first step and lifted, no problem. Ten steps up she was leaning on Wade more.

"We're going to get in trouble for this." Wade whispered and looked down into the kitchen.

"Do you care? I don't." Sadie said firmly, she was determined to make it up the steps and into the boy's room. She wanted to know what was wrong.

"Nope."

She stopped near the top and stared at the last few step.

"You OK?" Wade asked concerned.

"Yep." She took another step, her back muscles were starting to tighten up.

"We're free and clear." Wade said as they reached the top.

They walked slowly towards the boys' room.

Sadie had no idea what she would be looking for to see what was wrong with Reilly. Why so sad, upset, or whatever he was that was causing the frowns? He had been such a happy cousin since Aunt Dru and Jack got married.

Details…when did he start looking so distant? Since the first day Little Ghost and Scarecrow were brought to her window…that's when Sadie noticed it…but was it before that? She didn't know.

They reached the room and Wade opened the door.

"Reilly?" Sadie called out.

No answer.

She took a deep breath and walked in the room…to Reilly's half of the room.

Details…the shelf with his mother's pictures, the pictures of Reilly and Jack riding Rufio and Cooper, a rodeo picture of him and Grace team roping, more pictures…they were all there.

Sadie took a deep breath and let it out in frustration. Bed, chair, end table, lamp, alarm clock…. She stopped and looked back at the end table.

"Where is it?" Sadie asked quietly, looking at the spot it should be.

"I don't know." Wade answered.

Sadie turned. They were the only two in the room, no one had followed. Grace knew.

"Why did he do it?"

"I don't know."

"He didn't say anything to you?"

"It was gone right after your accident."

"Before I came home?"

"Yes."

No anger switch flipped but she could feel a slow burn…of disappointment and hurt.

"I don't understand, Wade." She said trying to calm herself down…her back starting to tense and ache.

"You have to ask him."

"OK, where is he?"

"I don't know, I've been with you."

Sadie turned and walked from the room a little faster and more determined.

At the top of the steps, she held the banister tightly and Wade held her casted arm.

With each step, the ache went through her back and her temper and disappointment increased.

Halfway down, she saw Reilly in the kitchen.

"Reilly!" She yelled.

He jumped and turned quickly; looking with wide eyes up the stairs at her.

"What?" He asked.

"Where is it?" She glared down at him.

His expression froze, then dropped. Without a word he turned and walked out the door.

"Reilly!" She yelled as loud as she could.

"Sadie!" Her dad walked into the kitchen; his face registering anger and disbelief. "What are you doing up there?"

Sadie gripped the banister tighter and Wade gripped her tighter.

"Where did he go?" Sadie asked her dad; he was racing up the stairs towards her.

"You know you aren't supposed to be going up those yet." He said angrily and bent over and lifted her with one arm wrapped around her thighs.

"Where did he go?" Sadie repeated, looking down at her mom, Aunt Dru, and Cora as they stared at her in disbelief.

He set her down on the floor, then with hands on hips turned to her. "What is this all about and why were you upstairs? Wade, why did you take her up there?"

"Trying to find out what was wrong with Reilly." She answered and looked at Aunt Dru. She could see her aunt knew something was wrong. "Did you know it was missing?"

"What?" She asked.

"Where is he?" Sadie asked her.

"I just saw him run out to the barn." Aunt Dru answered. "Do you know what's wrong?"

"No…but I have a clue." Sadie said as she walked through the kitchen.

"What is going on here?" Her mom asked as Sadie walked out the back door.

Aunt Dru followed to help her down the steps.

Sadie walked angrily across the driveway.

"Hold your temper." Aunt Dru said from beside her.

"I'm not angry…I'm mad and disappointed."

"OK…"

Rufio and Cooper's stalls were the first ones in the barn. They were empty since the horses were all out in the pasture. He was sitting in the back of Cooper's stall, arms resting on his bent knees. His head was down and didn't raise it as she opened the stall door.

She took a step in and Aunt Dru materialized with a stool.

"Sit." Her aunt ordered.

Sadie sat. Aunt Dru closed the stall door and stood on the outside, her arms resting over the doors.

"Where is it?" Sadie asked trying to keep her voice calm but firm.

"Under the bed," He answered without looking up.

"What?" Aunt Dru asked.

"The Zorro statue I gave him." Sadie looked up at her and saw the look of surprise then concern cross her face.

Sadie turned back to her cousin and sighed. So now she knew, for sure, that his mood was because of her. She was hurt that he would put it away, and upset that his depression was her fault. Just more guilt…

"Why, Reilly?" Sadie tried to keep her voice calm, but it shook from frustration.

"I'm not a hero." Reilly whispered.

"Why would you say such a thing?" Sadie felt her throat tighten.

"But I wasn't." He raised his head, his blue eyes shimmering with unshed tears and his voice shook. "I didn't save you, Sadie. I ran as fast as I could…I couldn't get there…I didn't save you..." The tears fell from anguished eyes.

Her shoulders drooped and the pressure in her head grew. She felt the tears coming again; she was so tired of tears and guilt.

"Nobody could have, Reilly." She whispered.

"A true hero would have saved you." He sniffed and wiped the tears away with his sleeve. "It just kept reminding me that I didn't save you…I just couldn't look at it anymore."

"Reilly," Sadie sighed, guilt burning. "Even if you were on Cooper, you couldn't have gotten to me in time. I lived it, watched the video, it happened too fast."

"Before you even kicked her to run…I was running to you, behind the fence, I yelled as loud as I could."

Sadie shook her head, "I heard you on the video, and if I wasn't so deep in my own head…thinking too hard, trying to decide…I would have heard you at the arena."

He leaned his head against the wall and looked at her through half closed eyes. "I've played it in my mind a million time."

"And each time you couldn't get to me because Scarecrow is faster than you." Sadie tried to smile. His expression didn't change. "There was absolutely nothing anyone could have done, not Dad, not Uncle Scott, not Batman, nor the original Zorro. The only person who could have saved me…is me." She shrugged, her whole body tired from the guilt.

He shook his head. "Sadie…I should have gotten to you."

"I wish I'd heard you Reilly, I really do, but it's my fault I didn't…not yours."

He sighed. "But a true hero would have been able to save you."

"A true hero isn't always there to save the day…if they were, the movies would be pretty boring." She smiled, and earned a smirk. "A true hero is what happens after the battle, crash, or tragedy…how they handle it and what they do."

He shook his head and turned away from her.

Sadie stretched her back, and closed her eyes. As she leaned against the wall, they opened.

"Reilly, what is the most important thing to me beside my family?"

He turned and stared at her, Sadie was sure he was trying to figure out what angle she was trying to work.

"Scarecrow and Little Ghost," He finally answered.

"Who took care of Scarecrow when I wrecked?"

"I did."

"Who took care of them while I was laid up in the hospital?"

"I did."

"Who…" She took a deep breath. It shook as she exhaled; she thought back to the moment Little Ghost pushed his nose on the screen to get to her, and a tear fell. "Who came up with the idea to get me back to my horses, through the window?"

"I did." His eyes glistened.

"You have no idea how much I needed that." She wiped away the tears. "But then again… I think you do."

He didn't respond.

"Who convinced me to eat so I could get to my horses faster?"

"I did."

"Constant food," Sadie smiled at him.

They sat quietly a moment while Sadie tried to put to words what she was feeling. "Reilly," She said softly. "No one could have saved me from the crash, but YOU were the one that took care of my horses, got me back to them." She looked at him in earnest, her voice low, quivering with emotion. "You got me my horses Reilly…that will always make you my hero. You will always be my Zorro."

They stared at each other in silence.

"You understand?" She pleaded with her eyes. "You did it for me…and I would have done it for you."

He rolled his lips together and nodded.

"Will you put it back?" She asked softly…hopefully.

His eyes changed…from agonized to relief; a little of the guilt released from her.

"Will you put it back?" She asked again.

"Yes," He sighed and stood. "Are you sure you're twelve?"

"Sometimes I feel like I'm a hundred and twelve."

He chuckled. "You need to rest your back. Going up and down those stairs couldn't have done it any good."

"They were actually a really good exercise for it." She said as he helped her stand.

When they turned to the door they stared in surprise. They had both forgotten Aunt Dru was standing at the stall door.

She smiled at the two of them and opened the door without saying a word.

"Can we check on Libby and Kit before I go in?" Sadie asked.

Both horse's bodies were huge and they looked miserable from their pregnancy. They could see movement on their sides when the babies moved.

"How long?" Reilly asked his mom.

"Any day," She answered and wrapped her arms around Libby's head. The horse had leaned into her body, needing love and support. "They are both waxing up."

Sadie shifted her weight from one foot to the other trying to get the ache out of her back.

"Come on," Reilly turned his back to her. "I'll give you a piggy back ride to the house so you don't have to walk."

Sadie giggled. "What about the wheelbarrow?"

"It'll bump on the ground too much. I'll walk slowly."

"I'll walk behind him to make sure you're safe." Aunt Dru chuckled.

Reilly had to bend all the way down for her to climb on his back. Aunt Dru helped brace him so he could stand.

"I'm too heavy." Sadie laughed as his arms wrapped around her knees and hers around his neck.

"You're a pencil," He answered and took a few tentative steps. "We're good."

With Aunt Dru following closely, they made their way across the driveway.

He lowered her down at the bottom of the steps, then stuck out his arm for support as she walked up to the deck.

They all three were laughing until they walked into the kitchen.

"Your parents want to see you in the no-media room." Cora informed her.

Sadie's mood plummeted.

CHAPTER TWELVE

Now what? Sadie looked up at Aunt Dru who opened her eyes wide and shook her head…she didn't know why her parents wanted to see her. Shoulders drooping, she walked to the hallway. She was going to get yelled at for breaking the rules and going upstairs.

Wade was in the living room with Grace. She quickly detoured to him.

"Did you get in trouble?" Sadie asked nervously.

"They weren't happy." He shrugged. "You fix Reilly?"

"As fixed as he can be…Zorro will return."

"Good," Her sister and cousin said in unison.

"Well, I guess I have to go face the music now." Sadie turned.

"It's the no-media room…won't be no music in there." Grace called out.

"That's what I'm afraid of," Sadie walked down the hall.

She stopped just before the door and slowly peered around the door opening to see what her parents were doing. They were standing looking out the windows; her mom leaned into her his chest and his arms rested comfortably around her.

Loving or comforting?

"Get in here," Her dad said without turning around.

How did he know she was even there? She had been so quiet. Details…she looked quickly…they would have seen her reflection in the window.

She walked in and sat in the big chair across from the small couch. It was her usual spot when she was in trouble; her in the chair, her parents on the couch facing her.

"You're not in trouble." Her dad smiled.

"Then why am I here?" She tilted her head and watched them sit.

"A couple of things," Her mother said.

"We were called to your school."

"I know." Sadie shrugged, she wasn't worried about that.

"Evidently all your homework was perfect." Her mother said.

"So? I knew I had it right."

"That's the problem." She said.

"They thought I CHEATED?" Sadie felt the switch go off and she stood quickly. "I don't CHEAT!"

Four hands raised in the air to calm her down.

"Sit back down," Her dad said gruffly. "Dang, you're going to have to learn to control that. They don't think you cheated."

"Then what's the problem?" Sadie let out a frustrated exhale and sat back on the chair.

"Nobody taught you some of the stuff on your test…" Her dad started to explain.

Sadie shrugged, "I helped Nora a couple of years ago with it, I already knew how to do it." What was all this fuss about?

"That's just it." Her mother smiled.

"What?" Sadie was getting more confused.

"The teacher said you are more of an assistant teacher in the class, helping other kids, than a student." She answered.

"I don't tell them the answers, I show them how to figure it out." Sadie defended herself.

"That's what your teacher said." Her parents glanced at each other.

Sadie couldn't read the looks on their faces; there were NO details to follow. She hated that!

"We met with more than just your teacher; there was also the principal and the superintendent."

Sadie's eyebrows rose. "I didn't do anything!"

They both chuckled, which confused her more.

"Sadie, they want to move you up in grades so you're doing work that challenges you." Her dad smiled.

Sadie stared in disbelief. "Not go to school with Wade?" Her voice rose in shock.

Her dad shook his head. "You go to school to learn, not spend more time with your cousin."

"I don't want to go up a grade. I want to stay with Wade!" Sadie started to feel the stress in her stomach.

He shook his head, "Sadie, you tutor an eleventh grader."

"So?" She felt the dang tears rising again, this time out of frustration.

"They want to take you up two grades, to 9th grade next year." Her mother informed her quickly, realizing how upset she was getting.

Sadie stared in disbelief again. "Nora's grade?"

"Yes, to start." He said.

"To start?" Sadie felt the panic. "Why am I being punished?"

"Sadie, this is a good thing." Her mom said gently. "They have all the faith that you'll not only excel in the higher grade but may need to take college courses while you're a junior and senior."

Sadie was numb and confused. "So instead of 7th grade next year, I'll be going in 9th grade?"

"Same school as your friends and Wade, just in different classes." Her dad assured her.

"It's more important that you stay challenged and learn to your ability, not what the grades and your age restrict you to." Her mom smiled reassuringly.

Sadie slumped back in the chair and frowned at them. "I don't have a choice, do I?"

Her mother answered, "It's our job, as your parents, to do what's best for you. We honestly believe this is what is best for you."

What next? They said there were a couple things.

"What else?" She asked in despair.

They smiled, and her dad answered. "We also talked with your doctor today."

Sadie inwardly cringed.

When she didn't speak, her dad continued. "You have an appointment on Wednesday, if everything goes well, as we all expect it will, then you can start riding again full time."

Again she stared at them.

"Since you did it before, it will be good therapy for your back and neck as long as you take it easy to start." He said. "You'll build the muscles back up again. We trust Little Ghost and Scarecrow."

"So do I." Sadie whispered and turned to look out the window. It meant she was closer to the moment they would want her to race again.

She was still sitting in the chair staring out the window long after her parents left. Could she race again? Every time the wind blew or she heard a loud noise she heard Aunt Jordan's scream. She'd close her eyes at night and would see the wall come at her. Every time someone would talk about her in the hospital or recuperating she would feel the weight of guilt on her increase.

Could she race again? Did she want to take the chance of getting hurt again and putting her family and friends through such turmoil?

Wade and Nora joined her in the seats her parents had left.

"We heard." Nora smiled.

"I'm sorry, Nora." Sadie tried to smile.

"It's not your fault, Sadie." Her cousin leaned back on the couch cushions.

"But it seems like every time we turn around, I'm stepping on your toes." Sadie sighed.

"Or wearing my jeans…but you've out grown my jeans now." Nora chuckled.

"But I can still wear your shorts and all your shirts." Sadie leaned on the arm of the chair.

"It's just those dang long legs of yours." Nora pointed out.

"I'm really happy for you." Wade frowned.

"I'm not." Sadie said truthfully. "I told them I wanted to stay with you."

"Alex will still be there with me," Wade shrugged sadly. "It's going to be weird though."

Sadie nodded in agreement…no pain, she sighed.

***

Two weeks of trotting and galloping around the arena and trail rides at Hells Gate Park and the ranch. They had been working on the basics and slow barrel work. Nora competed at the Asotin horse show one weekend and then she and Grace competed at the rodeo the next weekend. At the same time the two girls were busy fulfilling their royalty duties at different rodeos and parades. Wade and Reilly were competing, too. Sadie didn't go, she didn't want to face all the contestants and families until she was ready…the bruising gone …until she could compete.

The cast had been removed the day before.

Riding Scarecrow and waiting for Wade to join her, Sadie turned and looked down the arena. She had placed the barrels in the clover leaf pattern she knew so well…just to look at them, not to race, she had told herself. Still, her pulse was racing and her back starting to ache from the tension.

She pushed Scarecrow into a slow gallop and enjoyed the rocking motion of her horse. They moved around the parameter of the arena, the barrels were in the middle. She watched them carefully, waiting…for what? For them to roll at her and attack? The barrels didn't cause the accident…the ground did. Sadie looked at the dirt in the arena, it was the same as always. Neither Scarecrow nor Little Ghost had ever slipped in it. Jack took good care of it.

She stared at the barrels again as she jogged around them. The ground caused the crash, but the crash happened because of the wall. She turned and looked…no wall, just fence panels. No wooden white wall to fly in to.

Sadie looked at Scarecrow's mane as it bounced to the motion. She could still see it flying in her face, but it didn't scare her anymore…it should have been the big thick muscular neck. Scarecrow would take care of her.

"Scarecrow will take care of me." She said out loud and slowed down to a walk. "Scarecrow will take care of me." She repeated at a whisper.

Sadie maneuvered the gold horse to the back of the arena and stared out at the three barrels. They looked so familiar but so…scary at the same time.

She looked back at the barn, no one was there, so she turned back to the white barrels. How many times had she run the barrels in this arena? They had the arena for over two years now, but she didn't ride Scarecrow until the spring, barrels in the summer. Two summers, two springs and two falls…estimating 18 full months, 72 weeks, at least 5 times a week doing slow work…sometimes more when she was younger and just learning. She ran the barrels at least once in full speed a couple evenings a week; more at practice speeds. 72 weeks, 6 times a week, at slow or fast work it was at least 3 times each night on the average…

Sadie sighed…her calculations said it was nearly a thousand times she had worked Scarecrow around these barrels, in this arena. There had been no slips, no rolls, no falls, and no walls to be slammed in to.

She looked back out to the barrels, imagined herself going around them.

"What are you doing?"

Sadie turned and saw Aunt Dru climbing up on the fence, sitting on the top with her feet resting on the cattle chute.

"Practicing," Sadie answered with a half-hearted smile.

"Scarecrow needs practice standing still?" Her aunt grinned.

Sadie chuckled and shook her head. "No, I'm running the pattern in my head, you taught me that."

"I did, and my mom taught that to me."

Sadie nodded and looked out at the barrels again, but she didn't budge. Hearing her aunt move she turned in time to see her walk along the fence, turn and slide a leg over Scarecrow and sit behind her. Sadie instinctively leaned back against her aunt who slid her arms around her and took the reins.

Aunt Dru touched Scarecrow's sides and moved the horse into a walk. They walked, riding double on the horse, around the parameter of the arena in silence.

"How many times do you think you've ran barrels in this arena?" Her aunt asked.

"I was just calculating that…around a thousand times."

"That's a lot." She felt her aunt nod her head.

Aunt Dru moved Scarecrow away from the fence and they looked out at the three barrels.

At a walk, they started towards the first barrel.

"It was my fault." Sadie sighed, the barrels scared her…but the warmth of her aunt surrounding her made her feel stronger.

"Why do you say that?"

"I didn't like the ground."

"What was wrong with the ground?"

"It was hard, shallow, and kind of pebbly."

"There was a rider that went before you."

"Yes, she slipped but I didn't know if it was the ground or if it was her inexperience."

"But you decided to go anyway?"

"I figured I could stop if I didn't like it."

"Did you ever have a time when you doubted the ground before?"

"No."

"But your gut was telling you not to run."

"Yes, and that's why it's my fault. You know, when you race it's just you and the horse. It's completely my decision on whether I run…I decided to run, risked Scarecrow…terrified Aunt Jordan…and look what I did to the rest of the family." Sadie sighed. "It was my fault."

"I agree with you."

Sadie felt the tears start to rise; tears of relief that someone finally agreed with her.

"So where do you go from here?" Her aunt asked as they walked around the first barrel and aimed for the second.

"I don't know. With it being my fault, I should be able to fix it. When everyone said it wasn't my fault, I couldn't, it was out of my control…that's scary."

"Do you still want to compete?"

"Yes."

"In barrels?"

"Yes."

"What is the biggest mistake you made?"

"Running."

"No, try again."

They walked around the second barrel.

Sadie thought back over the whole ride, starting from when she talked to Nora to slamming into the wall.

"Not listening to my gut."

"Good. You have to remember that no matter what you compete in, you always leave the gate thinking you're going to do your best, try your hardest…not telling yourself 'if I don't like it, I'll stop'."

Sadie nodded as they walked around the third barrel. Her aunt pushed Scarecrow into a slow trot as they made their way down the final stretch.

When they reached the end, Sadie looked up and saw Wade standing at the barn watching them.

Aunt Dru turned Scarecrow and they trotted the clover leaf pattern this time. When they made it to the end, Wade was gone.

She handed Sadie the reins and Sadie turned them to the barrels again and they trotted around again. When they rounded the third barrel, Sadie pushed Scarecrow into a gallop.

Sadie felt the enjoyment of riding start to take over the fear of running. When they ended the run; Uncle Scott and her dad where standing with Wade watching them.

Aunt Dru took the reins and moved them to the chute.

"Hop off," She whispered to Sadie and helped her slide off the horse and onto the top of the chute.

Sadie turned and watched her aunt trot the big palomino in a circle. Then, suddenly, she took off at a run towards the first barrel. A little wide, they headed for the second barrel. The turn was tight. As they aimed for the third barrel, Aunt Dru took the barrel tighter than Sadie usually did, but she didn't hit the barrel and came around it perfectly. She lowered her head and kicked Scarecrow into a fast run to finish the race.

Sadie yelled excitedly seeing her beautiful horse and aunt run the barrels together.

Aunt Dru trotted Scarecrow in circles, then she turned and ran the barrels again. When she returned, she slowed Scarecrow into a trot and moved down the arena and away from Sadie…her head was down blocking her face with the cowboy hat.

Sadie stopped in confusion and turned to see her dad and uncle walk through the gate, down the arena, and to their sister.

Wade walked up to Sadie.

"Wow." He said his eyes wide.

"I don't understand," Sadie frowned. "Wow, what?"

Her aunt walked the horse to her brothers and stepped down out of the saddle.

"Dad told me that Aunt Dru hasn't run barrels since the morning of the accident." Wade explained.

"What?" Sadie gasped and watched aunt embrace her brothers.

"Dad said it was because she associated running barrels with being told of her parents and grandparents dying."

Sadie slid off the chute and stood next to Wade.

"She really loves you, Sadie." Wade glanced at her.

Tears stung at Sadie's eyes as she watched her aunt smile up at her brothers. Then the Trio turned and walked towards Sadie and Wade.

"You've done a great job with Scarecrow," Aunt Dru smiled at Sadie. Her eyes were rimmed red from crying.

"Thanks…" Sadie smiled, loving her aunt more than ever.

"You ready to try it?" She held the reins out to Sadie.

Her hands shook nervously as she mounted the horse. She smiled hesitantly at her aunt and walked along the fence.

Sadie looked at the barrels…she could do this…Aunt Dru rode for her…faced her demons…Sadie could, too.

Taking a deep breath, Sadie turned Scarecrow in a big circle, visualized the barrels in her head, the pattern, one…two…three…

She took off at a slow gallop towards the first barrel. The pounding of Scarecrows hoof beats echoed the pounding in her lungs and heart. The first turn was wide, a little sloppy. She headed for the second barrel, her eyes starting to burn from staring and not blinking. Another wide turn, but faster than the first. She could barely breathe.

Normally she would kick Scarecrow to run faster as they turned for the third barrel…this time, she didn't.

Sadie looked up at the third barrel, her heart was racing, tears stinging at her dry eyes, lungs burning…as she rounded the third barrel, the wind in her ears echoed Aunt Jordan's scream of terror and rippled through Sadie's nerves. The scream rang out in her head again and again and again…her heart and lungs bursting in fear. Sadie closed her eyes and saw Scarecrow's mane flying into her face, then suddenly, she was flying toward the wall. Her hands gripped the saddle horn trying to stay in the saddle.

"Sadie!"

She heard the yell but couldn't get her eyes open to look…it could be her dad.

"Sadie!" She heard it again and felt Scarecrow slow down to a trot then stop.

Her eyes opened to see her dad, uncle, and aunt running to her, panic on their faces.

Sadie had leaned forward, gripping the saddle horn, and her whole body was tense.

Her dad was the first to reach her and pulled her out of the saddle. Her aunt and uncle went to Scarecrow's head.

"Are you, OK?" Her dad asked nervously as he set her on the ground.

Sadie nodded, trying to catch her breath.

"What happened?" Aunt Dru stood at her side.

"I heard Aunt Jordan's scream." Sadie exhaled, trying to get her heart to slow down.

"Her what?" Uncle Scott and Aunt Dru said in unison.

Her dad pulled her into a hug and looked at the pair.

"We watched the video of Sadie's crash. It wasn't as bad as we thought to watch…except the wall part." He explained. "But we had the audio on and at the end, Jordan screams Sadie's name, right next to the camera, panicked and loud."

"It was awful," Sadie sighed. "I came around the third barrel and heard it…then saw the wall."

"I'm sorry, Sadie." Aunt Dru looked worried. "I shouldn't have pushed you."

"You didn't." Sadie smiled hesitantly. "I can do it."

"You want to try again?" Her aunt asked in surprise.

"Yes," Sadie nodded. She had to…for her aunt who faced her demons, for her horse who saved her, and for her entire family that had suffered long enough. She had to race the guilt out of her.

Her dad helped her mount the horse.

Sadie trotted Scarecrow back to the fence and turned to the barrels.

A grin crossed her face.

Each of the Trio had gone to the fence by a barrel. Uncle Scott was at the first barrel, Aunt Dru at the second barrel, and her dad was standing at the fence behind the third barrel.

"They'll protect you." Wade said from the chute behind her.

Sadie turned to him and nodded…no pain.

"Just take your time." Wade smiled. "They'd stand out here all day for us."

Sadie turned Scarecrow and did her circle, counted to three and started at a slow jog to the first barrel. The horse had run a lot already and didn't want to push her hard anymore.

"Just think about Scarecrow's pace." Uncle Scott yelled at her as she turned the first barrel. "Move with her."

Sadie did as he said, and made it to the second barrel.

"Pay attention to your reins, to your seat." Her aunt yelled.

Sadie adjusted the position of her body and lowered her hands. She was at the third barrel.

"Watch the pocket! Tighter!" Her dad yelled. "Like Dru!"

Sadie did as he said and jogged the horse closer to the barrel and slid her hand down the rein and finished the turn tightly.

Her mind was so busy doing what they asked, that she was jogging for home before she could even think about it.

Wade was standing in front of the chute, yelling at her, with a grin.

Sadie smiled and turned towards the arena. They were still standing, waiting, so she did it again. They yelled out their instructions to her again. She made it around without a problem.

"Do it again!" Uncle Scott yelled out.

So she did, at a slow gallop. This time though, they didn't have to yell, she was paying attention to everything they had said plus more. She thought of Scarecrow's stride, of the reins, the barrels, the feel of her legs against the saddle and horse, and then she looked at Wade as she ran for the end.

Whistles and applause rang out through the arena as the Trio walked towards her.

Sadie's heart was racing in excitement. The joy of riding had taken over.

CHAPTER THIRTEEN

It was still dark out as Sadie walked to the barn. She looked back at The Homestead, no lights were on. Her parents wouldn't be too thrilled she was out there by herself, but she just had to check on Kit and Libby. Both horses had started leaking milk from their bags…which meant they were both ready to give birth to Aunt Dru's old barrel horse Jet's grand-foal and great-grand foal.

There would be another 4th generation baby coming from Libby, and a new 5th generation baby coming from Kit; Nan, Jet, Libby, Kit and then Kit's baby.

The black Libby was bred to a black stallion…Aunt Dru hoping for another black horse. The red bay, Kit, was bred to a palomino. The stallion was chosen for his roping blood lines; hand-picked by Matt. The foal was a gift from Aunt Dru to her son. Nan had been given to his grandmother by his grandfather, Jet was his mother's, and Libby was his mother's too, Kit was Nikki's.

These are special babies, Sadie thought…someday, she would gift her kids with Scarecrow's babies.

She made her way into the barn through the small door. A light was on that just barely lit up the aisle so she could make her way to the mares without turning on a light to disturb them.

At Kit's door, Sadie looked into the stall to see her standing in a corner, her side was tense and she was sweating. Kit was in labor!

Hands shaking, Sadie took out Grace's phone, which she had swiped off her sister's bed side table. She called her Aunt Dru. A phone rang in the barn and Sadie turned to see Aunt Dru and Jack walking towards her. Matt and Nikki were right behind them.

Her aunt grinned at the surprised expression then pointed to the ceiling. Sadie looked up. She had forgotten about the camera in the mare's stalls which sent images to the monitor in Aunt Dru's bedroom. Her aunt had been watching all along.

Sadie smiled at the three adults then turned back to Kit.

"We saw Libby go down on the monitor." Jack smiled.

Sadie looked at them in surprise, "No… I thought…it's Kit."

"She was fine," Aunt Dru looked into Kit's stall which was right before Libby's.

They all four looked at the sweating Kit in surprise.

"You're right." Aunt Dru turned to her with a grin then walked past her to Libby's stall.

Sadie followed her and they looked in the stall at the same time.

"The feet are already sticking out." Her aunt whispered loudly, her eyes wide in surprise. She turned quickly to her husband and kids. "Both! At the same time!"

They were bred within two weeks of each other but no one expected them to have the babies at the same time.

"That was fast." Jack said softly and shook his head slowly.

Aunt Dru stood at the corner of the stalls, so she could see in both horses at the same time. Sadie stood at Libby's door watching the special baby's birth.

Slowly, all the Tagger family joined them and stood quietly to watch.

Libby's sides tightened and she groaned; the foal's nose could be seen resting on the front legs. Another push and the whole head appeared, one more grunt and the front shoulders appeared. Sadie stood in awe of the whole process. Her body was tingling; tears in her eyes as she glanced up at her Aunt Dru. She too had tears.

One more final push and the little black foal slid out of its mother, the flimsy bag the horse had been protected in was torn away from its face, its mouth opening and closing, gasping at the first breaths.

Aunt Dru glanced into Kit's stall then made her way to Libby's door. She stepped in, cloth in hand, and bent down to her new foal. Libby, still lying down, looked back at her human and watched her wipe their little foal with the towel, cleaning it's mouth and nostrils. The baby bounced its head and stretched out its long front legs. Within just minutes of being born, the little foal stood for the first time, its long legs wobbly. Aunt Dru smiled happily and she laid her hand on Libby's rump, patting her gently. She looked under the baby and turned to the family that was watching closely.

"It's a filly." She announced, her blue eyes shining.

Sadie grinned, another girl! Which meant this baby could have another baby and keep the generations going!

Matt moved behind her and stepped into the stall with Kit. The red bay had lain down, the babies hooves already visible.

"This is unbelievable." Nikki whispered from behind Sadie. They stood together, holding hands and watched the next baby's birth. "Has this happened before?"

Sadie's dad nodded, "Jan, the breeder in Craigmont where we got Monty, has had it happen a couple times. She's even had three in a day before."

Matt knelt at the stall wall and watched without interfering in the birth. With a huge grin on his face, he had a towel in hand, ready and waiting.

Sadie's whole body trembled in excitement. Quickly, she glanced at all the family members, watching the little miracle of the two babies born minutes apart. Everyone was smiling.

Nikki's hand tightened on Sadie's. She looked back in the stall in time to see the front legs be pushed out. Two black front legs with black hooves…another push from Kit and light tan upper legs appeared with a little black nose positioned in between.

Another push…the head appeared, tan with a white star on its forehead and a black mane.

Kit lay out flat, groaned and pushed, nothing happened. Matt frowned; Sadie's heart skipped a beat.

Another push, nothing happened.

"Is it stuck?" Sadie whispered, looking up at her dad.

"Could be…this is her first foal." He answered.

Kit was still lying flat, her head away from Matt.

Matt moved the birthing bag away from the baby's legs and toweled off the front legs. He looked up at his uncle.

Sadie looked up quickly and saw her dad nod.

"As she pushes," Her dad whispered.

Matt turned and stared at Kit's side. As her ribs tightened and body tensed, trying to push the baby out, Matt gripped the foal's front legs and gave a little tug.

There was a slight movement and the tan shoulders could be seen.

One more time…one more tug…and the shoulders slid out of the mare.

Matt sat back and waited for Kit to finish.

Another push and the remainder of the foal slid gently from her mother. Matt reached over and cleared the bag and fluids away from the baby's muzzle.

Four black legs, black mane and tail, tan body…Matt turned and grinned. "We might just have another buckskin in the family."

He toweled off the new foal as Kit stood and turned to nose at her new baby. Matt stroked the mare's nose and talked softly to her.

"I feel like a grandmother!" Nikki said excitedly.

The new tan foal stretched out its legs and pushed to stand up. Matt caught it as the foal stumbled to the side, then it stood, with all four legs spread out wide and looked around.

Matt chuckled which caused the baby to look over at him and stick his nose on Matt's. Everyone laughed and the baby looked up at the crowd. Matt looked underneath the foal and turned to the excited family.

"We have a little colt." Matt announced and stroked the foal's neck. "Welcome to the Tagger family, Leroy."

"Oh, how cute!" Nora said from beside Sadie.

Sadie watched the colt nose his mother and then Matt then she made her way back to the other stall. The little black filly was already nursing on her mother.

"Do you have a name yet, Aunt Dru?" Sadie asked.

Her aunt grinned at her. "I do."

"What is it?" Sadie asked eagerly.

"Tell you in a minute." Her aunt said as she stepped out of the horse stall.

Aunt Dru walked to the other stall and checked in with Kit and Leroy.

"Just adorable," She said looking at Matt and Nikki who were standing by the stall door.

They grinned at their mother and stepped out of the stall to join the family in the aisle.

"I don't think I've ever heard of two horse's having babies at the same time; in stalls next to each other." Uncle Scott said. "That's just amazing."

Sadie got the lucky spot between the two stalls and could look at both babies.

She felt a hand slide into her own and looked down at the hand then up, it was Aunt Dru. Reilly was standing on the other side of her. Aunt Dru was holding his hand too.

"What, Mom?" Reilly asked.

"I want you to meet Libby's baby…" Aunt Dru kissed him on the cheek and looked at Sadie. "Her name…is Zorra."

"Oh, Aunt Dru!" Sadie hugged her aunt and looked up at Reilly. He grinned proudly at his mom then over to Sadie.

***

Sadie crawled up onto the fence, excitement running through her. She looked at the barn, they weren't there yet so she turned and looked at the south pasture. All the Tagger Herd was home for the weekend, including Trooper and Harvey.

"They're going to be so excited!" Sadie looked down at her dad; he was standing next to her, his arm protectively around her.

Her mother was there, smiling up at her. "I've got the camera ready!"

Sadie turned and looked at all the family and friends standing next to the fence…waiting.

"Here they come!" Wade yelled.

Sadie turned to see Aunt Dru leading Libby out of the barn and towards the North pasture. Baby Zorra was trotting nervously next to her mom. Right behind them was Nikki leading Kit with baby Leroy walking proudly at her side.

Matt was at the gate to let the new family members into the pasture for the first time.

Libby and Zorra were walked in first. Aunt Dru took them in about 30 feet then unhooked the lead rope to let them free.

Libby nosed her baby, making sure everything was alright then lifted her head up and looked at the people lined up watching them. Her neck arched, ears perked, and she sidestepped nervously as she looked into the South pasture.

Sadie turned, "Oh look!" She called out.

The entire Tagger herd had lined up next to the fence, heads leaning over, and watching the new baby. Whinnies and nickers were called out.

Sadie turned back and watched as Nikki walked Kit and Leroy out into the pasture. She unhooked the horse, and Kit nervously looked at Leroy and trotted across the pasture, to the far end, Leroy running after her.

"Why'd she do that?" Wade asked.

"She's still pretty nervous…it's her first baby." Aunt Dru answered as she joined the family at the fence. "She'll keep them over there for a couple days until she relaxes and isn't so protective."

Leroy and Zorra's heads rose high and alert. They stood close to their mothers as they looked over at the two herds, horses and human, standing and watching their first adventure to the pasture.

THE TAGGER HERD SERIES

Matt Tagger

RESCUE OR RECOVER

CHAPTER ONE

"Come on Trooper, we're running late." Matt encouraged the horse to trot faster up the mountainside. The sky was just starting to lighten…sunrise was just minutes away.

"If we don't get there in time they'll be gone."

The horse matched Matt's urgency and moved faster. They finally hit the top and Matt pushed him into a gallop across the field and by a cluster of curious Hereford cows.

"Only minutes away, big guy. Then you'll have some time to rest."

The drive from Riggins took longer than usual due to construction which caused him to be late. The exhilaration of saving the hikers from the cliff slowly ebbed away the longer he had to wait for the construction delays.

Rappelling was easily his favorite type of rescue. This time there were three hikers that tumbled in a rock slide and had to be rescued. All three were banged up a bit but were going to survive.

There was nothing worse than when the rescues turned into a recovery mission. Three weeks before, he helped find three kayakers that had set out for a day trip on the Spokane River and didn't wear their life vests. Mid-May, after a heavy winter snow, the river was running fast, cold, and dangerous.

Even with warning signs everywhere and free vests available to use, the men had decided to kayak without them. Foolish move for three men in their mid-twenties all losing their lives because they were too proud to wear a vest. Four little kids were now left fatherless.

Rescues, like yesterday's rappelling down a rock cliff, helped make up for the recoveries. Most of the people they saved, along with their family members, were so grateful, relieved and happy.

Matt's first rescue nearly killed him. He'd thought he was in shape from all the training that he'd done, but the training was just in technique and discipline. He climbed, kayaked, jumped out of planes, and scuba dived but didn't make sure he was physically fit; that his body and energy would hold up for long rescues.

It took twice as long and all his energy to rappel down the first cliff to save the teenage girl that had fallen. It took him days to recover.

Since that time, he'd cycled, ran, swam, or lifted weights nearly every day.

On a normal day, it was Matt running up and down the mountain side at the ranch and not his horse, although many times Trooper would run alongside of him. He made a point of running in the pasture with Trooper a couple times a week. Some mornings, Nikki's horse Harvey joined in. The best times were when he would race the horse on the straight stretch leading into the Circle 50 ranch house. No matter how fast he ran, the horse barely broke a sweat running next to him.

Matt looked ahead and could see his target so he moved Trooper into the trees to be hidden as they approached. At the perfect distance he stopped the horse and quickly dismounted. The horse's sides were heaving from the exertion. The sun was just starting to peek above the distant horizon. It was going to happen at any second. He had to hurry.

Grabbing Sadie's camera out of the saddle bag he ran up closer, knelt down, brought the camera up and clicked a couple times to make sure everything was working perfectly. This was a once in a lifetime event, he couldn't mess it up now!

Matt watched intently waiting for the right moment. The sunrise lit up the sky reflecting colors of light unto the clouds. It was a spectacular sunrise with beams of light shining across the sky. Then it started, camera up, he started clicking, it was over quickly. He looked down at the digital camera and scrolled through the images. There were at least a dozen usable photos. It was going to be tough to choose.

He hesitated, took in the scene in front of him and smiled. What a great morning!

Matt turned, and ran down the hill to Trooper. He quickly mounted and retraced their steps back to the ranch house. He unsaddled the horse as fast as he could then ran into the house and downloaded the photos. He chose the perfect one and emailed it in to be printed.

Then he raced to his truck and headed to town with only three hours to get the print framed. He had already been to the framers and chosen everything that was needed. He sent a quick text to them to let them know this was the morning so they were ready.

He received a text back stating they were ready and could have him in and out within a half hour.

Two hours and forty-five minutes later he received a text stating he had 15 minutes before they arrived. Matt ran through the backdoor of The Homestead with the framed print in hand. The kids were already at school so it was his parents, Cora and aunts and uncles that were there waiting for him.

"It's great to have you safe." His mom kissed him on the cheek. "And what did you call us all here for…you brought a picture?"

The framed print was covered in brown paper so his family couldn't see it.

Matt grinned excitedly. "Need a spot to hang this in the hallway." He told his mom. "Quick."

"What is it?" Nick asked.

"That…" Matt chuckled. "…is a surprise, of course. Need to hurry, they're almost here."

"Who?" Grayson followed him down the hallway with a nail and hammer.

The spot was chosen and it was hung with the wrapping intact…just in time. He saw their truck turn into the drive and moved all his confused family back into the kitchen.

Matt was so excited he felt like bouncing like Reilly.

The back door opened and Nikki walked in. She grinned at the group in the room. Lucas was right behind her with a matching her grin.

"Mom…" Nikki started with a smile.

"Just a second, Sis." Matt took her hand and pulled her into the hallway.

"But…" She started, obviously confused by his actions.

"I have something to show you." Matt smiled. "So hush."

After asking everyone else to stay in the kitchen, Matt led his confused sister and Lucas down the hallway to the picture.

"What is that?" Nikki asked her brother with raised brows.

"Take the paper off." He grinned so hard his cheeks hurt.

With the help of Lucas, Nikki tore the paper from the picture and gasped.

"Matt!" She cried out, hand to mouth, tears started flowing.

"What is it?" Her mother called out from the kitchen.

Nikki turned and waved the rest of the family to them.

"Nikki!" Their mother cried out when she looked at the picture.

"Thanks," Lucas whispered to Matt as embraces were given between Nikki and her mother, father, aunts, and uncles and, of course, Cora.

The small group smiled happily at the portrait that showed the most magnificent sunrise which lit the couple in front of it. Matt had captured the moment Lucas dropped to his knee and proposed to Nikki.

CHAPTER TWO

"Hey, Alex, ready to go?" Matt asked the grinning 12 year old.

"Absolutely!" Alex excitedly limped across the Barn and Breakfast main lobby. "I can't believe Mom is letting me go with you on a school night."

"Well, honestly, me either," Matt chuckled. "But, I guess she agreed that I need a driving companion to take the Tagger herd to the ranch and Wade was doing something for 4H. I promised I'd have you back early in the morning in time for school."

"Why are you taking the horses up there?"

"We're driving to Billings Thursday morning for the auction and we're taking the herd to Jessup to watch over until we get back. Memorial Day is the next weekend and we'll have them at the ranches anyway."

"How come Jessup's not going?"

"He didn't really say, but I think it has to do with a lady veterinarian." Matt grinned at the boy.

Alex laughed. "He sure likes her."

"Yeah, and I think's it is mutual." Matt looked around the luxurious wood and rock lobby. "Where's your mother?"

"I don't…"

"Dru, I'm sorry, but I just don't think I can go." They heard her voice approaching down the long hallway.

"Tessa, we've been planning this…actually, you've been planning this for us for over eight months." Matt heard his mother say in a very irritated voice.

"Like I said, I'm sorry." Tessa said as they entered the lobby. She was dressed in one of the long sun dresses that she and Leah always wore. Her light brown curly hair just barely touched her shoulders. His mother wore jeans and a white button up shirt; her hair in a high ponytail.

As his mother made her way into the lobby, her expression matched the irritated voice. She gave him a 'hello' hug and tried to smile.

Tessa smiled stiffly at Alex. "Your bag is in the back, let's go get it." She turned without a glance or word at Matt.

"What did I do?" Matt whispered. Tessa was usually pretty friendly to him.

"I have no idea…maybe it's because you look so much like Nick."

"What did he do?"

"I have no idea, but she avoids him like the plague. Five minutes after I told her that Nick got back from Boise in time to go, she said she wasn't going."

"Dang, Mom." He shook his head. "It's not going to help that Dad is going to be here any minute."

"Tell him to fix it!" She said gruffly, then walked back down the long hallway towards her office.

Matt stood dumbfounded. What was he supposed to do?

"I'm ready, Matt." Alex said excitedly as he and Tessa walked out of the small office behind the registration desk.

As they approached, Alex turned to his mother. "What are you going to do without me, Mom?"

She finally made eye contact with Matt and gave him a slight smile. Then glanced down at her son, "I'm going down to the Palomino room and inspect it for customers that arrive tomorrow. Then I'm off work, so I think I might just go down and have an evening ride on Star."

"It's nice out, it should be a good ride." Matt said…the words barely out of his mouth when Tessa glanced towards the door and her face stiffened.

Matt turned to see Nick stepping out of his truck and walking toward the door.

"You have a great time," Tessa said to Alex and gave him a quick hug and kiss. She looked at Matt. "In time for school."

"I'll have him back." Matt promised.

She turned and quickly walked down the hall towards the Palomino room.

Matt just sighed and watched her walk away. What the heck did Nick do?

"Nick!" Alex shouted as he walked through the door.

"Hey, Alex, I heard you were co-pilot tonight," Nick joined them and smiled at Alex, then grinned up at Matt. Sometimes…it was just bizarre to look at him…it was like looking into the mirror of the future. Same brownish-green eyes, dark brown hair that just touched the collar of his shirt, jawline…just about everything. "Good to see you back safe. Rescue or recover?"

"Rescue," Matt smiled then turned to Alex.

"Hey, why don't you go put your bag in the truck and I'll be right there?" Matt told Alex and his traveling partner limped his way out the door.

"I put the box of supplies for Jessup in the back of your truck." Nick told him.

Matt nodded. He didn't really know how to broach the subject of Tessa so he just blurted it out. "What happened between you and Tessa?"

Nick looked at him in surprise then shook his head with a frown. "I have no idea."

They walked to the large front window so they couldn't be overheard.

"What happened?" Nick asked.

"As soon as Mom told her that you were back in time for the trip, Tessa backed out."

"Seriously?" Nick shook his head and sighed. "I was afraid she would do that. I don't know what I did, but it must have pissed her off big time."

"She doesn't act like she's mad."

"I know. That's what's so confusing." Nick said and pulled out his phone. "Watch this."

"What is it?"

"It's the video Reilly shot at Christmas when we brought out the sleigh."

The video showed the family staring in curiosity then surprised expressions. Tessa was crying and smiling, she went up to the sleigh and talked to Alex, turned and threw her arms around Nick's neck. She kissed him on the cheek and he playfully lifted her and placed her in the sleigh. Laughter rang out during the whole video.

"I don't understand, she looks extremely happy." Matt looked at his dad.

"I know. I've watched it over and over trying to figure it out. Christmas was great too, then we came back, and she's avoided me ever since."

"No clue why?"

"None, but there was a moment when Sadie was hurt and I cradle-hugged her on the couch. Tessa was there and Sadie and I told her a story. When Sadie hid her face, hiding from any more questions, there was a moment Tessa placed her hand over mine…it was…" He exhaled and shook his head. "I got the impression, in those 30 seconds, that she actually liked me…then, she stood up quickly and walked away without a word. I've only seen her a handful of times since, but only when it involved Alex."

"If she didn't like you…she wouldn't let you take Alex to the ranch and on shopping excursions with Wade and Nora."

Nick looked at Matt with frustration, "I don't know what to do."

"How do you feel about her?" Matt asked, already knowing the answer.

"After the first day, meeting her and Alex at the grand opening last year, I stopped seeing Paige. I knew after just those couple of hours, I liked Tessa more than I would ever care for Paige." He paused and looked at Matt with a grin. "After she argued with me for 30 minutes over Alex's boots, I really liked her. She had pride, determination, and just a fierceness about her when it came to him. I like that.”

“And Alex?”

“He’s just like her.” He looked out the door that Alex had limped through. “Ever since Dru, I’ve avoided women with kids; wouldn’t even ask them out. But with Tessa…and Alex…?” He sighed. “I just want to bring them in.”

“No clue what happened?”

“None.”

“Well, Mom’s pissed and she told me to tell you to FIX IT.” Matt grinned.

“How? I’ve never had this problem before.”

“Women usually knocking down your door?” Matt chuckled.

He shrugged. “I haven’t had an issue in that department.”

“Must be the look,” Matt sighed. “I haven’t had an issue in that department either…mine’s more keeping an interest in them.”

“So how do I ‘fix it’?”

“Well, she’s down in the Palomino room doing an inspection or something. Go down and confront her. She already avoids you, so what could it hurt?”

“Come on, Matt!” Alex yelled from the front door.

“Go fix it,” Matt told his dad with a grin and pointed down the hall. “I’ll see you in the morning for breakfast.”

Nick just nodded with another big sigh.

When Matt reached the door, he turned to see his father walk down the hallway towards Tessa.

###

“Alex, start waking up.” Matt shook his co-pilot in the truck. The boy had slept nearly the whole ride back. “You’re not making a very good riding partner.”

“I tried,” Alex sat up and tried to open his brown eyes. “I did better going up to the ranch.”

"You're telling me!" Matt laughed. "I've never heard anyone talk as much or as fast as you did last night."

"I was excited." Alex smiled tiredly.

"So you're not so excited about going to school this morning?"

"Not at all, I'm not Sadie."

"She does like to learn."

"And remembers EVERYTHING!"

"Have you ever played one of the trivia games with her?"

"When we were snowed in at the ranch at Christmas, she clobbered us."

Matt chuckled. "That's because, after they bought the games, she went through the questions and studied all the answers; just to learn, not to cheat."

"Dang, I wouldn't be able to remember three or four of them, let alone the whole box." Alex was finally awake enough to look out the window as they drove into the parking lot of the B&B.

"Me, either." Matt admitted.

There were a number of cars in the parking lot from the employees and guests. Some guests were already walking down to The Stables for a morning ride.

"What time is it?" Alex asked.

"Six."

"I wasn't supposed to be back until six thirty….I could have slept for another half hour!" Alex complained with a smirk.

Matt laughed as he parked. Alex quickly slid out of the truck.

Matt glanced back at the truck he pulled in next to…it was Nick's. He was there? They were meeting later for breakfast at the waffle place, not here.

Alex was at the doors when he yelled. "Mom's already here!"

Matt turned quickly. Tessa's SUV was parked in the same spot as the night before, he looked back at Nick's truck…that meant…

"Alex!" He yelled just as the doors closed behind the boy.

Matt ran for the door. He searched the lobby and saw Alex standing and staring down the hallway where Nick had walked down the night before.

Matt quickly made his way to him and when he reached Alex, Matt stood as still as Alex…in complete disbelief.

Tessa had Nick backed up against the wall and was placing one heck of a kiss on him, her sandals in her hand and they were both wearing the same clothes from the night before.

Stunned, Matt reached for Alex's shoulder to pull him away.

"How about the steakhouse?" Alex asked loudly.

Matt was confused at his comment, but not as much as Tessa was shocked by his voice. She jumped away from Nick, touching her lips with a hand. Nick just grinned at Alex and didn't move from the wall.

"Alex!" Tessa cried out while turning bright red. "How long have you been standing there?" Her embarrassed eyes reluctantly met Matt's amused ones.

"Long enough that Nick said he was taking us out on a date tonight," Alex grinned. "Can we go to the steakhouse?"

"Anywhere you want." Nick chuckled and finally stood away from the wall.

"Oh, my…" Tessa's eyes rolled up and she looked exasperated at the ceiling.

Matt turned to see his mother standing to his left and Leah standing next to her. He started laughing at the women's shocked expressions, Tessa's red one, Alex's pleased one and Nick's contented one.

"I'm going to get ready for work." Tessa shook her head and started to walk past them.

"But Mom!" Alex said loudly.

"What?" She asked looking down at him.

"Aren't you going to kiss Nick good-bye?" He asked with a devilish grin.

Tessa's face turned red again as she stared at her son in disbelief then she sighed and giggled lightly. "That's what I was doing when you showed up."

"Oh," Alex chuckled. "Maybe you should do it again since we interrupted you."

Tessa exhaled loudly, handed her sandals to her son then turned back to a grinning Nick. Placing a hand on each side of his face, she leaned in, and gave him a very impressive good-bye kiss.

Stepping back, she smiled at Nick, her brown eyes shining, then looked down at her son. "Good enough?"

Alex laughed and nodded.

Tessa nodded to the entertained group, took her son's hand, and walked to the door.

After they disappeared, Matt, his mom and aunt turned back to his father.

"So," Matt smiled at his dad. "You fixed it."

"Yeah," Nick sighed happily as he walked past them. "I'll meet you for breakfast in an hour."

They watched him walk through the doors then looked at each other.

"Well, that's not what I expected." His mom chuckled.

"It makes sense though," Leah added. "Why she didn't keep Alex away from him, but kept away from him herself."

"But why did she fight it so hard?" Matt asked and saw the frown on his mother's face.

"You know something we don't?" He asked her.

She walked away towards her office. "It's not my story to tell."

"Ok, I'll respect that," Leah said as she and Matt followed. "But I'm guessing she'll be joining us in Billings and not needing her own room."

"So we have an extra room." They reached his mother's office.

If he ever had to have an office, Matt wanted one just like his mother's. She'd decorated it with a simple western style desk and a small conference table but it was the large picture on the wall of the majestic mountains at the ranch that he loved. Included in the photograph was Rider's Point where her parent's and grandparent's ashes had been spread. The picture covered the upper half of the entire wall and old barn wood covered the lower half.

She leaned against her desk. "I'm not sure we can cancel the room at this short of notice and get our money back."

"Well, why don't we take Grace and Reilly?" Matt suggested.

Leah nodded. "I'll talk to Grayson, I'm sure he would agree."

"I know Jack will. He wanted Reilly to go in the first place," His mom said. "We'll take Reilly and Grace on Thursday night, so you and Grayson can have a night alone together."

"And we'll take them on Friday so you and Jack can have a night out alone."

"And while you five couples are out on the town Saturday night, I'll take them with me." Matt offered.

"You sure?" Leah asked.

Matt shrugged, "I'm the odd man out when it comes to all you couples, so they can keep me company. I'm sure I can come up with something that will keep us entertained."

Leah laughed. "Just don't make it jogging…Grace would shoot you."

CHAPTER THREE

"Matt Tagger," He smiled at the cute brunette across the counter while handing her his ID and credit card. "The room cost should already be taken care of."

"Welcome to our hotel," Her smile was bright. "I have your group right here. Is everyone else here too?"

He shook his head with a grin. "I ended up flying in. They all have the pleasure of driving the nine hours."

She giggled softly…a bit flirty, as Grace would say. "How did you end up so lucky?"

Matt chuckled at her use of words and the cute brunette blushed.

"Last minute business took me to Coeur d' Alene before coming here, so I decided to fly instead." He leaned against the counter as she handed him the ID.

"So you have a few hours before the rest of your group comes in. Any plans?"

"Probably drive over to the horse auction site and see if any horses have arrived yet." He tilted his head with a smile and glanced at her name tag. "Unless, Cindi, you're off work soon."

Cindi giggled and smiled regretfully. "I'm here until mid-night."

"Just a shame," He grinned and took the hotel key from her.

"I agree…unfortunately, those are my hours all weekend." She sighed in disappointment.

"Just a shame," He repeated with a wink. "Could you call me a taxi?"

"Of course, it just takes a few minutes for them to get here." She smiled again and pointed to his left. "The elevators are that way, your room is on the third floor, half way down."

"Thank you, Cindi." He lifted his bags and nodded. "Have a great afternoon."

"That's my line," She laughed. "So you have a great afternoon."

Matt walked away from the counter with a smile. That's just what he needed after the horrendous recovery they had that morning. He normally didn't have issues with dead bodies…but when it was a kid…and this one looked so much like Nora when she was little.

Matt opened the door to his room, dropped his bags, and turned around and walked back out. There was no way he was going to sit around the room and think about the little girl. He needed to keep his mind busy.

Cindi was talking with more customers so he walked out of the hotel to wait for the cab.

As he waited, he pulled out his phone. He'd forgotten to turn it on after getting off the plane. There were three voice messages waiting for him.

First message was Kevin: "Tragic this morning, but wanted to let you know how well you handled the recovery and dealing with the distraught family. You have a compassion in you that I wish everyone had. Forget about it all and have a good time at the sale."

Second message was from Lucas: "Matt, call me as soon as you receive this message. I know you're there hours before us so I need to talk to you."

Third message was from Lucas too: "Matt, we're in Missoula, I don't know how the cell service is going to be so I'm just going to tell you. I just got word that Elena is in Billings. I don't know why…but keep an eye out."

Why would Nikki's birth mother be in Billings? The last time they had seen her she tried to get Nikki to back up her lies and accusations of sexual harassment against Jack.

Dead little girls with screaming and crying parents and Elena; could the day get any worse? Maybe he should go back and flirt with Cindi.

The cab arrived and he headed to the livestock market. He stared out the window.

There was nothing he could do about the memories of the little girl but keep his mind busy. But Elena? Why would she be in Billings of all places? Last time Lucas had updated him she was in jail in Nevada for cashing checks that belonged to one of her co-workers.

There was no doubt she would be at the auction looking for another cowboy to connect with but, why here? Why an auction and not at a rodeo somewhere?

What could possibly bring Elena to Billings? And why the one weekend that the Taggers were going to be there? Was it a coincidence? Matt had a gut feeling it wasn't.

"Here we are," The taxi driver announced.

"Thanks," Matt paid him and stepped out to look around.

His eyes went to the large Billing's Live Stock Commission sign with the Hereford at the top. A life size statue of a palomino horse stood at the base. Since he was young, he'd heard the story of how the Tagger Trio met and hired Jessup here. Matt was only three at the time and he couldn't remember life without the foreman. How different would the ranch be if they hadn't met?

Turning to look at the two story building, he took in a deep breath and let it out slowly. This building, so far from home, held a special part of history for the Taggers.

A slight wave of disappointment washed over Matt that Jessup wasn't on the trip with them, but he had no doubt that he and Kate were enjoying having the ranches to themselves for the weekend.

To the right of the building was a large pasture covered with multiple medal panel pens; an arena was on the other side of the pens. To the left and around to the back was the check-in area for the horses being dropped off for the auction. It led to even more enclosures and stalls; covered and uncovered.

First thing Matt did was scan the few people he could see for Elena, then internally groaned when he realized that was going to be the pattern the whole time. Instead of relaxing and enjoying the break and auction, they were going to have to worry about running into the wicked woman.

His phone alerted him to a text.

TEXT FROM GRAYSON: Three people recommended trainer named Frank. Find him, see what you think.

Grayson was also looking to hire a ranch hand who could also train horses to help him with all the horses at home and the ones being purchased during their weekend.

TEXT FROM MATT: Anyone you talked to here to narrow the search?

TEXT FROM GRAYSON: Jamie at the café. Did you get text about Elena?

TEXT FROM MATT: Yes, will go find Jamie.

Matt glanced over at the building. He wasn't ready to go in yet; he wanted to check out the horses first. Most horses would be arriving in the morning but there were a few already there.

He wandered through the pens and watched as a few horse trailers arrived and were unloaded. A couple horses caught his eye right away; including a tall sorrel and a stout blood bay gelding. He needed one good backup horse for the next couple years until Kit's colt Leroy was ready. Matt smiled at the image of the cute buckskin colt, already taller than his mom's filly.

His family was bringing three stock trailers; two 6 horse and one 4 horse. All should be full when they returned home.

His mom had approval for the horses to be used at The Stables and for the kid's clinics. Grayson had final approval on the ranch horses, for both ranches.

Of course, knowing his family, if anyone wanted a horse bad enough…they were going to buy it.

Matt scanned the few people again but didn't see any sign of Elena; time to go inside. He stepped through the door and into a hallway that led to steps and according to the sign, right into the auction arena. The café was at the end of the hallway and through a door to his right.

He stepped in and asked an older waitress for Jamie.

"I'm Jamie," She said over her shoulder as she delivered an order to a table.

Matt waited for her to finish and turn to him.

"What you need, Handsome?" The waitress asked.

"My uncle said he talked to you about a horse trainer named Frank."

"Grayson?" She asked and walked back to the kitchen.

"Yes."

"Yeah, told him Frank is the best trainer around and needs a job, bad."

"If he's so good, why doesn't he have a job?"

"Your uncle asked the same thing," She grinned. "Too many trainers around here; most ranches are looking for older ones, with more experience. They're not giving the younger ones a chance. Grayson said he's looking for a backup trainer and would give a young one a try."

"He will, he's the best trainer I know, but has too many horses and rodeo kids he's working with…along with all the ranch work."

"Frank will help, worked with ranch horses and did rodeos."

"Where do I find him?"

The waitress stopped and grinned at him. Matt had no idea why.

"In the front office, just around the corner," She said pointing with her elbow since her hands were full.

Matt nodded and left the café to walk across the hall to an open area. To the right was a counter that opened to a large room with desks. The sign indicated the buyer's cards would be picked up there and after the auction they accepted payment and handled the paperwork for registered horses. To the left were multiple small offices. Just outside of the far office there were three people talking; two men and one woman.

Matt stepped back into the café and looked at the waitress.

"Which one?" He asked.

"In the blue shirt." She chuckled.

The woman had the blue shirt on. He raised a brow to the waitress.

She chuckled with a wink. "Yep, blue shirt."

Matt grinned at her inside joke; appreciating her sense of fun. "Thanks, Jamie."

He walked back into the hall then stopped. Grayson probably didn't care if the trainer was a woman or man but he better check first before approaching her.

TEXT TO GRAYSON: Frank is a woman

TEXT TO MATT: Don't care as long as she's good

Matt smiled, just as he thought.

TEXT TO GRAYSON: Continually scanning crowd for Elena, nothing yet…getting old quick.

TEXT TO MATT: Lucas said he's working on it, be patient, Mate

Matt chuckled.

TEXT TO GRAYSON: Lucas and Nikki are riding with you?

TEXT TO MATT: Just Lucas, tricked them into riding separately, for some reason they didn't seem to care for it.

Matt laughed.

TEXT TO MATT: Nikki is with Nick and Tessa, none of them were happy about it

Matt continued to laugh to himself.

TEXT TO GRAYSON: Tagger Trio and spouses happy though

TEXT TO MATT: Took us an hour to stop laughing

Matt was grinning when he looked up and glanced at the few people again. No sign of Elena. Frank, who had her back to him, was now only talking to one person and they looked like they were ready to leave.

He started walking towards her. A worn black cowboy hat held back her long wavy dark hair that cascaded down her back. It stopped half way to a pair of old jeans that looked a size too big for her slender frame. Her boots were well worn too. That was a good sign.

Matt was only a few feet away when the man she was talking with walked away.

"Frank?" Matt said as she started to leave.

She turned and looked up at him.

Matt stared at her, stunned…he knew her…had stared at her picture. But the shock of seeing her didn't compare to the shock that he had when he realized, from the look on her face, that she knew who he was.

CHAPTER FOUR

"No!" She gasped and quickly looked around the room. "You can't be here..."

"Excuse me?"

"Elena is here." Her dark chocolate brown eyes were a mixture of disbelief and panic.

"I know."

"You don't understand."

"Yeah, I do."

"We can't be seen together."

Matt looked around then took her arm and stepped to the corner.

"What are you doing? Let go of me."

"I plan on it," He put her in the corner then stood directly in front of her and let go of her arm. "Can you see anyone?"

He was broader than she was, so she started to move to look around him.

"Without leaning…can you see anyone?"

"No," She looked up at him; her eyes confused.

"Then they can't see you," He frowned. Now what? What was he supposed to say?

She stood, arms crossed tightly in front of her, and shifted from one foot to the other.

So, she was the reason Elena was in Billings.

"Your name is Josey, why do you go by Frank?" He asked Nikki's half-sister.

"It's Frankie, Jamie must have sent you over."

Matt nodded.

"She likes to mess with people."

"How do you know who I am?" He asked her.

"How do you know who I am?" She countered.

"We had a run in with your mother, a year or so ago."

"You've known for that long?" She asked in surprise.

"Yeah…how long have you known who I was?"

"Two days," She sighed and shook her head. "This is so mind blowing."

"Two days?" Matt gasped.

"Yes, Elena told me about Nikki two days ago."

"You didn't know you had a sister until two days ago?" He asked in disbelief.

She shook her head. "Did she know about me?"

"No clue."

"But she's known about me for a year?"

"Yes, but there's more to that story," That was Nikki's story to tell and there was no way he could run into Josey and not tell Nikki.

"Is she here?" Josey's voice was shaky and unsure, yet hopeful.

"On her way."

Josey's arms grew tighter around herself and her shifting increased. It reminded Matt of Reilly's bouncing.

"Why did Elena finally tell you about Nikki?"

She had been staring at his shirt, but glanced up at him. "She heard your family was coming here."

"How?"

"I'm not sure, something about Facebook."

Matt frowned, he was going to have to talk with Leah and Jordan to see if they could find out what happened. They had been pretty good at protecting the family's personal information.

"Why did she care? What did she want?"

Her eyes darted up at him then down again. She looked nervous.

"I didn't really give her a chance to tell me her plan. I just told her I wasn't going to help her with anything."

"Her plan…?" Matt felt his stomach tighten.

"Matt, we can't just stand here in the corner, I'm sure you look pretty odd from behind."

Matt looked at her in bewilderment. It was odd hearing his name from her.

"I'm sure it does." But he didn't really care. He didn't have enough answers from her yet.

"Matt?" She said tentatively.

He looked into her hopeful eyes.

"Do you think I could meet Nikki?" She hesitated. "Do you think she would want to meet me?"

"She would kill me if I didn't introduce you."

Josey inhaled sharply then let it out slowly. "You have no idea…"

"Well, like you said. We can't be standing here in the corner all day." He looked at his watch, about two hours before they arrived.

"Where are you staying?"

"Holiday Inn Express on Midland."

"Trapper's Café is about half way between. I can meet you there in 20 minutes." She offered.

"You'll show up?"

"I want to meet my sister. It sounds so weird to say that." She nodded. "I swear, I'll be there."

"I'll turn around and scan for Elena. If I start walking means she's not around. It'll take a few minutes for a taxi to get here but I'll meet you there in 20 minutes or as close to as I can get."

She looked up at him and nodded, her arms finally relaxed and she dropped them to her sides.

Matt started to turn then looked back, "Josey, I'm serious, Nikki will kill me if you disappear."

"Frankie…I'm Frankie. I promise, I will be there."

Matt turned, scanned the small room, no sign of Elena. Without looking back, he started walking. His heart raced as he waited for a taxi and on the drive to the café. He continued looking around him to see if Elena was following or if Josey was there. He saw neither.

When he entered the café, Josey wasn't there. He turned and looked out the door to the parking lot; no one driving in.

"Nikki's going to kill me," He whispered harshly to himself and sat at a table in the back of the building facing the door. Checking his phone…there were no messages.

For another fifteen minutes he sat staring out the window to the parking lot. The waitress, a very unfriendly one, brought him coffee and the sandwich he'd ordered after realizing he hadn't eaten anything all day.

A small old blue truck drove into the parking lot. He stuffed the last of his meal into his mouth and stared at the truck, willing it to be Josey that stepped out. It was.

A huge sense of relief ran through him as the waitress picked up his plate without saying a word.

His phone alert went off.

TEXT FROM GRAYSON: Find Frank?

TEXT FROM MATT: Yes

TEXT FROM GRAYSON: Well

TEXT FROM MATT: Just sitting down to talk

Well, Matt sighed. It wasn't a lie.

Josey saw him as soon as she walked in the door. There were only a few other tables in use and as she walked across the café, she glanced at the food on the tables.

He stood and pulled out a chair next to him. Her eyes widened in surprise.

"I can't remember anyone ever doing that for me. Are you sure you don't want me across the table?"

"I don't want to have to talk across the table for everyone around us to hear."

"There aren't very many people in here."

"Not right now, but the dinner crowd should be coming in soon. You hungry?"

She shook her head. Matt frowned, it was obvious she was.

"Can I get you anything?" The unfriendly waitress asked Josey. Matt silently wished she was Jamie or Cindi…friendly people.

"No, I'm fine." Josey shook her head again.

"Large fries, onion rings and a plate of BBQ sliders." Matt told the waitress who looked back at him in surprise.

"Hungry much?" The waitress grumbled then walked away.

"Not the nicest lady on the planet," Josey half-smiled at him. "But the food is good."

They sat quietly looking around.

"I don't know where to start." Matt admitted.

"Can you tell me about Nikki?" She asked quickly.

"Elena told you about Nikki…how did you know about me?"

"I went to the library and used their computers to Google Nikki and found the Facebook page on the horses." She looked at him sheepishly. He just nodded, a lot of people did that. "I also found the article in a western magazine that had you and Nikki's picture in it."

"So, what did your investigative work find out about her?" He was curious how much information was actually out there.

"Not much. The Facebook page had pictures and all, but not much on the personal stuff…which is actually good." Josey looked up at him shyly. "She is very…beautiful."

"I agree, but I'm biased." He chuckled.

"That's about as much as I know. I stayed until the library closed and haven't had a chance to get back. I just looked at the pictures…looking for every one with her in it."

"You said Elena knew we were coming because of Facebook." He said and she nodded. "Did you see anything on there that said we were coming here?"

Josey shook her head making her brown hair wave down her back. Her black cowboy hat made her eyes look like dark chocolate.

The waitress brought the food just as his phone alerted him with a message.

TEXT FROM GRAYSON: Well

TEXT FROM MATT: Not very patient, are you

TEXT FROM GRAYSON: NO

Matt chuckled. Then debated to himself how and who to tell right now about Josey. He looked up and she was sitting, hands in her lap looking out towards the diner.

"Eat," He said looking back down at his phone. "I can't eat all of that."

"Then why did you order it?"

"To share."

TEXT FROM MATT: Is this Grayson or Leah typing

TEXT FROM GRAYSON: Grayson, Scott's driving

TEXT FROM MATT: Keep between you and Scott, wife's OK. Do NOT say anything to Lucas

TEXT FROM GRAYSON: About what?

TEXT FROM MATT: Frank

TEXT FROM GRAYSON: What about him

TEXT FROM MATT: Not a word to Lucas

TEXT FROM GRAYSON: Why

TEXT FROM MATT: Don't want to interrupt his and Nikki's reunion tonight

TEXT FROM GRAYSON: ??

TEXT FROM MATT: Frank is Elena's daughter Josey Franklin

Matt looked up as he waited for his uncle's response. Josey had already finished two of the sliders and a good portion of the fries. She gave him an embarrassed smile.

"No onion rings?" He chuckled.

Again, the shake of the head and her hair waving down her back, "I don't like onions."

"Well, get something to drink."

"Water's fine."

"Seriously, Josey. Do you think a coke is going to break me after all this food?"

"Frankie." She said and turned to the waitress.

Matt watched her while she wasn't looking. Why couldn't he get himself to call her Frankie?

TEXT FROM GRAYSON: Are you messing with me?

TEXT FROM MATT: No

TEXT FROM GRAYSON: What are you doing?

TEXT FROM MATT: Feeding her lunch and talking about Nikki

TEXT FROM GRAYSON: Is that why Elena is there

TEXT FROM MATT: Yes

TEXT FROM GRAYSON: Not good

TEXT FROM MATT: Not good

TEXT FROM GRAYSON: Your impression of her?

TEXT FROM MATT: Not sure, come to Trapper's Café when you get in

TEXT FROM GRAYSON: About a half hour out, be there in an hour

TEXT FROM MATT: Scott and wives only

TEXT FROM GRAYSON: Understood

He put his phone down.

"Do you mind if I ask who you were texting with?" She asked between bites of the fries.

"My uncle…Grayson."

"Not Nikki?"

He shook his head. "This isn't something to text about."

She nodded, finally sitting back in her chair and looking out at the crowd of people coming in. He realized she was watching the door.

"Grayson is looking for an assistant horse trainer."

Josey turned to him with wide eyes. "That's why you were looking for me?"

Matt stared at his drink and nodded slowly…realizing that this may not be the best thing. He knew Grayson's heart well enough that he would hire her from the recommendations of the people but mostly because she was Nikki's sister. As much as Matt liked her already, he didn't want to take Elena's daughter to Idaho with them. He didn't even know her enough to trust her…maybe she was working with Elena.

"Matt?"

"What?"

"That's why you were looking for me?" She repeated.

Matt glanced up at her, breaking his trance. "Yes, he heard from a couple people that recommended Frank."

"Frankie."

"He said Frank." Matt looked at her and smiled. "Are you sure there isn't a Frank out there that I'm supposed to be looking for?"

She gave him a quizzical look. "No…I'm a horse trainer looking for a job."

"You're sure?" He grinned.

Finally realizing he was joking with her, she giggled and her eye's sparkled. Matt's heart skipped a beat.

He looked back down at the drink. That wasn't good…

CHAPTER FIVE

Matt didn't tell her that his uncles were going to join them. He didn't want to scare her off…but then again her desire to see Nikki would have kept her there, too.

"How many times are you going to look at the door?" Matt asked which made her turn back to him quickly with a guilty look.

She sighed. "I'm just worried."

"About?"

"Elena walking through the door," She looked at him with a frown. "She seriously cannot see us together."

"Why?"

"I just don't know what she would do."

"She can't hurt you unless you let her." He was shocked to see tears come to her eyes. "What?"

The tears fell and she quickly wiped them away.

"Josey, what happened?" He felt his gut tighten at her tears.

"Frankie…Matt."

"What did she do to you?" He ignored her.

"It's been two years since she was here," She started in a low voice he could barely hear. "I was just getting ready to graduate high school and go to college in the fall. We spent a great week together. I thought she was here for me…"

She looked back at the door.

"What happened?"

"My dad's parents left me enough money in their will to go to college, $50,000." She stopped and looked down at her hands. Another tear fell and was wiped away. "She convinced me that there should be another name on the account, in case of an emergency."

"She didn't…"

"We went to the bank on Thursday afternoon and she signed the paperwork." Josey leaned back and closed her eyes. "A week later, five minutes after they opened, she withdrew everything but ten dollars and disappeared until two days ago."

"Dang." Matt just shook his head. How could someone do that to their own child?

Josey wiped away the tears and took a drink. "My dad was furious at me for not talking to him first. I was eighteen so technically I didn't need his permission…but…" She looked up at Matt. "I just didn't…" She sighed. "He, my stepmother and stepbrother moved two weeks later and I have no idea where they are."

"What?" Matt was stunned.

She sighed again, sat up in her chair and looked over at him. "I guess he didn't trust me anymore. She'd stolen from him before because of me, and he didn't want it to happen again. So he left."

"Josey…" Matt just shook his head.

"I graduated high school while living with one of my friends until she went to college. Then I started taking odd jobs at ranches and training girls on barrels and other games. I ran barrels from the time I was six and was a High School State Champion, so that helped get the jobs."

"Where's your horse?"

That question really started the tears. "The next spring, I did my taxes, and I had to pay taxes on the money she stole, plus a huge early withdrawal fee, plus penalties."

Matt handed her napkins.

"Thanks," She sniffed. "I had to sell my horse to pay the taxes. I'd had him for ten years…since I was eight…I won the championship on him."

"Dang, Josey. I just don't know what to say."

"That's when I met Jamie." She smiled slightly as she wiped away the last of the tears. "I trained her nieces on barrels, and helped her buy a horse for herself. She tried helping me out by getting me a job at the café, needless to say…I don't make a good waitress."

"Why?"

"Two problems…I broke and spilled more than I earned, so I was a cost liability to them."

Matt smiled at the light coming back into her eyes.

"Then, Jamie found out that I don't have patience for stupid people."

Matt leaned back and relaxed. "I'm with you on that one."

Josey glanced at the door again, then turned to Matt, then turned back quickly to the door. Her eyes opened wide. "That's…" She turned back to Matt. "That's your uncles!"

Matt looked over and nodded at Grayson, Leah, Scott, and Jordan as they walked through the café. All four were staring at the brunette that looked like Nikki.

"You didn't tell me they were coming." She looked at him like he betrayed her in some way.

"It's OK, Josey." He whispered and stood to adjust the tables and chairs to make room for everyone.

Josey stared at the four newcomers then turned to Matt. "Is Nikki…?"

"She and Lucas disappeared as soon as we checked in," Grayson chuckled. "I think they were afraid we were going to put them in separate rooms, too."

Everyone laughed except Josey who just stared at the foursome.

"I'm Grayson," He held out a hand to her and she took it firmly, which, by the look on his face, impressed him. "This is my wife, Leah."

"It's nice to meet you." Leah smiled.

"I'm Scott." He shook Josey's hands firmly too. "And this is my wife, Jordan."

"Great surprise to meet you," Jordan greeted her. "You look a lot like Nikki."

"I do?" Josey's eyes widened in surprise.

"Yes." Jordan smiled.

They took their seats with Josey moving over next to Matt. Grayson sat next to Josey with Leah on the other side. Jordan sat next to Matt with Scott on the end. They sat in a horseshoe pattern with the end opening to the café. Josey nervously looked towards the door.

"So…" Leah started then stopped. "You go by Frank?"

Josey smiled as Jamie's joke seemed to steam roll. "No, Frankie, except Matt seems to have a hard time remembering that."

They all chuckled, Matt just shrugged.

"Who's Lucas?" Josey asked Leah.

"Nikki's fiancé," She answered.

"She's engaged?" Josey's surprised eyes looked at Matt.

"Just last Monday," He answered with a nod then looked up at Grayson. "How did you get them in separate trucks?"

The foursome started laughing.

Grayson grinned, "Dru and Jack had Reilly and Grace so they took off. Scott and I got in the front of my truck, told Lucas that he and Nikki could ride with us…so, he got in the back while Nikki went in the house for something."

"Leah and I quickly jumped in on each side of him and shut the doors quickly." Jordan giggled. "There wasn't a thing he could do as Grayson gunned the engine and we flew down the driveway, leaving Nikki walking out of the house with only Nick and Tessa to ride with."

"I've never heard such language!" Scott laughed. "And that was in the phone call from Nikki!"

They all laughed again.

Josey sat quietly smiling at their laughter.

"She yelled that she didn't have enough time with him anyway and she was going to get even someday." Leah added with a smile.

"Why don't they have enough time together?" Josey asked Leah.

"Lucas lives in Australia. He's only been here since Saturday." Leah explained.

Josey sat back in her chair and looked around the happy group then shrugged. "Newly engaged and apart for nine hours…at least they'll appreciate tonight more." She grinned.

They all laughed again.

"That's what we thought too," Grayson nodded. "Good to know you have the wicked humor your sister does."

Josey just stared at him in surprise.

"What?" He asked, suddenly concerned.

"She's only known about Nikki for two days." Matt explained when Josey didn't answer.

The new foursome sat stunned when the not so friendly waitress came over.

She took the orders from the four then looked at Matt. "You want even more?"

Matt chuckled and shook his head.

"Two days?" Leah shook her head. "How did she keep it from you for so long? And why?"

"Her and Dad broke up when I was five. I only saw her a couple times a year, normally on my birthday or Christmas…which are only a couple weeks from each other so I didn't see her very much." She glanced nervously at Matt. "I don't know why she hid it. Did Nikki find out why?"

"No, Elena shut down any time it was mentioned…wouldn't even say if you were a boy or girl." Matt answered.

"How did you find out?" Josey asked.

"Nick, Nikki's and my dad questioned some old rodeo friends and found you." Matt replied.

"So, Nikki's dad raised her too?" Josey's eyes widened in surprise.

Matt shook his head. "No, he came back about a year and a half ago."

"Who raised Nikki?"

"My mom, Scott and Grayson. Nick brought Nikki to my mother's family right after I was born so we could be raised together." Matt looked around the table at the group, they were still watching Josey. "Nikki should be in on this conversation." He told her.

"When?" Josey looked around at her sister's family.

"Good question," Jordan responded. "Does Nick know?"

Matt shook his head. "No one but you four, I didn't want to interrupt Dad and Tessa's evening. Mom and Jack have Grace and Reilly so I thought we could deal with it in the morning."

"Who's Tessa?" Josey asked. "I think I need a drawing to keep everyone straight."

"She's Dad's girlfriend," Matt smiled. "…as of Tuesday."

"It's been a busy week for your family." Josey sighed with a half-smile.

"Speaking of…" Scott turned to Matt. "We heard about this morning in Coeur D' Alene. Is that where you were?"

Matt nodded, his mood taking a plunge when he envisioned the little brunette girl.

"Bad one?" Leah asked with a concerned frown.

"Really bad." Matt answered.

"I feel so totally lost here." Josey sighed. "But what was this morning?"

"Matt does search and rescue," Scott told her. "Little eight-year-old fell in the river last night, they found her this morning."

Josey's eyes went wide in shock as she turned to Matt. "How awful!"

Matt nodded then looked around. "Next topic."

They all nodded in understanding.

Josey turned to Grayson. "Matt said you're looking for up to 16 horses."

"We are." He answered.

"What type are you looking for?" Josey asked.

"Mainly for use on the ranch, a couple for clients at The Stables," Grayson answered. "Plus we need some ponies and extremely gentle horses for a kid's clinic we host. You know any good ones that will be at the auction?"

Josey nodded. "Yes and no. Most horses come in from out of the area but I know a couple ponies. The best ones are for sale, but not at the auction."

"What makes them the best?" Grayson asked.

"I teach kids to do barrels and other gaming events. One of the families I work with has twin ten-year-old girls. One of the girls races barrels and is doing a great job. The other twin was born with special needs. She can't ride, just sits on the pony and they walk her around. The pony is wonderful with her. She'll stand and pet or brush the pony for hours. Both girls are growing too big for the ponies and the family is looking to sell them to purchase a couple larger horses."

"Reasonable price?" Grayson nodded in interest.

"Very, in fact, if they know that you're using the ponies for a kid's clinic, they would even give you a better deal. They just want to make sure the ponies get a good home." She answered enthusiastically.

"We have the horse competition tomorrow afternoon. Can you get us out there tomorrow morning?"

"Yes, I'll call them tonight." She smiled.

"Thanks, Frankie." He said.

"Matt said you were looking for an assistant horse trainer." She stated.

"I am." Grayson nodded.

"Do I have a chance?" She asked hopefully. "If everything goes alright with Nikki?"

"Why wouldn't it go alright with Nikki?" Grayson asked as his phone started ringing. Looking down at it, he frowned. "It's Lucas."

Just as Grayson answered the phone, Josey inhaled sharply.

Matt looked down at her and saw her face had gone white, she was staring straight ahead and was pushing her chair back, as if to leave.

He followed her gaze, as did everyone at the table. Elena was standing in the middle of the café staring at Josey; a look of suspicion on her face.

"No…" Josey whispered sharply and started to rise.

Matt instinctively grabbed her arm and kept her down as he stared at Elena. The woman switched her stare from Josey to Matt, it changed from suspicion to accusing, which made Matt stand. Grayson and Scott rose, too.

Elena looked up at the three men, eyes wide, then turned and nearly ran out of the café.

Matt was trapped between the wall, the table, by Jordan and a shaking Josey.

"I know, we just saw her." Grayson was talking into his phone as he left the table and walked to the front door, Leah and Scott right behind him.

Josey turned to Matt. "This is bad…I just know it is, I told you we couldn't be seen together." Her voice was shaking in fear. "And with your whole family!"

"It's OK, Josey," Matt assured her, taking her hand. "There isn't anything she can do."

"I've heard that before." Josey closed her eyes and shook her head.

Matt had to admit to himself, that he had, too.

"Grayson and Scott will make sure she can't hurt you." Jordan added in concern.

Grayson, Leah and Scott returned. "She's gone, left in a little red car." Scott told them.

"I've spent two years hiding from her and she finds me twice in one week." Josey shook her head in amazement.

"How would she have known you were here?" Matt frowned. "If she was following you, then she would have come in an hour ago."

"I'm afraid it wasn't Frankie she was following." Grayson answered, holding up his phone. "Seems as though she followed us here; she probably didn't have any idea that Frankie was in here too."

"My truck," Josey sighed, her hands still shaking.

"So she followed you, saw Josey's truck, and came in to see if we were all together." Matt nodded.

"There's nothing she can do to you." Jordan tried to console her.

"How did she find you the first time?" Scott asked.

"I'm not sure, I changed my name to Frankie after the last time I saw her." She glanced up at Matt. "I don't have a Facebook page or anything…but she still showed up at my apartment the other night."

"What happened? If you don't mind me asking." Leah asked.

"She came in and we talked for a while, about the last two years. She didn't mention the money, so I didn't either. Then she announces I have a sister named Nikki Tagger and that she and her family were coming for the auction." Josey rolled her eyes. "I was just…shocked. With my dad disappearing, I've been alone for two years, not knowing I had a sister."

"Frankie?" Grayson looked at her in confusion.

"What?" She looked up at him.

"I have a couple dozen questions stemming from the five sentences you just said." He looked at her with a tilt of the head.

"Me, too." Scott, Leah, and Jordan said in unison.

"Most importantly…how did she know we were coming here?" Leah asked in concern.

"She said something about seeing it on Facebook." Josey answered.

Leah and Jordan looked at each other in surprise. "There hasn't been a thing out there about any of our schedules in a year." Leah said firmly.

"I don't know then." Josey shrugged.

"I'll look at everyone's Facebook page when we get home." Leah frowned.

Matt had listened to their conversation but his mind was going to Josey's comment about her mother going to her apartment. If Josey was worried about her mother and hiding from her the last couple nights, then would she have stayed at her apartment? He didn't think so.

"Josey?" Matt interrupted their conversation.

"What?" She asked, turning to him.

"Where have you been staying the last couple of nights?" Matt looked at her in concern.

Her eyes widened in surprise then she started turning red in embarrassment. Just what he thought, she'd been sleeping in her truck.

He reached in his pocket and withdrew the key for the hotel which listed their phone number. Phone in hand he called the front desk. He smiled when Cindi answered.

"Cindi, Matt Tagger."

"What are you doing?" Josey frowned.

"Yes, I found something to entertain myself with…how's your afternoon been?" He flirted with Cindi and ignored Josey.

"Matt, what are you doing?" Josey whispered.

"Yes, it would have been fun. Yeah, next time you'll need to have a better schedule." Matt chuckled. "We've had an unexpected family member join us and I wanted to know if you would possibly have an extra room for the next couple of nights."

"No, Matt, NO!" Josey gasped.

"Frankie?" Grayson said. He was the only one listening to their conversation, the others were talking about Elena and Facebook.

"What?" She turned in a mortified whiney voice.

"For the weekend." Grayson said.

"You have a room? Great, the next three nights?" Matt said to Cindi while looking at his uncle in concern.

"For the weekend what?" Josey asked confused.

"I'll hire you for the weekend as a consultant." Grayson whispered.

"What?" She looked between Matt and Grayson.

"Yes, she'll be checking in tonight." Matt said to Cindi and looked between Josey and Grayson.

"I'll hire you for room and board the next three nights, and $150." Grayson told her, staring intently at her then glancing at Matt.

Matt finally realized what his uncle was doing; giving Josey a chance to say yes to the hotel room without feeling like it was charity.

"Do you have any welcome baskets prepared for last minute guests?" Matt asked Cindi.

"Are you serious?" Josey was near tears as she listened to Matt's conversation and the offer from Grayson.

"You've already helped with the lead on a couple of good ponies for the clinic. I'm offering you the weekend position to help me out." He glanced at Matt then back to her. "You have 30 seconds to say yes or no."

"What?" Josey said in a strained voice. She looked at Matt in confusion.

"Yes, great." Matt said to Cindi. "A snack basket would be great and the special toiletries basket would be perfect, it's last minute so she wasn't completely prepared."

"Twenty seconds." Grayson told Josey. "We have a 7:00 private breakfast meetings for the next three days to talk over what's needed for the day. You'll need to be there."

"Grayson…" She looked at him in desperation.

"Thanks, Cindi. Yes her name is Josey…."

"Ten seconds." Grayson smiled.

"Matt?" Josey turned to him.

"Yes." Matt said to Cindi. "Josey Franklin."

"Five seconds." Grayson smiled.

"Fine!" Josey nearly yelled, drawing the attention of the three others and the tables around them. Her face turned red in embarrassment.

"Yes," Matt chuckled at his uncle. Then spoke to Cindi, "Can you put it on the group account or do you need my credit card?"

"For what? Who's he calling?" Scott asked.

"How much cash do you have on you?" Grayson asked Scott as he pulled out his own wallet. He tossed sixty dollars in front of Josey who just stared at it.

"Cindi," Matt said into the phone while watching Scott, Leah and Jordan dig in their wallets. "We have a meeting room setup in the morning for breakfast. Yes, you found it? Do you have another small meeting room close by that we can use for about a half hour, at 6:30?"

CHAPTER SIX

"Do you think she'll like me?" Josey turned nervous eyes to Matt.

They were the only two in the meeting room, waiting for Lucas and Nikki to arrive.

With permission from the not so friendly waitress, who was friendlier after the large tip she received, they left Josey's truck at the café then stopped at a store for her. With part of the $150 she bought clothes for the next few days.

Now she stood nervously, arms crossed in front of her; in the protective mode. Her hair was pulled back into a pony tail that lay down her back over her new black sleeveless button-up shirt. She was wearing new jeans that actually fit her.

"Why wouldn't she like you?" Matt asked.

"I'm Elena's daughter."

"So is she."

Josey looked up at him. "I keep forgetting that…I…three days…."

"Nikki is a fierce, wonderful, beautiful, and compassionate woman."

"Matt," Josey whispered as she looked up at him with nervous, desperate eyes. "I've been alone for two years…no one." Tears shimmered. "I just want her to like me so much."

Instinctively, Matt took her hand and squeezed, it was a natural move that he had been raised with, when someone hurt, you reached out to help. He looked at her with comforting eyes.

"There's no reason she won't like you." He whispered back.

"Matt?" It was Nikki's voice.

He turned quickly and looked at his stunned sister. The first time Nikki saw her sister, her brother was holding her hand and staring into her eyes…probably not a good start, Matt sighed.

"Nikki." He said and dropped Josey's hand.

Josey inhaled sharply as she looked at her half-sister for the first time. Lucas closed the door behind them and stood behind Nikki who was staring in disbelief. He was glaring at Matt. No one had told them why they were coming to the meeting room.

Matt expected Nikki to step forward and greet her sister with open arms. Instead she took a step backwards and into Lucas' arms. He gripped her upper arms tightly, protectively.

"Matt?" Nikki turned her stunned eyes to him. "What…why?"

As Matt told his sister the previous day's events, she stood protected in her future husband's arms. Josey stood silently, alone, in her protective stance; tears threatening to fall. Matt's heart ached for her.

When he finished with booking the hotel room for Josey and Grayson offering her the weekend job, Nikki turned her eyes from Matt to Josey. Still she said nothing.

Matt turned to Josey. She looked at him in misery and disappointment, a tear fell.

"I should go," Her voice shook. "Tell Grayson I will live up to the bargain, but I'll meet him downstairs to go see the ponies."

Matt didn't know what to say. Nikki's reaction was just…so unlike her. He was stunned.

"No," Matt sighed in confusion. He wasn't really sure what he had expected but this silence wasn't it. "We'll go into the breakfast as you told Grayson you would."

Josey started to shake her head when Matt grabbed her arm and drug her from the room without looking at Lucas or Nikki.

"I don't understand." Josey whispered as they walked to the room where everyone else had gathered for breakfast.

"I don't either." Matt sighed. "I'm sorry."

They turned the corner and ran into Nick and Tessa in the hall.

Matt had called his mother and Nick an hour before to fill him in on the details.

Josey stared at Nick then looked at Matt.

Matt chuckled. "I forgot to warn you. Some people seem to think we look a lot alike."

Josey smiled at Matt then turned to Nick and held out her hand. "I'm Frankie."

He shook her hand firmly. "Nick." He returned her smile. "This is Tessa."

The women shook hands and smiled politely.

"How did it go with Nikki?" Nick looked behind them. "I thought she would be with you."

"Not well." Josey answered softly.

Nick looked at her in surprise, then looked at Matt, who shrugged.

Nick turned back to Josey. "Well, it's a pleasure to meet you. I understand you're going to be working with Grayson for the weekend."

Josey's shoulders lowered; "Yes, I have a friend that has some ponies…"

Matt's mind drifted as they walked down the hall. He turned to see if Lucas and Nikki were following, they weren't. What the heck was Nikki thinking?

As they walked into the breakfast, Nick and Tessa led Josey to the buffet then over to Grayson and Leah who greeted her warmly.

Matt walked to his mother and Jack who were sitting and watching the new addition.

"You OK?" His mom asked as he greeted them.

"I'm fine," Matt answered and looked at the group gathering around Josey. Reilly and Grace were excited about meeting Nikki's sister. The reaction he expected from Nikki.

"She's not what I'm talking about." His mom looked at him in concern.

Matt sighed and looked between his mother and stepfather finally realizing she was asking about the recovery the day before. "I don't know on this one, Mom," He admitted. "It's one thing when they're adults…but this little girl…she looked so much like Nora when she was eight."

She took his hand and squeezed. He squeezed back, thankful for the love and support.

"What did Kevin say?" Jack asked.

Matt took out his phone, found the message from Kevin and let them listen to it.

"I'm so sad for the girl and her family," She said. "But I am so proud of you for helping them."

Matt nodded and sighed again. "I'm really having a hard time compartmentalizing this one."

"Have you talked to Kevin about it?" She looked at him like there was no one else in the room.

Matt shook his head. "No, I left as soon as the parents were clear and haven't really stopped since."

"Call him," She told him. "He's been through this, he can help."

Matt nodded. "I know, I will later."

"Soon, Son." She said and looked towards the door then sat up straighter.

Matt turned to see Nikki and Lucas standing in the doorway. His sister was staring at Josey.

He saw Josey looking for him. He knew she saw him as an anchor but he just had time to stand when Nikki approached her. His mother and Jack rose to stand next to him.

Josey wrapped her arms into her protective mode.

"I'm sorry." Nikki finally spoke to Josey, her voice shook.

Everyone stopped and watched the sisters.

Josey shook her head, "You don't have anything to be sorry for…we kind of ambushed you."

Nikki took in a deep breath. "No, I do need to apologize."

"I don't understand." Josey whispered.

"I am the one that made the decision last year to not reach out to you." Nikki admitted.

"I don't understand." Josey repeated.

"When Nick found you…I didn't want to interrupt your life, I thought it was good. I didn't know what you went through, I didn't know about your dad…that Elena stole your future, your money." Nikki took a step towards her sister. "Can you forgive me?"

"Forgive you?" Josey whispered, tears streaming down her stunned face. "There is nothing to forgive. I've known about you for three days." Josey's voice quivered. "I've thought of nothing else. I searched the web for every picture I could find of you. I found the number for The Stables, but I was so afraid that you wouldn't like me, that I didn't reach out to you."

"Why wouldn't I like you?" Nikki asked as a tear escaped.

"Because I'm Elena's daughter."

"So, am I." Nikki sighed and opened her arms. Josey stepped to her and the sisters embraced for the first time.

"You know what this means," Matt's mom turned to him.

"Nikki's not leaving Josey behind," Matt nodded, unsure of how he felt. "And she'll bring the threat of Elena with her."

###

Matt jogged around the corner from the hotel; the music of Nickelback blaring in his ear buds and setting his pace.

He'd left the breakfast soon after Nikki and Josey spoke. He needed to run, get the anxiety out of him. Elena was there…a clear threat…and Nikki would never leave Josey in Montana…essentially bringing the threat to Idaho…home.

He jogged down the road toward the park trails the hotel clerk had suggested. The road was clear of traffic so he took off and ran as fast as he could, his heart rate soared as he imagined he was at the ranch with Trooper running next to him. Sweat started dripping down his back, his hair was already soaked but it felt good, his endorphins were on fire.

He found a grass clearing at the park and did sit-ups, push-ups, lunges, squats, then took off running again. The anxiety and stress started to drain from his body. The more sweat came out of him, the better he felt.

He turned around to make his way back to the hotel. There was just enough time to shower and change before meeting up with his mom and Jack. They had decided to split up in groups until the ranch competition started, then they would meet up at Miller's Horse Palace arena to watch together. Josey was leaving with Grayson, Leah, Grace and Reilly to see the ponies.

He hadn't talked to Josey after she spoke with Nikki, he'd grabbed a plate of fruit and left. He rounded the corner of the hotel and stopped in front of the doors, jogging in place while he waited for a group of people to exit before he could enter.

Matt smiled at the group as they exited and received an extra big smile from the last young woman in line, which made him chuckle inside. That always made him feels better.

As the lady stepped away from the door, Matt looked past her and straight into Elena's eyes; she was only 30 feet away. He stopped jogging and stared at her in disbelief that she was actually there. Slowly, he pulled the ear buds of his ears. She had a slight smile on her face that looked more like Josey than Nikki. Her hair was darker than both the sisters. She tilted her head, narrowed her dark brown eyes, and her lips turned into a sinister grin. It was a look of knowing…of dislike…it was ominous of what was to come.

Matt took a step towards her and she took a step back. He walked faster towards her…she turned and nearly ran around the corner of the building. He stopped at the corner and looked to see her sitting in her car, engine just started; the evil smile looking at him through the glass of her window.

She drove away as his phone rang. He unhooked the phone from his arm band and looked at the caller.

"Lucas?"

"What the heck is the matter with you people?!" He yelled into the phone.

Matt chuckled in confusion. "What are you talking about?"

"I can't keep Elena away from you guys if you won't stop running into her!" His voice vibrated with irritation.

"That was fast." Matt chuckled as he stood on the sidewalk and looked in the direction Elena had disappeared. "I went for a run; she was at the door when I got here."

"She wouldn't have made it in the door. I had that covered."

"Well, get her the heck out of town and I'll feel much better."

"I've got that covered too. She wasn't supposed to be out of Nevada and is about to get a call from her parole officer saying she has to be in his office by the end of the day or a warrant will be issued for her arrest."

"Good one." Matt smiled as he walked into the hotel. "Can she make it in time?"

"Only if she leaves now and drives really fast." Lucas chuckled. "By the way, thanks for the heads up on Frankie this morning."

"I figured you knew."

"We weren't worried about her, it was Elena they were tracking."

"How's Nikki?"

"In shock," Lucas sighed. "After you and Frankie left the room, I thought she was going to kill me."

"Why?"

"Because I should have known what the girl was going through and told her."

"Nikki said she didn't want to know, you weren't supposed to tell her a thing."

"Yeah, well, she forgot about that." Lucas' voice, which was usually full of energy, was sounding forlorn. "To protect Nick's identity here in the States and watching for those people who are a danger to you and your family, we check backgrounds for criminal history, what their current living and work situations…who they hang out with. Frankie's was fine a year ago, so it seemed."

Matt reached the elevator and stepped in, at the last second he saw Josey and Nikki in the lobby as the doors closed. "I thought you and Nikki were together today."

"No, after you left, Nikki decided she was going with Grayson and Josey for the day."

"Sounds logical."

"Well, after Reilly offered to go with Jack and Dru so I could go too, Nikki said no, he could stick with his plans of staying with Grace."

"Making it clear she didn't want you around." Matt grimaced for his future brother-in-law.

"Exactly…after being ticked off yesterday when the Trio pulled their little truck trick and separating us, she was eagerly getting rid of me today."

Matt chuckled as he stepped off the elevator and walked to his door. "She'll get over it. Just give her time."

"I leave on Tuesday for two weeks, Mate. I want to spend that time with my future bride."

Matt sighed, nothing he could do to help Lucas now. "So what are you doing today?"

"Riding with Nick and Tessa, I guess. I'm sure they aren't going to be too happy to have me around either." He sounded dejected.

Matt laughed. "I'll ride with you, then we can split from them when we get there, we'll do some brother-in-law bonding together. How long before you meet Dad?"

"We meet in 10 minutes."

"See you there."

CHAPTER SEVEN

"So, you two know how to tick off my daughter." Nick grinned at them as they met at his truck in the hotel parking lot.

"Me?" Matt asked in surprise. "I know how Lucas ticked her off, but how did I?"

"Thanks, Mate." Lucas frowned at Matt as they both slid into the backseat.

Nick chuckled at his future son-in-law. "You left before she had a chance to talk to you."

"Josey didn't seem too happy you disappeared either." Tessa said to Matt.

"Ahhh…" Matt said, grinning at Lucas. "I feel so wanted."

Lucas glared as Nick and Tessa laughed.

"Well, maybe that will clear you up to drive for me." Nick said to Lucas.

"Why would I be driving for you?" Lucas asked.

"I brought over a trailer for the Tagger's, if they fill up all their trailers, I may need to buy a truck and trailer to haul my horses back."

"What?" Tessa looked at him in surprise.

"You're buying horses?" Matt asked.

Nick nodded. "I'm buying Tessa a horse to ride and one for Alex."

"You are not!" Tessa gasped.

"Yes, I am." Nick chuckled at her reaction.

"I like Star…you're not buying me a horse."

"Well, Dru won't sell Star to me…and I didn't say I was buying YOU a horse. I learned my lesson when I bought Alex the boots. I said I'm buying one for you to ride." Nick said firmly.

"You asked Dru to buy Star?" Tessa asked in surprise.

"Yes," He nodded. "She said that Star is too good of a client horse to sell."

"You're not buying a horse for me or Alex." Tessa said firmly.

Matt and Lucas looked at each other and grinned.

"Like I said, I'm not buying you a horse, it's for you to ride." Nick argued lightheartedly.

"It's the same thing and you know it." Tessa retorted.

"Tessa?" Matt said from the backseat.

"What?" She said tersely. "Sorry that was a little harsh…what Matt?" She said again in a light airy tone.

"You need to pick your battles." Matt told her.

"Excuse me?" Tessa turned in the seat to look at him.

"You need to pick your battles," Matt repeated with a smile. "This one?" He shook his head. "You're not going to win, so you might as well go along with it."

Tessa turned to look at Nick, he raised a brow and shrugged with a smirk. She turned back to Matt and Lucas with a smile. "I think you're right."

They all laughed.

"So you pick out what you like and I'll find a good, dependable one for Alex." Nick smiled at her, a light shining in his eyes. "Deal?"

"Deal." Tessa relented.

"And if my bride is still mad at me, then Matt can ride back with me." Lucas nodded solemnly.

"Deal." Matt agreed.

*****

Matt laughed again as Tessa picked out another horse and Nick said no. It was the fifth one in a row. They were walking through the holding pens to the right of the livestock building.

"I thought you said I can pick my horse." She frowned while laughing.

"It's not your horse, it's mine. You just get to ride it." Nick grinned then leaned down and kissed her quickly. She giggled and took his arm affectionately. They continued down the rows of pens.

"I'm not sure I can take much more of this," Lucas sighed. "My bride's mad at me and Nick actually has a girlfriend."

Matt laughed.

"Not all the horses are here yet," Nick told her.

"I know but…Oh MY!" Tessa let go of Nick's arm and ran ahead of them. "Look at her!" Tessa's voice was full of excitement.

There was a pretty mare standing alertly in the middle of the pen.

"Oh Nick!" Tessa turned, her eyes bright. "Isn't she wonderful?"

Matt looked over at his dad and saw the grin. It was a happy, satisfied grin; she finally had the reaction to a horse he was waiting for. "That she is, Tessa." Nick said softly as he walked behind his lady.

Matt leaned on the fence and looked at the beautiful, elegant palomino paint. The mare had a light, nearly white mane, cropped short. She was deep golden with large white splotches decorating her muscular body. A wide white blaze highlighted her gentle and alert brown eyes. She looked positively feminine.

"Please, Nick." Tessa turned hopefully to him. "Can you buy her so I can ride her for you?"

"Are you sure?" Nick teased.

"Oh, yes." Tessa sighed as she turned back to the horse.

"Well, find her in the catalog and we'll see what we can do." Nick handed her the book but she grabbed his wrist instead and pulled him down to kiss him, solidly.

"I can't take much more of this." Lucas rolled his eyes at Matt, with a half laugh.

"Alright, we're out of here." Matt chuckled and they turned away from the pair.

"I don't even think they noticed we left," Lucas laughed. "…and I couldn't be more happy for Nick."

"Me either." Matt nodded as they weaved around the pens full of horses.

"Find any you like?" Lucas asked looking at a corral full of mules.

"Couple of them," Matt nodded and grinned at Lucas. "But I didn't have the reaction to them that Tessa just had with the little mare."

"Good to know, Mate." Lucas laughed. "I feel sorry for anyone trying to outbid Nick on that filly."

Matt nodded as he looked around at the growing number of people. "I spent as much time yesterday looking for Elena as I did looking at the horses."

"Well, she's officially out of Montana now."

"Think she'll make it on time?"

"Doesn't really matter," Lucas said with a wicked grin. "If she gets there in time, she'll walk into an office full of people wondering what the heck she's doing there."

Matt looked at him and laughed. "The parole office didn't call?"

"No, I had someone call her and pretend they were from the office." Lucas chuckled. "If she doesn't get there in time, she'll spend the whole weekend looking over her shoulder wondering when she's going to be arrested."

Matt laughed heartily as they walked across the front of the building and toward the back pens. They made their way through the covered stalls then out to the back pens where the open stock horses were beginning to arrive. Although some were trained, most weren't and would be pushed through the auction pen and sold quickly and without details, unlike the horses that were listed in the catalog.

The Taggers would be purchasing from the less expensive open stock horses, too. Grayson wanted a mixture of trained, ready to ride horses as well as those that would need trained. It kept the cost down since they were buying so many.

There was a mixture of good quality horses and some that were obviously just off an open range and had probably never been touched.

They met up with Nick and Tessa in time to ride over to Miller's Horse Palace where the ranch horse competition was being held.

The parking lot was full of trucks and trailers. Horses were tied up alongside the trailers, in pens, and being warmed up in an open arena to the back of the building.

Nick and Tessa went in the building while Lucas and Matt walked along the side to look at the horses.

"Watch the trailer ahead and to the left," Lucas said softly.

"Why?" Matt asked as he watched the horse trailer pull into a stop and the passenger side door open.

"Just doing you a favor, Mate." Lucas chuckled.

A long, jean encased leg stepped out of the truck, a well-worn pink cowboy boot hit the ground; then another. Long blonde hair swayed under a straw cowboy hat as the cowgirl turned back to say something to the driver.

Matt chuckled, "Probably talking to her UFC fighter husband."

Lucas shook his head, "Not quite…I saw them pull in a few minutes ago."

Another woman appeared at the back of the trailer. She had long red hair pulled back into a braid, a well-worn straw cowboy hat nearly hid her beautiful eyes from view.

They both looked like they stepped out of a ranch magazine cover.

Lucas and Matt walked next to the trailer as the blonde joined the red head and she lifted the handle to the trailer gate.

There was a bang, a whinny, and a few swear words from the cowgirls as the trailer gate flew open. The gate hit the blonde causing her to fly back into Matt's arms; he kept her from hitting the ground.

Lucas wrapped an arm around the waist of the redhead to pull her out of the way while grabbing the rope of the escaping horse with the other arm.

Matt had to admit, the Australian looked like a hero from a romantic western saving the girl and the horse in one swoop.

The blonde turned surprised eyes up at Matt as he set her upright.

"Thanks," She gasped then smiled…brightly.

Matt grinned at her and turned to Lucas who had made sure the red head was steady on her feet then let her go to concentrate on the large bay horse that was prancing nervously.

"Easy, brumby," Lucas talked softly to calm the horse.

"Well," The redhead stepped to the horse and held out a hand for the lead rope. Her smile widened when she got a good look at her tall hero. "I can't thank you enough."

Lucas nodded as he handed her the rope then stepped back away from her.

"His explosive unloading the reason you're selling him?" Matt laughed as the blonde stayed right next to him.

The blonde laughed and turned so her shoulder rubbed against his. "He's my brother's horse and not going to be for sale."

"He may want to reconsider that," Lucas said and both women turned surprised eyes to him.

"Australian?" The red head asked. Her eyes sparkled even more.

"Yes," He smiled and casually took a half step back away from her.

The blonde looked up at Matt.

He laughed, "No, I'm from Idaho."

"I like Idaho," The blonde grinned.

Matt chuckled.

The redhead and blonde exchanged looks then turned back to their pair of heroes.

"After I get Snapper to her brother, can we take you two out for a beer to thank you?" The redhead asked. Her voice was calm but her eyes were a bit anxious.

Matt chuckled again and glanced at his future brother-in-law.

Lucas shook his head but had a thankful smile, "Sorry, I don't think my bride would appreciate it."

"Oh…" The redhead's shoulders lowered, the disappointment very clear in her voice. "You're married…"

"Engaged," Lucas grinned.

Both girls turned to Matt. His stomach tightened and his neck warmed at the look in their eyes.

"I would love to ladies, and under any other circumstances I would join you, but I'm with family this weekend." He hoped his voice sounded calm and apologetic.

Both girls sighed and nodded.

"Well, thanks for catching us." The blonde said and turned to leave.

The redhead looked back at Lucas, her eyes giving him one more chance.

He shook his head and chuckled, "My bride is the absolute love of my life."

"Well, thanks again," She sighed, nodded, and led the horse away behind the blonde.

The two men grinned at each other and turned to walk back to the building.

They were stopped by two brunettes. Nikki was grinning ear-to-ear at her groom and Josey smiled at Matt then looked at Lucas.

Nikki and Lucas stepped to each other and within a blink of the eye, their lips met and he had her tipped into a grand movie kiss; her hair brushed the ground.

When the kiss ended, the love was radiating from them again. Nikki's arm wrapped around his and they walked together toward the building.

Matt and Josey quietly walked behind the newly reconciled pair. He felt a bit guilty and didn't know why.

"So, did we buy some pretty little ponies?" Matt asked to break the awkward silence.

"They did, both of them." Josey smiled excitedly. "Your uncle is a charmer."

Matt chuckled. "He's been called that before…along with a few other things."

Josey giggled and Matt looked down at her. The light was back in her eyes. She looked relaxed and happy…so much different than their first meeting with Nikki that morning at the hotel.

"Have a good time with Nikki?" He asked in a low voice.

"She's just awesome," Josey's eyes widened. "You were right."

"Usually am." He teased.

Josey giggled again. He was beginning to like that sound.

****

To the right of the entry door of the indoor arena was a set of bleachers. Directly to the left, tucked into the corner was the concession stand. A few tables were scattered in front of it. Along the side of the building to their left was another set of bleachers that led to the large back door where the horses would be led in. Straight in front of them was a long counter attached to the arena panels with old padded bar stools in front of it.

Sitting at the counter were the Tagger Trio and spouses along with Grace, Reilly, Tessa and Nick. The foursome joined them and pretty much filled the counter.

Matt sat between his mother and Josey to watch the competition.

Tessa cried out in excitement when she saw the little mare she picked out come into the arena. The woman riding her showed the horse off well. The painted palomino did everything the woman asked and looked elegant and beautiful while she worked.

"Maybe we should buy her for the ranch." Matt's mom told Nikki.

"I think you're right, she'd be perfect as a backup to Harvey." Nikki agreed.

Tessa's head swung over to the two women. "No, you don't!" She said with a warning glare then realized the two women were teasing her.

The entire group laughed.

"Remember the story of Blue?" Nick looked over at his ex-wife and daughter with a warning grin.

She and Nikki laughed even more.

"What happened?" Josey asked Matt.

"Nora, my little cousin, was with them. Dad gave her the paddle, told her to hold it up in the air until they won the horse." Matt explained with a smile.

"Oh wow." Josey said in surprise. "He must be a special horse."

"He is." Matt answered as he thought of the horse pulling the Christmas sleigh.

Scott, Matt, Grayson, and Josey spent the afternoon watching the competition and marking the catalog with the horses they were interested in for the ranches. His mom, Nikki, and Jack worked on the horses for The Stables.

Dinner at the hotel steakhouse was consumed by talk of the horses.

Matt sat across the table from Josey who was sitting between Grayson and Nikki. They were deep in conversation about the horses they had seen, which ones needed work, and which they thought would go for too much money.

It was clear to Matt that Grayson was going to hire Josey. It concerned Matt more than he thought it would. The vision of Elena's sinister smile danced through his mind. She would follow Josey, and that, Matt was sure.

Josey hadn't stopped Elena from trying to get to the Taggers, she just delayed it. Elena would come back and use Josey to get to them.

He heard a giggle and turned to see a table with parents and three kids. One of the girls had long dark hair…like Nora's…like the little girl he had pulled out of the river. His head began to ache.

"I'm going to go for a jog." Matt announced and stood quickly and left before anyone could react.

Stepping on the treadmill in the hotel fitness center, he ran. His heart raced, blood pumped, sweat dripped…but no matter how fast he ran, he couldn't out run the images of the little girl and the sinister grin. The impending doom rested on his heart. He had to protect his family.

Turning down the treadmill, he looked at the distance he'd covered. He had run ten miles…not a good thing late in the day on a full stomach.

He stepped down and worked on the weight bench before he realized how very exhausted his body was.

Wiping the sweat off his face, Matt made his way across the hotel lobby to the elevators.

"Matt?" His mother was walking to him. She had obviously been waiting for him.

"What are you doing here?" He asked in surprise.

"It's ten o'clock at night and you're working out."

"I didn't realize it was so late," He sighed as they stepped into the elevator.

She quietly took his hand, squeezed hard, and looked into his eyes. Her blue eyes radiated the concern she had for him. "Call Kevin."

The fear, anxiety, exhaustion, images of little girls and sinister smiles, and his mother's love finally caught up with him and he could feel the emotions fight to get out. They caught him by surprise.

"What can I do?" She whispered.

He just shook his head. "Just what you are…" He whispered with a constricted voice.

She leaned her head on his shoulder and squeezed his hand. The elevator door's opened at his floor and they didn't move. The door's closed, and they remained silent.

CHAPTER EIGHT

"I spent two hours on the phone with him last night." Matt assured his mother the next morning at breakfast.

"Did it help?" She asked in concern.

"Yes, in fact, he cussed me out for not calling him sooner."

She slapped him playfully on the arm, "Next time, you listen to your mother."

"I will." He chuckled and leaned to give her a kiss on the cheek.

They sat quietly watching the rest of the family prepare their plates from the buffet. Josey was in a sleeveless light blue western shirt today. She and Jordan were laughing at something.

"I talked to Grayson about Frankie." His mother said in a low voice.

"He wants to hire her, doesn't he?" Matt sighed.

"Yes, he's very impressed with her."

"She brings Elena with her."

"I know and he understands."

"He's willing to take that risk?"

"He's agreed to take it to a vote."

"Really?" Matt was surprised.

"He understands it could affect all of us."

"When?"

"Tomorrow morning after breakfast, before we pick up all the horses."

"There is something I haven't told you, just Lucas knows."

He told her of the run-in with Elena the morning before and how Lucas got her out of town.

She shook her head. "Grayson and Scott need to know."

"I know. I'll tell them sometime today."

"Matt!" He heard Grace yell from behind them.

She was skipping excitedly to him. "What are we doing tonight?" Reilly bounced in behind her.

"What's tonight?" Matt frowned in fake confusion.

"Seriously?" Grace laughed. "You're taking Reilly and I while all the adults go 'out on the town'."

"Ohhh….that…." Matt teased. "I have plans for you two."

"Can Frankie come?" Grace asked hopefully. "She's not 21 until January." She paused, then looked back at Josey. "When's your birthday?"

"What?" Josey asked and walked across the room.

"When's your birthday? You and Matt both have birthdays in January." Grace informed her.

"The 8th." Josey answered and looked at Matt.

"The 9th." Matt smiled.

"Dang!" Grace laughed and announced the new information to the room.

"That's funny." Jordan joined them. "Scott's is January 2nd and mine is January 3rd."

"And Reilly's is the 23rd." Grace added then looked at Matt. "So, can she go?"

He shrugged, "If she wants."

"Will you go with us?" Grace turned to a surprised Josey.

"Go where?" Josey asked while looking a Matt.

Matt just grinned and shrugged.

"Matt is taking Reilly and I while all the couples go out on the town." Grace told her. "Frankie, please go with us!"

Josey looked anxiously at Matt. "Is it OK?"

"Of course," He nodded with a mischievous grin.

They arrived at the auction yard early to walk around the pens again to see the horses that had arrived the night before.

Scott and Jordan were staying outside to watch as the horses were prepared for showing to judge their disposition. They would text if there was a problem with a horse and warn the bidders in the family.

While the loose stock was quickly auctioned, Matt's mother, Jack, Grace, and Reilly were at the outside arena watching sellers show off their horses with team roping and cow cutting. Nick and Tessa disappeared to talk with the sellers of the palomino paint mare.

Matt watched the untrained horse auction with Josey then Grayson to his right and Nikki then Lucas to his left.

At least twenty horses went through before Grayson flipped his card to bid.

"Frankie, why that one?" Grayson asked of the buckskin horse.

"Alert eyes, good balanced body, neck and head in proportion and he seemed curious not scared." She answered quickly.

"Would you have bid on him?" Grayson asked as the horse was pushed out of the show ring.

"Yes," She nodded then turned to him. "You going to test me all day?"

Grayson chuckled and turned amused eyes to her as he flipped the card a final time and won the horse. "Yes," He answered honestly.

"Bring it on," She challenged.

Matt chuckled as Josey leaned back, arms crossed with a determined look on her face.

Five horses later, while a sorrel was trotting back and forth across the show ring, a red dun with flaxen mane and forelock stuck his head over the entry gate. It looked like he was watching the sorrel and the crowd. He didn't seem worried or nervous at all.

"He's got a nice head…strong and masculine," Josey murmured, "Hopefully his body matches."

The sorrel ran out the exit door and the entry door was opened. The red dun trotted out and lapped the show room floor. He had a strong back, broad chest, deep withers, a large rump, and he looked well balanced. The auctioneer stated he was trained, used on a ranch the last couple years, and was seven-years-old.

Josey's body stiffened, "Bid on him."

Neither Grayson nor Matt moved.

"Why aren't you bidding?" Josey's voice was anxious as she turned to Grayson. Her knees started bouncing.

Grayson looked at her with no expression so she looked back at the horse that had stopped in the middle of the pen; head up and looking around at everyone watching him.

His body was muscled, balanced…he was beautiful with an intelligent mind set. She looked back at Grayson. "Aren't you going to bid on him?"

He ignored her and just looked down at the catalog…ignoring her and the horse he should be bidding on!

"Why?" Josey turned to Matt. He kept his face calm.

The horse was pushed out of the arena.

"Sold to 434," The auctioneer said quickly and moved on to the next horse.

"Why?" She turned back to Grayson.

He finally chuckled, "Because Nikki did."

Josey turned to her sister and laughed.

Nikki grinned, "I put dibs on him this morning when we saw him in the corrals. He'll be Harvey's backup."

Nick and Tessa joined the group; taking seats on the bench right behind them.

The registered loose stock horses were brought out one at a time in quick order. After grilling Josey on each pedigree stated, Grayson won two three year old green broke horses and a four year old.

"Nora's projects," Grayson told Josey. "She's Scott and Jordan's daughter. Only fourteen, but a heck of a horse woman. She'll get them finished while I work on the others."

"She'll love that," Matt nodded. He couldn't wait to see the look on his cousin's face when she was told.

"She's working with Bodi, too." Nick added.

Everyone joined the group as the auction for the horses in the catalog started.

Twenty horses in, Nikki won a couple of horses for The Stables and Grayson won three more for the ranch.

"Oh, this is a sad one." Josey sighed as a dark bay horse was ridden into the arena by a teenage boy. His father stood by the door; neither the boy nor man looked happy.

"Why?" Nikki asked.

"His dad had a heart attack and they need the money for the doctor bills. If they don't get enough out of the gelding, they'll have to sell more of their horses. The dad is a local team roper and has been riding this one for the last couple of years. He wasn't going to have anyone else in his family lose their horse because of him, so he's sacrificing his own." Josey sighed and watched the boy ride the horse around the small auction ring.

Nick took out his phone and typed in a message, Jack and Grayson's phones alerted them and they read the message and turned to Nick with slight smiles.

The bidding started and Nick bid few times. The bidding started to slow down at $400; the devastation was evident on the boy's face as he looked at his dad. Jack bid, Nick bid again, then Grayson, Nick then Jack.

Josey looked at the three men in confusion, then turned to Matt, who was grinning. Her face lit up when she realized what the three men were doing.

Grayson bid at $1000, then Nick, then Jack.

The man who was working with the auctioneer in spotting bids knew that the three men were together and was smiling in understanding.

The teenager in the arena had stopped and was looking at the crowd trying to see who was bidding. His sad face had started to brighten.

Jack bid at $2000, Nick, then Jack, Grayson, Nick, the bid was up to $3000.

The crowd was starting to murmur…those who knew the story, realizing what was happening, others just confused why this bay horse was receiving such high bids.

Matt laughed as Nikki's excitement got the best of her and she couldn't help but bid at $3500.

Jack, Grayson, and Nick stopped bidding which made Nikki start giggling; knowing they were trying to make her worried. Just as the auctioneer was ready to call the winning bid, Jack bid, then Grayson, Nick, Jack, Grayson, Nick, Jack…the bid was $4500.

The young boy in the arena had started to grin and looked at his dad, who was nodding in excitement. Matt guessed they had bid enough to cover what the family needed.

Grayson bid, Jack bid, then Nick bid…no more bidding. Grayson and Jack turned and smiled at Nick…they knew who had the bigger bank account.

Nick won the gelding for $5100 and tipped his hat to the boy in the ring. The boy grinned, waved, patted his horse, and walked out of the show ring.

Nick turned to Tessa. "I hope Alex likes bay horses."

"He's going to love him!" She laughed and hugged him happily.

The rest of the afternoon was uneventful while Nikki and their mom won three ponies to go with the other two bought the previous day. Grayson and Matt bought enough to fill the trailers.

Matt picked up the one that he liked as a backup to Trooper; the big stout blood bay that did well in the ranch competition. He wasn't a quarter horse and didn't come with papers but he had a great look and disposition. His size made him perfect for a pack horse, especially hauling fencing supplies up and down the steep mountainside.

One of the last horses brought in for the day was Tessa's little mare. She bounced excitedly in her seat and squeezed Nick's arm.

"Not much of a poker face." Matt told his dad with a chuckle.

Nick waited until the bidding slowed down then he bid on the mare, Tessa bounced again in excitement which caused all of them to laugh.

He won the mare for $4200.

"Oh…" The excitement was bubbling out of Tessa. "She's mine?"

"No," He shook his head with a grin. "She's mine."

"Nick…" She giggled playfully. "Will you let me ride her?"

"Maybe…" He teased.

Matt just shook his head and laughed.

###

Matt pulled into the department store.

"Stay here, I'll be right back." He told the confused trio in the truck. They had just finished a large dinner at a barbecue restaurant and now it was time for their 'activity'.

Chuckling to himself, Matt ran into the store, bought supplies and headed back out. He tossed a bag into the back seat to Grace and Reilly.

"I'm not going jogging!" Grace yelled when she pulled the pink sweat pants out of the bag.

"I will." Reilly laughed at his best-friend's reaction and pulled out a black pair for him and threw a pink pair to Josey.

"I'm starting to regret my decision to join you three tonight." Josey looked at Matt cautiously.

Matt pulled into the parking lot of a large building.

"It's nine o'clock, they looked closed." Josey said looking around at the empty parking lot.

"They are," Matt said as he opened the door of his mother's truck.

The trio followed him, looking around nervously.

"Matt…have you gone bonky?" Grace asked him.

Matt smiled at her as he pounded on the front door.

After a few minutes the door opened and a tall man with lots of blond hair greeted them.

"You must be Matt." He stuck out his hand and they shook eagerly. "And these are our victims?"

Matt and the man laughed as Grace, Reilly and Josey stepped backwards; with alarm on their faces.

"Yea," Matt tried to contain his laughter and introduced the three 'victims'.

"I'm Chops," Their host shook hands with each. "Let's get out of the doorway before someone thinks we're open and wants to join the fun."

"What are we doing?" Reilly asked as they stepped into the building.

When they walked around the corner the three 'victims' stopped and stared.

It was Reilly that turned to Matt first with a huge grin on his face. "AWESOME!"

Josey and Grace looked at each other, then to Matt. "Cool!" They yelled in unison.

In front of them was a huge building full of climbing walls. Multi-colored pegs decorated the geometric walls which were painted in bright colors. The padded floors were going to be much appreciated.

"I pulled in a couple favors for this," Matt told his group. "We've got the place to ourselves for the next couple of hours so you better enjoy."

"Are you kidding me?" Josey turned to Matt, her voice rose two octaves and her brown eyes shone in excitement. "I've always wanted to try this!"

He smiled at her sense of adventure, "Well, let's get you all changed and on the walls."

Chops supplied safety gear and lessons to the three while Matt started climbing the walls.

For the next two hours the four climbed, laughed, teased, challenged, joked, and at one point lay quietly flat on their backs on the padded floors.

"I'm exhausted." Reilly laughed as they stared at the ceiling.

"Ready to leave?" Matt had to tip his head back to look over at his stepbrother.

"Not on your life. You're going to have to drag me out of here kicking and screaming." Reilly answered with a laugh.

"I thought that's what we were going to have to do to get you in here." Chops chuckled.

"How long have you been climbing?" Josey turned to Matt.

"Couple years," Matt answered; twisting his head on the floor mats to see her.

"What other surprising things do you do?" She asked.

"Scuba dive, cycle, sky-dive, rappel, kayak, raft, and anything else I can think of that's outdoors and I might have to use while doing search and rescue." He answered and smiled at her look of amazement.

"And he's an EMT." Reilly added proudly.

"Well, come on, Mr. Outdoors Man." Grace jumped up and looked at Matt. "I'll race you to the top of that wall." She pointed to her left.

"I'll give you a 1 minute head start." Matt grinned as he stood.

She took off running with Josey and Reilly next to her. Even with the minute head start, Matt easily reached the top before any of them. He sat on the top of the wall and grinned down at his companions. Grace and Reilly made their way back down and raced each other up another wall.

His attention moved to Josey who was balancing on the colorful pegs just below him. She was looking up at him with a warm smile. There was something in the way she was looking at him that seemed to relax him. He returned her smile, which caused her eyes to sparkle. Grace's laughter broke them from the moment as they both turned to the 'life is good' sound.

Thoroughly exhausted and happy, they said good night to Chops and left the building.

"I'm hungry!" Reilly declared as they climbed in the truck.

"Of course, you are!" Grace laughed.

"I know of a place!" Josey said excitedly. "It's an ice cream shop only a mile down the road."

"Are they open this late?" Grace turned excitedly.

"They are!" Josey turned to Matt. "Can we go?"

"Show me the way." He laughed.

###

It was one o'clock in the morning when they arrived back at the hotel. Six hours later, Matt walked into the breakfast meeting and all three of his dinner companions were already there talking excitedly to Grayson and Leah.

"You got in at what time?" Leah looked at Grace in shock then, looked at Matt in concern.

"One o'clock," Grace said proudly. "What time did you guys get in?"

Grace's parents looked at each other and laughed. "Ten." Leah finally admitted. "I think we're getting old."

Laughter ran through the room as the rest of the family arrived.

"Tessa and I are going out this morning to find a truck and trailer." Nick said as they walked up to them.

"You really don't need it do you?" Jack asked.

Nick shook his head, "Never hurts…I could always sell it back home."

"Grace and Reilly are getting out of the junior rodeo age and need a new outfit to get their horses around to rodeos; especially when they are at college. The three of us will go with you and I'll buy it for Reilly."

"Deal," Nick nodded.

As the morning plans were made, Matt finally let himself think of the upcoming vote. Josey was sitting next to him, his mother on the other side. As the morning progressed, Josey had grown quieter…her deal with Grayson coming to an end.

Matt stared out the room window and thought of Josey. He liked her and knew Nikki would be talking to her about coming to Idaho with them. Nikki was waiting until after the vote to know if she was coming as a Tagger employee or as a sister.

Matt thought of Elena…seeing her only thirty feet away. Why was she even trying to get into the hotel? Why had she followed the Tagger's to the café? Why had she tracked down Josey after everything she had done to her daughter?

Elena was brazen or desperate to go through all that trouble. If she didn't have a plan before seeing him in front of the hotel, she did when she left. That was the look she gave him…the wicked knowing grin. Whatever it was, Josey was her key to unlock the door to the Taggers.

But why was she going so far out of her way to target them? Why would she be coming after them again? Revenge for Nikki kicking her out of her life after her failed attempt at trying to blackmail Jack?   And what if she found out about Nick's life in Australia; what length would she go to get her hands on that money?

After the plans for the morning were set, the business voting meeting was called. Everyone left but the Trio, Nikki, Matt, and Lucas.

When the door was closed, Grayson turned and faced everyone. "I want to hire Frankie as the assistant horse trainer."

They all nodded, since they already knew.

He continued, "I know she comes with the threat of her mother, so I agreed with Dru that we should all discuss and vote."

"Just so you know," Nikki looked around the room. "I will be bringing her back, one way or the other."

Lucas sighed with a grimace and Nikki gave him a defiant glare.

Matt watched his mother lean back in her chair and cross her arms. "There is a difference between her being your sister and being an employee." She said to Nikki. "As your sister, there is limited threat. As an employee, it opens up the whole company to liability; both ranches."

"She'll be an employee of Circle 50." Nikki argued.

"That's why the contract was written per Lucas' recommendation." Scott nodded. "To protect one if something happens to the other."

"I'm not willing to risk that, Scott." His sister stood. "Over one employee, it's not worth it."

"There is no clear threat right now, Dru." Grayson replied.

She turned to Lucas. "Frankie works for Circle 50, trains a horse for Tagger Enterprises that is used at The Stables. Who is liable?"

"The entire company, all three business'," Lucas frowned.

"She's not going to do anything Dru." Grayson argued. "It would be the same as anyone else that took the job."

"But she's not just anyone. Elena is behind her, whether she likes it or not." She responded.

"With the protection of our family, Elena can't use her." Nikki pointed out.

"Nikki," Her mother turned. "We have to protect our family, our company, our employees…not just Frankie. We have half a dozen friends that we can call right now that will give her a job in Idaho, close to you. Why does she have to work for us?"

"Because there isn't a reason she shouldn't." Grayson answered. "She's more than qualified for what I need help with, and she can help with training the kid's horses. It's not her fault that Elena is there."

Matt watched his mother shake her head, his own mind racing with the impending vote.

"I won't be changing my mind." She said. "I vote no on the hiring, but we can help her find something else close by."

"I vote yes." Grayson nodded.

"I vote yes." Nikki added.

Grayson looked to Matt. "If you vote with Nikki, then your votes counts as three, and with my vote she becomes an employee. If you vote no it will be a tie…Scott makes the call."

Matt looked out the window and thought of home…Circle 50, Tagger Enterprises, the B&B, The Stables, The Homestead…most importantly the kids.

He thought of the terrifying phone call he received after Sadie crashed at the barrel race…she may have a broken neck…the terrifying ride to the hospital. He thought of the nights, standing over her, broken, bruised and in pain. His mind went to Nora, her face taking over the face of the little drowning victim as he first saw her, held her, and as he brought her to shore in front of the screaming parents.

His mind went to Grace facing the grizzly, Reilly falling over a cliff, and Wade breaking his arm…crawling through the blackness of night to save Monty.

As hard as he tried, he wouldn't be able to save the kids and his home, the company, from everything…but he would do everything he could to save them from Elena and anyone like her.

Matt looked around at his mother, uncles, Lucas, then to Nikki, who looked at him hopefully, expecting him to say yes.

"I vote no." Matt told her.

"Matt!" She cried out, he knew she felt betrayed. "I thought you liked her."

"I do like her, as a person," He told her. "But she is a threat, she will be…someday…a tool that Elena will use to get to us. My vote is to protect this family and our company. I agree with Mom, find her a job close, but not with Tagger Enterprises."

"Scott?" Grayson turned impatiently to his brother.

Scott sighed then did the same thing Matt had done; turned and looked out the window.

Matt looked at his mother. She was leaning against a table, staring at Scott, probably willing him to say no.

Scott turned, looked at Matt then to Nikki. "I will put my trust in her, and in you two," He looked between Grayson and Nikki. "I vote yes."

CHAPTER NINE

"You're taking my Frankie and leaving?" Jamie looked at him in concern.

"I am," Matt smiled. "We've hired her at the ranch."

"She'll be good," Jamie sighed. "She has a good heart."

Matt just nodded. He was still upset with the vote.

"Jamie!" Josey joined them. "I'm going to miss you."

Matt stepped back and let them say good-bye. Nikki had taken Josey to clear out her apartment while they loaded the horses in the four horse trailers. Their group was outside waiting in the trucks for them to say goodbye to Jamie.

"There is something I need to tell you." Jamie looked between Matt and Josey. She took a deep breath then looked at Josey. "Mary, the other waitress in the café, is the one that told your mother where to find you."

Josey and Matt looked at her in surprise.

"She was trying to help a mother and daughter reconnect. She had no idea about your history."

Josey smiled and hugged the woman again. "Things have worked out for the best. If it wasn't for that, I still wouldn't know I had a sister."

"Well, that's true." Jamie smiled; the relief easily visible on the older woman. She turned to Matt. "Take care of her."

"I will, thanks Jamie, and since they are all waiting for us…we need to go." He hugged the woman and headed for the door, giving the two women a private moment.

As he stepped through the front door, he stopped and sighed. All the trucks and trailers were gone except the new truck and trailer Jack had purchased. Grace and Reilly were in the back seat waving and grinning. He was supposed to ride with his mom while Josey rode with Lucas and Nikki in this truck.

"Where'd they go?" Josey said from beside him, looking at him in confusion.

"I guess they decided we're going back together." Matt sighed heavily and walked to the truck.

"It won't be that bad." Josey frowned while glancing at him with hurt in her eyes. Matt didn't answer as he checked his phone for messages. One text from his mother;

TEXT FROM DRU: Sorry, my idea. You needed your mind busy during the ride and Grace and Reilly will do that to you…Grace wanted Frankie to ride with them.

TEXT FROM MATT: Thanks for loving me, Mom. I love you too.

TEXT FROM DRU: Heart and soul

As he drove out of the parking lot, he looked at Josey sitting in the front passenger seat staring out the side window with a sad expression. Her arms were wrapped around her front, in her protected mode.

It was going to be a long nine hour drive back if he didn't let his anxiety and anger go and just relax.

"Josey?" Matt said.

She turned dejected brown eyes at him.

"I'm sorry, I didn't mean it that way."

"Are you sure?"

"The four of us had a great time last night, didn't we?"

She smiled and her eyes lightened. "Of course, we did."

"Then we should have a good time on the ride back." He smiled reassuringly.

She relaxed and her arms dropped to her sides.

"Where did you put all your stuff?" Matt asked her.

She grinned with a blush, "Well, the apartment was actually a small room in the back of an older couple's house, it came furnished. It took about ten minutes, a garbage sack for my clothes, and three boxes to pack."

"Really?" Matt chuckled.

"Yeah, I'm not much of a collector of things, but…" she grinned. "…I have four saddles."

Matt and the teenagers in the back seat laughed.

"A garbage bag, three boxes and four saddles?" Matt smiled at her.

"And one of the boxes is full of my bridles and halters." She giggled again.

They all laughed.

"You have four saddles?" Grace asked.

"There is my State Championship saddle, training saddle, barrel saddle, and one I've had since I started riding. I couldn't get myself to sell them."

"Cool!" Grace said excitedly. "You must be good."

"Yeah…I have four saddles and no horse… I had to sell him." Her tone was heavy in regret.

"So, back to the original question," Matt said loudly to lift her spirits back up. "Where is all your…one garbage sack, three boxes and four saddles?"

"In the horse trailer, behind us," She answered, leaning back against the headrest and looking at him. "It just happened to have an empty tack room that would fit four saddles."

Matt chuckled.

"Sadie is our barrel racer," Grace told her. "I do it too…we can't get Nora to do it, she says its Sadie's thing. They have this weird thing between the two of them. Nora does poles, starting on goat tying and cutting too but she mainly likes to show horses instead."

"Sadie's just getting back into it." Reilly added.

"What? Why?" Josey said and turned to them.

For the next few hours, they talked about Sadie's crash and rodeos.

Matt stopped in Missoula to let the new bay gelding and golden painted mare out and stretch.

"Nick hired me to ride both of them to make sure they're good for Tessa and Alex." Josey told them. "I'm looking forward to meeting Alex."

"He's a great kid." Matt nodded.

The next hour, after getting back on the road, they discussed the kid's clinic until Reilly and Grace fell asleep.

Josey stared out at the majestic mountains as they passed over the border into Idaho occasionally letting out a quiet oohhh or an ahhh at the view.

Matt's mind wandered to the road itself. He knew that his grandparents and great-grandparents' accident was on this road but didn't know exactly where since his mother and uncles wouldn't tell anyone. He could have researched the accident but felt like that would have been disrespecting the Trio as well as the four that perished. Their memories would remain at the ranch, not here so far from home.

What did the Trio think when they drove by the actual spot on the mountain pass where the truck driver had fallen asleep and hit the car, sending it over the edge?

"How long do we follow the river?" Josey asked and pulled him out of his thoughts.

"For quite a while; this is the Lochsa. We'll turn in Kamiah and head over the prairie to take the horses to the ranch instead of going to The Homestead. If we went to Lewiston, we'd follow the Clearwater all the way in.

"It's beautiful, so peaceful in some parts then just raging in others…powerful. Do people raft it?"

"All the time."

"Have you?" She asked and finally pulled her eyes from the river to glance at him.

"A couple of times."

"I would love that." She went back to staring at the river.

"Have you ever been rafting?"

"No…thought about it a lot, but just never had the opportunity."

"Well, other than the river at the ranch, there is the Clearwater and Snake Rivers by Lewiston."

"So, maybe someday," She nodded. "Oh, look! Elk!"

A small herd was crossing a shallow part of the river. Most were cow elk with a few calves at their sides but a few small bull elk mingled in with them.

Matt glanced at her to see her smile and dark brown eyes were lit with excitement. Her hair was down cascading over her shoulders and not covered with a hat. The black shirt she was wearing, along with the dark eyes, and hair seemed to give her a sultry look.

He stared out the window and finally had to admit it to himself… she was beautiful. Not just beautiful, but the most beautiful woman he had ever seen.

Josey looked like Nikki, but just enough to see they were related but there was a slenderness to Josey's jaw and her eyes were different; darker…more…sultry. The sisters were both beautiful but it was different with Josey.

"What were you going to go to college for?" Matt asked her, trying to distract his own thoughts.

Josey frowned and didn't answer.

"What?" He asked in surprise.

"I don't want to tell you." She said honestly and looked out the side window.

"Why?"

"Because you won't believe me…now."

"What does 'now' mean?"

"Nikki told me about the vote."

"I figured she would."

"I don't want you to think what I say is because of the job Grayson gave me."

"That's confusing."

"The papers are in my boxes, I saved them…just to remember what I lost."

Matt turned the truck and trailer into the first roadside pullout.

"What are you doing?" She asked, turning to him as the truck came to a stop.

"Go get the papers."

"What?"

"I'm curious and I'm not going to be able to think about anything else until I know why you don't think I'll believe you."

She hesitated…looking at him…debating.

"Fine," She slid out of the truck and went to the trailer and hauled back a box.

She pulled a few folders out of the box and set them on the seat.

"They must be in the other box." She turned and walked to the trailer.

Matt looked down at the file folder. A piece of paper was sticking out the side. He looked back at Josey, then to the folder, and slid the paper out. Using his phone, he took a quick picture of the paper, then slid it back in just as she returned. He didn't know why he did it, but his gut told him to.

"Here," She flipped the folder over to him.

It was a folder from The University of Montana Western, the paperwork was for a Bachelor of Science Degree in Business Administration-Equine Management.

"This is one of the colleges and degrees Grace is considering." Matt was impressed…then confused. "Why wouldn't you think I would believe you?"

"Isn't that what Grayson does for Tagger Enterprises?"

Matt looked at the description of the degree. "To a point…him, Mom, and Nikki."

"Would you have believed me, without seeing the paperwork?" She stuffed the files back in the box and put them back in the trailer tack room.

When she returned and he started down the road again, she turned.

"Aren't you going to answer?"

"I don't know if I would have believed you or not." He answered truthfully. "Why wouldn't I. As far as I know, you've never lied to me."

"I haven't."

"So…I don't know."

"Thanks for being honest."

"I'm always honest."

"Then tell me why you voted against me."

Matt frowned, he figured Nikki would have told her.

"Elena…she's not done yet, she'll come after my family…she was pretty determined in Billings…she's a threat to my family."

"I'm not Elena…"

"No, but you are the connection between my family and her."

"What are you two arguing about?" Grace asked from the backseat.

"Nothing." They answered in unison.

"Fine then," Grace sighed and looked out the window. "Hey, aren't we close to the Weitas?"

"The whatas?" Josey asked.

For the remainder of the trip, Reilly and Grace told Josey about the horseback ride that turned into a rescue of Adam and Amy from the plane crash.

Matt barely listened…his mind went back to Elena, it made him tired.

Close to home, as they reached the top of the mountain grade where their phones received cell service, he received a message.

TEXT FROM KEVIN: Need Trooper this time

TEXT FROM MATT: Where

TEXT FROM KEVIN: Meet us in Grangeville

He pulled into Circle 50 and handed the keys to Reilly.

"Take them over to the ranch, everyone will be waiting." He told him.

"Where are you going?" He asked in surprise.

"Loading up Trooper and headed out to meet Kevin."

"You just drove for 9 hours…" Grace reminded him.

"Another hour won't hurt." Matt answered, hugged Grace and nodded to Josey who was staring at him with a stunned expression.

Matt entered the barn to retrieve his horse's halter. As he stepped out he looked at the truck as it drove away. Josey was looking out the side window towards him. Seeing her moving away from him, caused an ache in the pit of his stomach.

He turned and walked to the pasture to an excited Trooper.

###

"Are you alright?" Matt looked over the edge of the bluff and into the brush…blackberry brush. It was thick with thorns that grabbed at your clothes, hair, and skin. They dug in, stinging, to make a person immobile.

"No," Came the voice in the brush. "Do I look like I'm alright?"

"Couldn't really tell…I can't see you." Matt answered honestly; glad the man couldn't see the grin on his face.

"Every time I move, they dig into me…it's like being stabbed by thousands of little knives."

"I'm guessing you were on the trail above and somehow ended up over the edge and fell into the middle?" Matt tied Trooper to the nearest tree then slid a hand down his neck and over his shoulder.

"Pretty much tells the story." The voice said. "How long have I been out here…I keep falling in and out of sleep."

"Three days."

"My wife has to be pissed."

"No, but she is pretty scared."

"It'll turn into pissed…once she finds out I'm OK."

"Why?" Matt asked as he took his knife out of his saddle bags, slid on his thick leather gloves and started cutting at the wicked bush.

"She told me I was stupid to come out here by myself to hike…be one with nature…as I so stupidly put it."

Matt chuckled.

"I heard that." The voice said accusingly.

"You'll chuckle too in a couple days."

"I imagine you're right. But right now…I'm hungry, thirsty, and tired of being a pin cushion."

"It will take me awhile to get you cut out."

"Do you have food and water?"

"I always carry energy bars." Matt grinned. "Water, too."

"Is there anyone with you?"

"Not right now, they're on their way."

"Who were you talking to when you found me?"

"Trooper, my horse."

"I rode one, once."

"Well, you'll get another chance once we get you out of there."

"Really?"

"Unless you want to walk."

"I don't think I could."

"The trees are too thick here to get a helicopter in to fly you out. We'll have to walk up a ways to a clearing up on top."

"You have two horses?"

"No, just Trooper, you can ride him, I'll walk."

"Ok, as long as you promise not to trip on a rock, go over the edge and land in the middle of a huge blackberry bush."

Matt laughed.

"I heard that too." The voice finally chuckled.

"Keep your spirits up," Matt encouraged him. "It will help. My name's Matt Tagger."

"Well, nice to sort of meet you, Matt. I'm Gary…but you already knew that since you called out my name earlier. How did you know I was here?"

"I tracked your footprints…after I finally found one. Next time, tell someone *exactly* the trail you're going on."

"If there is a next time… Can you even see me yet?"

Matt looked around and under the bush. "Not even a toe."

"Just so you know…"

"What? You're not going to tell me you're naked in there are you?" Matt teased.

"No," The man laughed. "I have shorts on."

"Ouch." Matt grimaced, thinking of all the bare skin being pierced by the thorns.

"And…I've kind of…"

"I know…don't worry about it. There is a creek not too far away that you can clean up in before we meet up with everyone."

"Did you bring extra pants too?"

"No, but we'll wrap you in a blanket so no one will know."

"It's got to be a hundred degrees out here."

"So you don't want the blanket?"

Gary chuckled. "I'll take the blanket."

"I see your hand."

"Oh, thank goodness." The hand waved.

It took Matt another half hour of cutting to get the man loose from the vicious tentacles of the bush.

"You look like you were put in a room with a dozen angry cats." Matt grimaced at the thousands of scratches and gashes covering him from forehead to ankle.

"I can't thank you enough." Gary smiled. "Does my wife know I'm OK?"

"Yeah, I radioed in after I found you."

"Well, she can get the mad out by the time we reach them."

"Anything broken?" Matt held out a hand to help him step out of the brush.

"No," He stepped gingerly out of the brush. "Where's the food and water?"

Matt helped him walk to the waiting horse.

"Well, there is one good thing." Matt said as he handed Gary a second bottle of water.

"What?"

"At least you weren't upside down."

CHAPTER TEN

It was 1:30 in the morning when Matt drove down the long driveway of The Homestead. The building was completely dark.

As he led Trooper to the barn, low whinnies greeted him from the side corral. He put Trooper in his stall with plenty of hay then walked back to the corral. He could just make out the three auction horses that Grayson had stated were Nora's to train; two sorrels and a grulla. He was disappointed that he wasn't there to see her meet the horses. With an exhausted sigh, he made his way to the house.

Every bone and muscle seemed to ache. He had walked 2 miles uphill leading Trooper with Gary riding before they found a good spot for the helicopter. Then it was another couple of hours of riding to get back to his truck and trailer.

There was no sound from the house as he took off his boots at the back door and quickly made his way to the guest bedroom. He stretched out on the comfortable bed and closed his eyes. From the rescue of the hikers, to the recovery of the little girl, the trip to Billings and the days trying to find Gary; it had been a very long two weeks.

When his eyes finally opened, Sadie and Nora were standing at the doorway whispering. Sadie was twelve and Nora fourteen but Sadie was at least four inches taller than her cousin.

"What are you two doing?" He asked without moving.

"Matt!" They cried out and ran to him.

"You've been sleeping forever!" Sadie informed him as she sat at the foot of the bed. Her long blonde hair was pulled back into a pony tail. Nora, with her long dark hair in two low ponytails, sat on the edge of the bed next to her.

Matt stared at her. She was safe, happy, relaxed, and right in front of him. He hadn't seen her since before the recovery of the little eight-year-old.

"I need a hug," Matt told them and slowly pushed himself up into a sitting position. Someone had placed a blanket over him.

Both girls crawled to the top of the bed next to their cousin and hugged him. They comfortably tucked themselves under his arms.

"Was it a bad one?" Nora asked, her live dark brown eyes looking into his own.

Just seeing her helped ease the image and memory.

"No, it just took us some time to find him." Matt answered.

"So it was a rescue not a recovery?" Sadie asked.

"It was." Matt pulled them tighter into him then told them about the man that fell off a trail and into the huge blackberry bush. Wade and Alex joined them, sitting up on the bed and leaning against the wall. Wade turned the TV on and the small group sat quietly and watched cartoons.

Matt sighed with a smile, just what he needed…kid therapy and Bugs Bunny. You can never be too old for Bugs Bunny.

He looked at the clock, it said 8:00. Looking outside, he could see it was daylight. So he either slept for seven hours or nineteen hours.

"What day is it?" Matt leaned his head on top of Nora's.

"Saturday of Memorial Day Weekend" She answered with a giggle. "You slept all day yesterday and all night."

"Wow, no wonder why I'm hungry." Matt chuckled.

"Aunt Dru said you were mentally exhausted." Nora said.

"You probably have to go to the bathroom too." Wade informed him with a smirk.

"Food and bathroom is exactly what I need." Matt nodded.

"We'll get you some breakfast." Sadie offered.

By the time Matt made it back to the bed, the girls had a large tray of fruit, toast, ham, milk, orange juice and coffee for him.

"You two are my favorite ladies." Matt thanked them.

"Hey, what about me?" Grace teased as she and Reilly joined their group by sitting at the foot of the bed, affectively filling it.

"You bring me food, and you can be a favorite lady too." Matt teased.

Grace walked back into the kitchen and returned with a muffin, which she threw at him.

It hit his chest and rolled down onto the tray.

"There," Grace giggled. "I'm a favorite too."

"Competitive much?" Matt teased just seconds before half the muffin disappeared into his mouth.

While Matt ate, the group of seven watched Elmer Fudd chasing Bugs Bunny again.

###

"You're riding all three already?" Matt asked Nora as she trotted the dark grey grulla gelding around the arena.

"Yes," She grinned proudly. "Uncle Grayson was with me the first time, just in case. This one was a little snot at first but all three are learning really fast."

She demonstrated by having the horse move his front quarters in a circle then the back quarters, a good straight backup, and she finished with a side pass to the left then to the right.

"Whoever did the initial ground work and desensitizing did really good." Nora said. "I worked them in the round pen at The Stables. On the ground first but was able to move into the saddle pretty quickly."

"Did you name them?" Matt asked.

"The Three Amigos," Nora smiled. "Martin and Steve are the sorrels, and this is Chevy."

"From the movie?"

Nora nodded with a grin.

Wade and Alex walked up to the fence and watched quietly for a few minutes. Nora moved the horse into jog. He looked pretty smooth and the gelding was responding to her cues quickly.

"Can Alex and I ride with you up to the ranch?" Wade asked. It was Memorial Day weekend and the whole family would end up at the ranches by the end of the day.

"I can always use the company." Matt nodded. "But you have to ask Tessa about Alex."

Three hours later they were pulling into the Circle 50 driveway.

"Looks like a ghost town." Matt looked around at the small house, large barn and corrals. He was very glad to be home. Although his dad had purchased the property for him and Nikki, it would always feel like Andy and Clara's house. He had memories going back to when he was three and four years old at this ranch since Clara would watch them when the Trio couldn't take them to work. It had always felt as home to him…as much as the Tagger ranch house did.

"Mom said they've been working with the horses all week." Alex informed him with a smile. "Frankie is riding my new horse."

"She is?" Matt's stomach tightened at the mention of her name.

"Yeah, Nick's paying her to work both horses they bought." Wade added.

"No names yet?" Matt looked at Alex.

He shrugged. "I'm not good at coming up with names. I've never named an animal before."

"What does he look like to you? The first time you saw him." Matt asked.

"I was just so excited." Alex admitted with a sheepish grin. "He looked like the best thing on the planet!"

They all three laughed as Trooper was released into the horse pasture. They left Circle 50 and drove to the Tagger ranch. It was time to see her again.

"I only got to see him for a couple hours the other day. I can't wait to be out of school." Alex sighed. "But it was so funny…"

"What?" Matt asked.

"He tried to eat my candy bar." Alex giggled.

"What kind was it?" Matt asked.

"A Snickers bar." Alex answered.

"Well, there you go…sounds like a good name to me." Matt smiled.

"Me, too." Wade laughed.

"What?" Alex asked confused then his eyes lit up. "Snickers! My horse's name is Snickers!"

"What about your mom, did she name the little mare?" Matt asked.

Alex and Wade started laughing.

"Nick won't let her," Alex grinned. "He said it's his horse and he'll name her."

"That's got to drive Tessa nuts." Matt laughed.

"It is. She's kind of pouted about it all week." Alex chuckled.

They drove into the driveway of the ranch just as Josey and Grayson walked out of the barn carrying saddles.

"Looks like we got here just in time," Wade said excitedly.

Matt took a deep breath and exhaled slowly. Seeing Josey, at the ranch, and looking like she'd been there forever. She had on her black sleeveless button up shirt that she bought in Billings and her black worn cowboy hat; her hair in a ponytail. She looked absolutely beautiful and took his breath away.

He nearly jumped when Wade slammed the truck door.

"I named my horse." Alex said excitedly as he limped to the waiting pair. "Matt helped me name him."

Matt slid out of the truck and walked to the group. He hid his inner turmoil of seeing her again, giving her a slight smile and a nod and then to Grayson.

Wade knelt down and greeted Grayson's puppy, Pepper, when it ran up to him.

"And what's the name?" Josey asked, her dark brown eyes shining.

"Snickers!" Alex told her.

Josey and Grayson both nodded.

"Sounds like a great name," Josey handed him the halter. "Why don't you go get him?"

"Really?" Alex hesitated. "All by myself?"

"Frankie's worked with him the last couple days, making sure he was ready for you this weekend." Grayson told Alex with a glance to Matt.

Matt and Grayson leaned against the fence and watched Josey, Wade and Alex walk to the bay horse.

"Bad one this time?" Grayson asked.

"No, just took us a couple days to find him, he'll be fine."

"Dealing with the other?"

"Yeah, seeing Nora this morning really helped."

They heard a truck approaching, and turned to see Nick and Tessa in the front seat. Red, the little cow dog, was sitting on the middle console like a queen.

"Those two are nearly inseparable." Grayson chuckled.

"I'm glad, they're good for each other."

"Ever find out why she fought it so hard?"

"No."

"Are you sure that's safe?" Tessa called out to them as she watched Alex walk up to his horse.

"Wouldn't let him do it unless it was," Grayson answered, lowering down to greet the puppy, Red, as she ran to him excitedly.

"I know…" She smiled hesitantly. "Sorry…I've just spent so much time protecting him by myself, I forget when to back off sometimes and let you guys do it."

Grayson nodded then turned to the group in the corral. "Frankie, bring in the paint mare for Tessa."

"I am so excited, my first ride on her!" Tessa grinned at Matt.

Already knowing the answer but wanting to stir the pot, Matt asked; "Did you name her yet?"

Tessa's face blushed and nodded towards Nick. "HE won't let me."

"Seriously, Dad?" Matt teased.

"It's my horse, I'll name her." Nick answered with a smart ass grin.

"Well, I've had a couple names for HIM this week." Tessa informed Matt with raised brows.

"We've all had a couple names for HIM." Grayson laughed.

Snickers and the paint mare were quickly saddled.

Matt watched Josey instructing Alex as he rode. She was so relaxed and happy and… Dang! She was just beautiful! His fingers started hurting; he looked down and realized he was gripping the fence so hard his knuckles were white. He relaxed his hand, hoping no one else noticed. He glanced around and saw both Grayson and Nick looking at him. By the raised eye brows and smirks, they both knew. He sighed heavily as the heat rose up his neck and into his face. Without a word he looked out to the horse and rider.

Once Alex was done, Tessa walked into the corral to ride the mare.

Nick untied the mare from the hitching post and walked her to the middle of the corral. When Tessa stepped up to the saddle, Nick stepped in between the woman and the horse.

"What are you doing?" Tessa giggled in confusion.

"You want to ride this horse?" He asked with a tilt of the head.

"You know I do, Nick." She placed her hands on her hips.

"There is only one way that I'm going to let you ride my pretty mare." He said.

"Watch what you say in front of the kids!" Grayson shouted out to them. Josey and Matt joined his laughter.

Nick turned and grinned. Tessa turned red.

"What do I have to do to ride your pretty mare?" Tessa asked politely with a smile.

"You have to accept her as a gift from me." Nick said seriously.

Tessa's smile faded. "Nick…" She whispered.

 No one spoke. The only sound was a horse walking in the adjoining corral.

"You know how I feel about that." Tessa said in a low voice.

"I do," Nick nodded. "But it's time you realize how I feel about you, and that I will be buying and giving things to you and Alex for a long time to come. I plan on taking care of the two of you…whether you like it or not."

Tessa wiped away a tear as they looked intently at each other.

"You are worth it, Tessa." Nick whispered.

Matt felt like he was intruding, but he couldn't get himself to look away.

"I love you, Nick." She whispered, wiping away another tear.

Nick stared at her long enough that Matt didn't think he was going to say it…but then realized his dad was trying to check his emotions first. Nick leaned into Tessa's ear and by the light in her eyes, the blush on her cheeks, and the smile that crossed her face, he said exactly what she wanted to hear.

Matt glanced over at Alex who was staring at his horse's nose; tears were sliding down his cheeks.

"So," Nick said after clearing his throat. "Are you going to stare at my horse, or ride your horse?"

"I think," Tessa smiled. "I will ride my horse." She touched his cheek with a gentle hand and kissed him tenderly.

"Well, dang." Grayson whispered and turned to Matt. "I didn't see that coming."

"Me either." Matt shook his head.

Nick helped Tessa onto the mare and smiled happily at her as she rode the horse away from him. Matt looked at Josey, she was wiping away a tear. He glanced at Wade, he had his head down, playing with the two puppies.

Nick walked to Alex.

The twelve-year-old looked up at him as he wiped away the tears. "Mom didn't think anyone would ever love her again." His voice cracked from emotion as the tears started falling again. "Thank you for loving my mom and making her happy again." Alex dropped the horses lead rope and threw his arms around Nick's waist. Nick returned the embrace, his back to the group at the fence.

"Well, dang." Matt whispered and turned to Grayson. "I didn't see that coming."

"Me either." Grayson nodded.

Matt took a deep breath and let it out quickly to release the emotions, "So," He said loudly to his uncle. "How are the other horses doing?"

CHAPTER ELEVEN

Matt spent the next week working with Scott in preparing the equipment for the first hay cutting of the season. The Circle 50 equipment either needed repaired or replaced and took up most of their time. He rode fences and checked on the cows. They had rebuilt and mended fences the summer before. This summer would be focused on replacing miles of fencing on the property before it fell. They would also need to rebuild the lower pasture corral system.

He'd barely had a glance of Josey as she remained at the Tagger ranch working with the horses.

Saturday was the Tagger Herd anniversary barbeque party at The Homestead and Sunday, weather permitting, the fields would be ready to cut.

"Do you want to drive down together?" Nikki asked as she dismounted from the red dun purchased at the auction.

"Yeah," Matt answered as he stepped off the stout blood bay he had purchased. The horse had been impressive in the ranch horse competition and he was more impressive under saddle. Trooper was still young at five, and had a lot to learn. The blood bay was nine and had been used on a working ranch before the auction.

"He seemed to do pretty well, but he's got a different gate about him. You look like you're bouncing."

Matt nodded with a smile. "He didn't start walking until half way through the ride. It's kind of a prance or jig."

"Is it annoying?"

"No, it's pretty comfortable. Try him out." He said and handed her the reins.

"Dang, he's tall." Nikki commented as she stepped up into the saddle.

She took the gelding for a trip around the pasture. The horse's hooves seemed to kick out as he walked, causing the slight bounce.

"I could do this all day!" Nikki grinned down from the horse.

"I think so too, it's a bit faster than a walk but not as choppy as a trot. We could cover some ground with him. We could use a dozen of him."

"I wonder what breed he is." She asked as she slid out of the saddle.

"Between the prancy walk, hairy fetlocks, and tweaked ear tips, I'd guess he's a draft mix...we could always do a DNA test."

"Got a name yet?"

"I think we go with Jiggers."

"Fits him perfectly!" Nikki nodded.

Matt poured the grain for the horses. "How's your gelding? You decide on a name yet?"

She held the gate for him then shut it after he passed through. She looked back at the dun who was eagerly eating his food.

"He's real handsome to look at and will be a wonderful horse but he trips a lot so I don't think he's used to a rocky hillside."

"So, his name is Trip?" Matt chuckled.

Nikki laughed, "Fits him for now. I'll pasture him in the west pasture that has the rocky ground. It'll help him learn to pick up his feet when he walks."

They hung the halters in the barn and walked to the house.

"Everyone else has already headed down. This is Frankie's first trip to town, she's been at the ranch all week. She's going to work with Sadie and Grace this morning on barrels and all the girls on poles."

Matt nodded. A little disappointed and a little relieved that he didn't have to ride the two hours with Josey.

"I can't wait to see the babies; I wish they were up here with us."

"Mom wouldn't let that happen." Matt smiled. "Even if Kit belongs to you and Leroy belongs to me."

Nikki nodded, then glanced at her brother. "Frankie's doing well."

"I know, Grayson told me…tells me, every chance he gets."

Nikki chuckled as she headed into her room.

A half hour later they were driving down the road to The Homestead.

When they arrived, Matt stepped out of Nikki's truck and was greeted by four grinning fathers.

"What?" He asked Jack, Scott, Grayson, and Nick.

"Prepare yourself." Jack smiled.

"For what?" Matt frowned.

"Leah and Tessa took Frankie shopping for an outfit for the party." Scott answered with his eyes twinkling mischievously.

"So?" Matt shrugged as he and his fathers walked towards the barn.

Halfway there, Matt stopped and stared at the ground. Tessa and Leah were notorious for their summer sundresses, basically their uniforms at the B&B. Which meant…Josey was in a dress…not her sleeveless shirts, jeans, and cowboy hat; and by the look on all their faces, she looked good.

Matt exhaled loudly, which caused all four men to burst out laughing.

"She's out watching Sadie ride barrels and Nora do poles." Nick informed him.

"Yep," Matt said and turned towards the house.

All four men laughed again.

"So what time does this thing start?" Matt asked Cora as he greeted his favorite cook.

"Around two." She gave him a welcoming hug. "It's good to see you."

"You, too." He jumped up and sat on the empty portion of the counter to talk with her. "So what are you fixing?"

"All the sides; Grayson and Jessup are barbequing steaks and burgers."

"Looks like you're almost done." He looked around at the clean kitchen.

"I am, baked all last night."

"Apple pie?"

"Of course," She washed the last dish and put it on the counter to dry. "Now, you can accompany me up to the arena."

Matt's heart skipped a beat. Already? He was hoping to delay it longer.

"I told Sadie I would come up and watch my golden girls ride with Frankie helping her."

"OK," Matt sighed and slid off the counter. He couldn't avoid her all day. At least it would just be with Cora.

But it wasn't, when he rounded the corner, the whole family was standing there watching Sadie ride. Nora had already ridden and Cooper was back in the barn. Josey was hidden from his view behind the cattle chute.

"Looks like everyone was curious," Matt said, his voice calmer than his stomach.

"Frankie must be feeling the pressure." Cora chuckled.

Matt kept his eyes from Josey as he watched Sadie ride and his mother turned to greet him.

"Hello, Son." She smiled.

"Hello, Mother." He smiled back and kissed her cheek. "How are they doing?" He kept his eyes on Sadie.

"They're just about done," She answered. "It's amazing the little things that Frankie has pointed out; they will definitely help Sadie and Nora's time. They're going to work more this week…Grace too…Winchester is coming up. I'd like to make it a family event like we did last year and Sadie will need the support."

"Great, that was fun surprising Wade." Matt nodded and looked up to see his fathers looking at him, all holding back smiles, but their eyes were twinkling in humor.

Wade opened the gate and grinned up at Sadie as she rode out. "Good job, Sadie."

"That was awesome." Sadie nodded and the two walked toward the barn.

Matt's heart was pounding as he saw Josey walking through the gate. She was smiling at Nora as they turned and walked to the family.

Josey's dark brown hair was hanging loose around her shoulders; large curls caused it to bounce as she walked. The form fitting dress was cream colored with little straps over her shoulders. Pretty blue flowers decorated the hem of the dress that stopped mid-thigh. Matt recognized Grace's blue dress cowboy boots she was wearing… walking… toward him… She looked like she just walked out of the cover of a western clothing magazine.

Matt's eyes went back to her smile. She turned and caught his eye, her chocolate brown eyes shining with laughter.

"That's quite the outfit for training." Matt teased as his pulse raced.

Josey blushed and giggled. Dang…

"Doesn't she look beautiful today?" Nora smiled at Matt.

Matt looked at his cousin then back to Josey. He knew everyone behind him was waiting for his answer.

"Well, Nora," He started. "She looks beautiful everyday…today is just a different beautiful." Matt answered honestly and smiled at the woman in question.

Her blush deepened and her brown eyes sparkled as she grinned at him.

"Oh, Matt!" Nora's eyes widened. "That was so nice!"

He smiled at his cousin as the group behind him chuckled and they all walked towards the house.

"You just melted the hearts of every female that heard that." Nick laughed as he met up with him. "You must get that from me."

"No, had to be me." Scott walked up next to them.

"He definitely learned it from me." Grayson argued. "Just ask Leah."

"I'm pretty sure Dru would agree…he learned it from me." Jack laughed.

Matt rolled his eyes at his fathers and walked into the house with a grin.

It was a lot of work to keep from staring at her. Grace was dressed nearly the same as Josey, the flowers on her dress were pink, as well as her boots. They had quickly become close friends.

Matt's phone alerted him to a text;

TEXT FROM JACK: no message…it was a picture of Josey and Grace posing for the camera, showing off their boots… which basically was their legs.

Matt shook his head and looked across the kitchen to his step-father. Jack was grinning.

A few minutes later:

TEXT FROM NICK: no message…it was a picture of Josey, Sadie and Nora grinning happily for the camera

Matt took a deep breath and put the phone in his pocket.

A few minutes later he was digging it out again…

TEXT FROM GRAYSON: no message…it was a picture of Josey standing next to Sadie and Scarecrow. Josey's long legs showing beautifully and both Sadie and Josey were grinning.

Matt looked over at Scott…phone in hand …and waited.

Scott looked up at him, chuckled like a little kid, looked at his phone and typed.

Matt looked at his phone when the alert went off.

TEXT FROM SCOTT: The picture was of Josey standing between Reilly and Wade; all three grinning. Her arms were up and around their shoulders…which meant her dress was even higher on her thighs, showing more leg.

Matt turned off his phone, set it on top of the refrigerator and walked away from the roguish chuckling of all four men.

Smiling, he walked into the living room just as Tessa and Nikki were walking in the front door.

"There you are, Matt." Tessa smiled. "Would you mind? I'd like to talk to you and Nikki for a few minutes."

Matt shrugged. "No problem."

"Somewhere private?" She asked tentatively.

"How about the island out in the pasture?" Nikki suggested.

Tessa nodded and the three of them walked out to the fenced in benches in the pasture. The shade from the oak trees was needed for the warm day.

Matt sat next to Tessa with Nikki on the bench across from them.

"Is everything OK with you and Dad?" Nikki asked.

Tessa nodded with a grin. "It's funny talking to my boss about her dad."

Nikki nodded. "Right now…I'm not your boss, I'm your boyfriend's daughter." She informed her.

Tessa giggled, "Boyfriend…that sounds so odd."

"Especially thinking of Dad as a boyfriend to anyone," Matt chuckled.

"Well, that is what I wanted to talk to you two about." Tessa took a deep breath, it shook when she exhaled.

Nikki and Matt waited quietly for her to speak.

Tessa looked at Matt. "Nikki is a little ahead of you on this one."

Matt nodded with a frown, glancing up at Nikki; she was looking intently at Tessa.

"When she and Dru offered me the job at the B&B, I had to tell them…" She paused and looked worriedly at him. "I don't talk about this…"

"It's OK Tessa." Matt encouraged her; having no clue what she was about to say but realizing how much she had in common with his dad.

"A few years ago…I was sick." Tessa rolled her eyes. "Sick…that's true and not true…"

"Tessa, just spit it out." Matt took her hand and squeezed.

She grasped his hand and looked down at it. "I love that habit your family has…reaching out to hold hands when someone needs that extra support."

"Tessa…you're stalling." Matt smiled at her.

She giggled, "You're right…I am. OK…just spitting it out." She paused, took a deep breath, looked at Matt straight in the eye and said…nothing.

"Tessa…does Dad know what you're about to say to me?" He asked and she nodded. "Has he run away screaming?" He smiled when she chuckled and shook her head. "Well, neither will I…so just say it."

"I had breast cancer…I am a survivor of breast cancer, two years now." Her voice shook and her eyes dropped.

"Good for you." Matt smiled and glanced at his sister with a confused raised brow. Nikki was frowning.

"Why do you have such a hard time saying it?" Nikki asked.

Tessa nodded, "That's what I want to talk to you about…about Nick…he…" Tears sprung to her eyes.

Matt and Nikki waited in silence.

Tessa shook her head as if to clear her mind. "Let me start from the beginning." She paused, and spoke with her eyes closed. "Ok, when I was 29 I was diagnosed with cancer, I went through chemotherapy and had a single mastectomy. My support system was my brother and my mother." She opened her eyes and looked at Nikki. "They live in Moses Lake, I was living in Spokane at the time, so we were close to Shriners Hospital for Alex's leg."

"I've never heard you speak of them." Nikki told her.

"I don't…their support…didn't end up well." Tessa sighed.

"How can family support go bad?" Matt asked.

Tessa sighed heavily. "When I decided to have the mastectomy instead of just relying on chemo and radiation, they informed me that I wouldn't be a whole woman without my breast."

"WHAT?" Both Matt and Nikki cried out in disbelief.

Tessa nodded. "It got pretty ugly, and in my condition, mentally and physically, it ate at my self-esteem and I became depressed."

"Tessa, there are so many organizations to help…people that have gone through the same thing…" Nikki said, her eyes full of compassion.

"I know, and I was given all the information…but…they were my family…the people that are supposed to be the most honest with you." She sighed again. "After my hair grew back and I started to get back on my feet, I realized how controlling they had become. While

I was going through chemo, they had papers drawn up for me to give them custody of Alex."

"WHAT?" Both Matt and Nikki cried out again.

"I had refused, of course, but they figured that I would have a hard time taking care of myself, let alone a special needs child."

"He doesn't have special needs," Matt argued. "He just limps."

Tessa smiled up at him. "I wish they would have thought that. So just before I met you, just days in fact, we moved here to Lewiston to get away from them but still be close enough to Spokane and Shriner's Hospital."

"And within a week you were working for us." Nikki smiled.

"It was the most…wonderful thing that could have happened to me…but also the most terrifying."

"Why terrifying?" Matt asked.

"Your dad," She smiled timidly. "The first time I met him and your uncles, I didn't even think of him as anything but this nice guy teaching us to rope and ride. Then, when he asked to take Alex shopping, I nearly had a heart attack. Then he bought the boots, and I was furious!" She chuckled. "He had to talk me off the ledge!" They all chuckled. "That night…after I calmed down," Tessa smiled. "I realized that he was just this great guy trying to help, not take over my son."

"That's funny, if you know Nick's history with kids." Matt chuckled.

"I know now…but I didn't know then." Tessa leaned back against the bench. "Each time I saw him I relaxed and just started to like him being around. And then came Christmas." Her eyes widened and she shook her head with a wry grin.

"What happened at Christmas?" Nikki asked.

"Well, first was the sleigh…that beautiful sleigh." Tessa's eyes sparkled. "He had Wade hend Reilly ask me if Alex could help…smart man. It was a Christmas surprise right out of the movies…with Alex driving! He'd taken the time to teach Alex how to drive it…to be part of the whole process and surprise…not have him stand off to the side because of his limp."

"That was one of the best surprises." Matt agreed.

"Then came the puppy, Red," Tessa sighed with a smile. "He put up such a fight for all of 30 seconds when Dru handed him the puppy. I was watching him and Alex play with the puppy out in the snow…Nick and Alex's eyes were just glowing with happiness as they talked and played." She paused and looked between Matt and Nikki. "I realized, at that moment, that I was falling in love with your dad."

"Tessa, that's wonderful." Nikki smiled. "But why…?"

"I wasn't the woman he thought I was…I wasn't a whole woman," Tessa sadly reminded her. "Because of the mastectomy, my mother and brother…what they said, how I felt…so self-conscience about the scar, the missing breast." She closed her eyes, inhaled deeply and exhaled slowly. When she opened her eyes, she continued, "The first couple times I told anyone I had breast cancer, I thought they just looked right at my chest to see if they were real or not…so I quit telling anyone." Her hand subconsciously moved to her chest. "I had a weight problem when I was in high school, so I have always been self-conscience about my body. I had just lost a lot of weight before I found out about the cancer and lost more during the chemo, I've never come to terms with it in my head." She glanced down at her and Matt's entwined hands then up to him and Nikki. "I just couldn't see a man like Nick, loving someone like me, wanting to be with a woman…that wasn't whole…I wasn't worth it…worth him."

"Oh, Tessa," Nikki wiped away a tear.

Matt squeezed Tessa's hand tighter. His own stomach tightened and throat constricted in the emotion she had chosen to show them…to trust them with.

"I did everything I could to keep away from him," She smiled at the two of them. "When Sadie was hurt, and I saw how compassionate he was with her as he cradle-hugged her. The story they told…I, just for a second, thought maybe he could…" Tessa shook her head. "Anyway, before Billings, when Matt sent him down to 'fix it' we had quite the battle." She blushed.

"I don't think we want to hear all of that." Nikki sat back on the bench and shook her head.

"Not all of it," Tessa giggled, turning more red. "But when he finally got it out of me, about the cancer, the mastectomy, the scar…" She looked towards the house. "Honestly, if it wasn't for Sadie and his persistence, I don't think I would have said anything."

"Sadie?" Matt asked in surprise.

Tessa smiled; "When we rode together during branding, she told me about her love for Little Ghost…and her love for every inch of his scars. She said the scars were a symbol of the fight…the battle he had in staying alive." Tessa looked up at Matt, her eyes still moist but content. "She started crumbling the wall I had up. I started believing that my scar was a symbol of my battle…who I was…a survivor."

"We'll have to thank her." Matt whispered softly.

Tessa nodded, "She had no idea what the comment meant to me…and Nick..."

"How did he…" Nikki started.

Tessa rolled her eyes and grinned. "He said his scars were more impressive than mine, and if he showed me his, would I show him mine so he could prove it."

"Just the scar on the back of his arm is ugly but impressive." Matt chuckled.

"Yeah, it's pretty bad." Tessa nodded. "That's what you get for having a drunk veterinarian stitch your tear from a bull horn."

"And the knee, the ribs, the inside of his other arm…" Nikki continued.

"Bull rider!" Tessa giggled. "He asked me if they bothered me…which they didn't…he asked if his scars made him less of a man…which of course they didn't. Then it was just convincing me that my scar didn't make me less of a woman. Which…" Tessa turned red. "Is the end of this story!"

They all three laughed, each a little embarrassed.

Tessa took a deep breath and let it out. "I wanted you two to know about the cancer, what happened with my family, Alex, and why I fought the feelings I had for your dad." She smiled between the two of them. "I just didn't want to hide this from you anymore. It is something I work on all the time…to heal inside too. That way, if I do something, or say something, you'll have an idea why I react the way I do."

"Tessa," Matt looked at her in concern. "You have to know that Dad has as many scars on the inside as he does on the outside."

"I understand that…we've gotten into some good discussions about it." Tessa nodded. "We both want to help the other heal on the inside, too. We'll just have to be patient with each other." She smiled. "Which is why I named my horse,Patience."

"Oh, I love that." Nikki smiled.

"Patience the palomino paint." Matt laughed.

Nikki reached out and placed her hand over Matt and Tessa's that were still clasped together. "You need to share, not hold these things in, it will help."

Tessa nodded. "I'm going to talk to Dru, Jordan, and Leah next, but I wanted you two to know first."

"This had to be hard on Alex." Matt frowned.

"And Nick knows…and now you…" She nodded. "He's talked to Nick about it a couple of times, I think it's really helped him not having to hold it all in."

"I'll let him know he can come to me if he needs someone." Matt assured her.

"Thanks, Matt." Tessa squeezed his hand tightly. "Alex has been through so much, and my making him hold it in and him having to deal with me and my insecurities…?" She shook her head, tears falling again. "He is my life…" Her voice trailed off.

Matt pulled her to him and wrapped her in a strong embrace…sometimes holding hands wasn't enough.

CHAPTER TWELVE

Matt checked the straps on the full load of hay on the truck, then the trailer he was pulling. Good quality hay, Matt sighed in satisfaction and looked at the threatening sky.   After a week of cutting, raking, baling, and hauling, the large round bales were already wrapped for protection.   The large square bales were stacked and covered. All they had left was clearing the fields of the small bales that were sold or stored and fed to the horses belonging to Tagger Enterprises.

Every family member was driving or bucking bales as fast as they could to get the hay in the barn before the rain started.

Matt turned to Wade and Reilly, "You two head over to the north lower pasture where Mom is baling. Nora's driving truck with Scott and Grace bucking bales. Help them out while I take this to the main barn at Tagger Ranch."

They quickly jumped in Reilly's new truck and drove away.

Matt looked at his watch as he slid into the driver's seat. The ranch hands they had hired to help for the summer would be waiting for him at the barn.

As he came within sight of the ranch buildings, he could see Josey standing between the barn and a truck that belonged to Conner, one of the hired ranch hands. Matt didn't see the second ranch hand, but what he did see concerned him.

Josey was standing with her arms wrapped in front of her; her protective mode. Conner took a step toward Josey and she stepped backwards, her head turning to look at Matt and the truck. Conner turned, saw Matt approaching, and disappeared into the barn.

When Matt stopped the truck next to Josey he looked at her in concern but she just turned to open the barn doors. He turned the truck and backed the trailer into the barn.

Without a word to each other, the hired men unhooked the straps holding the hay down.

"You OK?" Matt whispered to Josey as they balanced on top of the load and handed the bales from the trailer to the men on the ground.

"Yes," She said quickly and grabbed another bale.

Matt caught the eye of the other hired hand, Kyle, who frowned at Matt then turned away.

How was he supposed to interpret that? The four continued to work in silence.

When the trailer was unloaded, Matt walked to the truck and Josey followed. She stood outside the barn while Matt unhooked the trailer then backed the truck into the barn to unload the hay from it. Josey stayed out of the barn until Matt climbed out of the truck. He looked at her in concern.

She didn't respond, just crawled up on the truck to hand the bales down to Kyle. Matt handed bales down to Conner.

"We can get another load in here," Matt told the group. "Conner, Kyle, you two meet up with Jessup in the south field where he is working on the small bales to fill up the remainder of this barn. The rest goes to Circle 50. Do you know where he is?"

"I do." Conner smiled innocently and jogged to the truck.

"I'll drive." Kyle pushed him out of the way and Conner laughed nervously and ran to the passenger side. He climbed in without looking at Matt or Josey.

As soon as they left, Matt looked at Josey. "What happened?"

She shook her head, "Nothing."

He cocked his head to the side and looked at her intently, letting her know he didn't believe her.

"He just asked me out tonight." She sighed.

Matt didn't move; he waited for her to continue.

"I told him I wasn't old enough. He said it didn't matter, he could get me in the bar anyway, no problem," She looked up at Matt. "I said no, I wasn't interested, and he was trying to convince me."

"How?"

She frowned. "He's not good, Matt."

"What do you mean?"

"I've been around enough people like him…he's going to be trouble and not just with me."

"Have you talked to Grayson?"

She shook her head.

Matt looked up at the sky. The dark grey clouds were rolling in quickly; the rain could be seen at a distance. "We'll be done bringing in the hay tonight, just before it rains. Grayson wants to ride in the morning to check on the fence in the heifer pasture before we move them in there. We'll talk to him in the morning and let Conner go."

Josey nodded and they left to help clear the fields.

The rest of the afternoon was uneventful with all the hay loaded in all the different barns well before the rain hit. It was a downpour for the first few hours, then quickly declined and stopped after dark.

###

Matt lay in bed thumbing through the book Sadie and Leah had put together of all the pictures taken during branding. He couldn't get enough of it…especially the cover shot of the group picture with the first calf to be branded with the Circle 50 brand. What a rough looking group of characters…his family…he laughed to himself.

Lucas had been overjoyed by the book of pictures Sadie had taken of Nikki. He had only expected one picture but couldn't have been happier with the collection Sadie gave him. Matt had to agree, they were stunning pictures of his sister. He'd only seen it once before it was taken to Australia.

His phone alerted him to a message.

TEXT FROM GRAYSON: Went home last night, will be up later to ride

Matt rolled out of bed and looked out the window. The weather was still grey and dismal but not raining.   It was too muddy for a run. He sure wished they had space for a fitness room at the ranch but the house was too small. Andy and Clara had raised three boys in the house but Matt had never realized how small it actually was until he and Nikki had moved in.

Nikki had stayed at The Homestead the night before with plans on working with their mom for the day. Jessup and Josey were at the Tagger Ranch so he decided to drive down to the heifer pasture and check the road for later.

He poured himself a large bowl of cereal and thumbed through the branding picture book again. Quickly getting bored after the last page was flipped, again, he quickly dressed then stomped through the mud to his truck and drove down the road. His mind went to Josey's posture when Conner was talking to her. He was beginning to really hate seeing her in the protection mode.

He crested the mountain and headed down the dirt road to the heifer pasture. There was a truck in front of him. Matt leaned forward and his eyes narrowed as he concentrated on the truck; something was off.

As he neared the truck he could see it wasn't moving…it was just off to the side of the road and tilted into the ditch. It was a Tagger Enterprises flatbed truck with wood slat stock racks on the back for hauling horses or cattle. Why was it out here?

He was within 50 feet when he saw something that made his heart stop, then race. A movement from the back of the truck; there were animals in the back! The truck was sitting at a steep angle which was dangerous to the animals inside.

He stopped his truck within feet of the ditched one then opened the door and stood on the side rail…there were horses inside! Tagger horses! But as high as he could stretch, he still couldn't tell which ones.

Matt reached for his phone. The closest person to help would be Jessup and Josey.

Jessup didn't answer but Josey did.

"Josey, where are you?" Matt asked as he stepped out of the truck and headed around to the back of the tilted one.

"At the training corral."

"Find Jessup, get to the top of the heifer pasture road as soon as possible, Jessup will know where it is." His voice was strained and gruff.

"Matt?" She asked concerned. He could hear her boots hitting the ground as she broke into a run.

"The stock truck is in the ditch with horses in the back." Matt climbed on the top of his truck and looked in the stock racks. "Four horses, they are at a pretty odd angle, leaning against each other."

"Jessup!" He heard her yell.

"Josey, get here fast." Matt ended the call and climbed up on the racks and maneuvered to the side.

The first horse, leaning on all the others was one of the new horses from the auction. He lifted his head and turned pain-filled eyes towards Matt. It caused a groan from the other horses. The second horse was one of Andy's older horses, a bay with a long blaze down his nose. He had just looked at the horse in the branding book…Jordan had ridden him. His head was up but resting over the third horses head. Matt climbed up higher. It was a grey horse…Little Ghost was at The Homestead and Tagger Enterprises only had one other grey horse…

"Monty!" Matt yelled and made his way to the front of the racks to climb on the top of the cab and looked down over the racks that rose three feet over the cab. "Monty!" He yelled again, his heart racing…nearly panicking.

The second horse moved his head which gave Monty room to lift his. Matt leaned down over the rail and reached down to the horse; his breathing was labored from the weight of the other two horses on him.

He reached for his phone.

Scott answered and Matt quickly filled him in.

"Is he all right?" Scott's voice was as panicked as Matt's heart.

"His breathing is bad. Jessup and Josey are on their way here."

"Who else is in there?"

"One of the auction horses, Andy's old bay gelding, Monty, then…"

"Matt?"

Matt reached over the rail to grab the fourth horse's halter and lifted. "Freddy, the sorrel Alex rode at branding…Andy's last horse…he's bad, barely breathing. He's…" Matt gasped.

"Matt!"

When he had lifted Freddy's head, he glimpsed a fifth horse lying underneath him.

"There's a fifth horse…it's a buckskin." Matt's heart nearly stopped. "It's dead."

"Is it Eli?" Scott yelled.

CHAPTER THIRTEEN

Matt tried to move the 4th horse's head to get a clearer look at the horse underneath.

"Matt, is it Eli?" Scott yelled again.

"I can't tell," Matt answered, his heart racing. "He's jammed underneath and I can't tell. I gotta go Scott so I can get them out of here. I'll call as soon as I know."

"I'm on my way…I'll call Dru and Grayson."

Matt tossed the phone behind him and looked over the outside edge of the stock rack. The buckskin's side was pushed against the slats of wood that created the rail. He could just see the coloring of the hide and a portion of the black tail but still couldn't tell if it was Eli.

He sat back up and looked at Monty and the other horses. He had to concentrate on getting them out, before he lost them, too. There was nothing he could do about the buckskin now, whether it was Eli or not.

His phone rang.

"Is it Eli?" Grayson's voice was strained and desperate.

"I don't know yet. He's jammed underneath two of the others." Matt sighed. "I didn't even know he was there. Grayson," Matt tried to contain his rising fear. "Was he pastured with Monty?"

"Yes." Was the abrupt answer which made Matt's insides quiver.

"Was there any other buckskin pastured with him?" Matt asked, nearly holding his breath for the answer.

"No," Grayson answered in a low gruff voice.

"They've been out here all night. It slid off the road. It looks like it happened during the rainstorm. Why are they here?"

"I told Conner to load five of the newer horses and take them to the heifer pasture corral this morning. Neither Eli or Monty should have been in that truck, let alone Andy's older geldings."

"Conner did this?" Matt felt the anger rise in him but pushed it down; there wasn't time for that now. "I gotta go Grayson, I'll call as soon as I know." He ended the call.

Jessup and Josey appeared over the hill. Both burst from the truck as soon as it stopped. Behind them was Warren, the foreman of the neighboring ranch. He jumped out of his truck, too.

"I need rope." Matt yelled at Jessup and the older man turned and stepped into the back of his truck, the tool box in the back opened.

Josey climbed up on Matt's truck then leaned over into the stock rack. Her eyes widened in shock. "Is that Monty?"

Matt nodded.

"Monty's in there?" Jessup hollered, as he limped up to the truck.

Matt nodded again. "There's a fifth horse underneath Monty and Freddy." He took a deep breath and looked at Jessup. "It's a buckskin."

Shock registered on Jessup's face and Josey gasped.

"Eli?" Jessup's face tensed.

"I don't know. We need to get the others out…concentrate on them."

"What can I do to help?" Warren asked.

Matt looked around and accessed the situation. "Move all the trucks around and out of the way. Back mine up to this one so we can pull it out when ready."

"What do we do?" Josey asked.

"If we back out this truck, then the horse underneath rolls into the legs of the others." Matt told them. "We have to secure the buckskin so he can't roll."

"How?" Josey asked.

Matt stared at her then looked down into the horses. "You'll have to go in, Jessup and I are too big."

"OK." Josey said without hesitation and walked along the side of the rail toward him.

"Jessup, the rope." Matt took one end and handed it to Josey.

"The horse isn't all the way down; his head is tucked underneath him. You'll have to find a way to get the rope around him and get it to Jessup on the outside."

Josey nodded and Jessup limped to the other side next to the exposed hide of the buckskin.

"If you can get it through, then you'll tie him up to brace him. Twice around him is better." Matt told them.

"OK." They said in unison.

Josey stepped over the rail and lowered herself over the edge and slowly slid in front of Andy's older bay. Matt stepped over the rail and slid his boot tips into the slats just above the horse's heads. He leaned down to make sure he could reach her. "If anything happens, I'm yanking you out."

Her brown eyes looked up into his; they reflected full trust in him. They nodded to each other and after a deep breath she turned to the horses. She spoke softly to them, reassuring them.

Just as she dipped underneath Monty's neck, Matt's phone rang. He ignored it.

"Talk to me, Josey." Matt said, staring down toward her.

"I can't tell if it's Eli, but I can get an arm underneath his neck." She said and Matt saw the rope start to move.

"I see it." Jessup confirmed. "Move it up…more…got it."

"Wrap it around one of the wood slats then feed it back through." Matt told him.

"Got it," Josey confirmed. "Across the body this time, Jessup, to hold him more secure."

"Ok." Jessup sighed.

"This is awful," Josey whispered from below.

"Sorry, Josey," Matt sighed. His eyes went to Monty who was just below him. The horse's breathing was labored. They had no choice; he needed help now.

"Not your fault. How did they get here? Who did this?" She asked from under the horse.

"Conner," Matt told her, then heard a string of words from her and Jessup that he'd already said in his head.

"I got the rope, tying it off." Jessup hollered.

"There's blood down here." Josey informed them.

When she stood, there was blood down her left shoulder and across her back.

Matt took a firm grip on the back of her belt, lifted her up and stepped over the rail to help her out.

"Got it Jessup?" Matt yelled.

"Got it." He answered.

Matt turned and looked at the trucks; Warren had everything ready to pull the truck out of the ditch and was watching from the hillside on the opposite side of the road. Jessup slid into Matt's truck.

"Josey, get in this truck. Guide it back as Jessup pulls us out." Matt said then looked across the road. On the other side was a smaller ditch but it was at the base of a rise in the hill. "Josey, look." He pointed.

She nodded.

"If you back us into that ditch, the door to get the horses out will be even with the hillside, or close enough to get them out without having them fall three feet down."

"Got it, but Matt?" She turned with a slight smile. "You have to let go of my jeans."

He immediately let go of her and she slid off the truck and into the cab.

He leaned over the rail and stretched out to Monty. The horse's breathing was even more labored. Then he reached out to Freddy, Andy's older sorrel gelding. He was bad…breathing was raspy and strained.

"Almost boys," Matt whispered. "Just hold on."

"You all ready?" Jessup hollered.

"Ready," Josey and Matt said in unison.

Matt stared into the darkness between Freddy and the rail…waiting to see…dreading…Eli had been pastured with Monty…

The truck jerked, the horses jolted over to the other side and the truck leveled out. Monty inhaled deeply when the pressure of the two horses was removed from his side.

Matt slid himself along the rail to look down at the buckskin. He reached for his phone.

"Is it him?" Grayson answered.

"No." Matt felt his whole body shake in relief…they hadn't lost one of the Tagger herd.

Grayson was silent.

"It's the little buckskin from the auction."

"He grabbed horses from two different pastures? I just don't understand where is mind was." Grayson said in disbelief.

"Probably in a can or a bottle." Matt sighed.

"I'll be there in 30." Grayson told him.

Matt ended the call and then called Scott as Jessup unhooked the chain from the two trucks. He repeated the news.

Then he called his mother and repeated the news.

"Conner is in jail," She said. "Probably for the best, before one of us got ahold of him."

"What's he in jail for?"

"From what I've found out so far, he was in the bar when Grayson called him and he decided to move the horses last night instead of in the morning, so he didn't have to get up early. After he went into the ditch, he caught a ride and went back to the bar…without telling anyone about the horses. At two o'clock he picked up a girl and was driving her car. When the sheriff pulled him over and was arresting him for the DUI, Conner got belligerent, so they got him for resisting arrest too, but he still didn't tell anyone about the horses."

"If he'd just told someone…" Matt sighed as he sat up.

"I know," She said. "I'm right behind Grayson, we'll be there in about 10."

He ended the call just as Josey turned sharply and put the truck's back wheels into the ditch; the truck was level. Matt carefully lowered himself over the rail and slid into the back of the truck.

He ran his hand over the first horse's back. It shivered but didn't panic, so he slid along the side and behind the horse to reach the door.

"There's a gap." Josey called out.

"How big?" Matt asked. A small gap between the truck bed and the dirt would be OK.

"About a foot and a half…just enough for one of the horses to drop a leg down." She answered.

Matt heard a groan and turned to see the old sorrel start to tremble. He needed to get them out before that horse went down into the other horse's legs.

"Josey, there are boards in the back of my truck." Matt said.

"Got it!" She ran to his truck, climbed in the back and handed them to Warren and Jessup.

"They have halters on but I need lead ropes." Matt called out to her.

"On it!" She yelled and ran to Jessup's truck to pull out a number of ropes out of the tool box.

The boards were placed to create a bridge over the gap.

Matt slowly opened the door so the horses didn't try to bolt. He walked across the 'bridge'.

"It feels OK…strong enough to hold their weight…briefly. It'll be easier to get Monty out first since he and the door are in the middle. Josey, handle the door."

She tossed him the lead ropes then jumped on the racks to grip the door.

Matt slowly made his way to the front of the horses.

Monty's breathing was better, but he had blood smeared down his side. He couldn't tell if it was Monty's or not.

"OK." Matt nodded to Josey and she opened the gate.

The big grey horse slowly backed out of the truck but he had an obvious limp.

Andy's sorrel gelding groaned again, and he stumbled sideways.

Matt quickly backed out the old bay horse and the auction horse. Freddy groaned again but remained upright. Matt took his halter, turned him, and walked him out, handing Josey the lead rope.

He turned back to the buckskin. "Jessup, untie the buckskin. I don't want to leave him this way."

After the buckskin was released, his body relaxed and spread across the truck bed. Matt ran his hand down the dead horse's neck and shook his head. He was the first horse Grayson had bid on at the auction. "Sorry, boy…you should have had a better and longer life than this. *You leave us now…To fly in the sky…Green pastures to run…Under a warm sun to lie. Fly High My Friend.*"

Matt slid a hand across the horse's shoulder and sighed. He walked out of the back of the truck, across the makeshift bridge, and watched Jessup and Josey check over the horses.

"Most of the damage is on their legs." Jessup informed him. "Stepping on each other and trying to fight to get out. I called Kate, Grayson had already called her. She's on her way…right behind Dru." There was no doubt they would need the veterinarian's help.

"Matt?" Warren asked.

"Yeah?" Matt looked over at his concerned expression.

"What can I do?" He asked.

"Take my truck to Circle 50 and get the stock trailer at the side of the barn." Matt answered and the man took off at a run to the truck.

Matt jumped down off the side of the hill and headed towards Monty. He ran is arms over him.

"He's got a few cuts on his legs, not bad though. The limp is gone…he just needed to stretch it out." Jessup informed him. "I'm more concerned about the damage on the inside of him, from the two horses laying on him all night. "

"The others?"

"The first one from the auction is doing well but it looks like he fought the most, probably because he could actually move. He has more damage on his legs and face." Jessup answered. "The second, the bay horse had blood on his sides and down his legs from cuts and scratches, which is what's on Monty. There's about a seven inch round, one inch deep gouge out of his hide on his rump and he has a worrisome cut along his hock."

"Andy's sorrel?" Matt asked.

"Not good." Jessup answered with a sigh.

"Better get him up the road and out of the way of the vehicles." Matt sighed.

"On it," Josey said and slowly moved the horse up the road then up to the flat field. She spoke quietly…soothingly to the horse.

Matt walked over to the second horse that had the gouge in his rump. "That's ugly."

Jessup nodded. "The circle will slowly enclose itself, it'll heal with just a little scar. Horse hides are odd that way."

"Matt!" Josey yelled.

He ran up the hill at the same time the three T3E trucks drove around the corner to them; the vet's truck right behind them.

Matt turned to Josey who was kneeling next to Freddy. The horse had gone down and was gasping for breath. Josey's eyes were wide and pleading as she looked at him.

Kate's truck passed the other three and drove right to the downed horse. The Trio jogged up towards them.

"Freddy…" He yelled out to them.

Josey moved out of the veterinarian's way and next to Matt. She leaned against him so he slid his arm around her waist and pulled her in tight. He meant to comfort her but he found her touch helped ease the anxiety inside himself.

After a few minutes, Kate looked up and shook her head sadly. "There's damage inside. I don't think we could save him even if we were at the clinic."

The horse groaned, gasped…then was gone. They all remained silent for a moment, each realizing the great loss of the big horse.

Matt stepped away from Josey and instantly felt cold.

He knelt next to Freddy and ran a hand across the horse's jaw then down his neck. Images of Andy riding the horse flashed in his mind and his breath shook. "Sorry old boy, this is no way to go after so many years of service. I hope you find Andy on the other side of the rainbow bridge…rest peacefully, Freddy." Matt wiped away the moisture in his eyes and took a deep breath; his voice shook as he spoke. *You leave us now…To fly in the sky…Green pastures to run…Under a warm sun to lie. Fly High My Friend.*"

They were going to have to bury two horses now because of Conner's drunken stupidity. Matt stood, looked at Kate, "Monty was the next in the pile."

She nodded.

"I'll move your truck down." Josey offered as she wiped away tears.

The Trio, Kate and Matt jogged down the hill.

"He's doing better." Jessup announced.

Scott went directly to Monty's head and the horse leaned across his chest. Scott wrapped his arm around the horse's nose and neck, holding him tightly, comforting him. He spoke softly and watched the veterinarian examine his prized horse.

Matt's mom and Grayson walked to the truck and looked at the buckskin. Matt knew they were confirming, in their minds, that it wasn't Eli. Matt would have done the same thing.

They heard a truck and turned to see Warren pulling in with the truck and trailer.

Josey slid out of the vet's truck, "Is there anything you need?" She offered to Kate.

"My portable ultra sound." She answered.

Josey opened the doors, "Where is it?"

Kate sighed and walked to the truck. They all stood patiently while she searched for the machine.

"It's not here," She grumbled and returned with a stethoscope. When she stepped away from the grey horse she nodded to Scott. "Everything sounds good inside, but I'd like to take him to the clinic and get the ultra sound done."

Scott nodded.

"Take my truck and trailer." Matt told him and watched as Scott walked his horse toward the trailer.

"I'll go with..." His mother kissed him on the cheek, squeezed his hand and followed her brother.

"Is there anything else I can do?" Warren asked.

"No, we've got it from here." Grayson offered a hand. "Thanks for your help, Warren."

"Sad thing, needless...that gelding up there? Seen Freddy work hard over all these years...he was a damn good horse that took care of Andy right to the end. He didn't deserve to go like that." Warren sighed and shook Matt's hand. He nodded to Jessup and Josey then turned away.

Kate quickly examined the other two horses. "They're good, just needing stitches on the leg a couple places and just cover the gouge with anti-fly antibiotic medicine."

"I got this Kate," Jessup nodded. "You go take care of Monty."

The woman reached out and laid her hand on Jessup's forearm and squeezed. He placed a hand over hers and nodded. "I'll call later." He said in a low voice. Their eyes registered the emotion they had for each other and for the desperate situation with the horses.

After Kate left, Matt, Grayson, Josey and Jessup looked at each other then to the horses.

"We'll bury the two here and let the kids do their service this weekend." Grayson said. "Alex was the last one to ride him...he's going to be pretty upset."

"I'm sorry, Grayson." Josey whispered, tears in her eyes again.

"What are you sorry for?" Grayson asked.

"Conner, he was bad." She looked at Grayson for forgiveness. "I should have said something."

"I was going to talk to you this morning then let him go." Matt added.

"What happened?" Grayson asked in concern.

Josey told him what happened the day before and surprised Matt with information that she hadn't told him; rude and inappropriate comments in the previous days.

Grayson turned to her. "This is not your fault. I hired him." Grayson held up a hand to cut her off when she tried to speak. "If anything like that happens again, WITH ANYONE, you contact me, Jessup, Matt, ANY of the Tagger family directly…I…WE won't stand for that behavior. Understood?" He asked sternly, looking directly at her.

"Yes. I will." Josey nodded taking in a deep breath.

"What about Kyle?" Matt asked her.

"He's good." She nodded. "Most the time he buffered us when it was just the three of us. He stopped the comments."

Grayson glared at her then walked away.

"I think he's mad at me." Josey watched him walk away then turned to Jessup and Matt, who were also glaring at her. "Ok…so you all are…message received."

###

Just as they finished burying the two horses, Matt's phone rang out.

TEXT FROM SCOTT: Monty is fine, will keep him at Homestead overnight

TEXT FROM MATT: Relieved; Thanks for letting me know.

TEXT FROM SCOTT: Thank you Matt

Matt relayed the information to the rest of the group.

Grayson exhaled slowly and looked out at the mountains. "I need to ride."

"I'll go with you." Jessup offered. "You catch up Eli and one for me. I'll go doctor these two."

Matt and Josey went with Jessup and he helped their foreman while Josey went in the ranch house to shower off the horse blood.

Grayson arrived just as they finished with the two horses.

Matt watched the two men drive off…Grayson needing to spend time with Eli, assuring himself the horse was OK.

****

Matt slowly lowered himself on the stack of hay in the barn. How could anyone do that to a bunch of innocent horses? Good, dependable, hard-working horses?

He leaned back and stretched, trying to release all the tension of the last couple hours.

His shirt was streaked with horse blood so he took off his cowboy hat long enough to pull the shirt over his head and toss it in the corner. He had a backup shirt in the truck.

He leaned forward, resting his elbows on his knees and thought about the day…about Josey. She was fierce today. He could see the love she had for horses and the temper she had for the drunken fool who had caused the accident. She hadn't stopped, listened to everything he said, and reacted fast. If it wasn't for the horrible reason they were there…he would have enjoyed working with her.

He could still remember the warmth of her touch when she leaned into him for emotional support and the calmness it created in his own stomach.

Matt sighed, she was Elena's daughter, the link between them and that horrible wicked woman. Josey was a ticking bomb that Elena was going to set off at any moment.

A movement at the barn door caught his eye and he looked to see the ticking bomb walking towards him. He straightened his back, suddenly aware of being shirtless.

Josey was walking with determination straight at him. Her dark hair was wet from the shower and hung down her back and shoulders. She wore clean jeans and a white sleeveless western shirt. But it was the look in her eyes that caught him off guard.

Without a word, she stepped up to him, a hand on both sides of his face and placed her lips on his. Matt's heart raced from the unexpected action and the emotion it generated inside him. He grabbed at her shoulders, intending to push her away but somehow he pulled her closer. His movement caused her to wrap her arms around his shoulders and intensify the kiss.

His hands ran down her sides then around her waist, a hand going up her back and under the wet hair to hold her even tighter. The aroma of lilacs entranced his senses.

He didn't think, he just felt. It went on forever…but not long enough, as she broke the kiss by moving just inches away from his lips. He could feel her breath as she spoke.

"I walked around the corner…jeans…cowboy hat…no shirt… it was as if you stepped out of one of those hot cowboy calendars." She whispered.

"Josey…" His hands slid up her arms, he tightened and started to push her away.

"No." She shook his hands off and wrapped her arms around his neck pulling him into another intense kiss. She leaned into him with such force he fell back against the hay.

Matt's heart continued the kiss. His mind, fighting the reality of the situation, kept his hands resting on her hips; not pushing her away to end the kiss, nor wrapping his arms around her to deepen the kiss.

He could feel her bare arms across his bare back, her fingertips slid lightly down his spine causing his body to shudder against her. She giggled into the kiss. Matt's mind and heart were in an intense battle. He knew he should stop but he didn't want to let go of her.

Elena's evil grin flashed in his mind.

He turned his head to break the kiss, "Josey…" He whispered.

"Matt…" She whispered against his ear, her breath against his skin caused fireworks through his mind and heart.

It was too much and he roughly pushed her away, stood, and stepped away from her.

"What's wrong?" Her eyes were dark with emotion and slanted in confusion.

"This will never happen…we will never happen." Matt glared at her, his heart still racing.

"I don't understand." Josey crossed her arms in front of herself, gripping her upper arms. Her protective move, he hated it, but caused it. "We…just…"

"No, Josey." He turned to walk out of the barn.

"Matt! Stop!" She yelled at him with a fierce intensity that caused him to stop and turn. Her face was red and her eyes blazing. Her hands had moved to her hips. "Why?" She fumed. "I don't understand why not?"

"Because I don't want it to happen," He lied then wondered why he lied.

"You're lying."

See…even she knew he was lying.

"Matt, you said you would always be honest; so you cannot tell me, after the last 5 minutes, that you don't want it to happen. So give me a better reason than that."

"I was just kissing a girl that kissed me." He turned to walk out.

"Oh, please!" She spit out, obviously not believing him. When he didn't stop; "Dang it, Matt, stop and talk to me…why are you doing this?" Her voice rang of hurt and desperation.

He stopped, but didn't turn. He couldn't tell her the truth, that she was Elena's ticking bomb that could jeopardize millions of dollars and thousands of jobs. He had to say the one thing that would hurt her, hopefully making her stop her inquisition. "I do not want to be with Elena Pelten's daughter."

She didn't respond so he took another step.

"Your sister is Elena Pelton's daughter." She said in a low angry voice.

Her tone showed his words had done the damage.

"But Nikki shut Elena down and kicked her out of our lives."

"And because I was a fool and believed in her?"

"Exactly…" He answered; his back still to her. "You don't compare to Nikki."

He heard her intake of breath.

"She took everything from me," Her voice quivered this time. Matt wanted to turn and hold her over the words he had used to hurt her. "Why would you think I would do it again?"

"I don't have any reason to believe you wouldn't," Taking a deep breath, Matt turned and looked at her, narrowing his eyes to reinforce his gruff tone. "Let it go, Josey. I voted against you even being here…I don't want you here…so let it go. You're nothing more than an employee to me."

She returned his stare until doubt flickered in her eyes. Slowly, her shoulders lowered in defeat. Her face turned red, then her gaze dropped as her arms wrapped in front of her.

Matt quickly turned and walked away before he lost his nerve and ran back to her. He made it to a truck without turning around and drove quickly away from the ranch without a destination in mind. Stomach turning, blood cold, and heart sinking he drove until his phone rang.

"Matt? Kevin. We have a couple rafters missing."

"Where?"

CHAPTER FOURTEEN

Matt stepped out of the truck and looked around at the other vehicles at The Homestead. His mom, Scott, Grayson, Nikki and Lucas were all there. His dad wasn't, so it must be a business meeting. He glanced towards the barn. Monty had fully recovered and was back to work at the ranch. The horse with the circle gouge was still recuperating from his injuries at Circle 50 under Nikki's care, of course. The bay horse was fine and back in the pasture and to work.

He had the urge to go greet the horses first but decided people were waiting; he'd do equine therapy later.

After returning from finding the missing rafters, with the help of Alex, Wade and Reilly, Matt had concentrated on replacing fence and had avoided any chance of seeing Josey. He was at the ranch store loading more fencing supplies when he got the call for the meeting.

His mom met him in the kitchen with a loving 'welcome home' hug and smile.

"What's this all about?" Matt asked as the two of them made their way to the library.

"I have no idea, but Lucas looks upset."

"Well, when your attorney looks upset…that just can't be good." Matt grinned at her.

"Truer words have never been said, Mate." The Australian greeted them with a frown. He closed the library door behind them.

"I'm really beginning to hate those closed doors." Nikki commented with a smile to her brother.

"Alright," Lucas took his seat next to Nikki then looked across the room at Matt, his face stern and unreadable. "Brace yourself."

Matt groaned inside. "Should I be sitting down for this?"

"Wouldn't be a bad idea," Lucas nodded solemnly.

Matt sat in the chair next to his mother, suddenly feeling like he was going to need her.

"I was forwarded a document that, from my understanding, will be filed on Monday." Lucas said, still looking at Matt. "It is a complaint of sexual misconduct and harassment in the workforce against you."

"Me?" Matt looked at him in shock, his stomach tightening in disbelief. "I haven't done anything."

"Is this legit?" His mom leaned forward towards Lucas.

Lucas nodded, "All reliable resources."

Matt looked around the room at his frowning and stunned family. "I haven't done anything wrong."

"Not one person in this room would ever believe you did." Grayson assured him.

Scott turned to Lucas. "Who's accusing him?"

Lucas leaned back in his chair and returned Scott's frown. "You…brace yourself."

"Why? Am I being accused too?" Scott asked gruffly.

"No," Lucas told him then looked at Matt. "Josey Charmayne Franklin."

"Frankie?" A group gasp of astonishment echoed through the room.

"She would never do that." Nikki turned to her stunned brother.

Matt sat frozen. Josey? She did this? The only thing should could use was the kiss in the barn, but she started the kiss. Was this the reason why? Did she only kiss him so she could file this complaint?

"Matt?" He turned his gaze to his mother. "Are you alright?" She asked taking his hand; deep concern in her eyes.

Matt nodded numbly. "I didn't do anything to Josey."

"She didn't do this." Grayson said firmly with Nikki agreeing again.

Lucas slid the paper over to Grayson to review. His uncle roughly flipped through the paperwork then threw it across the table. "She wouldn't do this."

Scott reached over and picked up the documents. "I took a leap of faith and voted for her. I'm the reason she is here."

"She didn't do this!" Nikki leaned towards her uncle, her voice firm. "There is no fault. There is something wrong here."

Scott stood as he placed the paperwork on the table. He began pacing while he looked at Matt. "I'm sorry, Matt. I should have listened to you. Dru, I'm sorry."

"SHE DIDN''T DO THIS!" Nikki yelled and reached for her phone.

"Nikki!" Lucas turned to her. "Do not call her."

"This is my sister and my brother you're talking about, and you want me to sit on the sidelines when I know this isn't right?" She turned fierce eyes to her fiancé.

"Nikki!" Lucas turned red.

"Josey? Where are you? The Stables?" Nikki said into her phone. "Can you come over to The Homestead right now?" A pause. "Good, see you in 20 minutes."

"Nikki," Lucas shook his head at her. "This could backfire…big time on you and Matt if she did this and you confront her now. You're jeopardizing your ranch as well as Matt's reputation."

"I'll take the chance on the ranch and his reputation will take a hit as soon as the papers are filed." She sat back in the chair and crossed her arms. "I believe in both of them. HE did nothing wrong and SHE didn't do this!"

Matt took a deep breath and let it out, his mind going back to the kiss in the barn. There was more there than someone planning a law suit. He and Josey wouldn't have had the argument afterwards if there was. It was raw emotion from her that couldn't be faked.

"Don't let emotions rule your thinking." Lucas warned her.

"What you're saying is, I voted for her because of my feelings, not for what was best for Tagger Enterprises." Nikki retorted.

Lucas didn't answer, which confirmed her belief.

Matt sighed. Why couldn't life just be easy? He didn't want this to happen, that's why he voted against Josey. He was sure something was going to happen…he just didn't think this would be it. He didn't think it would be a personal attack. The look on Elena's face in front of the hotel came back to him. That's what it was, she decided then and there to use him to get to at the Taggers. Elena had decided to make it personal.

Matt felt his anger rising and tried not to show anyone. They were as upset as he was. Even if the papers were against him, they were an attack on the whole family. He just sat quietly trying to maintain the anger and listened to his family discussing the papers.

Scott walked to the library window. "She's here."

Nikki stood and walked to the door. Lucas followed.

"I can talk to my sister alone." Nikki frowned at him.

"Not right now you aren't," He grumbled. "You're not talking to her without your attorney present."

"I'll try to remember you're my attorney right now and not my fiancé." She muttered.

Nikki stopped at the door and turned to her family. "Do not attack her." She said looking at Scott. His lips thinned in anger as he started pacing again.

Matt sighed again. He reached across and picked up the paperwork. There were the names; Josey Charmayne Franklin against Matthew Scott Tagger. He just wanted to leave and go running, or leave and go rappel off a cliff. Maybe leave and jump out of a plane…just leave and do anything besides facing Josey right now.

Matt stared at the paperwork, not really seeing it as they walked into the library.

"Is something wrong?" He heard Josey ask as she entered the room.

He could just imagine her expression and nerves facing a group of angry Taggers.

Lucas grabbed Nikki's arm and pulled her around the table, leaving Josey by the door standing by herself.

"What's the matter?" Josey asked glancing around the room.

"If you really want to do this now," Lucas frowned. "Give her the papers."

Matt hesitated; he didn't want to do it now…he didn't want to do it ever.

"Matt," Grayson said across the table. "Give her the papers so we can get this over with."

Matt forced himself to look up at Josey. Her long brown hair was loose down her back, held back with a wide black head band. She was wearing a blue T3E t-shirt and jeans. Her brown eyes were looking at him in total confusion. She just looked young, beautiful, and clueless.

"Give her the papers." Grayson repeated.

"What papers?" Josey asked him.

He slowly handed her the papers, then watched as she read them.

Her eyes went from confusion to wide. Her coloring changed from red, to white, to red again as she flipped through the papers. When she reached the last page, that had her signature on it, she gasped.

She slowly lifted her gaze to Matt. "Never…" She whispered, her face a deep red. She looked around the room at all the people staring at her, watching her reaction. "I didn't do this." Josey said looking back at the paper. "I didn't…"

"Look at the signature, the name…" Scott said as he paced the room.

Her eyes quickly went to him. "I didn't Scott, I swear, I didn't…it's not my signature." Her voice was full of desperation.

"I believed in you Frankie…" He shook his head in disbelief.

"Scott." Grayson looked at his brother. "I don't believe she did it either."

"It's a legal document." Scott glared at him.

"They can be forged." Lucas said quietly from his seat at the table. Matt glanced over at him, wondering if her reaction changed his mind.

"Please, believe me Scott. I know you stood up for me…voted for me…I didn't do this. I wouldn't do this to you…or to any of you." Tears started to well in her eyes.

Matt turned away. He couldn't look at her desperation.

"Matt," Josey said. "Please don't…please don't believe this."

He looked at his mother. She was staring out the library window…she had barely spoken since Lucas read the document, her face was tense.

"I still don't believe she did this." Nikki stood.

"Of course you don't." Scott glared at her.

"Scott, do not attack our own." Grayson said gruffly.

"You're right," Scott sighed and looked at his niece. "I apologize…it's just so frustrating."

Matt sighed inside. Why? Why did this have to happen? He looked at his phone, silently wishing it would ring…Kevin on the other side…needing his help so he could leave. If not Kevin, then the sheriff's department. Matt felt a twinge of fear run through him… the sheriff's department. He stood in frustration and walked to the window. Exhaling loudly he closed his eyes, a hand coming up to cover them as if it would keep out the pressure.

"Matt?" His mother stood. "What?"

"It just hit me," He said with exhaustion and devastation. Everything he'd worked for the last couple years was on the line…he felt like throwing up. "Most of the search and rescue I do is with the sheriff's office. If this happens…I'm out."

"No!" Josey cried. "It won't happen, Matt, I swear."

"We fight this. You know we will." His mother walked to him and squeezed his arm tightly.

"What do we have to do?" Grayson stood and started pacing with his brother.

"Frankie, it says Matt sexually harassed you." Lucas said with renewed energy.

Matt turned and looked at her. Her eyes went wide in embarrassment and her face turned red again. She glanced at Matt then back to Lucas.

"He didn't, I swear, he didn't." She said firmly, looking at the attorney.

"Have the two of you ever…." Lucas asked in a calm voice.

"No!" Josey and Matt said in unison.

Lucas stared at Josey, his eyes narrowed slightly, then he glanced over at Matt. Matt looked at his uncles. They were looking at her too…with expressions of doubt. Trying to keep himself calm, he turned to her. She was looking at the table; her face had gone from red to white; an anxious look in her eyes.

He knew what she was thinking about; the kiss in the barn…the fact that she basically attacked him. She would be mortified to have to tell this group that fact. He wasn't going to let that happen. No one but he and Josey would ever know everything that happened.

"We kissed once." Matt admitted, looking only at Lucas. He could feel the heat rise up his neck.

"I kissed Matt." Josey said quickly.

"It ended up mutual." Matt exhaled, determined Josey wasn't going to look bad in front of people she admired. He felt the heat rise and knew his face was red.

He had been staring at Lucas, but when his future brother-in-law's stoic expression cracked with a slight smile, Matt looked away from him to Grayson. There was no way he was looking at his mother, sister, or Josey.

Grayson had stopped pacing and was leaning against the wall, staring at the table.

"No one knew…" Josey added in a low voice. "I didn't tell anyone."

Nikki turned to Lucas, who shook his head slightly at her. She knew if Matt had told anyone, it would have been him.

"Matt?" His mother said.

He reluctantly turned to her. She had her poker face on again…showing no emotion.

"Did you tell anyone?" She asked.

"No one," He answered firmly. "And we've barely seen each other since."

"Why?" Scott asked.

Matt turned to Josey, she was near tears; her face red in embarrassment. His mind went back to that night, pushing her away and telling her there would never be anything between them. The words he used to hurt her…

"That's between me and Josey." Matt said looking back to his uncle who nodded.

"This doesn't matter." His mother said firmly. "We need to focus on the paperwork, the fact that it's signed by Frankie."

"It's not my signature!" Josey cried out. She walked to the computer desk. Grabbing paper from a drawer and a pen from the desktop she sat at the table and wrote her name. She wrote it a number of times then slid the paper to Lucas who took it and compared the signature to the one on the document.

"This is my signature," Josey stood and walked to the door. "I'll go get my reports out of Grayson's truck. They have my signature on them, if you don't believe that."

"Stay here." Matt ordered, loud enough it stopped her and everyone in the room turned to look at him.

"I can prove it…I just need to go get…" Josey started to turn.

"No, you don't," Matt told her firmly as he turned to face her. "That doesn't matter."

"What do you mean is doesn't matter?!" She asked in disbelief. "It MATTERS to me. I didn't do this and I don't want any of you thinking I did!" She yelled, as her anxious brown eyes searched the room.

"Josey…" Matt started.

Josey turned and looked at him, her eyes angry. "I DIDN'T do this."

"I know," Matt said softly and her expression changed to shock.

"What?" Scott turned sharply. "You believe her now?"

"I never said I didn't." Matt pointed out.

Matt glanced at Josey, a tear finally escaped her and she quickly wiped it away. He was sure it was from relief.

"What makes you think it wasn't Frankie?" His mother asked, looking at him with a quizzical tip of the head.

Again he glanced at Josey, a knot forming in his stomach. He glanced at his uncles, then Lucas and Nikki.

"Josey wouldn't have come after me. Like I said, we barely see each other. You all know that." Matt stated and looked at Grayson.

His uncle's face was grim when he realized what Matt was saying.

"She would have gone after Grayson, who she's with, by herself, most of the time." Matt continued as he turned to his mother. "It would have been her word against his."

"Oh, dang." Nikki whispered.

"He's right." Lucas nodded.

There was silence in the room as each processed the information.

Matt tried to stop himself, but he couldn't. His eyes went back to Josey. She was watching him with relief in her eyes. He turned away and looked out to the horses in the pasture.

"The papers haven't been filed?" His mom asked.

"No," Lucas answered leaning forward on the table. "My understanding is they are to be filed tomorrow morning."

"Frankie," Scott drew her attention. "I'm sorry it's…"

"It's OK." She whispered. "But I didn't have anything to do with this. I would never do anything like this, ever."

"I'm sure it was Elena," Matt said without turning around. The look she gave him in Billings…the evil wicked smile.

"The picture Warren posted on Facebook." Nikki nodded. "Somehow Elena must have seen it. It states clearly that you're Josey's employer. It just showed the two of you…you holding the back of her jeans."

Matt nodded then turned to Josey. "She got you to sign over your college fund. I'm sure she thought you would go along with it once it hit the courts…to protect her." He looked back out the window…trying to escape…at least in his mind.

"I wouldn't." She said firmly. "Matt?"

He turned and looked at her, he felt his heart constrict when he saw the anxious look in her eyes.

"You believe me, don't you?" Her voice, just over a whisper.

Matt didn't answer, he just turned back to the window.

"Is everyone in the room in agreement that Frankie didn't sign this?" Grayson asked.

Everyone nodded.

"Then what's the next move?" Grayson asked Lucas.

"Drawing up the papers isn't illegal." Lucas told them. "We have to wait to see if they file, if they don't…" He shrugged. "If they file, it will be up to Frankie to stop the claim. Plus there will be one heck of a long look at the attorney that took the case without verifying the person making the claim."

"I will fight it...absolutely." Josey said firmly and looked around the room.

"Then what?" Matt turned to her with more force then he meant.

She stepped back. "What do you mean?"

"You stop the claim…OK, that's good and the right thing to do." He stepped toward her and took a deep breath to stay strong and not react to her intimidated expression.

Elena made this personal…he had to return the favor, but unfortunately he was going to have to use Josey to do it.

"What happens next time Elena comes after us?" Matt asked her. "When we don't have a clue that it's coming? Because she knows you're here?"

"Matt…" Josey's voice shook and she nervously looked around the room.

"That's why I didn't want you here, Josey," He straightened his back. "Because you brought that woman back into our lives and it threatens my family."

"Matt!" Grayson said sharply.

Matt glanced at him but quickly turned back to Josey.

"I told you when we met in Billings that we shouldn't be seen together, but you insisted." Josey said and stood taller.

"So, you're saying this is my fault?" Matt asked in disbelief.

"No, I'm not." She took a step closer to him, fire in her eyes. "But you can't stand there and point the finger at me and say this is all my fault!"

"I agree with her, Matt." Grayson said.

"And I agree with her." Matt surprised everyone in the room when he turned to his uncle with a determined expression.

Grayson stiffened. "Matt, if you're saying this is because of me..."

"It's not all her fault because we ALL let it happen." Matt cut him off. "I stated why I didn't want her here. And what I feared... happened. It was a little more of a personal attack than I expected, but it still happened." He turned back to Josey. "So now what?"

"I don't know what you're asking." She answered, her eyes looking intently into his.

The look made his nerves tingle, butterflies fluttered in his stomach.

"She took $50,000 from you just two years ago." He reminded her. "Now she's after more."

"But I'll stop her." Josey countered, but was clearly confused.

"But what about the next time and we all know there will be a next time...while you're still here." Matt pointed out again.

Josey's eyes widened in shock; her voice quivered when she spoke; "You want me to leave?"

"No!" Nikki stood. "You're not leaving."

"Matt, you're not telling her to leave." Grayson said firmly.

Josey pulled her eyes from Matt's then turned and slowly walked to the door. "He's right. As long as I'm here, Elena will continue to attack. She's risking everything Matt's worked for...and there's the kids...I can't imagine hurting the kids...risking them? I'll be gone in the morning."

"No." Scott, Nikki, Grayson, and his mother said firmly.

Matt was surprised at his mother's reaction, but it confirmed what he was going to say next.

As her trembling hand hit the doorknob, he spoke.

"You can't leave, Josey." He stated loudly.

"You just said she was going to continue to attack your family if I'm here. So what can I do but leave?" She didn't turn around.

"You need Lucas to protect you from her, and my family to back you up." Matt answered.

"Why?" She turned.

"You are the only one that can stop her." Matt tried to remain calm.

"How?" Josey frowned.

Matt looked at Lucas.

Lucas stared at Matt for a moment then looked between him and Josey. "You could file a fraud or identity theft claim against her. I'll have to review Idaho law with the family attorney."

Matt turned back to Josey. She was staring at the floor.

They remained quiet, letting her decide.

Finally, her head came up and she looked at Matt with no expression then turned to Lucas. "It will put her in jail?"

Lucas nodded. "She's on probation for identity theft already. That, with other priors she's racked up, it probably will. For quite some time if you get the right judge."

Josey took a deep breath. "Can stealing my college fund be used against her?"

Matt looked at her in surprise. He hadn't expected her to be willing to prosecute her mother.

"It depends on all the details. I doubt there is a way to get your money back, since you said you signed the papers willingly. I can review them and you could use them if you're willing to testify against her." He answered.

"I am." Josey said. She looked determined but Matt could see her hands shaking.

"This is a big, Frankie." Nikki said to her sister. "Are you sure you don't want to take the time to make a final decision?"

Josey shook her head vigorously. "Is Matt right? Will you help me?" She asked Lucas.

"Absolutely," He nodded.

"We'll back you up." The Trio said in unison.

"Are you sure?" Nikki asked.

"I wanted to do something before…to finally make her pay for stealing from my dad…breaking us apart. Then stealing from me, my education, my future…I had to sell my horse..." Her voice shook, but she sounded firm on her decision. "I didn't know how or who could help me."

Josey paused then looked at Matt. "I didn't chose my mother and I tried to protect you from the moment we met, from before we met. If this is the only way to protect her next victim, then this is what I have to do."

Matt's emotions were in turmoil. He had pushed the issue hoping, but not believing, she would follow through. Now that she had? He didn't know what to do next. She looked scared…he wanted to hold her, let her know it would be OK and he would be there for her…but he couldn't. He was upset this all happened. He knew it would and no one but his mother agreed. There was so much at stake…not just money…but jobs…everything his Dad had worked for.

"Matt?" Josey's voice reached him through his thoughts; he had been staring at her. She was looking at him as if something was wrong.

He shook his head to try and shake off the turmoil.

"So now what?" Matt turned to Lucas.

"We wait until tomorrow to see if the papers are filed, and to be sure it's Elena filing them. If it is, then Frankie needs to respond immediately, before the evening news. The media will eat this up. The family that took in the Tagger Herd is now being accused of sexual harassment." Lucas leaned back in his chair and looked at Josey. "Do you have anything at all that has her signature on it?"

Josey nodded. "I still have the forms where she signed to get on my college savings account."

"Get me a copy and we'll compare to this signature." He held up the paper. "Matt, Josey, you both need to be here tomorrow morning so we can react fast."

"Does Elena have to be there when the papers are filed?" Josey asked nervously.

"No, but you will have to face her at some point." Lucas answered.

"And we'll be there with you to support you." Nikki added.

"But she could be anywhere right now." Josey sighed.

"I know where she is." Lucas informed her without elaboration.

"You do?" Josey asked surprised. She looked around the room and realized no one else was surprised. "Do you all know?"

"No," Scott answered. "Just Lucas."

"How do you know?" She asked Lucas.

"I'm Nikki and Matt's attorney," He reminded her. "It's my job to protect them from any threat."

She looked confused. "Then how did this happen? Wasn't I considered a threat?"

"You, yourself, are not a threat to them." Lucas answered.

"It's what you bring with you...that is the threat." Matt's mother stared at her. "If you weren't here...if you weren't an employee...those papers couldn't even have been drafted, let alone filed."

"But it's not my fault." Josey looked at her. "I didn't choose her as a mother, I tried to hide from her. I tried to forget she ever existed."

"And that's why I voted for you." Grayson told her.

"We're off track." Matt's mother headed for the door. "There's nothing we can do until Monday."

"I'll call you as soon as I hear anything." Lucas told Josey as he grabbed Nikki's hand and they walked to the door.

Josey nodded, then looked to Matt. He could see the turmoil and fear in her eyes.

Matt turned back to the window as he listened to people leaving. He wanted to assure her...but he was angry...he wanted to hold her...but she was Elena's daughter, a clear threat to his family. Until that threat was over...

"Matt?"

"What?" He asked with more force then he meant…it was his nerves, he told himself.

"I…" She started. "Us?"

He reluctantly turned back to the room. They were the only two left and the doors had been closed. Her brown eyes searched his for an answer. He could see the hope and it pulled at his heart.

"I want to strangle you… and I want to hold you." Matt said truthfully.

Josey just stared, bewildered. "I don't know what to do with that." She tried to smile but it faded.

"I don't either."

"You know how I feel."

"I do." He looked into her eyes. He'd dreamed of a woman looking at him the way she was now. It was the way Nikki looked at Lucas. It tore at him, the anguish was gut wrenching.

"Then what am I supposed to do?" She asked, her eyes starting to glisten. "What do we do?"

"We just take it one day at a time until one emotion takes over the other." He answered and saw the disappointment in her face.

His heart ached and his stomach trembled. He thought of Elena's wicked evil smile. There was no letting go until he knew his family wasn't in danger anymore from her mother, if even then. There was so much more to protect than Josey could ever imagine. It wasn't just the two of them.

"Can I ask you for one thing?" She asked in a low voice.

He nodded; afraid to speak.

"No one else is here and the doors are closed." Josey took a deep quivering breath. He could see the hurt and fear in her. "I just…I need…" She closed her eyes then shook her head.

Without another word, she turned and walked to the door.

His heart was racing, it felt like it was going to explode. If he held her now…he wasn't sure he could let go. But she needed him…if only for a moment.

"Josey," He whispered as his pulse quickened at the thought of holding her. She turned slowly, a tear was sliding down her cheek.

Matt opened his arms to her.

More tears and an anguished cry escaped as she ran into his embrace. She was trembling as he wrapped his arms tightly around her. It was something he had wanted to do since the moment he had left the barn after their kiss. He just wanted to hold her and he didn't want to let go.

Her head tucked just under his chin, Matt could feel the tears as they soaked into his shirt. He squeezed his arms tighter around her, trying to comfort her as much as he could in the short time he allowed himself this moment of weakness. His mind went back to the barn, watching her walk to him.

He closed his eyes to concentrate on her touch. She smelled of flowers…of lilacs. His arms moved from her waist and up her back to rest under her hair. His arms tightened, she responded with a surprised gasp and she leaned into him.

"Matt?" She whispered and started to lean back to look up.

"Don't." He spoke into her hair. "I wouldn't be able to stop from kissing you."

"I want you to."

"It's not the right time."

"Will there ever be a right time?"

"I don't know." It took all his inner strength to let go of her. She hesitated then finally dropped her arms.

When she stepped back and out of his arms, he instantly felt cold…inside and out.

She slowly walked to the door but just before opening it, she turned. "I never thought there could be anything worse than Elena tearing my dad and I apart. But this is worse Matt." The hope and desperation replaced with sadness. "She's taken everything from me…please don't let her take the possibility of us away too."

His heart told him to run to her and wrap her in his arms…never letting go. His mind reminded him how much was at stake; his family, everything Nick had worked for…thousands of jobs, and the millions of dollars that Elena would kill to get her hands on.

CHAPTER FIFTEEN

Matt shook his head to clear the emotions of the last hour. He needed something to do, he had to do something physical. He needed to run…literally.

When he walked into the kitchen they were all there.

"Where is she?" Nikki asked worriedly.

"She left out the front door." He answered.

Jack walked by him, stopped and looked at Matt's shirt. Matt looked down and saw a large wet circle from Josey's tears with her makeup smeared inside it.

"I had a shirt like that once." Jack said lifting his gaze to Matt's. "And it was caused by the same woman."

Matt turned to Nikki, remembering her sadness and tears after her meeting in The Stables with Elena when she tried to talk Nikki into blackmailing Jack. If the woman would do that to her own daughters, what would she do to everyone else?

It strengthened his resolve; he needed to stay away from Josey, not giving Elena a chance to get in.

"Matt?" Nikki stood. "Can we talk?"

He shook his head and walked towards the back door. "I'm going for a run."

His mother stopped him, wrapped her arms around his neck and pulled him in close. In a low voice, meant only for mother and son, she whispered. "I know what you're doing. I don't know if it's the right thing or not. But what I do know is that you're hurting and it tears me apart. I want you to know, that I love you with all my heart and soul. I'll be here for you if and when you need me."

Tears stung at his eyes and he pulled her closer. He used the warmth and strength from her to heal the unraveling edges of his heart.

Ten minutes later he was running down a dirt road…running away from everything that happened and what was about to happen.

Why did she have to be Elena's daughter? Why couldn't they have met in normal circumstances? He wanted to be with her…but everything his dad had worked for, all the jobs on the line… if Elena knew…if she found out…

He had to protect his family. Elena had taken everything from Josey and there wasn't anything he could do about it.

But maybe one thing… He stopped running and took out his phone to flip through the pictures. He found the one he was looking for and sent it to his mother.

TEXT FROM MATT: Can you find it?

TEXT FROM DRU: On it

The phone call from Sheriff Wendt came in at 9:15 in the morning.

"Matt? Where are you?"

"I'm at The Homestead just getting ready to head to Circle 50." Matt answered.

"Stay there, I'll be there as soon as I can."

It took the officer 27 minutes to pull down the driveway of The Homestead. Matt was sitting on the tailgate of his truck waiting for him. Lucas had come up with a plan and Matt was about to put it in action.

There were two officers in the car.

"Matt, this is Officer Burling." Officer Wendt introduced them and Matt shook the man's hand.

"What's up?" Matt asked, as if he didn't already know.

"I have to serve you papers." Officer Wendt frowned and handed Matt the official filing of the sexual harassment suit.

"What are they for?" Matt tried to look concerned.

"Read them, then we'll discuss." His friend asked. Matt could see the true concern in the officer's expression.

The other officer leaned against the front of their car.

"Sexual harassment?" Matt feigned surprise. "Is this a joke?" He looked up at both the officers.

"Keep reading." Officer Wendt sighed heavily.

Matt thumbed through the papers as if he'd never seen them.

"This is real?" Matt asked the two officers as he looked at the last page…still the same signature as on the papers that Lucas held.

"To the legal system…yes." Officer Wendt nodded. "But real? As in do I believe the allegations? No."

Matt sighed and nodded. "Thanks…and I can guarantee you that I didn't do anything like this. I don't see Josey enough for this to happen."

Both officers nodded.

"Matt, the date that is listed as the first date of sexual harassment doesn't quite work out." Office Burling informed him.

"What do you mean?" Matt asked in feigned confusion. After reviewing the papers more thoroughly, Lucas had noticed the dates too.

"The date listed is the day you were plucking Gary out of the blackberry bush." Officer Wendt frowned.

"What do I do?" Matt asked the officers.

"Do you know Josey Franklin?" Officer Burling asked.

"Sure I do, she's an employee, works with our horses." Matt nodded.

The officers glanced at each other. "Matt," Officer Wendt started. "You can't do anything to her to retaliate."

"I wouldn't dream of it." Matt nodded. "You should know that she's in the house."

"She's in The Homestead right now?" Officer Wendt looked at the house in surprise.

Matt nodded. "The family just had breakfast and talked about the horses, and the work needed this week." Which was actually true.

"Why would she be in the house, working with you, if she knew these were going to be filed today?" Officer Burling looked bewildered.

"Want to ask her?" Matt asked him.

"Matt, you have to cut off all communication with her." Office Wendt told him.

"She's my employee, works with my family, and she's Nikki's sister." Matt told them.

"What?" They said in unison.

"She's Nikki's sister?" Officer Wendt gasped.

Matt nodded, "They share a mother." He looked at the papers, then to the house, then to the officers. "I don't think she did this."

"Why?" Officer Burling asked.

Matt frowned. "The only time she has been down from the ranch is when we had The Tagger Herd anniversary party a couple weeks ago, on a Saturday." Matt flipped the papers as if he was looking for something. "The signature isn't right."

"You know her signature?" Officer Wendt asked.

"Of course, she writes progress reports on the horses…this doesn't look right." Matt slid off the tailgate. "I don't know what's going on here but I have a couple of the reports in my truck if you want to see."

The officers looked at each other. "OK." Officer Wendt nodded.

Matt pulled out the reports he had just placed in the truck and handed it to Officer Wendt.

"Matt?" The officer said after comparing the signature to the reports.

"Yeah?" Matt frowned at him.

"I'm going to take a huge risk here…and I could get in a lot of trouble…but you're a good friend, and I don't believe these charges." Officer Wendt looked at the house. "She's really in there?"

"Yes." Matt nodded.

"See if she'll come out and talk." Officer Wendt sighed.

Matt sent a text message to Lucas and Josey.

After a few minutes, they walked out the back door.

"Is that Lucas?" The Officer Wendt looked at Matt in surprise.

"Yeah, I just got served papers, figured I need my attorney since he happens to be here." Matt tilted his head as if he was confused.

"Your attorney just happens to be here?" Officer Burling asked, his bewilderment increasing.

"He's engaged to my sister, Nikki." Matt explained to him.

"What's up, Mate?" Lucas asked as they approached, looking concerned at the officers.

Matt handed Lucas the papers.

"What the…" Lucas frowned and looked over at Josey as if she just killed someone.

Matt had to work on not smiling at him.

"What's wrong?" Josey asked, in surprise. She looked nervously at the officers, Matt and Lucas.

She had been nervous, not sure she could pull off the charade.

Lucas handed her the papers, her hands shaking as she took them.

"I don't understand…" She looked from the papers to the officers.

"Did you file a sexual harassment claim against Matt?" Officer Burling asked her.

"Of course not!" Her eyes widened. "He's never done anything like that."

"You're Josey Charmayne Franklin?" Officer Wendt asked.

"Yes, I can get my ID…but I didn't do this." She said with more force.

Officer Wendt looked over at the other officer then back to Josey. "Can I see your ID?"

Josey went to Grayson's truck and retrieved her wallet. "I hope I'm not in trouble for it but I haven't changed from a Montana license yet, I haven't been down here during the week."

The officers glanced at each other then Officer Wendt took her license. He reached for the papers she was holding and compared the signatures; leaning over, he showed them to Officer Burling.

"Would you mind coming downtown with us?" The officer asked Josey.

"What?" She asked in honest fear.

"It's OK." Officer Wendt said. "We just need to review this as soon as possible. I'm fond of Matt and what he's done for our department, so I want to get this cleared up before his reputation is destroyed."

"Of course, then." Josey looked nervously between the two officers. "Can Lucas come with me?" Both officers nodded.

"What do you want me to do?" Matt asked Officer Wendt.

"Stay put." Officer Wendt ordered.

"OK." Matt said and within minutes Lucas and Josey were in the back of the sheriff's car and headed down the driveway.

The Trio, Cora and Nikki stepped out of the house and joined him at the truck.

"How did it go?" His mom asked as she took the seat next to him on the tailgate.

"Pretty much the way we thought it would." Matt sighed.

###

"You're a local hero." His mother said as she walked into the guest bedroom where Matt was hiding from the world as the news media announced the story.

"I'm a what?" He asked, pausing the movie he was watching.

She turned the newspaper to him so he could read the headline: Local Hero Falsely Accused of Sexual Harassment

There were four pictures accompany the article; Matt with the Tagger Herd when they were first rescued, Matt with Josey rescuing the horses in the truck, Matt rappelling down a cliff to rescue a hiker that fell, and Matt in scuba gear searching in the Spokane River. He didn't know which search that was for, but he knew where they got the picture.

"Kevin must have given them the last two." Matt smiled at his mom then scanned the article. "They even interviewed Gary the blackberry bush guy."

She sat in the chair next to the bed and looked at the movie he was watching.

"*Cliffhanger*? Turn it up." She said and stretched her legs out. Matt tossed the paper to the end of the bed and turned up the volume. They sat quietly and watched the movie together.

Halfway through, Matt received an alert on his phone.

TEXT FROM LUCAS: Elena arrested, positively ID'd as the one filing the papers. Preliminary hearing set for next week."

Matt handed his mother the phone. She read it, smiled, then turned back to the movie. They finished watching the movie together then Matt left for the ranch for the next week.

He'd be there until the morning of the preliminary hearing.

***

All the adult Taggers were there to support Josey as they sat with her in the court house.

Matt sat towards the back of the room, his mother at his side with Jack on the other side of her. Scott, Jordan, Leah, Grayson, Nikki and Lucas were in the benches in front of him; Josey on the end next to Lucas so she would have a clear path to take the witness stand. She would be the first to testify. Matt was told that the prosecuting attorney may also call him to testify.

When Elena was ushered into the room, she kept her face stoic and looked straight ahead. She looked at no one in the room except her attorney and the judge.

When she was called to take the stand, Matt heard Josey take a deep breath and let it out slowly. She nodded to Lucas and walked up to the bench and took the seat next to the judge. She started at the beginning with Elena stealing money from her dad when Josey and Elena went to visit him. Then she told of the college account…her paperwork was presented to the judge. She spoke of the meeting in her apartment in Billings when Elena told her about Nikki and the Taggers and asked for her help against them.

Josey was calm and spoke confidently; her voice getting louder and stronger the longer she spoke. She looked from her mother to Lucas and Nikki.

As she started to discuss working for Tagger Enterprises and her connection to Matt, the back doors of the court room opened and three sheriff's officers walked in, looked around at the crowd and spotted Matt.   Officer Wendt slid onto the bench next to Matt and the other two officers stood at the door.

Officer Wendt listened to Josey for a few minutes talking about working with Grayson then turned to Matt.

"How's it going?" He whispered.

"Seems like it's OK." Matt shrugged.

"Do you think you'll have…" Officer Wendt started.

"Excuse me." The judge said loudly. "Officer Wendt?"

Officer Wendt's head shot up and he looked startled at the judge. "Yes, Sir?"

"Is there a problem that can't wait until we're done here?" The Judge asked.

Officer Wendt stood, looked down at Matt then up to the judge. "We've had a couple hikers get caught in a rockslide." The Office nervously smiled. "Matt's been our go to man in these situations, he's our best at rock climbing. We were checking to see if he was going to be available. We need to move now, sir."

Matt looked up at the judge, then his eyes flickered to Josey who was looking at her hands that were resting in her lap.

The Judge looked at Elena, her public defender, the prosecuting attorney, then he pointed at Matt. "Mr. Tagger."

Matt stood.

"I don't see the need for you to testify, everything is pretty clear here. Please, go with the officers." The Judged nodded.

Matt turned to his mother and gave her a kiss on the cheek. The rest of his family turned and nodded.

"Mr. Tagger?" The judge called out.

"Yes, Sir." Matt stopped at the door and turned.

"Good luck to you and the hikers…please be safe." The judge nodded.

"Will do." Matt nodded with another look at Josey. Her head was still down.

He walked out the door.

CHAPTER SIXTEEN

Matt turned and watched the ambulance drive away. He sighed in exhaustion and near heat stroke.

"It has to be 110 degrees out here." Kevin said after downing another bottle of water.

"I agree," Matt nodded and lay back on the ground and looked up at the blue sky; his legs still dangling over the edge of the rock bluff. "I'm not sure which I'd prefer; 110 degree heat or the icy waters of the winter river."

"Flip of the coin on that one." Kevin chuckled as he coiled his rope.

"Matt?" He heard someone call his name so he twisted his head up to look. It was Kevin's boss, Sam.

"Yeah?" Matt answered.

"You have company." The man smiled.

"Seriously? Up here?" Matt frowned.

Sam nodded. "She said her name is Josey."

Matt stared at him, stunned that she was there and shocked that she introduced herself as Josey.   He looked back up at the sky.

"Isn't she the one…?" Kevin started.

"Yeah," Matt sighed.

"You're going to just lay there when you have a lady like that sitting at your truck?" Sam asked with a wry grin.

Matt just shook his head and sighed. For a couple of hours…just for a couple of hours he had escaped…Elena, the court, and his conflicting feelings for the woman waiting for him.

"I don't mind keeping her company while you lay there like a lump." The man informed him.

"Is she in a sundress?" Matt asked without looking at him.

"No…but I sure would love to see that." Sam chuckled.

"It is quite the sight," Matt smiled, thinking of her walking towards him, hair bouncing, eye's laughing.

"Then why are you laying there?" Kevin asked.

"Delaying…delaying facing reality," Matt sighed.

"She is reality, that's for sure." Kevin nodded. "Good or bad?"

"I don't know." Matt smiled over at him.

"Matt, if you're not going to get up…I'm headed over there." Sam warned him.

"Alright," Matt stood and started coiling his rope. He glanced over at his truck.

She had changed out of her court clothes and was wearing denim shorts and a white t-shirt. She was sitting on the tailgate with her knees pulled up to her chest and her arms wrapped them. Hair in a ponytail, her head lay peacefully on her knees. She was watching the people putting away their equipment.

She looked beautiful and sad.

"See you later." Kevin called out.

Matt watched her as he approached his truck. His mind went to the shared smile on the climbing wall in Montana, then the comforting feel of her when the horse died. Then there were the emotions when they kissed…the entrancing lilacs…

Why couldn't they have met under different circumstances? Where was the reset button to start this all over again?

Her eyes shifted and she saw him approach but she didn't move and her expression didn't change.

He threw the equipment in the back of the truck and walked around to stand in front of her. He glanced around looking for a vehicle that she would have driven but he didn't see one.

Without moving, she looked at him and gave him a slight smile.

"How did you get here?" Matt smiled back.

"I can't tell you that."

"Why?"

"It's to be explained to you in person."

"Really? Huh."

"Why didn't you ever call me Frankie?" She tilted her head up, just resting her chin on her knees.

"It's not who you are, it's who you had to be." He said honestly.

She nodded, tears just rimming her eyes. "They're going to extradite her to Nevada. Since she broke probation she'll be in jail for five years. Lucas figures she'll make a deal for two years here too, to run after the Nevada time."

Matt leaned against the tailgate next to her and looked out at the people gathering equipment and driving away. The wicked woman was out of their lives…it had to be hard on Josey and, if she would admit it, Nikki.

"You OK?"

"I'm a bit numb."

"What can I do to help?"

"I don't know…I just wanted to tell you what happened, I just wanted to see you." She sighed and closed her eyes.

Matt watched her for a moment, then walked to the passenger side of his truck, opened the door, and reclined the seat as far back as it would go.

When he lifted her off the truck, her arms encircled his neck and she rested her head on his shoulder. Dang…it felt good to hold her.

"This must be the cradle-hugging that Sadie was talking about." Josey whispered tiredly. "I agree…it's comforting."

Matt chuckled and set her on the seat and buckled her in.

As he crawled in behind the wheel, Josey turned towards him, eyes still closed, and hand held out to him.

Matt started the truck and headed down the road. He reached out, took her hand and held it all the way to The Homestead.

When they arrived, she was sound asleep, so he carried her to the house.

"Is she alright?" Cora whispered as she opened the backdoor.

"I believe Mom calls it 'mentally exhausted'." Matt answered as he walked Josey to the guest bedroom.

Cora folded back the covers and Matt lay her down gently. He pulled the blanket over her shoulders then gently lifted her hair away from her face. He stood quietly for a moment and listened to her breathing and gazed at her serene beautiful face. He could stand there all night, but forced himself to turn away and turn off the lights.

Matt sat on top the fence and watched as Wade released the steer from the chute and Grace and Reilly bolted out of the box, ropes swinging. Both hit their marks and stretched the steer.

Grayson nodded with a pleased grin.

"It's Sadie's turn now." Scott called out to the laughing teenagers.

Matt climbed down from the fence and grabbed a barrel and stepped off the paces. He looked up and made sure it was placed correctly with the ones Leah and Jordan were setting up. Sadie was back to competing…but not winning. She was having a hard time in unfamiliar arenas. He silently hoped that Josey could help where the rest of the family couldn't.

Matt turned and looked back at Sadie and Josey talking just outside the arena gate. Josey's arms were working imaginary reins as she described the positions to Sadie, who was nodding with a serious expression.

He climbed back on the fence and looked down at the barn to see his mother standing at the corner looking up at him, she nodded.

Matt turned and nodded to Grayson.

Grayson smiled and turned to Sadie. "Come on in."

Josey opened the gate and let Sadie and Scarecrow into the arena then followed.

They walked to the first barrel as Josey motioned with her arms the angle Sadie should be running. Sadie nodded.

"Wouldn't be easier if you just ran the pattern for her?" Grayson called out to Josey.

Josey shrugged. "This will work, she's getting it."

"I am, Dad." Sadie glared at him.

"I know, Sadie Girl." Grayson smiled at her. "But I think if Josey was on a horse she could help you better."

"It's OK, Grayson." Josey turned to him.

"How about this one?" Matt's mom asked as she led a tall dappled palomino gelding through the gate.

Josey turned and stared as her face turned white. Her legs started shaking as her hand shot out to Scarecrow to use her as a brace.

"What is it?" Sadie asked and looked in the direction Josey was staring.

"It's my Apollo." Josey whispered, voice quivering and tears had started sliding down her cheeks. "My boy…"

"That's your horse?" Sadie said excitedly. "He's beautiful…a big boy!"

Josey nodded, a sob escaping…her chin trembling.

Apollo was led into the arena with Josey's saddle and bridle already on. He pranced excitedly and tossed his head making his white mane fly.

When he was released, the tall horse trotted around the parameter of the arena then made his way to Scarecrow. The dappled gold gelding and the pure gold mare sniffed at each other then Apollo turned his attention on Josey. His long nose stretched out to her. Josey's hand shook as it reached for the muzzle of the horse, touching him lightly as if he were a ghost.

"My boy…" Josey laid her head on the horse's neck, her shoulders shaking from the sobs. The horse pushed his nose against her side. "I didn't…I thought you were gone forever."

As Matt watched the reunion, his mother walked to him and leaned against the fence he was sitting on.

"Hop on, let's see you ride." Jordan called out.

Josey hugged the horse, then quickly stepped to his side and mounted. She instantly fell over to the horse's neck and ran her hands down the length of it. When she sat up, her hands covered her face and she started crying again…shoulders shaking.

As she cried into her hands, with just her legs, she moved the horse forward and turned towards Matt and his mother. When she was close enough, she unburied her face and wiped away as much of the tears as she could.

With red rimmed eyes, she looked down at his mother, "I never thought I would see him again…thank you, how did you know?"

His mom looked up at Matt then walked away.

Josey smiled at him as she maneuvered the horse next to the fence. He reached out and stroked the neck of the yellow gelding.

"I'll pay you back." She whispered with a smile, her eyes sparkling. She reached out a hand.

He took her hand and squeezed. "No, you won't. Now go ride."

"I can't thank you enough." There was pure joy in her smile.

"Go ride." Matt smiled.

The family watched as Josey rode Apollo around the arena with Sadie and Scarecrow at their side. They were already discussing the battle of the blondes.

He didn't know why he had taken the picture of the horse's registration papers when they were coming back from Billings, but watching her ride the gelding with a truly happy smile across her face, he was really glad he did.

Matt turned as Nora climb up on the fence next to him. She was wearing her riding clothes, her long hair pulled back into two long pony tails just at the base of her neck.

They watched the pair ride for a few minutes in silence.

"Did you know that the first time Candace spoke to me, she said I was ugly?" Nora asked, looking at him with a tilted head.

"What?" Matt asked in surprise. "But you're friends and you're not ugly."

Nora shrugged. "We weren't friends then, and I believed her and it really hurt."

"Nora, I don't know what to say, but you're not ugly."

She smiled. "Reilly told me that, but it took a while to believe it."

"Why are you telling me this now?"

"The reason Candace said I was ugly was because she didn't like me. She didn't like me because her mother kept comparing her to me…wanting her to be better than me…so Candace started to hate me…because of her mother." Nora looked up at him, waiting.

Matt stared at her for a moment then he shook his head in disbelief. "You brought Josey up to the mountain to me?"

Nora nodded with a slight smile. "Candace and I are best friends because we got past what her mother did."

"You're wise beyond your years, Miss Nora." Matt sighed. "But you're not old enough to drive. Who was the chauffer?"

Nora smiled mischievously; her dark brown eyes twinkling with the secret.

"I've figured it was one or all of my so-called fathers." Matt raised a brow.

Nora slowly shook her head.

"No? Hmmm, that's surprising."

She climbed down from the fence and grinned up at him. "I'll give you one clue."

"OK." Matt smiled. He was enjoying her game.

"We rhyme." She grinned and walked away.

Matt laughed so hard he nearly fell off the fence. He turned and looked for his favorite devious cook. She was standing next to Scott and Grayson. When Nora approached Cora, the older woman looked at her then up to Matt. She gave him an innocent wave.

###

Matt leaned on the railing of the deck behind the house. He watched her leading the gold horse into the barn.

He pushed the button on the phone.

"Matt?" Josey answered.

"Is this Josey Franklin?" He asked.

"Of course, it is."

"Josey, this is Matt Tagger, we met in Billings a couple of months ago."

"OK…"

"I was hoping you would remember me."

"I do."

"Good, I was wondering…if you weren't busy…if you would like to go out on a date Friday night."

"A date?"

"Yes, if you're interested…I guess I should have asked if you were single first."

"I'm single, and if I remember right, you're not that bad looking either…and you have a really nice horse."

He laughed, "Well, I hope that works in favor of you saying yes to the date. I'd like to get to know you."

"You would, huh. Well I think it could be interesting. What would we do on this date?"

"I was thinking dinner at the Italian restaurant just across the river, then maybe a bike ride on the levee path."

"Well, that sounds just lovely."

"Is that a yes then?"

"Yes, Matt Tagger, I would love to go on the date with you."

"I'll pick you up at six on Friday night."

"It's a date."

They ended the call…she walked out of the barn and looked for him…their eyes met and they smiled.

Reset button…pushed.

THE TAGGER HERD SERIES

Nora Tagger

THREE HORSES AND A DREAM

Gini Roberge

CHAPTER ONE

"Nora! Get your right leg off him!"

"Nora! Get control of his speed!"

"Nora! Straighten him out!"

"Nora! Cow side only!"

"Nora! Stop him square!"

"Nora! Outside rein! Outside rein! Pick it up….hold him!"

Nora! Started hating her name…it had truly become a four letter word for her. She took a deep breath and kept her mouth closed. She listened intently to each order that was yelled at her and tried to react as fast as she could.

"Wait until he's at the hip!"

"Get in front of the cow!"

Maybe he realized he didn't have to say her name to know who he was yelling at…since they were the only two in the whole arena. Mouth closed…concentrate…

"Straighten him out!"

"Listen to me!"

"Black cow, black cow, black cow!"

"Stay on your horse!"

"Sit down on him!"

"Work up to the cow!"

"Nora, stay down on him!"

"Nora, use your feet!"

Dang…he remembered her name. Mouth closed…this was taking forever!

"Find a good spot and break it off."

She trotted Cooper over to Casey, her cutting coach, expecting him to be angry with her since he yelled so much.

"Good job." He nodded.

Her eyebrows shot up in surprise as she turned the black gelding to look out to the cattle in the arena. He always wanted to talk about the calves at the end of the training.

"It was a bit more intense training today since you're leaving tomorrow." Casey smirked at her surprised expression.

Nora and her mom had decided that Casey looked a lot like Dennis Quaid. He was a National Champion and had been competing and training students in reining and cutting for over forty years. Her parents had been assured that he was the premier trainer in the Northwest.

"We're headed down to Nampa for this weekend, then in two weeks we're at Pocatello." Nora reminded him.

"I'll be in the arena with you on both."

Nora rolled her lips together and nodded.

He grunted. "I promise I won't yell at you in front of everyone."

Nora glanced at him with a slight smile. "Thanks. I'll be taking Arcturus and Isaiah too, the horse show is this weekend too."

"You're going to be a busy lady. Are you still in royalty?"

"Just finishing out the reign for princess with the club, Grace was the queen. Then I have tryouts for the Northwest Youth Rodeo in mid-October but it starts in January if I'm appointed to their court."

"That seems a lot to make your mother haul you around to."

Nora stared at him, forcing herself to keep her face calm…like Aunt Dru's poker face. She didn't respond to his comment.

"You've only been competing in cutting for 6 weeks and second place in Caldwell a couple of weeks ago is pretty darn good. You're good at THIS." His arm swung to the cattle.

His yelling echoed in her head as she raised a brow to him.

He frowned at her. "Nearly everything I yelled at you, you were already doing. I was just reinforcing what you were doing."

She shrugged. "Maybe it's from watching Mom and Dad practice and compete. Plus I study a lot on the internet."

Casey stared at her long enough she thought something was wrong. He just nodded and pointed towards the cattle. "When you choose your cow…"

Chit chat was over; back to training, that was the way Casey worked.

An hour later, she stepped out of the saddle as Casey walked out of the arena. Her best friend, Candace, met her at the gate.

"Scott said to leave the cows in there, he's going to come out and practice in a little while."

Nora nodded.

"Why do you have a coach if your dad and mom know how to cut?"

Nora rolled her eyes. "If they yelled at me like that, I'd QUIT!"

Candace laughed which made her blonde curls bounce and her brown eyes shine.

"I need to work out the stress." Nora told her as they walked to the barn. "I think I'm going to take Arcturus on a walk and practice halter…he's never gotten better than third."

"Wish Lola was here…do you want me to walk Isaiah with you?"

Nora nodded and Candace ran ahead of her and Cooper to get the halters.

Cooper was brushed, grained, and loved on so she closed the stall door and took the lead rope for the other black horse. She reached up and touched his star. He leaned into her and she breathed in deeply to release the tension. Arcturus fed her energy and she started feeling better.

They slowly walked out of the barn and down the driveway.

Casey was sitting in his truck talking to her parents out the window. He stared at the horses as they walked by.

"Do you like him?" Candace asked when they were far enough away she knew they couldn't be heard.

"Not really," Nora admitted. She wasn't used to not liking people and really didn't say things like that out loud.

"Why?"

"I've never had anyone yell at me like that." She also didn't like his comment about making her mother haul her around.

"Wish I could say that."

Nora turned to her friend, remembering the horrible night they rescued her from the rodeo grounds when she was abandoned by her parents after months of emotional abuse.

"I'm sorry, Candace."

"Don't be. It's been over a year and I owe a lot to you and our friendship."

"You may not believe it, but I owe you just as much." Nora sighed. If it wasn't for Candace calling her ugly, she may still believe she was; then there was Nora's friendship with Sadie.

Another half hour of practice, with Candace critiquing her work with both horses, they decided to take a break and made their way to the pasture island. They climbed the fence and slid onto the horse's bare backs. Nora wiggled to Arcturus' hips then lay forward over his back and let her arms and legs dangle freely as he started grazing. She was glad she was wearing the Tagger Enterprises cap instead of the cowboy hat so it didn't get in the way. Her black hair was in a Sadie braid down her back.

Candace copied her position on Isaiah and the girls looked at each other and grinned.

"I don't think there could be anything more relaxing than this." Nora closed her eyes. All the stress from being yelled at was being melted from the warmth of the horse underneath her and the hot July morning sun beating down on her back.

Her mind went to the competition in Nampa that next weekend. She had already downloaded the patterns and memorized them. As she lay on the horse, she envisioned riding him around the pattern. Her hands and feet twitched as she practiced the movements of hand and body. She straightened her spine in anticipation of the ride. Then she imagined the pattern again but this time on Isaiah since she was going to compete with both of them.

In her imaginary practice, she was just headed to the gate obstacle, moving her feet to the cues she needed to give the horse, when she heard his truck. She knew it was his, having taught herself a long time ago how to listen and identify different trucks…the Trio's in particular. Then there was Reilly's blue truck, Grace's Trail Boss, and now Billy's.

Her eyes opened slightly as he turned into the driveway and slowly drove up the length of it. She could see him watching them but she didn't move or make any indication that she could see him. From his view, she had to look like she was asleep.

Nora watched him, watch her. Since she kissed him on Reilly's birthday, she had barely seen him…her choosing. He was a distraction. Even now as she was trying to practice he was distracting her…the imaginary gate didn't get opened.

"Who is that?" Candace broke the silence when his truck engine turned off.

The horses had moved apart as they grazed so she couldn't see her friend.

"Reilly's football friend." Nora closed her eyes.

"How old is he?"

"Seventeen, same as Reilly and Grace."

"Is that too old for us?"

Nora smiled. She had asked herself that a thousand times. "We're going to be in 9th grade and they are seniors."

"Did that answer my question?"

"Right now yes, in four years, no."

"That sucks."

Nora didn't reply even though she had the same opinion. The truck engine started and she opened her eyes again and watched it go down the driveway. Reilly was looking out at her from the passenger seat. His arm was hanging out the window and his hand flipped out in an unseen wave by the driver. Nora flipped her hand out in return. He understood and always made sure to never leave them alone and did his best to meet Billy away from The Homestead when she was there.

"Where do you think they are going?"

"Probably to the gym. Reilly has been going with them to build his upper body strength so he can throw the rope harder."

"Where's Grace?"

"With Josey and Sadie at The Stables. They are practicing barrels and poles over there since the cattle are here."

"Are Josey and Matt still dating?"

"I don't know. They went on their first date when we were in Caldwell a couple weeks ago." Nora opened her eyes and looked into the South pasture where Libby and Kit were pastured with their babies. The foals, Leroy and Zorra were grazing peacefully.

"Nora!" Her mother's voice interrupted them.

She flipped her head to the other side of Arcturus and looked towards the barn.

"Come in, your dad's going to practice."

Nora sat straight up. "Can I yell at him like Casey yells at me?"

She heard her mother laugh as she disappeared into the barn.

Nora clucked Arcturus into movement and used her legs to guide him to the small corral where she slid off him. They led the horses into the barn then headed up to the arena.

"I'm sure glad they finally put some portable bleachers out here." Candace said as they climbed up the short bleacher section and prepared to watch the practice.

Aunt Dru riding Rufio and Uncle Grayson riding Dollar joined her dad and Little Ghost in the arena.

Nora's mom and Cora sat on the bleachers next to her and Candace.

Wade and Alex were with Nick at Circle 50.

As the Trio warmed up the horses, her mother turned to her.

"Casey said you're doing quite well." She said proudly.

Nora shrugged. "I guess we'll find out this weekend."

"Don't let his yelling make you nervous." Her mom frowned.

Two and a half minutes to cut three cows…it happened so fast that his yelling actually made her focus more, but she wasn't going to tell anyone that. "I won't."

"Are you coming with us this weekend, Cora?" Nora asked.

The older woman shook her head. "I'll be with Leah taking Wade and Sadie to the Winchester rodeo."

"I'm gonna miss that one." Nora scrunched her face. It was a lot of fun last year as the Queen.

"Me, too." Her mom rested her elbows on her knees and a chin in her hand. "Things are changing…next year Reilly and Grace will be eighteen and out of the youth association."

Nora stared at her dad as he and Little Ghost danced with a cow. She thought of Casey's comment about her mother hauling her around to the rodeos, horse shows, and royalty events. She had never really thought about 'making' her mother haul her to all the events. She quickly glanced at her mother then back out to her dad. Did her mother really want to spend all the time away from him just to haul Nora to all the extra events that the other kids weren't doing? Was it fair to her mother or her dad?

She was only fourteen now and had planned on running for Miss Rodeo Idaho when she was twenty, like Cambria Weber had done. That was SIX more years. After she had her driver's license and learned how to pull a trailer she could haul herself around, but that was still two years of her mother hauling her. Was that fair? Was her quest for Miss Rodeo Idaho selfish? She'd tried so hard to be a good person. Would a good person make two people that loved each other spend so much time apart?

"Scott! Straighten him out!" Her mother yelled and broke her out of her haze.

CHAPTER TWO

"Are you ready?" Casey said without looking at her.

Nora nodded as she watched the little palomino miss the block of the cow as it trotted back to the herd. The rider yelled out from frustration.

"Don't ever do that," Casey ordered.

"I won't."

Nora took a deep breath and let out all the tension. She was more nervous in this competition than she was in any other she'd ever done.

"I can yell at you if you think it would help."

Her eyes shot up to him. His stoic expression was broken by the hint of humor in his eyes.

"Relax." He shrugged as if he were bored. "The world will not end if you don't do well. It's only your third competition."

Her back stiffen. She didn't go through all his yelling just to make an excuse of her inexperience and not do her best. Not everyone could win, but everyone could do their best.

"It's time." He nudged his horse forward.

Nora glared at the back of his head and pushed Cooper through the gate with Casey closing it behind her.

She quickly glanced around the whole arena, keeping herself from looking for her parents in the bleachers.

"Pay attention to the cows." Casey said gruffly.

Her lips rolled together and her stomach tightened. She really didn't like him.

She looked at each of the cows and slowly walked Cooper towards them.

"Remember to be aware of the turn back men but concentrate on the cow. To your right, little black with white spot." Casey told her.

Nora nodded and walked calmly into the calves, her eyes staring at the white spot on the cow. It rushed out of the crowd of its buddies and trotted out. The two riders in the middle of the arena blocked its path, forcing the cow to face Nora and Cooper.

Her hands lowered to Cooper's neck and the dance was on…

The cow shot out to her right and Cooper jumped towards it, she barely had to touch the horse to cue him back onto his haunches anticipating the turn of the cow. Cooper was set and pushed off to block the cow's turn.

She tried to make sure that any movement she made to direct Cooper was unseen. The more the judges could see her directing the horse, the more points were deducted from her score.

She could hear Casey talking firmly to her and tried to follow his direction as best she could. Back and forth the cow ran and Cooper blocked each move.

"Good." She heard Casey call out.

Nora waited until the cow stopped then pulled back on the reins to walk back in for another one.

"Little white one all the way in the back, this is the one to go deep in for." Casey called out.

Nora made her way deep into the pack and walked the little white one out. This one stayed in the middle of the arena and bounced back and forth. Cooper bounced, matching it's every move. Her body was jerked back and forth but she lowered her heels in the stirrups and pushed against the saddle horn to help keep in the saddle.

"Watch your seat." Casey hollered. "Good."

Again she waited until the cow stopped and she pulled back and went for another.

Her eyes hit a little red one that was at the edge of the herd, it looked full of energy so she went for it before Casey told her which one to cut.

"Watch him…thirty seconds…" Casey called out.

The cow trotted out farther away from the little herd than the others did which gave Cooper more room to move. The turn back rider pushed the cow towards her and Nora anticipated it would move right and, with a minuscule movement, she cued Cooper onto his haunches and was relieved when the cow moved right and Cooper was ready for it. They ran forward, the cow turned sharply, and Cooper turned as sharply, jerking Nora to the side. She held onto the saddle horn. They ran forward, Cooper leaning toward the cow so she barely lifted her outer leg up and pushed with her cow side leg. Cooper adjusted his path and ran straight to block the cow. She and Cooper turned with the cow and the buzzer went off.

"Good job." Casey called out just as the crowd erupted. Her dad's voice rang out over all the others.

Holding in her elation, she turned Cooper away and reached down to pat his neck. Her heart was racing in excitement and her eyes shot up to her coach.

He had a slight smile and was nodding his head in approval.

They both turned to the score board. There would be two judges each scoring her from 60 to 80 then the score added together. She received a 73 and a 74, total 147! She was in front of the three competitors that went before her, and there were only two left. So she at least had third.

They moved out of the arena and stood quietly watching the next rider.

No matter what Casey said, she knew she did good and it was exciting, exhilarating and heart pounding…it was one of the most exciting things she'd ever done!

"Your mom said she would record it."

"She always does so we can critique ourselves." Nora tried to keep her voice calm.

"I'll be over Monday afternoon to review it and work out a practice plan for the next two weeks."

Nora nodded. He still talked like he was bored. She rolled her lips again…still not liking him.

The buzzer went off, they looked at the scoreboard and waited…72 and 72, total 144…she at least had second and tried really hard not to let her excitement show.

She leaned forward and stroked Cooper's neck as the last rider rode into the little herd.

Nora was sure the next two and a half minutes was actually thirty. Her hands shook while she fiddled with his mane. She judged the rider and horse herself and was sure she did better.

She glanced at Casey. He was leaning against the saddle horn staring at the rider, probably judging them too.

The buzzer went off and their eyes immediately went to the scoreboard and patiently waited…70 and 71, total 141.

The elation ran through her as Nora grinned and looked over at her coach. She expected a bored look but was excited to see a smile as he nodded at her.

They could hear her parents screaming for her.

Nora stepped into the trailer, locked it, and quickly pulled off her boots. What a day! She had first in cutting, three firsts with Isaiah, and two seconds with Arcturus plus another third place showing in halter for him. That was just for Saturday! She still had more on Sunday.

She grabbed her phone and sat up on the bed. Her parents were checking on the horses one more time…or making out in the truck again.

First she sent a text to Nick letting him know her day's accomplishments.

Then she called Cora's phone. Nora's day had been so busy she nearly forgot that Sadie was running a race. Sadie was still having problems running in arenas away from home and had only come in third and fourth in the two she had run.

Cora didn't answer. Nora jumped off the bed and started pacing and dialed again. No answer. UGH!!!

She stood frozen and stared at the phone. She imagined Cora racing to it and seeing she'd missed Nora's call then calling her back…nothing.

Three quick knocks on the door and she looked through the window to see her parents. Her mother was on the phone.

Nora unlocked the door and opened it. "Is she talking with Cora?" She asked her dad.

He grinned. "Yes."

"That's why she didn't answer the phone." Nora looked at her mother's expression. She was frowning. "How did Sadie do?" She interrupted.

"Be patient." Her dad said calmly, also trying to read the expression on his wife's face.

"Wade won." Her mother smiled.

"Sadie?" Nora asked, holding her breath. Wade had won or come in second in nearly every event this year so she wasn't worried about him.

The smile disappeared, she shook her head, and held up three fingers.

"Third," Nora plopped onto the bed and looked at her dad. "She placed first in that one the last two years. It was one of Scarecrow's very first races ever and she won it." Nora lay back on the bed. "She HAS to do better in these next ones or she won't make it for the finals."

"How many are left?" He whispered.

"Two double headers then the final." Nora sighed. "I'll be with her next week. She HAS to do good on those or she won't have enough points to qualify."

Her mother hung up the phone. "She placed second in breakaway but that third barrel is giving her problems."

"It hasn't been that long since her accident…just barely four months." Her dad reminded her. "The important thing is she is back racing…whether she's winning or not."

"I guess." Nora sighed.

Her phone alerted her to a message.

TEXT FROM NICK: 85!

Nora giggled. It was the score that their bull riding friend Dude received when a bull kicked him in the butt. She showed the message to her parents.

"Well, you may be a kick in the pants, but you kicked butt today." Her dad grinned. "Did you enjoy it?"

"Oh yeah!" Nora nodded as she grabbed her pajamas and headed for the bathroom. "Except Arcturus' halter class."

"What did Casey say?" Her mom asked.

"That he would be over Monday to watch the video and set up a training plan for the next two weeks." Nora answered.

"No good job or anything?" Her dad asked.

"Yeah, I guess." She closed the door and quickly changed. When she opened the door, they were kissing again. "Stop that."

They all three chuckled. She loved seeing her parents happy.

Nora found her patterns for the next day and studied them while her parents prepared for bed. She was in the lower bed, the table converted to a bed, and her parents shared the upper bed.

"I kind of like you being with us." Her mother said to him as she crawled into the bed next to him. "I wish Wade was here so it was a family trip."

"Second cutting is coming up. After we get the hay in, we'll have to grab a day and do a family vacation somewhere." Her dad turned off the light.

Nora placed the papers on the table and tucked herself under the covers.

She closed her eyes and thought of her mother hauling her around…keeping them apart. It wasn't fair…she really was being selfish. A good person wasn't selfish.

Should she put her dream on hold and stop royalty until she could do it herself?

CHAPTER THREE

"How did you do Sunday?" Casey asked as they waited for the barn office computer to turn on.

"Arcturus won first in Reining, second in Western Pleasure, and third in Ranch Pleasure. Isaiah won in Trail and second in Reining."

"So YOU placed first and second in the Reining?"

"Yes."

"How many horses in that class?"

"Twelve."

The computer was finally on and she played the video from her winning ride. He critiqued her every bad move for the next 20 minutes. How could she possibly have won if she did nothing right?

Nora heard someone walk into the barn but didn't turn to look.

"You did a good pick with that little red cow at the end."

Finally!

"Was it luck or did you know what you were looking for?"

Bubble burst.

"He was energetic and I needed one that was a little more challenging for Cooper so it balanced the other two."

"Good."

Hoof beats caught her attention so she glanced out the door. It was Sadie leading Scarecrow.

"She the one that got hurt?" Casey asked as he leaned back in the chair.

Nora leaned back too and nodded.

"She's back to competing?"

"Yes, but she's not the same."

"What do you mean?"

Nora didn't know how to describe it so she leaned forward and grabbed the computer mouse. She played a video of one of Sadie's races.

"Here's last year." She told him.

They watched as Sadie bolted out of the alley and around the barrels then flying down the final stretch to victory.

"Do you have the accident?" He asked.

Nora played the accident with the volume off.

His arm twitched when she hit the wall, but he didn't say anything.

"New race?" He asked.

"This is from Saturday."

When it finished; "Play it again."

So she did, three times.

"She has a problem with the horse." He stated flatly.

"With Scarecrow?" Nora asked in disbelief.

"If that's the horse she's racing there."

"She has complete faith in Scarecrow…everyone does."

He shook his head. "She has a problem with what she's asking the horse, not what the horse is doing."

Nora sat back and stared at him then to the computer. "She's afraid of hurting Scarecrow?" Nora guessed that was what he was saying.

"She needs to get out of the arena and build up her trust between the horse and her…or her in what she is asking of the horse."

"How do you fix that?"

"You're a smart girl, Nora." He nodded. "You're a tremendous equestrian, even at fourteen."

"Well…thanks?" She lifted a brow.

He chuckled and stood. "I'll be back in the morning. Be ready by six, it's supposed to be in the triple digits the rest of the week so we'll stay away from late afternoons."

After he left, she walked to the corner of the barn to watch Sadie. She and Wade were trotting around the arena, their laughter floated in the air. Needing quiet to think, she walked down to the south pasture and the new babies, Leroy and Zorra.

Kit and Libby ignored her as she approached their babies. Aunt Dru had been working with the foals and they were quite friendly. She rubbed them down and laughed as they tried to push each other out of the way to get her attention.

Nora rubbed the black Zorra's chest and giggled as the horse's nose scrunched and twitched and her head bounced. The little buckskin colt did the same when she scratched him.

They bored with her quickly and moved close to their mothers; plopping to the ground for a nap.

Nora climbed onto the fence and watched the mares graze and the babies sleep. She thought of Sadie.

Trying to help Sadie, her family had hauled her around to all the local arenas and some private arenas to practice in. But Casey said to get her out of the arena.

"Amazing how long you can sit and stare at two small horses sleeping."

Nora turned to her Aunt Dru. She had her long blond hair pulled in a high ponytail and no hat today, her blue eyes looking out to the two sleeping foals.

"I agree." Nora nodded.

"What's going on in that head of yours?"

"Nothing but horses," Nora smiled.

"You're a bit of an equine fiend this summer, aren't you?" Her aunt leaned against the fence next to her.

"Eat, breath, sleep, think, talk, walk…"

"Jessup, Jack and I rode your little trio of horses from the auction the last couple of days. We pushed the cows to the lower valley and tried them out on different terrain. You did a great job, we were all impressed. I believe Jack has put his dibs on the little gruella you called Chevy."

Nora grinned at her. She had been surprised and excited when Uncle Grayson told her the three were hers to train and had loved every moment of it. Learning the horse's personalities was always fun but the best thing…was always the first ride.

"So you're out here clearing your brain by looking at horses?" She chuckled.

"Yeah," Nora laughed which made both foal's heads raise and look at her. They quickly went back to sleeping.

"You had a great weekend, are you ready for next weekend?"

"Arcturus and Isaiah have the weekend off but I need to practice goat tying more on Cooper. We're getting better but he's ready for the poles."

"Funny, isn't it?" Her aunt chuckled.

"What is?"

"When we had the meeting in the bunkhouse before the horses were trained, I told you, you couldn't have three horses to show." Her aunt looked at her proudly, "But you're doing very well on all three."

"Three horses," Nora smiled and her heart warmed as she thought of the three geldings. "I love all three…I love all horses."

Nora looked out at Kit, Libby and the babies. She wondered about talking to her aunt about Sadie.

"Just spit it out."

Nora smirked; of course she would know she wanted to talk. Aunt Dru was smart like that. "Are you going to the ranch tomorrow?"

"I wasn't planning on it. Do you need me to?"

"What would you think of an all-girl trail ride?"

"On a Tuesday?"

Nora nodded and told her aunt of her plan to help her cousin.

"Well," Aunt Dru grinned. "It's good to be the boss."

"This is fun!" Sadie declared; her blue eyes shining bright under her straw cowboy hat.

"I agree." Josey swung her saddle on the back of her gold horse, Apollo.

Nora tightened the cinch on Arcturus. He wasn't going to the rodeo over the weekend so she decided to have a fun trail ride on him, getting him out of the arena, too.

She stepped up into the saddle and looked around at their fellow riders.

Her mom on Cooper, Grace on Eli, Aunt Dru on Trooper, Aunt Leah on Rufio, Tessa on Patience, Cora on Dollar, Nikki on Harvey, and, of course, Sadie on Scarecrow. Nora's dad was practicing on Little Ghost so Sadie couldn't use the horse like she wanted. Of course, he was only following Nora's request.

"How come we've never done this before?" Aunt Leah asked.

Nora smiled as she listened to all the banter. Only Aunt Dru knew the plan and Nora sure hoped it worked.

"Ladies! Are you all sure you don't need me to come along?" Jessup hollered from the steps of the ranch house.

"You just put your feet up and eat a couple bon bons." Aunt Dru waved as they started down the road.

"So where are we headed?" Josey asked.

"We'll take a shortcut over to Circle 50." Nikki told her sister. "I have a surprise for us."

"Oh, fun!" Grace called out.

"Then we'll come back over by the Ghost town." Aunt Dru told them.

"How long will it take?" Cora asked.

"We'll be back by dinner." Aunt Dru told her. "And Jessup promised to have it ready for us."

"Terrific." Cora clapped.

The afternoon ride to Circle 50 was uneventful but a lot of fun with all the excited non-stop talk.

After her morning session with Casey and practice, Nora needed an afternoon of fun. He had yelled at her more than usual. For some odd reason, since she had won and did a good job, she didn't think he would be so loud or gruff. There was no friendly chit chat or talk of Sadie at the training. He came, he yelled, he left.

When they reached Circle 50, Nikki dismounted and ran in the house to return with a big box of ice cream bars, to the delight of everyone. They all laughed as they each took two.

Ten minutes out from the ranch, Aunt Dru put Nora's plan into action.

"Let's do follow the leader?" Her aunt called out.

"Sounds like fun." Aunt Leah agreed.

"What's that?" Tessa asked.

"Some off trail riding," Nikki explained. "Everyone takes a turn leading the group through obstacles or fun routes."

"Everyone has to do it?" Tessa asked in concern.

"You'll be fine." Aunt Dru assured her. "You've become quite the rider the last couple of months. It'll be good for you and Patience."

Tessa smiled anxiously in thanks and reached down to run a hand down the neck of her new palomino paint horse.

"Who first?" Nora asked; already knowing the answer.

"Let's go from oldest to youngest." Aunt Dru answered.

"Oh, yeah! Me first." Cora laughed and turned Dollar off the road and down into the trees.

"Me, last!" Sadie shouted with a laugh.

Cora led them for the next fifteen minutes into ditches and around trees. They had fun and ended on the road.

"My turn!" Aunt Dru called out. "Follow me, ladies."

She led them down a steep mountain side that made them lean back in the saddle. Tessa was nervous so her aunt stayed close. "Trust your horse." She told her. Tessa nodded and was smiling by the time they reached the bottom.

It was a very good training session for Tessa and Patience. It helped build trust in each other.

"Now we go up," Aunt Dru called out and she led them straight up the hill, no zig-zagging which made it more difficult.

Nora was in the middle of the pack with Sadie riding next to her. She glanced at her cousin who was frowning instead of smiling like everyone else.

"What's wrong?" Nora asked her.

"I'm just worried about hurting Scarecrow." Sadie said in a low voice.

Proof that Casey was right.

"We've done this dozens of times." Nora reminded her.

"I know."

"Look at Tessa and Patience."

Sadie's head turned.

"Tessa's never done this before and she's having fun." Nora pointed out.

Sadie nodded and Nora could tell she was trying to relax but her shoulders were up high.

When the walked onto the road, they took a short break to let the horses rest after the climb.

"My turn!" Aunt Leah called out. She started trotting and moved into the trees, weaving through them.

Nora watched Sadie; her shoulders were still up and she looked like she was near tears.

"She'll be OK." Nora whispered to Sadie.

Sadie glanced at her with concerned eyes but nodded in agreement and kept moving.

"Why are you so worried?"

"I don't want to hurt her."

"There's nothing you can do to hurt her. She'll protect herself…as well as you."

Sadie turned; her eyes looked like she was beginning to understand what Nora was saying.

"Sadie, look at Scarecrow," Nora tried to make sure no one else heard them. "She's having fun…she's enjoying getting out of the arena."

Sadie nodded and her shoulders started to relax.

"My turn!" Nora's mom called out and she walked down the hill and toward a creek. They weaved in and out of the creek as they made their way down a ravine between the mountainsides.

"This is so much fun." Tessa called out as Patience lunged up the side of the creek to a cow trail.

Everyone laughed in agreement.

Nora turned to Sadie. Her shoulders were down, her face tense, but there were no sign of tears.

"My turn!" Tessa laughed, "But I have no idea what to do right here. Can I pass and go last?"

"Sure." Aunt Dru nodded and turned to Nikki.

"My turn!" Nikki called out and made her way back up the hill. When they got to the top, she turned her mare, Harvey and made her backup into the trees, following another cow trail.

"Oh, this one is interesting!" Tessa said as she tried to get Patience to go down the trail backwards.

Aunt Dru moved up next to her and started showing her how to get Patience to move smoothly.

Nora was in front of Sadie so she was able to watch her cousin maneuver Scarecrow backwards towards her. Sadie's face was relaxed and she had just a hint of a smile.

"All your horses are so good at this!" Josey said in amazement as Apollo walked backwards.

"We've been doing this with The Tagger Herd for the last couple of years." Nikki explained. "It's great training and conditioning for them…and a whole lot of fun for us. They all need to get out of the arena now and then."

"My turn!" Grace called out as they reached a long stretch of the road and she kicked Eli into a gallop. Nora knew she would, Grace was so predictable.

The horse's hoof beats echoed throughout the mountains as the ten horses galloped down the dirt road. They were accompanied by a round of laughter from all the riders. Nora turned to Sadie, relieved to see the grin and bright blue eyes looking back at her.

Nora waited until they hit a section of the road that had a wide trail shooting off the side. It also had a small ravine that had a cow trail cut through it.

"My turn!" She yelled and slowed her horse down to a walk. "Can I do something different?" Nora asked, already knowing what Aunt Dru would say.

"Sure. What's your plan?" Aunt Dru grinned as the riders came together to listen.

"Can we do a loop ride?" Nora asked, excitedly.

"What's that?" Tessa and Josey asked in unison.

"Show us the loop." Aunt Dru said and turned to the duo to explain while Nora walked the trail.

She went straight down the elk trail then cut left and Arcturus had to slide down a small dirt trail that led to the narrow ravine. She trotted between two trees and Arcturus leapt up a rise in the hillside to the next trail. Nora swung to her left and around the top of the ravine which led back to the group.

"Fun!" Josey hollered and headed down the loop at a trot.

Aunt Dru took off when Josey returned but she did it at a slow rocking gallop. Matt's horse, Trooper was well practiced in these mountains.

Each of the ladies took a turn at the loop; Sadie was last.

Aunt Dru rode up next to Nora as Sadie started at a trot. They glanced at each other and patiently waited to see Sadie's expression when she returned from the loop.

Sadie was smiling when she returned.

"My turn!" Sadie laughed and turned Scarecrow to do the loop at a gallop in the opposite direction. After going around the top of the ravine she had to turn Scarecrow sharply off the trail to make the leap down the embankment then through the trees. Scarecrow jumped up onto the trail and ran back up the elk trail towards them.

"That was fearless!" Josey hollered at her and kicked Apollo into a run around the loop.

Nora was elated. Sadie would not have done that at the beginning of their ride. She turned quickly to her aunt who was also grinning. Each of the riders did the loop at a gallop, even Tessa who was laughing nearly the whole time.

"One more round at the same time?" Nikki yelled and pushed Harvey into a gallop down the first portion of the loop. Josey took off just behind her then Cora, then Aunt Leah. The riders continued joining until all of them were on the trail running the loop together creating a living carousel.

They went around the loop four times together until Aunt Dru headed down the road at a trot and everyone followed. As the horses started to cool down, they slowed to a walk.

"My turn!" Tessa called out.

Everyone turned to see what the newest rider had come up with.

Tessa turned her horse, glanced up at Josey, who had been helping her work with Patience, then she sidestepped a dozen steps moving to her left, she moved the painted horse's hips in a 180 degree turn, so she was pointed in the opposite direction, and continued to side-pass down the road to her right.

"Good job, Tessa!" Cora yelled out and sidestepped Dollar down the road.

They all maneuvered their horses back and forth then sideways.

They all ended with a laugh.

Nora rode up next to her aunt.

"That was fun." Nora grinned.

"I have to admit, it was!" Aunt Dru laughed. "I haven't had that much fun riding in years."

Nora glanced back at Sadie who was laughing with her mom and sister.

"Do you think it worked?" Nora asked her aunt.

"We won't know until this weekend when she races."

"I don't know what else we can do if it doesn't." Nora looked out at the stretch of dirt road in front of them.

"I don't either." Aunt Dru nodded with a sigh.

CHAPTER FOUR

"When is the wedding?" Nora asked Nikki as they rode down the forgotten road towards the ghost town.

The future bride beamed. "We haven't decided yet. We're thinking November or February."

"Why then?"

"Down season for the B&B so we can use the rooms for wedding guests, it's before branding, and out of show season and rodeos for all of you." She answered.

"Sadie's and my birthdays are in November plus Thanksgiving." Nora reminded her. "And isn't there a lot of calving in February?"

Nikki laughed. "That's the problem we're having, there is so much going on with all of Tagger Enterprises and family all year round. We thought of January but there are five birthdays in January, plus the chance of the bad snow again."

"Wouldn't you rather have it in the spring?" Aunt Dru asked as she rode up next to them.

"Yes, but that's such a busy season." Nikki sighed.

"Nikki, pick what weekend YOU want and everything can be scheduled around it." Aunt Dru chuckled.

"No one's going to change one of the kid's rodeos or shows just for our wedding." Nikki laughed.

"There's LOTS of rodeos and shows, Nikki." Nora told her. "We can skip one for the wedding, like we're going to do for the kid's clinic next month."

"Well, that's true." Nikki nodded. "I really wanted to do the first weekend in May, when all the wildflowers are in full bloom.

"Are you having it here at the ranch?" Nora asked.

Nikki shook her head and smiled with a blush. "At The Homestead."

"Like Aunt Dru and Jack's?" Nora asked.

Nikki's cheeks reddened as she shook her head. "Actually, out the back door."

"What?" Aunt Dru asked in surprise.

Nikki laughed as she explained. "He wants me to have the wedding of my dreams so he left all the decisions to me. His only insistence was where the wedding was held."

"But out the back door?" Nora chuckled.

"That's the first place Lucas saw you!" Aunt Dru's eyes widened in realization.

Nikki's brown eyes brightened as she nodded.

"That's so romantic!" Nora grinned at her cousin.

"That's what I thought!" Nikki's shoulders raised and lowered in excitement. "I just LOVE that moment…I remember it like it was yesterday. Just seeing that grin through his whiskers and his amber eyes peeking out from below his hat, I started falling for him THAT moment!"

Nora smiled at the love radiating from her cousin. When she grew up, she wanted a love like that. Her mind instantly went to Billy. She remembered the moment he walked into the library with his brother and Reilly so Sadie could tutor Brady. She had just stood and stared at him in shock until Sadie moved forward to grab the books out of Brady's hands.

She was used to big men because of her uncle and dad, but he was huge in her eyes. She barely glanced at Brady…which was odd since they were twins. Billy had looked at her with his blue eyes and they just seemed to wake the butterflies in her stomach. The butterflies had stayed all day and all night until she kissed him. Then they turned to bumble bees and shot through her stomach, her veins and to her head. What was she thinking kissing him like that!?

"Nora!"

Nora jumped and turned to see Grace next to her. "What?"

"What were you in such deep thought about?" Grace grinned.

Nora glanced around her. Nikki and Aunt Dru had ridden ahead of her and she was now riding between Grace and Josey.

"Nikki was talking about the wedding." Nora explained with no intensions of saying anything about Billy.

"That's going to be so much fun." Grace nodded in excitement and turned to Josey. "You should have seen Aunt Dru and Jack's wedding. It was in the South pasture and all the Tagger herd were walking around during the wedding ceremony."

"A dream wedding," Josey laughed then turned to Grace. "Why aren't you riding Buttercup today?"

Grace rolled her lips and shook her head. "She's not a mountain horse."

"Really?" Josey asked.

Grace nodded. "She had a couple bad crashes, so Dad tried to train her up here but she just couldn't relax." She shrugged. "She's perfect in the arena and that is what's important."

Josey nodded in understanding. "If Grayson can't help her, no one can."

Nora looked down at Apollo, Josey's horse. He was a big golden gelding with dappled coloring unlike the solid gold of Scarecrow. Nora remembered seeing all of Josey's saddles she won. Two were from her barrel racing.

"Why aren't you barrel racing?" Nora asked her, accidently interrupting the two girls' conversation. "Oh, sorry." She grinned in guilt. "I started that thought in my head."

Josey chuckled. "I do that all the time…drives Grayson nuts."

"So why aren't you racing?" Grace asked.

Josey shrugged.

"You don't work seven days a week, do you?" Nora asked.

Josey smiled and shook her head.

"Is Matt keeping you busy on your days off?" Grace teased.

Josey's smile disappeared and she looked straight ahead of her. A hand quickly went down to stroke the gelding's neck. A sign of needed equine therapy which meant something was wrong.

"Aren't you still going out?" Grace asked in surprise.

Josey glanced over at the Nora and Grace and shrugged sadly.

"What happened?" Grace asked in concern. "You guys seemed so happy about your date."

Nora frowned. They seemed perfect for each other. That's why she and Cora had taken Josey up to the mountains to be with Matt after his rescuing the hikers from a rock slide. Josey had been so sad. Matt had said she was beautiful and his face just lit up when he saw her.

Besides, she wanted to see the look on people's faces when Nikki told them that her brother was going on a date with her sister!

Josey shrugged again. "We went out three times, then…" Another sad shrug. "He stopped calling. When we see each other, which isn't very often, he doesn't even mention it."

"Do you?" Grace asked.

Josey shook her head. "I don't know what to say."

"CO…MU…NI…CATE!" Grace said loudly.

All three girls chuckled at the confused looks thrown their way.

"Ask him out." Nora told her.

She smiled and blushed. "I've picked up the phone a dozen time to do that."

"Why didn't you?" Nora asked.

"Too scared on what the reason is…that I can't fix it to get us back on track." Josey admitted.

"Josey, you're off the track right now." Grace pointed out. "If you don't push it back on, you can't go forward…you just stay crashed."

Josey just nodded and stared at the road ahead.

Relationships were hard at any level, Nora thought.

"So, back to the original question." Nora turned to Josey. "Why aren't you racing?"

"I've been training the new horses and hiding out at the ranch since the news articles hit the paper about my testimony against my mother for fraud." Josey said.

"Well that's enough of that!" Grace said declared. "You can't become a hermit on the mountain forever. You need to just get out there."

Josey frowned as she glanced at Grace.

"Josey?" Nora turned to her.

"Yeah?" Josey answered.

"You know that Grace and I are royalty of the local club." Nora asked and Josey nodded. "The weekend after we get back from finals in Philomath, the club is hosting a day of barrel racing for all ages at the arena."

Josey raised a brow, showing her interest.

"We're all going to ride. Why don't you get Apollo ready and ride with us?" Nora asked. "No pressure, it's just going to be a really fun day."

"Please do! Try it out, at least, and see what happens." Grace said excitedly. "Everyone there will be thinking barrels and will probably not even think of your testimony…besides who cares…you were brave and you'll be there with a bunch of us Taggers. We'll sick The Dingo on them if they give you a bad time."

The three girls giggled and looked at Sadie who was talking with Tessa.

Josey reached down and stroked Apollo's neck then turned to the girls with a grin. "Yes!"

"And what are we excited about over here?"

Nora turned to her mother. Nora listened as Grace and Josey told her mom about their discussion. Her mom's eyes lit up.

"Terrific!" Her mom said to Josey. "These kids will suck you right in and you'll be hauling Grace and Reilly next year." She laughed. "If Nora is appointed Queen or Princess for the NWYRA then we'll be concentrating on going to the events she needs to attend and those that Wade and Sadie can participate in."

Nora slowed Arcturus so she couldn't hear the conversation about hauling and next year's plan. Her mood plummeted as she calculated the extra hours her mother hauled her around.

###

They walked around the remains of the old ghost town and took a break from their ride.

"That follow the leader was just the funnest," Tessa smiled at Nora. "And I loved your loop."

"That was fun," Nora agreed readily. "All of us going around at the end was exciting."

"I wish we had pictures, but we were all having too much fun."

"I bet it would have looked cool."

"I'm going to have to talk to Nick about creating a course like that for me to play in at his property."

"I have no doubt he'll do it for you. Alex will enjoy it too." Nora nodded.

"And I know just the perfect place for it!" Cora trotted up next to them. "Wes and I…"

Nora's mind drifted as the two women talked and made plans for Nick. Pretty soon, they remounted and made their way back to the ranch. Nora rode next to Sadie as they neared the ranch buildings.

"I loved today." Sadie smiled.

"I loved the second half of the day." Nora chuckled.

"You don't like cutting?"

"I love cutting and any chance to ride a horse." Nora admitted.

"We've done lots of clinics but, except Dad with roping, I've never had a coach until Josey came to help…but she's not really my coach."

"And she doesn't yell at you."

"So having a coach isn't good?"

Nora shrugged. She wasn't going to admit that she didn't think she would be improving or have the confidence without him. "It's OK, just different."

"Thanks for talking to me out there." Sadie glanced at her.

"She'll take care of herself and you." Nora nodded. "Just let her do her job."

"Hey, Ladies!" Jessup yelled from the front steps of the ranch house. "Miss me?"

They all laughed.

"Weren't you right there when we left?" Aunt Dru teased. "Just been standing there pining away for us?"

Jessup laughed. "Been cooking away in here for ya."

"Good, I'm hungry!" Aunt Leah informed him as she stepped off Rufio.

It didn't take long for all the riders to have their horses unsaddled, brushed and let loose in the corral. Just as they were walking from the barn to the house, Matt drove in.

Aunt Dru and Nikki walked to his truck as everyone made their way through the door of the house. Josey stood at the door and stared at the truck, sighed and walked into the house.

"Talk to him." Grace whispered.

"Talk to him." Nora elbowed her.

Josey inhaled deeply and exhaled sharply, "If I get a chance, I will."

After eating the barbeque chicken that Jessup had prepared, Nora stepped out of the house and walked to the barn.

As much as she loved everyone, all the talk was starting to make her head hurt. Needing peace and quiet she walked into the barn and to the outside stalls. She crawled up in one of the large wood built-in hay feeders, sat with her back against the wall and her legs stretched out in front of her. She took a deep breath and relaxed. All the horses were standing quietly or lying stretched out sleeping in the sun.

She felt as tired as they looked. The alarm went off at 5:00, she was dressed and in the barn by 5:15. Before Jack left for The Stables, he helped her move the cattle from the back pasture into the corrals. At 5:55, she was warming Cooper up in the arena when Casey arrived.

He pointed, ordered, yelled, and stood looking bored for over an hour. Then, after he left, she moved out all the cattle, while Reilly saddled Rufio and Wade saddled Dollar. They practiced cow and goat tying for another two hours. Cooper was hosed down, brushed out, fed, loved on and led into the horse trailer.

Then Arcturus was caught, loaded, and they headed for the ranch. Sadie was so excited, she talked all the way to the ranch.

Now, Nora leaned her head against the feeder wall, closed her eyes and listened to the peace and quiet of the ranch. Her mind wandered to Arcturus and his halter class. Everything depended on his conditioning and his willingness to do the patterns. With Nikki's feeding program and Nora's exercise program he looked beautiful to her. Even after nearly dying of starvation, he had come back to full physical condition. She couldn't understand why he wasn't getting better than third place. He was willing to do anything she asked, so what was she not seeing that was holding him back?

She desperately wanted him to win in that class. It would symbolize his comeback from his short time in Cora's barn that nearly led to his death.

"Nora?" Matt called in the barn.

"I'm here." She answered behind closed eyelids.

"You OK?"

"Just need peace."

"Just checking, you were quiet during dinner. I'll see you later."

"Matt?" Nora heard Josey's voice and opened an eye just enough to see her walk in and close the door behind her.

"What?" Matt asked and glanced to Nora.

Her eyes closed again.

"We need to talk." Josey told him.

"Not right now, Nora's over there trying to sleep."

"She's one of the reason's I got brave enough to say something to you."

"What?"

"She and Grace told me to push you back on the track. It's the only way we can move forward."

"Josey, not right now."

"YES, now!" She said firmly.

There was a pause. "OK, fine. What?"

"What happened? Why did you stop calling?"

"You know why. We talked about it on the last date."

"But I don't understand what you were asking of me."

"I was asking for Josey, not Frankie."

"I'm the same person."

"No, you're not." He exhaled heavily. "Josey, you need to take the time to find the old Josey and let go of Frankie."

"I can do that with you in my life."

"No, you can't." Again the heavy sigh. "When we were together, you did…dang, Josey, I don't know how to explain it."

"Then how do you expect me to understand and fix it."

"It's not like a truck you can fix and take off in, Josey."

"Matt…"

"Josey, when we were together it was all about me, you took a backseat in everything, YOU put yourself in my shadow. That's not Josey, that's Frankie hiding."

There was silence.

"Look at the way you're standing." Matt said and Nora couldn't help herself, she opened her eyes.

Josey was standing with her arms crossed in front of her.

"That's your protective mode…that's Frankie…Josey doesn't need to stand like that because she's strong and independent."

"How do you know?"

"Because I recognized it the moment we met…I never called you Frankie." He reminded her. "When you stood toe-to toe-with Grayson and took his challenge at the horse auction; strong and independent…that was Josey. Racing me up the climbing walls, that was Josey. When you yelled at me in the library and told me it wasn't all your fault…that was Josey. THAT'S who you need to find and you weren't doing it with me. You were using me as a shield."

"I don't know how to do that." She said in a low confused voice.

"I can't tell you how to do it…I don't know." Matt sighed. "Go backwards…who were you before…in high school…?"

"I was a barrel racer; drove myself and Apollo where ever we needed to go."

"That's a fierce independent woman…that's Josey." He smiled encouragingly.

"I told Nora and Grace that I would join them at a barrel race next month." Her voice was stronger.

"That's awesome, Josey." Matt grinned. "That's your first step."

She nodded as her hands dropped from her sides and she hooked a thumb in a pocket and her stance relaxed.

"I understand," She sighed like the weight was lifted from her shoulders. "I don't know how long it will take."

"I'll be here waiting." He assured her. "I'm ready to go on adventures with Josey, I just don't want to pull Frankie along with me and out of the shadows everywhere we go."

"I want those adventures." Her voice was determined as she grinned at him.

They stood smiling at each other.

Nora shook her head in disbelief. "Just kiss her, Matt."

"What?" They said in unison and turned to her. They had forgotten she was there.

"Give her something to look forward to…or you kiss him Josey…give him something to look forward to." Nora chuckled. "I'll close my eyes."

Nora dramatically flung her arm across her face as they stepped into each other arms. If she couldn't kiss Billy, then at least Josey got a kiss from Matt…or vice-versa. After a few minutes, she heard them open and close the barn door.

Just as she started to relax again, the corral gate opened. Her mother was walking through.

"There you are." Her mom grinned. "It's time to load up and head home. We need to get back. You have practice early in the morning again."

"Yipee," Nora sighed as she drug her heavy legs out of the feeder.

If she knew what the next morning held for her, she would have refused to leave the feeder.

CHAPTER FIVE

"What was THAT?!" Casey's voice was low and vibrated in disbelief.

That was worse than the yelling.

"Answer me. What happened?" He walked out into the arena between her and the steer.

"I thought it was going to go left instead of right."

"Cooper was headed right, he anticipated better than you did." He shook his head. "You're supposed to be a team, he has a mind too. He THINKS too."

"I need to trust him more."

"You need to work WITH him more." He headed for the gate between the cattle pen and the arena. "Let's go to the other end of the arena and work with the flag."

Nora's shoulders drooped and her lips pressed together. She would NOT let him see her cry.

A half hour later, it got worse.

"Nora, get off the horse and get something to drink." He said gruffly.

She slid down, put the reins in his outstretched hand and walked to the cooler that was placed under the bleachers. She drank down a full bottle of water and turned back to her coach.

"Better?" He asked, almost human like.

She nodded…which wasn't exactly the truth.

"OK, we'll move to the horse and flag to work the basics again. Then we'll work the cattle and give you one run."

Nora nodded and listened carefully to what he said. He wasn't yelling, which she wasn't sure was good or bad, but she was able to concentrate on his words.

They rode back to the flag and she was a bit more relaxed chasing it back and forth across the arena. Then they slowly walked back toward the cattle. Taking a deep breath, she walked in to pick out the right steer to give her and Cooper a good dance.

When she was done, she knew she wasn't perfect…or very good…but she was better than the first session.

"Drink more water tonight and in the morning." He ordered and walked out of the arena.

Nora walked Cooper to the gate of the cattle pen, opened it and the steers quickly trotted through and into their pasture. She slid off the horse and walked him into the shade.

The plastic roping goat was next to the chute so she grabbed it, walked out twenty feet, and threw the fake animal to the ground. She stared at it and had the ridiculous feeling of guilt so she gingerly picked up the plastic goat and set it up on its four legs.

After retrieving her goat string, she walked back to Cooper's side. Pretending she jumped from the horse she ran to the goat, flipped it onto its side then knelt on the plastic animal to tie three of its legs. In a grand gesture, she threw her arms wide to stop the imaginary clock.

She repeated the procedure twice. On the third run, she tripped. Knees hit first, then face, then hands, classic face plant into the ground. Dirt was inhaled up her nose and in her mouth. She had to blink hard to clear her eyes.

Legs straight out behind her, Nora pulled herself up onto her elbows and rested her forehead in dirt covered hands. Even the ground was against her today!

"Nora?"

How in the world could he show up at this moment? Dirt filled her nose, mouth, ears, and covered her clothes. Tears rimmed her eyes and her long black ponytail had to look tangled and dirty where it hung under her cowboy hat.

"What?" She said into her hands.

"Are you alright?" Billy's voice was full of concern.

"Yes. I just needed a rest."

"Kind of a hard way to get yourself into a resting position."

"You saw me fall?" How mortifying!

"Yes, but it actually looked pretty graceful." He chuckled.

She didn't lift her face out of her hands as his voice got closer.

"How long have you been standing there?"

"I was curious and watched your last ride with Cooper…just before your coach left."

"Wonderful." She muttered.

"Are you going to get up?"

"I haven't figured out a way to do it without you seeing all the dirt in my nose, mouth, ears…everywhere."

"You're a kick, Nora." He chuckled.

What an odd thing for him to say…so close to what Nick says to her.

"We played a football game last year in Sandpoint when it was raining. We were mud from head to toe, slipped all over, and had fun."

"Sounds like fun."

"But do you know what was best about it?"

"The shower afterwards?" She smiled into her hands.

"It was the feeling…like you'd been through a battle. You don't come out of a battle unscathed. It made us feel pumped up and energized us."

"I feel like this morning was a battle." She lifted her head and looked down the dirt floor of the arena. She wiped as much dirt off her face as she could. "When do I start feeling energized?"

Billy was standing behind her. "Well, your coach said something to Scott about you drinking more water. So maybe after you get more water."

Nora pushed herself up so she was kneeling on the ground and sitting on her heels. "I need to wash down Cooper. He got the brunt of the work for my horrible practice this morning."

A large hand appeared at her side. The butterflies in her stomach woke up. As long as she kept them from turning into bumble bees…she should be good. Slowly, she slid a hand in his so he could help her stand. Once it was there…she didn't want to let go and she didn't.

Nora looked at her small hand in his large, strong and warm hand.

"Want me to get your goat?" He asked in a terrible southern drawl.

Without thinking about the dirt covering her face she looked up at him with a grin.

Billy's wide smile made his blue eyes twinkle in humor. "You going to make a billy goat joke, Pig Pen?"

Nora burst out laughing and dropped her hand from his. They laughed together as he lifted the goat and they walked to Cooper.

Halfway to the barn, Reilly came around the corner towards them.

His eyes widened in surprise then he laughed at Nora. "What the heck happened?"

"Billy pushed me down." Nora joked. "Beat him up for me."

Reilly grinned at Billy, who stood 5 inches taller and weighed a good 80 pounds more. "I'll get right on that."

Nora quickly unsaddled Cooper as Reilly and Billy watched. Billy took the saddle and headed to the tack room.

"You OK?" Reilly whispered while he was gone.

She shrugged and glanced at the tack room door. "I'm too stressed and dirty to think about it right now."

She walked the patient black horse into the wash room and tied him up. Cooper loved the water and as she lifted the hose he sidestepped into her trying to get closer. He hit the end of the hose causing it to spray out and into her face. Water dripped from her hat, nose and chin. Nora shook her head and glanced at the door. At least that wasn't seen.

She really needed to get herself together.

One more step and she tripped over the hose and landed on her butt. Cooper sidestepped away from her as her hat went flying. The water flowing from the hose was now soaking her legs while the water on the ground soaked into her jeans from the ground. She lay back onto the ground and stared up at the ceiling. The water soaked into her clothes and her hair.

Cooper lowered his head to her and she ran her hand down his nose then his leg which was at her elbow.

"Which day?" She heard Billy out in the aisle.

"I have a rodeo this weekend, won't be back until late Sunday," Reilly answered. "So it has to be Monday."

"Ok, you call Marla and I'll call Christina." Billy answered.

Nora felt like she was kicked in the stomach, all the butterflies were crushed. They were arranging a date. Billy was going out with a girl named Christina.

Why should that bother her? She's only fourteen, couldn't date until she is sixteen and even then he would be nineteen…illegal and just wrong. Was he supposed to wait until she turned eighteen? That would make him twenty one. That wouldn't be right or fair to him…even if he did like her.

She ran her hand up Cooper's leg and down around his knee. It seemed warm, she needed to put ointment on it when she put him in the stall. His nose came down to her hand so she rubbed the velvety end softly.

"Nora!" Reilly ran in next to her.

"I'm fine." She assured him as she looked up at him. She ignored his outreached hand.

"Are you sure?"

"Yeah," She looked up at the ceiling while Reilly turned off the water. "Casey said I needed more water."

Reilly chuckled. "On the inside, not the outside."

"Christina, this is Billy." They heard his voice in the aisle.

Reilly's eyes shot to the door then back to Nora. His brows coming together in concern.

"It's OK." She tried to smile; her throat constricting and stomach trembling.

"Nora…"

"Reilly," She inhaled deeply and let it out slowly. "Please, just let me have this moment…this really bad moment."

"Nora…" He frowned and shook his head down at her.

"Sometimes a person just needs to embrace the bad, get it over with, so they can allow the good back in…and appreciate it more." The tears were waiting, but she wasn't going to let them come out with him watching. "Please go."

He rolled his lips into a grimace and took a deep breathe. He finally nodded with sad blue eyes and walked out of the room.

Flat on her back, lying in a puddle of water on the cement floor, she rubbed Cooper's leg and let the tears slide down the side of her face and into her hair.

Nora waited patiently for the tears to stop…hoping the bad luck was flowing out with them. When she finally felt the tears slowing, she sat up and pushed herself back against the wall. She bent her legs and crossed her arms over her knees.

Every inch of her was wet.

There was a movement at the door and she glanced over to see Sadie.

Her cousin walked to her, slid down the wall and sat next to her, mimicking her position and ignoring the water on the floor.

"Reilly said you needed a friend," Sadie whispered and took her hand and squeezed.

Nora leaned over and rested her head on her cousin's shoulder.

"What time is it?" Nora said in a low voice.

"Nine."

Nora's heart plummeted. "It feels like it should be at least two or three."

"Long morning?"

"Yeah."

"What do you want to do now?" Sadie asked without moving.

"Cooper needs some ointment on his knees."

"Then what?"

Nora shrugged.

Sadie stood, "I'll take Cooper to his stall if you want to grab the ointment."

###

Nora's eyes slowly opened and she stared at the television. After she and Sadie took care of Cooper, Nora took a long warm shower. When she made it to the living room, Sadie and Cora had started a movie with a bunch of snacks, soda, and lots of water. The three of them sat and watched the movie, a comedy, together then started a second. Nora had fallen asleep at the beginning of the movie and the credits were now running.

"Feel better?" Cora asked with a smile.

"Yeah." Nora answered without moving.

"What now?" Sadie asked as she started popping through the channels on the TV. She stopped on a movie…*Wyatt Earp*…which starred Dennis Quaid as Doc Holliday. Dennis Quaid…who looked just like Casey.

"Sadie…" Nora said accusingly.

She heard her cousin's wicked little giggle before she turned the channel.

"I need to check Cooper's knees." Nora answered Cora. "I should also oil my gaming saddle."

She pushed herself up and looked over at her companions.

"You may want to do something with that hair." Cora grinned.

Nora automatically reached up to it. She had fallen asleep with it wet from the shower. It was all the way down to her waist and was beginning to be a real pain. She didn't know how Sadie could stand that long of hair. All Nora could do with it, when she wasn't in her princess curly hair mode, was to put it in the braid so it didn't get everywhere.

"Do you think Mom would let you cut it for me?" Nora asked the older woman.

"I don't know what Jordan would say, but I'm not doing it." Cora shook her head with raised brows. "I'll cut the boys because they aren't so worried about theirs and they wear hats all the time."

"Would you take me into a salon if I ask Mom?" Nora stood and headed for the phone.

"How much do you want cut off?" Sadie asked in surprise.

"Just mid-back." Nora dialed her mother. "I just need a change."

Her mother said yes and Cora drove the two girls into Lewiston. Cora treated the girls to a manicure and pedicure, too.

"A nap, trip to the salon, and some retail therapy." Cora grinned at the girls as they walked out of the western clothing store. "It can't get any better than that."

"Thanks for the shirts, Cora." Sadie smiled as they buckled up in Cora's car.

"Yeah, thanks!" Nora smiled. "Now we have matching shirts for this weekend."

"All three of us, Grace and your mothers!" Cora laughed. "I have one more idea."

"Really?" The two girls grinned.

"Dairy Queen downtown for some ice cream." Cora drove down the road.

Nora scooped another bite of banana split and smiled at Cora. "You're the best."

Cora crinkled her nose and smiled back. "I really enjoy taking you girls out. Fills me with energy, we need to do it more often."

Nora nodded. She felt totally different from the crying girl that morning and was glad she'd let herself have a moment of depression, she needed to get it out of her body and mind. Holding it in just made it worse, but now her mind was clearer and she seemed more focused.

She needed the nap and now half her hair was gone, she felt pampered from the salon visit and the new red sparkling shirt that Cora bought her. Now she was looking forward to the weekend and the rodeo.

Watching Sadie practice that night, she could see a difference in her attitude also. Sadie didn't run Scarecrow at full speed in the heat, so they would have to wait until Saturday to know if their trail ride had worked.

Early Friday morning Nora, Sadie, Wade, Alex, Grace, Reilly, Aunt Leah, Cora and her mom loaded into two trucks pulling horse trailers and started the six hour drive to Vancouver.

CHAPTER SIX

Nora sat nervously on top of a calm Cooper. There was a long line of pole riders in front of her. Grace was six riders behind her. Much to the delight of Grace and Reilly, Kelly was there too and was running right after Grace.

Sadie had placed second in her division and was now waiting for barrels. Nora just wanted to finish her pole ride, watch Grace and Kelly then put Cooper away so she could watch Sadie's barrel run from the bleachers.

After they were done with the pole bending, she would watch Grace and Sadie run barrels, then she would need to get ready for goat tying. Then she was done for the day and she could sit back and watch everyone else. Not that she could relax because she was always more nervous for them then herself.

Nora and Cooper moved forward in the line.

The rider in front of her took off into the arena. Nora trotted Cooper to the front of the ally and watched the runner. Cooper's energy increased. He understood they were close to the start. The rider and horse knocked down two poles and was swearing when she rode by her.

"Focus." Nora whispered to herself. She heard her name called and barely leaned forward and Cooper was in a dead run. He was the fastest horse Tagger Enterprises owned, but his turns weren't as tight as Buttercups. They were both good at changing leads and weaving through the poles.

Cooper's thundering hoofs seemed to vibrate through her body as she ran down the length of the arena to the end pole. It seemed like they barely started when she was already pulling him to turn. He did better than normal and they weaved in and out…made another tight turn, and weaved in and out.

She made the last turn to make the run back to the finish line. As they flew by the poles, she was relieved to see all of them still standing.

Nora pulled on the reins and leaned back to slow Cooper down. His whole body was vibrating…he loved to run and this never seemed long enough for him.

The announcer called out her time, 21.855, she was in first thanks to Cooper's speed!

She turned and trotted back to the fence so she could watch Grace and Buttercup.

"Good luck!" Nora called out to her cousin.

"Way to go!" Graced waved back with a hearty, 'Life is good', laugh.

Nora rode to the fence and when Grace was up she stood on her tip toes in the stirrups to watch. Grace pranced on Buttercup then suddenly they were running. Nora's breathing froze…straight down the arena, fast quick turn, weaving between the poles, another tight turn, weaving back, and as she turned around the last pole all the poles remained upright and Grace was kicking Buttercup wildly. As she ran out of the arena Nora exhaled.

Grace's time was called out, 21.835. Grace took over first place, knocking Nora to second. She had been hoping for her first belt buckle win!

"Ugh!" She called out with a grin to her cousin. Grace laughed and rode up next to her.

"You staying here for Sadie to ride?" Grace asked.

Nora shook her head. "Headed up to watch with Mom."

Kelly was in and out of the arena with her red and white paint horse in 22.355 seconds.

They watched the next six riders go. Last rider in…and out…they held their first and second and Kelly placed fourth. After a grin and a high five, Nora turned Cooper towards the trailers. She tied him up and ran to the bleachers.

Her mom was talking on her computer tablet when she arrived.

"What's going on?" Nora asked her grinning aunt.

"Congrats!" Aunt Leah hugged her. "She's talking with The Trio, Nick and Tessa."

"Really?" Nora leaned over her mother's shoulder and looked at the tablet screen to see the five adults standing in Aunt Dru's office of the B&B. She waved at them and they laughed and waved back.

"Congrats! We saw your run." Aunt Dru told her.

"Thanks!" Nora grinned at them. "We have to make it through Pee Wee Barrels before Sadie's run."

"That's what Jordan said." Uncle Grayson nodded. "But we wanted to make sure everything worked; besides we got to see that black horse fly."

Nora nodded. "He loves to run."

"Alright," Her mother interrupted. "I'm going to clamp this thing on the tripod so I don't have to try and hold still."

Nora looked around at the group of people sitting with them. She smiled at all the parents she recognized.

"Fingers crossed for Sadie." One of the mothers said as she held up a hand with actual crossed fingers.

"She did better this week." Nora smiled politely.

One of the other mothers nodded. "It's great to see she came back so soon after the accident. We were praying for her."

Nora nodded and saw all the other parents nodding and smiling.

"Almost there!" Aunt Leah announced.

Nora turned and stared out the entry area. She could see Sadie was second out and grabbed her mother and Cora's hands for support. They squeezed tightly.

Sadie walked Scarecrow back and forth. She reached down and stroked the palomino's neck.

"She looks so calm." Aunt Leah whispered in anticipation.

Sadie glanced up at the rider running into the arena. She was next.

Nora ignored the other rider. It didn't make any difference what anyone else did…it was important that Sadie returned to form and did the best she could…no holding back.

The other rider ran out of the arena.

Nora couldn't help it…the anticipation was too much…she stood up to watch.

Sadie was at the ally…she looked out into the arena…did a circle and turned.

Scarecrow was at a full stride as she entered the arena; running for the first barrel. The angle was perfect and they turned sharply without hesitation in the stride.

"Yes!" Nora started bouncing. A good first barrel was always crucial.

The run to the second barrel was fast and the turn nearly perfect with both horse and rider looking to the third barrel.

"Go, Sadie!" Nora screamed along with all the parents around her.

Cora was nearly screaming in Nora's ear as she cheered alongside her in their matching shirts.

Third barrel, Sadie ran just to the right of it, swerved out and then back around with barely a hesitation. She couldn't have come any closer to the barrel without actually hitting it.

The crowd around Nora was standing and cheering. The energy was insane as Scarecrow was digging deep and flying. There was no hesitation in anything Sadie did…she was full out competing as she rode Scarecrow high over her neck like a jockey at the racetrack.

Nora screamed louder and jumped higher, tears filling her eyes as she watched the run to the end. Scarecrow fed off the energy of the crowd and stretched out further and ran harder.

Sadie ran to the end of the arena and circled her beautiful palomino to slow her down and come to a stop. She twirled in the seat to look at her time.

The crowd around Nora was hollering and cheering, they all understood, that insane run told them all that Sadie had returned!

They could barely hear the announcer over the intercom tell the screaming crowd that "the blonde express" that just ran through was not only a return of an injured barrel racer but she returned with such gusto that the horse and rider had set a new youth arena record and was within 2 hundredths of a second from breaking the overall record!

Nora hugged her mom and aunt, turned to the mothers around them, grinned and tried to thank them but she didn't think they heard her. They were all clapping wildly and were giving Sadie a standing ovation.

After a quick wave into the computer, with everyone grinning and waving back at her, Nora ran down the stairs and back to the stalls. When she got to her cousin, Sadie and Grace were embracing from the back of their horses. Reilly, Wade, and Alex had already congratulated her and were headed back to the warm-up arena.

Sadie saw her and jumped off of Scarecrow and the cousins hugged.

"That was awesome!" Nora said excitedly.

"My heart is still racing!" Sadie grinned as they walked away from the line of barrel racers and toward Cooper.

"Let me have Scarecrow and go see our moms." Nora told her. "Everyone is so excited for you."

Sadie turned and looked at the bleachers.

"Go!" Nora told her.

Sadie took off at a run and Nora walked Scarecrow around the area to cool her down. When her breathing returned to normal she led the palomino up to Cooper and tied him to the trailer. The horses nosed each other then ignored each other.

Nora ran back to watch Grace run. She and Sadie were in different divisions so there was a possibility of both of them winning.

Buttercup's turns were great but she wasn't the fastest horse and they came in third. Kelly was ecstatic to come in second!

Grace still had to compete in goat tying, breakaway, and team roping. If she kept placing, she would win all-around again.

Buttercup may not be a mountain horse, but she had turned into a tremendous all-around horse in the arena.

Nora waved at Alex, Reilly, and Wade who were back on their horses. Alex and Wade had started team roping together…as well as Alex doing breakaway.   Wade was winning at tie-down and breakaway but Alex had yet to catch the calf.

Nora stood by the trailers and looked around the people and horses. She liked it here; all the camaraderie and seeing her cousins compete…it was fun. Maybe the royalty wasn't the only thing she should give up. If she did the same thing that the other kids did, it would save her mother half the traveling time.

Arcturus and Isaiah would have to be trained differently. It would be so different for them…and for her. The rodeos had an energy and a loud volume that the horse shows didn't. Not competing in trail or halter classes, she couldn't imagine that…but maybe…

"Excuse me."

Nora turned to the sweet voice behind her and all she saw was the big gold crown wrapped around the black cowboy hat. It felt like someone had thrown cold water into her face.

She forced herself to move her eyes from the crown to the smile that was beaming at her.

"Hi, I'm Allison." The current Queen of the NWYRA said.

"I'm Nora." She put on her 'perfect' smile, the one that hid her true emotions, and stretched out a hand.

Allison took it firmly and shook her hand.

"I noticed you had on the same shirt as Sadie, the rider of the palomino."

"She's my cousin." Nora explained, keeping her eyes from moving to the crown.

"Oh, nice." The girl smiled and it made her eyes bright. "I saw her accident, it was terrible. I was literally in tears for her."

"It took a long time for her to recover."

"My sister had an accident too and hasn't come back." Allison sighed. "Physically she's fine but she just doesn't want to race anymore."

"Does she do anything?"

"She does breakaway roping."

"Well, at least she's still riding."

"That's true." Allison smiled. "I remember you were dressed up that day…a princess?"

Nora nodded as she swallowed hard. "My cousin, Sadie's sister, Grace is the queen."

"She has the red shirt on too…oh, how fun," Allison giggled. "I wish my sister would have done it with me."

"It is fun." Nora nodded and glanced quickly at the crown.

"Have you thought of running for NWYRA queen?" She smiled…it looked genuine.

"Yes." Nora said before she could stop herself.

"Wonderful! I think you would be great; your family is into rodeo and the country way of life. You would represent very well."

"Thanks," Nora forced her 'perfect' smile a little wider.

"Come on, Nora!" Sadie yelled from behind her. "We need to get ready for goat tying."

"Well, good luck, Nora." Allison smiled and waved to Sadie.

"Thanks." Nora whispered and turned to Cooper, her smile faded before she did the complete turn.

She could do this…she could let it go…for her mom and dad. Lots of people let go of dreams…she could, too.

Sadie's division ran first and she won second place while looking graceful when she jumped from Scarecrow.

Nora was next…the last rider of her division. She watched the rider in front of her jump from the horse and face-plant before she got up and ran for the goat.

"Oh, heck, don't let me do that out here." Nora sighed, her stomach filling with dread and she suddenly wished she was on top of Arcturus or Isaiah in a quiet arena where no one face-planted.

She moved Cooper to the end of the entry aisle, his head perked and neck arched as he looked into the arena. As the arena workers quickly replaced the previous runner's goat with the goat Nora had to tie, the horse's energy seemed to triple and vibrate into her legs and to her heart.

Her hand went back to check the tie rope end that was tucked in her jeans, the other end in her mouth. They announced her name and she loosened Cooper's reins. He bolted out down the lane and toward the goat making Nora's heart fly into her throat. He was faster than at home in the arena practicing and it made her pulse scream. She envisioned herself falling and breaking her face as she landed but she lifted her right leg over the saddle and pulled herself up by the saddle horn to release her left leg from the stirrup.

Cooper was aimed just to the right of the goat so when she hit the ground she would be propelled directly at it. Holding her breath, Nora hit the ground already running at full speed. She straddled the rope so the goat couldn't run and barely had time to stop before she reached the goat and flipped him quickly. She pulled the tie out then wrapped and tied as fast as she could, then jumping back with her hands in the air. Her heart was pounding!

Her breathing was rapid as she waited the required six seconds to make sure her tie held. After the seemingly long wait, she ran back to the goat to get her rope then turned to run to Cooper. They announced her time, 10.41. She won ! It was her turn to beat Grace who had an 11.2.

She wasn't going to admit it to anyone…but she never wanted to do that again! But it was only Saturday and she had to do it again on Sunday.

Nora smiled and nodded politely at all the people who congratulated her.

Reilly greeted her with a big hug and grin as he stroked the neck of his black Cooper. "He's fast!"

Nora nodded with her 'perfect' smile on her face.

As she made her way up to the trailer to tie up Cooper for the day, she ran into Sadie.

"What's up?"

"Buttercup." Nora put the 'perfect' smile back on.

"Stop that smile." Sadie glared. "I hate that smile! What's wrong?"

Nora's eyes widened in surprise.

"Yeah," Sadie nodded. "I can tell the difference…so what's wrong?"

Nora turned and looked around her. "He was faster than I expected." She finally admitted.

"Did he scare you?"

Nora shook her head, "I think I psyched myself out…too worried about face planting, but don't tell anyone."

"Why not?" Sadie looked confused.

"Because it's my first win." Nora smiled proudly. "I don't want everyone to think of me being scared instead."

Sadie nodded. "I understand that, but what are you going to do tomorrow?"

"Try to win again." Nora put the 'perfect' smile back on and the two cousins laughed.

Twenty four hours later she jumped off the too fast Cooper and ran to the goat. Her heart was ready to explode as she tied the goat again and threw her arms in the air and silently congratulated herself for not face-planting.

Jogging towards Cooper, they announced her time…10.49. There were two more riders after her. By the time she exited the arena from the far end and trotted back to the front, the other riders had run, and they announced Nora winning the division. She had two wins in goat tying and one in poles for the weekend, since she had beaten Grace earlier in that race.

Sadie, who had won her barrel race again by nearly breaking her own record, greeted her at the trailer. They both laughed at Nora's 'perfect' smile.

Sadie trotted out to prepare for breakaway and Nora headed to the bleachers to spend the rest of the day watching Alex, her brother and cousins compete.

Wade won breakaway, placed second in chute dogging and placed third in calf tying.

Alex missed his throw in team roping, with Wade good heartedly laughing it off. It mattered that they were there…trying. They would win someday Wade had told a disappointed Alex; reminding him that Wade had tried for over a year before he won his first gold buckle. With a more positive, good natured attitude, Alex was fifth in breakaway. He caught the calf for the first time in competition…that was what was important.

Sadie won barrels, poles, and placed second in breakaway, third in goat tying.

Reilly won team roping with Grace, second in chute dogging, and fifth in calf roping.

Grace won the roping with Reilly, first in breakaway, second in poles and barrels, and third in goat tying. Due to both day's accomplishments, she was leading in points to win the year's all-around buckle again.

At the end of the day, Nora tied Cooper into the trailer and stepped out so Reilly could load Rufio.

She stood with Cora and watched the remaining horses load. "Cora?" Nora turned to her.

"Yes?" The older woman smiled.

"Your husband sure knew what he was doing when he bought horses."

Cora took her hand and squeezed tightly. Tears sprang to her eyes as she smiled proudly.

CHAPTER SEVEN

Nora was in the barn when Casey arrived. Cooper was still in his stall.

"You're early." She said with wide worried eyes.

He nodded. "How did the weekend go?"

She walked to Cooper's stall, halter in hand, as she told him the results of their weekend.

"When was the last time Cooper had a day off?" Casey followed her to the stall but kept her from opening the door.

Confused, Nora lowered the halter. "Between practice and competition? Probably two, almost three weeks."

Casey nodded. "Let him have the day off then."

Nora looked at him bewildered. Why was he there if Cooper was going to have the day off?

"Saddle up Isaiah," Casey told her and walked out of the barn.

Nora stood frozen and stared after him. She had no desire or inclination to work Isaiah with the cows. She had no doubt the horse could do it, but she didn't want him to. They didn't even do it at the ranch!

Now what? Had he discussed this with her parents? Surely if he did they would have said something to her. Should she confront him?

She couldn't stay in the barn forever. Taking a deep breath she walked out of the barn and headed to the arena.

Casey was sitting on the bleachers…which caught her by surprise; he was always standing in the arena.

"Where's the horse?" Casey asked with a frown.

"In his stall." Nora rolled her lips and took another deep breath. "Why?"

"I don't want him working with the cows." She tried to sound confident and mature.

"He's not going to."

Nora tilted her head and frowned at him.

"Nora, I'm a two time world champion in reining."

Nora's eyes opened wide, she had forgotten about that. "You're going to coach me in reining?"

He nodded, "Go get Isaiah. We'll work with him today and Arcturus tomorrow."

Nora hesitated, looking at him warily, then turned. Her time with her two horses was a peaceful time for her, relaxing…her time away from the world. She didn't want him yelling at her as she rode her two geldings. It would shatter that solitude.

She glanced at the house as she walked around the corner of the barn. Her parents were in there…should she go to them? Did they know?

Nora hesitated...she looked from the house and into the barn. How many fourteen-year-olds had the opportunity to train with a two time world champion? She turned to the barn and walked to Isaiah's stall.

If it turned out bad today, she would talk to her parents.

Ten minutes later, she rode Isaiah out of the barn and into the arena. She stopped him in front of Casey, who was still sitting on the bleachers.

"He's a beauty." Casey nodded.

Nora didn't know what to say, so she said nothing.

"Do you remember the pattern from your last reining competition?" He asked.

She nodded.

"Warm him up then show me."

Five minutes into the ride, her back muscles relaxed and her breathing matched the tempo of the horse's canter. She forgot Casey was there and smiled at Isaiah's willingness to do what she asked. His dark red hair glistened in the morning light and his perfectly combed mane bounced and flowed like silk. She let the pounding of the hoof beats lull her into a world of her own; one she had loved since she was eight while watching her uncle train the ranch horses.

When Isaiah was ready, she ran him through the pattern three times before Casey's voice interrupted her solitude.

"Bring him here." Casey called out.

It wasn't a yell, just an order. She turned to the bleachers but he wasn't there. She turned looking around the whole arena before she saw him at the end leaning on the cattle chute. She was so far into her own world, she hadn't seen him move.

Nora walked the horse next to the fence and looked down to her coach.

"You enjoy this."

She nodded.

"Why would you want to do anything else?" His tone was calm, dark brown eyes soft and inquisitive.

"I like doing other things, too."

"These last thirty minutes you've been the happiest I've seen you since I started coaching you."

She wasn't sure what to say so she just nodded.

"Grayson taught you?"

"Yes."

"And you taught Isaiah?"

"Yes, and Arcturus."

Casey shook his head slightly and sighed.

"Trot to the other end of the arena, turn right then come back directly at me; repeat but turn left next time."

Nora did as he said then stopped in front of him.

"Do you realize that you lean slightly when you turn to the right?"

"I do?" Nora was stunned. "I've never seen it in the video Mom takes."

"She is shooting you from the middle so you run crossways to her, not directly on."

"Do I lean going left?"

He shook his head. "Try it again without trying to correct yourself, but watch your position, feel your body as you go around the turn."

Nora did as he said and could feel herself tilt when she turned. She looked up at him and nodded, went around again and corrected herself.

For the rest of the lesson, Nora listened carefully and Casey's voice never rose over his normal bored tone.

Ninety minutes later, she watched Casey descend the bleachers and walk away.

She stood in the middle of the arena on top of Isaiah and realized how much he had taught her in such a little amount of time. She could barely wait for the next day and she could ride Arcturus for him. And the weekend show! She could hardly wait.

Why wait? Looking up at the morning sun, she decided she had more time so they practiced the moves Casey had taught her. She took Isaiah to the barn and saddled Arcturus. He'd had three days of rest. She could practice on him today so she would be ready for Casey in the morning.

Nora was lost in her own world with her two beautiful horses for another couple of hours.

When she finally slid off Arcturus for the day, she sprayed both of them down in the barn wash room. She thought how different her morning was from what she was expecting…Cooper, the cows, and the yelling.

She led both horses out to the north pasture to join the rest of the herd. Even after all their practice and exercise that morning, they took off at a run, instigating a whole herd run around the pasture. Libby, Kit and their babies began running in the south pasture.

Nora leaned against the fence and wondered why her parents didn't tell her about the change in coaching. Why didn't they? How irritating it was becoming that everyone else seemed to be making decisions in life for her…except her?

The calmness within her while riding her horses slowly faded. She turned to the house and the irritation grew with each step because she knew it wouldn't do any good talking to them. They made the decision…she would just have to live with it.

###

"Casey decided to give Cooper a day off?" Cora asked.

Nora nodded from the deck chair while picking at the lunch in front of her and watching Cora finish her yoga exercise.

"So what did you do this morning? He was here most the morning."

"Worked with reining on Isaiah."

"I thought he was just your coach for cutting with Cooper."

"Me, too." Nora put her feet up on a chair and stared at her boots, the bad mood getting worse.

"It started that way." Nora's dad walked up the stairs to the porch and sat in a chair across from her. "Casey recommended adding the reining and Jordan and I agreed."

Nora glanced at her dad, trying to keep her face calm. Why didn't they bother to tell her?

"Both horses?" Cora asked with a glance to Nora. Nora could tell the older woman was trying to see if she was upset.

"Yes, we work with Arcturus in the morning." Nora smiled, trying to hide her inner irritation. "I worked with him this morning after Isaiah so we would be more prepared."

"Always the over achiever," Cora chuckled as she rolled up her yoga mat.

Her dad put his feet up on the chair next to Nora's and playfully bumped her boots with his. Normally, she would have bumped back but now she couldn't even muster up a smile.

"Casey is impressed with both horses." He said with a confused look to her.

"Scott…seriously…isn't everyone?" Cora chuckled and headed to the back door. "It'll just take me a few minutes then I'll be ready."

"Ready for what?" He asked after Cora shut the door.

"She's taking me to The Stables so I can work with Bodi."

"Well, I can take you."

Nora shook her head. The irritation was growing and she needed away from him and her mom until she had a chance to calm down and let it go. Even Cora understood that it would upset her…why couldn't they see it?

"What?"

"What, what?" She asked and looked from her boots to him.

"What's the matter?"

Nora bit her lip, shook her head, and looked back to her boots. It was never a good idea to argue with a parent, especially when you were in a bad mood. Besides, when they put their 'foot down' it really didn't matter what she said.

He pulled his feet off the chair and leaned forward, towards her. "What's the matter?"

"Nothing, Dad." She said a little more tersely than she meant to.

"Yes, there is." He argued. "What did I do, that you won't even let me drive you to The Stables?"

"Cora said she would." Nora moved her eyes from her boots and out to the pasture…totally opposite of where he was sitting.

"Look…at…me." He said very calmly but she could hear the irritation in his voice.

She had no choice but to look at him…because that was the way parenting worked…when they said something, you were supposed to just do it. Whether it was making all the decisions when it came to her horses and her training…or simply where she looked…it was up to them!

Her head felt like it was moving through thick mud as she turned…*forcing* herself to turn to him. With every inch of the turn, her irritation with him increased. By the time she was looking at him she was scowling…unintentional, but it happened and his jaw clenched and eyes narrowed.

They glared at each other.

"Talk to me." He said through gritted teeth.

Nora felt her stomach tighten in anger…it should have been nerves for looking at him the way she was…but she was just MAD.

"What do you want me to say?" She returned with a low tone of irritation. He might as well tell her what to say too.

"That's enough, Nora," He fumed. "I have no idea why you're mad at me, so if you want to clear this up, you have to talk to me."

She rolled her lips together and started to turn back to the pasture.

"Don't you turn…," He sat up straighter.

She forced her eyes back to him, her back muscles tightening and her jaw clenching to the point it began to hurt.

"Spit…it…out." His voice was no longer calm…it was pissed.

No good would come of her arguing with him so she remained silent.

The backdoor started to open.

"What is the problem, Nora?" He asked in rising frustration and anger.

The back door closed, whoever was coming out changed their mind quickly.

Nora's stomach tightened, her blood felt like fire through her veins. She had never been this mad and it was at her dad!

"Speak Nora." He ordered. "We will not be leaving here until you do."

And there it was! The ultimatum that meant a kid HAD to do what a parent told them.

She felt like she was going to burst and tried desperately to keep her voice calm instead of yelling.

"Why didn't you tell me about changing Casey to a reining coach?"

"That's what this is all about?" He nearly shouted.

Nora nodded.

"Just because you don't like him…"

"That has nothing to do with it!" She matched his tone and volume which caught both of them by surprise.

"Then what's the problem? He's a 2 time world champion! You should be thanking us."

Nora's feet dropped to the ground with a thud.

Her voice quivered in anger. "I thanked you before you hired him…I thanked you when you hired him…I understand that I am fortunate to have Casey training me."

"Then what's the problem?" He shouted in exasperation.

"Why didn't you tell me about changing Casey to a reining coach?" She yelled, her eyes blazing at him.

"It was just a logical transition, Nora." He yelled back. "Casey suggested it after seeing the horses the other day and hearing how your competition went."

"Why didn't you talk to me about it?" She forced herself to remain seated, she wanted to stand and stomp her feet. "Why did I have to be blindsided with it this morning by Casey?"

"Just because you don't like him…."

"IT DOESN'T HAVE ANYTHING TO DO WITH THAT!" Nora shot out of the chair, took two steps and spun back to him.

"Then what does it have to do with?" He stood; towering over her.

"Why didn't you talk to me about it?" She repeated; glaring up at him.

"Why would we?"

"Exactly!" She threw her arms in the air.

"Exactly what?" He asked, his expression clearly confused.

"I'M NOT FOUR! I'M FOURTEEN!" Her hands went to her hips, she knew she was going to get in trouble for yelling and talking back to him but she couldn't get herself to stop. "Casey yells at me that Cooper has a brain, I should work WITH him, not force him to do what I want."

"What…"

"I have a brain too! I have feelings and I have opinions…I CAN THINK! I should have input on things that make a difference in my horses and in my riding and in my competitions."

"I…"

"Even if you 'put your foot down' and say I have to do it anyway…at least you talked to me about it!"

"NORA!" He shouted.

She stopped yelling, her whole body vibrating. Taking deep breathes to calm the shaking, she dropped her hands from her hips so her stance wasn't so combative.

"We never thought of asking you Nora." His voice was a forced calm. "It just seemed like a natural move."

"I wouldn't have had a problem with it, even if I don't like him yelling at me, I just should have been part of the discussion. It has to do with ME."

"You're right…it does have to do with you…and we probably should have talked to you about it." The tension in his body decreased.

She didn't know what to say or do next…she hadn't expected him to say that. She hadn't expected to yell at him either and was sure she was going to get in trouble.

Her shoulders lowered and her eyes went to her boots.

"Chin up." He said quietly.

Nora raised her chin but looked at the back door, wondering who had attempted to come out.

"Look at me."

Nora scrunched her face and held it tightly. She hated when they told her that!

"Relax, Nora." He exhaled loudly, his patience wearing thin.

She relaxed her face and tried to relax her back muscles.

Before he ordered her to do it again, she looked up at him.

"I will talk to your mother," He said calmly. "And we'll make sure you're included in conversations about coaching, the horses, and your competitions."

Nora took a deep breath and let it out slowly. Well…that was unintentional but it worked…now what was she supposed to do?

He turned and started to walk away then stopped and looked back at her. "Why do you hold these things in? Why didn't you just come and talk to us?"

One shoulder went up in half-shrug, "Why didn't you just ask me what I wanted?" She sighed, the tension leaving her body.

He stared at her, without speaking, then finally turned and walked into the house.

Nora walked to Cora's car and waited to be driven to The Stables.

Something was going to happen from the confrontation…it probably wouldn't be good.

CHAPTER EIGHT

Nora stood in the middle of the round pen at The Stables and watched Bodi run around the parameter. She had loved this horse since the day she and Nikki bought him at the auction for Nick when he was only six months old. He had grown into quite a beauty.

Nikki, Jack and Aunt Dru were standing on the outside watching. They all three knew how to train horses, it was part of Jack's job and he always had a few going on the same time. Knowing they were watching her every move did not help her mood.

She stepped ahead of the blue eyed, cream colored two year old and he quickly turned, inward with his head toward her…which was good. He had spent the first couple minutes of the training turning with his butt to her, which was bad.

She made him turn again by stepping ahead of him and stepping backwards, he turned in…he jogged a full circle around the pen and she stepped ahead of him again. He turned in so Nora lowered her head and took a step back from him. He stopped immediately, looking at her…waiting for the next silent command.

Nora turned her back to him, just slightly, and Bodi slowly walked to her, stopping just inches from her. She turned and spoke softly to him, running her hand down the length of his nose and down around his round jaw.

She stepped away from him, said "Back" loudly and the horse took two steps back. "Good job." She smiled and his head bounced as she reached to stroke him again.

She repeated the words but this time kept him walking backwards until he had crossed the pen. She was following him but she didn't touch him during the process until she was ready for him to stop completely, then she praised him with a rub down the length of his nose and neck. She turned and walked away, he followed calmly and politely.

Nora stopped…he stopped, if she took a step, Bodi would take a step. She ran her hands over his entire body, talking to him softly. She lifted each hoof and used her hoof pick to clean out dirt…which was very little.

She walked over to the tack she had in the corner, Bodi followed. Putting the bridle on him was easy…it wasn't his first time so it went quickly and without incident. Then the saddle pad and saddle.

He still wasn't used to the cinch around his ribs and twisted toward her when she tightened it.

Nora had never been on him, no one had. He was basically hand fed from the time she and Nikki won him at the auction. She was sure that Bodi wouldn't do anything if she stepped into the saddle now.

She moved back to the center of the round pen and gave the horse directions to run to her left, and he did without hesitation. Another ten minutes of him running left and right…all with his head turning toward her and he simply ignored the saddle.

Nora stopped him, told him to 'back' from thirty feet away and he did. She smiled. Arcturus didn't even do that.

Turning her back to him, she peeked behind her and watched him walk calmly to her. She turned and congratulated him on a job well done.

Nora was the first person on the backs of the three horses brought back from the auction for her to train. Uncle Grayson had been close by, ready to react if something happened. The gruella was the only one that gave her a problem. He had bucked a few times. She found it exciting and hadn't been scared at all.

The horse had even reared up once and though her uncle had stood away from the fence and was ready to run to her, he let her handle the situation. She didn't panic and the horse quickly relaxed. There were no more issues with him. He was patient and learned quickly after that.

She looked at Bodi…then deciding she was already in trouble for yelling at her dad, so they could be mad at her for this too…without warning to her audience, she stepped to his side, pulled the rein closest to her so his nose was pointed to her. She reached for the saddle horn as she put her foot in the stirrup.

"Nora!" They all three called out and she could see them walking up to the gate. Jack unhooked the lever just as she pulled herself up to a standing position in the stirrup.

Bodi sidestepped but she held her position and pulled the rein in closer to her. He tried to walk forward but it just sent him in a circle since his nose was pointing towards her. She waited patiently until he stopped then she stepped down, patted his nose and repeated the procedure until he didn't move.

Truly believing the horse wouldn't do anything, Nora stepped up and surprised her audience again by lifting her leg over the saddle and sitting on top of Bodi for the first time. He didn't do anything but turn his head to look at her. She smiled down at him and lightly stroked his neck. The first time was always exciting.

Nora looked up to see Jack walking toward her with a bit of a glare from his blue eyes. Without a word, he clipped a lead rope to Bodi's halter and started walking him around the round pen.

Keeping a tight hold of the saddle horn, just in case Bodi spooked, she ran her free hand down his cream colored neck and over his rump. She was so used to riding two black horses and a deep red bay that the light color was quite odd to her.

Jack stopped and without a word, Nora stepped out of the saddle and stroked the horse's neck.

"You going to do that again?" Jack asked with a frown.

Nora shook her head without looking at him and walked Bodi back to the center of the pen to strip him of the tack. He shook his entire body when she lifted the saddle off his back.

"You just wait, little Bodacious," She laughed at him which made his head bob up and down. "That was nothing compared to your future rides."

Finally in a good mood, she walked him to the gate and was met by three very upset faces. Her good mood dissolved quickly.

"Let me put him away before you yell at me." She sighed and walked him to the stalls. She stayed with him for a half hour to delay the inevitable scolding for getting on him without warning them…or even getting on him at all.

Rooster and Bodi shared a stall so she played with the sorrel wishing she had more time so she could ride him.

Rooster was being used for the hippotherapy program through Nikki. It was one of the reasons she was down from the ranch today. She was working with Gary, the speech therapist, and Jeremy, the little boy they met at last year's kid's horse clinic.

Jeremy loved Rooster and came to ride him a couple times a week for therapy and sometimes just for fun.

"Stop delaying and get out here." Aunt Dru called from outside the stall.

Nora stared at the door without moving. She didn't really want to go face them but couldn't figure out how to get out of it.

It was only Aunt Dru waiting for her as she exited the stall.

"Scott called."

Before she could stop herself, Nora shrugged then cringed inside. She glanced at her aunt to see her reaction.

"Wow." Her eyebrows raised in surprise.

Nora stood silently, waiting…

"You want to talk about it?"

Nora shook her head.

"If you had talked about Casey with your parents, maybe there wouldn't have been a yelling match."

"If they would have thought I had a brain then maybe there wouldn't have been a yelling match." Dang! Why did she keep saying things like that…she just needed to shut up!

"What's your issue, Nora?" Her aunt stood, hands on hips, blue eyes glaring out from under her straw cowboy hat.

Nora shook her head and tightly rolled her lips together.

"You're shutting down now, aren't you?"

Nora nodded.

"Let's go." Her aunt turned and walked away. "I'll take you home and you can sit in the truck for 20 captive minutes while I tell you why you shouldn't have gotten on Bodi like you did."

Nora followed, sat quietly while her aunt lectured her, then when she got home she searched out her parents so they could take their turn. She couldn't find them so she went to the no-media room and waited.

There wasn't really anything but the back deck and the hay barn visible through the windows where she was sitting. She leaned back and closed her eyes to imagine the pattern for the upcoming weekend's competitions.

When she opened her eyes, it was dark outside. What the heck?! She sat straight up and looked around her. The clock said it was ten o'clock.

Why didn't they wake her up? She was never going to be able to get back to sleep. With a deep sigh, she walked out of the room and down the long hallway. She was in socked feet since she left her boots at the back door when she arrived home.

Nora could hear someone talking from the large dining room so she headed to the voice.

Different voices chimed in and became louder. She stopped at the base of the steps…just out of sight of the people in the room.

"I won't say anything to her," Uncle Grayson was talking. "That's up to you, but she is very capable of training Bodi."

"Of course she is." Her dad said.

"That wasn't the point, Grayson." Aunt Dru added. "It's the fact that she got on him with no warning to us so we had time to react if something happened."

"She wouldn't have gotten on him if she thought something was going to happen," Uncle Grayson argued for her. "She's smarter than that."

"Still not the point," Her dad said. "It's the fact she would not have gotten on him…risked getting in trouble…if she wasn't already in trouble for the yelling match on the porch."

Nora nodded, he was right.

"You didn't talk to her at all about the change in coaching?" Uncle Grayson asked.

"Not in the change…nor what he said about her, no." It was her mother that answered.

What did Casey say about her?

"Well, you can get pissed at me if you want…but I'm siding with Nora on that one…I would have been upset too." Uncle Grayson said and Nora smiled slightly.

"Why didn't you say anything to her?" Aunt Dru asked.

"It never crossed my mind," Her dad admitted. "We're just so used to making the decisions and don't always talk to Wade and Nora about it."

"They are getting to that age…" Uncle Grayson started.

"That they have a brain and can think too." Her dad finished sarcastically. "Trust me, I heard that this afternoon."

Nora could hear chuckles but couldn't tell who they were from.

"It's a transition age…parents holding on, kids trying to get more independent. That age was tough with Matt and Nikki…boys and girls go through it a whole lot different." Aunt Dru said.

"We're not perfect parents and we did handle it badly." Her dad sighed. "I just don't know how to handle it now. I'm certainly not going to reward her for her actions. I didn't even want to be around her by the time we were done."

Nora cringed. THAT made her heart ache.

"I have no idea what to do or say besides we were wrong." Nora's mom said.

"Wrong or not, her attitude…the way SHE handled it was not right." Her dad added.

"It's hard at that age to figure out how to handle all the emotions." Aunt Dru pointed out.

"You didn't hear her, Dru." Nora's dad said gruffly.

"It's just so unlike her." Aunt Dru sighed.

"She's always been such a good girl." Her mother said.

Nora's heart nearly stopped…if she wasn't a good girl…she was bad. She felt the tears begin to rush to her eyes as her chin quivered. She turned and went up the stairs as fast, but as quiet as she could. When she reached the top, she heard the backdoor open.

Nora ran down the hallway and into her room. Sadie and Grace were sleeping so she quickly stepped out of her jeans and crawled into bed, throwing the blankets over her head and burying her face into the mattress and under the pillows. She let the tears soak into the mattress.

Her mind went to the morning ride…just her and Arcturus cantering around the arena, just the two of them in the morning sun. It was peaceful…heaven…her world. The image…the feeling…slowly melted away as she thought of her mother's words and how they pierced her heart like a dagger.

How did it go so bad? How could she fix this? How could she hide the bad person inside her that nearly everyone saw today? Tears soaked into the sheets of her bed.

She heard footsteps walking down the hallway and she held her breath…waiting…

But they didn't stop at her bedroom door, they walked past. She heard the boy's bedroom door open then close.

It was Reilly…today was Monday…the night he and Billy had the date with Christina and Marla.

Nora screamed in her head! So loud she didn't hear the other footsteps coming down the hall and nearly jumped out of bed when she felt the hand on her arm.

"Nora," It was her mother. "Come with me."

She tugged on Nora's arm and held a pair of pajama bottoms for her to put on. After pulling them on, she was led out of the room, across the hall and into her parent's bedroom. Her dad was waiting for them with a scowl on his face.

The tears increased from the yelling match, Aunt Dru's lecture about Bodi, her mother's words, and thinking of Billy on a date with another girl. He would go on many more dates…maybe even marry before she was old enough.

Nora stared at the look on her dad's face, it was obvious he didn't want to be there. She tried hard to stop the tears, but started to gag on them instead. Her mother barely got her to the bathroom before she vomited. There wasn't much because she slept through dinner.

"Nora, darling…what is going on with you today?" Her mother whispered as she held her hair back.

"I don't know." Nora said honestly between the gags. "I'm sorry, Dad."

"Nora…" He sighed.

"I should have talked to you but I was so upset." Nora gasped.

"Nora, let's get your head out of the toilet before we start talking about this." He said and left the bathroom.

When her body started to relax, her mother gave her water to drink, her dad handed her the toothbrush he had retrieved from the girl's bathroom.

"I don't think she's even eaten today." Her dad said. "She pecked at her lunch then didn't eat it before they left for The Stables."

"Let's get you something to eat." Her mother pushed her toward the hall door.

"It's too late to eat." Nora argued, her stomach still queasy.

"You need something in your stomach." Her mother argued back.

"You have a brain, Nora. Think it through." Her dad said tartly.

Nora cringed at the comment and nearly ran out the door.

"You can stay up here." Nora heard her mother say and the door slammed behind them.

And there she did it again! Made her parents argue about her! Why couldn't she hold her tongue? Why did she have to be so selfish? She wasn't just bad, she was horrible!

Nora remained quiet and stared out into the dark as she tried to eat. Her mother leaned back in her chair and closed her eyes.

"You can go to bed, Mom." Nora said, hoping she would go up and reconcile with her dad. "I can turn off the lights and go to bed myself."

Her mom leaned forward and looked at her with a frown.

"Nora, it wasn't just the fact it was disrespectful, it's the fact that you let it get that bad without talking to us."

Nora lowered her fork and placed it on the table. She forced herself to look at her mom.

"It all happened so fast…I tried to be quiet but he kept pushing and I just…" Nora said softly, trying to sound calmer than she was.

"This all started because of Casey working with you on reining this morning?"

"Yeah…I didn't know…and it just upset me that you didn't even talk to me about it." She felt the irritation returning and tried to bury it down deep so her mom couldn't see it again.

"We didn't do it on purpose…it was an honest mistake."

Nora nodded, she had to remain calm, keep the irritation hidden.

"Until we figure this all out…and you and your dad talk about what happened, you will not be working with Bodi."

Nora gasped, eyes wide, but she managed to remain quiet as she stared at her mother who stood and walked slowly across the kitchen and up the stairs.

She leaned back in the chair and stared at her plate then to the clock. It was eleven o'clock. Maybe he would be awake, he normally was this time of night but she needed her phone. She didn't have it all day, so it must still be on the charger in the library.

She retrieved the phone and made her way back to the small kitchen table.

TEXT TO NICK: Are you awake

TEXT TO NORA: Yes, what's up

TEXT TO NICK: Buttercup

TEXT TO NORA: Have a good day

TEXT TO NICK: No

TEXT TO NORA: Want to talk

TEXT TO NICK: No

TEXT TO NORA: Anything at all good happen

TEXT TO NICK: I worked with Bodi

TEXT TO NORA: Was he good

TEXT TO NICK: Yes, I sat on him

TEXT TO NORA: He mind his manners

TEXT TO NICK: He did

TEXT TO NORA: Are you working with him tomorrow? I'll come watch

TEXT TO NICK: No, got in trouble, grounded from him

TEXT TO NORA: You got in trouble that bad

TEXT TO NICK: Yeah

TEXT TO NORA: Need a visit?

Nora stared at the phone, he would come tonight if she asked, even if he was 45 minutes away. She was very careful what she typed into the phone because her parents read it all the time. But she needed to talk to him about her dark side…the bad within her…he was the only one that knew, understood, and didn't judge her for it.

TEXT TO NORA: No answer? That bad?

TEXT TO NICK: It will probably be better tomorrow

TEXT TO NORA: What do you expect will make it better?

TEXT TO NICK: Dad will cool down and talk to me

TEXT TO NORA: Just need time?

TEXT TO NICK: I hope so, I don't like him being mad at me. Plus I want to ride Bodi again

TEXT TO NORA: It was fun?

TEXT TO NICK: First ride is always fun

TEXT TO NORA: Are you OK tonight

TEXT TO NICK: Yes, you need to go? Tessa there?

TEXT TO NORA: Not if you need me, yes and Alex

TEXT TO NICK: They move in yet

TEXT TO NORA: I almost have her talked in to it

TEXT TO NICK: Why the hold up

TEXT TO NORA: Her place is closer to the B&B

TEXT TO NICK: Ahhh, but your place is closer to you

TEXT TO NORA: Ha! I will remind her of that

TEXT TO NICK: Good night…thank you
TEXT TO NORA: It will be better, you are good, good night

She lay the phone on the table and ate all of her dinner. He always made her feel better…he believed she was good.

CHAPTER NINE

"You practiced," Casey commented when she finished her last pattern run with Arcturus. He was sitting on the bleachers while she sat on the horse and looked up at him.

The morning was beautiful with a gentle warm sun and a slight breeze. The sky was light blue with no clouds. These were the mornings that Nora loved to get lost in her ride. She wanted the practice to end so she could disappear into her own world.

"Yes, of course." Nora looked warily at him. She wasn't sure if he was upset or not. "I want as much practice as possible with what you showed me for this weekend's show."

Casey nodded, he seemed to be pleased…but she had never seen his pleased look so she wasn't really sure.

He stood to leave then sat back down and looked at her.

"Yesterday you said you didn't want to work Isaiah with cows. Does that include Arcturus?"

"Yes."

"Why?"

"Arcturus doesn't like cows, and we just never have with Isaiah." Nora answered; worried he was going to force the issue. "He's been my show horse and we're careful not to get scratches on him for the showmanship classes."

"Have you seen reined cow horse competitions?"

Nora nodded.

"And never thought of moving Isaiah in that direction?"

Nora shook her head.

"Any reason why?"

"I've been working on the horse shows."

Casey nodded, "It's something to consider, we could always just try him out next week after we get back." He stood and started to walk away. "You cutting with Isaiah would allow you to give Cooper back to Jordan to compete with."

Nora stared at him as he walked away…she felt like her heart had sunk into her stomach. She had to be the most selfish kid on earth! Her mother had been competing with Cooper for over a year and Nora had, without hesitation, taken Cooper from her.

Arcturus shifted and Nora looked around. No one was in sight so she turned him and circled the arena at a canter. She needed to escape…get away from reality…get away from the world. There was no way she could have another day like the one before.

Lowering in her seat, she cued the horse to a slow jog. He had just completed a great practice session and didn't want to work him any harder, nor punish him because she needed to escape.

Nora was so lost in her world she nearly ran over her mother. Arcturus sidestepped around her and Nora looked up in surprise. No one was awake when she left the house except Jack and they only spoke of his clients at The Stables; a safe topic.

Her mom stroked the black horse's neck and looked up at her with a smile. "Put Arcturus away and change your clothes into something lighter then meet me in the kitchen."

She turned away before Nora could ask why.

An hour later, Nora had Arcturus bathed, his summer sheet placed on him to protect him from the sun's rays, and in the pasture with the other horses.

She showered and put on shorts, a button up sleeveless shirt and slid on sandals. She guessed that if she dressed wrong, her mother would tell her what else to wear.

"Where are you going?" Sadie asked while sitting in the middle of Nora's bed.

"I don't know."

"I heard the argument yesterday." Sadie whispered.

Nora looked at her in surprise then realized she didn't see Sadie at all yesterday.

"How can we live in the same house and not see each other all day?" Nora smiled, not wanting to talk about the yelling match anymore.

Sadie shrugged. "You were riding here…I was riding there…then you slept all afternoon."

"Took me forever to get to sleep last night." Nora kicked off the sandals and grabbed another pair.

"You're going to be really tired later."

"Probably." Nora shrugged and tried on the third pair of shoes.

"Here," Sadie stood and walked to her portion of the room and returned with pink slip on walking shoes that matched Nora's shirt.

"Thanks, that's better." Nora slid them on and tried walking in them. "We wear the same size everything but pants."

"Makes it convenient…unless you're wearing something that I want to wear." Sadie giggled.

"I better go." Nora smiled nervously at her cousin.

"I hope it's something fun." Sadie returned her smile.

Nora walked down the hallway and headed down the stairs, glancing over the railing to see if her mom was there…she was…and so was her dad.

She kept her face calm with just a slight smile as she descended the steps.

"I think that's the first time I've seen you in summer clothes in weeks." Her mother smiled.

Nora tried to smile and glanced at her dad. He was forcing a smile, too. That wasn't good.

When she reached her parents, her mother handed her father a piece of paper.

"Here's your list. I'll see you two this afternoon." She turned and walked toward the library. Nora nervously looked at her dad.

"Your mother has decided we're running errands together for the trip this weekend." He smiled at her and turned toward the back door.

Nora silently followed him to his truck, he opened the door for her and she hesitantly smiled at him; her stomach felt like a rock.

She took a deep breath and let it out slowly as he walked around to the other side of the truck.

"Did you eat breakfast?" He asked and started the engine.

"No."

"You really should before you ride, it'll make you feel better."

"OK."

"So where do you want to go to breakfast?"

Nora glanced over at him as he drove down the long driveway. "I like the waffle place downtown."

"Good choice," He turned onto the main road to town then glanced at her. They rode silently for a while until he finally spoke. "Let's just get it out so we can enjoy the day."

"OK." Nora swallowed hard and her stomach started to hurt.

"Dru told me she had you for 20 captive minutes after the Bodi ride yesterday."

"Yes."

"Do I need to tell you anything more than what she did?"

"No, she was pretty thorough. Until he has more training, I won't do it again without letting someone know."

"Good." He nodded and sighed. "Now the other."

"I'm really sorry."

"Me too, I shouldn't have let my temper take over and we should have talked to you about Casey."

"I shouldn't have been so disrespectful," Nora said honestly. "I love you and Mom and really appreciate what you do for me."

"We love you too, Nora Bug."

"So, what's my punishment?" Nora asked nervously. She was really worried about her reaction if they kept her away from Arcturus.

"We've had a hard time with that one," He admitted. "It doesn't make sense to spend the practice time and coaching money for your horse shows then take that away when you're in trouble."

"Ok?" Nora couldn't think of anything else that would bother her if they took away from her except her phone…which was her only connection to Nick. They wouldn't do that….would they?

"If you're on the computer, you're looking up horse competitions and videos that help in your shows, so it's not logical to take that from you."

Nora bit her lip in anticipation.

"Even with Tessa and Alex, Nick relies on you to keep him company when he travels, so it would be punishing him too to take the phone…besides you only talk with him and Candace. It would be punishing Candace, too."

Nora internally sighed in relief. She couldn't think of anything else that would bother her if they took it away…besides Bodi and they already did.

"So what would you suggest?"

"What?" Nora looked at him in surprise.

"We couldn't think of anything…so what would you suggest we do to punish you?"

Nora stared out the window, mulled it over then looked up at him. "Your being mad at me and not wanting to be around me was the worst thing. Mom being mad…that was just awful."

He parked at the restaurant and looked down at her. "So, to punish you…your mother and I have to stay mad at you?"

"There really couldn't be anything worse than that." She said honestly. That was why she hid the darkness inside her and only shared it with Nick. She didn't want her parents to be disappointed or dislike her because of it.

"It's really hard to stay mad at you when you say things like that." He smiled, the love back in his eyes.

"So now what?" She smiled back.

"Waffles covered in whip cream and blueberries." He reached for the door handle.

###

"How are you doing?" Jack asked as he handed her a bowl and set one down on the counter for himself.

"Fine," Nora placed her phone on the table and took the bowl to fill it with cereal.

"You don't normally eat breakfast before going out."

"I know, but Dad said it would give me more energy in the morning."

"Did it work yesterday?" He joined her at the table and poured milk in both their bowls.

"I guess. The training with Arcturus and Isaiah went well, but it was more low key than working with the cows and Cooper like we are this morning."

"It's five thirty."

Nora nodded. "Casey just texted and said he would be here at seven."

"Dang, you could have slept in."

She shrugged, "I was lying in bed thinking of Arcturus anyway."

"Something wrong with him?"

"No, he's healthy. I just don't know how to get him above third place in halter. I looked at all of Mom's videos yesterday from this year. Then on the computer for the ones I could find on YouTube of the professionals and I can't figure out what's going on."

"Halter is pretty specific to his confirmation, conditioning, and his personality."

"Yeah…but to me…I can't see what's wrong."

"Want some help?"

Nora smiled, "You would help me?"

He rolled his blue eyes and his dimples deepened when he smiled at her, "Of course, I would. I've been around showing all my life, grew up with it at my parent's stables in Texas. Reilly's mom showed for a couple years before he was born. That was how we met."

"Can you help this morning? I work with Cooper today then we leave on Friday morning." Anxious to get to the barn, she quickly shoveled cereal into her mouth.

"Sure, Grace was coming in early to the Stables this morning, she can take Trail Boss over and I'll go when we're done."

"She'll love being the morning boss." Nora grinned and took her bowl to the sink. "I'll go get him ready."

"Fix him up like you would for the show…except his hooves…don't worry about those."

Nora stepped out the back door and ran to the barn. This was exciting; she got to postpone being yelled at by Casey and had the chance of helping Arcturus.

She brushed him and sprayed him with his conditioner that made his black hair slick and shiny. Then his mane was brushed and sprayed and the shiny show halter was placed on him.

Jack was already standing in the arena when she arrived. He had placed a starting cone just in front of the cattle chute.

It was another beautiful summer morning with a few puffy clouds gliding by in the slight breeze. The sun was up, just warming the morning; it would be hot in the afternoon, another triple digit day.

"I didn't clip him, we'll do that Friday night."

"That's fine. Just follow my commands then we'll talk about it."

Nora followed every command as if she were showing to a real judge. Arcturus seemed alert. When his attention would wane she would click to him to get his attention.

"Let's reverse roles." Jack suggested with a smile.

"Did you see something?" She asked excitedly.

He chuckled at her enthusiasm. "Let's see if you see something."

Jack followed each of her commands. She really enjoyed pretending to be a judge and she watched the black horse's every move then walked around him, judging his confirmation and stance.

Nora looked at Jack and shook her head. "I just don't see anything; he's beautiful."

Jack laughed. "Have you ever heard that love is blind?"

"Yeah…" She said hesitantly. "You're saying he's not beautiful?"

"No, I'm saying you look at him differently…you love him so much you love everything about him. You see no flaws."

She looked at him warily and he handed the leather lead back to her.

"I'll be right back." He said and turned to walk to the barn.

Nora turned her attention to her beloved Arcturus. Love him too much? She rubbed a hand down the horse's face, around his jaw, under his eye and up to his star. She leaned her forehead on his, closed her eyes, and took a deep breath to fill her lungs with the morning air and him.

Pure love.

They stood quietly in the middle of the arena with the sun warming their backs. The breeze tangled her loose hair with his. Her black shirt blended with his black body. For a moment, she felt as one with him in her heart.

She never wanted that moment to end but knew Jack would be returning so she slowly opened her eyes. He was standing at the gate smiling at her. He had an arm behind his back.

"I didn't want to disturb you."

Nora thanked him with her smile as he approached.

"Turn around." He instructed so she stepped away from her horse and turned.

Ten minutes later she was starting to get nervous.

"Casey is going to be here soon, I need to get Cooper ready."

"Yeah…whatever," Jack chuckled. "Walk out about ten feet and when I tell you to, turn and tell me what you think."

Nora took ten steps, shifting from one foot to the other, anxious to see what he was doing.

"Ok."

She turned quickly and stared at her black horse.

He had changed the show halter from a thinner strap to a broader strapped halter. It made his head look stronger…more masculine.

Then he had braided the horse's mane up off his neck.

"His neck looks so…big." Nora whispered in awe.

Arcturus' whole look changed with just those two adjustments.

"It's a fast, rough braid, but it gives you the look you want."

"You're right…he looks magnificent."

"Which is how you describe Isaiah," He reminded her.

"Oh my gosh! You're right!" The excitement ran through her.

"You've never thought of putting his mane up before?"

"No, I like it down for all the western classes."

"Cutting it short an option?"

Nora shrugged, "I'd have to think about that."

"Well, band it this weekend, see how it works then make a decision." Jack suggested.

"The halter needs some attention; it must have been one of Nikki's. Thank you, Jack." Nora gave him a big hug before he left for The Stables.

She could hardly wait for the next few days to pass. She was ready, but anxious for Arcturus.

CHAPTER TEN

Nora lowered the clippers, stepped back, and looked at Isaiah. She just smiled, he was so handsome. The horse turned and dipped his nose to her so Nora spoke softly and ran a hand over his newly shaven muzzle.

"Nora!"

She jumped and turned, wide eyed, "What?"

Her mother was shaking her head. "I swear this whole equestrian park could implode and you wouldn't know it when you're around those horses."

Nora chuckled and walked the red bay horse to his stall. Before shutting him in for the night, she double checked his blanket, making sure it was tight. She checked his water and his hay.

"Come on." Her mother sighed. "He's fine, Cooper is fine, and Arcturus is fine."

Candace and her aunt appeared next to her mother. Just the four of them had ridden to the show together. Casey was meeting them in the morning for the reining classes which were first on the show schedule.

One more glance in Cooper and Arcturus' stalls she finally relented to walk to the trailer for dinner.

When they walked in the trailer, there was a white box on the table with a big red bow.

"What's that?" Nora turned to her mother and was greeted with a smile.

"Check it out." Her mother answered.

Waiting for her three companions to sit at the table, Nora reached for the envelope attached to the top of the box.

"Your payment for working with Bodi. Kick butt this weekend. 85!"

"Who's it from?" Candace asked.

"Nick," Nora giggled in excitement. "He wasn't supposed to pay me for working with Bodi."

"Don't complain!" Candace said excitedly. "Open it up!"

Nora slid the red ribbon and bow off of the package and hung it from the wall hook holding back the curtain. She planned on keeping it for a long time. She tipped open the side of the box…just a little…and peeked inside. All she could see was white tissue paper.

"Oh, you're killing me!" Paige rolled her eyes.

Nora laughed and threw the lid off and tore back the tissue paper.

Her laugh stopped and she stared.

The other three gasped.

With just the tip of her finger, Nora gently touched the brand new show halter. The sterling silver plating had gold bead trim and an intricate engraving with black inlay and the black leather that would match Arcturus perfectly. It had the same broad strap as the one Jack had placed on her horse.

"That's fantastic." Her mother exclaimed.

"Just beautiful." Paige added.

Nora gently lifted the halter out of the box. She could hardly wait to see how it looked and to send Nick a picture. "Can we go try it on him?"

"Let's get dinner first." Her mother stood. "I can't wait to see it on him either."

All four quickly ate the pre-cooked meal that Cora had prepared for them and headed back to the stalls. As they neared the outside stalls they found three men standing in front of Isaiah's door looking in at the horse. Nora didn't recognize them.

"Can I help you with something?" Her mother asked warily and stepped protectively in front of Nora; Paige did the same with Candace.

Nora glanced around nervously looking to see if there was a guard or someone to help. There were lots of campers she could scream for.

"Is this your horse?" A man in a large grey Stetson asked.

"Yes," Her mother said, sounding calm. The man wasn't very tall but he was broad and stocky. He looked…sophisticated. The other two men stood quietly behind him.

"Is he for sale?" The Stetson man asked.

"No." Her mother answered as Nora's eyes widened in surprise.

"Would you consider selling for a…" The man started.

"No, he's not for sale for any price." Her mother said firmly.

"Can I at least give you an offer?" The man smiled showing perfect teeth.

"I don't think you should waste any time with that." Her mother smiled politely.

"It's not a small amount." The man countered.

"It doesn't matter. He isn't for sale." Her mother repeated.

"Maybe I should talk to your husband." The man tilted his head with a frown and the two men next to him just shook their heads and took a step back.

"Well, isn't that a rude sexist comment you just said to four females." Her mother's back straightened and her voice lowered. "And if my husband was here, he'd kick your ass for saying such a stupid thing."

Nora managed to hold back the giggle but the grin spread across her face.

The Stetson man chuckled; "My wife would too, but I had to give it a shot." He looked at Isaiah and back to the four females standing in front of him. "Can I give you my card in case you change your mind?"

"Don't waste a card." Her mother shook her head.

Stetson man grinned; "Alright, I'll give up. Good luck with him tomorrow." He said looking right at her mother.

"He's my daughter's horse." She corrected him.

The man's eyes went straight to Nora; his brows rose in surprise.

Nora felt her cheeks redden at the sudden attention, but she kept her back straight and tried to look as confident as her mother sounded.

"Well," The man nodded. "I look forward to what you do with him the next two days."

"Reining first…" Nora smiled innocently. "Then some halter, showmanship, trail, western pleasure…"

The man laughed, a big booming laugh, "You're killing me, young lady." He looked back to her mom. "No sale?"

"No sale." Her mother grinned proudly.

The man sighed, touched the tip of his hat and nodded to the four females. "Good luck."

With that, the three men left.

When they rounded the corner and were out of sight, Nora's mother turned with eyes wide and a grin across her face. "Goodness!"

"Way to go, Jordan." Candace chuckled.

"Love the part about Scott." Paige said proudly.

"My mom is such a bad ass." Nora laughed and checked in on Isaiah and Cooper before opening Arcturus' stall.

The halter fit him perfectly and he looked strong and masculine.

Her mom took a picture of her standing with the black horse and his new halter. Nora sent it to Nick, Sadie, and her dad.

"Now I can't WAIT for tomorrow!" Nora beamed as her horse nudged her with his nose.

###

"Watch your lean." Nora told herself as she turned to the right at the end of the white canvased covered arena. She sat straight and Arcturus turned perfectly. One more run down the middle of the arena ending with a KILLER sliding stop that made her heart race…spin to the left…spin to the right…back up ten steps, stop and sigh in relief.

Nora grinned as she finished and walked out of the arena to the applause of the crowd. She and Arcturus won the class.

There were two riders between her and the ride with Isaiah. Because she had shown Isaiah a year longer than Arcturus, Isaiah was in a different class.

Casey stood with the bay horse. "Good job."

"Thanks, it felt really good." Nora slid off the black horse and switched reins with Casey. She quickly moved her saddle to Isaiah as Casey switched her competitor number from Arcturus' number to Isaiah's.

"Not much I can say to improve the pattern." Casey actually smiled at her as she stepped into the saddle.

Nora chuckled and turned the horse to watch the next competitors.

The rider finished strong, her spins at the end were just short of four full turns.

"How did my spins look?" Nora turned to Casey.

"They were good." He assured her.

Nora nodded and watched the next rider; a boy on a palomino. He looked good until his final sliding stop which was short. The first spin she counted three, the second spin was four.

"Did he miss that?" Nora asked.

"I counted three and four." Casey nodded.

Nora walked to the main entry gate.

"You got this." Casey called out just as she entered the arena at the excruciatingly slow pace that was asked for.

She made her way down the side of the arena, turned halfway down, they stopped in the center. She stepped backwards four steps then moved directly into a canter to her right…four circles large to small at different paces…transition lead change…repeat circles to her left…ride to the end of the arena…turn to the center… speed up all the way to the end…sliding stop…roll back to the left…light canter back to the other end…turn to the center…speed up all the way to the end…sliding stop…roll back to the right…light canter to the other end…turn right to the center…final sliding stop down the middle…four turns to her right…four turns to her left…step back ten steps…sigh…grin…reach forward with both hands and stroke the sides of the red bay's neck.

Nora could hear her mother and Candace over the rest of the audience.

Her final score from the three judges; Arcturus was 216, Isaiah 217. She won first in both divisions. The coaching Casey had given her the first of the week escalated both horses up a level in their performance. She also admitted that it had improved her performance and confidence.

Casey was smiling as she rode out of the arena. He walked next to her as they headed back to the stalls to prepare for the halter classes.

"Thank you, Casey."

"You're welcome."

"What are you going to do the rest of the day?"

"Thought I'd stick around and see how the boys do in halter and western pleasure."

"Careful," Nora warned. "They'll get under your skin and not let you go."

"So…they're contagious?" He looked up at her with a smirk.

"Yep."

###

"Arcturus' class is right before Isaiah's." Nora quickly checked herself in the mirror. Her black jeans were clean and looked good; she wore a sparkling black and silver shirt that looked good with both horses. Her hair was slicked back and into a long straight ponytail. A black cowboy hat was placed perfectly on her head.

These were the times Nora really appreciated she received her mother's Native American looks instead of her dad's tall and blonde looks. Her nearly black eyes, darker complexion, and the black hair blended well with the horses but stood out in the arena.

"I'll have Isaiah waiting and ready when you walk out of the arena." Her mom said.

They headed for the stalls.

Her mother helped prepare both horses. Arcturus' new show halter shimmered to match Nora's shirt. His mane was tightly banded for the first time.

Nora walked into the arena behind a beautiful chestnut; she was fifth in line, ten more followed her and Arcturus. Her hopes and anxiety were pushed to the back of her mind as she listened intently to the judge and the commands. There were three judges that walked around each of the horses. Arcturus' head was up and watching the judges and the audience. Nora smiled proudly inside, but kept her face calm with her "perfect" smile.

The first moment she ever saw Arcturus flashed in her mind; the black, scared, skeleton of a horse that looked at her with hope. She had been afraid to even touch him in fear of hurting him. He had come so far and every fiber in her body wanted this win for him.

They walked the pattern and stood back in line. Arcturus only took two attempts to place his hooves correctly. He was having a good day which was evident in his curious attitude as he watched the people in the arena.

The judges finished reviewing each horse then walked back into the middle of the arena. The lead horse of the group placed third. Nora nearly jumped as they turned towards her and motioned for second…but it was for the chestnut in front of her. Nora's heart plummeted…for thirty seconds as they pointed to her and her black horse as the winners of the class, winning first from all three judges. She nearly screamed in delight and grinned proudly.

As she left the arena she fought off the tears for her horse. Nora forced herself to stop thinking of the past and concentrate on Isaiah as she and her beaming mother switched horses. Her back competitor's number was switched.

She quickly led Isaiah to the line entering the arena.

Twenty minutes later she was leading him out again…as the winner of his class.

Now she had two horses qualified for the Grand and Reserve Champion Class.

"You can't show two at the same time." Her mother looked worried. "What now?"

"Only another youth can show for me." Nora told her; she had read the whole rule book but had only dreamed, yet never believed, both of her boys would qualify. "Can you find Candace?"

Her mother reached for her phone but Candace was already running to them. She and Lola had already competed in the mare division and placed second in reining and third in halter.

"I can help!" Candace beamed. "Which horse do you want me to take?"

Nora's heart nearly stopped. She wanted to be with both of them.

"Nora, take Arcturus." Her mother decided for her. "And go."

Candace and Isaiah entered the arena in front of Nora and Arcturus.

No matter how hard she tried, Nora couldn't stop her hands from shaking. She was so excited and overjoyed that both horses won their class and especially for Arcturus. The grin stayed on her face through the whole judging.

Her heart jumped for joy when Isaiah won Grand Champion.

Twenty minutes later she was standing between her prized horses grinning happily for the camera. Her mother took pictures with her own camera and with Nora's cell phone.

"Are you going to tell everyone before we get home?" Her mother smiled.

"No way!" Nora laughed. "I want to see their reactions."

###

Cooper shot to the left in front of the calf…his nose went down, stretched out and faced the animal. They shot to the right and Nora had to brace herself to the sudden jolt. The calf jumped back and forth, Cooper and Nora matched his every move. It stopped so

Nora pulled back and turned into the small herd looking for the third calf.

"Check the white face in the back." Casey called out.

Nora searched for the calf and nodded.

"Forty five seconds." Casey announced her remaining time.

Nora got aggressive and moved in quick. The white face calf and a red buddy shot out from the others. Cooper followed. It took half her remaining time to get the red calf to split from their target but the last 15 seconds was a whirlwind. They ran back and forth then stayed in the middle with Cooper bouncing between his right front leg and his left. The buzzer rang just as the legs finally moved together and shot to the right to chase the calf.

"Nice ending." Casey nodded as they left the arena.

Nora nodded, the energy of the day was still racing through her.

There were three judges this time; total score 218. She was in second place with one rider left.

"I was too aggressive with the last one?" Nora asked.

Casey nodded. "It's part of the learning. The good thing is you recognize it yourself and I don't have to point it out."

"I do a lot of studying."

The last rider finished and Nora was pleased to place second in the class.

"You've had a good day." Casey commented as they made their way back to the horse trailer. The cutting arena was across town from the show arena.

"Yep," Nora nodded with a grin. In Showmanship, she had placed first with Arcturus and second with Isaiah. In Western Pleasure, she placed second on both horses since they were in different divisions. "Trail class in the morning then we head home."

When they reached the horse trailer, the man with the Stetson was talking with her mother, Paige, and Candace.

Stetson turned and looked up at Nora with a smile and a shake of the head. "A third horse?"

Nora nodded as she stepped off Cooper. She quickly glanced at her mother to gauge her expression. "He's not for sale either."

Stetson laughed, then surprised her by holding out a hand to her coach. "Casey, good to see you."

"You too, Roger." Casey shook his hand.

"So, you're working with the horses?" Roger asked.

"No, working with Nora, she works the horses." Casey answered. Nora was surprised at his description…and very pleased.

"Who trained the horses?" Roger looked between Casey and Nora.

"I did." Nora said proudly.

"How old are you?" Roger smiled in disbelief.

"Fourteen," She smiled. "My Uncle Grayson taught me how to train."

Roger looked to Casey.

Casey smiled. "I started working with Nora and Cooper a couple months ago with cutting. We just started this week on reining with the other two." He looked between Nora's mother and Roger. "You tried to buy Arcturus and Isaiah?"

"The red bay," Roger nodded.

"Isaiah," Nora said.

"Didn't get very far, did you?" Casey chuckled.

Roger returned the grin, "No, didn't even get an opportunity to give a number."

"Well, Roger," Casey looked at Nora then to Stetson man. "Nora can do as well with Isaiah as your team could."

Nora and Roger's eyes opened wide in surprise.

"That's quite the praise coming from you." Roger nodded while reaching in his pocket to withdraw a card. He held it out to Nora.

"None of them are for sale." Nora didn't take the card and glanced at her mother who stepped in closer to her.

Roger smiled. "It's not for the horses."

"Then why would I need your card?" Nora asked.

"It's for you." He informed her.

"What?" Nora and her mother said in unison.

"When you finish school, give me a call. I would like to offer you a position on my training team." Roger stretched his hand out farther to her.

Nora looked at him in shock then looked to her mother.

"Are you serious?" Her mother asked in concern.

Casey answered, "Roger wouldn't offer it if he wasn't serious." He took the card out of Roger's hand and handed it to Nora.

Out of respect for her coach, she reluctantly took it but didn't look at it.

"Well, you've had a long successful day and I won't hold you up." Roger tipped his hat to her mother, Candace, and Paige then looked to Nora. "I'll be seeing you at future shows."

He and Casey nodded to each other then Roger walked away.

Nora slid the card in her pocket and loaded Cooper into the trailer.

When she stepped out of the trailer, Casey was just leaving.

"Casey?" Nora stopped him. "Who is Roger?"

Casey smiled, "He owns one of the top quarter horse ranches in Oklahoma and one in Texas."

"Have you known him long?"

"I was one of his first trainers when he started his business," He nodded. "I won my first World Championship on one of his horses."

Nora's eye brows went up in surprise. "Small world."

"Narrows a bit when you compete at AQHA shows. He likes to travel to the shows and look for horses." Casey's eyes narrowed and he stared at her. "There are very few people that get the chance that you were just offered. Take it as a great honor Nora, and consider it."

Nora nodded, but remained quiet.

"Nora? Do you know why I yell at you during practice with Cooper?"

She slowly shook her head.

He looked in the trailer at the horse then back to her, "You have a natural ability with horses, especially Arcturus and Isaiah, but with others too."

Confused, Nora just nodded.

"When you ride, you escape into your own world," he smiled.

Her eye brows shot up in surprise that he noticed it.

"I do the same thing. You have to be able to escape to block out the distractions of everything that's happening in the crowd and arena, and concentrate on the horse and task at hand." He shut the door of the trailer and lowered the lever. "You can't do that in cutting. You have to be alert to everything, not just your horse…to the cows, to the four riders helping push the cows and to that timer."

Nora nodded in agreement.

"When I yell, it's to keep you out of your own world and keep you in this one." Again, he smiled slightly.

Nora's dislike of him melted away and she smiled because he was right.

"I'll see you in the morning," He tipped his hat to her and turned away.

"So what do you think?" Her mother asked as she stepped into the truck for the ride back to the equine park.

"About what?" Nora yawned. She was suddenly very tired, the energy and excitement of the day finally wearing off.

"The offer." Her mother chuckled.

"I'm going to college and starting a super horse business with my cousins." Nora answered and leaned back against the seat.

"You should consider it." Her mother told her.

Nora didn't answer. She just looked out the window at the fading daylight. If she took Roger up on the offer, she would be giving up on her dream of being Miss Rodeo Idaho…but hadn't she already decided that?

They pulled into the parking lot at the equine park and slowly approached the horse stalls. Nora turned to Candace to see if she was awake and saw tears silently gliding down her friend's cheeks.

CHAPTER ELEVEN

Nora took her hand and Candace squeezed tightly while wiping away her tears with the other.

"What's the matter?" Nora whispered.

Candace shrugged. "It's stupid."

"What?"

"I just wanted him to win so bad today." Again, the tears pooled in Candace's eyes.

"Which one?" Nora smiled hesitantly.

Candace softly giggled. "Isaiah."

"Why him and not the other two? And why not Lola?"

"Lola wasn't in the gelding class. I wanted him to win so bad I thought my head was going to explode from wishing so hard."

Nora had felt the same way about Arcturus in the halter class. "Why?"

"Because he's special to me," Candace admitted shyly.

"Really? I didn't know that."

"If it wasn't for Isaiah, we wouldn't be friends."

Nora nodded, now she understood.

"If you didn't win that class that day at the show where me met…I wouldn't have said anything to you, especially something so mean." Candace wiped away more tears.

"It all turned out good." Nora reminded her. "Besides, if it wasn't for the Tagger Herd coming into our lives, I wouldn't have been there. We were there the year before but Mom didn't know if we would go there again because I only showed Libby in a couple classes."

"That's just it." Candace sighed. "If you weren't there and I didn't speak to you so we became friends…where would I be right now?"

Nora had never thought of that.

"Where would my parents have abandoned me?" Candace whispered, her eyes looking sad but the tears were gone.

"Oh, Candace. They would have made sure you were OK."

Candace shrugged. "Maybe…but still…just think how different it would all be if it wasn't for Isaiah."

Nora smiled encouragingly. "Well, I'm glad you were with him today when he won his first Championship at an AQHA show."

A satisfied smile spread across the blonde's face. "I am too, though I wish you could have been too."

"I was with Arcturus in his first try." Nora reminded her and squeezed her hand tightly. "As Wade said, the Tagger Herd came into our lives for a reason…mine was to make you a friend."

"And to have an opportunity like Roger offered you tonight." Candace nodded with a slight smile then turned to watch the sun descend over the stalls. "And to save me."

###

"Have you considered it at all?" Her mother asked as they turned down the driveway to The Homestead.

"No." Nora said honestly. She was too tired to think of anything when they finally made it to bed the night before and this morning was a rush to prepare the horses for the trail class. Arcturus placed first and Isaiah was third because Nora let the gate slip out of her hand when she maneuvered him through the obstacle. They recovered well but it wasn't enough.

She had slept nearly the whole nine hour drive coming home and Roger's offer did not enter her mind at all.

"We'll discuss it with your dad tomorrow and see what he thinks."

Nora glared at the back of her mother's head. Shouldn't the decision be up to Nora? But at least they were going to include her this time.

As excited as she was to tell everyone how the weekend was, she also dreaded coming home to reality. It was so easy to forget all the world's trouble when you were away from home.

With all the stops they made to give the horses a break from the trailer, it took ten hours to get home. Since they didn't leave until noon, it was ten o'clock at night and dark out when they pulled in the driveway. Still, the back deck was full of Taggers and friends and they all descended on the trailer to help unload the horses and find out what happened.

Nora knew no one would mention the weekend's results before she did and when she rounded the corner of the trailer and saw the lineup of family. She couldn't stop the grin on her face.

There was one person she had to go to first and he was grinning wide and proud in front of her. She wrapped her arms around his neck and whispered; "Thank you, thank you, thank you so very much, Uncle Grayson."

They squeezed each other tightly before she stepped back and looked up at him.

"It was a good weekend?" He asked with a chuckle.

"Yes, it was very good." She beamed.

Nora thanked Nick for the beautiful halter and Jack for his help. Everyone was extremely happy to hear Arcturus won his first halter class.

Out of the corner of her eye, Nora saw her dad and mother embrace in a big movie kiss, breaking away with a grin to each other. The pang of guilt ran through her stomach, they were so happy and she kept them apart. Not anymore…she sighed…her dream was slowly ebbing away.

Reilly proudly walked Cooper out of the horse trailer with a beaming grin to Nora.

"He had us in first place, but I messed up and got us second." She admitted.

"You'll get it next time." He laughed. "There's always next weekend!"

Nora's stomach turned as she thought of the goat tying. She had no desire to jump off a speeding Cooper ever again.

Reality was making its way back.

Nora gripped the chute handle and looked between Grace and Reilly.

"Just do it!" Grace laughed making Buttercup prance.

She yanked the handle and let the steer loose.

Buttercup and Rufio took off. Grace's rope flew and caught the steer around the horns; she quickly pulled the steer to the left to give Reilly a good shot at the back hooves. His lariat flew at the target and came up with one hoof short.

"Dang!" He hollered and shook the lariat to release it from the steer.

Wade trapped the steer in the exit gate and released Grace's rope from the horns.

"Ya can't get 'em all the time." Wade hollered at Reilly with a grin.

"Yeah, yeah, yeah…" Reilly muttered and repositioned in the roping box.

"Score this one." Grace hollered at Reilly. "Buttercup anticipated."

Nora looked down at the steer in the box to make sure it was positioned correctly then pulled the lever…it took off running and Buttercup bounced out of the box.

"One more time." Grace yelled.

Nora released the next steer and Buttercup held her position.

"Ok, 70% Reilly." Grace nodded over at him.

Nora let the next steer out and they took off at a gallop to the animal but didn't give it a full competition drive.

Both ropers hit their targets.

Three more rounds and three more steer successfully captured.

"OK, my turn." Wade hollered and stepped up onto Dollar.

Nora turned to check the next steer and saw her parents walking towards the arena. Dang! She knew what they wanted and had managed to avoid them all morning.

Her parents climbed on the bleachers and watched as Wade roped three calves in good time for breakaway.

"Reilly, can you push in a couple tie-down calves?" Wade hollered.

Wade and Reilly took turns on a dozen tries as Nora handled the chute and Grace pushed in the calves.

Sadie arrived from practicing barrels with Josey at The Stables and rode Little Ghost in to practice breakaway.

The morning was full of cows and horses.

Nora saddled Cooper while Grace and Sadie put the poles in place. Her parents sat quietly for another hour and watched the three girls practice.

They kept a full cooler of water just under the bleachers so when they took a water break the riders were lined up in front of her parents.

"Nora, stay here." Her dad said as they headed back out to practice before the temperature escalated to the triple digits.

Nora sighed and watched her brother and cousins ride away.

"Your mother told me about Roger." He said.

"Did she tell you that she threatened to have you kick his ass?" Nora grinned and hoped to start the conversation on a good note.

"Yes," He laughed. "And I would have too, what a comment!"

Her parents turned to each other with love in their eyes causing Nora to sigh heavily. How can their love for each other keep causing her such pains of guilt?

"Since you went to bed late and were out here by six, I know you didn't look him up on the internet." He said.

"I want to go to college and raise super horses with my cousins." Nora repeated what she had told her mother. Why can't they just let it be?

"You refuse to even consider it?" Her mother asked, sounding a little frustrated.

Nora just looked between the two; it was obvious what they wanted.

"I can't say anything more or different." Nora told them honestly.

"Well, we think it should be left open for consideration in the future." Her dad said firmly.

"Ok." Nora sighed.

"To do that, you can't mention your feelings to Casey so it doesn't get back to Roger." Her mother said. "We don't want the offer taken off the table in case you change your mind."

"Fine," Nora nodded. It was aggravating, but at least they were talking to her about it instead of making the decision for her.

"Casey will be here later to review the videos." Her mother informed her.

Nora frowned…the pressure just continued… "I thought he wasn't coming until tomorrow morning."

"He wants to discuss something with you and watch the videos." Her dad said.

Nora nodded tiredly. She was hoping to have a quiet afternoon.

They had just put the horses in the pasture when Casey arrived.

Nora walked in the barn to start up the computer. When he didn't join her, she stepped out of the barn and saw him standing on the back porch talking to her parents.

She leaned against the opening of the barn and waited…aggravation starting to grow again.

He finally turned and walked to her. She met him at the computer.

He slid in the chair next to her and handed her a few pieces of paper.

"What's this?" She asked and looked down at the riding patterns on the paper.

"It's a pattern I worked out when I did an exhibition a couple years ago."

"It's not a normal pattern, there's lots more to it." She studied the paper and walked through the pattern in her mind.

"Wasn't meant to be, but it would be a good training pattern so the horses don't get stale with the normal."

Nora nodded and continued to study the pattern. "Can you talk me through it?"

They spent the next half hour reviewing the pattern before saddling Arcturus and walking to the arena. She broke down the pattern in different stages before attempting it all in a row.

"That's a lot more than usual but it's interesting." Nora smiled at him as she trotted to the bleachers. He handed her a bottle of water.

"Keeps your mind fresh, too," Casey nodded, seeming pleased. "Have you considered Roger's offer?"

Nora was surprised by the change of topic but hoped it didn't show. Her good mood from the ride plummeted…she knew what he wanted. "We've discussed it." She said truthfully.

"Are you still planning on doing the royalty thing next year?"

Nora shrugged and kept her face calm as she fought the urge to yell at him. Couldn't they just leave her alone and let her decide her future?

"Think out of the box and out of this town, Nora." He stood. "You aren't limited to regular shows and royalty…the sky's the limit with your talent and those horses."

Nora swallowed hard and tried desperately not to glare at him while he was looking at her.

"Have you considered giving your mother back Cooper and working with Isaiah on the cows?"

Nora felt like she was going numb; why did he keep doing that? She felt bad enough already and had considered moving Isaiah to the cows to give her mother Cooper because that's what a good person would do.

"Yes." She finally managed to admit.

"Want to try him in the morning?"

"Sure." She nodded.

"OK, I'll see you in the morning." He stepped down the bleachers and walked away.

Nora turned the horse so she could look out into the farmer's fields at the end of the arena.

Give Cooper back and stop royalty…stop her dream of being Miss Rodeo Idaho.

She wanted to yell and scream at him…how could he just stand there and tell her to give up on her dream? But he was right…wasn't he? The darkness started taking over inside her as the frustration and anger began to increase. Just finally admit it and give it up, she told herself and felt her head begin to ache.

"Nora?"

She looked at the gate and saw Billy. The butterflies flew through the darkness.

Why was he here?

Nora stared for a moment then she finally cued the horse forward. She stopped next to the fence but didn't make a move to get down.

"You look really good on that horse." Billy smiled, his blue eyes looked anxious.

"His name is Arcturus." She said coolly, her stomach was getting queasy.

"I'm sorry about the other day."

She frowned…he didn't do anything.

"My phone call…" He took in a nervous breath.

Nora's heart nearly stopped…did Reilly tell him she was upset? Why would he do that? She was going to kill him!

She looked at Billy with the poker face she had been practicing and didn't say a word.

Billy took another deep breath and looked at the ground. "Maybe I shouldn't have come up here…or said anything."

He hadn't said anything…but then again…she didn't either. Her mind flashed to the kiss in the barn on Reilly's birthday, her neck and cheeks warmed; she was sure she had turned red.

Billy looked back up at her then quickly looked down the arena behind her.

"Reilly wanted to ask Marla out, but was nervous so I offered to ask out Christina and make it a double date." His eyes flickered back to her then to the horse's nose.

Nora sat like a statue, but her insides were a raging river.

"I start football practice soon." He didn't look at her.

What did that have to do with anything?

"The games start the Friday before the first day of school." He looked back down the arena. "Have you ever gone to a game?"

Nora slowly shook her head. "No, but I watch it on TV with my dad." She was thankful her voice sounded calm.

He glanced up at her then down the arena again. "Brady and I decided to go to college together."

Nora stared at him a moment; she wasn't understanding this conversation at all, "That's good. Sadie and I will be going to the same college too." If she had her way.

"Reilly said she was moved up a couple grades. To yours?" He finally looked up at her.

"Yes. So we'll be going to college at the same time."

"She's really helped Brady…that's why he and I can go together."

Nora nodded; she was really confused about this conversation.

"We were looking at Oregon," Billy looked away from her.

"Which one?"

"The Ducks, in Eugene." He looked at the ground then back up. "Corvallis has a really good equestrian program."

Nora stared into his anxious blue eyes, not knowing what to say. Billy had looked into an equestrian college for her?

"They are less than an hour apart." He continued.

Nora's eyes widened, he was trying to keep them close after she went to college…when she was older.

"I'll have to discuss it with Sadie." Nora finally managed to say as her heart raced.

Billy looked up at her, smiling…more relaxed. "Once practice starts, I won't be around much. I have to concentrate on football and school…to keep my grades up."

Nora nodded and smiled. "Maybe I can talk Reilly into taking me to watch one of your games."

Billy returned her smile, his blue eyes looked happy. "I'd like that."

"Billy, let's go!" Reilly yelled from the barn.

They nodded at each other in understanding and Billy turned to jog down to Reilly. Nora returned Reilly's wave then turned Arcturus around to canter him around the arena.

###

"What are you talking about?" Sadie glared at her from across their bedroom.

"College," Nora sighed, her stomach hurt just bringing it up. Why did she? It wasn't right.

"Oregon? We talked about Colorado State University in Fort Collins. They have a great Equine Sports Medicine program, plus rodeo and a club for you. It has everything we both want."

Nora just lay on the bed and stared at the ceiling. Why was she doing this? Why was she even mentioning this to Sadie? CSU was perfect for what Sadie wanted, why would she try to make her change so Nora could be closer to Billy? In four years! What kind of a selfish person was she turning in to?

"Nora? Do they even have a rodeo program?"

"Never mind, Sadie," Nora threw her arm over her eyes. "Just forget I said anything."

"What made you think of changing to Oregon?" Sadie continued.

Nora felt queasy and knew her cousin wasn't going to stop until she broke down and told her.

"Just forget it Sadie, please. I'm going to go help Cora with dinner."

She walked out the door and looked down the long hallway. It had been a long time since she had the inclination to run and slide…what was wrong with her!?!

She slowly walked down the hall and felt the dark feelings in her rise. It caused her to get angry with herself, with Billy, Casey, her parents, and Sadie. Why did everyone want Nora to DO what they wanted. Want her to BE what they wanted?

Cora was the only one in the kitchen and welcomed Nora's help.

Her dad walked in from the library just as the back door opened.

Nora bit her bottom lip as she heard Reilly, Brady and Billy laughing. They walked into the kitchen and Nora kept her eyes on the large bowl of pasta salad she was stirring.

"You boys staying for dinner?" Cora asked the grinning trio.

"We don't want to intrude." Brady answered.

"We have plenty." Her dad answered.

"Grayson and Dru won't be back from the ranch until late." Cora added. "So there is more than enough, but it's too hot to eat outside so we'll be in the dining room."

Nora pushed the large bowl of pasta towards her dad and smiled at him.

"Subtle hint." He grinned back and carried the bowl to the table.

Keeping her eyes from the group she retrieved the French rolls from the counter and turned to hand it to her dad, too.

"Anything else?" He chuckled.

"I'll think of something." She smiled.

Sadie and Wade bounced their way down the steps and into the dining room. Nora's mom and Aunt Leah appeared from the library.

"Is this it for dinner tonight?" Reilly asked.

"Yes," Aunt Leah answered. "Paul is out of town so Jack and Grace are working late at The Stables. Tessa, Nick and Alex should be here in a while for a visit but they said not to hold up dinner just for them.”

They all settled around the table, Nora was safely tucked in between her parents so she didn't have to sit next to Billy…but he was in Grace's chair across from her.

“You boys decide on a college yet?” Nora's dad asked.

Nora's heart skipped a beat.

“Looks like Oregon.” Brady answered.

“You're going to be a Duck?” Wade grinned. “In those bright yellow and green uniforms?”

There was a round of chuckles from the group.

Nora tried to keep her eyes down but she could just see Sadie on the other side of her dad. Her cousin had bent over and looked at her. Nora glanced over to see Sadie frowning…that quick, and Sadie knew why Nora had suggested they change their college.

“I think Grace and I decided on Missoula…or Pullman…or Moscow.” Reilly chuckled while grabbing more bread.

“Sadie and Nora had considered Colorado…Fort Collins.” Nora's mom added.

Nora's heart raced. Why did she have to say that?

Nora's eyes flickered to Billy. He glanced at her then down to his plate. Her eyes went to Sadie who was looking at Billy then moved to Nora. Her eyes narrowing just enough Nora's heart skipped another beat.

She gritted her teeth…waiting for The Dingo to appear…waiting for Sadie to say something…but she didn't.

“Why Colorado?” Brady asked.

“Sadie wants to go into equine sports medicine and they have a great program there.” Wade answered.

“One of the best.” Aunt Leah added.

“You would be great at that.” Brady grinned at Sadie then looked to Nora. “What are you going to study?”

Nora swallowed hard trying to force down the lump that had been rising through the whole conversation.

"I'm not sure yet…it'll probably be in horse training and judging." She answered, trying to keep her voice calm.

"Nice…that would be good for you, too." Brady said and reached for more pasta.

Nora's eyes flickered back to Billy. He was looking at Sadie with an expression Nora couldn't read. His eyes moved back to Nora then he calmly reached for more bread. Nora didn't know what to do or what to say. It felt like all the blood had raced to her head.

"Scott, are you going with the group to Cottage Grove to the rodeo this weekend?" Cora asked.

Nora was glad the college conversation ended but cringed at her dad's answer.

"No, the weather's been good this year. We'll work on getting the second cutting in tomorrow and will be picking it up over the weekend."

"Do you need some help bucking bales?" Billy asked. "It's always good exercise."

"How would you know, city boy!?" Reilly laughed.

Nora ignored the easy banter around the table and thought again of her parents. Next weekend was rodeo…her mother would be gone with all of the kids. Two of the last three weekends Nora's show schedule had kept her mother away from home and her father. Then there were the evenings and upcoming dates for the royalty program.

Nora stared at her plate. She'd barely taken a bite. How could her mother even like her when Nora continued taking away so much from her?

First the college talk…then this…could it get any worse? Yes…

CHAPTER TWELVE

"Nora," Her mom said and she turned to look at her. "I spoke with Kristen's mom and she suggested we get together while we're in Cottage Grove so Kristen can give you some insight into running for the queen position in October."

Nora's heart plummeted to her stomach.

"Who's Kristen?" Cora asked.

"She was queen a couple years ago…she thinks Nora would be great." Nora's mom answered and smiled over at her. Her smile slowly disappeared. "Are you OK?"

Nora nodded, she didn't know if she could speak.

"Oh, I saw Nora speaking with the current queen when we were at the last rodeo." The older woman turned to Nora. "How did that go? Did you tell her you were going to run for next year's court?"

Again, Nora swallowed hard but she just shook her head and stared at the barely touched dinner on her plate.

"Nora?" Her mom said.

Nora looked at her and couldn't think of what to say.

"What's wrong?" Her eyes looked concerned.

Nora took a deep breath. This wasn't exactly the circumstances she wanted to announce her decision. She wasn't even really sure what she wanted…she needed time…the pressure made her head hurt. Why did they have to ask her now?

"Nora, what's wrong?" Her mother repeated.

Maybe if she said it out loud it would all go away…the anger would go away…the pressure…

"I don't…" She started meekly then stopped to clear her throat. "I don't think I'm going to try out."

Her mom's eyes widened in surprise. "What? Why not?"

Even though she was only looking at her mom, she knew everyone around the table were looking at her…waiting for the answer. The pressure didn't go away…it increased.

Nora didn't want to answer her, but knew there was no way to get out of it. She also didn't want to lie…but didn't want to tell the whole truth either…the pressure pounded behind her eyes.

"Nora, answer me." Her mother frowned. "You've been planning this one for a year…why don't you want to try out?"

"Things change," Nora finally managed to say. Why couldn't her mom stop? She didn't want to announce this in front of Billy…or anyone else! The anger started to take over again, she couldn't let it loose…not twice in a week!

"Casey would be happy if she didn't run," Her dad said; which caused her mother to glare at him. "What?" He said innocently. "He thinks she should be focusing on the horses."

"That's for Nora to decide," Her mother said gruffly and looked back to Nora. "Why?"

Nora's stomach churned. It was bad enough she took her mom from her dad so much, but they continued to argue because of her.

Her mind raced trying to come up with something. Her eyes landed on Wade who was sitting on the other side of her mother. He tilted his head to her in confusion. She tried to mentally ask him for help.

His expression changed and he nodded slightly.

"When do you start football practice?" Wade asked the twins.

"Next week." Brady answered then turned. "Mr. Tagger?"

"Geez…don't call me that!" Her dad laughed. "Call me Scott."

The group laughed…everyone but Nora. She glanced at Wade to thank him, he smiled then looked to Brady.

"We were looking through the football records at the high school Friday and saw you and Grayson were in there."

"WHAT!?!" Wade nearly yelled.

Nora turned surprised eyes to her dad. She knew he had played football but had no idea he set records. He was just staring at Brady with a blank expression then his eyes slowly turned to his wife.

Nora turned to her and she was looking at him with understanding, she turned to Brady.

"The week of the Lewiston and Clarkston game, when he was a senior, was the week his parents and grandparents were killed in a car accident." She said softly. Both brothers inhaled sharply. "He didn't play that game, which meant he didn't have enough time on the field that year to break Grayson's record."

"What record did you break?" Reilly asked so low they barely heard it.

"My father's," Her dad answered after clearing his throat. "My dad had set the record for most passing yardage in a season and in a game. Grayson broke the record for most in a season and I broke the record for most in a game."

"It was the game the week after the funeral." Her mom told them.

"Kind of a Brett Favre game." Wade said.

"Exactly." Their dad smiled at him. "But Brett didn't miss a game when his dad died."

"I want to break your record, Dad." Wade announced. Nora turned to him in surprise. He had a wicked grin.

"Really, Son?" Their dad chuckled.

"I want to break your record…AND I want to break Uncle Grayson's record."

"Competitive much?" Cora chuckled.

"You have to play football to do that." Their dad teased.

"Mike and a couple of the other guys wanted me to play this year since I've grown. Practice starts in a couple weeks." Wade answered, still grinning. "I'll be going to the gym with Reilly and the twins tomorrow."

Everyone chuckled, even Nora.

"So," Her dad smiled. "You're going to start tomorrow, to break our records in five years?"

"Yes," Wade said loudly and firmly with a devilish twinkle in his eye.

Her dad leaned against the table to look squarely at Wade. "You may say that Grayson is a better roper than me, but I was a better quarterback than him."

"Well," Wade continued to grin. "I guess you're going to have to become my quarterback coach and help me break those records so you can prove that to Uncle Grayson."

"Ooohhh!" Aunt Leah laughed. "He knows how to push your buttons!"

"And we know where the competitiveness comes from." Reilly chuckled.

"I think I started something here." Brady grinned.

"And in five years," Her dad smiled at him. "You can come back from your fancy college and watch Wade break those records."

Nora felt the twinge in her stomach again and her smile faded. She looked to Billy but he was laughing at Wade.

She finally managed to eat part of her dinner and rose to take her plate to the kitchen. Silently, she was wishing Billy would follow so she could talk to him but he remained seated.

Not wanting to go back to the table and face her mother's interrogation, Nora walked up the steps to her room. There was no one else upstairs so it was quiet…just what she needed.

As she sat on her bed, she looked at the picture on the wall that Nick had sent her after their weekend together at the bull event and horse show. The picture was Nick, the bull rider Dude, and Cambria Weber, wearing her hat with the large crown.

Nora stared at Cambria…wondering what it would be like to wear the crown and show all the people that she was a good person…they wouldn't give the crown to someone that wasn't.

Her shoulders slumped as she thought of not running for Miss Rodeo Idaho, her dream for the last two years. But she couldn't put her mother through all those years of hauling her around to all the extra events. She couldn't keep her parents apart. It wasn't right; Nora realized that now. The first step was accomplished; her parents knew she wasn't going to try out in October.

It would be years before she had to admit her dream was gone. She would have to concentrate on the super horse business…or even consider Roger's offer.

"Why didn't you just tell me?" Sadie said from their doorway.

Nora's head started to hurt again and her back tensed. She deserved Sadie's anger and was surprised The Dingo didn't appear at dinner.

"I'm sorry." Nora whispered and continued to stare at Cambria's frozen grin…such a happy person.

"I'm not changing my plans for him." Sadie walked past Nora and to her own section of the room. "You can change yours…which I would hate…but I'm NOT changing mine. You need to remember what YOU want in life Nora, not what other people want for you."

Nora closed her eyes…tears threatened to rise. She needed to leave.

"I'm sorry." Nora whispered again and walked out of the room.

Why was life so hard? Why couldn't it be easy? She just wanted to ride her horses and let the world pass her by…but she couldn't, and all the decisions and questions seemed to be suffocating her.

When she reached the bottom of the stairs she turned sharply into the hall hoping no one had seen her but came face to face with her mother.

"There you are." With a determined look, her mother stepped between Nora and the backdoor, purposely stopping her exit. "I let Wade interrupt at dinner, but now you're going to tell me why you changed your mind."

Nora swallowed hard trying to quell the nerves running through her. Her instant reaction was to yell at her mother…like she did her dad…but she couldn't…not again.

"Please don't." Nora whispered.

"What?"

"Please, just let it go…let me go."

"Nora…" Her mother looked irritated and concerned at the same time.

The backdoor opened and Nora could see Tessa and Nick walk through. His eyes instantly connected with Nora's. From his expression he knew something was wrong.

"Talk to me, Nora. Why did you decide not to run?" Her mother pressed.

Nora looked at her mother, fighting the glare she wanted to give her. "Mom, stop."

"Stop telling me that and talk to me." She ordered.

Nora took in a deep breath and fought the words starting to rise. Her eyes looked desperately to Nick.

His lips moved but no words came out…he said it again, silently. "It's OK."

Nora's eyes went back to her mother…then to Nick.

"It's OK." He silently told her again.

"Something's wrong," Her mother continued. "Let's go in the no-media room and discuss this."

Nora suddenly felt claustrophobic…the anger fought to get out…she started to panic.

"It's OK." Silently spoken again.

"Mom, please don't." Nora whispered again…anxiety causing her lungs to compress.

"Why not? You need to talk to me."

"You have company…later, please Mom…later." Nora tried to keep the desperation out of her voice.

Her mom turned to Tessa, Nick and Alex as they walked from the backdoor to the kitchen. Nora took the opportunity and stepped behind her mother and headed to the backdoor from the hallway.

When she stepped out the back door, Billy's truck was gone. He'd left without her having a chance to explain…the pressure in her head increased.

She ran across the porch, jumped down the steps and turned to the barn. To her surprise she didn't run in the barn and to Arcturus, she ran behind it…to the empty arena. She quickly climbed on the bleachers, sat on the bottom bench, and rested her cowboy boots on the top rail of the fence.

The sky was a deep blue with not a cloud in sight to block the heat from the sun. It was so hot, she could already feel her skin moisten and her jeans stick to her legs. It had to be over a hundred degrees but she didn't care, maybe the heat would melt all the bad feelings that had made their way back.

Her eyes slowly moved around the arena. The cattle were lying peacefully on the other side in their small pasture, in the shade of a small cluster of trees. The barrels were knocked over and laying with the gaming poles next to the fence. The practice goat was on its side by the chute. It was all the evidence of their busy morning…but now it was silent. Her anxiety eased and the tension behind her eyes evaporated. She took deep breathes to relax her muscles and mind.

She closed her eyes and thought of cantering around the arena on Arcturus…her body rocked to the memory of the rhythm. Her eyes opened as the anxiety released.

How could she change everything that seemed to be piling up on her? Casey, Billy, Roger, Sadie, her parents…they all wanted her to change to what they wanted…but what did she want?

A slight breeze pushed her loose hair across her face so she leaned her head to the right to push the hair away; it allowed her to see Nick walking through the arena gate.

CHAPTER THIRTEEN

He walked straight up in front of her and rested his arms across the top of the fence. If she tipped her boots to the right, they would touch his arms.

His eyes looked concerned.

"What's up?" She asked him, trying to smile.

"Buttercup," His voice was calm. "Lonely?"

She shook her head, "Just alone."

"You didn't go to Arcturus."

"Weird isn't it?"

"Yes."

She looked into his concerned eyes for a moment then looked passed him to the cattle.

"How do you keep from changing who you are and becoming someone that other people want you to be?"

"Inner strength, belief in who you are, and what you want."

Nora nodded as she thought back to Matt and Josey's conversation. Josey had become Frankie because of Elena. Was she becoming someone else because of Casey? Or because of Billy? Was it a bad thing? Were they trying to make her better?

"Is it other people or life that is changing who you are?" He asked.

"What's the difference?"

"Well, look at the Trio." He started. "Their life was great but *who* they were was changed when the accident happened. All three of them are different than the people I knew when Dru and I were married."

"So life got in their way."

"Yes…an example of people changing you would be what Elena did to Josey. She changed Josey and now Josey is trying to find herself again. But she'll never be the same innocent Josey that she was before Elena stole from her or tried to use her against Matt and the Taggers. She'll always be more wary of people, more distrusting."

"Change isn't always bad." She glanced back to him. "You became someone else."

"But it was of my choosing," He nodded. "I was a kid who didn't want to sleep on the ground and wanted a full stomach at least once a day. I didn't have close friends growing up because I didn't want anyone to know about my home or my parents. I fought to change that kid."

"And you did."

"But it took a long time…you know that. Until our weekend trip, I didn't really let that lonely kid go or let him finally be happy. If it wasn't for that weekend, I don't think I would have allowed myself to be happy with Tessa and Alex." His voice cracked and his eyes glistened.

"I changed that weekend, too." She whispered.

"You were always a good person."

Her chin quivered. He knew what she meant…he always did. "But I didn't really believe it until that weekend." A tear escaped and slowly slid down her cheek. "I thought I was ugly…inside and out."

"You're beautiful…inside and out."

Another tear escaped as she tried to smile. "So I can't be pretty at twelve but I can be beautiful at fourteen?"

He smiled. "Just be fourteen."

She nodded with a sigh.

"Do you want to change?" He asked.

"I didn't think so."

"What makes you think you do now?"

She shrugged and wiped away the tears with her shoulders.

"I don't want the person I want to be…to be at the expense of others." Another tear fell. She took a quivering deep breath to relax her tightened lungs.

"I don't understand. You wouldn't do that."

She sniffed and swallowed hard. "I've tried really hard to be a good person. I feel like I fight every day…and I thought I was being good…but I didn't know I was doing it…but I was…"

"Who?"

Nora turned away from his eyes and looked down the arena.

"Nora?"

She shook her head and gritted her teeth to stop more tears from falling.

"Do you want me to crawl over this fence and shake it out of you?" He asked firmly.

Nora felt the emotion roll from her stomach to her heart and put pressure in her lungs. She tried hard to force herself not to cry but it wasn't to be stopped. She closed her eyes, lowered her head, and just let them roll.

Nick placed his hand on her leg, which made her cry that much more, because he wasn't running away like he did the first time on their weekend trip. He stood quietly comforting her with a gentle touch while the emotions released from her.

"I'm going to walk over to the cooler and get you some water."

She nodded without looking up.

Taking deep breathes she opened her eyes and looked up to the sky wishing the heat would evaporate all the tears. Using the sleeve on her t-shirt she wiped them away.

Nick handed her the water bottle and she swallowed half of it trying to drown the emotions.

"Tell me," He said softly. "What makes you think the bad is back?"

Nora sighed, the tears finally stopped.

"Did you hear about the argument between me and Dad?"

"Is that what happened when you couldn't work with Bodi?"

Nora told him about the argument.

"That makes you angry…not bad."

She shook her head, "It's not just about the argument." She had finally admitted it to herself…she needed to say it out loud. "I'm not mad that I yelled at Dad."

Nick's brows came together in confusion.

She looked straight into his eyes and admitted the truth. "He made me mad…he just kept pushing…I wanted to be left alone to deal with the frustration but he wouldn't let me…he just pushed so I pushed back." She sighed heavily and looked out at the quiet arena. "I don't want decisions made for me. I should have a say in my life."

"I agree."

She looked back to him.

"And it doesn't make you bad, Nora." He said in a quiet but firm voice.

"I should be upset I yelled at my Dad."

"It doesn't make you bad, it makes you strong."

"What?" She gasped in disbelief.

"Nora, you're a little slip of a young lady." He smiled.

It was her turn to look at him in confusion. "Thanks?"

Nick chuckled. "He pushed and you stuck up for yourself. You knew what you needed…time to work it out…but he didn't give it to you. You pushed back, you stood up for yourself."

"What does that have to do with me being little?"

"Because you're little, people are going to think they can push you around…bully you." He nodded. "But you're becoming stronger inside, which is why you stood up for yourself when it came to your Dad pushing you."

"When it happened…I was upset. But the more I look back on it…I'm not…and I should be."

"Why?"

"Because he's my DAD! I love my dad and everything he and Mom have done for me and my horses. I shouldn't be yelling at him."

"I'm not saying you should yell at Scott, just talking calmly to him would have been better, but no matter who it is, you have to stick up for yourself. You can't let people bull doze over you because you're little or because you're quiet."

Nora thought of her mother. She was even smaller than Nora, yet she had stood up strong and confident when Roger first appeared at Isaiah's stall.

Her mom was strong…Nora was different.

"I couldn't control it." Nora admitted. "I felt it happening and couldn't stop it."

"You hold it in too much…you hold it until it builds and explodes. You need to let some of the stress and frustration out before it gets to that point."

"But it would be showing everyone…all the time…" Nora said worriedly.

"You're not bad, Nora…you're human." He smiled. "We all get frustrated and angry sometimes."

She shook her head and could feel the tears returning.

"What?" He asked.

"But, it's not just the yelling match with Dad. It's…I'm…hurting people without realizing it just so I can have what I want." She took another deep breath and let it out slowly. "Aunt Dru told us once that if we want something with all our heart to look at the consequences of it. If it's going to hurt someone then I have to weigh the decision on whether it's worth it…whether I should continue."

He smiled slightly, "Dru would probably be pretty happy to hear you were listening when she told you that."

Nora nodded and wiped away a tear that escaped.

"But, who do you think you're hurting?"

"Mom…Dad…Sadie..." She said quickly before she couldn't speak.

His brows furrowed in confusion. "How are you hurting them?"

She shook her head and sighed, wishing the dark emotions to go away.

"You have to tell me so I can help."

Nora didn't know what to say so she didn't say anything.

"Alright, one at a time, Sadie."

Nora closed her eyes and took a deep breath. "I tried to persuade her to do something that wasn't best for her, for something I wanted…or thought I wanted..." She opened her eyes and looked for the disappointment on his face. There wasn't any. That was the good thing about Nick…he never judged her.

"Did it work?"

She shook her head. "I felt sick just bringing it up."

"Then why do you feel like you're using Sadie to get what you want?"

"Because I tried."

"Nora, you didn't try very hard and knew it was wrong while you were doing it. That doesn't make you bad."

"But I feel so guilty."

"Again, that shows you're not bad." He gave her a slight smile. "If you didn't feel guilty…then I'd be worried."

She swallowed the lump in her throat and nodded.

"How are you hurting Jordan?"

She sighed and looked back at him. "All the extra shows she has to take me to because of my horse shows and the royalty stuff."

"She does that because she loves you and wants to."

"Because she has to…because of what I want…not what she wants."

"How do you know what she wants? Have you asked her?"

"She's my mom. She's not going to say I'm a burden to her."

"So you've decided to remove that burden, without talking to her."

Nora shrugged.

He stared at her a moment then his eyes narrowed. "That's why you decided not to try out for the royalty thing in October?"

She nodded and took a deep breath.

"Is it just the October one you're giving up on?"

Nora's jaw dropped and she stared at him in surprise. She thought she had years before having to tell anyone.

"Miss Rodeo Idaho?"

She frowned, "It's an awful lot of extra work on Mom and I don't know if it's who I want to be anymore. I don't know if I should be holding onto that dream."

"Who do you want to be?" His tone was calm.

"I think…" Her throat constricted. "I don't know."

"Who is trying to make you someone you're not?"

She didn't answer.

"Why do you suddenly feel like you're a burden to your mother?"

She didn't answer.

"Did someone say something to you?"

She nodded but didn't say anything.

"Who?"

Nora shook her head then jumped when he exhaled sharply.

"You've never held back from me before. Why now? Is who you're protecting more important than our friendship?"

Nora's eyebrows shot up in surprise. "Of course, not."

"Then let me help you figure out what you want. I need to know, so we can work it through."

"Casey."

"Your coach?"

She nodded.

"Ok, what did he say?"

"That I was making Mom haul me around to all the extra shows and royalty commitments."

"What else?"

"He said that I'm good at cutting and reining… saying I should be focusing on that."

"And give up on royalty and the rodeo events?"

Nora nodded.

"Anything else?"

"He pointed out that I took Cooper from Mom." Nora rolled her eyes. "I didn't even think about that! I wanted to get into cutting, Reilly mentioned Cooper, and I just took him without even thinking about her."

Nick rolled his lips and stared at her for a minute before talking.

"I don't think Casey was trying to be mean. He probably didn't realize that he was hitting a tender spot with you, something you've battled within yourself."

She nodded and swallowed hard. Casey didn't say any of it to be mean, he just pointed it out to her.

"You're a great equestrian, Nora. You'll do well in any of the disciplines because of your determination and understanding of horses."

"Casey said that, too."

"So your first question was how do you keep from changing who you are and becoming someone that other people want you to be?" He asked and she nodded. "You're afraid Casey is changing who you are to what he wants you to be?"

"Yeah."

"What do you think he wants you to be?"

"Shows…reining and cutting only."

"Is that what you want? To get rid of the rodeo and royalty?"

"I don't think so." She shrugged. "I just don't really know any more. If I wasn't doing the royalty, it would be easier on Mom."

"Is the thought you're a burden to your mother swaying that decision?"

"Yeah, kind of."

"Don't you think it would be fair to her, to ask her?"

"She wouldn't say that I'm a burden."

"Maybe not, but you're basing everything off of incomplete information."

"What?"

"You need all the information to make an educated decision. We've talked about that before. Make sure you have all the questions answered before making the decision."

"Like you do with buying companies?"

"Exactly," He answered. "I wouldn't be any good at it if I didn't make sure I had all the answers first."

Nora nodded.

"You're not letting your mother defended herself. Don't you think that's unfair to her?"

"Well…I guess." Nora shrugged.

"Can I call her out here so she can plead her case?"

"She won't admit it, Nick."

"But you're not giving her a chance. You're going to make the decision without telling her why. Don't you hate it when people do that to you?"

Her parents had made the decision to make Casey her reining coach without discussing it with her…look how that ended.

"Well?" He asked again.

He was right. "Yeah…Dad, too." Nora nodded.

"What did you do to your dad?" Nick asked as he typed into his phone.

"Besides the yelling match? I kept Mom away from him."

He put his phone back in his shirt pocket.

"How do you feel about Arcturus, seeing him every day?"

"I love that. I get up in the morning anxious to get in the barn and see him."

"When you're away from Arcturus a long time, how do you feel when you return?"

"Overly anxious to see him, it's like he's all new and …" Nora grinned. "I just get excited."

"Do you think, that maybe, that's the way your parents feel when they are apart on the weekends and see each other when she returns?"

"That it makes seeing each other more special?" Nora had never thought of that.

He nodded and glanced towards the barn. She followed his gaze and saw her parents were nearly at the arena already.

"That was fast." She said in surprise.

"They were probably in the barn looking for you."

Holding hands, her parents walked into the arena and stood next to Nick so she was looking down on all three of them. Her mother looked so tiny between the two men.

They both looked at her in concern.

"Are you, OK?" Her mother asked.

Nora nodded and tried to smile but seeing them together just made her feel guilty again and Nick's explanation was just lost to her.

"Nick said you needed to ask us something." Her dad looked between her and Nick. "What is it?"

Nora's throat tightened and she didn't think the words would come out without a bunch of tears following them. She looked to Nick, hoping he would understand.

He nodded and turned to her parents.

"She has concluded that the horse shows and royalty commitments are putting extra work on Jordan and keeping the two of you apart."

"What?" They both turned to her in surprise.

"That's why you don't want to run for NWYRA royalty?" Her dad asked and she nodded.

"Nora, that's crazy!" Her mother nearly shouted. "I love taking you and I'm so proud of you."

Nora stared at her boots, then glanced at Nick…as if to tell him 'I told you so'.

Her parents turned to Nick.

"She said you would never admit she was a burden." Nick explained with a raised brow.

"I'm not sure whether I should laugh or be pissed?" Her mother was instantly upset. Her dark eyes bored into Nora. "Why would you think I see you as a *burden*?"

Nora's lungs tightened…she was suddenly nervous. "I…you…"

"Just spit it out!" Her mother fumed…nearly screaming at her.

CHAPTER FOURTEEN

"Jordan!" Her dad turned to her mother and grabbed her arm. "Take a breather…step back a minute." He pulled her into the arena.

Nora's eyes widened and she looked to Nick who was looking down…which meant he was just as confused as she was.

Nora wrapped her arms in front of herself. It was the pose that Josey had when she was talking to Matt…the protective mode.

Nick lifted his head. "Relax." He whispered. "She loves you and would do nothing to hurt you."

Nora moved her hands to the bleachers on each side of her, gripping the edge tightly. Her parents had their backs to her so she couldn't tell what was happening. She looked back to Nick, her chin quivering.

"Evidently, she has an inner demon too." Nick whispered.

That shocked Nora…she had never seen anything like that from her mother before.

Her parents turned and walked back to the fence. Her mother's demeanor was more relaxed.

"Why?" She asked Nora in a soft controlled voice.

Nora stared at her a moment, trying to read her face. Why did she have that reaction? She turned to her dad, he had the poker face on. He wouldn't give her a clue.

"You have to haul me around to all the extra meetings, shows, and commitments that being in the royalty have." She whispered from nerves.

"I don't consider it hauling you…I consider it taking you. There is a difference." She answered in a controlled calm. "There are also chaperones that will help."

"I keep you away from Dad more." Nora continued.

"I adore and love your father with all my heart. But I love you too and feel lucky that I get to spend this much time with you."

"But I take you away from things you love to do and people you want to be with." Nora frowned.

"There is nothing I love to do more than watch you and the rest of the kids compete. I love spending all the hours driving with you kids. Listening to your stories and ridiculous jokes on each other…it fills me with joy, Nora." There were tears in her mother's eyes. "Do you think there is anything in the world that would have been better than watching Sadie at the rodeo regain her glory? Or watching Wade in Winchester when he won his first competition? Or Grace and Reilly enjoying their friendship as they compete? Do you think I would miss out on one minute of Arcturus winning his first halter class or miss out on the pride in you and that horse I had at that moment?"

Nora's throat was tight and the tears had risen inside her and were sliding down her cheeks. She just shook her head.

"Tell me one thing, in this world, that I could possibly love more than that?" A tear slid down her mother's face and she slowly wiped it away, not moving her eyes from Nora's.

"Dad." Nora whispered.

Her mother chuckled, "Well, you kind of got me on that one." She turned to her husband and smiled with love shining. "But I get him the rest of the week and we make those moments count." She turned back to Nora. "I quit my job…a job I loved, to take you kids to the rodeos and shows. I am very lucky to be able to do that…there are a lot of mothers and fathers that wish they could do what I do." She grinned. "I wear the buckle you kids gave me for Christmas proudly...and show it off all the time."

Nora took a deep breath and let it out.

"You would deny me all those memories?" Her mother asked with a tilt of the head and a lift of a brow.

Nora shook her head the anxiety started to ease from her muscles.

"But I took Cooper from you." Nora sighed.

Her mother shook her head; "I can compete on him if I wanted to, I will next winter. He's a remarkable horse, he can handle both of us…three of us since Jack rides him for team penning…four of us since Reilly ropes on him too." Her head tilted and eyes narrowed, "What happened that would make you feel this way?"

Nora noticed she didn't say the word 'burden'.

"I'm…just…confused." Nora admitted.

"About what?" Her dad asked.

"Everything." Nora sighed.

"Nora, I understand how confusing life can be." Her mom said.

Nora didn't mean it to happen but her eyes dropped down to the ground. Her mom had everything…how could she…

"Nora, look at me." Her mother said firmly which made Nora's eyes fly back up; a little afraid that she would yell at her again.

"Do you remember what it was like when I still worked at the paper mill, after the horses came into our life?" Her mother asked.

Nora's eyes opened wide and she nodded. Her parents fought all the time; that was horrible.

"I understand what being confused is like." Her mother assured her. "I was so confused, it nearly cost us our family." Her eyes softened. "I know what it's like to be confused."

Nora nodded.

"Do not hold it in," Her dad told her. "Talk it out. Whether it's with me, your mom, Sadie, Candace, Nick…or with anyone. Don't hold it in, talk it out. Before it explodes or eats you up inside."

Nora nodded and took a deep breath; it was the same thing Nick had already told her.

"Does knowing that I love to take you to your shows and royalty events help?" Her mother asked.

Still, she didn't use the word 'burden'. Nora nodded.

"Do you want to try out for the royalty in October?" Her dad asked.

Nora looked to her mom.

"It is my dream, to have my daughter achieve her dreams." Her mother smiled warmly. "My time will come in a couple years when all you kids have left the nest."

"Nora," Her dad said and she turned to him. She could see the love and caring in his blue eyes as he looked at her. "There will be a lot of obstacles rise that get in the way of your dreams; whether it's Miss Rodeo Idaho or the super horse business. YOU have to work through them and focus on what YOU truly want. Don't give up on your dreams…fight for them. It is the only way to reach them." They smiled at each other.

"So you'll reconsider?" Her mother asked.

"YOU decide what YOU want…about all your goals." Nick said.

Nora's eyes shifted from her mom to Nick then back to her mom. The weight lifted from her shoulders, she nodded.

"What else are you confused about?" Her dad asked.

"College…Roger…super horses…" Nora answered, just talking to the three of them really helped but she wasn't going to mention Billy. They would say it was just a crush…and she really didn't know if it was or not.

"You're fourteen, you don't have to decide for another four years. Don't get hung up on it now." Her dad told her. "We just don't want you closing the door with Roger until you're absolutely sure what you want…when the time comes. Things will work themselves out."

"Anything else?" Her mother asked.

Nora shrugged, looked down at the three of them from her perch above the fence and smiled.

"What's the smile for?" Her mother asked while returning the smile.

"From up here, you look so tiny between them." Nora grinned. "I get an idea of what Uncle Grayson sees."

"Just don't tell her about the grey hair." Nick's eyes were lit with humor.

"WHAT?" Her mother's eyes opened wide, one hand went to the top of her head and the other smacked Nick on the arm. "I don't have grey hair!"

Nora and the men laughed.

Her mom turned to her dad, "I don't have grey hair," She repeated with a hand still resting on the top of her head. "Tell him I don't have grey hair."

"She doesn't have grey hair, Nick." He said as he was told but was grinning when he did it.

"Scott!" She nearly shouted…then started giggling at herself. She lowered her hand from her head but smacked Nick again. "I don't have grey hair."

"My mistake," Nick chuckled and gave Nora a wink. "Must have been how the light hit all the black hair making one or twelve look grey."

She pushed him with both hands, "Nick!"

Nora and her dad laughed.

"Nick, quit picking on my wife." Her dad chuckled.

All the tension released from Nora, she felt relaxed and the happiness began to return to her heart.

"Other than Nick being blind…" Her mother chuckled. "Are we good here…are you OK now?"

Before Nora could speak…

"Why didn't you go to Arcturus?" Nick asked, catching Nora off guard.

Her parents turned to her in surprise, obviously they hadn't thought of that.

"You always go to him." Her dad stated.

"I don't know why." Nora shrugged. She loved the horse, and now had the urge to go to him…but why didn't she go to him when she needed him the most?

"When was the last time you had a day off from horses?" Her dad asked.

Nora's eyebrows rose…what?

"Cooper had a day…actually two days off." Her mother stated. "Between the three horses, rodeos, horse shows, cutting, ranch work, I can't remember the last time you had a day off."

Nora just looked between the three of them. She knew exactly the last time she had a day off from horses. It was when Sadie was in the hospital, four months before. Helping take care of Scarecrow and being with Arcturus had helped her get through the tough time worrying about her cousin.

"I have the Cottage Grove rodeo this weekend." She reminded them.

"Is that what YOU want?" Her mother asked in concern.

Nora hesitated; she liked the rodeos more than expected but didn't like jumping off Cooper in the goat tying. This would be her way out of that without having to tell them why. Only Sadie would know and she'd never tell anyone.

"Well…" Nora said, trying to keep her voice calm. "I really like going with you and the kids to the rodeos…and I really like running poles with Sadie and Grace."

"And the goat-tying?" Her dad asked.

Nora shrugged a shoulder.

"You only do what you WANT to do." Her mother told her.

"I could give up goat-tying," Nora nodded nonchalantly. "That saves some practice time for Isaiah and the cows."

"What?" They all three asked in surprise.

"Casey suggested trying Isaiah with cows tomorrow for the reined cow competition."

They all three just stared at her.

"What?" Nora asked in concern.

"You've never wanted to work Isaiah with the cows." Her mother pointed out.

"Is that what YOU want or what Casey wants?" Nick asked.

"I don't know...I think so…" Nora responded truthfully. "I don't think it would hurt to try him. He might like it. I love cutting…it's so exciting." Both her parents grinned in understanding which made her smile at them. "And I love reining, so putting them together just seems like the right thing to do. I think Isaiah and I will both really like it."

"You're beaming and your voice is excited." Nick smiled at her.

Nora grinned, she hadn't really thought much about the reined cow event since Casey had mentioned it…but talking now…to her parents and Nick…the excitement was building to give it a try.

Her mom stepped to the fence and placed her hands over Nora's boots. She looked up with a smile. "I want that grin and look with everything you do."

"You too, Mom." Nora giggled and was rewarded with the happy light in her mother's eyes.

"So we're all good?" Her dad asked.

Nora nodded. She felt better than she had in weeks!

"Well, come on then." Nick held out a hand.

He took one hand and her dad took the other. They braced her as she jumped off the fence and into the arena, the dusty dirt puffing at her feet.

"It must be 105 degrees out here." Her mother shook her head as she put her arm around Nora's. They walked ahead of Nick and her dad as they headed for the gate.

"It'll be cooler where you're headed." Nick said.

"Where's that?" Nora turned to her mother. She didn't know they were going anywhere.

Her mother stopped and looked back at him with a questioning glare.

Nick grinned wickedly. "The hair salon…"

"I do not have GRAY HAIR!" Her mother kicked dirt at him; it was so dry and dusty it covered both men.

Nora burst out laughing.

***

Her alarm went off…it was actually just a vibration alarm so she didn't wake Sadie and Grace. She quickly grabbed it and turned it off. Her eyes opened…something didn't seem right, the room was too light…she was too rested.

A quick glance at her phone and her heart nearly stopped. It was 7:00! She was an hour late in meeting Casey!

Nora threw the covers off and reached for her jeans. Pulse racing she slid her socks on and grabbed the first shirt she could find.

She ran halfway down the long hallway then jumped into a slide and slid all the way to the banister. She laughed out loud when she stopped and started jogging down the stairway. Hopefully Casey wouldn't blow her good mood.

Nora slid her boots on and pulled open the door. Casey's truck wasn't by the barn. She turned and ran down the deck…when she reached the steps…she stopped in confusion.

Nikki's truck was at the bottom of the steps blocking her path and she was sitting in the driver's seat grinning at her.

"What's going on?" Nora frowned and looked to the barn. Where was Casey?

The back door of the truck opened revealing two smiling blondes; Nora's best friends, Sadie and Candace. Grace leaned around Nikki. She had run out of the room so fast, she didn't realize Sadie and Grace weren't in there.

Nora smiled hesitantly her eyes glancing to the barn again.

"Get in." Nikki smiled.

"I have practice." Nora glanced to the barn again.

"Not today," Grace laughed. "Aunt Jordan changed your alarm time."

"Come on, Nora!" Sadie and Candace shouted in unison.

Nora took a step toward them…her eyes going to the barn.

"Jordan said to tell you, she's making a 'mother' decision and you need a day off so she called Casey and canceled practice for today and tomorrow."

"What?" Nora's heart lurched.

"She already packed your suitcase…it's in the back." Nikki said.

"For what?" Nora gasped.

"Silverwood! We're going to the waterpark and do all the rides!" Sadie laughed.

"For two days! Just the five of us!" Candace said excitedly. "We're spending the night in a hotel!"

Nora felt the excitement build…just the five of them…her eyes glanced to the barn.

"If you even try to go to the barn," Nikki grinned wickedly, it looked so much like Nick's wicked grin. "The four of us will tackle you, tie you like a goat, and throw you in the back."

Nora burst out laughing and ran to the truck to crawl in next to her best friends.

CHAPTER FIFTEEN

"Are you ready?" Casey asked her.

Nora turned and looked at him. The grin slowly spread across her face.

"Yes," She answered.

"Stop grinning." He ordered.

"I don't think that's possible." Nora laughed.

He grinned from the top of Isaiah. Nora was on Arcturus and they stood in the middle of The Stables large arena.

"Whose idea was this?" He asked.

"The ride was my idea, but it was all your fault." She chuckled.

"Gonna blame it on me?"

"Sure! You're the one that showed me the pattern for the exhibition you did and riding it with the horses was a lot of fun…especially when you rode it with me."

"I think the horses liked it, too." He nodded.

"Your grandkids are here…so they'll enjoy the outfits…which were Wade's idea." Nora chuckled again.

"I was going to say that they are the only reason I agreed to this but after seeing all these kids at the Kid's Clinic here…well, it's heartwarming…they'll enjoy this."

"And they'll enjoy it more with your outfit." Nora laughed.

She glanced at him again, to see the large red clown nose that bounced when he wiggled his lips. She had to dip her chin to her chest to see over her really large red clown nose.

He shook his head backwards trying to get the long strands of the orange wig out of his face which made Nora laugh. He wore an oversized white and blue polka dot clown suit and his face was painted white except the large blue smile…and red nose.

Nora chuckled again. Her wig was blue and spikey…way up in the air. Her clown suit was tie-dyed pink, yellow and red with a little blue. It was pretty wild. Her face was also white but she had a big pink smile.

There were brightly colored strands of ribbon in the two gelding's manes and tails. Red and white paint circled their eyes and a bright red nose was attached to the noseband of their bridles. Nora and Casey grinned at each other when they heard Jack make the announcement of the special riding exhibition.

"This is one of the funnest things I have ever done." Nora said as she sat straighter in the saddle and prepared for the music to start.

"Me, too." Casey chuckled.

The music started; she and Casey moved the horses into a trot at the same time. The kids erupted in clapping and laughter. They did a complete circle around the arena, side-by-side. When they reached the end, they turned and ran down the middle to complete two perfect sliding stops next to each other. There were shouts and laughter from the crowd.

The horses moved away from each other then came together in the middle of the arena…facing each other. To the beat of the music they side-passed, stopped, twirled once, then side-passed the other direction, stopped, and twirled again but twice this time. They trotted next to each other…cantered and moved into flying lead changes…all to the timing of the music and the laughter of the children and adults cheering them on. They came together at the end of the arena again and danced the horses across the dirt floor to the delight of the crowd. Their wigs were bouncing wildly.

When they reached the far end, they turned in unison, broke into a fast run and slid to a stop in front of the crowd…dirt flew! They backed the horses ten feet then completed spins in unison. When they stopped, they were facing a screaming crowd.

Nora smiled at her coach, who was grinning and waving at his excited grandkids. She looked for all her family in the crowd and the joy within her increased at the sight of their proud grins and laughter.

Arcturus and Isaiah had their heads held high; soaking in all the attention they earned.

She and Casey stepped off the very excited horses and walked them to the fence so the excited kids could greet them. When she made it to the end of the row of people she looked up to see Reilly and Grace, and right behind them, Brady and Billy. The twins were wearing their purple and gold football jerseys…much to the delight of the kids attending the clinic.

"That was awesome, Nora!" Brady smiled at her.

"Thanks," She grinned.

"We gotta get back to the roping." Grace pulled Reilly away and Brady followed.

Nora nervously glanced at Billy. She hadn't seen or spoken to him since the disastrous dinner a few weeks before. Arcturus leaned his head across her so she wrapped her arms around his nose and stroked his neck gently.

"You're the best looking, blue haired clown I've ever seen." Billy grinned.

Under the white makeup Nora turned red, she had actually forgotten about the wig. He opened the gate for her and walked with her to the stable.

"I checked," Billy said in a low voice when they walked into the stalls. "It doesn't cost much to fly between Portland and Denver." Nora smiled slightly and tipped her head up to the very tall teenager to see his blue eyes smiling shyly. "But you have to wear the blue wig on the plane."

Nora's giggles echoed throughout the building.

THE TAGGER HERD SERIES

Grace Tagger

The Past and the Future

Gini Roberge

CHAPTER ONE

"Grace, you know that doesn't work."

"I know, Mom, but it makes me feel like I'm at least trying."

Grace twisted the phone in the air again. Seeing no bars indicating she was receiving reception, she brought her arm back in the window and rolled it up quickly. The cold October air caused a shiver down her spine.   It was just Grace and her mom riding back home from the ranch. She looked down at the phone in her hand and patiently waited for the spot on the mountain where they received cell service.

"You know she's happy for you."

"I know," Grace sighed. "I talked to her before I tried out for the royalty court. She really wanted me to."

"She was overjoyed when you won queen."

"Yeah, I can still remember her screaming in excitement," Grace grinned. "I just hope Nora gets queen of the Junior Rodeo Association so my winning the Lewiston Roundup Queen doesn't turn into salt in a wound."

"She will remain happy for you either way." Her mother smiled into the dark night. The lights of Tessa's borrowed SUV lit their way over the mountain. Other than the gravel covered road, they could only see silhouettes of trees on the left and nothing but the black night on the right.

Grace shrugged. "Do you think Candace has a chance with the Junior Rodeo royalty?"

"Of course," Her mother frowned at her. "There is no way Nora would have suggested she try if she didn't believe in her. Kristen and her mother have been very helpful for both of them."

Grace stopped staring at her phone and leaned back against the seat headrest and could see the first turn of the steep, winding grade come into sight. "Kristen was a good queen; I think she's trying out for Miss Rodeo Oregon next year. What do you think Nora would do if Candace won queen and she was princess?"

"Knowing Nora? We would never know."

"That's true, she sure can hold it all in."

"You all can…which drives me nuts."

Grace's phone alert rang out into the night.

"STOP!" Grace yelled and poked at her phone to unlock it. Her mother stopped the SUV in the middle of the road.

"Three messages!" Grace said excitedly.

TEXT FROM JORDAN: Candace is princess!

Grace and her mom quickly exchanged smiles then she swiped to the next message.

TEXT FROM JORDAN: No message, just a picture of Nora standing next to Arcturus. She was wearing a black hat with the queen's crown proudly displayed. Nora's smile was wide and happy!

"Queen and princess together!" Grace bounced excitedly. "They are going to have so much fun!"

Her mother laughed and started moving the SUV forward. "I'm sure Jordan and Paige are already overwhelmed."

"Oh Mom!" Grace grinned. "I am so happy for both of them."

"I'm thrilled for Candace. This is really going to help with her self-esteem and confidence."

"The other message is probably a picture of them together." Grace looked down at her phone then suddenly fell forward; her seatbelt digging into her shoulder.

She looked up in confusion and had to brace herself on the dash of the vehicle to keep from bashing her head against it.

"Grace! Hold on!" Her mother yelled; her voice panicked.

She turned to see her mother having to push herself off of the steering wheel.

"We're going over!" Her mother gasped in fear. They had just started to descend the long winding grade and now they were going over the side!

The SUV tilted heavily downward and to the right; the back of the vehicle high in the air. Grace's phone fell to the ground as she used her hands to brace against the dash and window.

"Mom…" Grace was gripped with fear, the visions of the steep mountain side with the rock bluffs flashing through her mind.

They did a full turn to the right and the vehicle's back tires slammed onto the ground, but they were still moving down at a steep angle. Grace braced herself on the dash, her legs straight out pushing against the floorboards. Panic gripping her lungs.

"I can't stop…it's just sliding…the mud…" Her mother's whispered voice shook. "Hold on, Baby Girl."

Her leg pumped the brakes to try and stop.

"When I hold the brake down it starts to turn us…I'm afraid of flipping…if I can keep it straight and flat we can ride it down to the bottom. If it angles or hits something…it will tip us…we may tumble…"

"Mom…" Grace clenched her jaw to keep in the scream. She looked in front of the car at the ground and rocks visible in the headlights. They were at a terrifyingly steep angle. She was shocked they didn't flip over.

A large rock suddenly appeared in front of them…there was a loud bang…the vehicle slowed down…a terrible metal screeching sound from underneath…the floor vibrated… they were moving again.

"I love you, Baby Girl." Her mother said through clenched teeth.

"I love you, Mom." The tears of fear and disbelief started to rise.

A row of trees appeared in the headlights.

"I'm going to try to slide into the trees. The airbags should protect us." Her mother said in what Grace knew was false bravery.

Grace leaned back as far as she could and used the center console and door grip for a brace. She didn't want the airbags to go off with her arms braced against the dash.   Her mind went back to the plane crash she had witnessed in the mountains. They had landed into the trees; branches busting through the window killing the parents. Her stomach quivered in fear.

It seemed to take forever as the trees loomed closer. Her mother tried to turn the wheel to move the SUV to them. Her foot pumped the brakes.

"Hold on, Baby…hold on…" Her mother whispered.

The trees came closer and closer, Grace couldn't tear her eyes away from them…she leaned back farther, but it was just inches. The front of the SUV fell causing them to bounce and fly forward, then the back wheels slammed down. They flew backward just as the front of the vehicle hit the trees.

The airbag released and all Grace could hear was her mother scream.

"Mom!" Grace fought the white flimsy bag. It seemed to have a life of its own as it kept grabbing at her arms. "Mom!"

The SUV had stopped, but she could hear her mother gasping.

"Mom!" Grace finally pushed the bag out of her way and looked to her mother. She was leaned back, her face writhed in pain.

Cold air streamed through… a window must have broken. Grace glanced at the front window. It was still intact and the head lights showed nothing more than broken trees over the hood of the vehicle. Turning quickly, Grace looked behind her. All the windows on her side were intact; it had to be from her mother's side.

"Mom…" Grace unfastened her seatbelt.

"Are you OK?" Her mother whispered through a grimace.

"Yes, what's wrong?"

"My leg," She gasped. "Turn off the engine…just in case there's gas leaking."

Grace turned the key, the dashboard's lights turned off and everything went black.

"I can't see anything." She nearly panicked.

"Give your eyes a minute to adjust." Her mom whispered.

"I've got to get the flashlight out of the back."

"Grab the whole emergency box while you're there."

"Anything else besides your leg?" Grace asked as she leaned her own seat all the way back then crawled over the seat, trying to avoid touching her mother. The box was in the far back of the SUV. She knelt on the second row of seats and stretched her arm into the back and was relieved to feel the box. She pulled it into the back seat and slid off the top. The flashlight was right on top.

The light burst on and shown out the broken backseat passenger window and lit the tree that was twisted into it.

Wiggling back into the front seat, Grace turned the light to the ceiling so she didn't flash it in her mother's face.

"Grace," Her mother whispered.

"I didn't hit you did I?" Grace said anxiously.

"No. I'm just so thankful you're alright." She grimaced.

Grace set the flashlight on the dash and shot the beam between them to the back. She took a good look at her mother.

Her head was leaning back and even with the bad lighting Grace could tell she was pale.

"Look at me." Grace told her mother.

She turned her head slowly and squinted through the beam of light. Her eyes looked alert. "Are you ordering me around, young lady?" Her mother teased.

"Yep, for now." Grace couldn't even fake a chuckle; her face muscles were too tense to try a smile.

The window next to her mother was arced inwards; it looked like it was on the verge of breaking. The side airbag had deployed but the door was still pushed against her mother.

"How is your side?" Grace asked.

"It took a shot, but I can move my arm so it's not broken, the ribs may be though. Grab the light and shine it to my leg."

"Is it still hurting?" Grace knew it was a stupid question the second it left her mouth. She gripped the light and pointed it underneath the steering wheel.

The light shown on the jean encased legs and the knee-high snow boots. The side of the SUV had crushed into the space and all the way to the brake pedal. The left leg twisted at an odd angle just under the knee. It was perched over the top of the right leg.

"Obviously broke." Her mother leaned back against the seat. Her body visibly shuttered.

Grace turned quickly to the emergency box and pulled out the silver emergency blanket. Folding it out, she placed it over her mother as tightly as possible.   Back to the floor of the backseat and Grace grabbed the blanket that she had spotted earlier.

"Tessa was well prepared." Grace told her mother.

"Matt made sure she and everyone else had a good winter emergency box."

"We'll have to thank him."

"You'll have to go get him."

Grace turned quickly to her mother. "Leave you?" Fear ran through her.

"Yes, I can't go…you'll have to and soon." She turned worried eyes to her.

"I can't leave you." Grace's voice vibrated in shock as she stared into her mother's pain filled eyes.

"Grace, it's supposed to snow up here tonight. Can you imagine what would happen if we have a snow storm like we did at Christmas last year?"

Grace's body trembled. They could be snow covered for days.

"It wouldn't be dangerous for just us, but those looking for us, too. You know the road…all you have to do it follow the tire trail we left on the mountain to get there. We were within minutes of cell service…or you can run down to Parson's Ranch." Her voice was low and stressed.

"OK, Mom, I know…I understand, but first I need to check to see what it looks like outside, get you set, then I'll go."

Grace turned back to the box and aimed the flashlight into it.

"There's energy bars and water in here. Plus some easy-light gel to make a fire…matches…gloves…" Grace grabbed the gloves and stuffed them in her pocket. She would need those for the climb out.

"Is there a rifle?" Her mom's voice was soft.

"I don't see one." Grace crawled into the backseat to see what other supplies she could find. "All the windows are intact back here, except the one right behind you."

She shown the light into the back, "There's a saddle blanket back here." She pulled it out and placed it into the broken window trying to block the incoming cold air. "It will help if I can stop the air." Grace took duct tape from the box and taped the blanket over the window trying to cover any gap where the air could sneak in.

"Good idea. If we had the truck…there is a rifle, but I don't know about Tessa's."

"I'm looking…" Grace took a deep breath to calm her nerves and continued to look.

"If we had the truck…I have no doubt we would have flipped."

"Thank goodness we brought Tessa's." Grace said. She found green emergency lights in the box and broke one to activate it. A spooky green hue shown through the vehicle.

"I'll have to take the flashlight, Mom, but these sticks last for hours."

"Good plan."

"There are flares! We can use them to show where we are, they'll really light up the sky out here."

"Matt will be proud of you."

"I'm glad I listened to all his search and rescue mumbo jumbo."

She tried to think of everything Matt would do in this situation. "I wish I had a horse to ride out."

"Thank heavens we weren't pulling a horse trailer." Her mother sighed.

"What happened?"

"I don't know…we just suddenly dipped and slid."

Grace continued her search. "There isn't a rifle in here."

"I don't think I'm bleeding." Her mother told her. "Shine the light and see if you can tell."

Fear gripped Grace's gut. The bears would be hibernating but the mountain lions were all over the property. The smell of blood would attract them.

She wiggled back into the front seat. "Are you warm?"

"Quite, the two blankets do a good job."

Her mother's black, fur trimmed hat held her blond hair back and was long enough to cover her ears. It would help keep the heat in her body. "When I leave, pull the blanket over your head."

"Yes, ma'am."

Grace tried to maneuver around the seat to take a better look at her mother's leg but couldn't get a good angle.

"I'm going to have to open the door." Grace sighed. "I haven't even looked out yet."

She turned the flashlight out the window.

"Trees on that side?" Her mother whispered.

Grace turned back to her pale mother. "I can't see anything."

She smiled gently. "You're doing great, stay strong."

"I will." Grace returned her smile, hoping to reassure her.

She turned to the door, beamed the light out, and pulled the handle.

Great relief ran through her as the door opened but the cold flash of air diminished it quickly. She zipped her coat up completely and pulled the hood over her head. The coat was only to her waist.

"My winter coat is in the back seat, it will go down to your knees. You'll need to wear it over the top of yours." Her voice was low, barely above a whisper.

Grace flashed the light around the mountain side.

"Well?"

"Nothing but more downhill mountain on this side, two trees in the front of the SUV…Tessa's gonna be upset with you." Grace tried to keep a sense of humor to keep from freezing in fear.

"I have a feeling she'll forgive me."

Grace took in a deep lungful of air then knelt down and looked under the vehicle.

"No fuel smell, that's good. I don't see anything dripping from the car either."

"That's a relief."

She took out an emergency light, broke it and tossed it on top of the car. It lit up the area around her and the vehicle.

"You're completely in trees on your side. You did a good job, Mom. If we didn't hit those two trees…we would have slid a whole lot farther."

Grace looked into the car to her mother. "Still warm?"

"Yes, I'm fine, just sick to my stomach that you have to climb up that mountain in the dark."

"I'll be fine, Mom." Grace leaned back into the SUV and beamed the light to her mother's legs. The bend in her leg made Grace's stomach turn as she lightly touched the bottom of the leg…no moisture. "No blood."

She pulled the blankets down lower over her legs and tried to wrap them the best she could without touching them. "I can't tell if it's your knee or your shin bone that's broken."

"The whole leg hurts…could be both. I'm glad there isn't any blood. Keep up with the good words, Hon." Her mother smiled.

"I'll try." Grace crawled back into the seat and shut the door. She turned to her mother and took her outstretched hand, squeezing it tightly.

"Take the gloves."

"I will, and your coat…flares, emergency lights, a couple of the energy bars and bottles of water. I'll keep my hood on to keep the warmth from escaping out the top of my head." Grace took a deep breath and let it out slowly. Her mother was pale and looked tired, she had to go soon to get her help. "You'll be safe in here, Mom. The trees are blocking the broken window and the saddle blanket should keep out most of the cold air."

"You've got everything handled, Sweetheart, and I'll be fine here, tucked safely away, while you're out in the cold, climbing a mountain in the dark." Tears rimmed her eyes.

"It's OK, Mom." Grace swallowed hard to keep the rising tears at bay…she had to stay strong for her mom. "You saved us this far." She squeezed her hand tightly. "It's my turn now."

"I don't know what happened." Her mother whispered; her blue eyes full of distress.

"I'll find out when I get up there, Mom. It wasn't your fault." Grace leaned to her mother and tried to hug her as gently as she could. "You saved us."

"I love you, Baby Girl." She felt her mother's gentle kiss on her temple.

"I love you, too." Grace leaned back and smiled warmly at her mother. "You'll be OK; I've left you a few emergency lights. I'll place some on the ground as I go up the mountain so it will light our way back down."

She reached into the emergency box and pulled out the energy bars. "I'll put them here close."

"We had a big dinner with Lucas, Nikki, and Matt…I'm good."

"Well, just in case."

Grace flashed the light around the inside of the vehicle. There was nothing left to do but walk up the mountain and get help.

She turned back to her mom, "I have to go now," Their hands squeezed tightly. "You keep warm and I'll be back as soon as I can."

"I'm so sorry, Grace."

Grace wiped away the tear sliding down her mother's beautiful, yet frightened face.

"I'll be OK." She smiled. "You just take a nap and I'll be back before you wake up."

Her mother chuckled through the tears.

Grace leaned forward, kissed her mother's forehead then turned quickly to the door and climbed out, gently closing the door behind her.

She turned back and put her hand on the window, looking at her mother. The green light enabled her to see that she had leaned back against the seat and closed her eyes.

Taking a deep breath, Grace pulled her mother's coat over the top of her own. Her own knee-high snow boots stopped where they met the coat. She was thankful she had worn her flat boots instead of the higher platform ones. They weren't meant for climbing mountains; she hoped they held up to the rocks.

Digging into the pockets, Grace double-checked her supplies then turned and walked to the back of the SUV. The mountainside was slightly visible in the moonlight and showed they were a long way down; it was going to take her hours to get up to the top.

Beaming the light on the ground, she found the tracks of the vehicle in the thick mud and took her first step to retrace them just as the first snowflakes started to fall.

CHAPTER TWO

One foot in front of the other, keeping her mind from worrying about her mother, from thinking of mountain lions, from how far she had to climb, and from her burning muscles and lungs. She focused on the tracks of the SUV's path…she climbed and climbed and climbed.

In her mind, she was on Eli, executing the pattern that won her the horsemanship competition for the roundup royalty. Nora had been proud. In fact, without a doubt, Nora would have beaten her. The coaching from Casey was polishing the years of work Nora already had on Arcturus and Isaiah. They had won or placed in every competition they entered. They had just started a winter's break when Nora went to compete for the royalty court. For the winter, she and Isaiah would continue their training for the next season of the reined cow horse competitions. Both horse and rider thoroughly enjoyed chasing the cows.

Grace stopped and pointed the flashlight up the mountainside. She couldn't make out the top yet. Turning, she could barely see the emergency light she had tossed on top of the SUV. The vehicle was nearly hidden on the edge of the trees. She cracked another emergency stick to light up the area around her then placed it on the nearest rock. Hopefully the snow wouldn't cover it up before she returned. It wasn't a heavy snowfall, just little crystal flakes that glistened when the beam from the flashlight touched them.

She continued her uphill climb. At times, it was so steep she hardly had to bend over to touch the ground with her hands. They were so lucky the back of the SUV didn't flip over the front.

Her mind went to Wade playing football. One of his new passions was to beat quarterback records set by his dad and uncle.

During his first game, the coach didn't let him play the first half of the game and he barely played the second half but Wade was patient. His coaching with his dad was building his confidence and he knew his time would come. It was the third play of the second game that Wade had his chance.

Wade was in the running back position, but the play called for a throw into the end zone. The quarterback fumbled the ball and Wade picked it up. He threw a perfect touchdown throw into the end zone to the receiver. They didn't win the game, but Wade had become quarterback for the rest of the season. He made his mistakes but he improved every game. Their season had just ended. Grace couldn't wait to come back from college the next year to watch Wade play.

She stopped and looked out into the darkness around her and tried to remember anything that would tell her how far they had slid down the mountain. It happened so fast, yet it seemed to last an eternity. Halfway they had hit a rock that scraped the bottom of the SUV and slowed them down. When she ran into that, it would help judge her progress.

She didn't find it until a half hour later. She turned and barely saw the emergency light she had placed down the hill so she put another one on the metal covered rock.

She estimated at least another hour of climbing. The boots had begun to hurt her feet, but that pain didn't compare to the leg muscles burning.

"I hate climbing uphill." Grace muttered out loud.

The sound of her voice seemed to echo into the darkness. She began to sing softly. Trying to remember the words kept her from thinking of her mother, hurting lungs and muscles, or being scared.

She turned; the halfway point was barely visible. Another emergency light was placed.

It would be daylight before the green lights would darken.

One step in front of another…her muscles burned and her lungs were on fire. She coughed trying to clear them but it didn't help.

The only skin susceptible to the cold air was her face…why hadn't she worn a scarf?!

She looked up and was sure she could see the edge of the road. The mud was deeper the farther she climbed up the mountain. She tried to find a spot off to the side where she could still see the tracks but didn't slide in the mud.

She was close now, so she had to make a plan. They hadn't driven very far from the point she had received the text messages so she knew she was close to cell service and could call…

Grace stopped, anxiety suddenly taking over…and anger. She had left her cell phone in the SUV!

The tears started to rise. How could she be so stupid!?! Now it was going to take longer to get her mother help. She would HAVE to jog to Parson's ranch house for help…miles away!

Her parents always gave her a bad time that she was glued to her phone…and the one time she really needed it…she left it behind!

She tried to stomp to let out the frustration but her legs refused to give her that much energy. Shaking her head, denying the tears, she continued to climb. The longer she stood still, the longer it would take to get help.

Back to the climbing and thinking of her mother, hopefully she was sleeping. From the point Grace had fought the air bag and first laid eyes on her mother, she hadn't moved, other than the inch or two to look down her leg the first time. She didn't move…at all.

Grace stopped and turned to look back down in the direction of the SUV, as if she could see her mom. She said her ribs were broken… Grace's hand went to her sore shoulder where the seat belt had kept her from flying forward. It would have been the same for her mom, except the steering wheel…and the side of the car twisted into her.

Grace rolled her lips tight and glared into the darkness. She knew her mom well enough that she would have walked herself, drug herself up the hill to keep Grace from doing it. But not if she was badly injured…as in…broken ribs…internal injuries.

Grace turned, suddenly deathly afraid for her mother. Her steps were wider and faster, she didn't care how bad her legs screamed at her.

She placed another green light on a rock. There were only two left…and the three flares. The flares would burn out faster so she wanted to use those last.

Step after step, trying desperately to move faster with each step…until she heard it…a truck or car engine…somewhere above her in the dark.

Grace beamed the light up the hill. She could see the edge of the road only fifty yards up. Her heart raced when she saw the lights of a vehicle making their way down the grade.

She tried to run, but it was no use, the muscles were exhausted, her lungs abused from the cold air.

She had to get up there before the car passed on the road. Again, she tried to run…it wasn't happening.

The flare! It would be brighter than the green lights and stand out in the middle of the dark night; no one could miss it out here.

Her dad had taught all the kids how to check their oil in the vehicles, how to change tires and also how to light the flares in an emergency.

Grace lit it quickly. She squinted against the brightness of the red light that took over the night sky.

Looking up to watch the headlights as they weaved their way down the steep grade, she continued climbing while waving the flare. There was no way someone could miss the bright red glow.

The lights disappeared as they went behind the mountain then reappeared just to her left.

Grace held her breath and frantically waved the flare. They had to see it! Her mind flashed at the moment she was yelling at her dad when they were fighting the fire at the ranch, and Eli was on the other side of the mountain. Her dad had seen her and was able to get to Eli and use him to get to the top of the mountain and save the ranch.

Grace kept moving upward and staring at the headlights…that finally stopped! The lights flashed on and off, their way of telling her they saw her!

Relief raced through her as she continued her climb.

"Hello!" She screamed out when the car door opened and shone a light inside.

"Hello?" The male voice rang out.

"We need help!" Grace yelled, tears threatening again.

"Who are you? What happened?"

"Grace Tagger."

"Grace!" She could see the figure headed to the edge of the road. "It's Warren." The foreman of the neighboring ranch.

"Mom's hurt!" Grace cried out.

She was only fifteen feet from the top when he reached her. He wore a thick coat and a black cowboy hat that sheltered his face from the falling snow crystals.

"How bad is she?" Warren asked and looked down the hill. "How far?"

He pulled her to the top of the hill and she nearly fell to the ground when she reached the flat ground.

"I've been climbing for at least two hours." Grace turned to look at him as his eyes moved past her and widened in shock.

"Grace, look!"

She turned to follow his gaze. Ten feet in front of his car the road disappeared.

"It's a mudslide." Warren shook his head as they walked to the twenty-foot wide ditch that used to be road.

"That's what happened." Grace gasped. "We didn't even see it. All the sudden we were dipping then turning then sliding all the way down the mountain. The mud just carried us down." The light of the flare shone on the SUV's tire marks as they dropped into the ditch.

"I'd be in it too if it weren't for seeing your light."

Grace stared at Warren's shocked expression then turned to his car, back to the ditch, down the hill, then back to Warren.

"I'll put a flare on both sides so anyone else coming up here can see it." She said. "You have to go back after Matt."

"Of course," Warren turned to his car then looked back to her. "How bad is Leah?"

Grace took in a shaky breath. "She has a broken leg." She stopped and concentrated on her mother. "She didn't move or even try to move after the accident…so she's hurt worse than she told me." Grace rolled her lips. "She said her ribs were broken too…could be internal."

Grace lit a second flare and tossed it across the ditch to protect drivers coming from the other direction. Even if Matt got to them…they couldn't drive past that ditch.

"Warren?" Grace turned back to him just before he shut his door.

"What?"

"You'll have to call someone from below to drive up here to get her."

Warren looked down the road then to Grace. He nodded his understanding. "I'll call Parsons."

"I'm headed back down to Mom." Grace turned to slide off the side of the mountain.

"Be careful, Grace." He told her.

"You too," Grace hollered out to him. "Don't crash! You're the only one that knows we're down here."

He yelled something to her but Grace couldn't hear what he said, she was concentrating on the hillside and the rocks as she tried to jog, which turned out to be a slide down the hillside and back to her mother. The boots rubbed relentlessly on blisters she knew had formed on her ankles and heels.

She counted the green lights as she passed them. How many five…six? The metal covered rock they had hit appeared then disappeared as she hurried by it. Half way…she was making much better time going down the hill. Then she realized she was going to have to walk back up again.

"Someone will have to carry me!" Grace shouted into the night which made her cough; a deep lung rumbling cough.

She flew by another light; it was the first one she'd placed. Her eyes stared down the hill trying to see the light on top of the SUV. Her foot hit something hard and she fell forward…she tried to stop the fall but there was no hope…she hit the ground with both hands then tucked in her shoulder to protect her head and rolled. Her mind flashed to Buttercup tumbling down the hill during the kid's cattle roundup. Oh, she wished Buttercup was there now.

Grace stopped rolling and lay still for a moment looking up into the dark, starless sky. The light snowflakes fell gently on her warm cheeks. After a few deep breaths, she pushed herself up into a sitting position and looked around at the darkness. Her mother's coat and the gloves had protected her from the rocks and brush. The flashlight had fallen a couple of feet away and shone on a rock bluff to her left. She reached for the light and focused its beam on the bluff that had a thirty foot sheer drop off from the top. If the SUV had dropped over that…?

Grace shuttered and looked back down the steep hill. She could just make out the light on top of the SUV. Up and jogging down the hill, the beam of the flashlight just in front of her so she didn't tumble again.

She coughed again to try and clear out the cold air from her lungs…no use, they continued to burn.

As she approached the SUV she slowed down so she didn't scare her mother.

"Mom! I'm back!" Grace yelled out and made her way to the door. She glanced in before opening the door, hoping to see her mother looking back at her.

She was in the same position as when she left; eye's closed.

Fear ran down Grace's spine as she reached for the door.

There was a loud click as she lifted the handle, her mother's eyes flew open and she turned wide eyes to her.

"Mom!" Grace yanked the door open.

"Grace! What's the matter? Why are you back so soon…is something wrong…are you hurt?" Tears filled her frightened eyes.

"No, Mom. I'm OK." Grace pulled the door closed and grabbed her mother's hand; squeezing it tightly…it was so cold. "You're freezing."

"I'm OK…what happened? Couldn't you get up the hill?"

Grace looked confused at her mother, then she felt the urge to laugh but couldn't from the strain in her muscles and burning lungs.

"Mom, I've been gone for almost three hours." Grace tried to smile at the shocked expression looking back at her. "See, you did sleep."

Her mom relaxed back on the seat.

"I ran into Warren just before he slid into the ditch on the road that we slid into."

"What?"

"The road was washed out…that's how we ended up down the mountain; the mud grabbed us and pulled us down. If Warren hadn't stopped when he saw my flare, he would be down here with us."

"Oh, Grace." Her mother gasped, the mist from her breath showing how cold it was in the vehicle.

"Mom, we have to get you warm." Grace frowned.

"Grace…"

"Stop saying you're fine…I know you aren't." Grace ordered and was surprised when her mother just nodded.

That scared Grace even more, but she wasn't going to show it.

She aimed the light into the emergency box to see if there was anything else to help. Her eyes landed on the easy-light gel.

"I'm going to build a fire," Grace announced. She looked back at her mother; her eyes were closed again. "Do you think you can move enough we can get you out of here and to a fire?"

"I don't know." She whispered.

"I'm going to get it built. Even when Matt gets here, it may take a while, we'll need to be kept warm."

"I'll just hang out here." Her mother smiled.

Grace finally released a sigh and chuckle. She was so relieved just to be back with her mother and knowing Matt was coming to rescue them. Grabbing the gel, she left the vehicle and made her way into the trees to start collecting pine needles and dried limbs.

Twenty minutes later she had a fire blazing. Now it was time to try and move her mother.

She quickly climbed back in the SUV and shut the door. Her mother's eyes turned to her, then past her. "That's a good looking fire."

"I didn't want it too close in case there was gas leaking that we didn't know about. Can you move to get to it?"

"I've been too scared to try after the first time." Her mom admitted with a sad look.

"I don't think we should move you." Grace decided. "You're protected from the snow and wind, plus we could hurt you worse."

"They'll be here soon…I'm OK."

"I said stop that, Mom." Grace ordered as she beamed the light into the box again. She saw something that made her smile.

"What?" Her mother asked.

Grace reached in the box and pulled out a small camp frying pan like she had in the mountains the week of the airplane crash.

"Going to cook me something?" Her mother raised a brow in humor.

"No, better." Grace smiled. She turned back to the box and pulled the large knife out of the bottom.

She climbed into the back of the vehicle and lay down all the seats except the one behind her mother. She used the knife to tear a large piece of carpet from the floor to expose the metal underneath.

"Tessa's gonna be upset with you." Her mother smiled.

"I think she'll forgive me after she sees what you did to the front end." Grace giggled. "I'll be right back."

She stepped out of the car and looked around the ground. She found a couple relatively flat rocks and returned to the SUV to place them on top of the metal she had exposed. Then she headed for the fire, frying pan in hand.

She turned and looked up the mountain, hoping for lights…nothing.

Using the frying pan, she dug out the red coals from the fire and quickly made her way back to the SUV. When she crawled in the passenger seat, she placed the hot frying pan full of red coals on top of the rocks. The warmth could be felt immediately.

"Grace, that's brilliant." Her mother grinned. "I am so proud of you."

Grace smiled. "I didn't want to put it on the carpet. I was worried about the glue so it's on the metal then rock. I don't think it will be bikini weather in here, but it'll keep you warm enough."

"You've done a great job."

"Well, except one thing." Grace admitted and looked to the floor at her feet. It was lying just under her seat. "I forgot to take my phone. It's a good thing Warren showed up or I would be jogging to Parson's Ranch right now."

She unlocked the phone, surprised to see it working. "Guess what?" She grinned at her mother.

"What?"

"No service down here." She chuckled.

Her mother chuckled and grimaced. "Don't make me laugh."

"Sorry," Grace smiled and tucked the phone in her pocket. "I'm going to get a refill." She put on her glove and gripped the handle of the frying pan. "Thank goodness the handle isn't metal."

She was on her third refill, the coals keeping the vehicle warm, when she spotted a light.

She stared in confusion…the light wasn't coming from up the mountain. It was coming out of the trees next to her. She froze in place and stared at it.

"Hello?" Grace called out anxiously.

CHAPTER THREE

"Grace?" The female voice called out.

"Nikki!" Grace dropped the pan on the ground and ran toward the light.

It seemed to bounce slightly and was high…and for a reason. Nikki rode in on Harvey while leading Trooper. She had a wide black cowboy hat on and her long winter coat covering her body and legs.

Grace stopped and turned back, "I'm gonna tell Mom you're here." She called over her shoulder.

"Where is she?"

"In the SUV, it was safer."

Grace informed her very relieved mother as Nikki found a tree to tie the horses.

Grace filled the pan with coals then crawled in the back seat while Nikki sat in the passenger side. She pulled off her black hat releasing her dark hair.

"How are you?" Nikki asked worriedly as she pulled off her gloves and pressed a hand on her aunt's forehead.

"I'm OK."

"Mom, knock that off." Grace frowned.

Her mother glanced back at her then to Nikki. "My leg has gone numb; it's broken…knee or bone. My ribs are broken but I haven't moved since the crash…it's…very…extremely painful. I'm afraid of internal injuries."

"Where are Matt and Lucas?" Grace asked.

"They're coming from the top to follow your trail. I dropped down the ravine a ways back and found a cattle trail to see if I could find an easier path to get you out of here."

"It was a lot faster; I didn't see their lights at all." Grace wiggled to the back and looked out the window and up the hill. "I see them now."

"I saw your fire and was on a good trail so I could gallop for a ways here." Nikki answered. "We've ridden both horses in the dark."

"Nikki?" Grace's mom's voice was low…they could barely hear it. "Grayson?"

Nikki reached out and grasped her aunt's hand tightly. "Matt called Josey. She and Grayson were at the indoor arena practicing roping with the boys. Josey and Cora are driving The Trio to the hospital to wait for you."

Her mom nodded and closed her eyes. Even from the backseat Grace could see the tears sliding down her mother's face.

Her own tears started rising, Grace's throat constricting.

"I'm going to refill the pan." Grace's stepped out of the door and walked to the fire. Relief ran through her as she watched the two lights making their way down the mountain. She scooped out the red hot embers from the fire then tossed more tree limbs on the fire to use as a beacon to the men.

Grace opened the door and showed Nikki what to do with the pan.

"That's brilliant, Grace." Nikki smiled at her through tense facial muscles.

"I'll wait by the fire." Grace closed the door, stepped in front of the fire and watched the flashlights grow closer.

She started shaking in excitement as the men's shapes started to form. She could tell they were carrying something but she couldn't see what it was.

"Grace?" Matt called out and Grace's very tired legs tried to run to her cousin and she threw her arms around him. His arms engulfed her and his strong embrace made her feel safe.

"Where's Leah?" Matt asked as he stepped away from her. The fire reflected in his worried eyes.

Grace nodded at Lucas and looked back to Matt. "I kept her in the SUV it was safer. I took the fire to her to keep her warm."

"You have a fire in there?" Lucas asked.

Grace nodded. "Slide in the back but be careful and close the door quickly to keep the heat in there."

Lucas hugged her quickly then both men went to the SUV.

Grace stood quietly by the fire. She leaned over the heat and breathed in the warmth trying to fill her chilled lungs. It caused her to break out in a fit of coughs.

She stared at the vehicle…every inch of her wanted to be with her mom but she knew the three of them needed to be with her now.

Her eyes moved to the equipment Matt had dropped. There was a snow sled included. It caught her by surprise until she realized how close the long narrow sled looked like the carriers he uses in his search and rescue.

The door finally opened and Nikki and Lucas stepped out. Matt slid into the front seat as Nikki walked to Grace and wrapped her arms around her protectively.

"Are you alright?" Lucas asked.

Grace nodded, her whole body started to shake, but not from cold.

Nikki squeezed tighter. "She'll be OK."

"I know." Grace whispered, refusing to let the tears out. She started another round of coughing.

"That doesn't sound good. You weren't coughing at the house." Lucas said.

"Just started when I climbed the mountain," Grace nodded. "What is Matt doing?"

"He leaned the seat back so he could examine her side and leg before deciding how to get her out." Nikki answered.

"Then what?" Grace felt totally out of control and she hated it.

"We'll go back the way Nikki came in." Lucas answered. "It's not as steep. She'll ride Harvey to lead the way. You'll ride Trooper."

"Thank goodness I don't have to try and walk out….and Mom?" Grace turned to him.

"We're going to wrap her in the sled and pull her with Trooper." He answered.

"She can't bounce on the ground!" Grace's spine straightened and her eyes widened.

Nikki quickly shook her head. "She won't. Lucas and Matt will be holding the sled above the ground to make it as smooth as possible. Tying it to Trooper will allow him to take the majority of the weight so we can get out faster."

The door to the SUV opened.

"Grace," Matt motioned for her and she walked as quickly as she could to the vehicle. He turned to Nikki. "Grab Harvey's saddle bags. I need the brace I put in it for her leg when we wrap it. Lucas, grab the tarp we brought down. We're going to have to remove the sun roof. Luckily, it's pretty good sized so we should be able to lift her up and out. We'll use the tarp to cover Leah and keep her protected in case the glass breaks."

Grace and Nikki stood next to the fire and watched the men move in and out of the vehicle as they prepared to remove the glass. Matt crawled to the top of the SUV with Lucas in the vehicle in case it dropped. They tossed the glass to the side and Matt slid through the open roof to his patient. Lucas exited the vehicle and opened all the doors that weren't blocked by trees.

Grace went to her mother who was leaning all the way back in the seat.

"Almost out." Her mother tried to smile bravely.

"I love you, Mom." Grace smiled and took her hand.

"I love you too, Baby Girl. You've done a tremendous job tonight."

Grace nodded, "So did you by saving us, Mom."

Matt appeared next to Grace and looked down at her mother.

"With the driver's side crushed into the trees, we either have to take you out through the passenger side or through the roof." Matt said. "Through the roof we can keep you as straight as possible and not have to bend you and take a chance on your damaged ribs." He turned and looked at Grace. "You'll have one of the toughest jobs. You'll have to brace her leg and try to move it around the steering wheel."

Grace's eyes opened wide and she looked at her mother.

"It won't be easy and it will be painful." She squeezed Grace's hand tightly. "Do what you need to do to get me out of here."

"Ok, Mom." Grace nodded and swallowed hard.

Nikki crawled in through the back and made her way to lean over their patient. She had removed her long coat to be able to maneuver better. "I'm going to grip you under the shoulders and help slide you back and up to Lucas on the roof. He has wiped it down to dry it off as much as possible."

Matt crawled into the side of the vehicle, behind Grace. "I'm going to brace your back to keep as much pressure off your ribs as possible."

"Just get me out of here and to my husband." She grimaced and gripped Nikki's arm.

Matt looked to Nikki, she nodded, then to Grace.

"We can do this." He whispered.

Grace took a deep breath, and looked into his eyes. "We can do this." She whispered in return, his words helping give her the strength.

"Leah, if you need to scream…scream. None of us will hold it against you." Matt told her and she nodded but gritted her teeth.

"Grace, get ready." Matt instructed.

Grace knelt on the seat and leaned under the steering wheel. She placed one hand under the knee and the other just down the leg from the weird angle in the leg. Her stomach turned.

"One, two, three…." Matt said and they moved as one to lift her mom.

Her mother groaned deeply, Grace worked hard to keep her mind closed from the sound and focus only on the leg. She needed to keep her movements separate from the reality that she was hurting her mother.

The good leg slid around the bottom of the steering wheel towards Grace so she tried to slide the broken leg with it but it wouldn't move far enough…another distant groan… she had to push it away and slide it between the wheel and the smashed door. To her relief, as Nikki and Matt lifted and pulled her towards the back of the vehicle, there was just enough room that the leg slid free.

Matt's arm slid under Grace's to help brace the leg as he lifted it to the hole in the roof then into Lucas' waiting arms. Grace cradled her mother's calves and followed her over the seat and up through the window. Her mother let out another low, guttural groan.

"I got her." Lucas said from the roof.

"Nikki stay here and support her legs while I get the sled up to Lucas. Grace the blankets; take them to the fire."

They all moved quickly. Grace pulled both blankets behind her as she walked briskly to the fire. She stared at the men on the top of the vehicle placing her mother onto the sled.

"Careful, don't tip her." Matt said to Lucas as they lifted the sled off the roof and down to the ground. There was a quivering in Grace's heart and stomach as she saw her mother finally carried away from the mangled SUV and to the fire.

The snow started falling in larger flakes that stuck to the ground and caused a white carpet around them. The air was brisk and Nikki quickly slid her coat back on. The fire felt good as Grace laid the regular blanket over the top of her mother then gripped her hand tightly while Matt wrapped the brace around her leg.

"I'm guessing a broken leg, not the knee." Matt told them. "How are you doing Leah?"

"I'm fine." She said through gritted teeth. "It's starting to turn back to an ache."

"The ribs?" He asked and pulled the blanket over the legs and tucked it around them.

"They hurt, but on the outside…not the inside…does that make sense?" She answered.

"Yes, and that's a good thing but, honestly, it doesn't guarantee that nothing's wrong." Matt glanced down at her and she nodded in understanding.

Grace bit her lip nervously. They had to get her mother out and to help fast!

He reached out for the emergency blanket and quickly had it tucked around her. The hat covered her head and the blankets covered her all the way up to her chin. Only her face was visible.

"Lucas and Nikki grip the ends of the sled; you'll lift so I can wrap the rope around her." Matt instructed. "Grace, on the other side and help me get the rope around the basket."

"Basket?" Grace hesitated.

"Sled," Matt chuckled. "It's normally a stokes basket that we use."

They finished wrapping her mother into a cocoon then moved to get the horses.

Two long leather straps were wrapped around the saddle horn of Trooper's saddle, then under the skirt of each side so Grace wasn't sitting on it. A rope was tied to the straps that ran down the length of the horse's tail. A few feet out and Matt tied it to the tip of the sled.

"Grace, mount up." Matt ordered.

Grace walked stiffly to the side of Trooper and gripped the top of the saddle. She tried to lift her leg but it only came up a few inches before the pain screamed out at her. She leaned against the horse.

"I can't get my leg up," She chuckled nervously. "I'm afraid the climb got the best of them."

Lucas helped her on the horse and carefully slid her boots into the stirrups for her. She leaned forward to run a hand down the length of the horse's neck; her body relaxing with the knowledge she didn't have to walk out.

Lucas and Matt stood at the back, gripped the sleigh straps and prepared to lift.

"Grace, take about ten steps forward." He nodded. "Let's test this."

The men lifted as the horse moved forward. The sled leveled out with Trooper's rope bracing the front of the sled and the men holding up the back; her mother was carried forward.

"How is that, Leah?" Matt looked down as they walked.

"I feel like I'm swinging in a hammock." She answered. "With both your ingenuity…you and Grace could rule the world."

They all chuckled.

"Stop." Matt looked up at Grace with a grin.

She pulled Trooper to a stop and grinned back.

"The pain is getting to you," Lucas shook his head down at their passenger as they set her on the ground. "You're starting to get delusional."

Her mother chuckled then groaned. "Don't make me laugh."

Matt stood and looked around. "Is there anything you need from the SUV?"

"I hate to sound so stereotypical female…but could you grab my purse?" Her mother smiled up from her hammock.

"I'll get it." Nikki walked back to the SUV and returned with the bag and the green emergency light from the top of the vehicle. She placed the light on top of the sled to keep their passenger lit and placed the purse in her saddle bag.

From her perch on top of Trooper, Grace watched Nikki mount Harvey and the men put out the fire. An eerie calm went over the group as its light diminished. The only light around them were the flashlights they each held and the green glow from the light on her mother's blanket.

"You OK, Mom?" Grace asked.

"Yes, Hon. Just ready to be out of here." She answered.

"It's going to take at least an hour or two to get to the top." Grace predicted.

She was right. They walked slowly, stopping occasionally so the men could switch sides of the sled and rest their arms.

Grace continually looked between Nikki and Harvey calmly leading the way into the dark night and her mother who was swinging comfortably behind Trooper. She had fallen asleep just after they started walking.

Grace worked hard to keep the coughing quiet so she didn't disturb her mother, but the cold still gripped her lungs. When they arrived at the road, they continued walking toward the ditch. They took a break and photographed the area. Matt took more flares from his truck and lit them to replace the ones Grace had placed.

Warren and Jessup were there to check on Grace and her mother. They were going to remain on the mountain to repair the road when daylight rose.

Nikki promised to keep him updated, then led the group to the left, up and over the mountain to by-pass the mudslide and road. Parsons was waiting for them on the opposite side; his truck was turned and ready. There was a canopy on his truck giving the group a covered sanctuary for the ride to town. Matt and Lucas transferred the sled and it's passenger into the back. Grace was lifted in next to her, followed by the other three.

Parsons had brought blankets and the cold group thankfully wrapped themselves. The windows between the cab and the back were left open so the heat from the truck could flow through.

"Warren and Jessup will take care of the horses and trucks." Matt told Grace and wrapped his arm around her. His warmth felt good. She turned into his shoulder to muffle the sound of the next coughing fit. When she turned, her mother was looking at her in concern.

"That's gotten bad." She whispered.

"Not as bad as broken ribs and leg." Grace smiled.

"Touché." Her mother sighed.

The truck moved and they all settled into the ride.

"Do you know what this reminds me of?" Nikki smiled down at her aunt.

"Sadie's birth." Her mother answered.

Grace and Matt nodded.

"How could this possibly be like a baby being born?" Lucas asked in bewilderment.

"She was born in the fall branding pasture." Her mother tiredly smiled up at him.

"Little Dingo was born out in the wilderness?" Lucas laughed. "Well, that explains a lot!"

"And, I promise to tell you the story when we get home." She sighed from her cocoon sled.   "But for now, I just need Grayson." Her eyes closed as a tear escaped. No one mentioned it.

Matt cut the rope from around the sled and Grace quickly found her mother's hand and held it tightly. She turned into Matt's shoulder to try and hold back the coughing. It felt like Jack Frost had entered her lungs and was scratching to get out. Another round of coughing couldn't get rid of him.

CHAPTER FOUR

"Matt, I don't want to be moved, I don't want to be picked up, I don't want to be poked, prodded or anything else." His aunt glared at him from the sled. "Just tell Parsons to drive straight to the hospital in Lewiston where my husband is waiting for me."

"Leah, the ambulance…" Matt started, returning her glare.

"NO, tell him to drive to St. Joe's, no stopping." She lowered her voice, trying to demand with her tone and eyes.

"Matt," Grace turned to her cousin, "It's not going to help her by getting her upset, it will make things worse, please stop."

Matt exhaled sharply and rolled his lips tightly. "If we get you in the ambulance, they can go faster."

"NO!" Her mother yelled causing Grace to jump. "I don't want to be moved."

"Matt, stop." Grace gripped his arm.

"Matt, just let her have her way this time." Nikki added in concern.

He sighed and shook his head. "Fine," He grumbled and crawled up to the window between the cab and the canopy. "Drive to St. Joe's, no stopping."

"Thank you." Grace sighed.

They rode in silence until they reached the top of the canyon and came within cell service; all their phone alerts going off at the same time.

Grace quickly reached into her pocket while she held back another cough. Her phone was ringing…it was her dad.

She quickly unlocked the phone and accepted the call.

"Daddy!" Grace answered, her mother's eyes turned quickly to her.

There was silence at first, then a long shaking sigh. "Are you, OK?"

"I am, just a cough, Mom did good. She saved us."

"Gracie…" His voice shook causing goose bumps to rise on her arms.

"I know, Daddy." The tears started to rise again. "You need to talk to Mom…she needs you too. Just a sec…"

Grace placed the phone in her mother's shaking hand.

"Grayson…" Her mom closed her eyes tightly. "Yes…I know…I did what you told me to do if it ever happened…yes…just my leg and ribs…Matt is hopeful there isn't any internal injuries…Grace was a hero…you'll be so proud."

Grace swallowed hard, not allowing herself the tears yet. She needed to be in control and strong for her mother.

"We're just going through Cottonwood; we'll be there in an hour or so." Her mother's eyes opened and looked up at her in concern. "Yes, let them know…where is Sadie…OK…tell her we love her…we'll be there soon…I love you, too." She handed the phone to Grace.

Grace ended the call and looked at her phone, there was a message open. It was the third message she had received prior to the crash. She had thought Jordan sent a picture of Nora and Candace together. It wasn't, Grace chuckled which caused another round of coughing.

"Grace?" Her mother looked in concern.

Grace shook her head and held the message up for her mother to read.

TEXT FROM REILLY: Be Careful, bad feeling

"That boy…" Her mother smiled. "Tell him to be quicker and more specific next time."

Grace smiled and typed the message to him.

She didn't receive a text back from him…the phone rang.

They spoke most of the way into town as she told him and the group in the truck about her climb up the mountain.

Just before they hung up, Reilly informed her that the entire family, Nick, Tessa, Dr. Mark, and more were in the hospital waiting room. "We're waiting for you, Gracie." His voice was reassuring and warmed her inside, which made Jack Frost wake up in her lungs. He ended the call as another round of coughing wracked through her. Matt embraced her tightly.

When they neared the hospital, Matt moved to the window to speak with Parsons.

"What are you doing?" Nikki asked.

"Told him where the ambulance bay is so he can back down it." Matt answered.

"Why?" Grace frowned.

"Because I want the doctors to see you before the family does." Matt said firmly.

"Matt…" Her mom looked up at him. "I…"

"No discussion, Leah." Matt said gruffly. "I let you have your way last time…not this one."

"Matt, I want to see my husband." She glared.

"You spoke with him." Matt countered.

"Matt…" She argued.

"Leah, it's more important for the doctors to see you first. I'll face the wrath of Grayson and the family over this one." He sat back down next to Grace and glared down at his aunt.

"Matt…" She continued to glare.

"If you're not going to do it for yourself," Matt said firmly. "Then do it for the pneumonia that is making its home in Grace's lungs."

Grace gasped, as did her mom and Nikki.

Her mother stared at her in shock then nodded at Matt, "OK." She said softly.

******

Grace sat cross-legged on the emergency room bed and watched the nurses wheel her mother back in the room after getting x-rays. She wanted to move to her but the oxygen tube around her head and up her nose kept her connected to the bed.

"Mom?" Grace called out softly.

She turned and smiled. "I'm fine. The doctor will be in soon to let us know."

The tears started to rise again which put a strain on Grace's lung…another coughing fit started… her mother frowned and looked to the nurse.

"The doctor is working on it." The nurse assured her. "The oxygen will help, and they took x-rays to check for pneumonia, he'll be back in a few minutes."

Grace pulled the blanket up to her shoulders. "Why do they keep it so cold in here?" She asked the nurse.

"I'll get you a warmed blanket and socks for your feet." The nurse responded and turned to her other patient. "How about you?"

"I could use one too." She smiled at Grace.

The nurse left the two of them alone.

"Are they going to keep us here or can we go home?" Grace whispered.

"I'm hoping they send us home."

Grace heard footsteps and, expecting the doctor, she leaned around her mother's curtain and down the hall; her heart raced when she saw her dad; relief on his face as his pace quickened.

Grace threw the blankets off and stretched up for his embrace. His arms were strong around her…squeezing and squeezing tighter. He felt so…safe…so anchored.

"You OK?" He asked leaning back and looking down at her. His blue eyes were anxious.

"Yes," Grace smiled, hoping to reassure him. She took a deep breath, which caused another round of coughing.

His arms wrapped around her tightly; holding her while she coughed.

"That sounds awful." He whispered into her hair.

"It's getting better." She leaned into his chest and they held each other quietly. He felt so warm and made her feel so loved.

She realized he hadn't seen her mom; she would have been hidden behind the curtain so Grace leaned back and looked up at him.

"Mom's behind you." She whispered and his eyes widened in surprise, he turned quickly.

"They said you were getting x-rays." He said as he stepped away from his daughter and toward his wife.

Grace looked around him and saw her mom leaning back onto the pillows. Her lips pressed firmly together and her eyes seemed to plead as her composure began to crack. Tears started to fall as their shaking hands touched.

Grace pulled the oxygen tube over her head and stood quickly to close the curtain; hiding her parents from the world.

"What are you doing?" The nurse appeared at her side.

"My dad…" Grace answered. "They need some time together."

"I understand," The nurse helped her replace the oxygen tubes and Grace crawled back on the bed as the nurse wrapped her in the warm blanket.

"Oh, that's nice." Grace smiled at her.

"I don't think I've ever seen our waiting room so full of people." The nurse smiled as she slid the socks over Grace's feet. She carefully maneuvered them over the bandages which covered a multitude of nasty blisters.

"Can one more come back?"

"How do you choose out of all those people?"

"My sister, Sadie. Mom really needs to see her…so do I." Grace looked hopefully at the nurse.

"I'll see what I can do." She said and disappeared down the hall.

Grace waited…watching…hoping…then a sense of relief flooded through her as Sadie came running down the hall; her long blond hair flying behind her and tears rolling down her cheeks. Grace scooted to the far edge of the bed and her sister climbed up and they hugged tightly.

"That was terrifying." Sadie squeezed.

"It was." Grace sighed.

"Where's Mom?" She leaned back, her blue eyes wide in concern.

"With Dad." Grace nodded to the curtain.

Sadie turned and looked at the curtain. "He was so scared, we all were." She turned back, her blue eyes shimmering from the tears. "They stood in the corner and held hands…they were like statues staring out the window."

"Who?"

"The Trio," Sadie sighed. "Jack wouldn't let us go to them but he sat with us so it was OK. Aunt Jordan and Nora just got here."

"Oh, Sadie," Grace pulled her sister into another hug. "I totally forgot that's how their parents and grandparents died…a crash over a mountain."

"It was really hard, even for Jack, but everyone knew they needed each other. Dad needed them."

The girls sat quietly holding onto each other and staring at the curtain that blocked them from their parents.

The doctor arrived and pulled the curtain back so the sister's caught a glimpse of their dad touching their mother's jaw lightly; caressing. It was a loving touch they had seen between the two a hundred times but none as poignant as this one.

They both looked to the girls and smiled. Sadie ran to her mother as their dad came back to sit with Grace. They listened intently to the doctor; broken leg and ribs…no internal injuries. Grace had acute bronchitis; they would need to watch to make sure it didn't turn into pneumonia.

It took two hours for the temporary cast to be placed on their mom's leg, her ribs to be wrapped carefully and all the paperwork to be completed. Grace was given medicine and strict instructions to get plenty of fluids and rest.

A pair of wheelchairs appeared with nurses standing patiently behind them. Sadie's eyes opened wide and she laughed at the memory of the nurse wanting to roll her out of the hospital after her barrel racing accident; their dad heroically picking her up and walking her out.

Grace grinned; her legs and feet didn't want to take another step so she had no problem crawling into the wheelchair and held her mother's hand as they were wheeled down the hall and to their awaiting family.

******

Grace leaned against the door of the guest bedroom. Aunt Dru's arms were wrapped around her and Sadie was standing next to her, they held hands tightly.

Her dad gently lifted his wife onto the bed. It was 4 o'clock in the morning and they were all in their pajamas getting ready to go to bed for the night…morning.

"All the way over," She smiled up at him. "So the cast is against the wall."

"Why?" He chuckled softly.

She just smiled at him.

When she was happy with her placement she looked at her girls. "Sadie, come here."

Sadie carefully climbed on the bed next to her mother.

"Grace." Her mother smiled.

Grace stiffly walked forward; her dad had to lift her into the bed.

"As far as you can, make room for your father." Her mother whispered and smiled up at him.

Her dad chuckled, eyes looking lovingly at his wife. He placed the covers over the top of his girls and slid in next to Grace. He lay on his side, facing the three of them then his arm stretched across his daughters and held his wife's hand.

"You better be careful, Dru." Her mom smiled.

"About what?" Aunt Dru asked.

"This hasn't been a good year for the women in Grayson's life. He may lock you in a padded room for the rest of the year." She sighed and closed her eyes.

"I may just put myself in there willingly." Aunt Dru smiled, turned off the light and closed the door.

Grace lay safely…warmly wrapped in the love of her family. In the few moments her eyes were open, she realized there was no other place she wanted to be…and would never leave…not even for college.

CHAPTER FIVE

It was so warm…and quiet…she couldn't be more comfortable and refused to open her eyes. But then she moved causing shoots of pain through her leg muscles and up into the small of her back. She froze and sighed. It really did happen, it wasn't just a nightmare. Images of the mountainside flying by flashed in her mind and the image of the trees approaching…then the moment of impact and her mother's scream.

Grace's eyes flew open to check on her mother; luckily she was facing her and didn't have to move.

She was sleeping soundly, her chest rising and falling in deep breathes. Sadie was curled up next to her, she was awake, staring at the ceiling…tears slowly sliding down into her blond hair.

Grace reached out and touched Sadie's arm; her sister turned tear filled-eyes to her then rolled as Grace pulled her close. Small, quiet sobs, escaped Sadie as she tucked her face into Grace's shoulder.

Grace tried to reassure her but started quietly coughing instead. Her dad's arm came across them and he pulled them in closer, holding them tightly until Grace's coughing and Sadie's tears stopped.

Grace checked her mother's breathing…still sleeping.

"Are you OK, Gracie?" He whispered.

Afraid she would start coughing again and wake her mother, she just nodded.

"Sadie?" He whispered.

"I'm OK. I just got scared and sad." She whispered.

"Let's go in the kitchen so Grace can have some food and take her medicine." He slowly slid out of bed and helped Grace stand.

"My legs really hurt." Grace grimaced. "Now I wish I had gone jogging with Matt and gotten in shape."

"I promise, we won't tell him that." Sadie giggled and their dad smiled while watching his wife, making sure she remained sleeping.

"What about, Mom?" Grace asked; concerned about leaving her alone.

"I bet there are a dozen people out there that will come sit with her for a few minutes while you eat." He helped her walk to the door.

"I wasn't left alone for days." Sadie reminded them.

As soon as the door was open, Nikki, Aunt Dru, Tessa, Aunt Jordan, and Cora hurried down the hall.

Her dad and sister were on each side of Grace as she walked down the hall; each gently holding an elbow. The abused muscles and sores from the blisters on her feet and ankles screamed at her. Her feet felt like they were ten times the size of normal. They felt so heavy…like she was trying to lift buckets of water from the bottom of the ocean.

"She's still sleeping." Her dad whispered to the women. "I gave her a pain killer about an hour ago so she'll be out for a while."

They nodded and after some gentle hugs from Aunt Dru and Cora the two women walked into the guest room.

"I'm going to have to sit on something soft." Grace sighed.

"We'll get you in the living room on the nice soft couch." Her dad gently lifted her and carried her into the room.

"I'll get you something to eat." Aunt Jordan turned to the kitchen.

"Can I go back to Mom after I eat?" Grace asked, she already felt the strong desire to see her…even if it had only been a minute.

"Yes, you'll need to get some more rest." He nodded.

Twenty minutes later she had food in her stomach, the medicine taken and was lying back in the bed with her mother. She stared at the rising and lowering of her mother's chest. She was still in a deep sleep. That was good…she wouldn't hurt that way. Grace's eyes closed.

She heard whispering and her eyes flew open. Her mother was looking over the top of her then glanced down to her.   Her eyes were stressed, as if in pain.

"Are you OK?" Grace asked and grimaced when she went to move. The pain shot through the muscles in her legs and up into her back.

"About the same as you." Her mother said softly.

Grace rolled onto her back and looked up into the eyes of her dad.

"How's my girl?" He asked with an exhausted smile.

"Tired," She whispered, which started her throat to tickle and her lungs to hurt…the coughs rolled out and lasted a good five minutes.

Her mother reached for her hand, her father knelt by the bed and they waited patiently for the coughs to cease.

"Sorry…" She whispered.

"Here…" He helped her sit up, put a pillow behind her back and handed her a coffee cup. "It's hot…well very warm tea. Cora said it will help keep things cleared up in there."

Grace took a few sips then nodded as she looked back to her mother. "Are you OK?"

She nodded, "I hurt…which would be shocking if I didn't."

"It's barely been 24 hours." He informed them.

"We slept all day?" Grace asked in surprise.

"Yes, and you'll sleep all night tonight and then all day tomorrow." He ordered with a smile.

"I got no problem with that." Grace smiled.

"It must be the pain killers speaking…but I don't have a problem with that either." Her mom sighed and closed her eyes.

Grace took another sip of tea and handed it to her dad. She smiled then rolled onto her side and cuddled into her mother's arm…making sure not to hurt her.

******

She could hear whispering again but didn't open her eyes. Every time she woke, her dad was there, hovering, taking care of them, and getting more stressed. Now she understood what Sadie had said about the whole family looking tired after her accident. As much as she loved him and needed him…he really needed a break.

Grace took the chance and opened one eye…her mother was awake, looking over the top of her again…but she wasn't the one whispering. So, Grace turned her head. Her dad and Sadie were sitting next to each other in the two small cushioned chairs reading a newspaper and talking softly. Sadie pointed at the paper and he shook his head.

"That's this Saturday," He whispered.

"I know…" Sadie answered. "We can pick one up and take care of it this winter."

"Pick what up?" Grace asked making both their heads look up in surprise.

Their eyes went to her then past her.

"You're both awake!" Sadie grinned but didn't get up.

"How are you feeling?" Her dad asked them, he remained seated too.

"Hungry." Grace answered.

"Me, too." Her mom answered.

"Well then," Cora said from the door. "I'll go fix you something to eat."

Grace hadn't seen her…she wondered who else was in the room and twisted her head around.

"She just walked in the door." Sadie smiled, understanding what she was doing.

"Good timing." Her mother said.

"What were you picking up?" Grace didn't move from her comfortable position on the soft mattress and under the warm comforter.

"There is a special Saturday horse auction this weekend at the stockyards." Sadie answered.

"You have plenty of horses." Her mother said.

"This would be for experience." Sadie explained. "We can buy one, take care of it and train it over the winter. Then sell it this spring; a project horse."

"We have to use our own money, split it evenly." Grace said. The thought was exciting.

"You, me, Nora, and Nikki," Sadie nodded. "The start of our super horse business."

"I know they would both agree." Grace ignored the aches and pains to roll onto her side, facing her dad and sister. "If we get one that isn't perfect now…needs help…and then present him for sale in really good condition…we could make a good profit. It'll show what we can do…even though we're still young."

Her dad smiled.

"Does that mean you agree?" Grace asked him and Sadie glanced up at him quickly.

"It means that I'm glad to see your sense of business come out." He answered.

Grace returned his smile. She had been working with Jack the last couple of years at The Stables. Between him and Aunt Dru, they were teaching her well…just like they did with Nikki.

She didn't need to go to college…she could just learn from family.

"We'll have to track everything we feed him and the cost." Grace told Sadie. "Anything we buy for his upkeep and the amount of time we spend with him."

"Can we?" Sadie looked over to her mom then up to her dad.

"As long as your father goes with you," Her mother answered which made him shake his head. "I will have enough people to take care of me…you can send me pictures so I can feel a part of it."

Sadie nodded excitedly. "But, you have to let us choose the horse." She looked up at their dad.

He was still frowning at his wife.

"It will only take a couple of hours…" Their mom said.

"It can take all day." He corrected her; he was well practiced at horse auctions.

"I will be fine." She stated flatly. "Between Cora, Dru, and Jordan; the three of them will have no problem taking care of me."

"Leah…" He sighed impatiently.

"Grayson," She returned with a 'don't fight me on this' look.

Grace and Sadie remained quiet; they had seen this 'war of wills' many times.

They were quiet long enough, staring at each other, that Grace finally decided to break it up. She moved the covers off her and slowly sat up.

Sadie and their dad rose to help her.

"I just need to go to the restroom." Grace hobbled into the room.

When she emerged, it was just her mom lying in the bed.

"Where did they go?"

"To fix us some lunch…or dinner…I'm not really sure what time it is." Her mother chuckled.

Grace checked her phone. "I think it will be breakfast." She grinned.

"Seriously…" Her mother sighed then looked at the two empty chairs with the newspaper sitting on one. "Hand me the advertisements."

"OK." Grace grabbed the whole paper then she slid back under the covers.

The newspaper was tossed aside and just a flyer was kept.

"Phone…" Her mom reached out a hand.

Grace handed her the phone then watched as she typed something into it.

"Who are you texting?" Grace asked when she saw the slight smile on her mother's face.

"Dru and Jordan."

Within minutes Aunt Jordan was walking through the door with the computer tablet. She too had a smile on her face.

"Breakfast will be a little delayed," She said then turned to Grace. "Everyone at barrels last night sent you best wishes and glad you're both alright."

"What?" Grace and her mother both gasped.

"That should be tonight." Grace said in surprise.

"It's Thursday morning ladies, not Wednesday." Aunt Jordan chuckled.

"He's been here all that time?" Her mom asked and knew she was talking about her dad.

Aunt Jordan nodded. "Full support of your plan."

"What plan?" Grace asked looking back at her mother.

"Is Scott around?" Her mom asked.

"He wouldn't leave either." Her aunt nodded.

"Anything you need?" Her mother asked her aunt.

"For what?" Grace was really confused.

"I'll be round 2 if this one doesn't work." Aunt Jordan grinned. "Dru said anything you want in the living room, she likes the no-media room the way it is, I do, too."

"I do, too." Her mother nodded and started working on the tablet.

Aunt Jordan left and Grace raised herself on the pillows to watch her mother. She started smiling and nodding when she saw what her mother was doing.

"Which one do you want? Pick one for Sadie and Nora." Her mother chuckled.

Grace dialed the number for her mother and listened to her for the next half hour and couldn't wait to see the look on her dad's face.

The phone call had ended and the computer was on the side table before Sadie and her dad appeared with two trays full of food.

"Sorry it took so long." Sadie said as she waited for her mother's tray to be placed in front of her, then she held out Grace's tray and their dad placed it carefully in front of her.

"Dru insisted we wait for biscuits…which Cora quickly made from scratch." Her dad said tersely.

The food smelled delicious and made her stomach rumble so she dug into it while watching her parents.

"You have about two hours before a delivery arrives." Her mother smiled sweetly at her dad.

His brows furrowed in confusion. "What?"

"I ordered some furniture while you were in the kitchen." She continued with her sweet tone.

He sighed and shook his head, "Leah…what could you possibly think you had to have right now?"

"Well," Her mother smiled at him. "Since this room seems to be sick bay; I ordered a sleeper sofa for in here."

He glanced at the two chairs, which Grace was sure he had been sleeping in, and nodded, "Sounds good."

"Oh, that's not all." Her mom smiled, her blue eyes shining with innocence.

He turned back and looked at her with narrowed eyes; he knew something was up.

"There are five new dressers for the kids coming, a new loveseat for the living room, and an entertainment center for the living room that will need to be assembled." The sweet smile remained.

"Is that all?" He asked in a very cool controlled tone.

"Well…no." Came the answer and his shoulders went up. "And a complete new bedroom set for us."

He stared. Grace couldn't quite tell what he was thinking but his jaw tightened and the muscles twitched.

"I get a new dresser?" Sadie said excitedly.

"I picked out matching ones for all three of us and boy ones for Reilly and Wade." Grace smiled, and then grinned when her dad's frown moved to her. She shrugged slowly and looked apologetically to him.

"Most of that goes up those stairs." He finally said.

"Really…hmmm…I guess I didn't realize that." Her mom gave him a slight innocent shrug. "They'll be here around 10:30."

He continued to stare at her.

"You may want to move the other stuff out before they get here." She said as an afterthought and took a bite of biscuit.

"I'll help, Dad!" Sadie said excitedly.

He looked down at her, "You won't be the only one." He turned and walked out with Sadie following. Just a few steps out the door he yelled, "Scott!"

Grace and her mother glanced at each other with guilty grins and finished their breakfast.

*****

"I think they're tired." Aunt Dru grinned from the doorway. Her stressed blue eyes were shining. "I told Jack to have Reilly go to The Stables after school. Nick is up at the ranch helping Jessup."

Grace and her mom chuckled.

"He'll complain, but inside he's thankful he has something to do." Her mom sighed tiredly.

"I'll sleep on that new sleeper sofa and let Dad sleep here with you." Grace suggested, having no desire to leave her mother's side. "At least he'll get a good night's sleep."

"I agree, Hon." Her mother nodded. "If it was him lying here, I wouldn't be sleeping anywhere else either."

"I don't know why we didn't think of changing out the two chairs last spring when Sadie was hurt." Aunt Dru said.

"Where did the chairs go?" Grace asked.

"Your room," Aunt Dru told her. "Sadie asked for them and there was room. The dressers are headed up to the bunkhouse to replace the older ones up there."

"I'm tired of this bed." Her mom sighed. "I need a bath. If I get to cuddle my husband tonight, I want to smell good."

Aunt Dru chuckled, "I'll get Jordan. Between the two of us we should be able to get you a bath. We just have to do it while Grayson is upstairs and busy."

While her aunts took care of her mother, Cora changed the sheets on the bed and Grace lay on the new sofa bed. She hadn't checked her phone messages since right after they were rescued. She thumbed through all the get well texts until she crossed a number she didn't recognize.

TEXT FROM UNKNOWN: Grace, are you OK?

The same text five times over the last couple days. She looked at the number again and didn't recognize it so she sent the number to Reilly. Within minutes he responded with an IDK.

She sent the number to a few friends from school. They didn't know either.

There were no missed calls from that number, just the text. She shook her head, if they were important they would call back. She moved on to her Facebook page that had 214 new messages and pictures sent to make her feel better. She didn't respond to any of them, she wasn't ready yet and if she responded to one, she would have to respond to all of them. Guilt would make her.

She typed in one status update to everyone thanking them for all the well wishes then quickly closed it down as her aunts helped her mother back into the bed.

Her mother had taken a pain killer before the bath so she promptly fell to sleep once she was comfortable.

Grace lay on the small bed and watched her sleeping…watched her breathing. The thought of leaving her mother…she didn't ever want to leave again…she didn't want to be away…in case something else happened.

******

"Hello, Your Highness."

"Well, hello Your Highness." Grace laughed as Nora walked into the room and plopped down next to her on the bed.

She had started wearing her long straight black hair in two pony tails that were captured toward the back and base of her neck. Her dark brown eyes were shining in humor.

"I can't believe you both are Queens!" Her mother smiled from the big bed. "Although the 'Your Highness' title may not work out in this family."

"Well, that's a bummer." Nora dramatically sighed. "Especially when The Princess joins us."

"Candace is coming down?" Grace asked.

Nora nodded, "Next week for Sadie's birthday. Paige already had plans for them for this weekend so she can't go to the auction with us."

"The auction! That's going to be fun!" Grace smiled at her mother. "Is Dad going with us?"

She shrugged her shoulders as he walked in the door.

"I'm not going anywhere." He said flatly and looked down at them.

"But Dad…" Grace sighed.

"How does the furniture look?" Her mother changed the subject.

He smiled at her then looked down at Nora. "Well, since you weren't involved in this…"

"In what?" Nora asked with an impending doom look.

"The furniture conspiracy…" He smiled wickedly at Grace.

Grace and her mother laughed.

"Be thankful Nora is here right now." He tilted his head and raised his brows.

"Why?" Grace asked…suddenly worried.

"Because she is the only reason I'm giving you a five second warning before I tell your mother what I think of the new bedroom set." He stepped away from the door.

"Dad!" Grace shrieked, she knew he wasn't joking so she threw the covers off.

"Oh gross!" Nora scrambled off the bed and turned quickly to help Grace.

"Now Leah…" He chuckled as he approached his laughing wife.

"It's not been 5 seconds!" Grace screamed as she and Nora barely made it to the door and slammed it shut behind them.

"Oh the horror!" Nora laughed.

"Just makes me shudder." Grace added as she stiffly walked down the long hallway to the kitchen. It was one time she didn't mind leaving her mother's side.

"What's going on?" Reilly appeared at the end of the hall.

"You truly DO NOT want to know!" Nora shook her head.

He looked down the hall at the closed door and laughed, "You're probably right."

"Sadie and I talked to Nikki about the auction while you were sleeping." Nora told her as they sat around the small kitchen table. "She's all for it and excited."

Grace nodded and looked at the clock; 5:00. Cora would be fixing dinner soon.

"When is Nikki coming down?" Grace asked. She hoped Nikki would sway her mom about not having to have her dad there if Nikki was at the auction with them.

"Not until Saturday morning; early." Reilly answered. "She has a couple horses she's taking care of and doesn't want to leave them by themselves too long. Josey will be going over a couple times during the day to check on them."

"Lucas is gone?" Grace asked.

"He and Nick left this morning for Australia." Reilly answered.

"Matt?" Nora asked.

"At the ranch right now, but he and Kevin were doing some training stuff for search and rescue this weekend." Reilly answered.

"Does everyone check in with you before they leave?" Grace laughed.

Reilly grinned and nodded, "I think they should…at least with Cora. We can have a big chart on the wall."

"Instead of 'Where's Waldo', it can be 'Where's the Tagger Today'." Nora joined the laughter.

Aunt Dru and Uncle Scott walked in the back door but walked down the hall to the guest room.

"Ya better knock first!" Grace called out to them.

They both turned and looked surprised she was in the kitchen then stopped before the door and hesitated. Aunt Dru's laugh echoed down the hall as she knocked.

Her dad opened the door and the two joined them…the door was then closed.

"Why do you think they closed the door?" Grace mused.

"I don't know." Nora and Reilly said in unison.

"It's not like you can overhear anyone from down there." Grace frowned.

"Sadie's birthday is next weekend…" Nora shrugged.

"I haven't heard anything on what they are doing for her." Reilly nodded as all three continued to stare at the closed door.

"Where is she?" Grace asked.

"Her and Wade are in the barn."

The bedroom door opened and her dad walked out, closing the door behind him.

Reilly's phone started ringing.

"Another family member checking in with you." Nora said as he answered it.

Grace smiled at the grin on her dad's face as he walked towards her.

"I don't think I've seen you move that fast in a long time, Gracie." He teased.

"That was just sick and wrong, Dad." She shook her head at him.

He looked up at Reilly and his grin disappeared. Grace turned…Reilly was looking at her dad with a shocked expression…something was wrong.

CHAPTER SIX

"What? Are you sure?" He said on the phone. Reilly's eyes were wide as he looked to Grace then to her dad again. "Ok."

Reilly handed the phone to her dad, who looked at him quizzically. Before putting the phone to his ear, he looked at the front of it then back to Reilly, his frown deepened.

"What?" He said gruffly into the phone.

Grace looked curiously to Reilly who just stared at her dad.

The conversation was completely one-sided since her dad didn't speak. He looked at Grace then to Reilly, back to Grace.

After a few quiet minutes he finally spoke, "Here only."

He tossed the phone to Reilly, turned without a word, and headed down the hallway.

"Dad?" Grace stood to follow him and glanced back at Reilly who had the phone back to his ear. He was looking out the kitchen window.

Nora shrugged; she looked surprised and confused, too.

"Stay there. I just need to talk to your mother." He walked into the guest bedroom and shut the door.

Grace stopped, turned to Reilly and held up her arms as if to say what.

He finally turned from the window as he ended the call.

"What?!" Grace asked, walking stiffly back to him.

"Levi."

"Levi, what?"

"It was Levi on the phone."

"Levi talked to Dad!?" Grace's jaw dropped and she stared at him. Reilly and Levi hadn't spoken since the New Year's Eve fiasco when Allen gave her alcohol without her knowledge. She hadn't spoken to Levi since their meeting at Home Depot a couple days later.

Reilly nodded, he wasn't smiling…nor was he frowning…she couldn't tell how he felt about it.

"So? What did he want?" Grace turned and looked down the hall at the closed door.

Reilly didn't answer so she positioned herself directly in front of him, toe to toe.

"Reilly, tell me. What did Levi talk to Dad about and why did Dad say 'only here'?"

"He asked Grayson if he could come over to visit you."

Again the shock ran through her. "Dad agreed?"

Reilly nodded and stepped around her. "He'll be here in an hour." He walked out the back door.

Grace turned as the door to the hallway from her mother's temporary room opened. Aunt Dru and Uncle Scott walked out, their face's unreadable. They turned and walked out the side door of the house.

Frustrated, Grace walked down the hall.

"I would really like to go upstairs to my own room." Her mother said as Grace walked in the doorway.

She looked at Grace. "Did Reilly tell you?"

Grace nodded and looked at her dad who was sitting on the edge of the bed.

"I should have asked if you wanted to see him first." He said.

"Of course I do." Grace nodded. She missed him. She had always liked Levi more than Allen and could never understand how she ended up with Allen...which turned into the huge mistake.

"There are conditions." Her dad stated.

"Only here." Grace nodded.

"He also said he would treat you with the up most respect you deserve…if he doesn't…" Her dad warned.

"He will." Grace nodded anxiously.

"This is his only chance." Her mother told her.

"He knows what he did wrong…and has been sorry from the beginning." Grace assured them.

"He said that," He nodded, looking at her in concern. "It's the ONLY reason I agreed to this. That and he asked me personally. He was concerned enough about you, to ask me, so he could see that you're OK."

"It shows he has honest concern." Her mother had a slight smile.

"Thank you, Dad." Grace smiled. "I promise, it will be OK."

"You best go do something with that hair then." He chuckled.

Grace's hands automatically went to her head. "Ack!" She turned and as quickly as her stiff legs would move she headed down the hall.

"Nora said Levi was coming." Sadie said as they met in the kitchen.

"Yes, he is…I have to get ready." Grace turned and looked up the stairs; she groaned.

Sadie took her arm and helped her up the steps.

"I'll go Dingo on him if he hurts you again."

"He didn't hurt me in the first place, Allen did."

"You know what I mean, Grace." Sadie said tersely.

"I do and I love you for it." Grace smiled.

She showered and carefully assessed what to wear. She wanted to impress Levi but didn't want to upset her dad. Black leggings which would cover the bandages on her feet and ankles; she would have to go without shoes. Then a brown loose fitting sweater dress that stopped just at the top of her knees. She was completely covered but still looked stylish. Both Levi and her dad should approve.

Then the makeup; just enough to highlight but not enough to make her dad uncomfortable, everything had to go perfect. She didn't want to make her dad upset so Levi would be able to come back. Hair was left loose and hung stylishly to her shoulders; the way both Levi and her dad liked.

Sadie had kept her company and walked with her down the stairs to help if needed. They had just made it to the bottom step when the lights to a truck shown down the driveway. The dark night was brightened when the large area light switched on, showing a red truck. Levi stepped out and was greeted by Reilly.

"He is cute." Sadie whispered.

"He is." Grace stared at him through the window. He had grown taller and seemed more mature than the last time she had seen him at a distance; about six months before at a rodeo. He had gone from cute…to handsome. She suddenly became nervous.

They waited in the kitchen as Reilly and Levi walked to the back door.

Her dad walked out of the bedroom and made his way to her; his expression showing his approval of her clothes.

He made it to her as Reilly, then Levi, stepped into the kitchen.

Levi grinned at Grace, his shoulders lowered as he relaxed when he saw her. He turned to her dad and quickly stretched out his hand.

"Thank you, Sir." Levi's voice was deeper and more confident then she remembered. His expression was tense.

Her dad nodded and shook his hand.

Levi's eyes went to Grace then back to her dad. "How is Mrs. Tagger?"

"It's been a tough couple of days but she's doing better." Her dad answered. "She hates lying around with nothing to do."

"I'm very relieved they are alright." Levi said and glanced, with a smile, to Grace. "I couldn't believe it when I heard about it. Did they get the road fixed?"

"Jessup worked on it." Her dad answered. "He had to cut into the mountain by quite a bit…they have a state engineer coming out to look at it."

They moved into the living room to sit. Sadie, Reilly, Levi, Grace and her dad talked comfortably for an hour about the accident, the ranch, and about roping. Cora appeared briefly, nodded, then went to the kitchen to start dinner.

Her dad finally excused himself and walked down the hall to her mother.

She grinned at Levi and he sighed happily. It had to be going well or her dad wouldn't have left the room.

"Come on Sadie; let's get everyone something to drink." Reilly took her by the wrist and drug her reluctant sister out of the room. Sadie glared a warning at Levi.

As soon as they were alone, Levi turned to Grace with anxious eyes. "Grace, you look beautiful."

She felt her veins warm…she just knew she blushed.

"I was so worried…I just had to see you." He continued.

"I'm glad you called," She said honestly, enjoying the look on his handsome face, his blue eyes…she remembered back to the first moment she met him at the roping clinic.

"I've been wanting to call…dialed your number quite a few times but never followed through."

"I understand…I did the same thing."

"I just thought the more time that went by; the easier it would be with your family." He said earnestly. "I didn't want to have to sneak around like we did at Home Depot."

"Me either."

"But after the accident…I realized life was too short. I couldn't wait any longer. I had to see you and take the chance with your family."

"Going directly to Dad was the right thing."

He nodded, his eyes looking concerned. "Is this what you want Grace?"

Grace sighed. After his mistake of not considering her feelings at New Year's and landing her in the predicament with Allen, that was the perfect question for him to ask.

"Yes," She smiled which caused his whole body to relax and his eyes to shine a little more.

Reilly and Sadie returned and the discussion turned to roping and rodeos.

Grace tried to assess the feelings between Reilly and Levi. As far as she knew, the last time they saw each other was the split second in Home Depot when Reilly had found them together. Before that, was at the party when Reilly threw Levi to the ground and broke his cheek bone in anger for Levi's part in Allen's attack on her.

They seemed calm and relaxed. She didn't feel any turmoil between the two of them…specifically Reilly.

"What about Sunday?" Reilly was asking her.

"What?" Grace chuckled. From the looks on their faces, they knew she wasn't paying any attention.

"How are you for Sunday's roping jackpot?" Reilly asked.

Grace shook her head. There was no way her legs and lungs would be healed enough to ride.

"How about you rope with Reilly?" Sadie suggested. She must have decided Levi wasn't a threat to Grace anymore.

Levi looked at Reilly, who nodded. That gesture made her feel good.

Levi turned to Grace, "Not without your dad's approval."

"My approval for what?" Her dad walked into the living room carrying her mom.

Levi quickly stood to make way for her on the soft couch which was next to the chair Grace was sitting on.

Grace and Sadie gathered pillows to place around their mother and under her casted leg.

Once she was positioned comfortably she turned to Levi. "Grayson's approval for what?" She asked warily.

"I can't ride at Sunday's jackpot," Grace started. "Sadie suggested Levi ride with Reilly to take my place for the day."

Her parents exchanged a glance and finally nodded.

"I think it's a good idea." Her dad agreed.

Grace wanted to grin but kept her face calm…poker face. She turned to Levi, "You're a header, you can ride my horse instead of hauling yours down if you want."

"You'll enjoy riding Buttercup," Her dad smirked. "Especially when you have to tell someone the name of the horse you're riding."

They all laughed softly.

"Luckily, most everyone there already knows her." Grace grinned.

As they discussed the details, Grace glanced around the room. Her mother was on the couch with her dad at the far end; his hand resting easily on the ankle of her good leg. Sadie and Reilly sat on the new loveseat across from her and Levi sat on the edge of the large recliner. They all seemed relaxed.

When Levi stood to leave, Grace slowly rose and walked with him and Reilly to the backdoor.   She and Levi smiled at each other and said goodnight.

The door closed and Grace turned to Reilly, "You OK with this?"

"I'm trying, Gracie." He nodded, his blue eyes looking concerned. "Honestly, I've missed him as a friend but I just don't know if I can get past what happened. One chance, Grace; that's all he's got."

"I agree." She sighed as they made their way back to the living room.

"That seemed to go well," Her mother was leaning comfortably into the cushions.

Grace looked to her dad; he nodded.

"I like the new loveseat." Grace said as she sat on it next to Sadie, "…and the entertainment center."

She giggled at the look on her dad's face.

"Which brings us to tomorrow and Saturday…," Her mother smiled at her husband.

"Leah…" He started.

"It's totally up to you." She smiled back at him.

"What is?" He frowned, knowing he wasn't going to like what she had to say.

"You have a choice. You, Dru, and Scott can either leave in the morning and go to the ranch for the day…"

"Leah, I'm not leaving." He sighed in frustration.

"Or, I can go furniture shopping again." She finished.

Grace's eyes opened wide and she rolled her lips together to keep from laughing.

He rolled his eyes, knowing she was serious. "You don't need anything more."

"That's true," She nodded innocently. "But Dru and Jordan were admiring the new bedroom set and are thinking they might need new ones too."

He chuckled and shook his head, "The furniture conspiracy expands? You brought them into it, too."

She stretched a hand out to him and he knelt next to her and took it gently. "They are as concerned about you and Scott, as I am. Actually, I'm quite concerned about Dru too…she has the poker face going. You three relived a terrible moment and you need to go see the road work and mountain mud slide for yourself. You need time on the ranch and with Eli. I am OK now and so is Grace." She assured him. "We will be right here, safe and sound while you're gone."

"Leah…" His voice trailed off, he was beginning to give in to her demands. He looked up at Grace with slightly anguished eyes then back to his wife.

"Grayson," She whispered and pulled his hand to her chest so she could look deeper into his eyes. "You have to let go a little. Trust that Jordan, Cora, Tessa…and the rest of them can take care of us. You have to let go, you have to trust them."

He swallowed hard and nodded. "I do, Leah. I do trust them, I just…" His voice trailed away as he leaned into her open arms.

Sadie, Grace, and Reilly quickly left the room.

CHAPTER SEVEN

"How do you plan to get up there?" Josey asked.

Grace stared at Buttercup and wondered why she suddenly looked 10 feet tall today. The cream colored horse was standing calmly eating her morning ration of grain.

"You can just boost me up like normal." Grace sighed. For a control freak, not having control of your own sore body was very frustrating.

"Why don't we get a ladder?"

Grace laughed, "Just pick up my foot and boost."

Josey bent behind her to cradle Grace's foot in her hands. In one, not so graceful lift, Grace was boosted up onto the patient horse's bare back.

"Uuugghhh…" Grace groaned as the sore muscles screamed at her. Laying on her belly, she dangled her head on one side of the horse and her slipper covered feet on the other.

"I told you." Josey laughed.

"Grab a leg and pull it over her rump," Grace sighed.

"It's a good thing you're in sweat pants so they stretch." Josey lifted Grace's foot up and over the horse's rump.

Grace twisted so she was laying on top her horse; arms resting on each side and her face resting on her withers. The warmth of the mare was soothing. She grinned at Josey who sat on the straw bale they had pulled into the stall for a seat.

Josey's brown hair was pulled back into a ponytail which made her dark eyes stand out. She looked like Nikki…sort of…but then sometimes she didn't at all.

"I love it up here," Grace grinned.

"I do that with Apollo," Josey admitted. "Sometimes there isn't anything more healing than the warmth and love of your horse."

They sat quietly for a moment.

"How's it going with you and Matt?" Grace asked.

Josey shrugged a shoulder, "Good and bad."

"What's that mean?"

"I love being around Matt and miss him when he isn't there. He is so much fun. We moved the Circle 50 heifers to the winter pasture last week; just the two of us. We forgot about everything and everyone and just had a great day." Josey leaned against the stall wall, stretched out her legs and stared at her boots. "I want that every day, that's why I keep trying. I know we have a future together, but I just…" She exhaled. "I don't know what the holdup is in my head; why I can't get my mother out of it."

"Matt said he'd wait for you."

"Yeah, but for how long?" Josey glanced at Grace. "I have to figure out how to walk at his side and not behind him. Once he pointed it out, I knew he was right and Grayson agreed with him, too."

"I hate to say it, but I have no idea how to help you." Grace sighed.

Josey smirked, "Well, what kind of a friend are you?"

They chuckled at each other then became silent. Buttercup finished eating and turned her head to Josey who quickly cupped her muzzle in her hands and stroked the soft hairs. Grace closed her eyes to concentrate on the warmth coming from the horse. Her mind went to her mother.

"Where's your head?" Josey asked.

"Wow," Grace chuckled and opened her eyes to grin at her friend. "You've been around Dad too much."

Josey laughed, "Yes, I hear that question a lot."

"I was wishing Mom was here so I could see her."

"She's on the sofa in the living room, cuddling with Sadie and Nora. Supposedly watching a movie but Leah's eyes are closed."

"I haven't slept this much in…forever." Grace sighed, her hand moving gently over the horse's hair.

"Well, your body went through a lot, so did your brain; making the climb and worrying about Leah."

"I guess…"

"How are you handling it all?"

Grace sighed, "I don't know…sometimes it just feels like a bad dream…until I move and the pain in my legs and back shoot through me. I ended up with huge blisters on my feet from the boots, too."

"I've never gone through an emergency thing like that." Josey said, nearly whispering. "Telling Grayson about it…I don't ever want to do that again."

"I'm sorry, Josey."

"It's not your fault the road washed out. When I hung up the phone with Matt I went to Grayson's jacket. He'd taken it off in the building and I took the keys out of the pocket so he wouldn't be able to drive."

"That was smart." Grace said. "I don't think I would have thought of doing that. What did you say?"

"I told him that you were both alright but you had been in an accident and Matt was taking care of you. He turned white and looked like he was going to throw up so I yelled at the boys to load the horses."

"Who was there?"

"Alex, Wade, and the boy with one arm."

"Vic?"

"Yeah, Grayson was helping him with a new horse he just bought." Josey said. "We loaded Snickers and Dollar then, while we drove to The Homestead to drop them off, I told him what actually happened."

"What did he say?"

"Nothing…he didn't say anything…just got the horses unloaded, trailer unhitched, and everyone that was in the house climbed into the truck and I drove them to the hospital. Cora had gone over to the B&B office and collected everyone there to drive them. When we got to the hospital, Grayson stood in the corner of the waiting room with Scott and Dru staring out the window and holding onto his phone…waiting.

"You know about the other accident?"

"Nikki and Matt had already told me."

They were quiet, deep in their own thoughts. Grace couldn't help but think about what could have happened.   The desire to see her mother increased.

"I want to go in with Mom."

Josey nodded, "I do, too."

******

Grace sat cross-legged on her sofa bed in the guest room and placed the phone in the middle of the circle created by her, Sadie, and Nora. Her mother and Aunt Jordan watched from the large bed.

"Can you hear us Nikki?" Grace leaned down to the phone.

"Yes." Nikki's voice boomed from the speaker on the phone.

"OK," Grace grinned. "This is our first official meeting for the super horse business."

She glanced around to see the very happy faces looking back at her.

"Yay!" Nikki's voice came from the phone.

Nora and Sadie clapped.

"OK," Grace said again, "As the business manager of our company, I will lead the meeting. Due to all our schedules, we promised to buy only one horse to start. So we need to decide how much we should spend. Then what type of horse we want that works for all three of you; one that needs a nutrition plan, exercise plan, and training. "

"If we buy this weekend, when do we sell?" Nora asked.

Sadie nodded, "How much time do we have to work with him?"

"We want to sell in a public forum instead of a private sale, so more people see what we accomplished." Nikki told them. "There is a spring auction in May at the stockyards or we can sell at the Horse Expo at the indoor arena in March."

"Well," Grace grinned at Sadie and Nora. "I happen to be busy the first weekend in May…I have a wedding to attend."

A very happy giggle boomed from the phone. "I'll be gone for a two week honeymoon after that."

"Plus graduation at the end of the month." Nora smiled at Grace.

"And, state rodeo finals then too." Grace nodded.

"So it's the March expo then." Sadie concluded. "That's best because we have a whole week to show it off, plus in a big arena instead of just the little show ring. The horse expo lets us show him off each night; Tuesday team roping, Wednesday is barrels, Thursday is team penning. Then, on Saturday, a preview where we'll have time to show him off really well."

"Do you think he can do all of that?" Grace asked.

"Sure," Nora nodded. "He doesn't have to be perfect; he just has to show he's willing."

"And another thing," Nikki said. "We need a gelding so we don't have a surprise pregnancy with a mare and definitely no stallion."

"Agreed," The three on the bed nodded.

"We have to be aware of how much trained horses sell for too," Nikki added.

Grace nodded, "We don't want to buy one for too much now, put a winter's feed and training in him and not be able to make our money back at the sale."

"Agreed," Sadie and Nora nodded.

They ended their first meeting after Nikki promised to be at The Homestead by 7:30 the next morning so they could be at the stockyards by 8:00 to preview the horses; the tack auction started at 10:00 and the horse auction started at 11:00.

They arrived at the stockyards at 7:55 very excited and anxious for the day.

Nikki drove with Sadie, Grace, and Nora as her passengers.

The Trio had arrived back to the house the night before and they, plus Jack, arrived in the truck right behind the happy business owners. And, much to the business owner's delight, Dr. Mark had joined them so he would be available if they had questions.

They slowly walked down each aisle and looked in each pen. The third pen made them stop. Inside was a red and white paint pony; only 14 hands tall. He was underweight, held his head low, and looked half asleep.

"He looks exhausted," Sadie whispered.

Grace stepped into the pen and stroked the horse's neck. A woman stepped in next to her.

"That's my kids' horse." The woman declared. "They've outgrown him."

"They?" Sadie asked with a raised brow.

"Yep, four of them. He's been a good pony for them. Doesn't do much but walk or run a trail but they had fun." The woman smiled.

The Tagger girls nodded and walked away.

"He probably needs more training to do more than just go from a walk to a run." Nora said.

"Plus nutrition and exercise; after a week or two of rest." Sadie nodded.

"Our first potential?" Grace looked at the three of them and they nodded in agreement.

A numbered sticker was placed at the base of the tail of each horse. The horses would be sold in numerical order. Grace made a note on the papers on her clip board of the number on the paint horse.

Three stalls down was a sorrel. He was very tall, very underweight, and looked pretty young.

Grace read the paper attached to the stall door. "He's only three, gelded, and has been green broke; registered quarter horse though."

Nikki stepped in the stall and greeted the red horse. "I like him."

Grace looked for the owner who was standing outside the pen gate watching them.

"Can we see him walking?" Sadie asked the man.

He raised a brow to her then looked at Nikki. Nikki tilted her head and looked at him with a "well?" look.

"Ok," He nodded.

Grace untied the horse and led him out into the aisle, thankful there weren't very many people in the aisles yet. Sadie walked to the end and squatted down next to the fence so she would have a good view of his gait. Grace led the horse away from her then toward her. Sadie stared at the horse's movement. She held up a finger for one more time.

Grace nodded at the horse's owner and walked the aisle one more time trying to avoid the other customers.

Sadie finally nodded, the horse was placed back in its stall and the Tagger girls met to review.

"He needs shod differently." Sadie told them. "Other than that, he looks good."

"So, he's another candidate?" Nikki asked as she looked over at him.

"I think so." Sadie looked to Grace and Nora; they nodded too.

"Great, we have two now." Grace made a note on the clipboard of his sticker number.

They wandered farther down the aisle, in the last pen in that aisle was a large brown horse with what would have been a black mane and tail, but all the hair was entangled in a mass of tan cockleburs. Even the forelock of the horse was tangle creating one long cocklebur patch on top the horse's neck. His tail was so full of the weed it looked like a club.

"Yikes." Nora made a face.

"But look at HIM." Sadie's eyes opened wide.

The horse, even though he was very underweight, was definitely not quarter horse. Grace looked at the information sheet at the stall opening.

"He's a mustang." She informed the group.

"Oh, cool!" Sadie and Nora said in unison.

The horse turned and looked at the four of them. Then his head jerked up and seemed to look around.

Nora giggled and Grace looked at her in confusion. What was so funny?

Nikki took the lead and walked into the stall. The horse was calm as she slid a hand down his neck and over his back. She stepped back when the horse's head bounced up again and he looked around.

Nora giggled again.

"What's so funny?" Grace asked her but Nora didn't have a chance to answer.

"He's a nice horse," A man from the door said. "Pretty gentle but has his quirks."

"Can we walk him down the aisle?" Grace asked and the man shrugged.

Sadie made her way down the aisle, squatted down and they repeated their routine. The horse walked with some energy but stopped a couple times and looked around. Every time he did, Nora grinned.

The horse was returned and the owners met again.

"Well, he works for Nora and Nikki; how about you Sadie?" Grace asked.

"Oh, yeah." She nodded enthusiastically. "He's different than the horses we have because he's a mustang. He'll have more endurance, I want to try that out."

"Anything wrong with his legs?" Grace asked.

Sadie made a face and shook her head. "No, he's got pretty tough hoofs and I didn't see a problem with anything else."

"OK, we have number three?" Grace asked and her partners all nodded.

While Grace made the notes on the clipboards, the three other's moved on. When she looked up she was being watched by a man in a plaid shirt. He startled when he realized she had seen him and his cheeks reddened.

Grace gave him a sweet smile which made his eyes light up.

She looked back down at the clipboard so her cowboy hat would hide her widening smile. She was a few months short of eighteen, but had been accused of looking like she was in her twenties. Knowing she was going to be around cowboys, she had worn just enough makeup to highlight but not too much so she didn't look like she was trying to look older. Her dark blonde hair was straightened and just reached her shoulders. The black cowboy hat she wore was down low, like Josey wore hers.

She wore her good Wranglers; that fit her snuggly but comfortably. Her denim T3E jacket was worn over a black hoody. Unfortunately, she had on her mother's cowboy boots that were a size too large. Thick socks and bandages were placed over the wounds left by the blisters making it tolerable to walk.

From the looks she had received from other cowboys, she knew she looked good. The man in the plaid shirt confirmed it when she looked up and he smiled. Even though he was too old, mid-twenties she guessed, she returned the smile and softly giggled. Because plaid shirt wouldn't be able to hear it, she practiced her flirty giggle that her dad hated.

"Grace, in here." Nikki stepped around plaid shirt.

His eyes opened wide when he looked between her and Nikki. "That's my horse."

"Really?" Grace smiled and walked past him and into the pen to see a dark bay gelding.

Sadie had one of his front hooves resting in her lap and she was poking on the bottom of it with a hoof pick. "Can we see him walk?" She asked plaid shirt.

He shrugged, smiled at Grace and walked the horse down the aisle. Sadie squatted down and watched the horse with a frown.

When man and horse returned Sadie was biting her lower lip. "Can you trot him?"

Again a shrug, glance to Grace, and he turned and carefully trotted the bay horse down the aisle. Luckily there were only a couple people in the aisle they had to avoid.

"Nikki, could you go see if Dr. Mark can come over?" Sadie asked from her squatting position. Her eyes didn't move from the horse.

"Sure." Nikki smiled and turned.

As soon as she was out of ear shot, Sadie stood and looked at Grace and Nora.

"Why are they doing that?" Sadie asked with a frown.

"Who doing what?" Grace raised a confused brow to Sadie then looked at Nora who looked confused too.

Sadie took the clipboard from Grace and flipped to the back of the papers until she found a blank sheet.

Grace leaned over her shoulder to see her sister drawing squares and wiggly lines.

"What is that?" Nora asked as she watched.

"This area is the walkway above us looking down into the holding pens." Sadie pointed at the paper with the pen. "These are the pens…the auction building…the enter and exit doors into it."

"Ok…?" Nora said.

Sadie looked seriously between the two of them then down to her drawing. "Aunt Dru is standing right here," She pointed at the paper indicating the middle of the raised walkway. "Jack is here." She pointed at the end of the walkway; about twenty feet from Aunt Dru and nearly above the three of them. "And at the exit door, here, is Uncle Scott…the entrance here, is Dad."

Sadie glanced up at Grace and Nora; her blue eyes concerned.

Grace casually turned as if looking at the horse pens. Out of her peripheral vision she could see the placement of her dad, aunt, and uncles. She turned back to Sadie and Nora with a frown.

"Why are they like that?" Sadie asked again.

Grace shrugged, "It looks like we're surrounded."

"More like a surveillance team for the President." Nora looked down at the paper then up to Sadie and Grace. "Why?"

"It's like they are watching over us." Grace nodded.

"But why? We've been here hundreds of times over the years and they've never done anything like that." Sadie pointed out.

"I don't know." Grace shook her head. It just didn't make any sense.

"Why did you send Nikki away before you pointed it out?" Nora asked.

 "She probably knows and is doing it too…just close to us." Sadie answered.

"Should we just ask them? They always tell us we should just talk to them." Nora shrugged.

"Let's see…" Grace smiled at them and turned. Looking in the horse pens she walked about half way down…just below her aunt…then looked up. Her aunt was looking down at her, grinning. "See anything you like?" Grace called up.

Aunt Dru shook her head making her blonde hair sway; her blue eyes twinkled in humor, "You girls said you didn't want help, so I'm not saying."

Grace looked over at Jack then back to her aunt, "Why are you guys standing so far apart? It's like you don't like him anymore."

"Some days…" Her aunt grinned and shrugged but didn't answer the question.

"Are you girls done looking at the horse?" The man in the plaid shirt asked. The bay stood quietly at his side.

Grace turned to him and smiled. He returned her smile; blushing just a little. "We wanted one more look. My cousin went to get Dr. Mark."

"The Vet? Why?"

"I'm not really sure." Grace shrugged.

He nodded with a frown and turned as Nikki and Dr. Mark approached then passed as they made their way back down the aisle to Sadie.

Sadie squatted back down and Dr. Mark, who was in his seventies, used the fence to help lower into her position. Sadie swirled her finger in the air…her signal to have the horse walk the aisle one more time.

"Would you mind?" Grace smiled at him again, making his cheeks redden again. "Half way to them so they can see from the front then away from them so they can see the back?"

"OK, you gonna walk with me?" He asked with a shy tilt of the head.

"If you insist..." Grace laughed which caused him to smile and his eyes to twinkle. "My name is Grace Tagger." She held a hand out to him.

He took it and shook firmly but let go quickly, "I'm Paul Adler."

They walked silently toward the squatting pair, with Nikki and Nora staring at the legs of the horse too, and then turned to trot away. When they reached the far end Grace looked back down the aisle. Sadie nodded so she turned to the horse owner. He started to say something but stopped himself when her dad appeared at her side, placing one shoulder in front of hers; purposely blocking them.

"How's it going?" Her very tall dad towered over the startled man.

"Good..." Paul said then nodded to Grace and walked away.

Her dad looked down at her with a wry grin.

"Subtle, Dad...real subtle..." Grace giggled and walked back to her sister.

"I can't even believe you know that," Dr. Mark shook his head at Sadie.

"What?" Grace asked, hating to have missed out on any of the conversation.

"Solar Keratoma." Sadie answered matter-of-factly.

Grace's brows furrowed and she looked at the older veterinarian for clarification.

"It's a tumor in the inner hoof wall that normally grows toward the toe, this one grows down."

"Curable, after a quick medical procedure." Sadie added quickly.

"But down for how long?" Grace asked them. It was her job to make sure their project horse was something they could all work with; not just one or two of them.

"Takes a couple of months before you want to ride too much," He answered.

Grace shook her head at Sadie, "We don't have that much time to turn this horse around if we're selling at the horse expo."

"He doesn't have much time…at all." Sadie said with a defeated sigh. "Anyone that see's that won't want to buy him…I don't want him suffering because of it…it's so simple to fix."

"I know, Sadie." Grace sighed, feeling helpless herself. "But we promised we would only buy one horse and it has to be the right horse for all of us."

"We already have three chosen." Nora reminded her, as she looked solemnly down the aisle and sighed, "I just want all horses."

Grace turned to Nikki, who was also looking down the aisle toward the pen the horse was being held. She turned back with a pensive look. "I did promise too…"

The four future business owners looked at each other then back down the aisle.

"Alright you, Tagger girls," Dr. Mark said and they all looked at him. "You buy your project horse and I'll buy that bay and be your first client."

"Seriously?" Grace grinned in excitement.

"Yes," He laughed at their relieved and happy expressions. "I have complete faith in all four of you and it would be an honor to be your first client."

He happily accepted their hugs of appreciation then walked away shaking his head.

She watched him walk to her dad at the door into the building, Grace glanced at the other door, Uncle Scott was leaning against a panel talking to the auctioneer…but he was still looking around at all the people.

She glanced up and saw Jack looking out into the parking lot…still in his spot at the end of the walkway. Aunt Dru was talking with the auctioneer's wife, her aunt's eyes looking around at all the people mingling in the aisle; she was still in the middle of the walkway.

That was one of the oddest and confusing things Grace had ever seen…when it came to her family.

Grace glanced quickly at Sadie and Nora, shrugged her shoulders, then took the clip board back from her sister. There wasn't anything they could do about it now…they just needed to focus on their project horse.

The four business owners reviewed the three horses; a long tall sorrel, a short tired paint pony, and the underweight cocklebur infested mustang. All three geldings, so there wouldn't be a surprise pregnancy.

"Who is your first choice?" Grace asked.

"Sorrel." Nikki said.

"Mustang." Nora grinned.

"Mustang." Sadie grinned.

"Paint," Grace added. "So the mustang wins out."

"Who is up first?" Nora asked.

"Sorrel, mustang, and then paint." Sadie answered before Grace had a chance to look at her notes.

"So what happens if we can afford the sorrel?" Nora asked. "Do we pass and wait on the mustang?"

Her three companions looked to Grace. As the manager, she was the one to make the decision…she hoped she made the right one. "We pass on the sorrel and wait for the one the majority wants." She told them. "Then if he goes for too much we hope on the paint."

They all three nodded their agreement.

"I hope the paint goes to someone good," Sadie sighed. "He really needs some time off away from kids."

"I just want to take all of them home." Nora nodded; her dark brown eyes looking sadly around the horse pens. "This is torture to leave any behind."

"We just hope they go to good homes." Grace nodded, understanding their misery.

"I agree," Nikki sighed. "But we have to stay focused."

"You may have a problem with that," Sadie told Nikki then nodded her head to the parking lot.

Three muddy and scared foals were ushered out of a plain white stock trailer. There were two small bays with wide blazes down their long noses and a sorrel paint that had a full bald white face and white legs. All three were only about six months old; same age as Leroy and Zorra.

"Ugh!" Nikki exhaled loudly and rolled her eyes. A scared little Bodi was brought home from the last auction Nikki had attended.

Aunt Dru's laughter could be heard over the entire area. They all four turned and looked up at her; their laughter joined in.

CHAPTER EIGHT

The auction arena was a long rectangular room with raised seating on both ends and along one side. The other side was the auctioneer's booth that had a large window so he could interact with the crowd. The first three rows were individual seating then behind those were bench style seating for another four rows. The animal show arena, which was 20 x 40 feet, was in between the long seating area and the auctioneer's booth.

The Tagger girls took their seats in the first row right across from the auctioneer. Even with the white metal rail separating them from the arena, they could almost reach out and touch the horses as they were being shown. Dr. Mark, Jack and The Trio sat right behind the four girls.

In a way, they were surrounded again, Grace thought. Maybe it was just a coincidence; how else would they be sitting?

Dr. Mark was the first to win his little bay horse.

"Forty-five day notice, ladies!" He informed them. All four Tagger girls clapped excitedly.

Paul Adler, the plaid shirt man, walked right in front of them and smiled up at Grace which made her giggle.

"Down girl…" She heard Aunt Dru behind her.

Grace just chuckled then silently watched the next three horses come in, sell, and exit. Then the sorrel was walked into the arena.

With $250 each in the purse, they had $1000 to spend…the sorrel sold for $950.

"I was thinking the mustang was going to go for more than the sorrel." Nora whispered worriedly. The four girls looked anxiously at each other.

"The little paint shouldn't be as much though." Sadie sighed.

"How many horses before the mustang comes up?" Nora asked.

Grace looked at her notes, "Ten horses."

"I need to use the restroom." Nora stood hesitantly.

"I'll go with." Grace nodded and they started to make their way down the aisle, apologizing on their way.

When Grace made it to the end, she looked up to see her dad at the doorway to the outer building. He had been sitting right behind her! She turned quickly. Uncle Scott wasn't there either. She glanced around and found him standing at the far side entry door.

It looked like they were guarding the room. What the heck?

"Come on, Grace." Nora grabbed her hand and they hurried down the hall to the restroom.

Her dad followed them and was standing at the door when they walked out.

"Dad?" Grace pushed Nora forward so she would go into the auction room.

"Come on." He stepped aside and motioned for her keep moving.

"What's going on?" She didn't move.

"What do you mean?"

"Nora and I have gone to the bathroom in this building a hundred times without being escorted."

He shrugged and didn't answer.

"Dad…" Grace frowned in confusion.

"Gracie…" He grinned.

She knew he was smiling to make her feel better but it wasn't working. She stared at him…waiting for him to answer her…he wasn't going to. Frustrated, she walked by him then glanced back and saw him looking out the window of the front doors of the building. He was frowning so she glanced out. There were just a few older cowboys talking by a truck; nothing worthy of his concerned look.

"Dad?" She stopped again, just at the entry into the auction room.

"What?" He said off-handedly.

"What's going on?"

"Just worried about your mother," He said and pushed her into the room.

That was plausible, Grace told herself as she made it back to her seat. She had been so busy with the horses, the she had only occasionally thought of her mother…wishing she was there with them. Tessa was at the B&B, but Aunt Jordan and Cora were taking care of her…*she would be* OK Grace told herself as she took her seat again.

Uncle Scott was still standing by the door, watching the auction. She could hear Aunt Dru and Jack talking behind her, so she figured her dad was back at his post by the other door. She turned and looked. He returned her look…from the door. They stared at each other a moment before Grace turned back to the auction.

Sadie's leg nudged her own. Grace turned to her concerned expression.

"Wait until we get home," Sadie whispered. "You have to let it go for now."

Grace nodded and watched the bidding of a pair of large mules. They sold quickly with the winner shouting in victory.

That made Grace chuckle, and she started to relax. According to her notes, there were only two more horses before the mustang came out.

She took ahold of Sadie's hand and Nora's. Nora grabbed Nikki's hand. This was a special moment…it was the beginning of their business. Grace grinned at the three of them. They nodded and returned her smile, they understood too.

"If we win the mustang, we have to leave fast," Nikki leaned over and whispered to the girls.

Grace laughed, "So we get out before the foals come in?"

"Yes!" Nikki grinned.

The door opened for the next horse to enter…much to Nikki's dismay, the three foals were herded through the door.

"No…!" Nikki sighed dramatically causing her partner's and mother to laugh.

They had played rock, paper, scissors to see who would control the auction paddle. Nora had won and was holding the paddle tightly. She giggled and held it out to Nikki. Her cousin turned dramatic, defeated eyes to her, and took the paddle.

The auctioneer announced the foals would sell as choice. Which meant they were only bidding on one foal. The winning bid could choose the foal or foals of their choice. If they didn't want all of them, the second bidder could then purchase a remaining foal at the winning bid price.

Grace set her feet on the railing in front of her and wrapped her arms under her knees to watch the bidding. It started and no one bid. Grace turned to Nikki, she clutched the paddle tightly. The bidding was only $25 when Nikki finally raised the paddle. It quickly rose to $75 but then stopped. Grace turned again, Nikki was staring at the three foals who were huddled together just underneath the auctioneer window.

The auctioneer, who they had known for years, called her by name; "Nikki, are you going to let these little guys go for only $75?"

Nikki looked at him and her shoulders drooped; she slowly shook her head.

"So, does that mean you'll go to $100?" The auctioneer laughed.

She nodded slowly. The price quickly went up to $150 each and Nikki rolled her head back and stared at the ceiling.

"Nikki, are you going to let these three little colts go for only $150 each?" The auctioneer asked which caused the whole room to laugh. "They are registered…they are adorable…and look at those big beautiful eyes."

"Ugh!" Nikki called out and looked back at him.

"Is that a bid?" The auctioneer asked with a grin and the room laughed again.

Nikki nodded, finally returning his smile.

The bidding shot up to $200.

"Nikki…" The auctioneer started but stopped when Nikki shook her head firmly.

His eyes opened in surprise then turned to the last bidder, a woman with short brown hair in a yellow shirt. Grace recognized her as a local trainer. The woman wasn't smiling as Grace thought she should be.

Aunt Dru leaned in from behind and whispered to the girls. "She's afraid she just won a horse she really didn't want. She was just bidding to run up the price."

"Bid is $200 for choice, going once, going twice…" The auctioneer announced.

"$205." Nikki called out.

The yellow shirted trainer visibly relaxed in relief causing a low murmur of laughter in the room.

No one else bid and Nikki won choice.

"Now, Nikki," The auctioneer grinned at her. "How are you going to choose just one of those cute little fellas?"

"Just wrap them all in pretty little bows." Nikki shouted to him. Another round of laughter rang out as the auctioneer hollered "sold"!

One more horse then the mustang would be brought in for sale.

Grace turned to Nikki who was leaned back looking content.

"You would have gone higher?" Nora whispered high enough Grace could hear.

Nikki shrugged with a grin, "Probably, Mom won't let me bring Leroy to the ranch so now I have some babies of my own to take care of."

Grace chuckled at the excited look on her cousin's face.

The next horse sold quickly and the four partners gripped hands tightly. Nora let go of Nikki's hand and took control of the paddle.

The dark brown mustang was ridden into the building.

"Dang," Sadie whispered in dread, "I thought he was going to walk him in."

Grace sighed; he would sell for more if he was trained already.

Nora leaned forward; staring intently. "Wait for it…" She whispered.

Grace looked back at the horse…he was walking, but hesitantly. His ears were twitching from rider to the crowd. The room remained quiet as the horse slowly walked across the room and turned back. The rider only walked in a figure eight. There was no spinning, side-passing, trotting, reining…nothing but a figure eight.

The auctioneer was busy as the horse entered and walked the floor. When he turned and leaned to the microphone, Nora whispered again, "Wait for it…"

The horse was in mid-step when the auctioneer started talking and his voice rang out into the room. The brown horse stopped, his leg slowly lowering. When it hit the ground, he didn't move it again. The man calmly nudged the horse…but the horse didn't move his legs but his ears moved slowly forward and he looked left then right as if looking for something.

Grace could have sworn the horse turned and looked right at them. He was only five feet away; they could smell the horse's sweat.

The rider kicked harder but the horse still didn't budge.

"I want to jump over this rail so bad." Nora's whole body was tense as she leaned forward.

The rider finally gave up and stepped out of the saddle. He quickly took the saddle and pad off and set it to the side. Grace was surprised; most people did that to show off the conformation of the horse, but it didn't help with the mustang since he was so skinny. He looked better with the saddle on. The rider walked to the front of the horse and tugged on the bridle…the gelding didn't move. Nora's hand reached out and grabbed the rail.

The auctioneer told the audience the horse was adopted from BLM when he was a year old then, as a three years old, he had 90 days professional training on a ranch. The owner had taken ill and the horse had been put to pasture for the last two years…barely touched.

Nora was on the edge of her seat, staring at the horse she could almost reach out and touch. One hand gripped the rail the other gripped the paddle with their number on it.

The auctioneer started the bidding at $2000 and all four girls groaned.

Between the horse's underweight appearance, mane and tail completely tangled in cockleburs and the refusal to move no matter what the man did, the auctioneer couldn't get the bid higher than $500. Nora raised the paddle; the price moved to $600, she raised the paddle again the price went to $700.

"$725!" Someone behind them yelled.

Nora raised the paddle at $750. She raised her gaze from the horse to the auctioneer.

"$775!" The voice yelled out again.

Grace wanted to scream at them! Nora remained calm and raised the paddle again at $800.

"$825!" The voice called again and Grace forced herself not to turn and glare at the other bidder.

Nora raised the paddle at $850.

Silence.

"Going once, going twice, sold! To the little lady in the front row" The auctioneer smiled at Nora.

They all four jumped in excitement.

"Now if we can just get him out of here." The auctioneer laughed at their reaction.

"Stop talking!" Nora called out and folded both arms over the rail to stare at their new project horse.

"What?" The auctioneer asked her.

"Stop talking." She repeated.

He nodded with an understanding smile and leaned away from the microphone; the room went quiet.

The man kept trying to pull the horse to get him to move.

"Stop yanking on him." Nora said quietly and the man and horse turned to her.

It took a minute after the man stopped moving before the horse's body relaxed, and then it stepped sideways with his head moving around. Once the gelding decided the voice was gone, he nudged the man with his nose and took a step forward. The man smiled at Nora, tipped his hat to her then turned to lead the horse out of the room.

Nora leaned back and grinned at her partners. "We got him!" She bounced excitedly.

******

When they arrived at The Homestead, Grace was excited to see her mother sitting in a chair in front of the barn. She was in one of the deck lounge chairs; her leg propped on pillows and blankets piled over her. Cora and Aunt Jordan were sitting in chairs next to her.

"I wasn't missing this." Her mother grinned as she greeted each of the girls excitedly.

"Wait until you see him!" Sadie was bouncing in her boots.

"I watched the whole thing." Her mother surprised her.

"What?" The girls said in unison.

"Your father 'face timed' me as soon as the mustang walked into the building." She turned to Nora. "I thought they were going to have to physically restrain you from jumping in."

Nora laughed and nodded, "That was tough…I wanted to so bad!"

When the door to the horse trailer was opened, the three colts were huddled in next to the mustang that seemed to be protecting them.

"He looks like their big brother." Grace laughed.

Cooper and Rufio, who were in the first two stalls, were moved back to Trooper and Harvey's stalls since they were at Circle 50.

Her dad and Uncle Scott herded the three colts out of the trailer; they stepped gently down to the ground and looked around. Whinnies echoed from inside the barn and from the mustang.

"Nikki!" Grace's mother yelled.

"What?" Nikki said happily as she held open the trailer door and watched her new little charges.

"I want the bald face paint!" She said.

"Really?" Nikki laughed.

Grace's dad laughed, "I knew that was coming. She's always wanted a paint with that coloring."

"Then why didn't you just buy her one?" Uncle Scott asked as they stepped out of the trailer.

"I wouldn't let him," Her mother explained as she grinned at the colt. "I wanted to pick him out myself and I didn't see one I wanted until him." She looked at Nikki. "Can I buy him? I'll give you $25 more than you paid as a delivery fee."

Both women laughed as Nikki nodded happily.

Grace looked at the colt again. He had a black mane and tail and dark eyes instead of the blue that was common in bald face horses. The white ran up his legs and just at the top it started a speckled trail up to the light sorrel coloring of the body; which gave the hint of being muscular and refined. Once Nikki's supplement program was put in place, he would be a bull dog of a horse.

As the parents and Nikki focused on the colts, Grace saw Nora sneak into the horse trailer to the mustang. They had loaded them so quickly, she didn't have a chance to greet him at the stockyards. Grace stepped to the left so she could see Nora clearly as she approached the mustang. The brown horse was still tied to the trailer but he lowered his head toward her the best he could.

Aunt Jordan stood and took a step to the trailer just as Nora reached out to touch the muzzle. Grace's dad stopped her aunt.

"Grayson…" She frowned.

"She knows what she's doing…let her connect." He said. "The horse needs to trust…that's why he wouldn't follow the directions of the guy that was showing him. He didn't trust him." He nodded to Nora. "She understood and is taking the time now to connect before he's brought out into his new home."

They all quietly watched Nora stroke the horse's nose and talk softly to him. Her hand moved up his muzzle, nose, over his eye, stopped just under his eyes to caress the fine hair. The horse tilted its head to her, so she swept her hand under his rounded jaw then up to his ears, and his neck. With both hands she slowly caressed down his neck and side to move to the top of his back and down the length of it. She stopped at his back hip and lifted her left hand back toward the front of the horse. His nose came back as far as possible; just enough he could barely touch her fingertips. She stepped back to his head and cradled his nose in both her hands. After a few minutes of speaking softly, she untied the horse and he followed her calmly out the door of the trailer.

Nora stopped after all four of his hooves were on the ground and let him look around.

"Good job," Her uncle smiled proudly down at her. Nora grinned up at him.

"It's going to take hours to get those cockleburs out of his hair." Aunt Jordan said. "We had horses like that in Wyoming when I was a kid. We used cooking oil in a small bottle to squirt it onto their manes then slowly worked the hair out; saved from having to cut off the mane."

"Good idea!" Grace grinned. "We were going to start on it when we got back from the roping jackpot tomorrow."

Aunt Jordan's eyes flickered to her mother than back to Grace. "Don't forget to drop them in a bucket when you remove them then burn them so the seeds don't spread."

"Ok," Grace nodded and turned to her mother…she was looking up at her dad… "What?"

"Nothing, let's get the horses put away." Her dad said and turned to help escort the colts to the barn.

Grace looked around at the adults. Aunt Dru was wrapped in Jack's arms as they leaned contently against the barn. Her mother, Aunt Jordan, and Cora were sitting in their chairs and Uncle Scott was standing next to Nora and the mustang. They all quickly exchanged glances.

"NO." Grace nearly yelled, causing a few coughs to follow, the weird actions by the adults was bizarre and she'd had enough.

"Excuse me?" Her mother said in a very irritated tone.

Sadie stepped next to Grace; she must have seen it too.

"What was with the surveillance tactics today at the stockyards?" Sadie asked.

"The what?" Their mother asked.

"They strategically placed themselves around the stockyards so we were being watched over…like protected…like the secret service does for the president." Sadie answered.

"Walking us to the bathroom," Nora added with a glance to her uncle.

"Don't say you weren't doing it," Grace looked around at them. "We're all smarter than that."

Grace turned to her dad to see if he was going to deny it again.

"Alright," He nodded with a concerned expression.

Suddenly, Grace was nervous.

CHAPTER NINE

"Let's get the horses put away and Leah into the house first." Aunt Dru said as she and Jack moved forward to help with the colts.

Sadie and Nora glanced nervously at Grace as they walked to the barn. Her dad lifted her mom into his arms and carried her toward the house. Cora jogged in front of them to reach the door first and open it for them.

Grace looked at Nikki and from her expression, just as Sadie guessed, she knew, too.

By the time the horses were nestled into their stalls, Reilly and Wade returned home from the ranch. They all gathered in the no-media room.

Grace sat in the middle of the long couch with Nora then Wade to her right and Sadie then Reilly on her left. Both boys looked totally confused on what was happening. Her dad positioned his chair to face the girls and was next to the one her mother was settled into, her leg propped on top the ottoman.

All the other adults moved their chairs so they were all sitting in a circle.

When her dad finally spoke, he was looking directly at Grace.

"You received a handful of messages the beginning of the week that you didn't have programed into your phone." He said to her.

"Yeah, after the accident," Grace frowned and looked between her parents. "All they said was 'Grace are you OK?'."

"We traced the number." He told her bluntly.

"You're still checking my phone?" Grace was surprised.

"Not all the time," He answered.

Grace was a bit irritated, but her curiosity was peaked. "Who did the number belong to?"

"Allen." He answered, again very bluntly.

The irritation she was feeling quickly turned to shock…then anger…back to surprise…then to irritation at Allen this time instead of her parents. How could he possibly call her after what he did?

Sadie took her hand and squeezed, "Why does his calling have to do with what you all were doing today?"

Their dad sighed deeply and leaned back in his chair; "After some investigating, we found that he and his family had moved to North Dakota last winter."

"Ok…" Grace frowned. "So…today was…?"

"We received word that Allen was on his way here… to see you." He told her.

The anger returned and she knew her neck and face were turning red. Her stomach tightened as if it had been punched. He had affected her life again; caused her family grief. She felt like he was stealing her control again.

"We wanted you girls to have today…enjoy today and getting your first project horse before we told you." Her mother said, her eyes concerned but full of love.

Grace nodded slowly.

"Where is he?" Reilly asked. "Does anyone know?"

"He's here in town," Her dad answered. "But they aren't sure where."

"Who are "they"?" Sadie asked.

"We hired a private detective to find and follow him while he's in town to make sure he doesn't get close to any of you kids." He answered.

"But you can't find him?" Reilly asked.

They shook their heads.

Reilly pulled his phone out of his pocket and made a call before anyone could stop him.

"Where is Allen?" He said gruffly into the phone. Hesitation… "No, he's in Lewiston." Another pause, "OK, let me know if you hear anything."

Reilly looked up at her parents, "Levi…he didn't know he was here. He's calling around to family to see if anyone has heard from him."

Grace stared at her dad, "Alan won't hurt me."

He returned her stare, "And last year, would you have believed he would give you alcohol without you knowing and take you into a locked bedroom?"

Graced grimaced, "No…"

"We have no idea what he wants and what he will do." Her dad said. "Too many women have been attacked thinking an ex-boyfriend wouldn't hurt them. They end up in the hospital or the ground."

"Dad…" Grace glared.

"We error on the side of safety," Her mother added. "Our job is to protect you."

"Which brings us to tomorrow…," Her dad sighed as he turned back to Grace.

"It's the roping jackpot," Grace reminded him.

"Grace, we all agree that it's best you don't go." He said flatly.

Grace's back stiffened and the anger ran through her like liquid fire. She stood abruptly, hands on hips. "What? Yes, I am."

Her dad stood and looked down at her. "Grace, not until he's found."

"Am I to be a prisoner here in my own home? Because of him?" She nearly screamed in frustration which caused another round of coughing.

"Grace, calm down," Her mother took her hand.

"Mom," Grace felt the tears of anger rise as she looked down at her. "He can't do this to me again…he can't take my life in his hands again…he can't take me out of control again."

"Grace, we have to protect you." Her dad said, his worried blue eyes trying to convince her. "Until he is found, and we know his intentions, we have to keep you safe."

"Dad," Grace took his hand and squeezed both her worried parents hands tightly. "In my counseling…I'm supposed to rely on others to help me and not try to control everything."

"That's what we're trying to do." Her mother whispered, tears shimmering in her worried eyes.

Grace shook her head, "No, you're protecting me, but letting him control us and what we do. That can't happen."

"Grace…" Her dad said. "It's our job to protect you."

"But we can't do this. I can't be a prisoner of him anymore." Her voice started to regain its strength. "WE have to take control."

Her dad stared at her for a moment…looking into her determined blue eyes. "Once they find him…we'll take control."

"We take control by allowing him to find me." Grace told him, hoping he would agree to the plan that just formed in her head.

"Grace…" He said but stared at her thoughtfully.

"We let him find me under OUR conditions." She nodded firmly, determined now. "WE find out what he wants. Let him know that he isn't in control anymore; get him OUT of our lives permanently."

"You want to set a trap for him?" Jack asked.

Grace shrugged, "I guess you can call it that. We just don't change our plans tomorrow; we do the roping jackpot. If he shows up we deal with him. If he doesn't, we just have fun."

Her dad didn't say anything, he just stared at her. She knew he was considering it.

"I'm not riding. I'll be on the bleachers surrounded by a lot of people." She reminded him.

He looked down at her mother who looked worriedly back to him.

"Just get it over with under our conditions." Grace repeated again with a firm confident voice.

Her mother sighed and her dad nodded.

"You, Wade, Cora, Nikki, Nora, and Sadie will go to the Bed and Breakfast so you're surrounded by people and away from here; in case he comes here." He told her mother and she readily agreed.

******

Grace stepped out of her dad's truck and adjusted her black cowboy hat as her eyes scanned the people around her. Nothing unusual; just the same people and horses she had ridden with before.

She met her dad and Reilly at the back gate to the horse trailer to unload Buttercup and Rufio. Levi appeared with a not-so-calm smile on his face. Reilly had told him what was happening and Levi was worried for both Grace and his cousin, but agreed to go along with the plan.

No matter what the plan was for the day, she still couldn't believe Levi was there; back in her life. She busied herself by telling him about her horse instead of thinking about how tall he was or how broad his shoulders had gotten over the last year. They brushed up against each other a couple times which caused her to giggle. He was smiling, too.

"Get moving you two." Reilly chuckled behind them and followed Buttercup as they walked toward the building. He and Levi were to watch over Buttercup in case Allen saw the horse and tried to find Grace.

She watched as they stepped into the saddle and rode into the indoor arena building at the rodeo grounds. They entered through the gate and moved around the arena to warm up the horses. The arena covered the majority of the building but there were three sets of bleachers along the north side of the building. A food trailer selling hamburgers, chips, and pop, was placed in the corner to her left.

Grace looked around for the people she knew were there to protect her. It was heartwarming that they would do this for her but it was also irritating that they had to. Her dad was just inside the building's small entry door talking with a number of cowboys she recognized.

She walked calmly down the outside of the arena and toward the bleachers that were to her left. There were two tables setup that held the awards and trophies for the day's competitions. There was a brown, navy, and gold saddle pad that would look fantastic on Buttercup. What a bummer she didn't even have a chance to win it.

"Grace!" She heard a female voice call out.

She turned to see Marla and other school friends waving at her so she made her way up the bleachers to them and spent the next half hour talking about the accident while watching Levi ride Buttercup around the arena. It was odd seeing someone else riding her cream colored horse.

Reilly rode Rufio up to the edge of the arena across from her and Marla. He and Marla dated for six months but parted ways during the summer. They returned for their senior year of school as just friends, but today they started their flirting again. Levi rode up next to Reilly and he was introduced to the girls around them.

As they spoke, Grace looked around for her aunts and uncles. Uncle Scott and Aunt Jordan were at the back area where the cows were held and pushed into the cattle chute. Jack and Aunt Dru were at the first small door that was to the side of the two sets of bleachers. The only unprotected door was a wide door that slid up to open. It was closed and blocked by a truck.

The announcer started reviewing the rules with the competitors so Reilly and Levi joined the other riders at the chutes. Her phone alerted her to a text.

TEXT FROM DAD: You warm enough?

Grace was wearing the new western style coat her parents had bought her; a longer one like her mother's that she wore climbing the mountain the week before. It seemed so long ago. Her cough was nearly gone; the tightness in her lungs only occurred when she exerted herself. But the soreness in the muscles was only tolerable when she took aspirin. She was still taking the medication to keep from getting pneumonia.

Grace slid off a glove and typed:

TEXT FROM GRACE: Might need hot chocolate soon

TEXT FROM DAD: You getting it yourself or do you want me to do special delivery

Grace laughed and looked down the end of the building to her dad who was still standing by the door. He grinned back at her.

TEXT TO DAD: Love you Dad

She watched him look down at his phone then back at her. He smiled making his blue eyes shine. It was enough to warm her heart.

The door next to him opened and Grace caught her breath…the door closed. There was a man there that looked just like Allen. The door opened again, a man she hadn't seen before walked through. She looked back out to the arena; Reilly and Levi were up next. She tried to concentrate on them. Allen was starting to haunt her.

"Go Buttercup!" Grace yelled which caused her to start coughing. No more yelling, she told herself.

Reilly and Levi backed the horses into the box…just touched the back and Levi nodded. The calf was released and they took off down the arena. Levi twirled the rope, threw, and missed. Reilly pulled Rufio back and shook his head at his partner. He trotted past Grace and grinned.

Levi followed behind as he recoiled his rope, "I think he's missing you already."

"Well, quit missing the calf and he won't!" Grace called out and started coughing again…stop yelling, she told herself again.

Levi caught the calf the second time around and so did Reilly. Grace stood and clapped for them and her horse.

The rest of the day was draw for partners so Grace watched Reilly and Levi compete with different riders.

She glanced back down to her dad. He was talking with a couple of men but his eyes were constantly looking around.

She really needed to use the restroom, but didn't want to tell all the men so she stepped down the bleachers and headed to Aunt Dru at the small side door.

They exited out the side door together, laughing at Grace's embarrassment.

Her aunt's hair was rolled into a bun and was hidden under her cowboy hat. A dark blue scarf was wrapped around her neck and tucked into her black ranch coat. She was almost unrecognizable.

As they walked down the side road next to the arena building, they became separated by a group of horse and riders. Grace looked back and saw her aunt waiting for the horses to pass so she quickly walked to the porta-potty and stepped inside. Aunt Dru would catch up with her by the time she came out.

And she was right; her aunt was standing in front of the portable restroom. Across the road, her dad was leaning against the building watching her.

Grace giggled in embarrassment and walked to the portable washroom. As she reached for the towels a movement in front of her caught her attention. Allen stepped out from behind a horse trailer behind the restrooms. He was taller than she remembered. He was wearing a baseball cap instead of the normal straw cowboy hat. His eyes…they looked at her in desperation.

She stepped back and looked to her dad and aunt. They couldn't see Allen from their vantage points. Allen may have seen Aunt Dru, but probably didn't recognize her.

Grace quickly turned back to Allen; he was still staring at her, his hands in his jacket pockets. Why didn't she tell someone that she thought she saw him earlier!? Why did she convince herself it wasn't him? She took three large steps backwards which must have alerted her aunt because she was quickly at her side. That alerted her dad who was running across the road with his phone to his ear. Allen's hands came out of his pockets; Grace tensed and her aunt stepped protectively in front of her.

CHAPTER TEN

Allen lifted empty hands in the air to try and calm her. "I just want to talk…just want to apologize."

His eyes grew wide and he stepped backwards when her dad appeared at her side. Aunt Dru grabbed him to keep him from attacking the suddenly terrified teenager.

"I just want to apologize!" He yelled; hands still extended in front of him. "Please," Allen pleaded with his voice and eyes. "Just let me talk to her, apologize to her."

Grace turned to see her aunt, uncles, and two other cowboys running out of the building. Jack ran to his wife and the rest ran behind the horse trailer and stopped behind Allen. He glanced back then turned to Grace.

"Please…" Allen said softly, his eyes begging her father.

The sound of thundering hoof beats reached them as Reilly and Levi appeared from around the building and came to a stop next to the group. They both slid off the horses and Reilly walked to Grace while Levi walked to Allen. He approached his cousin with long strides and threw a punch that connected with Allen's jaw before anyone could react. Allen fell backwards but caught himself from falling to the ground. Levi stood motionless and glared at his cousin.

"Dang, I wanted to do that." Aunt Dru whispered.

It made Grace chuckle, which made part of the tension in her back release. No matter what happened next, she was well protected.

"Let me talk to him." She looked up at her dad.

Much to her surprise he nodded, "Alright."

Grace walked toward the cousins as she stuffed her hands inside the pockets of her long coat. She glanced between Levi and Allen as she placed herself halfway between her family and the cousins. Her eyes went back to Levi and she thought back to the voice message he had left her after the New Year's incident. *"I doubt you do, but if there is any way you would agree to talk, I want to personally apologize to you. This has changed my life forever…the guilt will be with me forever. I don't want it to do the same to you. You did nothing wrong. Grace…if you don't text or call…just know…I am so sorry…please tell Reilly I am sorry… your friendships are a great loss to me."*

"Before you say a word to me, apologize to Levi, and mean it." She said to Allen who was rubbing his jaw.

He nodded vigorously and turned to his cousin and took a deep breath. "When I asked you to distract Reilly I had no thought of hurting Grace. I just wanted to talk to her, persuade her to be my girlfriend. I was NOT asking you to be a part of what happened. I didn't know that it was going to happen…"

Levi's shoulders lowered.

"We were close growing up…we weren't just cousins, we were friends…best friends." Allen's voice was full of honesty and regret. "What I did…didn't just tear us apart but it also affected our entire family, causing my parents to move us to North Dakota. Dad hates it there…so does Mom. She hates being away from Aunt Lana." Allen sighed and shook his head slowly. "That hour…the decision to drink too much…to drink at all…to give it to Grace without her knowing has torn our family apart and it's my fault…all my fault, not yours. What happened was all my fault, not Grace's, not yours and I am so sorry…so very, very sorry."

Grace couldn't see Levi's face but knew he was struggling. He'd turned slightly when Allen had mentioned Levi's mother. His head lowered to the ground as the last words of apology were said.

Levi and Allen had been as close as she was with Nikki and Nora…to lose their friendships would be awful…heartbreaking.

Grace's heart constricted for both of them, she silently hoped that Levi would reach out to his cousin; they were both hurting. She sighed when Levi stepped to his cousin and wrapped his arms around him. Allen's face disappeared into his cousin's shoulder, his own shoulders rising and lowering as he cried.

Grace looked beyond the cousins to her uncle, aunt, and the cowboys watching them. Their stances were no longer defensive. They too realized that Allen was no physical danger to her.

Everyone stood quietly until Levi stepped back from Allen and said something so low that no one but his cousin could hear it. Using the sleeve of his jacket, Allen wiped away the tears and looked at Levi, a slight relieved smile crossed his face…his eyes moved to Grace…the smile disappeared.

Levi turned and without looking at Grace walked to stand next to Reilly.

Grace walked forward until she was within a few feet of Allen. Her hands still tucked in her long coat, black cowboy hat tilted up enough she could easily see him, and her resolve and confidence strong.

She spoke low so only he could hear her. "I don't know everything that happened."

He shook his head, his eyes desperate, he took her lead and whispered too, "Nothing Grace…I swear! I didn't take you there for anything to happen beside to talk to you and hopefully make-out without Reilly interrupting. I stopped before I heard his voice. I just stared at you, wondering what I was doing…how you got drunk so fast…how stupid I was…how out of control jealous I was."

"Jealous?"

"I always knew you liked Levi more than me," He sighed. "That's why I kissed you before he had a chance to. I wanted you to like me more; to be my girlfriend."

"You didn't think of what I wanted?"

He shook his head, "No, just what I wanted; then and at New Year's. I guess, in a way, even now. After I read about your accident on Facebook, I had to see you…to apologize to you before something happened again and it was too late."

"You texted."

"I did, but you didn't answer and even if you did you wouldn't have known it was me. I wanted to make sure you knew it was me apologizing…to truly understand how sorry I am."

"What you wanted…"

"Yes," He sighed. "What I wanted…needed…not what you wanted…"

"But what I needed." She finished and saw a flicker of hope in his eyes.

"You needed to see me?" He asked in disbelief.

"No, but I needed to know what you did. I needed to know that after the years of friendship we had, that you were really sorry for what you did."

"I truly am Grace…I am so sorry…"

"But you need to understand everything that you did." She swallowed hard knowing she had to relinquish some of the knowledge to him. "You took my control."

His eyes registered anguish not the superiority she had feared all these months. He hadn't wanted to control her. She paused and stared at him…from the words he'd said and his actions, she realized that she was now in control of his life. Was she going to abuse that?

"I'm not telling you this to make you feel worse," Grace explained. "I'm telling you this so you can truly understand what you did to me physically and mentally."

"I'm sorry, Grace."

"I know," She nodded because she truly believed he was. "You took control…took my control. I am a control freak. I need to be in control of my life; in what happens to me. I take charge. You touched me in here," She lifted a hand to her head.

He nodded, his eyes looking regretful.

"What you do affects others…you can't just think of what YOU want…you have to think of how others feel." Her voice had risen; she didn't care if anyone heard the rest of what she was going to say.

"Except for this…me coming here…I've been working on it…counseling…."

"You've apologized and since I believe that you are sorry for what happened…I am accepting that apology." She said loudly and firmly. She felt a sense of relief flow through her.

The tears in his eyes rose again. She heard a noise behind her and turned to see Levi with his head rolled back and looking at the sky. His body was slumped… as if he was relieved.

She glanced at her family; they nodded to her in support so she turned back to Allen.

"Now," She sighed, "You have to move on."

"What?" He frowned.

"People make mistakes, Allen. I'm not diminishing what you did, but you have to move on with your life. Stop letting this affect you and your family's lives by focusing on the past. Learn from it and now improve your life from it. Tell your dad to move back home. Tell your mother to reconnect with her sister. They shouldn't be punished for this… family is important."

"If it wasn't for my parents…" He whispered then stopped; overcome by emotion.

"Turn things around, Allen."

"I will Grace… I needed you to understand before I could."

She nodded, "Go home Allen, turn things around."

"I will Grace. I promise… I will." He looked at Reilly. "I am sorry, Reilly; so very very sorry to betray your trust and our friendship."

He turned to her dad, Aunt Dru and Jack. "I am sorry, please tell Leah." He turned around to Aunt Jordan and Uncle Scott and apologized to them. Then he nodded to Levi, walked to a small white truck, and drove away.

Her dad walked up to her, took the hat off her head and handed it to Aunt Dru. He then wrapped her in a strong hug, squeezing tightly, then that little bit tighter. She relaxed.

"I didn't realize he had become a victim of his own actions." She whispered to him.

"I didn't either… you did good."

"Thanks," She stepped back. "Now let's go back in and watch Levi miss again."

"Hey!" He smiled, "I only missed once."

******

"My fingers hurt." Grace looked down at the tiny poke marks at the end of her fingertips.

"Mine, too." Nora nodded.

Grace and Sadie were working on the mane while Nikki and Nora concentrated on the tail.

"We're almost done." Nikki pulled another sharp pointed cocklebur out of the mustang's tail and tossed it in the bucket.

"I can't believe how much hair he has," Sadie pulled the comb through another loose strand of mane. "Aunt Jordan's trick really worked but now he's all oily. We'll need to wash it out."

"I don't think he'll care." Nora giggled and looked at the brown horse's head. They were standing in the middle of the aisle of the barn with the other horses leaned over their doors watching. The mustang's head was low and relaxed. "He's got a great disposition."

"He seems pretty smart." Sadie nodded. "I read that mustangs were really intelligent, loyal, as well as being good at endurance."

With relief, Grace pulled the last cocklebur out of the mane and Sadie slid the mane rake through the hair; up and down the neck one more time. There was a lot of hair but it was weighted down by oil.

"We're done," Sadie announced.

"Almost there," Nikki smiled.

Within minutes Nikki and Nora stepped away from the horse. The girls switched ends so they could see how the other pair did.

"It looks good," Sadie declared.

"We didn't lose much hair." Nikki looked into the bucket at the pile of weed heads but only a small amount of long black strands of hair.

"But I think I lost all feeling in my fingertips." Nora giggled.

"I can feel every poke in mine." Grace laughed.

"I don't think we should use the hose yet." Nora decided. "Let's just use buckets to wash him off."

It took three shampoo sessions and a good conditioner to get the oil out of his hair. It lay limp against his brown neck but it reached down to his shoulder, nearly to the top of the leg.

"What should we call him?" Grace asked.

"How about Mustang?" Nora smiled.

"Call a mustang, Mustang?" Nikki asked with a raised brow.

"Remember when Jessup had that orange cat up at the ranch?" Sadie asked with a grin.

"You mean Orange Cat?" Nikki laughed.

"Orange Cat the orange cat, Blue the blue roan, Bay the bay horse, Red the red dog…" Nora nodded.

"Mustang the mustang." The four girls said in unison and laughed.

"Hey, he looks good." Wade said as he, Reilly, and Levi walked into the barn.

"We have the fire pit going." Levi told them with a smile to Grace.

She felt herself blush. In just the few hours since the conversation with Allen, their relationship had relaxed. Even her dad's attitude toward Levi was different; more accepting.

They finished running the towels over a very patient Mustang to dry him off as much as possible. He was returned to his stall with plenty of hay and his new supplements mixed with oats that Nikki had put together to get the weight back on him.

The three colts were missing from their stall. They had been so busy with bur removal they didn't see anyone take the colts.

"Where are they?" Nora asked in surprise.

"Leah had them put in the small corral so she could watch her new colt play." Reilly led them out the door and to the corral.

Her mother was sitting in a chair at the gate of the corral. She was sitting at the opening, straddling the gate with her broken leg outside the corral and her good leg inside.

Grace and her group laughed at the sight but stopped moving when they saw the bay colt with the crooked blaze hesitantly walking to her outstretched hand. He stopped and leaned his nose as far out as it could get but was still inches from the grain cupped in her hand.

The other bay with the wide blaze and the bald face colt were at the back of the corral watching. Her dad was standing inside the corral fifteen feet from her mother. With his long legs, he would be able to get to her quickly if something happened.

The crooked blaze bay took another step and leaned so far he nearly fell. His lips twitched as he finally reached the grain cupped in her hand. He took a step back as he ate the few kernels. A more confident step got him another bite. He stepped back quickly when she lowered her hand to the bucket in her lap, but stepped closer as the hand came out with a pile of grain on top.

The bald face colt's head came up alertly as he watched his friend eating the grain. He quickly walked across the corral and stood at the back end of his buddy. The other bay colt remained in the back watching.

"Come get some," Her mother said to her colt and his ears twitched to her. They twisted so much that Grace thought they looked unattached to his head.

The crooked blaze bay stepped back and bumped into the bald face, who sidestepped away from him which got him closer to the man standing at the fence. The bald face colt jumped back which brought him closer to her mother.

Her colt took a quick bite of grain from her hand then trotted to the back of the corral; the crooked blaze bay followed.

Her dad picked up his smiling wife and Wade jogged forward to shut the gate for them.

"I don't want to go inside yet." Her mother complained.

"We have the fire pit going." Grace told her.

"Do you mind?" She smiled at her husband.

"Whatever you want." He grinned and altered his path.

"You keep saying things like that; I may just fall in love with you." Her mother chuckled and kissed his cheek.

"Ewww! Stop!" Grace and Sadie yelled out, their faces scrunched in false horror.

They all laughed as they settle around the fire on the makeshift log chairs. Within minutes the entire family was gathered around the roaring fire.

The sun set as delivered pizza was passed around the group. After dinner was done, Levi stood and smiled around the family.

"I need to be headed home, but I want to thank everyone for today. The majority of it was a lot of fun." He nodded to Grace's parents then aunts and uncles.

Grace stood with Reilly but didn't look at her parents as she followed them to Levi's truck which was in the driveway on the other side of the barn.

After Levi and Reilly shook hands and joked about the day's events, Reilly stepped to the front of the truck. Grace and Levi were blocked by his open door.

"Thank you for today, Grace." Levi smiled softly at her, the light from his truck reflected in his blue eyes.

"Well, thank you for riding Buttercup for me." She was tall enough that she nearly matched his height.

They stood quietly a moment until Grace realized that Levi wouldn't make the first move to kiss her…she would have to. She laid a hand on his arm and took a step closer to him.

"Are you sure Grace?" He whispered.

"Yes."

CHAPTER ELEVEN

Sadie picked up the #1 candle from the cake tray and put the frosted covered end into her mouth. She picked up the #3 candle, dipped it into the frosting and handed it to Dr. Mark with a giggle. He laughed, but promptly sucked the frosting off the end.

"Time for presents!" Aunt Dru called out.

Sadie grinned, took Dr. Mark's hand, and they walked down to the no-media room together. The entire family, Paige, Candace, Nick, Tessa, and Alex followed.

Grace walked next to Lucas as they followed the pair.

"I was surprised to see Dr. Mark here." Lucas whispered to her. She smiled at his accent. It didn't matter how long he had been in the family, she still loved hearing it.

"Why?" Grace looked up at him.

"I don't think he's ever been to anyone else's birthday; that I've been here for." He answered.

Grace giggled; she forgot he didn't know the story. "Remember that Sadie was born in the fall branding pasture?"

"Oh, yeah." Lucas nodded slowly.

"Dr. Mark delivered her." Grace smiled.

His booming laughter echoed down the hall. "Well that just seems appropriate for Little Dingo. That's why he calls her 'my Tagger'?"

Grace nodded. She had really been jealous of the nickname the veterinarian had given her sister. Once she was old enough to understand the meaning, she was OK with it and loved him saying it.

Once they were all settled around the room, with Sadie front and center, Dr. Mark handed her the first gift; the box was wrapped in white paper with a bow that was just as large as the box.

"That's tradition; he always gives her the first one." Grace whispered to Lucas.

Sadie smiled at the vet and carefully removed the ribbon and handed it to Grace to take care of.

"She has a box in our closet that contains all the ribbons from all the gifts he's given her." Grace explained and Lucas nodded.

Sadie opened the box and grinned. She looked at Dr. Mark with love shining in her eyes then lifted a leather journal from the box.

"It's time for you to start your own set." Dr. Mark smiled, his eyes shining too. His own hand written journals had held the secret to save Arcturus two years before. Nikki had helped him publish the journals which allowed him to retire.

She opened the journal and flipped through the empty pages then lay it on the table next to her so she could rise and wrap her arms around his neck. When Sadie returned to her seat Grace handed her sister the gift from her.

Sadie thanked her then unceremoniously ripped the paper off and looked inside. Her face showed confusion as she lifted three round wooden circles from the box. They were painted blue, pink, and white with a horse shoe in each.

Sadie looked at her in confusion. "OK…thanks, Grace?"

Grace grinned as Reilly handed her his gift.

Just as unceremoniously, she ripped the paper off and opened that box. She pulled out a wooden letter S; it was about 2 feet tall and painted blue.

Sadie started laughing and reached out for the gifts from Nora and Wade.

"You know already?" Wade asked in surprise.

Sadie nodded and lifted the T and A out of their boxes. She placed them on the floor in front of her with the dots Grace had given her after each one:

S.A.T.   Which stood for Sadie Ann Tagger.

"That's too funny." Matt laughed.

"Those will go above my bed," Sadie declared, then giggled. "Or maybe they will go above our new chairs and I'll put them as: SAT…

The whole room laughed with her.

Next, she was given a small box from a grinning Uncle Scott.

She opened the box and pulled out a slip of paper.

"It's time." She read the note. "Time for what?"

"Time to look behind the little brown sofa," He told her with a devilish chuckle.

It was the sofa that Wade, Candace, and Paige were sitting on and set right in front of the large wall of windows. Sadie stood and hesitantly looked behind it, stretching out her neck as far as she could. Then she jumped in excitement and ran to the back of the sofa and pulled out a brand new saddle.

All the kids joined in her excitement. When she placed it on the ottoman as if it was the back of a horse; she slid onto it excitedly.

"It's not a barrel saddle." Reilly pointed out.

Sadie looked down at it, then stood and examined it a little more. Her eyes widened and she looked at her parents then uncle.

"What?" Wade asked.

"That looks like my saddle," Nora's eyes widened. "My CUTTING saddle."

Sadie's head whipped around from the saddle to her uncle.

"It's time." Uncle Scott grinned.

"I can CUT?" Sadie turned to her parents with a hopeful expression.

"You've done a great job with Scarecrow so it's time to add the cutting now that Scott has Little Ghost trained for you." Her dad grinned.

"Will you teach me?" She asked her uncle.

"Of course," He answered.

"Don't yell at me…" She warned with a dingo gleam in her eyes.

He laughed, "I wouldn't dream of it."

She quickly hugged him and her parents then returned to her saddle; running her hand gently over the tooled pattern. "I want to go put it on Little Ghost."

"One last gift," Her mom announced and nodded to Nora.

Nora stood and handed Sadie a small long box then turned to return to her seat.

"Stay up there." Aunt Jordan said and Nora hesitated.

"Why?" Nora asked in surprise.

"Because your birthday is in a week, so we thought we would combine this one." Her mother smiled.

Nora and Sadie's smiles disappeared and they looked at each other in shock then to their parents in dismay.

"You bought us something we have to share?" Sadie looked mortified.

"That never goes well." Nora's voice was low and just as stressed as Sadie's.

"Believe me, girls," Uncle Scott nodded and looked at Aunt Dru. "We know exactly what you mean."

"Hey!" Aunt Dru laughed. "I share."

"But not very well and certainly not willingly," Her brothers laughed.

Both girls stood quietly, too stressed to even smile at the family joke.

Sadie lifted the box and lowered it again, she sighed as she looked at Nora.

"Just open it!" Alex yelled.

Sadie slowly stood from the saddle and they hesitantly looked at each other then ripped the wrapping paper off and opened the box.

Both girls stared in silence, then Sadie started bouncing, then Nora joined her.

"What is it?" Candace asked; excited for them even though she didn't know what it was.

The girls looked at each other, squealed in delight, wrapped their arms around each other, and started bouncing higher.

"I guess it's good." Wade lifted a brow and looked at his parents.

"We're going to horse camp in June!" Sadie squealed and wrapped her arms around her mother's neck then to her dad.

"You could TEACH horse camp." Matt huffed.

"But it's at the University of Colorado in Fort Collins!" Nora stopped bouncing and ran to her parents to throw her arms around them.

"Isn't that where they picked to go to college for the equine sports program for Sadie?" Nikki asked.

"Oh, yeah; that makes sense." Matt looked impressed.

"Do we get to take our own horses?" Sadie looked up hopefully.

"We decided with both of you going, you can." Her mom answered.

It created another squeal from the girls.

"I'm taking Arcturus!" Nora said excitedly.

"Ohhhhh, I don't knowwww." Sadie moaned. "I want both to go!"

"Just one," Her dad shook his head with a grin.

Grace watched her sister and cousin reading through the camp information. They had moved onto what clothes that would be taking with them. Candace had risen and joined them at looking at the information; she was quiet and trying hard to hide the jealousy. Sadie glanced at her and the excitement started to fade.

"Oh, Candace…I wish you could go with us." Nora said after noticing Sadie's reaction.

"It's OK." Candace swallowed hard. "You can send me pictures."

"How about you send me pictures?" Paige said.

"What?" Candace looked hopeful to her…tears welling in her eyes.

"Jordan and Leah told me what was going on and offered to haul Lola with the girl's horses. I called immediately, and got you registered for the camp with them." Paige grinned.

Candace stared in disbelief. It wasn't until Sadie and Nora squealed and brought her into a hug that the reality set in and Candace screamed in delight and the three started bouncing again.

******

"I've never heard such screaming." Dr. Mark shook his head as the family gathered around the large fire pit behind the barn.

"It was pretty high on the Richter scale." Grace grinned as she stared into the flickering flames of the fire.

"It will be a good one for Sadie. I've known some colleague's that went to that school. I'll see if I can pull a favor or two and make sure they get a complete tour of the school instead of just the camp." He nodded.

Grace didn't know if Candace had a plan yet but at 13 and almost 15, her cousin and sister had their college plans settled. And Grace hadn't gotten brave enough to tell her parents she wasn't going to college. She had a feeling this was going to force the issue.

"Which college did you decide on?" Dr. Mark asked her.

Grace froze inside; dang!

Grace didn't answer so Reilly did. "We're trying to decide on Dillon, WSU, or U of I."

"Not too far away from home." Nikki smiled.

"How far is Dillon?" Lucas asked.

"About seven hours." Reilly answered.

Lucas nodded and looked to Grace, "What are you going to study?"

She just shrugged and diverted her eyes to the three girls.

"Grace?" Reilly looked at her in concern.

"What's wrong?" Her mother asked. She was in one of the deck lounge chairs, her leg propped on pillows.

"Nothing," Grace answered and looked around the family. Everyone was relaxed and happy so this would be the time to make her announcement; she wouldn't have to repeat it over and over. "I've decided not to go to college."

"What?" Reilly blurted out.

"Grace," Her mother looked at her in surprise. "You're going to college."

"I don't need to." Grace said firmly. "I can learn all about equine business from Jack, Aunt Dru, and Nikki."

"It's not the same." Aunt Dru frowned.

"You didn't go to college," She pointed out to her aunt. "And look at what you've accomplished. I've learned a lot from you already from working at The Stables. There is no reason to go to college and spend all that money when I can learn it from you three."

"It's not just about the school work," Nikki said. "It's about the people you meet, the contacts you make from all the classes. I use a number of them still in starting my business."

"Grace," Her dad said and she slowly turned to look at him. "When did you make this decision?"

She shrugged, "I don't see any reason to be gone," Her eyes flickered to her mother. "I don't want to go and I'm not going to."

"Grace…" Her mother looked at her in disbelief.

"I've made up my mind; I have no intentions of going to college." Grace repeated to her surprised parents.

"But Gracie…" Reilly's voice was low and stunned.

She turned to him and saw the hurt in his eyes. Their years of dreaming about going to college together were over; it caused a small crack in her wall of determination.

Grace stood and walked away from them before her composure broke.

CHAPTER TWELVE

She didn't hear anyone following her but when she entered the house the door was pulled from her hand and she felt a small push on her back.

"Into the no-media room," It was Uncle Scott.

"I'm not changing my mind. I'm not going to college." Grace repeated and stopped at the junction where the hall to the outside and the hall to the bedrooms met.

"That's between you and your parents." He said and pointed down the hallway.

"Why bother going in there then?" Grace said defiantly.

His brows furrowed together and there was no amusement in his normally relaxed expression.

"It doesn't have anything to do with college…it has to do with you and Leah."

"What?"

He tugged on her arm and they moved together down the hallway. She didn't want to go, but she wasn't going to be rude and pull her arm away either. Once she was inside the room he closed the door behind them and motioned for her to sit on the couch.

He could talk all he wanted. Didn't mean she had to talk so she sat on the couch and waited for him to give her every reason there was for her to go to college. She still wasn't going to.

Her uncle sat on the opposite end of the couch. He pushed his blonde hair back away from his blue eyes then turned to her.

"Your accident with Leah was in October of your senior year of high school."

Grace glanced at him as if he were crazy…she already knew that.

"It was September of my senior year of high school when I lost my parents and grandparents in an accident similar to yours."

Grace's head fell back against the couch and she closed her eyes tight to stop the nearly instant flow of tears that rushed to her eyes. He knew why she was refusing to leave; she didn't think anyone would understand. She was so wrong. He would understand the fear that had gripped her.

"It's the thought of not being there when she needs you, to miss out on a second of time, even just a fleeting moment that you could have been together if something were to happen to her."

"Or Dad." She whispered and opened her tear filled eyes to look at her uncle.

His eyes were filled with understanding. "It is the same fear that Grayson, Dru, and I had to overcome too."

"How did you get through it?"

"Well, it wasn't easy and it wasn't quick…it took us a long time and a thorough talking to by Andy plus some trickery between him and Leah."

Grace turned to face him. "When I think about leaving…I just have this fear that she'll be gone when I come back."

He nodded. "I've been there."

"How did you get over the fear?"

He slowly shook his head, "I'm not over it. After living through what we did…how fast they were gone? I don't think we'll ever get over the fear."

"But you don't look like it. You look fine."

"We've worked on that over the years." He turned in his seat and raised a knee across the cushions to face her. "At first, other than school, we could barely be apart; hence the nickname 'The Trio'. We did EVERYTHING together even if it was just going from the ranch house to Andy's house to get supplies."

"What happened to make you stop?"

"Pretty much Andy and Leah," He shrugged with a smirk. "The first months, if Grayson and I weren't in school, we were at Dru's side. The first summer after they died, from the moment I graduated, we were inseparable. Leah was in the picture by then but she was in California for the summer with her family until school started back up. Then we'd see her every weekend when she came to the ranch with Grayson." He chuckled. "It had become so automatic for us to get up, get Nikki and Matt taken care of and ready for the day then we just went about our business. If we couldn't have the kids with us them Clara took them for the day. Their kids were teenagers at the time and she really enjoyed having a 1 year old and 3 year old to take care of."

"Whether it was riding, going to the stockyards, cattlemen's meetings, grocery stores, doctor's visits, sales…everything…we were together. I couldn't imagine being away from either of them for more than thirty minutes." He chuckled. "It got pretty crazy and we all three FELT it but couldn't really SEE it until Leah and Andy pointed it out."

"What happened to make it stop?" Grace asked. She had never heard this story before.

"The next year, after they were out of college for the summer, Leah asked Grayson if they could stay at the ranch while Dru and I went into Lewiston for fencing supplies." Scott grinned. "You should have seen the look on Grayson's face…I'm sure Dru and I had the same look."

"What happened?"

"He told her no, she got pissed, and we took Matt and Nikki and left her behind."

Grace's eyebrows shot up, "Mom must have been mad."

"Furious!" Scott nodded. "She was at the ranch alone when Andy showed up and she asked him what she should do. Andy managed to calm her down and between the two of them, they came up with a plan to show us what we were doing."

Grace turned to face him, pulling her knees up around her chin and wrapping her arms around them.

Uncle Scott grinned. "They had Zanger call me about a bull that we had been trying to buy from him, had Dr. Mark call Grayson about helping with a couple of horses he had to doctor, then had the attorney call Dru. They wanted us to meet them all at the same time."

"Lewiston for the attorney, Riggins for the Zangers, where for Dr. Mark?" Grace grinned.

"Nezperce," He chuckled. "Andy and Leah were standing there when we got the calls, purposely coming in at the same time."

"What did you do?"

"Well, we all accepted, not knowing the other two were accepting the meetings too. When we got off the phone and told each other…we just stood and stared. I swear, we all three turned white as snow at just the thought of not going together."

He looked at her with a wry smile, "We started trying to decide who to call back and say we couldn't go when Andy pointed out what we were doing. It had been a year and a half since our parents died…we were blind to it even when people would joke about it."

"Could you see it when Andy pointed it out?"

"To a point, but we didn't see what was wrong with it until he pointed out that we were living in fear." He smiled gently at her. "That's what you're doing now…living in fear."

"But I can't get myself to stop."

"Did you talk to your therapist?"

She shook her head. As much as she hated going to a therapist to start out with, he had really helped her deal with the New Year's incident with Allen, the loss of Levi as a friend, and more importantly, the unknown of what Allen had done while she was unconscious.

"Why?"

"Because I didn't want to admit it out loud that I was letting something control me again." She sighed.

"It doesn't make you weak."

"I know…or keep telling myself that."

"Well, we let our fear control us." He sighed. "Even as hard as we fought Andy and Leah as they tried to tell us what we were doing wasn't good for us, and we insisted there wasn't anything wrong with it, we knew we were letting the fear win. Leah and Grayson were already engaged and she asked him if he intended on bringing me and Dru on the honeymoon." He chuckled, "I think that was kind of the real eye opener. He really didn't want us there and we REALLY didn't want to be there."

Grace smiled.

"Andy pointed out how much in life we were going to miss if we continued. He wanted us to quit living with the fear that something was going to happen every day and instead to enjoy life as an adventure because the day would come that one of us would die. Whether it was the next day or in sixty years, we would eventually die."

"That's a terrible thought."

He nodded, "But it's true. It is up to us to make sure the time we have on this planet, together or not, is spent wisely and we treat it as an adventure. No matter what we did, if it was meant for us to have long lives then that would be the way it was meant to be. If not, then there wasn't anything we could do about it. We just had to accept that and move on."

"You obviously did."

"It was a long uphill battle." He admitted with a grimace. "We took short trips away from each other to start so the anxiety didn't take over. Then it got easier to do but the fear is never gone. It will always be with us."

He turned back to her again.

"Every time Jordan takes off for a trip with you kids, I get anxious on whether she is going to get back. I have the fear in my heart, placed there by my parents and grandparents loss, and it will never go away. I've just learned to deal with it. When she fell in the fire a couple of years ago…how close she was to being gone? I realized that all the fighting we had been doing was taking away from all the love we should have been giving each other."

"You guys did change after that, everyone noticed it."

He nodded. "We still have our battles but we never, ever, part each other without letting each other know that we still love each other. We'll always battle; it's just who we are…two hot heads that want their own way." He grinned.

She nodded. "Is Dad and Dru the same way?"

"Dru had Andy the first year and he really helped her. I know Grayson had problems at college that he never talked to us about. I had friends call me saying they were worried about him."

"Really? What was wrong?"

"He was angry…like we all were. Dru and I buried it in work. Grayson didn't have that when he was at school."

"Angry?"

"Oh, Grace," Scott sighed and turned so he could stretch his legs out in front of him and lean his head back against the couch. His eyes went to the ceiling. "Anger… My parents were Dru and Grayson's age, early fortys….it was so unfair they were taken from us. There was anger at everything we didn't have time to say, at everything they didn't have a chance to teach us, everything that we never got done, and it just continued through the years. It became anger that they never got to meet you kids…that you didn't get to meet them and have grandparents." He stopped when his voice cracked and tears glistened in his eyes. "Every time Wade or Nora…any of you would accomplish something great it was so hard not to have them here so they could share…they could see…just how wonderful all you kids are. The day I married Jordan…when each of you kids were born…they should have been there." Tears slid silently down his cheeks.

His voice was anguished and the emotions so raw. Grace's tears fell.

"There are so many times I wanted to call them and say 'Mom, what should I do? Or 'Dad, how do I…?', but I couldn't." He swallowed hard. "When Nora and I got in the screaming match on the back porch?"

"Yeah?" She whispered.

"I was so angry, but not at her. I was angry at my parents for not being there for me to talk to. To ask them how to handle the situation. I wanted them so bad my heart physically hurt to the point

I wanted to reach in my chest and just pull it out." More tears escaped and he just ignored them so Grace did too. "I just got angry and, unfortunately, Nora got the brunt of the anger."

She sat quietly while he stared at the ceiling before speaking again. "Raising kids isn't easy; we haven't done it before. We didn't know what to do. We made a mistake, but I didn't know how to recover from it. I got angry and luckily have the best wife in the world that has patients and love for me and can help me through the bad times. Grayson and Dru help too, but they tend to just get angry with me instead of helping me deal with it. I just don't know what I'd do without Jordan."

"You two are so different than Mom and Dad." Grace said honestly.

He just chuckled and glanced at her. "They are a lake, serene with a deep love."

"That sounds romantic." Grace teased.

"That's what Jordan says…just repeating her words."

"Then what are you two?"

"We're like the Snake River. We can be calm and beautiful, floating along without a care in the world or we can be raging rapids that are ready to kill you at any moment." He grinned with a twinkle in his eyes. "That's how my wife describes our marriage."

Grace laughed.

He looked back to the ceiling. "When we hit the rapids, we just hold on until we get to the calm waters because they are so worth it."

"Now, that sounds romantic." She smiled and his phone alerted him to a message.

He pulled the phone from his pocket and read the message.

"Leah is about to tell Lucas about Sadie's birth." He leaned back on the couch and looked at her thoughtfully. "Don't let fear run your life and don't let anger run your life. One day at a time, Grace. Enjoy every minute of it while you can because it can change so fast. Go on your adventure to college and rodeos with Reilly, we'll be here…Leah and Grayson will be here…if that's what's meant to be."

Grace swallowed to get rid of the emotions creeping back up. She reached a hand out and he took it and squeezed tightly. "I'm sorry, Uncle Scott, that you had to dredge up your past for me."

He smiled warmly, "It's OK, the past happens so we can help make the future better."

She leaned across the couch and gave him a big hug. "Reilly will thank you."

"Yeah, he owes me now," He chuckled as they stood. "I'll make sure he knows that."

They stopped in the kitchen and splashed water on their faces to wash away the tears then left the house to hear the story of Sadie's birthday.

CHAPTER THIRTEEN

"Grayson, it will be fine, stop worrying." Leah said for what had to be at least a dozen times.

"Yeah…you've said that." He grumbled and pulled in behind Dru's truck at the fall branding corral. "Stay there until I open the door."

He stepped out with a glance to the people in the middle of the corral and the cow bellowing from inside the chute.

"It's about time!" Scott yelled from the group of people.

Grayson hurried to Leah's door before she attempted to get out herself. "As much as I love you, I wish you would have stayed at The Homestead with Jordan and the baby. Remember, you were early with Grace."

She smiled lovingly at him as he gently helped her to the ground. The cold November air bit at Grayson's skin so he pulled the emergency blanket off the backseat of the truck.

"Yes, I remember, but that was two weeks. I still have four weeks to go and the doctor said yesterday that everything looks normal." She assured him and took his arm firmly in her hands as he held her tightly. "Besides, I was in labor with Grace for sixteen hours before she finally decided she wanted to join us."

Scott, Dru, Jessup, Dr. Mark, and Andy turned away from the cow and turned surprised eyes to the very pregnant Leah.

"Why are you here?" Dru asked her sister-in-law with a glare.

Leah just grinned and took a seat on the cooler that Scott rushed to her; a safe distance from the cow in the chute. Grayson laid the blanket over her legs.

"I'm fine," She said again. "We're only here to bring the medicine then head back."

"So hurry up and give this to Dr. Mark," Grayson tossed the bag with the medicine to his brother. "I want to get her back home."

"Grayson, go help," Leah swished her hand to the cow. "I'm not leaving until they're done so you might as well help them out."

"Leah, look at me." He ordered.

She turned her beautiful blue eyes up to him with a raised brow. Her blonde hair flowed down her back over her coat and a black fur trimmed hat framed her face.

"There are five people with that cow and each one of them can give it a shot. They do not need me." He said flatly. "I have NO intentions of leaving your side."

Her eyes twinkled in delight as the smile crossed her face. "I love you." She said softly and slid her hand into his.

Grayson returned her smile until the sound of hoof beats reached them.

They turned to see Nikki and Matt galloping their horses down the road. The ten and seven-year-olds loved to gallop anywhere they rode.

"I love watching those two," Leah said softly. "I can't wait until our kids are that age and riding all over this ranch."

"Me, too," He squeezed her hand. "Parson's should be here any minute with Grace so we can take her home with us."

"I love that she can go play with his grandkids, but I hate being away from her." Leah said and ran a hand over her enlarged belly. "Do you think that will ever change?"

"I hope not," He chuckled. "She'll grow up just like you."

"And that would be…?" She asked with a raised brow.

"Strong, confident, and in charge," He grinned down at her.

"I thought you were going to say bossy." She smiled.

"I'm sure she will be that too." He teased. "But Grace and little baby there would be very lucky to grow up to be like you."

"And you." She smiled lovingly. "There is a reason I fell in love with you."

"You…" He started then turned when the cow bellowed loudly and the group around it hollered.

Grayson took a half step to them but stopped when her hand gripped his tightly. He turned back to see her head down to her chest and her arm curling around her belly.

"Leah?" Panic ran through him as he knelt next to her.

"The baby…" She gasped and wrapped her arms around her stomach.

"Dr. Mark!" Grayson yelled, then slid his shaking arms around his wife to keep her from falling. He gently lowered her to the ground.

"Leah?" He whispered, trying to keep the fear out of his voice; his heart was pounding.

"The baby is coming." She curled her body around her belly but fingers grasped his arm.

"You're in labor?" Dru asked as she ran to their side.

"No, the baby is coming NOW!" Leah cried out.

"Let me in," Dr. Mark ordered and quickly moved around everyone to get to Leah and lift her long maternity skirt.

"It's coming out," Leah gasped as she rolled onto her back. She clung onto Grayson's arm as her body arched.

"As in NOW!" Dr. Mark hollered. "Get the sanitary medical pads out of my truck…towels, blankets…anything! I need water and gloves." He ordered over his shoulder as he covered her with the blanket.

He barely had his hands washed and the gloves on before the baby made its appearance.

"It's a girl," Dr. Mark announced as he lowered the baby onto a towel.

Grayson tore off his coat and held it out for the veterinarian to place the baby into its warmth.

"I don't hear her." Leah cried. "Is she OK?"

Grayson looked down at the tiny pink baby he held as Dr. Mark cut the umbilical cord. She looked perfect, her eyes opening and closing, then looking up to the sky. Her fingers were reaching and her toes curled in then stretched out.

"She's OK," Grayson whispered but couldn't pull his eyes from the baby. "You're OK, Baby Girl." He whispered to her as his heart seemed to swell.

"Grayson?" Leah cried, her hand gripping at his arm.

"She's OK." He repeated and looked up at his frightened wife. Tears rolled down Leah's face as her desperate eyes looked at him. "She's perfect."

A shaky breath and a gasp escaped from Leah. "Why is she quiet? Why can't I hear her?"

Grayson moved forward and nestled the baby next to his wife.

"See?" He whispered. "She's fine."

They cuddled the baby between them as more blankets and coats were placed over the three of them.

The sound of an engine could be heard and Grayson looked up to see Parson's pulling in next to the corrals.

"He has a canopy on his truck," He said and looked up at Scott, Dru, and Jessup. "Clear it out and make her a bed. We'll take them to the hospital in it."

All three met the truck as Parson's lifted Grace out of the front seat. The four-year-old's eyes widened in worry as she ran to her parents.

"Mommy! Daddy!" The blue eyed blonde little girl cried.

Grayson lifted his free arm so she could cuddle under the blanket next to him.

"You have a little sister," Leah smiled up at her.

"A sister? I wanted a brother like Matt." Grace glared at the baby.

The only thing visible from the coat was the tiny pink face.

Grayson and Leah looked at each other and smiled.

Within minutes, the truck was backed up next to them. Dru pulled Grace away as Scott helped Grayson stand with the baby wrapped in his arms.

Scott and Jessup lifted Leah up into the truck and wrapped her in blankets.

Grayson handed the wrapped baby to Scott, who was kneeling in the truck bed next to Leah. He hesitated to look down into the pink face and smiled as he nestled her into Leah's arms.

"Why is she so quiet?" Leah whispered.

"She seems pretty content," Scott answered. "Her coloring is very good and breathing sounds just fine."

"We need to get going." Grayson said.

"Where are Matt and Nikki?" Leah asked.

"I have them with me," Dru answered.

"Is the baby OK?" Matt asked.

"Yes, come see her." Leah said and Grayson helped the two kids crawl into the truck.

Matt and Nikki knelt next to Leah and looked down at the baby.

"She's pink." Matt whispered.

"She's tiny." Nikki added.

"What's her name, Mommy?" Grace asked. She was standing on the back seat of the truck leaning through the window into the canopy.

"Well," Leah looked to Grayson. "We haven't really decided on a girl's name yet…besides Anne as the middle name."

Leah looked out the back of the truck to the group of people looking in.

"Dr. Mark? What is your mother's name?" She asked.

The veterinarian smiled through his large mustache.

✱✱✱✱✱

"So, you not only delivered her, but you named her." Lucas said as he grinned at the older man with the thirteen-year-old sitting happily next to him.

Grace looked at her sister and smiled at the laughter in her eyes.

"Yep," Dr. Mark answered. "Told Leah right then, that she was my first human delivery so she was mine, too…she's *my* Tagger."

"And I happily agreed," Her mother grinned. "And we got to the hospital with no problem. I worried about her all the way there because she hadn't made a noise."

"When they took her out of the coat, she screamed like a banshee." Her dad grinned as Sadie giggled. "She was pissed and let everyone in the hospital know it."

"First sign of that temper," Wade smirked.

Lucas turned to Grace, "And how long before you accepted having a sister instead of a brother?"

Grace laughed her 'life is good' laugh, "I still haven't!"

The Homestead

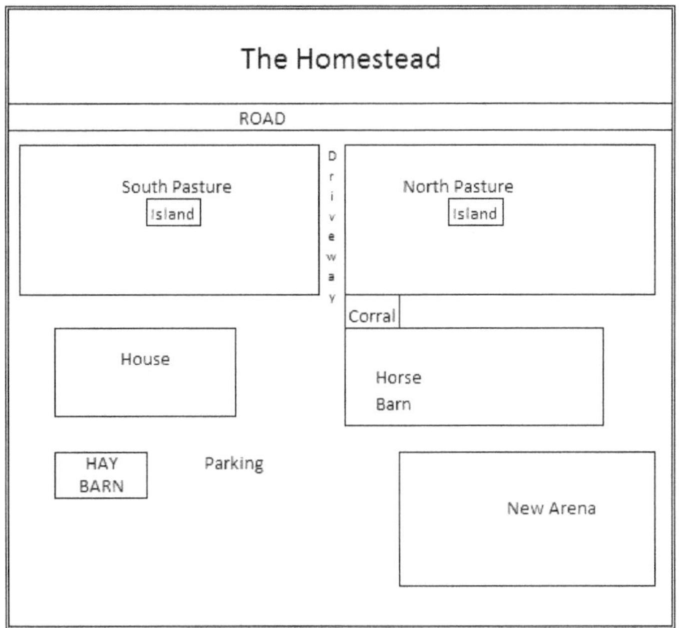

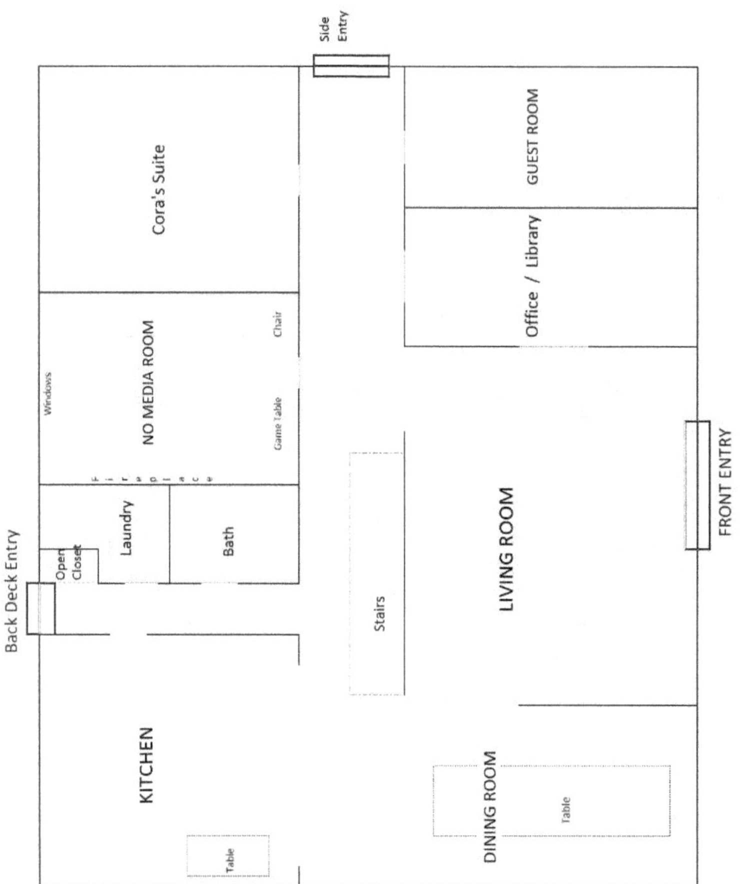

The Homestead Downstairs

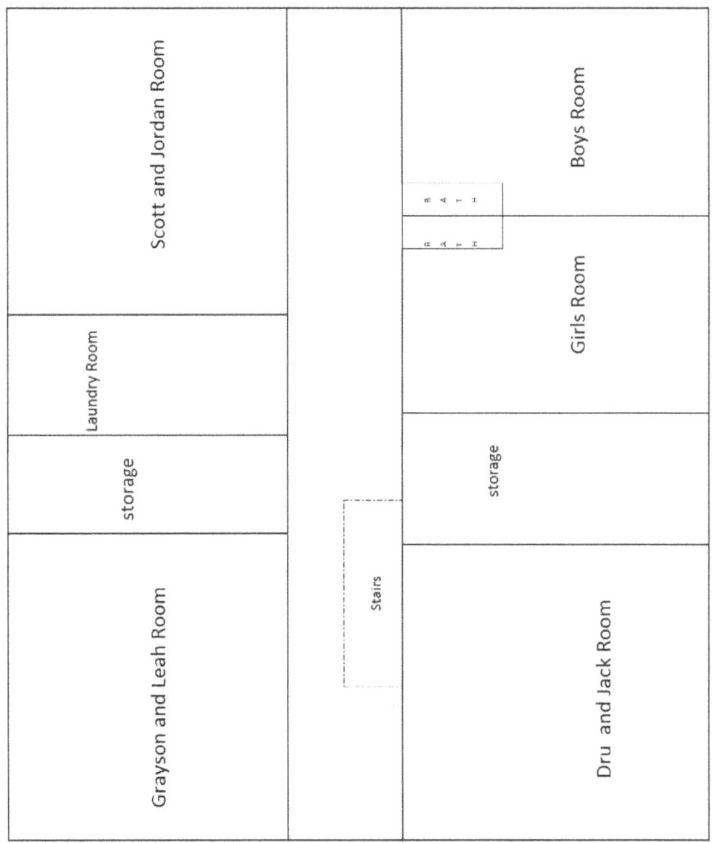

The Homestead Upstairs

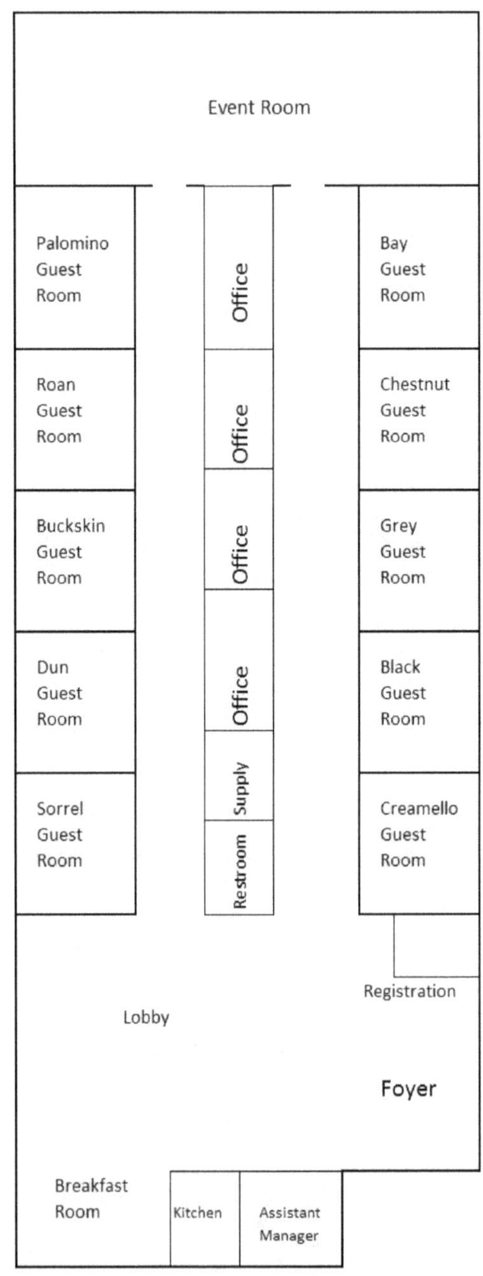

Tagger Enterprises Barn & Breakfast

The Tagger Family

Drucilla
    Nikki
    Matt —— Nick

Grayson
    Leah
        Grace
        Sadie

Scott
    Jordan
    Nora
    Wade

Jessup: Tagger Ranch

Jack Morgan: The Stables
    Reilly

Cora Smith: The Homestead

Tessa Elliott: Barn & Breakfast
    Alex

Tagger Property History:
Mathew and Grace
Anderson and Nora
Mathew and Anne
Grayson Mathew, Scott Anderson, Drucilla Anne

ABOUT THE AUTHOR

I was raised with Shetlands and ponies and have loved horses since I watched a Shetland colt born when I was four.

Growing up, the TV show Bonanza was my favorite. I loved that western life and wanted to be Little Joe and Hoss' little sister. I wanted to live at the Ponderosa. Watching rodeos on television and attending when I could, was the closest I could get to the cowboy way of life.

That changed when I purchased my first 'big horse' when I was twenty-one and living in Alaska. I now have the great-granddaughter of that horse in my pasture.

I am also a photographer specializing in the equine industry; shows, races, jackpots, and rodeos. With my photography, I create my own covers.

The Tagger Herd Series was my first venture into fictional writing and I love the family and horses in the series.

My first 'stand-alone' novel was Hoofbeats in the Wind which ventured into rodeo.

My next book, Coffee With Cowboys delved deeper into the rodeo world and researching for the book was an adventure. I have met wonderful people from fans, stock contractors, and competitors. I thank every one of them that have helped make that book a possibility. It will always be special to me because of the people I met.

Bijou Bay was inspired by Idaho's Black Rock Ranch and the a true story I was fortunate enough to be told.

Writing, researching, photography, my two dogs, Morgan and Tagger, and Kit in the pasture, fill my world and keep me busy.

www.ingramcontent.com/pod-product-compliance
Lightning Source LLC
Chambersburg PA
CBHW061044210726
48294CB00001B/24